M. C. Cooke

Handbook of British Fungi

Anatiposi

M. C. Cooke

Handbook of British Fungi

Reprint of the original, first published in 1871.

1st Edition 2023 | ISBN: 978-3-38212-695-7

Anatiposi Verlag is an imprint of Outlook Verlagsgesellschaft mbH.

Verlag (Publisher): Outlook Verlag GmbH, Zeilweg 44, 60439 Frankfurt, Deutschland
Vertretungsberechtigt (Authorized to represent): E. Roepke, Zeilweg 44, 60439 Frankfurt, Deutschland
Druck (Print): Books on Demand GmbH, In de Tarpen 42, 22848 Norderstedt, Deutschland

HANDBOOK

OF

BRITISH FUNGI

With full Descriptions of all the Species, and Illustrations of the Genera.

BY

M. C. COOKE, M.A.

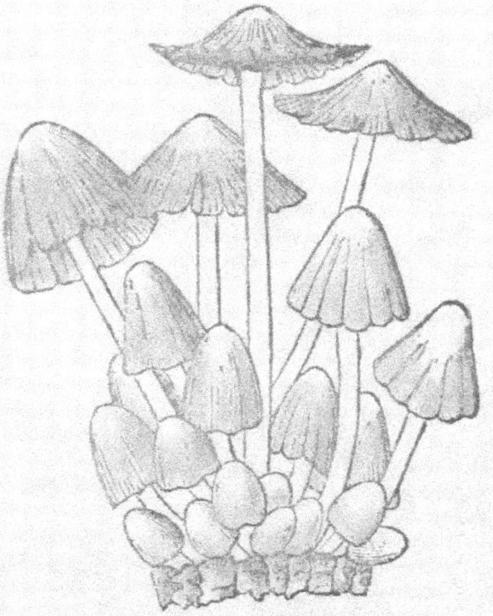

London and New York:

MACMILLAN AND CO.

1871.

PREFACE.

THIRTY-FIVE years ago one of the volumes of the "English Flora" contained full descriptions of all the species then known of British Fungi. Prior to this several floras, and especially Mr. Samuel Gray's "Natural Arrangement" and Withering's "Arrangement," included the fungi; but it was left to the Rev. M. J. Berkeley to collect the materials, and eliminate from them, a Mycological Flora of the British Islands. During the thirty-five years that have elapsed since the appearance of the last complete Mycologic Flora, no attempt has been made to revise it, to incorporate species since discovered, and to bring it up to the standard of modern science. No apology, therefore, is necessary for the present effort, since all will admit that the want of such a manual has long been felt, and this work makes its appearance under the advantage that it seeks to occupy a place which has long been vacant.

It was my intention at first to have added an introduction, treating of the structure and affinities of the different orders and genera included in the present volume, with an explanation of my own views as to the classification adopted, but as the work proceeded it so far exceeded the dimensions originally estimated, that it was found impossible to do justice to this portion of the subject here, and the "Introduction" has been postponed, in the hope that hereafter it may appear as a separate volume. It may suffice to state that, in the face of the bewildering chaos of new genera which have of late been proposed on the Continent, especially for Ascomycetous forms, I have endeavoured to avoid, as much as possible, encumbering these pages with a nomenclature often fanciful, seldom necessary, and which may, at best, be regarded as transitional. It is hoped that such changes as have been made will commend themselves to the student as facilitating the study of organisms by no means easy of comprehension.

The arrangement of the Hymenomycetes is based upon the latest views of the illustrious Fries, with such additions as were recommended by Mr. Worthington Smith in a recent volume of the "Journal of Botany." In fact, Mr. Smith's arrangement is adopted *in toto*, and I availed myself of his experience by associating him with myself in this portion of the work.

During the progress of this "Handbook" I have to acknowledge with gratitude the suggestions, and aid, of numerous friends, especially of Professor Elias Fries, the Rev. M. J. Berkeley, M. A., C. E. Broome, Esq., F.L.S., W. G. Smith, Esq., F.L.S., Dr. E. Capron, Dr. Bull, and H. C. Ravenal, Esq. For the measurements of the spores in the Agaricini I am indebted to Mr. W. G. Smith, as well as for the drawings of many of the woodcuts. North American localities have been inserted for some species, but I am aware that this portion of the work is very imperfect.

I am conscious that I have not produced a perfect work. Pursuing the study of Fungi as a recreation in the intervals of the daily business of life, it was no easy task to prepare and arrange the descriptions of nearly three thousand plants, compare specimens and figures, and measure their spores. It would be presumption to suppose that this has in all cases been done without error, although it is hoped, with some confidence, that the errors are few, and of no great importance.

Subscribers will not regret that, instead of 600 pages they will receive more than 900; and instead of 200 figures upwards of 400. No effort has been spared to make this work worthy of their confidence, and, by the publication of an occasional supplement, it is hoped to maintain it for many years as *the* "Handbook" for every student of British Fungi.

M. C. C.

Upper Holloway, July, 1871.

HANDBOOK

OF

BRITISH FUNGI.

DIVISION I. SPORIFERA. *Spores naked.*

I.	Hymenium free, mostly naked, or soon exposed.	*Hymenomycetes.*
II.	Hymenium enclosed in a peridium, ruptured when mature.	*Gasteromycetes.*
III.	Spores naked, mostly terminal, on inconspicuous threads, free, or enclosed in a perithecium.	*Coniomycetes.*
IV.	Spores naked, on conspicuous threads, rarely compacted, small.	*Hyphomycetes.*

Family I. HYMENOMYCETES.

Mycelium floccose, giving rise at once to a distinct hymenium, or producing a variously shaped, naked, or volvate receptacle, even, or bearing on its upper or under surface various folds, plates, prickles, &c., clothed with fertile hymenial cells. Spores naked, mostly quaternate, on distinct spicules. *Berk. Introd. p.* 351. *Outl. p.* 89.

Hymenium, normally inferior—

Fruit-bearing surface lamellose.	*Agaricini.*
Fruit-bearing surface, porous or tubular. .	*Polyporei.*
Fruit-bearing surface clothed with prickles.	*Hydnei.*
Fruit-bearing surface, even.	*Auricularini.*

Hymenium, superior or encirling—

Clavate or branched, rarely lobed.	*Clavariei.*
Lobed, convolute, or disc-like, gelatinous; (fertile threads not compacted into a true hymenium).	*Tremellini.*

Tabular View of the Subgenera of Agaricus. Pl. vii.

	I. Leucospori.	II. Hyporhodii.	III. Dermini.	IV. Pratellæ.	V. Coprinarii
* Hymenophore distinct from the fleshy Stem.	1. Amanita.	10. Volvaria.			
	2. Lepiota.	11. Chamæota.		26. Psalliota.	
		12. Pluteus.		27. Pilosace.	
** Hymenophore confluent and homogeneous with the fleshy Stem.	3. Armillaria.		19. Pholiota.	28. Stropharia.	
	4. Tricholoma.	13. Entoloma.	20. Hebeloma.	29. Hypholoma.	33. Panæolus.
	5. Clitocybe.	14. Clitopilus.	21. Flammula.		
	6. Pleurotus.	15. Claudopus.	22. Crepidotus.		
*** Hymenophore confluent with, but heterogeneous from the cartilaginous Stem.	7. Collybia.	16. Leptonia.	23. Naucoria.	30. Psilocybe.	
	8. Mycena.	17. Nolanea.	24. Galera.	31. Psathyra.	34. Psathyrella
	9. Omphalia.	18. Eccilia.	25. Tubaria.	32. Deconica.	

Gills adnate.
Plants parasitic on other Agarics . . . . xii. NYCTALIS.
Not parasitic.
Milky . . . . ix. LACTARIUS.
Not milky.
Rigid and brittle . . . x. RUSSULA.
Waxy . . . . vii. HYGROPHORUS.
§ Stem lateral or absent . . . . 6. *Pleurotus.*
‡ With cartilaginous bark.
Gills adnate . . . . 7. *Collybia.*
Gills sinuate . . . . 8. *Mycena.*
Gills decurrent . . . . 9. *Omphalia.*
* Plant tough, coriaceous, or woody.
† Stem central.
Gills simple . . . . xiii. MARASMIUS.
Gills branched . . . . xvi. XEROTUS.
† Stem lateral or wanting.
Gills toothed. . . . . xiv. LENTINUS.
Gills not toothed . . . . xv. PANUS.
Gills channelled longitudinally or crisped xvii. TROGIA.
Gills splitting longitudinally . . . . . . xviii. SCHIZOPHYLLUM.
Gills anastomosing . . . . xix. LENZITES.

II. Spores rosy or salmon colour.—*Hyporhodii.*
* Without cartilaginous bark.
† Hymenophorum free.
‡ With a volva . . . . 10. *Volvaria.*
‡ Without a volva.
With a ring . . . . 11. *Chamæota.*
Ringless . . . . 12. *Pluteus.*
† Hymenophorum confluent.
‡ Stem central.
Gills adnate or sinuate . . . . . 13. *Entoloma.*
Gills decurrent . . . . 14. *Clitopilus.*
‡ Stem lateral or absent . . . . 15. *Claudopus.*
* With cartilaginous bark.
Gills decurrent . . . . 18. *Eccilia.*
Gills not decurrent.
Pileus torn into scales . . . . 16. *Leptonia.*
Pileus papillose, subcampanulate.
Gills membranaceous, persistent. . 17. *Nolanea.*
Gills subdeliquescent . . . . iii. BOLBITIUS.

III. Spores brown, sometimes reddish or yellowish brown.—*Dermini.*
* Without cartilaginous bark.
† Stem central.
‡ With a ring.
Ring continuous . . . . 19. *Pholiota.*
Ring arachnoid, filamentous or evanescent.
Gills adnate, terrestrial . . . . iv. CORTINARIUS.
Gills decurrent, or acutely adnate, mostly epiphytal . . . . . . 21. *Flammula.*

‡ Without a ring.
Gills adhering to the hymenophorum, and sinuate . . . . 20. *Hebeloma.*
Gills separating from the hymenophorum, and decurrent . . . . vi. PAXILLUS.
† Stem lateral or absent . . . . 22. *Crepidotus.*
* With cartilaginous bark.
Gills decurrent . . . . 25. *Tubaria.*
Gills not decurrent.
Margin of pileus at first incurved . . 23. *Naucoria.*
Margin of pileus always straight . . 24. *Galera.*

IV. Spores purple, sometimes brownish-purple, dark purple, or dark brown.—*Pratellæ.*
* Without cartilaginous bark.
† Hymenophorum free.
‡ With a ring . . . . 26. *Psalliota.*
‡ Ringless . . . . 27. *Pilosace.*
† Hymenophorum confluent.
Veil normally ring-shaped on the stem 28. *Stropharia.*
Veil normally adhering to the margin of pileus. . . . . 29. *Hypholoma.*
* With cartilaginous bark.
Gills decurrent . . . . 32. *Deconica.*
Gills not decurrent.
Margin of pileus at first incurved . . . 30. *Psilocybe.*
Margin of pileus at first straight . . . 31. *Psathyra.*

V. Spores black, or nearly so.—*Coprinarii.*
Gills deliquescent . . . . ii. COPRINUS.
Gills not deliquescent.
Gills decurrent . . . . viii. GOMPHIDIUS.
Gills not decurrent.
Pileus striate . . . . 34. *Psathyrella.*
Pileus not striate . . . . 33. *Panæolus.*

Genus 1. AGARICUS, Linn. Syst. Nat. (1735).

Spores of various colours; gills membranaceous, persistent, with an acute edge; trama floccose, confluent with the inferior hymenium. Fleshy fungi, putrifying, and not reviving when once dried, hence differing from such genera as are deliquescent, coriaceous, or woody.

This genus is divided into five series, according to the colour of the spores, the subgenera in each series are arranged in the accompanying plates. Each series consists typically of three groups.

1.—Hymenophore distinct from the fleshy stem.
2.—Hymenophore confluent and homogenous with the fleshy stem.
3.—Hymenophore confluent with, but heterogenous from, the cartilaginous stem.

These three groups are kept distinct in the plates, the subgenera in each series corresponding in position with its analogues in the other series.

* Hymenophore distinct from the fleshy Stem.

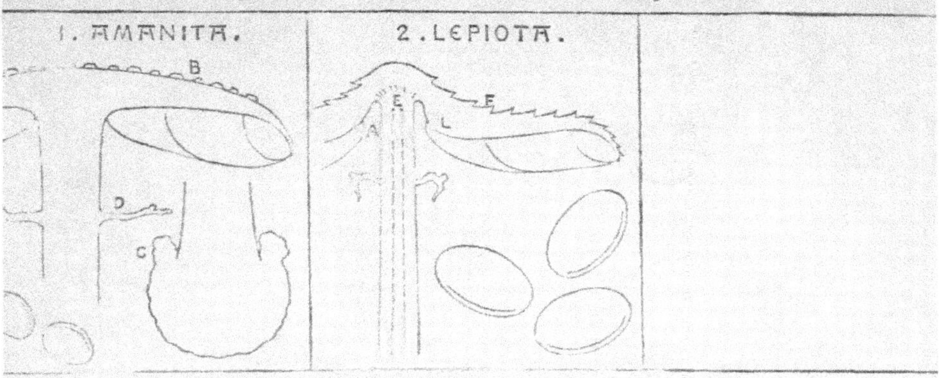

** Hymenophore confluent and homogeneous with the fleshy Stem.

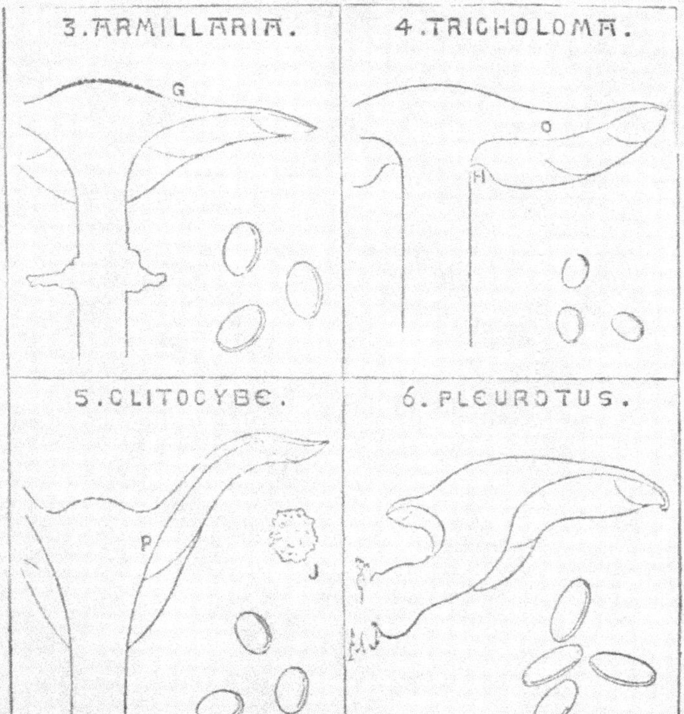

*** Hymenophore confluent with, but heterogeneous from the cartilaginous Stem

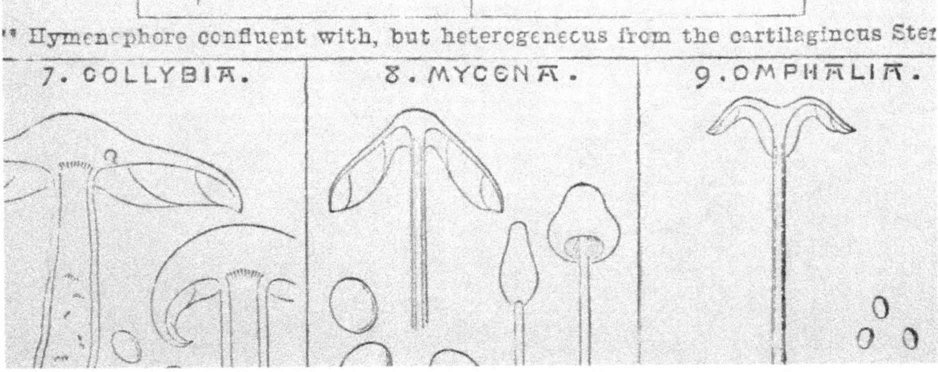

Series 1. **Leucospori.** Spores white (Plate ii).

The species bearing white spores seem higher in type than those producing coloured spores. Most of the former are firm, and many persistent, whilst, as we approach the black-spored Agarics, there is a greater tendency to deliquesce. The spores of the *Leucospori* are mostly oval, sometimes nearly round, generally very regular, but sometimes spinulose. They vary in size; and, while containing the largest as well as the smallest known spores, are as a rule *small*, generally white, but sometimes dingy, or with a suggestion of yellow, or pink. As a rule, none of the *Leucospori* grow on dung or in rank places, whilst in the darker and black-spored groups these habitats are the rule.—*W. G. S.*

Sub-Gen. 1. AMANITA. Pers. Syn., p. 246.

Veil universal at first, completely enveloping the young plant, distinct and free from the cuticle of the pileus; pileus convex, then expanded, not decidedly fleshy; stem distinct from the hymenophore, ringed or ringless, furnished with a volva, free and lax, connate with the base, or friable and nearly obsolete; gills free from the stem.—HAB. On the ground, mostly in woods and uncultivated places.—(*Pl. II., fig.* 1, *A. muscarius.*)

This subgenus is remarkable for the great development of the veil, which at first entirely envelopes the young plant in a thick clothy wrapper; as the fungus reaches maturity the veil is ruptured, and part remains in scattered patches on the pileus (B), whilst part forms a more or less complete cup or volva at the base (C); when there are no fragments on the pileus the veil has been ruptured in one place, and the whole mass remains at the base; this is often the case in *Agaricus phalloides* Fr. Some of the species have the stem furnished with a ring (D), which is part of the veil, whilst three species are ringless (or more properly, *the ring is adherent to the stem*). In some species the veil is thick, and greatly developed, whilst in others it is thin and friable, and both volva and patches are evanescent; the higher forms of *Amanita* stand alone, from the stem being furnished with a *volva* and *ring*. Some of the species are edible, others highly poisonous.—*W. G. S.*

Sect. 1. *Vaginatæ*—ring obsolete.

1. **Agaricus (Amanita) vaginatus.** *Bull.* "Sleek Amanita."

Pileus thin, campanulate, then nearly plane, margin membranaceous, deeply sulcate; stem fistulose, attenuated, fragile, flocculoso-squamose; volva sheathing, loose; gills free, white, then pallid.—*Berk. Outl. t.* iii, *fig.* 4. *Eng. Fl.* v, *p.* 2. *Huss.* ii. *t.* 34. *Bull. t.* 98, 512. *Vitt. Mang. t.* 16. *Lenz. f.* 2. *Kromb. t.* 1, *f.* 1-5, *t.* 10, *f.* 6-9, *t.* 30, *f.* 13-14. *Fl. Dan. t.* 1014, 2142, *f.* 2. *Gard. Chron.* (1861), *p.* 97. *Gonn. & Rabh.* i. *t.* 7, *f.* 1. *Barla. t.* 5. *Vent. t.* 5.

Var. albida. *A. nivalis, Grev. t.* 18. *Eng. Fl.* v. *p.* 3. *Paul. t.* 151, *f.* 1-2.

In woods and under trees. Common. [United States.]

Variable in size and colour. Pileus 4 in. or more, viscid when moist, shining when dry, at first there are a few broad scales, but these soon vanish; the cuticle easily peels off. Stem 6 in. or more high, ½-1 in. thick, attenuated upwards, obtuse at the base, where it is furnished with a volva, which is adnate for about an inch, and then, in general, closely surrounding it like a sheath, but sometimes the margin is expanded. The volva is easily overlooked if care be not taken to dig up the very base of the stem. Gills free, ventricose, broadest in front, often imbricated, white. Smell scarcely any.—*Eng. Fl.* Spores spherical ·00032 × ·00038 in.—*W. G. S.*

2. Agaricus (Amanita) Ceciliæ. *B. & Br.* "Grey ringless Amanita."

Pileus at first ovate, then campanulate, clothed with scattered subpersistent warts; margin grooved; stem stuffed, silky above, squamulose below: volva soon breaking up.—*B. & Br. Ann. N.H. no.* 663. *Berk. Outl. t.* 3, *f.* 5. *Fr. Icon. t.* 11? *Price f.* 112.

In woods. Aug. Sept. Common in Epping Forest.

Colour mouse-grey. Distinguished by its less perfect volva and stuffed stem, which does not simply contain a few cottony fibres, as that of *A. vaginatus.* Pileus at first semi-elliptic, densely and uniformly clothed with the thick mouse-coloured volva, which at length splits irregularly below from a slight prominence at the base of the stem, but by no means vaginate; then campanulate, obtuse, 3-4 in. across, margin sulcate, dingy yellow, either quite smooth, or more or less clothed with the depressed or even acutely warty remains of the volva. Stem 4 in. or more high, ¾ in. thick, attenuated upwards, above silky, transversely or obliquely rimose, below squamulose from fragments of the volva, spongy within, with occasional cavities, not truly bulbous; ring none gills thick, sometimes forked or anastomosing, the shorter ones abruptly truncate behind, quite free, at length remote, interstices venous. Smell none. Taste sweet.—*M. J. B.* Spores oval ·00034 × ·0006in.—*W. G. S.*

3. Agaricus (Amanita) adnatus. *Smith.* "Adnate gilled Amanita."

Pileus fleshy, firm, smooth, rather moist, convex, then expanded, buff beneath the cuticle; margin extending beyond the gills; stem stuffed, at length hollow, pale buff, rough, fibrillose; ring none; volva lax, adnate, or almost obsolete, white, pubescent, remaining in woolly patches on the pileus; gills white, crowded, truly adnate. *Saund. & Sm. t.* 20.

Woody places, amongst oak and holly. Kingsdon Wood and Alfoxen, Combe, amongst the Quantock Hills, Somerset.—(*J. A. C.*)

Pileus fleshy, very firm, not brittle, smooth, rather moist, pale buff-yellow, 2½-3 in. across, margin exceeding the gills; gills white, crowded, truly adnate; stem stuffed, at length hollow, pale buff, rough, and fibrillose, 2-4 in. high; ring absent; volva lax, adnate, or almost obsolete, white and pubescent, remaining in woolly masses on the pileus; flesh firm, almost rigid, as in *Russula,* white, stained sienna-buff under the cuticle of the pileus; spores slightly oval, ·0001 × ·0003 in.—*W. G. S.*

Sect. 2. *Phalloideæ*—volva free and lax.

4. **Agaricus (Amanita) vernus.** *Bull.* "Spring Amanita."

Pileus at first ovate, then expanded, rather depressed, viscid, white ; margin naked, smooth ; stem stuffed, equal, floccose, base bulbous ; volva closely embracing the stem with its free margin ; ring reflexed ; gills free.—*Bull. t.* 108. *Vitt. Mang. t.* 44. *Paul. t.* 156, *f.* 3-4. *Smith P. M. f.* 8. *Price f.* 3. *Gard. Chron.* (1861), *p.* 480, *fig.*

In woods. Early summer. Poisonous.

Altogether white. Distinguished from white forms of *A. phalloides* by its closer sheathing volva, and more ovate pileus when young, and from the white forms of *A. vaginatus* by the presence of a ring.

5. **Agaricus (Amanita) phalloides.** Fr. "Stinking Amanita."

Pileus campanulate, then expanded, obtuse, viscid; margin even, regular; stem hollow above, attenuated ; volva bulbous, free above, loose ; ring membranaceous ; gills rounded, ventricose.—*Sys. Myc.* i. *p.* 13. *Epicr. p.* 4. *Vaill. t.* 14, *f.* 5. *Paul. t.* 155, 156, *f.* 1-2. *Berk. Outl. pl.* 3, *f.* 1. (*right figure.*) *Smith. P. M. f.* 7. *Eng. Fl.* v. *p.* 1. *Kromb. t.* 28, *f.* 1-10. *Corda Sturm t.* 55. *Price f.* 28. *Barla, t.* 4. *Gonn. & Rabh.* i. *t.* 10, *f.* 1. *Vent. t.* 40. *A. bulbosus, Bull. t.* 2. *A. vernalis, Bolt. t.* 48. *A. verrucosus, Fl. Lond. t.* 312 ; *f.* 4-5.

Woods, and their borders. Aug.—Nov. Common. [Pennsylvania.]

Pileus 2-3 in. broad, irregularly scaly from the fragments of the volva adhering to the surface, variously coloured, white, straw-coloured, brownish, greenish, &c. Stem 3-4 in. high, ½ in. thick, fibrillose, attenuated upwards, bulbous below. Volva adnate at the base, with the margin free, more or less expanded. Odour powerful, and fœtid, especially as it decays. Considered poisonous. Spores spherical ·0003 in.—*W. G. S.*

6. **Agaricus (Amanita) mappa.** *Batsch.* "Delicate Amanita."

Pileus convex, then plane, without separable cuticle, margin nearly even ; flesh white ; stem stuffed, then hollow, cylindrical, nearly smooth, bulbous, nearly globose at the base ; volva with its free margin acute and narrow ; ring membranaceous ; gills adnexed.—*Fr. Epicr. p.* 6. *Gonn. & Rabh.* i. *t.* 11, *f.* 1. *Paul. t.* 158, *f.* 1-2. *Vitt. Mang. t.* 11. *Kromb. t.* 1, *f.* 6, *t.* 28, *f.* 11-12. *Ann. N.H. no.* 138. *Price f.* 66. *Vent.* 40, *f.* 1-2. *A. bulbosus, Bull. t.* 577, *F.D.G.H.M.* *A. venenosa, Pers. Com. t.* 2. *Schæff. t.* 241. *Sow. t.* 286 (*left figure.*) *Curtis t.* 312 (*right figure.*)

Under trees. Not common. Poisonous.

Colour variable. Habit like that of a small *A. phalloides*, from which it is distinguished by its less developed volva, which, instead of being cup-shaped, is little more than a mere rim fringing the bulb.—*M. J. B.*

Sect. 3. *Muscariæ*—volva cut round, lower part connate with the stem.

7. **Agaricus (Amanita) muscarius.** L. "Fly Amanita."

Pileus convex, then expanded, clothed with scattered warts, the remains of the volva, margin striate, flesh beneath the viscid cuticle yellowish ; stem stuffed, bulbous at the base ; volva adnate, concentric, scaly ; ring lax, deflexed ; gills reaching the stem and forming decurrent lines upon it.—*Grev. t.* 54. *Eng. Fl.* v. *p.* 4. *Huss.* i. *t.* 1. *Gard. Chron.* (1860), *p.* 169. *Kromb, t.* 9, *f.* 1-19. *Corda Sturm t.* 54. *Price f.* 56. *Barla. t.* 2. *Vent. t.* 1, *f.* 3-4. *Sow. t.* 286 (*right fig.*) *Smith, P.M. f.* 13. *Cooke, B. F. t.* 1. *Gonn. & Rabh.* i. *t.* 6.

Woods, especially fir and birch. Aug.—Nov. Poisonous. [Pennsylvania.]

Pileus 3-7 in. broad, orange, scarlet, sometimes brownish, beset with superficial conical warts, viscid when moist, margin thin and striate. Gills white, broad, ventricose, free or slightly adnexed. Stem 4-9 in. high, ½-1 in. thick, stuffed with cottony fibres, sometimes hollow. Bulb covered with close conical scales, the remains of the volva. Highly narcotic, producing intoxication, delirium, and death. Spores ·00032 × ·00025 in.—*W. G. S.* (*Pl. II., fig.* 1.)

8. **Agaricus (Amanita) excelsus.** Fr. "Tall Amanita."

Pileus convex, then plane, at first innato-fibrillose, clothed with irregular, mealy, evanescent warts ; margin nearly even ; flesh white ; stem stuffed, cylindrical, scaly below, bulbous, immarginate ; volva evanescent ; gills ventricose, free, rounded behind. —*Fr. Epicr. p.* 8. *Berk. Outl. pl.* 3, *f.* 3. *Eng. Fl.* v. *p.* 5. *Kromb. t.* 29, *f.* 14-17. *Paul. t.* 159. *Gonn. & Rabh.* i. *t.* 8, *f.* 1.

In woods. Quality doubtful. [Carolina, U.S.]

Colour brownish. Margin sometimes sulcate. Pileus 4 in. broad, slightly viscid, smooth, with a few more or less conical irregular scattered warts, easily rubbed off ; cuticle tough and clammy, easily peeling off ; gills obtuse before and behind, but broader in front, truly free, half an inch broad, the margin slightly uneven. Stem 6 in. or more high, 1 in. thick, going deep into the earth, scaly below the ring, scales thick and squarrose, above the ring the scales are closely adpressed, their interstices finely silky, apex striate, tolerably firm, juicy, white ; ring half way down, large, substriate within, externally downy. Taste pleasant.—*M. J. B.* Spores ·0003 × ·00022 in.—*W. G. S.*

9. Agaricus (Amanita) pantherinus. D.C. "Spotted Amanita."

Pileus convex, then expanded, margin striate, flesh under the viscid pellicle white; stem stuffed, then hollow, nearly smooth; volva at the base ocreate, with the margin entire, obtuse, and free; gills attenuated, free.—*Fr. Epicr. p.* 5. *Eng. Fl.* v. *p.* 4. *Fl. Dan. t.* 1911, *f.* 2. *Vitt. Mang. t.* 39. *Vent. t.* 3. *Kromb. t.* 29, *f.* 10-13. *Paul. t.* 160, *f.* 2. *Schæff. t.* 90. *Barla. t.* 7, *f.* 1-3. *Roques. t.* 21, *f.* 2-3. *Gonn. & Rabh.* i. *t.* 1.

In woods or pastures near trees. [Pennsylvania.]

Brownish, not red or reddish brown, as in *A. muscarius*. Pileus, 4 in. broad, with flat, mealy warts, which rub off with difficulty, glutinous when moist; when dry, soft to the touch like kid leather. Stem 5 in. high, half an inch thick, stuffed, then more or less hollow, silky, and even, or torn into reflexed scales; ring deflexed; volva quite smooth, connate, the extreme margin only free all round.—*M. J. B.* Not poisonous. Spores, ·0003 × ·00019 in.—*W. G. S.*

10. Agaricus (Amanita) strobiliformis. Fr. "Fir-cone Amanita."

Pileus convex, then expanded, with persistent warts; margin even: flesh compact, white: stem solid, floccoso-squamose, bulbous, base subterraneous; volva with the margin acute, concentric; ring torn; gills rounded behind, and free.—*Epicr. p.* 5. *Vitt. Mang. t.* 9. *Vent. t.* 4. *Paul. t.* 162. *Bull. t.* 593. *Berk. Outl. t.* 3, *f.* 2. *Smith E. M. f.* 10. *Gonn. & Rabh.* i. *t.* 7, *f.* 3. *Ann. N.H. no.* 662.

Borders of woods. Rare. Esculent.

Pileus when young subglobose, bulb of the stem conical below, rooting, its border sometimes incised all round, sometimes even, floccose above to the edge of the pileus; scales of pileus large, wart-like, with a brown disc, and white floccose border, persistent, angular. Pileus, when expanded, 8-9 in. across, at length quite smooth, margin extending beyond the gills, white, cinereous, &c. Stem 6-7 in. high, 1½ in. thick, firm, solid, bulb not properly scaly, veil large; gills rounded behind, the shorter ones denticulate at the base. Odour and taste pleasant.—*M. J. B.*—"It attains a very large size in well-grown specimens. The persistent patches on the top are not unlike the scales of a fir-cone, hence its specific name; the gills do not reach the stem. Average size of spores, ·00054 × ·00035 in."—*W. G. S.*

Sect. 4. *Validæ*—volva thin and friable.

11. Agaricus (Amanita) rubescens. *P.* "Reddish Amanita."

Pileus convex, then expanded; warts unequal, mealy, scattered; flesh becoming reddish; stem stuffed, attenuated upwards, squamulose; ring entire; gills attenuated, reaching the stem and forming decurrent lines upon it ; volva obliterated.—*Fr. Epicr. p.* 7. *Eng. Fl.* v. *p.* 5. *Vent. t.* 26, *f.* 1-3. *Kromb. t.* 10, *f.* 1-5. *Letell. t.* 677. *Trans. Woolh. C.* (1868). *Gonn. & Rabh.* i. *t.* 5. *Price, f.* 75. *Huss.* i. *t.* 23. *Vitt. Mang., t.* 41. *Schæff. t.* 91-261. *Paul. t.* 161. *Curt. Fl. L. t.* 312, *partly. Hogg & Johnst. t.* 1. *Smith, E. M. f.* 1. *Badh.* i. *t.* 12, *f.* 1, ii. *t.* 11, *f.* 3-5.

In woods. Common. Esculent. [United States.]

Margin of pileus in some instances with the appearance of striæ ; flesh turning reddish when cut or bruised ; gills broad in front, narrowed behind ; stem above the ring clothed with flat adpressed scales, below the ring the scales have their upper margin free and patent. Smell strong, taste not unpleasant. Spores ·0003 × ·00023 in.—*W. G. S.*

12. Agaricus (Amanita) spissus. Fr. "Clammy Amanita."

Pileus convex, then plane, rough with minute, adnate, mealy warts ; margin smooth ; flesh firm, white, unchangeable ; stem stuffed, firm, attenuated upwards, squamulose ; ring entire ; gills adnexed, with decurrent lines on the stem.—*Fr. Epicr. p.* 9. *Curr. Linn. Trans.* xxiv., *p.* 151. *Kromb. t.* 1, *f.* 7, *t.* 29, *f.* 1-5.

In woods.

Pileus 3 in. broad, umber with a greyish tinge, evidently viscid, smooth, with a few patches of the volva adhering, not in the form of warts, but irregularly ; epidermis tough and clammy, easily peeling off, margin not striate ; gills very broad, more than half in., ventricose and adnexed. Stem 3 in. high, 1 in. being buried in the ground, swollen and bulbous at the surface, narrower above and below. Ring deflexed and striate. Spores white, irregularly pear-shaped or balloon shaped, with a short stalk, colourless, about ·0005 in. long. —*F. Curr.*

13. Agaricus (Amanita) asper. Fr. "Rough Amanita."

Pileus convex, then plane ; warts minute, crowded, nearly persistent ; margin even ; flesh compact, brownish beneath the cuticle ; stem stuffed, then hollow, attenuated ; ring entire, distant ; gills rounded behind, free.—*Fr. Epicr. p.* 9. *Eng. Fl.* v. *p.* 6. *Vitt. Mang. t.* 43. *Bolt. t.* 139. *Bull. t.* 316.

In woods. June.—Oct. [Carolina, U.S.]

In many respects resembling *A. rubescens*. Pileus 2-3 in. broad, scarcely umbonate, reddish, with various tints of livid and grey, clothed with small acute warts ; flesh thick, permanent white, except immediately beneath the epidermis ; gills white, broad in front, with sometimes a little tooth behind running down the stem ; stem 2-3 in. high, sometimes 1½ in. thick at the base, often less, bulb rather rough, striate above the ring, silky below ; ring broad, striate. Odour strong, taste not unpleasant.—*M. J. B.* Spores ·00032 × ·00026 in.—*W. G. S.*

14. Agaricus (Amanita) megalodactylus. *B.* "Strong-scented Amanita."

Strong scented. Pileus soft, convex, smooth, reddish-grey; cuticle entire; margin even; stem somewhat bulbous, solid, fibrillose; ring very large, placed near the top of the stem; gills moderately broad, free, pallid, at length tinged with red.—*Berk. Outl. p.* 91.

In a wood near Stamford.

Pileus 3½ in. across; stem 5 in. high. The volva is almost obsolete, it is allied to *A. lenticularis*, but the solid stem is not squamulose, and the gills do not assume an olive tint.—*M. J. B.*

Sect. 5. *Denudatæ*—veil entirely obsolete.

15. Agaricus (Amanita) lenticularis. *Lasch.* "Smooth Amanita."

Pileus globose, then convexo-plane, soft, smooth, margin even; stem stuffed, bulbous, squamulose; ring broad above; gills free, becoming pallid.—*Lasch. Linn. no.* 18. *Paul. p.* 306, *t.* 149. *B. & Br. Ann. N.H.* (1866), *no.* 1104. *Fr. Icon. t.* 13.

In plantations. Oct. Coed Coch.

Remarkable for the great development of the ring, and the smooth pinkish tan pileus. Stem 4-6 in. long. Pileus 3-4 in. broad. Flesh soft, spongy, white, with a mouldy odour. Gills free, approximate, ventricose, broader behind, very much crowded, white.

Sub-Gen. 2. LEPIOTA. Fr. S.M., i. p. 19.

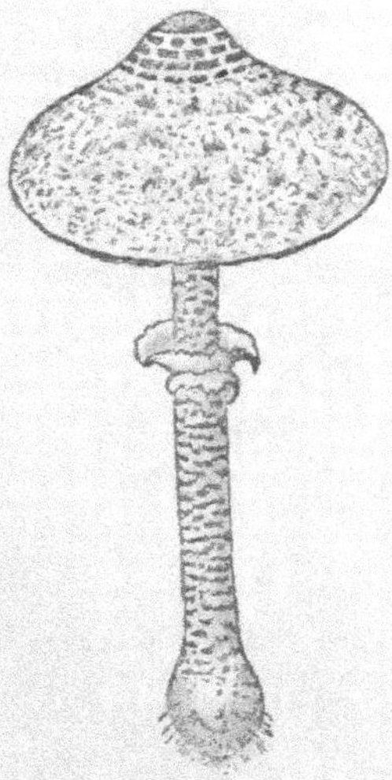

Fig. 35.

Veil universal and concrete, with the cuticle of the pileus breaking up in the form of scales (F); pileus never compact, often very thin, the flesh always soft and thread-like, and not only distinct from the stem, but often separated above into a peculiar cup; stem distinct from the hymenophore, generally hollow, full of threadlike fibres, rather sub-cartilaginous than fleshy, different in texture from the flesh of the pileus, hence it is easily removed, leaving a cup or socket at its point of juncture with the pileus (E), furnished with an annulus, which is at first continuous with the cuticle of the pileus, often moveable, sometimes evanescent; volva none; gills free; hence not sinuate or decurrent.

HAB. On the ground, mostly in rich grassy places, and more often in fields than woods.—(*Pl. II., fig.* 2, *Ag. procerus.*)

Several species as *A. clypeolarius*, Bull, *A. cepæstipes*, Sow., and *A. cristatus*, Fr., appear in hothouses all the year round. Lepiota is readily recognised by its *free gills*, annulated stem *without a volva*, and generally scaly pileus. Usually autumnal and edible.—*W. G. S.*

Sect. 1. *Proceri.*—ring moveable.

16. Agaricus (Lepiota) procerus. *Scop.* "Parasol Mushroom."

Pileus fleshy, soft, at first ovate, then expanded and umbonate; cuticle thick, torn up into broad scales; stem hollow, tall, bulbous, variegated with adpressed scales; ring moveable; gills very remote.—*Fr. Epicr. p.* 12. *Eng. Fl.* v. *p.* 7. *Trans. Woolh. C.*, 1867. *Badh. t.* 2. *Barla. t.* 8. *Schæff. t.* 22-23. *Fl. Dan. t.* 772. *Curt. Fl. L. t.* 69. *Vitt. Mang. t.* 24. *Price f.* 74. *Lenz. f.* 5-6. *Vent. t.* 6. *Paul. t.* 135. *Hogg & Johnst. t.* 8. *Cooke, B. F. t.* 2. *Huss.* i. *t.* 88. *Smith E. M. f.* 14. *Kromb. t.* 24, *f.* 1-12.

Pastures. Common. Esculent. [Pennsylvania.]

Pileus 3-7 in. broad, at first obtusely conic, at length campanulate, strongly umbonate, fleshy, cuticle velvety, red brown, broken into sub-reflexed scales, the whole resembling brown shaggy leather, margin white, or pinkish, silky, flesh soft, and cottony, except in the centre, when young. Gills perfectly free, separated by a considerable space from the stem, ventricose, margin serrated, pale, pinkish yellow, or white. Stem, 8-12 in. high, ½ in. thick, attenuated upwards, sunk deep into the flesh of the pileus, bulbous, scaly, hollow, but stuffed with a cottony web. Ring coriaceous, thick and spongy, convex below, moveable. Taste and smell pleasant.—*M. J. B.* Spores ·0006 × ·0003 in.—*W. G. S.* (Pl. ii., fig. 2 and fig. 35.)

17. Agaricus (Lepiota) rachodes. *Vitt.* "Large grey Lepiota."

Pileus fleshy, soft, at first globose, then expanded and depressed; cuticle thin, broken into persistent scales, stem hollow, attenuated, smooth, immaculate, bulb at first abrupt; ring lacerated, moveable; gills remote.—*Fr. Epicr. p.* 13. *Berk. Outl. pl.* 3, *f.* 6. *Price, f.* 104. *Huss.* ii. *t.* 58. *Vitt. Mang. t.* 20. *Ann. N.H. no.* 257. *Gard. Chron.*, 1861, *p.* 599. *Kromb. t.* 24, *f.* 15-16.

In shady pastures. Not common. Esculent. [Carolina, U.S.]

Flesh mostly red when bruised. Closely allied to *A. procerus*, from which it is distinguishable by the pileus being more globose when young, by the generally distinctly marginate bulb, and the stem being free, or nearly free, from the spots which give *A. procerus* a snake-like appearance.—*Gard. Chron.* Spores ·00018 × ·00025 in.—*W. G. S.*

18. Agaricus (Lepiota) excoriatus. *Schæff.* "Flaky Lepiota."

Pileus fleshy, soft, obscurely umbonate; cuticle thin, breaking up into scales; stem hollow, short, cylindrical, scarcely bulbous, smooth, white; ring moveable; gills rather remote.—*Schæff. t.* 18-19. *Eng. Fl.* v. *p.* 7. *Vitt. Mang. t.* 35. *Krombh. t.* 1, *f.* 9, *t.* 24, *f.* 24-30, *Vent. t.* 7. *Paul. t.* 135 *bis.* *Letell. t.* 609, *f. A. B.*

In pastures. May—Sept. Esculent.

Pileus $2\frac{1}{2}$ in. across, expanded, often a little irregular, carnose, umbonate, flesh spongy, cuticle cracked into small areolæ, silky between them, especially on the margin, pale fawn, the umbo dark, gills ventricose, free, so as to leave a broad space round the top of the stem, which is sunk into the substance of the pileus, dull white, slightly watery, unbricate when old, sometimes broader on one side of the pileus than the other, and sometimes stained with claret colored blotches. Stem $1\frac{1}{2}$-2 in. high. $\frac{1}{4}$-$\frac{1}{3}$ in. thick, attenuated regularly upwards, without a decided bulb, minutely fibrillose, hollow, but stuffed with a cottony web. Ring deflexed, moveable. Smell scarcely any.—*M. J. B.* Spores ·0005 × ·00035 in.—*W. G. S.*

19. Agaricus (Lepiota) gracilentus. *Krombh.* "Slender Lepiota."

Pileus rather fleshy, campanulate, then expanded, obtusely umbonate; cuticle thin, breaking up into adpressed persistent patches; stem hollow, elongated, slightly bulbous; ring thin, free, evanescent; gills remote, broad, pallid.—*Kromb. t.* 24, *f.* 13-14. *Berk. Out. p.* 93.

In pastures. Esculent.

Resembling *A. procerus* but more delicate. Stem 5-6 in. long, 4-5 lin. thick, obsoletely scaly. Pileus at first ovate, then campanulate, and at length flattened, spotted with brownish scales. Spores ·00043 × ·0003 in.—*W. G. S.*

20. Agaricus (Lepiota) mastoideus. *Fr.* "Bossed Lepiota."

Pileus rather fleshy, soft, ovate, then expanded, and acutely umbonate; cuticle thin, breaking up into scattered papillæ; stem hollow, equally attenuated from the bulb, weak, smooth; ring entire, moveable; gills very remote, pallid.—*Epicr. p.* 14. *Fl. Dan. t.* 2144. *Berk. Mag. Zool. & Bot.* i. *t.* 2, *f.* 1. *Kromb. t.* 24, *f.* 17-18. *Batt. t.* 10, *f. A.* *Letell. t.* 609, *f. D.E.*

In woods. Oct. King's Cliffe. [Cincinnati.]

Pileus $1\frac{3}{4}$ in. across, $\frac{3}{4}$ in. high, very strongly umbonate, with a depression round the umbo, sub-carnose, epidermis breaking up into small umber papillæ, which are larger and more scattered towards the margin; gills remote, rather narrow, yellowish; stem $3\frac{1}{2}$ in. high. slender, strongly attenuated upwards, incrassated at the base, sunk into the substance of the pileus, minutely villoso-squamose, filled within with cottony fibres. Ring deflexed, scarcely moveable.—*M. J. B.*

Sect. 2. *Clypeolarii.*—pileus shield-like.

21. Agaricus (Lepiota) acutesquamosus. *Wm.* "Squarrose Lepiota."

Pileus fleshy, obtuse, at first floccose, then bristly with erect, acute, squarrose scales ; stem somewhat stuffed, bulbous, below the ring rough or silky, pruinose above ; gills approximate, lanceolate, simple.—*Huss.* ii. *t.* 5. *Kromb. t.* i. *f.* 18-20, *t.* 29 *f.* 18-21. *A. Mariæ. Klotsch. Linnæa* vii. *t.* 8. *Berk. Eng. Fl.* v. *p.* 4. *Ann. N.H. no.* 139.

On soil in gardens, and in greenhouses. [Cincinnati.]

Generally tawny. Pileus 2-3 in. broad, with dark coloured scales. Stem tawny, pruinose 2-3 in. long or more, 4 lines to ½ in. thick. Ring white. Substance fleshy, tough, elastic, white. Spores ·0001 × ·00023 in.—*W.G.S.*

[AGARICUS (LEPIOTA) FRIESII. *Lasch.* recorded by B. & Br. Ann. N.H. (1866) No. 1105 was entered in error.]

22. Agaricus (Lepiota) hispidus. *Lasch.* "Hispid Lepiota."

Pileus fleshy, thin, umbonate, at first tomentose, then breaking up into squamose papillæ. Stem fibrillose, stuffed, thin, attenuated, above the ring floccoso-squamose ; gills approximate, ventricose, simple.—*Linnæa* 1829, *no.* 407. *Ann. N.H. no.* 901. *Fr. Icon. t.* 14, *f.* 1.

In shady woods, amongst pine leaves. Aug.

Stem about 3 in. long, 3-5 lines thick. Pileus 2-3 in. broad, umber. Smell like that of *Lactarius theiogalus.*

23. Agaricus (Lepiota) Badhami. *B. & Br.* "Saffron Lepiota."

Pileus at first campanulate, obtuse, then expanded, or depressed and umbonate, hispid with minute, velvety, ermine-like scales; stem bulbous, white, silky, stuffed with cottony threads ; ring firm, slightly moveable ; gills remote, ventricose ; whole plant when wounded of a saffron-red. *Ann. N.H. no.* 664. *Berk. Out. p.* 93.

Under yew trees. Sept. Apethorpe. Norths.

Pileus 2-4 in. across, at first campanulate, obtuse, at length expanded, often depressed and umbonate, hispid, with minute, velvety, fuliginous scales, but sometimes entirely fuliginous, without any distinct scales; stem 2-3 in. high, ¼-½ in. thick, attenuated above, bulbous below, white, silky, or floccoso-squamose, stuffed with cottony threads ; ring firm, erect, and deflexed, more or less moveable, beneath, frequently clothed with dingy granules ; gills truly remote, ventricose, rather broad. Spores elliptic, ·0003 in. long, flesh tolerably compact. The whole plant when wounded assumes a rich red tint. Smell rather disagreeable.—*M. J. B.*

24. Agaricus (Lepiota) meleagris. *Sow.* "Sowerby's Lepiota."

Pileus fleshy, thin, convex, then plane; cuticle broken up into black scales; flesh turning red; stem solid, squamulose, thickened downwards, and black; root reticulated; gills nearly free.—*Sow. t.* 171. *Berk. Outl. p.* 101, *no.* 50 (sub. *Tricholoma*) *B. & Br. Ann. N.H.* 1865. *Eng. Fl.* v. *p.* 9.

On hot-beds. May—Oct.

"It has a solid stem, and a curious, somewhat reticulated root, in drying it becomes of a blush-red all over, except the lower part, which retains the darker hue."—*Sow.* Stem about 3 in. long, ¼ in. thick, nearly equal, pileus 1½ in. broad. Stem stouter in proportion than in *A. clypeolarius.*

25. Agaricus (Lepiota) clypeolarius. *Bull.* "Fragrant Lepiota."

Pileus fleshy, soft, umbonate, at first with an even crust, at length broken into floccose adpressed scales; stem fistulose, thin, almost equal; ring evanescent, floccoso-squamose; gills free, approximate.—*Bull. t.* 405. 506, *f.* 2. *Tratt. Aust. t.* 26. *Paul. t.* 136. *Eng. Fl.* v. *p.* 8. *Fr. Icon. t.* 14, *f.* 2. *Berk. Out. p.* 94. *Vent. t.* 44, *f.* 3-4.

In woods and hot-houses. [United States.]

Sweet scented. Variable in colour, white, yellow, pink, rufous, brown, &c. Pileus 1½ in. broad, sub-campanulate, strongly umbonate, whitish, with reddish scales; gills numerous, quite free, nearly reaching the stem, ventricose; stem 2-3½ in. high, 2 lines thick, hollow, but stuffed with cottony fibres, whitish, pale brownish, or rufescent. the whole clothed with fibrillose scales. Ring sometimes remaining on the stem, but generally attached to the margin of the pileus, or evanescent. Inodorous and insipid.—*M. J. B.*

26. Agaricus (Lepiota) cristatus. *Fr.* "Stinking Lepiota."

Pileus slightly fleshy, rather obtuse, cuticle at first continuous, naked, then broken into sub-granulose scales. Stem fistulose, slender, even, equal; ring entire, evanescent; gills free, at length remote.—*Fr. Epicr. p.* 15. *Batsch. f.* 205. *Price f.* 105. *Grev. t.* 176. *Krombh. t.* 25, *f.* 26-30. *Berk. Outl. pl.* 3 *f.* 7. *Eng. Fl.* v. *p.* 9. *Huss.* i. *t.* 48. *Berk. Exs. no.* 1.

In fields, lawns, &c. Common. [United States.]

Pretty, and remarkable for its strong scent. Solitary or subgregarious. Pileus ½-1½ in. broad, expanded, umbonate, white, the cuticle broken into rufescent scales, which are either flat or reflexed, less frequent on the margin, ring sometimes attached in fragments to the margin, sometimes moveable on the stem, flesh firm, thin; gills remote, numerous, slightly ventricose, the margin uneven, often imbricated, tinged slightly with yellow. Stem 1-2 in. high, 1-2 lines thick, tough, composed of fibres, smooth or fibrillose, hollow but with a few cottony fibres, flesh towards the base reddish, with a rooting mass of branched fibres. Spores white, elliptic. Smell and taste strong and unpleasant.—*M. J. B.*

Sect. 3. *Annulosi*—ring fixed.

27. **Agaricus (Lepiota) vittadini.** *Moretti.* "Great white Lepiota."

Pileus fleshy, obtuse, rough with strong wart-like scales ; stem solid, cylindrical, stout, concentrically squarrose ; ring large ; gills free, ventricose, thick.—*Moret. Bot. Ital. t.* 1. *Vitt. Am. t.* 1. *Krombh. t.* 276, *f.* 1-14. *Huss.* i. *t.* 85.

In pastures. Rare. Norfolk, Northamptonshire, Hunts, &c.

A large species of a pure white ; extremely beautiful. Considered poisonous.

28. **Agaricus (Lepiota) holosericeus.** *Fr.* "Silky Lepiota."

Pileus fleshy, obtuse, soft, silky fibrillose, becoming even : stem solid, bulbous, sericeo-fibrillose, ring superior, persistent, broad, reflexed; gills free, ventricose, white, growing pallid.—*Fr. Epicr. p.* 16. *Smith Seem. Journ.* 1868.

In moist woods. Staplehurst, Kent. Esculent.

Large, inodorous. Pileus fleshy, soft, smooth, convex, then expanded, disc never umbonate, of a floccose silky texture, fragile, entirely uniform in colour, 3 in. or more broad, gills free, broad, ventricose, crowded, pallid ; stem solid $2\frac{1}{2}$-4 in. high, $\frac{1}{2}$ in. or more thick, bulbous at the base, soft, fragile, silky fibrous ; ring superior, membranaceous, broad, soft, pendulous and reflexed. Spores ·0003 × ·0002 in.—*W. G. S.*

29. **Agaricus (Lepiota) naucinus.** *Fr.* "Large spored Lepiota."

Pileus fleshy, soft, cuticle thin, entire, or breaking up into granules, somewhat umbonate and smooth in the centre ; stem almost hollow, thickened at the base, attenuated upwards, fibrillose ; ring large, at length evanescent ; gills approximate, whitish.—*Fr. Epicr. p.* 16. *Krombh. t.* 24, *f.* 20-23. *Paul. t.* 150, *f.* 1-2. *Batt. t.* 7-9. *Vent. t.* 48, *f.* 5-6.

In fields.

Delicate tan color, the gills at length assuming a dirty pink hue. The large white spores are very characteristic. Easily confounded with *A. cretaceus.*

30. **Agaricus (Lepiota) cepœstipes.** *Sow.* "Onion stemmed Lepiota."

Pileus sub-membranaceous, ovate, then expanded, mealy and scaly, disc fleshy and broadly umbonate ; margin plicate ; stem hollow, floccose, thickest in the middle, or at the base ; ring evanescent ; gills at length remote.—*Sow. t.* 2. *Grev. t.* 333. *Sturm. t.* 1. *Fl. Dan. t.* 1798. *Eng. Fl.* v. *p.* 7. *Gard. Chron.*, 1860, *p.* 47.

On tan and eaves in hot-houses.

White or yellow, stem variable. Gregarious or tufted. Pileus 1-3 in. broad, ovate conical when young, then campanulate, and finally nearly or quite plane, darkest in the centre, and more or less covered with small scattered fibrous scales, flesh thin, margin very thin, and semitransparent, plicate, substance tough. Gills numerous, thin, broad, rounded near the stem, and separated from it by a circular space, but the stem is not penetrating. Stem 3-6 in. high, straight or crooked, firm, even, smooth, narrow at the top, ventricose, then narrower at the bottom, somewhat pruinose, the centre at first stuffed, then hollow. Ring perfect, erect, persistent. In decay the pileus becomes brownish.—*Grev.* Spores ·0003 × ·00015 in.—*W. G. S.*

Sect 4. *Mesomorphi*—intermediate forms.

31. **Agaricus (Lepiota) granulosus.** Batsch. "Granular Lepiota."

Pileus fleshy, convex, then expanded, soft, mealy with innate granules, stem stuffed, then hollow, nearly equal, flocoso-squamose below the ring: gills crowded, reaching the stem, or free, white. —*Fr. Epicr. p.* 17. *Eng. Fl.* v. *p.* 10. *Sow. t.* 19. *Bull. t.* 362, 530, *f.* 3, *t.* 104. *Huss.* i. *t.* 45. *Batsch. f.* 24-97. *Fl. Dan. t.* 1677, *f.* 1, *t.* 1795. *Bolt. t.* 51. *f.* 2.

In woods and on heaths. [United States.]

White, pink, vermilion, yellow, &c. Always easily distinguished by its mealy granular aspect. Subgregarious. Pileus ½-1 in. broad, usually dull reddish yellow. Fleshy in the centre, at first convex, or obtusely umbonate, at length often plane or depressed, somewhat wrinkled, covered with furfuraceous scales. Gills white, or yellowish white, fixed to the stem, ventricose and sometimes nearly free. Stem 1-3 in. high, 1-4 lines thick, slightly incrassated at the base, solid when young, becoming hollow with age, stuffed at the base, sometimes slightly compressed, with a subfugacious flocculose ring about the middle, above which it is slightly fibrillose, beneath it scaly like the pileus.—*M. J. B.* Spores ·00012 × ·00015 in.—*W. G. S.*

It is the variety *Amianthinus*, which is found in this country.

32. **Agaricus (Lepiota) polystictus.** *Berk.* "Little brown Lepiota."

Inodorous, fleshy; cuticle continuous, or broken into scales; stem attenuated downwards, stuffed with cottony threads, scaly below the fugacious ring, silky above; gills crowded, rounded before and behind, free, white, with a pale-yellow tinge.—*Eng. Fl.* v. *p.* 9. *Berk. Out. p.* 95.

Amongst short grass by roadsides.

Pileus 1½ in. across, not at all campanulate, expanded, and broadly, obtusely umbonate, flesh thick in the centre, firm and tough, the cuticle broken into minute flat scales of a rich red brown. Gills numerous, unequal, rounded before and behind, broad, ventricose, quite free, the margin serrulate, white, with a slight yellowish tinge. Stem 1 in. high, ⅜ in. thick in the middle, divided into two distinct portions, the upper silky, of a pinkish hue, the lower scaly, like the pileus, but the scales browner, attenuated at the base, hollow, stuffed with fine silky filaments, with many branched fibrous roots. Ring fugacious, attached in minute portions to the edge of the pileus. Inodorous and insipid.—*M. J. B.* Spores ·0001 × ·00012 in.—*W. G. S.*

Sect. 5. *Illiniti.*—pileus viscid.

33. Agaricus (Lepiota) gliodermus. *Fr.* "Viscid Lepiota."

Pileus thin, soft, campanulate, convex, smooth, even, rufous, viscid; stem whitish, floccoso-squamose, stuffed with cottony threads; ring torn; gills free, white, approximate.—*Fr. Hym. Mon. p.* 31. *B. & Br. Ann. N.H. no.* 785.

In woods. Aug. Wothorp, near Stamford.

Pileus $1\frac{1}{2}$ in. across. Stem about 3 in. long, 2-3 lines thick, equal, dry, as far as the incomplete torn ring floccoso-squamulose, above the ring naked, whitish, or rufescent. Gills broad, crowded, white.

Sub-Gen. 3. Armillaria. Fr. S. M., i. p. 26.

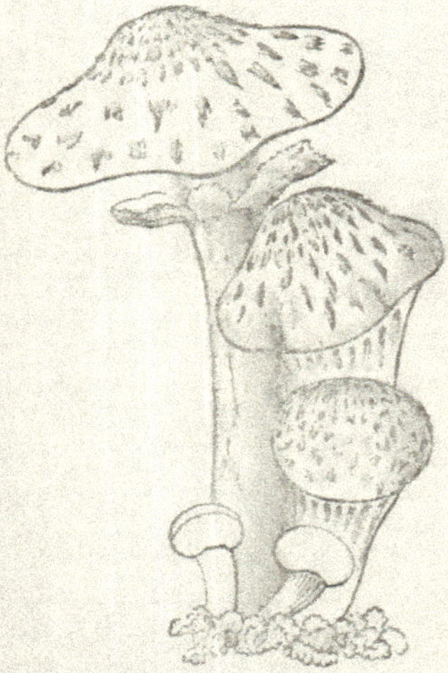

Fig. 36.

Veil partial, in infancy attaching the edge of pileus to the upper part of stem, and often forming flocci on the pileus (G); pileus generally fleshy; stem homogeneous and confluent with the hymenophore, furnished with a ring (sometimes absent in abnormal specimens), below the ring the veil is concrete with the stem, often forming scales upon it, similar to the scurfy scales on the pileus; gills broadly touching, or running down the stem.

Hab. On the ground, or on stumps of trees.—(*Pl. II., fig.* 3, *Ag. melleus.*)

This subgenus corresponds with *Pholiota* and *Stropharia*; it is also allied to *Tricholoma*, *Clitocybe*, and *Collybia*, amongst the white-spored Agarics. Fries subdivides *Armillaria* into groups, depending on their relations to one or other of these subgenera.—*W. G. S.*

Sect. 1. *Tricholomoideæ.*

34. Agaricus (Armillaria) constrictus. *Fr.* "White Armillaria."

Pileus fleshy, convex, then plane, obtuse, even, dry, with an evanescent silky lustre; stem solid, nearly equal; ring superior, evanescent; gills emarginate, crowded, white.—*Fr. Epicr. p.* 22. *Batt. t.* 7, *f.* 4. *Eng. Fl.* v. *pt.* 2, *p.* 11. *Fr. Icon. t.* 18, *f.* 1.

In pastures, where the ground is bleached with urine. Rare. Northamptonshire.

Pure white, odour very strong, like that of fresh meal. Pileus obtuse, plano-convex, broadly umbonate, fleshy, shining with a silky lustre, assuming a very pale yellow tint when bruised; gills close, very deeply emarginate, even when quite young; stem 2 in. high, ¼ in. thick, rather flexuous, fibrillose, solid, more lax and fibrillose within, very brittle; when young, with a delicate web-like curtain, which soon vanishes; spores white, subelliptic.—*M. J. B.*

35. Agaricus (Armillaria) ramentaceus. *Bull.* "Dingy Armillaria."

Pileus fleshy, convexo-plane, obtuse, villoso-squamose, dry; stem solid, unequal, scaly; ring inferior, of interwoven flocci; gills emarginate, crowded, whitish, then discoloured.—*Bull. t.* 595. *f.* 3. —*Berk. Out. p.* 96.

On the ground. Not common.

Whitish or yellowish, scales brown, odour unpleasant.

Sect. 2. *Clitocyboideæ.*

36. Agaricus (Armillaria) melleus. *Vahl.* "Honey-Coloured Armillaria."

Pileus fleshy, at length plane, clothed with fibrous scales; margin striate; stem spongy, stuffed, elastic, fibrillose; ring floccose, patent; gills adnate, ending in a decurrent tooth, somewhat distant, pallid, then mealy with the profuse white spores, and spotted with reddish-brown.—*Fr. Epicr. p.* 23. *Berk. Outl. t.* 4, *f.* i. *Cooke, B. F., t.* 3. *Fl. Dan. t.* 1013. *Vitt. Mang. t.* 3. *Vent. t.* 24, *t.* 25, *f.* 1, 2. *Lenz. f.* 7. *Price, f.* 16, 32. *Kromb. t.* i. *f.* 13, *t.* 43, *f.* 2-6. *Gard. Chron.* (1860), *p.* 5. *Badh.* i. *t.* 16, *f.* 3, ii. *t.* 9, *f.* 3. *Sow. t.* 101. *Batt. t.* 11, *F. B. Eng. Fl.* v. *p.* 12. *Gonn. & Rabh. t.* 3. *Barla. t.* 11. *A. laricinus. Bolt. t.* 19?

On dead stumps. Very common. [United States.]

Densely cæspitose, pale rufous, more or less shaded with yellow. Sometimes without a ring. Pileus 2-7 in. across, fleshy, at first convex, then plano-expanded, often sub-umbonate, variously lobed, dirty yellow, brownish yellow, or reddish, rough with reflexed scales, especially towards the centre, which are at first bright wax-yellow, at length dark brown; margin slightly striate, flesh firm; gills distant, adnato-decurrent, at first pale, at length reddish, mealy with the white spores; stem 2-8 in. high, swollen at the base, thinnest in the middle, fibrillose, with a slight yellow pubescence at the base, yellowish or reddish, occasionally somewhat scaly near the apex, firm and elastic, solid; ring large, yellow, tumid, spreading; odour agreeable; esculent, but not commendable.—*M. J. B.* Spores ·00035 × ·00023 in. —*W. G. S.* (Pl. ii., fig. 3 and fig. 36.)

Sect. 3. *Collybioideæ.*

37. Agaricus (Armillaria) mucidus. *Fr.* "Clammy Armillaria."

Pileus thin, soft, convex, then expanded, rugulose, glutinous; stem stuffed, rigid, thickened at the base; ring superior, reflexed, with the margin erect, striate; gills rounded, striato-decurrent, distant, white.—*Fr. Epicr. p.* 24. *Fl. Dan. t.* 773, 1130, 1372. *Gard. Chron.*, 1861, *p.* 576. *Tratt. Austr. t.* 27. *Eng. Fl.* v. *p.* 11. *Saund. & Sm. t.* 5. *Price, f.* 91.

On Beech. [United States.]

Pure white, or with a cinereous tinge; cæspitose. Pileus $1\frac{1}{2}$ in. broad, white, tinged with brown, hemispherical, clammy, uneven, radiato-rugose, tough; margin thin, somewhat turned in; gills broad, distant, rounded behind, but not in front, adnate, margin serrulate; stem $1\frac{1}{2}$–3 in. high, 1–2 lines thick, bulbous, attenuated upwards, often curved, white, brown at the base, with minute adpressed scales, juicy, solid, with a pale line down the centre; ring persistent; margin often brown, and slimy, adhering so closely to the stem by its upper portion as easily to escape notice in an advanced stage of growth.—*M. J. B.* Spores ·00063 × ·00053 in.—*W. G. S.*

[AGARICUS MILLUS, *Sow.* is doubtful. Berkeley refers it to *A. (Tricholoma) terreus*, and Smith, following Fries, in "Middlesex Flora," to *Armillaria.*]

Sub-Gen. 4. TRICHOLOMA. Fr. S. M. i., p. 36.

Veil absent, or if present, floccose, and adhering to the margin of pileus; pileus generally fleshy; stem homogeneous, and confluent with the hymenophore, central, and subfleshy, without either ring or volva, and with no distinct bark-like coat; gills sinuate, *i. e.*, with a sinus (or small sudden curve) near the stem (H).

HAB. All the species grow on the ground, the larger in hilly woods, and the smaller in pastures.—*(Pl. II., f.* 4.)

Most of the species grow in the autumn, some very late, but a group of which *A. gambosus*, Fr. is the type, is strictly *vernal*, and the species constituting it have long been considered special delicacies; the greater number of the remaining species are also edible, and have a pleasant odour like that of new flour, but a few are rank and suspicious, of which *A. saponaceus* is an example.

A. *Limacina*—pileus viscid.

Sect. 1. Gills white, not changing.

38. Agaricus (Tricholoma) equestris. *Linn.* "Fir-wood Tricholoma."

Pileus fleshy, compact, convex, then expanded, obtuse, flexuose, squamulose, viscid; stem solid, obese, sulphur coloured, as well as the free, crowded gills.—*Fr. Epicr. p.* 26. *Schæff. t.* 41. *Buxb.* iv., *t.* 10. *Price, f.* 92. *Berk. Out. t.* 4, *f.* 2. *Ann. N. H. no.* 665. *Krombh. t.* 1, *f.* 16-17. *t.* 68, *f.* 18, 21. *Harz. t.* 22.

Amongst fir leaves. Rare.

Pileus yellow, inclining to reddish, 3-5 in. broad, disc and scales darker. Variable in the length and thickness of the stem. Spores ·00023 × ·00015 in. —*W. G. S.*

39. Agaricus (Tricholoma) sejunctus. *Sow.* "Separating Tricholoma."

Pileus fleshy, convex, then expanded, umbonate, unequal, slightly viscid, streaked with black fibres ; stem solid, stout, ventricose, sub-squamulose ; gills emarginate, broad, rather distant, white. —*Sow. t.* 126. *Fr. Epicr. p.* 26. *Eng. Fl.* v. *p.* 19. *Berk. Out. p.* 97. *Fr. Icon. t.* 23.

In mixed woods. [United States.]

Pileus several in. across ; stem 2-3 in. high. Odour unpleasant, taste bitter, margin of the pileus thin, yellow. " Pileus dirty yellow or nearly white ; gills whitish and thickest near the stem, somewhat flattened, as it were, by separating from it in a peculiar manner, and partly adhering to each other."—*Sow.* Spores nearly spherical ·00025 in.—*W. G. S.*

40. Agaricus (Tricholoma) portentosus. *Fr.* "Dingy Tricholoma."

Pileus fleshy, convex, then expanded, sub-umbonate, unequal, viscid, streaked with black innate lines ; margin thin ; stem solid, stout, equal, striate ; gills emarginate, very broad, white, at length distant and pallid.—*Fr. Epicr. p.* 27. *Ann. N. H. no.* 666. *Fr. Icon. t.* 24*a*. *Harz. t.* 73.

In woods. Sept. King's Cliffe.

Closely resembling *A. sejunctus.* Stem 3, sometimes 4-6in. long, 1 in. thick, solid. Pileus 3-5 in. broad, livid or dingy, sometimes with a tinge of violet. Flesh scarcely compact, white. Spores ·00018 × ·00013 in.—*W. G. S.*

41. Agaricus (Tricholoma) fucatus. *Fr.* "Stained Tricholoma."

Pileus thin, conical, then convex, at length expanded, flexuose, viscid, streaked with innate lines ; disc fleshy ; stem solid, somewhat bulbous, squamulose ; gills emarginate, rather crowded, yellowish-white.—*Fr. Epicr. p.* 27. *Eng. Fl.* v. *p.* 116. *Fr. Icon. t.* 24*b*.

In pine groves.

The thin pileus, squamulose, sub-bulbous stem, and yellowish gills distinguish it from *A. portentosus.* Pileus slightly viscid, flesh thick in the centre, margin thin, yellowish, with cinereous fibrillæ, subrimulose, with a satiny lustre. Gills broad, emarginate, slightly wavy, moderately thick, not distant, scarcely connected by veins, with a slight tinge of yellow. Stem tinged with yellow, as is the outer flesh, punctato-squamulose, bulbous, attenuated upwards. Odour like that of new flour.—*M. J. B.*

42. Agaricus (Tricholoma) spermaticus. *Fr.* "Stinking Tricholoma."

White. Pileus rather fleshy, convex, then expanded, obtuse, repand, smooth, viscid; margin membranaceous, naked; stem stuffed, then hollow, elongated, twisted, even; gills emarginate, rather distant, eroded.—*Fr. Epicr. p.* 27. *Paul. t.* 45, *f.* 1-3. *Paul. t.* 45.

In fir woods.

Pileus several inches across. Smell strong, unpleasant.

Sect. 2. Gills discoloured.

43. Agaricus (Tricholoma) nictitans. *Fr.* "Spotted Gills "Tricholoma."

Pileus fleshy, convex, then expanded, obtuse, smooth, viscid, even; stem stuffed, dry, elastic, nearly equal, squamulose, yellowish; gills from the first rounded behind, free, yellow, crowded, obscurely spotted with reddish brown.—*Fr. Epicr. p.* 28. *Bull. t.* 574, *f.* 1. *Huss.* ii. *t.* 46. *Ann. N.H. no.* 667.

In woods. Sept.

Inodorous. Stem 3 in. long, ½ in. and more thick. Pileus 3-4 in. broad, viscid, yellowish, disc darker. Spores ·0003 × ·0002 in.—*W. G. S.*

44. Agaricus (Tricholoma) fulvellus. *Fr.* "Tawny Tricholoma."

Pileus fleshy, convex, then expanded, viscid, even, disc darker, punctato-rugose, stem stuffed, then hollow, fibrillose, whitish, then rufous, naked above; gills rounded, then emarginate, crowded, white, then rufescent.—*Fr. Epicr. p.* 28. *Ag. fulvus Bull. t.* 555, *f.* 2. *Ann. N.H. no.* 59.

In woods. Inodorous.

Considered by Fries (Epicr.) as a variety of *A. nictitans.* Sometimes the gills and inside of the stem are more or less yellow. Smaller than the last. Spores nearly spherical ·00015 in.—*W. G. S.*

45. Agaricus (Tricholoma) flavo-brunneus. *Fr.* "Yellow-brown Tricholoma."

Pileus fleshy, conical, then convex, at length expanded, subumbonate, viscid, clothed with streak-like scales; stem hollow, somewhat ventricose, fibrillose, at first viscid, yellowish within, tip naked; gills emarginate, decurrent, crowded, yellowish, then rufous.—*Fr. Epicr. p.* 29. *Letell. f.* 707. *Fr. Icon. t.* 26*a*.

In woods.

Odour that of new meal. Stem 3-5 in. long, ½ in. thick, rufescent or brownish. Pileus 3-6 in. broad, disc darker, dingy rufous, or reddish brown.

46. Agaricus (Tricholoma) ustalis. *Fr.* "Burnt Tricholoma."

Pileus fleshy, convexo-plane, obtuse, smooth, viscid; stem stuffed, equal, dry, rufo-fibrillose, apex naked, silky, nearly smooth; gills emarginate, crowded, white, at length with reddish spots.—*Fr. Epicr. p.* 29. *Mon. Hym.* i. *p.* 58. *Batt. t.* 17. *c.*

Chiefly in pine woods. Reigate (*W. G. S.*)

Pileus fleshy, not compact; hemispherical at first, umbonate, soon plane and obtuse, glabrous, edge not striate, dotted on the disc; gills emarginate, with a decurrent tooth, crowded, moderately broad, white, at length turning red; stem stuffed, at length hollow, two to three in. long, about half in. thick, equal, dry, fibrous, whitish or turning red, whiter and silky at the apex, but not mealy; scentless. Spores ·0003 × ·0002 in.—*W. G. S.*

47. Agaricus (Tricholoma) albo-brunneus. P. "White and Brown Tricholoma."

Pileus fleshy, hemispherical, then expanded, obtuse, viscid, streaked; disc papillose; stem solid, short, equal, white above and squamulose; gills emarginate, crowded, white, then brownish.—*Fr. Epicr. p.* 29. *Sow. t.* 416. *Schæff. t.* 38. *Eng. Fl.* v. *p.* 15. *Barla. t.* 12.

In woods. Smell like new meal.

Cæspitose. Pileus 3 in. broad, convex, flattish, very glutinous, dirty white, changing to a ferruginous tint. Gills white or brown, very broad, and slightly angular near the stem. Stem 3 in. high, ½ in. thick, generally swollen near the middle, attenuated above and below, towards the base highly ferruginous. When young covered with a shaggy wool, which soon disappears. Remarkably glutinous, so that leaves and sticks which are in contact can scarce be separated without tearing the pileus. The pileus appears when grown to be constantly smooth, but the stem, though occasionally smooth, generally has the apex pale and squamulose, and the lower part more or less marked with transverse scales.—*M. J. B.* Spores ·00014 × ·00016 in.—*W. G. S.*

48. Agaricus (Tricholoma) pessundatus. *Fr.* "Overturned Tricholoma."

Pileus fleshy, compact, convex, very obtuse, repand, viscid, granulose, spotted; stem solid, firm, at first ovato-bulbose, everywhere villous with whitish scales; gills free, or emarginate, crowded, white, at length spotted with rufous.—*Fr. Epicr. p.* 29. *Mon. Hym.* i. *p.* 58. *Sterb. t.* 8, *A.*

In pine woods. *(J.A. C.)*

Pileus compactly fleshy, convex, then expanded, very obtuse, bent, glabrous, never striate, but scaly, spotted, viscid, chestnut or red, paler at the circumference; gills deeply emarginate, crowded at first, very narrow, shining, then wider and reddish; stem solid, hard, at first bulbous, entirely villoso-scaly, at length nearly equal, 2 to 3 ins. long, 1 in. thick, nearly glabrous, white, odour strong, like new meal, taste pleasant, spores ·0002 × ·0001 in.; allied to *A. russula*, which is distinguished by its granular rosy pileus.—*W. G. S.*

[Fries places *Agaricus frumentaceus*, Bull. here, whilst Berkeley removes it to *Entoloma*, on the ground that the spores are rose-coloured.]

B. *Flocculosa.*—pileus dry, fibrillose.

Sect. 1. Gills whitish, not spotted.

49. Agaricus (Tricholoma) rutilans. *Schæff.* "Red-haired Tricholoma."

Pileus fleshy, campanulate, then expanded, dry, variegated, as well as the somewhat hollow, soft, ventricose stem, with purplish down; gills rounded, crowded, yellow; edge thickened, villous.—*Fr. Epicr. p.* 30. *Schæff. t.* 219. *Eng. Fl.* v. *p.* 17. *Sow. t.* 31. *Fl. Dan. t.* 1610. *Bolt. t.* 14. *Buxb.* v. *t.* 46. *Krombh. t.* 63, *f.* 10-12.

On pine stumps. Common.

Subcæspitose. Pileus 2-4 in. broad, at first hemispherical, or somewhat cylindrical, at length expanded, obtuse, more rarely plane, clothed with a short, dense, crimson-red or olive-purple down, margin involute, white; as the pileus expands the yellow cuticle becomes visible in the interstices of the down, which is then scattered. Gills free, broad, rounded behind, but often when old adnexed, sometimes forked, bright yellow, floccoso-serrate, margin turning sometimes to a rich yellow-brown. Stem 2½-3½ in. high, ½-1 in. thick, downy, like the pileus, only the down is shorter, very obtuse at the base, attenuated upwards, solid, then occasionally hollow. Odour strong. Taste bitter.—*M. J. B.* Spores ·00033 × ·0002 in.—*W. G. S.*

50. Agaricus (Tricholoma) scalpturatus. *Fr.* "Scratched Tricholoma."

Pileus fleshy, conical, then convex, and expanded, obtuse, breaking up into floccose, umber, or rufous scales; stem stuffed, unequal, white, fibrillose; gills emarginate, somewhat crowded, quite entire, white, then yellowish.—*Fr. Epicr. p.* 31. *Batt., t.* 15 *f. (young). A. argyraceus. Eng. Fl., No.* 36, *in part.*

Fir plantations, borders of woods, &c.

Stem solid, 2-3 in. long, ½ in. thick, firm, closely fibrillose. Pileus 2-3 in. broad, the cuticle breaking up in scattered, floccose, umber, or rufous scales Flesh whitish.

51. Agaricus (Tricholoma) luridus. *Schæff.* "Lurid Tricholoma."

Pileus fleshy, convex, then expanded, sub-repand, dry, smooth, at length breaking up into little fibres; stem stuffed, stout, unequal, smooth; gills emarginate, crowded, dirty white.—*Schæff.*, *t.* 69. *Fr. Epicr. p.* 31. *Batt., t.* 17. *B. Eng. Fl.* v. *p.* 16.

In woods. Common. [United States.]

Subgregarious. Pileus 3 in. broad, at first convex, then expanded, often lobed and waved, brown or greyish, with tints of yellow, sub-umbonate, fibrilloso-striate, fleshy; flesh firm. Gills broad, thick, rounded behind, nearly free, but annexed by a small tooth, connected by veins, much broken or notched. Stem 2-4 in. long, 3-5 lines thick, obese, nearly equal, or slightly attenuated, solid, minutely and closely fibrillose, pulverulento-squamulose above, where it is yellowish, undulated, sometimes of a beautiful red when bruised. Odour like new flour.—*Eng. Fl.*

52. Agaricus (Tricholoma) columbetta. *Fr.* "Dove-colour Tricholoma."

White; pileus fleshy, ovate, then expanded, obtuse, rigid, subflexuose, at first smooth, then silky, fibrillose, or squamulose; margin involute, at first tomentose; stem solid, stout, unequal, striate, nearly smooth; gills emarginate, crowded, thin, somewhat serrulated.—*Fr. Epicr. p.* 33. *Kromb. t.* 25, *f.* 6-7. *Letell. t.* 625. *Fr. Icon. t.* 29 *b. Sterb. t.* 9. *B. &c. Eng. Fl.* v. *p.* 19. *Ann. N. H., no.* 259.

In woods. Oct. [United States.]

Pileus 1½-4 in. broad, convex, silky, centre dilute mouse colour, lightly shaded off, border white when young, sometimes tinged with pink, cracking with age. Gills fixed, white, brittle. Stem 2 in. high, 3-6 lines thick, solid, white, cylindrical, often compressed, crooked, silky, central when young, not always so in a more advanced age.—*With.* Sometimes the pileus is white, spotted with reddish, or with a yellowish tinge. Spores ·00023 + ·00018 in.—*W.G.S.*

Sect. 2. Gills discoloured, or spotted.

53. Agaricus (Tricholoma) imbricatus. *Fr.* "Imbricated Tricholoma."

Pileus fleshy, compact, convex, then expanded, obtuse, dry, innato-squamulose; margin at first inflexed, pubescent; stem solid, stout, pruinose above; gills emarginate, adnexed, somewhat crowded, white, then becoming rufescent.—*Epicr. p.* 33. *Schæff. t.* 25. *Berk. Outl. t.* 4, *f.* 3. *Eng. Fl.* v. *p.* 17. *Fr. Icon. t.* 30.

In fir woods.

Gregarious. Pileus 2-3½ in. broad, dry, obtuse, at first subconic, then convex, expanded, sometimes plane, very broadly umbonate, fleshy, rich red brown, fibrilloso-squamulose, rimulose, the umbo darker, with the fibrils closer; occasionally the pileus is scarcely squamulose, but clothed with adpressed silky fibrils. Margin involute, paler, tomentose. Gills slightly rounded behind, subadnate with a minute tooth, or nearly free, umber when bruised, not very broad. Stem 2½-4 in. high, ½-¾ in. thick, firm, stuffed, at length more or less hollow, sometimes strongly attenuated, sometimes incrassated at the base, fibrillose, colour of the pileus, nearly white above, where it is, squamulose or pubescent.—*M. J. B.* Spores ·00023 × ·00018 in. —*W. G. S.*

54. Agaricus (Tricholoma) vaccinus. *P.* "Scaly Tricholoma."

Pileus fleshy, campanulate, then expanded, umbonate, dry, rough with floccose scales; margin involute, tomentose; stem hollow, equal, fibrillose; gills fixed, somewhat distant, white, at length rufescent.—*Pers. Syn. p.* 293. *Fr. Epicr. p.* 33. *Batsch. f.* 116. *Pers. Ic. & Desc. t.* 2, *f.* 1-4. *Eng. Fl.* v. *p.* 17.

In fir woods. Sept. Oct. [Carolina, U.S.]

Pileus 1-2 in. broad, campanulate when young, clothed with scales, those in the centre thick, broad, short, on the margin consisting of fasciculate hairs. Gills rather broad, emarginate, nearly free, at first dirty white, in age of a rufous hue, margin generally stained with rusty spots. Stem 3-4 in. high, ½ in. thick, beset with hairy scales, which mostly point upwards, paler than the pileus, whitish above, base clothed with white down. Veil fugacious. Taste bitter.—*Pers.*

55. Agaricus (Tricholoma) crassifolius. *Berk.* "Thick gilled Tricholoma."

Pileus flesby, waved, minutely adpresso-squamulose, umbonate, ochraceous; disc umber; stem solid, nearly equal, pruinose; gills thick, moderately distant, nearly free, at length yellowish, stained with brown.—*Outl. p.* 100. *A. pachyphyllus. Eng. Fl., p.* 16.

In fir woods.

Gregarious. Pileus 2-4 in. across, rather wavy, umbonate, at length often depressed, ochraceous, shaded towards the centre with umber, minutely squamulose, sometimes (when old) the epidermis cracks in broad scales, flesh very firm. Gills slightly adnexed or nearly free, acute behind, moderately distant, thick, fleshy, acquiring at length an ochraceous hue, here and there stained with umber. Stem 1½-2 in. long, ⅜ of an in. thick, solid, nearly equal, pruinose, much paler than the pileus. Odour rather strong.—*Eng. Fl.*

56. Agaricus (Tricholoma) murinaceus. *Bull.* "Mouse Colour Tricholoma."

Pileus thin, firm, brittle, at first campanulate, then expanded, cracked, streaked, silky, dry; stem stout, cracked, and streaked with minute black scales, solid; gills very broad, undulated, distant, more or less anastomosing, brittle, cinereous, often marked with raised lines ; edge at length black.—*Sow. t.* 106. *Bull. t.* 520. *Ann. N.H., no.* 261.

In woods. Sept. Not common.

Very different from *Hygrophorus murinaceus*, Fr. Pileus 4½ in. across, at first campanulate, slightly umbonate, then expanded, thin, firm, but very brittle, mouse-coloured, cracked and virgate, silky, not the least viscid, flesh white ; taste rather acrid ; smell not nitrous. Stem 3 in. high, 1 in. thick at the top, cracked and streaked, silky, with minute black scales, solid but fibrous, not the least stuffed or hollow ; gills very broad, undulate, distant, having a tendency to become forked and anastomosing, brittle, often marked with raised lines, cinereous, powdery, interstices slightly veined, edge at length black.—*M. J. B.* Spores ·00019 × ·00014 in.—*W. G S.*

57. Agaricus (Tricholoma) terreus. *Schæff.* "Grey Tricholoma."

Pileus fleshy, soft, campanulate, then expanded, umbonate, dry, clothed with innate, floccose, or scaly down ; stem stuffed, nearly equal, adpresso-fibrillose, whitish ; gills adnexed, with a decurrent tooth, crenulate, pale-grey.—*Schæff. t.* 64. *Fr. Epicr. p.* 34. *Letell. t.* 663. *Sow. t.* 76. *Paul. t.* 116. *Vent. t.* 45, *f.* 4, 5. *A. multiformis. Eng. Fl.* v. *p.* 18.

In woods, especially of fir.

Gregarious, often in large rings, or solitary. Pileus 1-2½ in. broad, conic when young, with a delicate arachnoid veil, then obtuse, expanded, quite plane, variously waved, sometimes minutely umbonate, thin, mouse-grey, or very dark cinereous, clothed with flat and matted down, with sometimes a few depressed or raised squamules of the same colour, margin inflexed ; flesh cinereous ; gills rather distant, broad, the margin wavy, more or less rounded behind, and attached by a tooth, more or less cinereous, especially when young, with a few indistinct connecting veins ; stem 1-3 in. high, ¼-½ in. thick, stuffed, at length hollow, fibrillose sericeous, sometimes a little pulverulent, white, the base occasionally sub-rufescent ; pileus and stem very brittle.—*M. J. B.* Spores nearly spherical ·0002 in.—*W. G. S.*

(Pl. II., fig. 4, *reduced.)*

c. *Rigida*—granulate or squamulose.

Sect. 1. Gills whitish.

58. Agaricus (Tricholoma) saponaceus. *Fr.* "Strong Scented Tricholoma."

Strong scented, firm. Pileus rather compact, convex, then expanded, obtuse, dry, smooth; then rimoso-squamose or punctate ; margin at first naked ; stem solid, unequal; gills uncinato-marginate, distant, thin, quite entire, white then pallid, sometimes greenish.—*Fr. Epicr. p.* 35. *Bull. t.* 602. *Sow. t.* 281. *Batsch. t.*

36, *f.* 203 *a. b.* *B. and Br. Ann. N.H.*, 1866, *no.* 1106. *A. argyraceus. Eng. Fl. (in part.)*

In woods. Sept.

Stem 2-3 in. long, ½ in. or more thick, unequal or curved, base attenuated, rooting. Pileus 2-4 in. broad, whitish, cinereous, greenish or blackish, margin thin, at first inflexed. Spores ·0002 × ·00015 in.—*W. G. S.*

59. Agaricus (Tricholoma) cartilagineus. *Bull.* "Cartilaginous Tricholoma."

Cartilaginous, elastic, rather fragile; pileus fleshy, convex, bullate, gibbous, undulated, smooth; cuticle rimulose, finely dotted with black; stem stuffed, equal, stout, lineato-striate, somewhat mealy; gills slightly emarginate, adnexed, crowded, pallid.—*Bull. t.* 589, *f.* 2. *Fr. Epicr. p.* 37. *Sm. Journ. Bot.* iii. *p.* 28.

In grassy spots.

Smell like that of new flour. Pileus 2-3 in. or more broad, stem short and firm, but fragile, 1-2 in. long.

60. Agaricus (Tricholoma) cuneifolius. *Fr.* "Wedge-gill Tricholoma."

Very brittle; pileus rather fleshy, convex, then plane, dry, smooth, but soon cracked; stem, hollow, attenuated downwards, white, pruinose above; gills thin, crowded, white, broad in front, obliquely truncate, attenuated behind, with a decurrent tooth.—*Fr. Epicr. p.* 37. *Eng. Fl.* v. *p.* 44. *Bull. t.* 580, *f. A.B. Batsch. f.* 206.

In pastures. Not uncommon.

Pileus about 1 in. broad, brownish or subochraceous, subcarnose, at first conic, obtuse, afterwards expanded, with a strong umbo, much waved and split at the margin, which is at first involute, and minutely tomentose, the surface rimose; gills distant, broad in front, ventricose, acutely arcuato-adnate, thick, connected and traversed by veins, white, with a slight reddish cinereous tinge; stem 1-1½ in. high, 2-4 lines thick, nearly equal, stuffed, at length hollow, pruinose above, with sometimes a few superficial squamules towards the base, smell like new meal.—*M. J. B.* Spores nearly spherical ·00018 in.—*W. G. S.*

Sect. 2. Gills rufescent or cinereous.

61. Agaricus (Tricholoma) colossus. *Fr.* "Colossal Tricholoma."

Large, very hard, pileus compact, very thick, hemispherical, then expanded, smooth, at length diffracto-squamulose, margin at first involute, at length unrolled and flexuous, stem quite solid, at first tuberous, apex constricted, smooth, white, below and within brick-red; gills rounded, crowded, thin, white, then broad, and of a pallid brick-red.—*Fr. Epicr. p.* 38. *Mon. Hym.* i. *p.* 47. *Icones. t.* 21.

Woods. Near Taunton.—*(J. A. C.)*

Pileus when young tuberiform, emerging from the earth in a bulbous form, narrowly involute at the margin, surrounding the narrow part of the stem; then hemispherical, at length unrolled, plano-convex and depressed, always very obtuse, when expanded a span or more wide, scaly. Gills rounded, free, but on account of the obliquity of the stem, emarginate, decurrent, at first narrow and crowded, white, then broader, more distant, entire, at length ½ in. broad, fragile, lacerated, pale brick red; stem solid, flesh everywhere similar and very compact, 3 to 4 in. long, ovato-bulbous at the base, but very much narrowed at the apex, 2 in. thick, the bulbous part glabrous, but fibroso-lacerated, tawny, the narrow part floccose and shining; veil obsolete, unless the flocci on the apex of the stem are considered a rudimentary one; flesh dry, very hard, extremely fibrous when broken, passing into a brick-red color, at first scentless, then with a smell of cheese, or fresh meal. Spores ·0002 × ·00015 in.—*W. G. S.*

D. *Sericella*—pileus at first silky.

Sect. 1. Strong scented.

62. Agaricus (Tricholoma) sulfureus. *Bull.* "Sulphury Tricholoma."

Pileus fleshy, convex, then expanded, rather umbonate, unequal, at first slightly silky, then smooth and even; stem stuffed, sub-equal, slightly striate; gills distant, arcuato-adfixed, sulphur-coloured as well as the stem.—*Bull. t.* 168. *Fr. Epicr. p.* 40. *Vent. t.* 23, *f.* 4-5. *Berk. Outl. t.* 4, *f.* 4. *Sow. t.* 44. *Smith, P.M., f.* 23. *Fl. Dan. t.* 1910, *f.* 1. *Paul. t.* 85, *f.* 3-4. *Eng. Fl.* v. *p.* 42.

In woods. Common.

Pileus 1-2 in. broad, fleshy, obtuse, at length expanded or depressed, with a slight appearance of an umbo, sometimes flexuous and irregular, dirty yellow, or ochraceous umber, darker in the centre, the margin at first involute, and minutely tomentose, the whole clothed with extremely minute silkiness or squamules, so as to give it a pulverulent appearance, retaining the impression of the fingers; flesh yellow; gills sub-distant, rounded, flexuous, emarginate, or arcuato-adnate; stem 2 in. or more high, 4 lines thick, occasionally sub-bulbous, stuffed, sometimes at length hollow, the surface of the cavity rather slimy, yellow within, furnished at the base occasionally with many rather strong, yellow, fibrous roots; odour disagreeable, taste unpleasant.—*M. J. B.*

63. Agaricus (Tricholoma) bufonius. *P.* "Toad-like Tricholoma."

Pileus fleshy, convex, then expanded, sub-umbonate, at first silky, then smooth, punctato-rugose, opaque; stem stuffed, equal, flocculose; gills arcuate, somewhat decurrent, rather distant, of a yellow tan-colour.—*Fr. Epicr. p.* 40. *Bull. t.* 545, *f.* 2-0. *Ann. N. H. no.* 786.

In pine woods. Nov. Coed Coch.

Pileus purplish, brownish, tan-coloured, &c; stem 2-4 in. long, flocculose; gills rather more crowded, and paler than in *Ag. sulfureus.*

64. Agaricus (Tricholoma) lascivus. *Fr.* "Tarry Tricholoma."

Pileus fleshy, convex, then expanded, obtuse, somewhat depressed, at first silky, then smooth and even; stem solid, equal, rigid, rooting, white, tomentose at the base; gills arcuate, adnexed, crowded, white.—*Fr. Epicr. p.* 40. *Eng. Fl.* v. *p.* 42.

In woods.

Pileus pale tan-coloured, 2½ in. broad, convex, at length depressed, firm, fleshy, under the lens minutely adpresso-silky, margin at first involute, flesh white; gills white, when young arcuato-adnate, nearly horizontal, when old sub-decurrent, very brittle, not very close; stem firm, solid, more or less fibrillose, or fibrilloso-squamose, fibrillæ curved up from below, paler than the pileus, rooting, downy at the base, not bulbous, apex pruinose; odour of gas tar.—*M. J. B.*

65. Agaricus (Tricholoma) inamænus. *Fr.* "Unpleasant Tricholoma."

Pileus fleshy, convex, then expanded, rather umbonate, slightly silky at first, then smooth and even; stem solid, equal, rooting, white; gills arcuato-adfixed, decurrent, very distant, white.—*Fr. Epicr. p.* 40. *Eng. Fl.* v. *p.* 43.

In woods. Oct.

Pileus 1-3 in. broad, convex, with or without an umbo, fleshy, but not very thick on the margin, under the lens adpresso-silky, white, with a slight tinge of ochre in the centre, often minutely cracked; gills broad, distant, emarginate; stem 2 in. or more long, 3-6 lines thick, equal, tough, not always rooting; odour strong.—*M. J. B.*

Sect. 2. Inodorous; small.

66. Agaricus (Tricholoma) ionides. *Bull.* "Purplish Tricholoma."

Pileus fleshy, campanulate, convex, then expanded, umbonate, even, nearly smooth, changing colour; margin at first flocculose; stem stuffed, elastic, attenuated, fibrillose; gills emarginate, with a decurrent tooth, crowded, thin, eroded, white, then pallid.—*Bull. t.* 533, *f.* 3. *Fr. Epicr. p.* 41. *B. & Br. Ann. N. H. no.* 902. *A. purpureus. Bolt. t.* 41.

In woods.

Pileus 1-3 in. broad; stem 2 in. long, 2-3 lines thick.

67. **Agaricus (Tricholoma) pæonius.** *Fr.* "Pæony Tricholoma."

Pileus fleshy, convexo-plane, sub-repand, very obtuse, even, silky, then nearly smooth, margin flocculose; stem hollow, soft, equal, fragile, persistently fleshy-red; gills rounded, free, ventricose, crowded, whitish.—*Fr. Epicr. p.* 42. *Mon. Hym.* i. *p.* 81.

Amongst grass and moss. Oct. Burnham Beeches.—*C.E.B.*

Pileus very obtuse, ½ in. broad, of a persistent red colour; stem about 1 in. long, 2-3 lines thick.

68. **Agaricus (Tricholoma) carneus.** *Bull.* "Flesh-coloured Tricholoma."

Pileus rather fleshy, hemispherical, or convex, then plane, or depressed, obtuse, even, nearly smooth, becoming pallid; stem stuffed, short, rigid, thickened upwards, pruinose, reddish; gills very broad behind, rounded, crowded, white.—*Bull. t.* 533, *f.* 1. *Fr. Epicr. p.* 42. *Eng. Fl.* v. *p.* 30.* *Krombh. t.* i. *f.* 30.

In pastures.

Pileus seldom exceeding one inch, plane, sub-carnose, often slightly umbonate, firm, shining rufous pink, rather undulated, flesh white; gills white, crowded, rounded behind, with a short decurrent tooth; stem 1 in. high, 1½ lines thick, same colour as the pileus, stuffed below, at length hollow, frequently splitting, minutely squamulose.—*M. J. B.* Spores ·0001 × ·00007 in. —*W. G. S.*

E. *Guttata*—pileus rivulose, &c.

69. **Agaricus (Tricholoma) gambosus.** *Fr.* "St. George's Mushroom."

Pileus thick, fleshy, convex, then expanded, undulate, obtuse, moist, smooth, spotted, at length cracked; margin involute at first; stem solid, stout, equal, flocculose at the apex; gills emarginate, with an adnexed tooth, ventricose, crowded, yellowish-white.—*Epicr. p.* 43. *Ann. N.H., no.* 140. *Berk. Outl. t.* 4, *f.* 5. *Sow. t.* 281. *Vent. t.* 11. *Huss.* i. *t.* 83. *Smith E. M. f.* 19. *Cooke B. F. t.* 9. *Krombh. t.* 63, *f.* 18-22. *Gard. Chron.* (1860) *p.* 672, *fig. Trans. Woolh. Cl.* (1868) *t.* 12. *Badh.* i. *t.* 1, ii. *t.* i. *f.* 1.

In pastures. May. June. Esculent.

Pileus white or slightly tinged with ochre, growing in rings; variable in size; smell strong. This is the *Agaricus prunulus* of some authors. Spores ·00052 × ·0004 in.—*W. G. S.*

70. Agaricus (Tricholoma) albellus. *D. C.* "Confluent Tricholoma."

Pileus at first conical, then expanded, smooth, moist, spotted as if with scales; disc compact, sub-umbonate; margin thin, even, naked; stem solid, ovato-bulbous, fibrilloso-striate; gills attenuated behind, and adnexed without a tooth, crowded, entire, white, broadest in front.—*Fr. Epicr. p.* 44. *Paul. t.* 95, *f.* 1-8. *Schæff. t.* 50. *Tratt. Aust. t.* 20. *Sow. t.* 122. *Smith. Seem. Journ.* (1866) *t.* 46, *f.* 45.

On the ground. Rare. Esculent.

The stem of the fresh plant has a slight inclination to be silky outside, becoming ultimately stuffed or inclined to hollow within, whilst the word "mottled" would give a better idea of the pileus than "spotted after the fashion of scales;" this part of the plant is very conical and fleshy. Spores very small, ovoid, ·0001 in. long.—*W. G. S.*

71. Agaricus (Tricholoma) monstrosus. *Sow.* "Monstrous Tricholoma."

Pileus fleshy, at first convex and umbonate, at length waved and lobed, opaque as if white-washed; margin inflexed; stem compressed, solid, streaked, opaque white, tomentoso-squamulose above, slightly rooting; gills moderately distant, scarcely rounded behind, but not truly decurrent, cream coloured.—*Sow. t.* 283. *Fr. Epicr. p.* 104.

On the ground. Probably esculent.

Often densely cæspitose, and then not compressed.

72. Agaricus (Tricholoma) immundus. *Berk.* "Dirty Tricholoma."

Cæspitose, fleshy, pileus at first convex, dirty white, stained with bistre, minutely silky; margin inflexed, silky or minutely scabrous, and squamulose; stem fibrillose, of the same colour as the pileus; gills sub-cinereous, with a pinkish tinge, marked with transverse lines, emarginate.—*Berk. Outl. p.* 103, *no.* 57.

Amongst short grass, on sheep's dung.

Pileus 2 in. or more across; every part blackish when bruised; border deflexed; spores white.—*M. J. B.*

73. Agaricus (Tricholoma) tigrinus. *Fr.* "Spotted Tricholoma."

Pileus fleshy, conical, convex, then expanded, contorted, or cracked, moist, smooth, spotted with black; margin even; stem solid, stout, somewhat pruinose, striate, swollen at the base; gills adnate, with a decurrent tooth, at length distant, white, then dingy.—*Fr. Epicr. p.* 45. *Schæff. t.* 89.

Under firs. Reigate.—*W. G. S.*

Odour fœtid; spores nearly round, ·0003 in.; pileus 2-3 in. broad; stem 1½ in. long, ½ line thick. Fries does not consider this distinct from *A. graveolens.*

F. *Spongiosa*—pileus moist, compact, or spongy.

74. Agaricus (Tricholoma) albus. *Fr.* "White Tricholoma."

Pileus fleshy, convex, then depressed, obtuse, smooth, even, dry; margin at first involute, at length repand; stem solid, firm, elastic, equal, smooth; gills rounded behind, fixed, crowded, thin, broad, white.—*Fr. Epicr. p.* 47. *Berk. Outl. t.* 4, *f.* 6. *Bull. t.* 536. *Batt. t.* 20, *f.* 1.

In woods.

White or shaded with yellow; variable in size; stem solid, 3 in. long, ½ in. and more thick; pileus 3-4 in. broad, tough, very dry, and smooth. Spores ·0001 × ·0002 in.—*W. G. S.*

75. Agaricus (Tricholoma) acerbus. *Bull.* "Bitter Tricholoma."

Pileus fleshy, convex, then expanded, obtuse, smooth, rather spotted; margin thin, strongly involute, sulcate; stem solid, blunt, yellowish, squamulose above; gills emarginate, crowded, pallid, then inclined to rufous.—*Bull. t.* 571, *f.* 2. *Fr. Epicr. p.* 49. *Ann. N.H. no.* 668. *Vent. t.* 38, *f.* 7-8.

In woods. Not common.

Pileus 3-4 in. across; white, tinged with yellow, at length stained. Remarkable for its bitter taste, and involute sulcate margin. Spores ·00017 in. diameter.—*W. G. S.*

G. *Hygrophana*—pileus thin, at length soft, moist, hygrophanous.

76. Agaricus (Tricholoma) grammopodius. *Bull.* "Ring Tricholoma."

Pileus fleshy, campanulate, or convex, then expanded or depressed, umbonate, smooth, moist; stem stuffed, elastic, sulcate, smooth, attenuated upwards; gills arcuate, adnate, crowded, white.—*Bull. t.* 548-585, *f.* 1. *Fr. Epicr. p.* 50. *Huss.* ii. *t.* 41. *Bolt. t.* 40? *Eng. Fl.* v. *p.* 37. *Ann. N.H. no.* 61.

In pastures forming rings.

Large, brownish grey; pileus 3-5 in. broad, fleshy, margin thin, rather brittle, convex, firm, campanulate, then somewhat plane, also depressed and repand: gills not decurrent, narrow, sometimes divided; stem 3 in. high, ½ in. thick, firm, of the colour of the pileus, thickened at the base, and villous.—*Fries.*

77. Agaricus (Tricholoma) melaleucus. *P.* "Changeable Tricholoma."

Pileus fleshy, thin, convex, then expanded, obsoletely umbonate, smooth, moist, changing colour; stem stuffed, thin, elastic, somewhat smooth, whitish, sprinkled with a few fibrils, thickened at the base; gills emarginate, adnexed, ventricose, crowded, white.—*Fr. Epicr. p.* 51. *Buxb.* iv. *t.* 12, *f.* 2.

On the ground.

Stem stuffed, then hollow, 2-3 in. long, 2-3 lin. thick, whitish, with darker striæ; pileus 1½-3 in. broad, dingy black, then livid brown, pale when dry; flesh soft, white.

78. Agaricus (Tricholoma) brevipes. *Bull.* "Short-stemmed Tricholoma."

Pileus fleshy, soft, convex, then plane, even, smooth, opaque when dry, umber, growing pallid; stem solid, firm, rigid, very short, sub-incrassated, brown; gills emarginate, crowded, ventricose, brownish, then dirty white.—*Bull. t.* 521, *f.* 2. *Paul. t.* 44, *f.* 1-2. *Fr. Ep. p.* 51. *Seem. Journ.* (1869) *t.* 95, *f.* 1-4. *Kl. Fl. Boruss. t.* 374.

In plantations. June. Esculent.

Pileus about 2 in. broad. Stem brown within and without, bulbous, very short. Spores ·00032 × ·0002 in.—*W. G. S.*

79. Agaricus (Tricholoma) humilis. *Fr.* "Dwarf Tricholoma."

Pileus fleshy, soft, umbonate, then convexo-plane or depressed, even, smooth, hygrophanous; margin thin, extending beyond the gills; stem stuffed, short, equal, fragile, pallid, villoso-pulverulent; gills rounded (with a decurrent tooth), crowded, ventricose, whitish.—*Fr. Epicr. p.* 52. *Buxb.* iv. *t.* 32. *A. blandus, Eng. Fl. No.* 41, v. *p.* 20. *Ann. N.H. no.* 260.

On the ground and amongst grass. [United States.]

Pileus 2½ in. broad, plano-convex, umbonate, very minutely pulverulento-tomentose, so that when touched the impression of the fingers remains upon it, not brittle, moderately fleshy, dry, the margin sometimes undulate, grey-lilac, with a tinge of brown on the umbo. When young sometimes browner, the edge white, and minutely downy; gills broad, rounded behind and nearly free, white, margin undulate, brittle, becoming rather brown at the edge as they dry. Stem 2 in. high, 2 lines thick, ¾ in. at the base, sub-bulbous, and brownish at the base, the brown colour penetrating the flesh to the centre, solid, rather brittle, pulverulento-squamulose at the apex, subfibrilloso-rimose below, with a little down at the base. Spores white, round.—*M. J. B.*

80. Agaricus (Tricholoma) subpulverulentus. *Pers.* "Lustrous Tricholoma."

Pileus fleshy, convex, then expanded or depressed, even, with an innate, white, pruinose lustre; margin inflexed; stem solid, equal, smooth, somewhat striate; gills rounded (without a tooth), crowded, narrow, white.—*Fr. Epicr. p.* 52. *Huss.* ii. *t.* 39. *Ann. N.H. no.* 669.

In pastures. Oct.

Pileus 2 in. across. Dirty white, or greyish, with a white lustre. Spores ·0001 × ·00018 in.—*W. G. S.*

Sub-Gen. 5. CLITOCYBE. Fr. S. M. i. p. 78.

Pileus generally fleshy in the disc, obtuse, plane or depressed, hygrophanous, or not hygrophanous; stem confluent and homogeneous with the hymenophore, elastic, with a fibrous outer coat, covered with minute fibres; gills acutely adnate, or decurrent.—*Pl. II., fig.* 5.

HAB. All are terrestrial.

The species are generally small, though some are very large; many possess an agreeable odour, but few only are known to be edible. Most of the species appear late in the autumn or in early winter.—*W. G. S.*

A. *Disciformes*—pileus flattened.

Sect. 1. Pileus cinereous or tawny.

81. Agaricus (Clitocybe) nebularis. *Batsch.* "Clouded Clitocybe."

Pileus fleshy, compact, convex, then expanded, obtuse, even, at first clouded with grey, then naked; stem stuffed, firm, fibrilloso-striate; gills somewhat decurrent, arcuate, crowded, white, then pallid.—*Batsch. f.* 193. *Eng. Fl.* v. *p.* 34. *Fr. Epicr. p.* 55. *Smith E.M. f.* 24. *Fl. Dan. t.* 1734. *Gard. Chron.* (1860) *p.* 145, *fig. Bull. t.* 400. *Ag. turgidus, Grev. t.* 9. *Huss.* ii. *t.* 9. *Badh.* i. *t.* 9, *f.* 1, ii. *t.* 4, *f.* 2. *Berk. exs. no.* 2.

In woods. Common. Esculent. [United States.]

Stem 3 in. long, about an in. thick, fibrilloso-striate, white. Pileus fleshy, 3-5 in. broad, clouded with grey, or dingy brown, at length grey, sometimes pruinose. Spores ·00017 × ·0001 in.—*W. G. S.*

82. Agaricus (Clitocybe) inornatus. *Sow.* "Grey Clitocybe."

Pileus fleshy, plane or depressed, obtuse, even, smooth; cuticle separable; stem solid, nearly equal, smooth, firm, grey, as well as the adnate, plane, at length decurrent, crowded gills.—*Sow. t.* 342. *Fr. Epicr.* p. 57. *Eng. Fl.* v. *p.* 37.

Amongst grass.

Pileus 3 in. broad, fleshy, plane, or subdepressed, margin turned in. Gills of the same colour as the pileus. Stem 2 in. long, ½ in. thick, paler than the pileus.—*M. J. B.*

Sect. 2. Pileus brightly coloured.

83. Agaricus (Clitocybe) vernicosus. *Fr.* "Varnished Clitocybe."

Pileus fleshy, depressed, obtuse, even, smooth, shining; stem stuffed, equal, short, yellow, as well as the adnate, slightly decurrent, rather distant gills.—*Fr. Epicr. p.* 60. *Berk. Out. p.* 108. *Sow. t.* 366.

In fir woods.

Not found since the time of Sowerby. Pileus 3 in. across, pinkish or tawny. Stem short, yellow.

84. Agaricus (Clitocybe) odorus. *Bull.* "Sweet Clitocybe."

Dirty green, tough. Pileus fleshy, at length plane, even, subrepand, smooth; stem stuffed, elastic, unequal, smooth, base incrassated; gills adnate, scarcely crowded, broad, pallid.—*Sow. t.* 42. *Price, f.* 70. *Bull. t.* 176, 556, *f.* 3. *Grev. t.* 28. *Fl. Dan. t.* 1611. *Fr. S.M.* i. *p.* 90. *Eng. Fl.* v. *p.* 36. *Krombh. t.* 67, *f.* 20-22. *Berk. exs. no.* 6.

In woods. Aug.—Nov. Strong smell of aniseed.

[Carolina, U.S.]

Pileus 3 in. broad, plano-convex, with or without an umbo, smooth, lurid pale green, sometimes here and there whitish, so as to appear zoned, fleshy, but rather watery, flesh dull dirty white, margin not striate, but sometimes transparent, in the young plant inflected, tomentose, gills pale, rather waved, decurrently adnate, the interstices wrinkled. Stem 2 in. high, 4 lines thick, firm, somewhat flexuous, subfibrillose, with a little scattered down, stuffed, attenuated towards the base, which is downy, and furnished with strong-branched, greenish, or whitish roots.—*M. J. B.* Spores nearly spherical ·00025 in.—*W. G. S.*

Sect. 3. Pileus white.

85. Agaricus (Clitocybe) cerussatus. *Fr.* "White-lead Clitocybe."

White. Pileus fleshy, convex, then expanded, obtuse, even, moist, soon smooth; stem spongy, solid, tough, elastic, naked;

gills adnate, very crowded, thin, then decurrent, unchanged in colour.—*Fr. Epicr. p.* 61. *Fl. Dan. t.* 1796. *Ann. N.H. no.* 670.

In fir woods. April.—Sept. Probably esculent.

Not umbonate as *A. opacus*. Often gregarious. Pileus 2-3 in. broad, a little convex, soon plane, and obtuse, rather shining. Gills not decurrent. Stem 2-3 in. high, somewhat thickened at the base, furnished frequently with fibrillose radicles.—*Fries*. Forming very large rings. Sometimes producing a merulioid hymenium on the top of the pileus.—*M. J. B.* Spores nearly spherical ·00013 in.—*W. G. S.*

86. Agaricus (Clitocybe) phyllophilus. *Fr.* "Leaf-loving Clitocybe."

White. Pileus fleshy, convex, then plane, soon depressed and umbilicate, even, dry; marked with a white lustre round the margin; stem stuffed, then hollow, spongiose and fibrillose; gills adnate, decurrent, moderately distant, white, then yellowish.—*Epicr. p.* 62. *Eng. Fl.* v. *p.* 34. *Fl. Dan. t.* 1847.

Amongst leaves in woods. Sept. [Carolina, U.S.]

Generally sweet-scented, sub-cæspitose. Pileus 2-3 in. broad, slightly fleshy, when young nearly plane, sometimes repand. Stem 2-3 in. long, obliquely rooted at the base.—*Fries*. Spores ·00024 × ·00013 in.—*W. G. S.*

87. Agaricus (Clitocybe) pithyophilus. *Fr.* "Fir-wood Clitocybe."

White; pileus fleshy, thin, becoming plane, umbilicate, smooth, growing pale; stem nearly hollow, round, then compressed, smooth (whitish tomentose at the base); gills adnato-decurrent, crowded, plane, always white.—*Fr. Ep. p.* 62. *B. & Br. Ann. N.H.* (1866) *no.* 1107.

In fir woods. Oct. Coed Coch.

Gregarious, sub-cæspitose; pileus 2-3 in. broad, even, smooth, flaccid, dirty white when moist, white when dry.

88. Agaricus (Clitocybe) candicans. *Fr.* "Whitish Clitocybe."

White; pileus somewhat fleshy, convex, then plane, or depressed, even, shining, with a thin dead white film; stem subfistulose, even, waxy, shining; gills adnate, crowded, thin, at length decurrent.—*Fr. Epicr. p.* 63. *Bull. t.* 575, *f. E. Fl. Dan. t.* 2021, *f.* 1. *Bolt. f.* 17. *Eng. Fl.* v. *p.* 36.

Amongst leaves in woods. [Carolina, U. S.]

Pileus 1 in. across; when moist white, when dry dead white, sub-carnose, tough, regularly deflexed at the margin, rarely sub-deformed; gills rather close; stem 1-2 in high, 1-2 lines thick, nearly equal, incurved at the base, rooted and villous, the rest smooth; aberrant forms numerous.—*Fries.*

89. Agaricus (Clitocybe) dealbatus. *P.* "Ivory Clitocybe."

White; pileus rather fleshy, convex, then plane, and revolute, even, smooth, somewhat shining; stem stuffed, fibrous, thin, equal, sub-pruinose above; gills adnate, crowded, thin, white.—*Fr. Epicr. p.* 63. *Eng. Fl.* v. *p.* 36. *Sow. t.* 123. *Cooke, B. F. t.* 10 *a. Gard. Chron.* (1861), *p.* 312. *Smith E. M., f.* 27. *Hogg & Johnst. t.* 10.

In fir plantations, &c. Esculent.

Gregarious; pileus 1 in. or more, sometimes cup-shaped, innato-pruinose under a lens, dirty white, cream coloured, or roseate; gills adnate, at first slightly emarginate, brittle, white, moderately broad; stem 1 in. high, 2 lines thick, often curved, farinaceous, stuffed, occasionally hollow above when old; odour fungoid; spores white, round. A variety sometimes occurs on old mushroom beds, which is cæspitose, 1-2 in. or more across, lobed and undulate. Spores ·00016 × ·00007 in.—*W. G. S.*

90 Agaricus (Clitocybe) gallinaceus. *Scop.* "Acrid Clitocybe."

White, acrid; pileus somewhat fleshy, convex, then depressed, even, dry, opaque; stem solid, equal, thin, even; gills sub-decurrent, crowded, thin.—*Fr. Epicr. p.* 63. *Bolt. t.* 4, *f.* 2? *Huss.* 1, *t.* 39.

In pastures. Common. Strong odour.

Pileus opaque, dirty white, about 1 in. across; stem 2 in. in length.

B. *Difformes*—pileus irregular.

Sect. 1. Pileus cinereous or dark brown.

91. Agaricus (Clitocybe) elixus. *Sow.* "Sodden Clitocybe."

Pileus umbonate, at first convex, at length variously depressed, dingy, minutely tomentose and streaked; stem even, nearly of the same colour as the pileus; gills decurrent, distant, white.—*Sow. t.* 172. *Berk. Outl. p.* 109, *no.* 82. *Ann. N.H. no.* 264.

In woods. Oct.

Pileus 2-3 in. across, at first strongly umbonate, obconical, at length flat, or even depressed, with the border flexuous, not the least involute; disc fuliginous, very minutely virgate, border whitish, with dingy sodden spots, not viscid; stem 1 in. high, ⅜ in. thick, or 2 in. high, ¼ in. thick, dingy, like the pileus, clothed with matted down, which reaches to the base of the gills, often smooth at the base, which is buried amongst leaves, solid, mottled within, slightly discoloured beneath the cuticle; gills very distant, decurrent, white, interstices more or less veined.—*M. J. B.*

92. Agaricus (Clitocybe) fumosus. *P.* "Smoky Clitocybe."

Sub-cartilaginous, rigid; pileus fleshy, convex, then expanded, obtuse, even, naked, turning pale, cuticle adnate; stem stuffed, unequal, somewhat pruinose above; gills adnate, rather crowded, grey, or whitish, as well as the stem.—*Fr. Epicr. p.* 56. *Eng. Fl.* v. *p.* 35. *Pers. Ic. Pict. t.* 7, *f.* 3-4. *Fr. S. M.* 1, *p.* 88.

In woods and waste ground. Solitary. [United States.]

Var. **polius.** densely and connately cæspitose; pileus convex, then plane, obtuse, smooth, grey; stem flexuose, smooth; gills crowded, whitish.—*Fr. Epicr. p.* 57. *Trans. Woolhope Club*, 1868, *p.* 246. *Saund. & Sm. t.* 13.

On charcoal heaps, in woods, round the wrekin. 1868.

Cæspitose. Pileus 2½-3 in. broad, fleshy, but thin on the margin, more or less wavy, slightly umbonate, with a thick skin, marked with little pits, so as to present the appearance of innate fibrillæ; bistre coloured; gills rather pale, variously adnate, rounded behind, or emarginate, sometimes almost decurrent; stem 1-2½ in. long, ⅜ in. thick, quite smooth, except at the apex, where it is punctato-squamulose, nearly equal, stuffed.—*Eng. Fl.* Spores nearly spherical ·00024 in.—*W. G. S.*

Sect. 2. Pileus pallid.

93. Agaricus (Clitocybe) opacus. *With.* "Opaque Clitocybe."

White; pileus fleshy, convex, then expanded, umbonate, repand, even, covered with a floccose shining film; stem stuffed, unequal, flexuose; gills adnate, decurrent, very crowded, white.—*Fr. Epicr. p.* 67. *Sow. t.* 142.

In woods.

Pileus white, opaque, smooth, nearly flat when expanded, but a little turned down at the edge, and a very small protuberance in the centre, cracking when old, and the skin readily peeling off, diameter 1½-2 in.; stem solid, white, cylindrical, 2 in. high, ¼ in. diameter, filled with a watery, and when old with a brownish pith; gills fixed, white, very thick set, and very fine, in pairs or in fours.—*Withering.*

C. *Infundibuliformes*—pileus funnel-shaped.

Sect. 1. Pileus innately flocculose or silky.

94. Agaricus (Clitocybe) giganteus. *Fr.* "Giant Clitocybe."

Pileus infundibuliform, not umbonate, slightly flocculose, white, opaque; stem equal, thick; gills white, then yellowish, shortly decurrent.—*Fr. Epicr. p.* 67. *B. & Br. Ann. Nat. Hist.* (1865), *no.* 987.

In very rainy weather on a grassy bank. Aug. Aboyne.

"Pileus slightly viscid when moist, broadly infundibuliform, without any trace of an umbo, 9 in. across, white, opaque; margin incurved, at length sulcate. Stem 2½ in. high, 1 in. thick, equal, obtuse, minutely flocculose; gills at first very narrow, forked behind, decurrent, at length slightly rounded, white, then yellowish."—*B. & Br.*

95. Agaricus (Clitocybe) maximus. *Fr.* "Sowerby's Clitocybe."

Pileus fleshy, thin, sub-flaccid, dry, silky or squamulose, broadly infundibuliform, disc compact, somewhat umbonate; stem stuffed, compact, elastic, attenuated, fibrilloso-striate; gills decurrent, rather crowded, whitish.—*Epicr. p.* 68. *Buxb.* iv. *t.* 1. *A. giganteus, Sow. t.* 244. *Eng. Fl.* v. *p.* 33. *Huss.* i. *t.* 79. *Letell. t.* 682. *Hogg. & Johnst. t.* 23.

Meadows and woods. Sept. Esculent. [United States.]

Pileus 4-14 in. broad, fleshy, often splitting at the margin, broadly infundibuliform, the base of the funnel sunk into the stem, with no trace of umbo, dirty white, with an ochraceous tinge, minutely adpresso-squamulose to the naked eye, sometimes guttate, the whole surface under a lens clothed with a fine matted silkiness, margin grooved, the grooves shallow. Gills close, forked, yellow-white, as broad as the flesh of the pileus. Stem 2½-3 in. high, nearly 2 in. thick at the base, firm, fleshy, elastic, quite solid, sub-bulbous, sometimes attenuated upwards, minutely but conspicuously pubescent, when bruised dirty rufescent. Odour strong.—*M. J. B.* Spores ·00022 × ·00013 in.—*W. G. S.*

96. Agaricus (Clitocybe) infundibuliformis. *Schæff.* "Funnel Clitocybe."

Pileus fleshy, thin, at first convex, umbonate, clothed with minute innate silky down, at length funnel-shaped, flaccid; stem stuffed, soft, elastic, thickened downwards; gills decurrent, moderately distant, white.—*Schæff. t.* 212. *Price f.* 69. *Fr. Epicr. p.* 68. *Berk. Outl. t.* 5, *f.* 2. *Eng. Fl.* v. *p.* 32. *Bull. t.* 286, 553.

On the sides of woods, amongst moss, &c. Common.

Pileus of a pale reddish tan, 2-3 in. across, dry, elastic, at first convex, then umbonate, depressed, or quite infundibuliform, with traces of the umbo, variously crisped and lobed, margin involute and downy, the whole clothed with a delicate closely woven web, which is often pinched up at the margin into little raised striæ, these generally vanish as the pileus becomes completely expanded. Flesh moderately thick in the centre, colour of the pileus. Gills white, attenuated, numerous, unequal, some of them forked at the base. Stem variable in length, 2-9 lines thick, attenuated upwards, elastic, stuffed, paler than the pileus. Odour strong but grateful.—*Eng. Fl.*

Var. **membranaceus.** *Fr.* In a fir wood. Torquay.—*W. W. S.*

Fries says this well-marked variety is intermediate between *A. squamulosus* and *A. infundibuliformis*, appearing earlier in the year than the latter.

All the parts are thinner, the pileus never at first umbonate, 3 in. across; stem equal, spongy, 4 in. long, ½ in. thick, sometimes cæspitose. Grassy places in woods. Spores pip-shaped, ·00027 long.—*W. G. S.*

97. **Agaricus (Clitocybe) trullæformis.** *Fr.* "Bowl-shaped Clitocybe."

Pileus fleshy, obtuse, at length infundibuliform, floccoso-villose, margin expanded, stem stuffed, elastic, equal, striate; gills decurrent, sub-distant, connected by veins, white.—*Fr. Ep. p.* 68. *B. & Br. Ann. N.H.* (1866), *no.* 1108.

In fir woods. Oct. Coed Coch.

The rather distant gills, which are connected by veins, and infundibuliform pileus, distinguish this species, which is not hygrophanous.—*B. & Br.*

Sect. 2. Pileus quite smooth.

98. **Agaricus (Clitocybe) geotrupus.** *Bull.* "Trumpet Clitocybe."

Pileus fleshy, convex, then broadly infundibuliform, obtuse, umbonate, compact, even, smooth; stem solid, compact, fibrillose, attenuated upwards, flesh white; gills decurrent, crowded, simple, white, at length of the colour of the pileus.—*Bull. t.* 573, *f.* 2. *Fr. Epicr. p.* 70. *Paul. t.* 112. *Sow. t.* 61. *Gard. Chron.* (1861), *p.* 734, *fig. Huss.* i. *t.* 66. *Harz. t.* 75. *Letell. t.* 670. *Grev. t.* 41. *A. infundibuliformis, var. Eng. Fl.* v. *p.* 33.

In woods and on their borders, often in rings.

[United States.]

Pileus white, tan-coloured, &c., 4 in. broad. Stem 6 in. long, nearly 1 in. thick, 1½ in. at the base, more or less fibrillose, sometimes with broad, transverse, closely-pressed scales. Spores ·00028 × ·0002 in.

(Pl. II., fig. 5, *reduced.)*

Var. **subinvolutus.**—*Batsch. f.* 204.

Spores spinulose, nearly spherical, ·0003 in.—*W. G. S.*

99. **Agaricus (Clitocybe) inversus.** *Scop.* "Brown-red Clitocybe."

Pileus fleshy, fragile, convex, then infundibuliform, smooth; margin involute, even; stem stuffed, then hollow, rather rigid, smooth; flesh pallid; gills decurrent, simple, pallid, then of the colour of the pileus.—*Fr. Epicr. p.* 71. *B. & Br. Ann. N.H. no.* 110.* *Schæff. t.* 65. *Bull. t.* 553. *Paul. t.* 66. *Sow. t.* 186.

In fir woods. In a ditch. Woodnewton.

Pileus 2 in. across, not flaccid, brownish red at first, then tan-coloured; often cæspitose. Spores nearly spherical ·0001 in.—*W. G. S.*

100. Agaricus (Clitocybe) flaccidus. *Sow.* "Flaccid Clitocybe."

Pileus rather fleshy, thin, flaccid, umbilicate, then funnel-shaped, even, margin broadly reflexed; stem stuffed, unequal, sub-flexuose, villous at the base; gills decurrent, crowded, arcuate, yellowish.—*Sow. t.* 185. *Fr. Epicr. p.* 71. *Eng. Fl.* v. *p.* 32.

In fir woods.

Often densely cæspitose; pileus bright in colour, sometimes streaked; flaccid when young, 2-3 in. broad, always of a peculiar form and substance, orbicular, depressed, rather plane than infundibuliform, by reason of the deflexed margin, very even and smooth, generally reddish, sometimes white; gills very much attenuated behind, very close, tender, and narrow, not running far down; stem 1-2 in. long, 2 lines thick, slender, generally equal, smooth, with a sub-cartilaginous bark, stuffed, soon hollow, not rooting, nor incrassated, and villous, except from peculiarity of situation.—*Fries.* Spores slightly spinulose, nearly spherical ·00019 in.—*W. G. S.*

D. *Cyathiformes*—pileus cup-shaped.

101. Agaricus (Clitocybe) cyathiformis. *Fr.* "Cup-shaped Clitocybe."

Pileus between fleshy and membranaceous, at first depressed, then infundibuliform, even, nearly smooth, moist, hygrophanous; margin for a long time involute, even; stem stuffed, elastic, attenuated upwards, fibrilloso-reticulate; gills adnate, then decurrent, united behind, dingy.—*Fr. Epicr. p.* 73. *Sow. t.* 363. *Huss.* ii. *t.* 1. *Bull. t.* 575, *f. M.* *Vaill. t.* 14, *f.* 1-3. *Bolt. t.* 145.

In meadows, &c. Common. [Cincinnati.]

Pileus 2 in. across, variable in colour, generally dark brown or bistre. Spores ·00033 × ·00018 in.—*W. G. S.*

102. Agaricus (Clitocybe) brumalis. *Fr.* "Wintry Clitocybe."

Inodorous; pileus between fleshy and membranaceous, at first umbilicate, then funnel-shaped, smooth, flaccid, hygrophanous; margin reflexed, even; stem at length hollow, equal, somewhat incurved, smooth, whitish; gills decurrent, distinct, pallid.—*Fr. Epicr. p.* 76. *Bull. t.* 248, *f. A. B.* *A. metachrous.* *Eng. Fl.* v. *p.* 67.

In woods. Oct.

Livid grey when moist, nearly white when dry; pileus 1-2 in. broad, in its earliest stage conic, gradually depressed, but not deeply infundibuliform, almost membranaceous, margin pellucid; gills of the same colour as the pileus, adnate, scarcely decurrent, not turning pale so fast as the pileus, often separating from the stem at the base; stem 3 in. or more high, at length hollow, outer flesh livid, inner white, downy at the base, minutely fibrillose above, apex pulverulent.—*Eng. Fl.* Spores nearly spherical ·00013 in.—*W. G. S.*

E. *Orbiformes*—pileus rounded.

103. Agaricus (Clitocybe) metachrous. *Fr.* "Ob-conic Clitocybe."

Inodorous; pileus somewhat fleshy, convex, then plane, depressed, rather smooth, hygrophanous; stem stuffed, then hollow, equal, tough, pruinose above; gills adnate, crowded, pale cinereous.—*Fr. Epicr. p.* 77.

In woods amongst leaves.

Pileus 1½-2 in. across, when young cinereous brown, then livid, whitish when dry; stem about 1½ in. long, 2 lin. thick, broader when compressed, grey, frosted with white above; gills adnate, not truly decurrent.

104. Agaricus (Clitocybe) fragrans. *Sow.* "Fragrant Clitocybe."

Fragrant; pileus rather fleshy, convex, then plane, or depressed, even, smooth, hygrophanous; stem stuffed, then hollow, elastic, smooth; gills sub-decurrent, rather crowded, distinct, whitish.—*Sow. t.* 10. *Fr. Epicr. p.* 78. *Pers. My. Eur. t.* 27, *f.* 5. *Letell. t.* 658. *Krombh. t.* i. *f.* 34-35. *Eng. Fl.* v. *p.* 67.

In woods. Common. Esculent.

Pileus 1½ in. across, ochraceous, with a sweet anise odour; convex, then plano-convex, minutely dimpled, dirty white, very rarely slightly zoned, when dry nearly white, margin thin and transparent, turned in when young, and minutely tomentose; gills very broad, decurrent, distinct, not pure white; stem 2-3 in. high, 2-3 lines thick, attenuated upwards, minutely fibrillose, villous at the base, sometimes pruinose above.—*M. J. B.* Spores ·00026 × ·00016 in.—*W. G. S.*

F. *Versiformes*—pileus variable.

105. Agaricus (Clitocybe) difformis. *P.* "Deformed Clitocybe."

Pileus somewhat membranaceous, convex, then plane, and sub-umbilicate, smooth, hygrophanous, striate when moist, even when dry, at length between squamulose and rimose; stem hollow, equal, smooth, shining; gills adnate, distant, whitish.—*Fr. Epicr. p.* 79. *Bolt. t.* 17.

In fir plantations. Near Halifax.

Stem tough, 2-3 in. long, about 2 lin. thick, smooth, and shining whitish, usually contorted and compressed: pileus variable in form, 1 in. and more broad, when moist striate and livid, silky and shining, whitish when dry.

106. Agaricus (Clitocybe) ectypus. *Fr.* "Copied Clitocybe."

Pileus rather fleshy, plane, at length depressed, and revolute, hygrophanous, finely streaked, with adpressed sooty fibrillæ; margin rather striate; stem becoming hollow, elastic, fibrillose; gills adnate, somewhat distant and pallid, at length stained with red, mealy.—*Fr. Epicr. p.* 79.

In meadows.

Stem 2-4 in. long, 3-5 lin. thick, sub-bulbous, dirty yellowish; pileus about 2-3 in. broad, honey-coloured, then rufescent; margin very thin, striate.

107. Agaricus (Clitocybe) bellus. *Fr.* "Pretty Clitocybe."

Pileus rather fleshy, convex, then depressed (dull orange), sprinkled with minute dark scales; stem stuffed, equal, tough, rivulose; gills adnate, sub-distant, connected by veins, yellowish, reddish brown, at length mealy.—*Fr. Epicr. p.* 79. *Eng. Fl.* v. *p.* 42.

In fir plantations. Fœtid.

Pileus 2½ in. broad, deep orange brown, becoming gradually pale; gills incarnato-ferruginous; stem 2½ in. high.—*M. J. B.* Often growing in company with *A. laccatus*.

108. Agaricus (Clitocybe) laccatus. *Scop.* "Waxy Clitocybe."

Pileus membranaceous, convex, then depressed, and somewhat umbilicate, variable, hygrophanous, mealy; stem stuffed, equal, tough, fibrous; gills adnate, thick, distant, brightly coloured, at length mealy.—*Fr. Epicr. p.* 79. *Schæff. t.* 13. *Bull. t.* 570, *f.* 1. *Grev. t.* 249. *Kromb. t.* 43, *f.* 17-20, *t.* 72, *f.* 19-20. *Batt. t.* 18, *G. I. Huss.* i. *t.* 47. *Berk. Outl. t.* 5, *f.* 3. *Bolt. t.* 63-64. *Sow. t.* 187-208. *Fl. Dan. t.* 1249. *Batsch. f.* 99. *Eng. Fl.* v. *p.* 41. *Price, f.* 122.

In woods. Extremely common and variable. [United States.]

Sometimes of a bright amethyst, usually reddish brown; pileus 1-2 in. broad, convex, the centre more or less depressed, often cracked or squamulose, with a mealy appearance, sub-carnose, turning pale when dry, margin incurved, often very much lobed and waved; gills more or less of the colour of the pileus, not changing colour, horizontal, broad behind, and adnate, thick, distant, sometimes forked above, mealy from the white spores; stem 1-6 in. long, thicker and downy below, fibrillose, tough, hollow, of the colour of the pileus, not becoming pale.—*M. J. B.* Spores globose and echinulate, ·00035 in. diameter; echinulate spores are unusual in *Agaricus*.—*W. G. S.*

Sub-Gen. 6. Pleurotus. Fr. Epicr. p. 129.

Veil evanescent, or none; pileus fleshy in the larger species, with a smooth or ragged margin from the remains of the veil; substance either compact, spongy, slightly fleshy, or membranaceous; stem mostly lateral or wanting, when present confluent and homogeneous with the hymenophore; gills with a sinus or broadly decurrent tooth.

Hab. Most of the species grow on wood, a few only on the ground.—(*Pl. II., fig.* 6, *and fig.* 37.)

Fig 37.

The species are large, handsome, and polymorphic, but some are small and resupinate; they generally appear late in the year, and return, year after year, to the same habitat more frequently than terrestrial fungi; all are harmless, and some edible. All the species become putrid when old, and never coriaceous or woody.—*W. G. S.*

Sect. 1. *Lepiotaria.*—pileus scaly.

109. Agaricus (Pleurotus) corticatus. *Fr.* "Large scaly Pleurotus."

Pileus compact, excentric, villous, at length floccoso-squamulose; stem firm, fibrillose, veil membranaceous, torn; gills decurrent, sub-distant, anastomosing behind.—*Hym. Suec. p.* 236. *B. & Br. Ann. N.H.* 1865, *no.* 995. *Saund & Sm. t.* 4.

On an old prostrate elm. Oct. Belvoir Castle.

Pileus excentric, 7 inches across, expanded, swollen in the centre; disc, especially in the centre, broken up into brownish grey silky scales, which are more minute towards the thin, strongly involute margin: veil woven, adhering slightly to the stem and margin; stem 3 in. high, 1½ in. thick, pitted and silky below the evanescent ring, firm and tough, mottled; gills rather broad, pure white, very decurrent, anastomosing behind, sometimes forked; edge entire. Smell rather strong; a large and noble species, perhaps too closely allied to *A. dryinus.*—*B. & Br.* Spores ·0005 × ·0002 in.

110. Agaricus (Pleurotus) dryinus. *P.* "Spotted Pleurotus."

Pileus compact, hard, oblique, variegated with dark spot-like scales; veil fugaceous, torn, white, appendiculate; stem lateral, stout; gills decurrent, narrow, nearly simple.—*Fr. Epicr. p.* 129. *Nees. f.* 177. *Huss.* ii. *t.* 29-33. *Vent. t.* 44, *f.* 1-2. *Schæff. t.* 233. *Eng. Fl.* v. *p.* 70. *Gard. Chron.* (1860) *p.* 832.

On trunks of ash, willow, &c. Oct. [U. States.]

Pileus ¾-3 in. broad, excentric, white, the surface broken into light brown adpressed scales, margin involute, with fragments of the broad woven veil adhering to it, flesh continued into the stem; gills white, not very broad, decurrent, forked, crisp; stem 3 in. high, attenuated downwards, firm, almost woody, tomentose, but not scaly. Taste like *Ag. campestris.* Spores ·00013 × ·00017 in.

111. Agaricus (Pleurotus) spongiosus. *Fr.* "Spongy Pleurotus."

Pileus pulvinate, soft and spongy, sub-tomentose, veil torn, fugacious, appendiculate; stem very short, excentric, tomentose; gills sinuate, adnate, crowded, white.—*Fr. Epicr. p.* 130.

In a rotten beech. Oct. Epping Forest.—*W. G. S.*

Sub-sessile, thick, pileus cinereous, with the habit of *Polyporus betulina*, 2-3 in. broad, persistently tomentose. Spores ·0004 × ·00018 in.
(Pl. II., f. 6, *reduced.)*

Sect. 2. *Concharia.*—pileus shell-shaped.

112. Agaricus (Pleurotus) ulmarius. *Bull.* "Elm Pleurotus."

Pileus fleshy, compact, convexo-plane, smooth, somewhat spotted, moist; stem rather excentric, stout, thickened below, subtomentose; gills adnexed (emarginate or rounded), rather crowded, broad, whitish.—*Fr. Epicr. p.* 130. *Bull. t.* 510. *Sow. t.* 67. *Vitt. Mang. t.* 23. *Cooke, B.F. t.* 7. *Eng. Fl.* v. *p.* 73. *Price. f.* 83.

On elm trunks. Sept.—Dec. Esculent. [United States.]

Pileus 3-12 in. broad, obtuse, smooth, subcoriaceous, but within very white, soft, yet compact, thick, sometimes marbled with livid spots; gills numerous, broad, white, adnate or sub-decurrent, irregular; stem excentric ascending 2-3 in. long, about 1 in. thick, solid, firm, incrassated at the base, white, sometimes furfuraceous, single or in tufts, varying a good deal in texture.—*Grev.* Spores nearly globular, length ·0002 in.

113. Agaricus (Pleurotus) subpalmatus. *Fr.* "Subpalmate Pleurotus."

Pileus fleshy, soft, convexo-plane, obtuse, even, smooth; stem excentric, incurved, equal, fibrilloso-striate; gills adnate, crowded, broad, rufescent.—*Fr. Epicr. p.* 131. *Sow. t.* 62. *A. palmatus. Eng. Fl.* v. *p.* 73.

On squared timber, old trunks, &c.

Pileus 3-4 in. broad, excentric, at first convex, the margin involute, then more expanded; cuticle thick, tough, elastic, gluey, but not moist, not easily separable from the flesh, distilling drops of a limpid reddish fluid, with a hot and astringent styptic taste, margin beautifully reticulated, of a pale orange buff or nankeen colour, pruinose, very fleshy, flesh mottled; gills paler, rounded behind, connected by veins, free, joined at the base by an obsolete collar. Stem 1-2 in. high, ½ in. thick, oblique, thickest below, smooth, whitish, of a fibrous structure, sometimes a little hollow.—*M. J. B.* Spores slightly echinulate, ·00017 × ·00023 in.

114. Agaricus (Pleurotus) craspedius. *Fr.* "Thick-stem Pleurotus."

Pileus fleshy, soft, convexo-plane, or depressed, undulato-lobate, sub-pruinose; stem solid, excentric, short; gills adnate, scarcely crowded, broad, whitish.—*Fr. Epicr. p.* 131. *Paul. t.* 44, *f.* 3. *Fl. Dan. t.* 891. *Saund. & Sm. t.* 7.

On the trunks of trees.

Cæspitose. Stem elastic, spongy within, unequal, pallid. Pileus more or less excentric, 3-5 in. broad, brick-red, pale tan, or greyish; margin at first involute, then opened, crenately lobed and waved, and fimbriate.

115. Agaricus (Pleurotus) fimbriatus. *Bolt.* "Fringed Pleurotus."

Pileus fleshy, thin, plane, then funnel-shaped, even, hygrophanous; margin at length sinuate and lobed; stem somewhat excentric, stuffed, compressed, firm, short, rootless, villous; gills adnate, thin, much crowded, slightly forked, white.—*Fr. Epicr. p.* 131. *Bolt. t.* 61. *Sterb. t.* 15, *B. Ann. N.H., no.* 672*. *Eng. Fl.* v. *p.* 37.

On trunks. Rare.

Gregarious, or tufted. Pileus 3 in. broad, slightly fleshy, plano-convex when young, often excentric; turning pale; gills very close, narrow and tender, often forked; stem about 1 in. long, smooth.—*Fries.* Most beautifully and repeatedly lobed and fimbriated.—*M. J. B.*

116. Agaricus (Pleurotus) lignatilis. *Pers.* "Beech Pleurotus."

Pileus fleshy, firm, convexo-plane or somewhat umbilicate, floccoso-pruinose; stem stuffed, then hollow, flexuose, sub-villose; gills adnate, crowded, narrow, white.—*Pers. Syn. p.* 368. *B. & Br. Ann. N.H.* (1865), *no.* 996. *Fl. Dan. t.* 1797. *Saund. & Sm. t.* 6.

On beech trees. Burnham Beeches, abundant in 1863.

With a strong mealy odour. Stem sometimes 2-3 in. sometimes only 3-4 lines long, thin, unequal, pileus usually more or less excentric, from 1 to 3-4 in. broad, repand, undulately lobed. Spores ·00015 × ·00012 in.

117. Agaricus (Pleurotus) circinatus. *Fr.* "Circinate Pleurotus."

Pileus fleshy, convexo-plane, obtuse, orbicular, glistening, slightly silky, becoming whitish; stem stuffed, elastic, short, equal, smooth, rooting; gills adnate (sub-decurrent), crowded, white.—*Fr. Epicr. p.* 132. *Secr. no.* 670.

On rotten wood. W. W. Saunders, Esq.

Solitary, beautifully regular, sub-central, tough, wholly white, not hygrophanous, odour faint, not mealy; stem 1-2 in. long, 3-4 lines thick; pileus about 3 in. broad.

118. Agaricus (Pleurotus) ostreatus. *Jacq.* "Oyster Pleurotus."

Pileus soft, fleshy, sub-dimidiate, conchate, ascending, growing pale; stem abbreviated (or obsolete), firm, elastic, strigose at the base; gills decurrent, rather distant, anastomosing behind, whitish. —*Fr. Epicr. p.* 133. *Huss.* ii. *t.* 19. *Sow. t.* 241. *Letell. t.* 695. *Vitt. Mang. t.* 4. *Lenz. f.* 19. *Vent. t.* 17, *f.* 3-4, *t.* 18. *Krombh. t.* 41, *f.* 1-7. *Tratt. essb. Sch. t.* O. *Tratt. Austr. t.* 40. *Cooke, B.F. t.* 8. *Smith, E.M. f.* 17. *Jacq. Austr. t.* 288. *Eng. Fl.* v. *p.* 71. *Badh.* i. *t.* 2, ii. *t.* 10. *Hogg. & Johnst. t.* 21.

On trees, especially laburnum. Autumn and winter. Esculent. [United States.]

Imbricated, large; pileus sub-dimidiate, very thick and fleshy, flesh white, dusky towards the surface, 1 in. deep, the border at first fibrillose, or squamulose, margin involute; as the pileus expands the white fibrillæ vanish, and the colour changes from dusky to bistre; margin paler and rimulose, the whole surface shining and satiny when dry, soft and clammy when moist, towards the base in age there is a little white down; gills broad, here and there forked, anastomosing at the base, dirty white, the edge serrated, umber. In large specimens there is often a distinct stem, clothed with a dense short white down, which runs up between the gills; when dry the pileus becomes pallid or yellowish.—*M. J. B.* Spores ·0003 × ·00015 in.

119. Agaricus (Pleurotus) salignus. *Fr.* "Willow Pleurotus."

Pileus compact or spongiose, sub-dimidiate, horizontal, at first pulvinate, even, then with the disc depressed, sub-strigose; stem short, white, tomentose; gills decurrent, somewhat branched, eroded, distinct at the base, nearly of the same colour.—*Fr. Epicr. p.* 133. *Letell. t.* 687. *Tratt. Austr. t.* 4, *f.* 8. *Paul. t.* 22, *Eng. Fl.* v. *p.* 72.

On trunks of trees. Oct.—Jan. [United States.]

Pileus convex, 4-6 in. broad, stem excentric or lateral, sometimes obsolete; fuliginous, white, or ochraceous, according to its stage of growth.—*Fries.* Spores ·00036 × ·00015 in.—*W.G.S.*

Sect 3. *Holopleurus.*—pileus dimidiate.

120. Agaricus (Pleurotus) petaloides. *Bull.* "Petaloid Pleurotus."

Ascending; pileus fleshy, spathulate, entire, disc villous, depressed; stem compressed, villous; gills decurrent, crowded, narrow, whitish.—*Fr. Epicr. p.* 134. *Bull. t.* 226, 557. *Vent. t.* 44, *f.* 5, 6. *Pers. Obs. t.* 4, *f.* 1. *Eng. Fl.* v. *p.* 72.

On the ground, amongst grass. Rare. [United States.]

Gills whitish, tender, decurrent; stem flat, often channelled, nearly erect; solitary, stem about 1 in. long, erect.—*Purton.* Spores ·0003 × ·00015 in.—*W. G. S.*

121. Agaricus (Pleurotus) serotinus. *Schrad.* "Yellowish Pleurotus."

Pileus fleshy, compact, viscid; stem lateral, thick, squamulose, with sooty points; gills determinate, crowded, yellowish, or pallid.—*Spic. p.* 140. *B. & Br. Ann. N.H.* 1865, *no.* 997. *Fl. Dan. t.* 1293, *f.* 2. *Buxb.* v. *t.* 2, *f.* 2.

On trunks of trees. Jedburgh. Bowood. [United States.]

Gregarious; pileus 2-3 in. across, yellowish, or dingy olive, reniform, or obovate, margin at first slightly involute, then repand; flesh whitish, insipid.

122. Agaricus (Pleurotus) mitis. *P.* "Kidney-shaped Pleurotus."

Pileus rather fleshy, tough, reniform, even, smooth, growing pale; stem lateral, compressed, dilated upwards, with little white scales; gills determinate, crowded, distinct, white.—*Fr. Epicr. p.* 135. *Berk. Outl. t.* 6. *f.* 9. *Eng. Fl.* v. *p.* 74. *Mag. Zool. & Bot. no.* 48.

On dead larch. Oct. Scotland. Notts.

Pileus ½ in. broad, at length almost sessile; gills distinct from the horizontal stem, very close, linear-lanceolate, pallid-whitish.—*Fries.* Firm, tasteless, white, or rufescent. in the young state spathulate, and the stem quite distinct, the pileus gradually dilates, the stem becomes obsolete, and the pileus reniform, the outer margins meeting, and the one overlapping the other; upper stratum gelatinous.—*M. J. B.*

123. Agaricus (Pleurotus) tremulus. *Schæff.* "Grey Pleurotus."

Pileus rather fleshy, reniform, depressed, tough, even; stem marginal, distinct, nearly round, ascending, villous; gills adnate, determinate, narrow, distant, grey.—*Fr. Epicr. p.* 135. *Schæff. t.* 224 (*except fig.* 1.) *Sow. t.* 242. *Eng. Fl.* v. *p.* 74.

Amongst moss. Rare. Malvern Hills. Scotland. Denbighshire. [United States.]

About 1 in. across; grey, turning pale, sometimes sessile, the base villous; gills distinct, distant.

124. Agaricus (Pleurotus) acerosus. *Fr.* "Lawn Pleurotus."

Pileus membranaceous, reniform, plane, striate, sub-lobate, hygrophanous; stem very short or obsolete, lateral, rather strigose at the base; gills determinate, narrow, crowded, simple, grey.—*Fr. Epicr. p.* 135. *Bolt. t.* 72, *f.* 3. *Ann. N.H. no.* 673.

On gravel, lawns, wood, &c. Rare. Hitchen, Suffolk.

Pileus membranaceous, striate, when moist grey, when dry silky white, very variable, 1-2 in. broad; gills horizontal, not decurrent, of the same colour as the pileus. Spores nearly globose, ·0002 in.

Sect. 4. *Omphalaria*—pileus at first resupinate.

125. Agaricus (Pleurotus) porrigens. *P.* "Pine Pleurotus."

White; pileus fleshy, tough, at first resupinate, then ascending from the extended base, ear-shaped, smooth above; gills very narrow, linear.—*Fr. Epicr. p.* 136. *Eng. Fl.* v. *p.* 72.

On old pine trunks. Rare. Inverary.

Imbricated, various in size, sub-flaccid, the base stretching forward, often tomentose, very rarely stipitate; pileus even, margin thin inflexed, lobed in large specimens; gills when young vein-like, somewhat divided.—*Fries.*

126. Agaricus (Pleurotus) septicus. *Fr.* "Thin Pleurotus."

White; pileus somewhat fleshy, thin, resupinate, then reflexed, even, pubescent; stem thin, incurved, pubescent, at length evanescent; rootlets byssoid; gills distant.—*Fr. Epicr. p.* 136. *Sow. t.* 321. *Eng. Fl.* v. *p.* 74. *Letell. t.* 706.

On twigs, decayed fungi, dung, &c.

Pileus 3-5 lines broad, at length free, slightly carnose; gills rather broad, distinct; stem 2 lines high, attenuated upwards, sometimes obsolete, as well as its radicles.—*Fries.*

127. Agaricus (Pleurotus) mastrucatus. *Fr.* "Imbricated Pleurotus."

Pileus fleshy, upper stratum gelatinous, at first resupinate, then expanded, sessile, lobed, squamulose; gills greyish white.—*Fr. Epicr. p.* 137. *Sow. t.* 99. *Eng. Fl.* v. *p.* 74.

On old trunks. Rare. [Cincinnati.]

Imbricated; pileus 1-4 in. across, lobed in large specimens, flaccid, rough with hairs, and rigid points intermixed; gills radiating from a downy knob.—*Fries.*

128. Agaricus (Pleurotus) atrocœruleus. *Fr.* "Blue-black Pleurotus."

Pileus fleshy, upper stratum gelatinous, at first resupinate, then obovate, reniform, tomentose; gills crowded, white, becoming yellowish.—*Fr. Epicr. p.* 137. *Schæff. t.* 246, *f.* 3, 8, 9. *Ann. N.H. no.* 674. *Saund. & Sm. t.* 6.

On trunks. Rare. Penzance.

Pileus at first resupinate, soon reflexed, obovate or kidney-shaped, 1-2 in. broad, villous, rugulose when dry, commonly dark bluish, rarely brown; flesh soft, upper stratum gelatinous. Spores ·0003 × ·00013 in.

129. Agaricus (Pleurotus) algidus. *Fr.* "Dingy Pleurotus."

Pileus fleshy, cuticle gelatinous, at first resupinate, then expanded, reniform, smooth; gills rather broad, crowded, pale, yellowish.—*Fr. Epicr. p.* 137. *Fl. Dan. t.* 1552, *f.* 1, *t.* 1556, *f.* 2. *Pers. M.E. t.* 23, *f.* 5.

On trunks. Linlithgowshire. [United States.]

Pileus about 1 in. across, reddish umber or cinereous, usually cæspitose and imbricated, somewhat kidney-shaped, smooth, viscid when young.

130. Agaricus (Pleurotus) Leightoni. *Berk.* "Leighton's Pleurotus."

Pileus at first obliquely conical, umber, then lead-coloured, furfuraceous, with short scattered bristles intermixed; upper stratum gelatinous; gills rather thick, tan-coloured, distant, somewhat forked at the base, slightly undulated; interstices scarcely reticulated.—*Ann. Nat. Hist.* xiii. *t.* 9, *f.* 1. *Berk. Outl. p.* 138.

On wood. Near Shrewsbury.

Pileus 5 lines broad, at first cyphellæform, obliquely conical, umber brown, gradually becoming paler, at length of a pallid lead colour, furfuraceous, especially behind, where there are a few bristles; flesh consisting of two distinct strata, of which the upper is gelatinous, and of the colour of the pileus, the lower white. Stem, none; gills of a pallid tan colour, thickish, distant, undulated, obscurely wrinkled at the base, the interstices scarcely reticulated. —*M. J. B.*

131. Agaricus (Pleurotus) cyphellæformis. *Berk.* "Pendulous Pleurotus."

Pileus cup-shaped, then dependent, upper stratum gelatinous, cinereous, very minutely strigose, especially at the base; margin paler, sprinkled with a few meal-like scales; gills pure white, rather distant, narrow, linear.—*Mag. Zool. & Bot.* i. *t.* 15, *f.* 3. *Berk. Outl. p.* 138.

On dead stems of herbaceous plants. Oct.

Gregarious. Pileus 2 lines or more broad and high, altogether stemless, cup-shaped, hanging down, cinereous, very minutely strigose, especially at the base; margin paler, sprinkled with a few meal-like scales. Upper stratum gelatinous, cinereous, beneath which the flesh is white and very thin. Gills pure white, rather distant, the alternate ones shorter, narrow, linear.—*M.J.B.*

132. Agaricus (Pleurotus) Hobsoni. *Berk.* "Hobson's Pleurotus."

Pileus membranaceous, reniform, or dimidiate, stemless, pale-grey, minutely downy; gills rather distant, pallid.—*Berk. Outl. p.* 139.

On larch stumps. Sept. Apethorpe.

Pileus 1-4 lines across; margin involute.

133. Agaricus (Pleurotus) applicatus. *Batsch.* "Little grey Pleurotus."

Dark cinereous; pileus submembranaceous, rather firm, resupinate, then reflexed, somewhat striate, sub-pruinose, villous at the base; gills loose, paler.—*Fr. Epicr. p.* 137. *Batsch. f.* 125. *Sow. t.* 301. *Eng. Fl.* v. *p.* 75. *Bull. t.* 581, *f.* 2. *Pers. M.E.* i. *t.* 28, *f.* 8.

On dead fallen branches. Common. [S. Carolina.]

Pileus about ½ in. across, when young cup-shaped, resupinate, slightly carnose, striate when moist, more or less villous; gills broad, distant, radiating, grey, the margin whitish, stem none.—*M.J.B.* (*fig.* 37, *nat. size.*)

134. Agaricus (Pleurotus) striatulus. *Fr.* "Striate Pleurotus."

Pale cinereous. Pileus very delicate, striate, flaccid, smooth; gills few, distant.—*Fr. Epicr. p.* 137. *Eng. Fl.* v. *p.* 75.

On firwood, hazel twigs, &c. Scotland. [S. Carolina.]

Scattered or gregarious, persistent. Pileus 3-4 lines broad, convex, wrinkled when dry; gills few, unequal, distant, sometimes dirty-white, sometimes the whole plant is brown.—*Fries.*

135. Agaricus (Pleurotus) hypnophilus. *P.* "Moss Pleurotus."

Resupinate, flat, white; pileus sub-reniform, nearly smooth; gills simple.—*Pers. M.E.* iii. *t.* 24, *f.* 5 *a. Berk. Outl. p.* 139. *Eng. Fl.* v. *p.* 75.

On the larger mosses and fallen leaves. Appin.

Exactly the habit of *A. variabilis*, but the spores are white, and in consequence the gills do not change colour.

136. Agaricus (Pleurotus) chioneus. *P.* "Snowy Pleurotus."

Snow-white, sub-resupinate, minute; pileus very thin, villous; gills rather broad; stem very short, villous, at length obsolete.—*Pers. M.E.* iii. *t.* 26, *f.* 10-11. *Berk. Outl. p.* 139. *Eng. Fl.* v. *p.* 75.

On wood or dung. Rare. Lytchett, Dorset.

Pileus 2 lines broad, extremely delicate and fragile, clothed with white down, fixed by a few downy threads, the margin involute; gills radiating, distant, with sometimes a single smaller one in the interstices.—*M. J. B.*

Sub-Gen. 7. COLLYBIA, Fr. Epicr. p. 81.

Pileus at first convex, with an involute margin; stem with a cartilaginous bark, of a different substance from the hymenophore, but confluent with it; gills adnate or slightly attached (not decurrent).

HAB. Most of the species are epiphytal.—*(Pl. II., fig. 7.)*

Usually small and tough, lasting far into the winter; few only are known to be edible, as *A. fusipes, Bull. A. esculentus, Wulf*, &c. *Marasmius* is closely allied to *Collybia*.

Sect. 1. *Striæpedes*—stem sulcate, fibrillose, or striate.

137. Agaricus (Collybia) radicatus. *Relh.* "Rooting Collybia."

Pileus fleshy, thin, convex, then plane, wrinkled, glutinous; stem stuffed, tall, attenuated upwards, rooting, rigid, smooth; gills adnexed, distant, white.—*Fr. Epicr. p.* 81. *Sow. t.*48. *Gard. Chron.* 1860, *p.* 265. *Grev. t.* 217. *Krombh. t.* 62, *f.* 6-10. *Paul. t.* 97, *f.* 3-4. *Berk. Outl. t.* 5, *f.* 4. *Eng. Fl.* v. *p.* 44. *Huss.* i. *t.* 15. *Price, f.* 98. *Vent. t.* 56, *f.* 1-2.

On old stumps, &c. Very common. [United States.]

Pileus 3-4 in. across, flat, more or less umbonate, radiato-rugose, smooth, at first slimy, carnose, tough and elastic, delicate, fusco-ochraceous, olivaceous, &c., often irregular; gills white, thick, distant, ventricose, adnate, with or without a tooth, sometimes almost decurrent; stem 4-8 in. high, about ⅜ in. thick, attenuated upwards, twisted, not smooth, but rather furfuraceous, sometimes striate above with raised lines, paler than the pileus, juicy, brittle, splitting longitudinally, sometimes tough, at length hollow, rufescent within, penetrating very deeply into the ground by a fusiform root. —*M.J.B.* Spores ·00041 × ·00068 in.

138. Agaricus (Collybia) longipes. *Bull.* "Long-stemmed Collybia."

Pileus fleshy, thin, conical, then expanded, umbonate, dry, slightly velvety; stem stuffed, tall, attenuated upwards, villose, at length sulcate; root long, fusiform; gills rounded behind, rather distant, white.—*Bull. t.* 232. *Fr. Epicr. p.* 81. *Huss.* i. *t.* 80. *Batt. t.* 20, *f.* A. *Corda. Sturm. t.* 52. *Ag. pudens, Ann. N.H. no.* 64.

On old stumps, &c.

Stem quite as velvety as in *A. velutipes*, and the pileus, especially its margin, more or less so, and by no means glutinous.

139. Agaricus (Collybia) platyphyllus. *Fr.* "Broad-gilled Collybia."

Pileus between fleshy and membranaceous, becoming plane, obtuse, moist, streaked with little fibres; stem stuffed, equal, soft, naked, striate, pallid, ending abruptly; gills truncate, adnexed distant, broad, white.—*Fr. Epicr. p.* 82. *Bull. t.* 594. *Paul t* 97, *f.* 1-2. *Buxb.* iv. *t.* 18. *Ann. N.H. nos.* 263, 323.

In woods, amongst leaves. Rare. [S. Carolina.]

Pileus 5 in. or more across, smooth, hygrophanous, expanded, with a broad umbo, sinuated and undulate, thin, except in the centre, umber shaded with bistre, more or less virgate, but by no means silky, though it has a sleek shining aspect, flesh brownish beneath the sub-cartilaginous cuticle, in other parts firm and white; stem 2½ in. high, ½ in. thick, nearly equal, obtuse, stringy, slightly twisted, streaked, smooth, not rooting; gills broad, truncato-adnexed, at first white, at length pallid, distant, smell strong, taste not unpleasant.—*M. J. B.*

The variety (*A. repens*), with a stout creeping mycelium, has also been found in Britain.—(*Gard. Chron.*, 1861, *p.* 926, *fig.*) Spores ·0005 × ·0007 in.

140. Agaricus (Collybia) fusipes. *Bull.* "Spindle-stem Collybia."

Tough; pileus fleshy, convex, then plane, smooth, even, or rimose, umbo evanescent; stem stuffed, then hollow, contorted, swollen, sulcate, fusiform and rooting; gills adnexed, nearly free, at length separating behind, broad, distant, connected by veins, white, then the colour of the pileus.—*Fr. Epicr. p.* 83. *Bull. t.* 106, 516, *f.* 2. *Sow. t.* 129. *Vent. t.* 19, *f.* 5-7. *Krombh. t.* 42, *f.* 9-11. *Schæff. t.* 87-88. *Fl. Dan. t.* 1607. *Batt. t.* 20. *B. Berk. Outl. t.* 5, *f.* 5. *Huss.* ii. *t.* 48. *Cooke, B.F. t.* 5. *Eng. Fl.* v. *p.* 45. *Price, f.* 85. *Hogg. & Johnst. t.* 14.

On stumps. Very common. Esculent.

Densely tufted; pileus 1½ in. or more broad, when young hemispherical, smooth, dull vinous brown, fleshy; margin incurved, then expanded, cracked, sometimes tesselated and warty, paler, but here and there towards the margin marked with dark patches, as if burnt; gills pale, umber, free, or only apparently adnate, sometimes rounded behind, and then separating from the stem, with a rather watery appearance, though dry, connected by veins, distant; stem 2-6 in. long, ½-1 in. thick, ventricose, rooting, paler than the pileus, marked towards the base with little dark specks, striate longitudinally, often cracked; substance within loose and fibrous, at length hollow; taste agreeable.—*M. J. B.* Spores ·0002 × ·00013 in.

Var. **ædematopus.** *Fr.* Gills unequally decurrent, pallid.—*Pall. Ross.* i. *t.* 9, *f.* 2. (*Pl. II. f.* 6, *reduced.*)

141. Agaricus (Collybia) maculatus. *A. & S.* "Spotted Collybia."

Pileus fleshy, compact, convex, then plane, obtuse, even, smooth; stem stout, ventricose, striate, attenuated below, abrupt; gills free, crowded, rather linear, white, as well as the stem.—*Fr. Epicr. p.* 84. *Sow. t.* 246. *Huss.* ii. *t.* 60. *Eng. Fl.* v. *p.* 45.

In fir woods. Not common.

Pileus 2-3 in. across, at first white, then spotted, as well as the stem, with reddish brown, even, smooth, truly carnose, rather compact, hemispherical, at first with an involute margin, then quite plane, margin often repand, white, here and there spotted with rufous, at length altogether dirty rufous; gills free, very close, narrow, scarcely above 2 lines broad, linear, dirty pallid; stem 3-4 in. high, but much drawn out when growing amongst moss, 4-10 lines thick, stout, unequal, more or less ventricose and attenuated below.—*Fries.* Spores nearly globular, length ·0002 in.

(Pl. II., fig. 6, small figure.)

142. Agaricus (Collybia) butyraceus. *Bull.* "Buttery Collybia."

Pileus fleshy, convex, then expanded, umbonate, even, smooth, moist, changing colour, flesh becoming white; stem stuffed, externally cartilaginous, conical, striate, reddish brown; gills nearly free, crowded, crenulate, white.—*Fr. Epicr. p.* 84. *Bull. t.* 572. *Buxb.* iv. *t.* 5. *f.* 1. *Batt. t.* 16, *C. Eng. Fl.* v. *p.* 46.

In woods, especially of fir. Common. [S. Carolina.]

Pileus 1½ in. broad, sub-carnose, convex, expanded, umbonate, sub-viscid, of a livid ochre, or dull green, when quite young of a livid brown, the margin sub-rufescent, but a portion below the umbo soon grows pale, so that the pileus appears of four colours; the umbo always dark, sometimes the rest of the pileus is pale, rufescent, or ochraceous, margin occasionally striate, flesh white, mottled with rufous; gills close, free, not ventricose, rounded, edge rather uneven and notched; stem 1½-2 in. high, ⅜ in. thick below, somewhat twisted, smooth, slightly striate, downy at the bulbous base, stuffed, white within, outer coat of a different structure and pubescent.—*M. J. B.*

Sect. 2. *Velutipedes*—stem velvety, floccose, or pruinose.

143. Agaricus (Collybia) velutipes. *Curt.* "Velvet-stemmed Collybia."

Pileus fleshy, thin, convex, then plane, obtuse, smooth, viscid; stem stuffed, velvety, rooting, dark-bay; gills adnexed, distant, yellowish.—*Fr. Epicr. p.* 86. *Curt. Fl. L. t.* 70. *Huss.* i. *t.* 56. *Bolt. t.* 135. *Krombh. t.* 44, *f.* 6-9, *t.* 62, *f.* 21. *Tratt. Austr. t.* 7. *Batsch. f.* 122. *Paul. t.* 104, *f.* 5-6. *Cooke exs. no.* 301. *Vent. t.* 25. *f.* 3-4. *Batt. t.* 22 *C. Eng. Fl.* v. *p.* 44. *Vaill. t.* 12, *f.* 8-9. *Bull. t.* 344, 519, *f.* 2.

On logs and trunks of trees. Common. [United States.]

Cæspitose; pileus 1-3 in. broad, smooth, slimy, of a beautiful tawny colour, convex. expanded, fleshy, margin thin, sub-transparent; gills ventricose, broad, scarcely adnate, ochraceous; stem 2-9 in. high, ¾ in. thick, incurved, velvety, rich tawny brown, pale above, often compressed and striate, fistulose. —*M. J. B.* Spores variable in size, nearly globular, average length, ·00027 in.

144. Agaricus (Collybia) caulicinalis. *Bull.* "Thatch Collybia."

Pileus somewhat fleshy, convex, then plane, umbilicate, clothed with velvety scales, or fibrillose; stem stuffed, then fistulose, tough, more or less hairy; gills separating, then free, ventricose, rather distant, white.—*Bull. t.* 522, *f.* 2. *A. stipitarius. Fr. Epicr. p.* 87. *Alb. & Sch. t.* 9, *f.* 6. *Berk. Outl. t.* 5, *f.* . *Huss.* i. *t.* 68.

On grass, old thatch, twigs, &c. [United States.]

Pileus clothed with tawny or brown hairs, or fibres, which sometimes form scales, 4-5 lines broad; stem 1-2 in. long, tough, bright brown.

145. Agaricus (Collybia) confluens. *P.* "Confluent Collybia."

Pileus somewhat fleshy, convex, then plane, obtuse, flaccid, smooth, hygrophanous; stem fistulose, slightly compressed, rufous, clothed with white, pulverulent down; gills remote, free, narrow, very crowded, whitish.—*Fr. Epicr. p.* 88. *Pers. Ic. Pict. t.* 5. *f.* 1. *Buxb.* iv. *t.* 20. *Batsch. f.* 104. *Eng. Fl.* v. *p.* 46.

Amongst leaves in woods. Common. [United States.]

Pileus 1 in. across, reddish brown, in rings or confluent masses; gills leaving a distinct area round the top of the stem; stems adhering to each other; densely tufted, at first convex, at length expanded, obsoletely umbonate, more or less irregular and compressed, the margin when fresh finely striate; gills distinct, perfectly free, linear, finely serrulate, pale, changing to cream colour; stem 2 in. high, or more, above 1 line thick, compressed, thickest upwards, pale rufous below, the whole covered with white mealy pubescence, not strigose.—*M. J. B.*

146. Agaricus (Collybia) ingratus. *Schum.* "Unpleasant Collybia."

Pileus rather fleshy, globose, campanulate, or convex, umbonate, even; stem fistulose, long, contorted, rather compressed, pulverulent or downy, especially above, umber below; gills free, narrow, very crowded, pallid.—*Fr. Epicr. p.* 88. *Berk. Out. p.* 117.

Var. **B.** Pileus convex, obtuse; stem villoso-pulverulent.—*Berk. Out. p.* 117.

In woods.

Differs principally from *A. confluens* in the gills not leaving a free space round the top of the stem.—*M. J. B.*

147. Agaricus (Collybia) vertirugis. *Cooke.* "Wrinkled Collybia."

Pileus tough, thin, radiato-rugose, minutely pulverulent, campanulate, then convex, at length plane; stem minutely velvety, strigose at the base, fistulose; gills adnate, white, with a yellowish tinge, connected by veins.—*Ag. undatus. Berk. Outl. p.* 117, *no.* 107. *Eng. Fl.* v. *p.* 51.

On dead fern roots.

Pileus not exceeding 1 in. across, dull brown, or cinereous, campanulate, at length convexo-plane, wrinkled in the direction of the gills, tough, submembranaceous, minutely pulverulent; gills truly adnate, ascending or horizontal, moderately distant, connected by veins, white, with a yellowish tinge; stem 2-2½ in. high, ½-1 line thick, strigose at the base, rufous, minutely velvety, fistulose, sometimes compressed.—*M. J. B.*

As *Ag. undatus* Fries. has precedence of this species, the name adopted by the Rev. M. J. Berkeley must be given up, and we therefore substitute another. According to custom this would be *Ag. Berkeleyi*, if that name had not already been adopted for an Indian species.

148. Agaricus (Collybia) conigenus. *P.* "Fir-cone Collybia."

Pileus somewhat fleshy, nearly plane, unequal, sub-umbonate, smooth; stem minutely fistulose, tough, pulverulent, becoming pallid, root strigose or fibrillose; gills free, narrow, much crowded, becoming pallid.—*Fr. Epicr. p.* 89. *Buxb.* i. *t.* 57, *f.* 2. *Sow. t.* 206. *Eng. Fl.* v. *p.* 50.

On fir cones. Oct. Nov.

Pileus about 1 in. across, reddish brown at first, pallid when dry, rather irregular, umbonate, expanded, often depressed, sometimes quite smooth, occasionally more or less lanato-pubescent, sometimes tinged with chocolate; flesh woolly when dry, firm when moist; gills very numerous, linear, free, or only adnexed, tinged with yellow, or of the colour of the pileus, the unequal ones very long; stem variable in length, ½-1½ lines thick, tough, pulverulento-pubescent, with a long, very strigose, rooting base, rufous, hollow, woolly inside.—*M. J. B.* Spores ·0001 × ·00015 in.

149. Agaricus (Collybia) cirrhatus. *Schum.* "Cirrhate Collybia."

Pileus rather fleshy, plane, silky, at length umbilicate; stem slightly fistulose, flexuose, equal, pallid, pulverulent; root twisted, fibrillose; gills adnate, crowded, narrow white.—*Fr. Epicr. p.* 90. *Batsch. f.* 95. *Berk. Out. p.* 117.

Amongst leaves, &c. [Cincinnati.]

Often attached to a little yellowish, nodular *Sclerotium.* Stem 1-2 in. long, filiform, pallid; pileus 5-6 lin. broad, rather silky, at length finely and concentrically rivulose, opaque, white.

150. Agaricus (Collybia) tuberosus. *Bull.* "Tuberous Collybia."

White; pileus slightly fleshy, convex, then expanded, umbonate, smooth, even; stem sub-fistulose, obsoletely pulverulent; root smooth, springing from a sclerotioid tuber, somewhat yellowish; gills adnate, crowded, slender, white.—*Fr. Epicr. p.* 90. *Gard. Chron.* 1860, *p.* 456, *fig. Bull. t.* 256. *Fl. Dan.* 1613. *Batsch. f.* 93. *Grev. t.* 23. *Eng. Fl.* v. *p.* 51. *Berk. Mag. Zool. & Bot. no.* 44.

On dead *Russulæ*, &c., and on the ground. Aug.—Nov.

Small; pileus 2-9 lines broad, sub-carnose, at first convex, then expanded, and sub-umbonate, sometimes depressed, white, shining, with a satiny lustre; gills numerous, close, acutely adnate; stem 1 in. long, very slender, white, or subrufescent, under the lens pulverulent, falsely fistulose; the stems have a tendency to become engrafted on each other; either attached to or without a *Sclerotium*.—*Eng. Fl.* Abundant in the tubes of a dead *Polyporus squamosus*, Epping Forest, 1869. Specimen in the British Museum. – *W. G. S.* Spores ·0001 × ·00007 in.

151. Agaricus (Collybia) racemosus. *P.* "Branched Collybia."

Pileus sub-membranaceous, convex, grey, somewhat tomentose, (sprinkled with racemose abortive pilei), stem stuffed, base sclerotioid, black; gills adnate, crowded, white.—*Fr. Epicr. p.* 90. *Sow. t.* 287. *Pers. disp. t.* 3, *f.* 8. (*Nees. f.* 190.) *Mag. Zool. & Bot. no.* 45.

On the ground, or on putrid Agarics. Very rare.

Turns almost black in drying.

Sect. 3. *Lævipedes*—stem naked, smooth.

152. Agaricus (Collybia) acervatus. *Fr.* "Tufted Collybia."

Cæspitose; pileus somewhat fleshy, convex, then plane, at length umbonate, smooth, hygrophanous; margin slightly striate; stem fistulose, equal, naked, rufous; base rooting, tomentose; gills free, narrow, much crowded, at first whitish.—*Fr. Epicr. p.* 92.

At the base of old fir stems.

Pileus when moist reddish, when dry whitish, 2-3 in. broad; stem 2-4 in. long, 1-2 lines thick, quite smooth, except at the base.

153. Agaricus (Collybia) collinus. *Scop.* "Hill Collybia."

Pileus rather fleshy, campanulate, then expanded, umbonate, smooth; stem fistulose, equal, abrupt, naked, even, growing pale;

gills free, ventricose, lax, white, becoming pallid.—*Scop. Carn. p.* 432. *Fr. Epicr. p.* 90. *Schœff. t.* 220. *Fl. Dan. t.* 1609. *Bull. t.* 403, *f.* 1. *Seem. Journ. Bot.* iv. *p.* 347.

On grassy slopes.

Pileus rather viscid, somewhat striate, shining when dry, 1-2 in. broad, smooth, tawny or tan colour, becoming pale; stem 3-4 in. long, 2-3 lines thick, hollow and rather fragile; gills free and rather distant, quaternate.

154. Agaricus (Collybia) xanthopus. *Fr.* "Yellow-stemmed Collybia."

Pileus rather fleshy, convex, then expanded, sub-umbonate, even, smooth; stem fistulose, equal, yellow, even; base equal, rooting, strigose; gills truncate behind, free, broad, thin, lax, crowded, whitish.—*Fr. Epicr. p.* 91. *Batsch. f.* 209, *var. Eng. Fl.* v. *p.* 46.

About the stumps of trees, &c. July.

Pileus 1-2 in. broad, tough, sub-convex, becoming pale; stem 3 in. high, rigid, strigose at the base.—*Fries.*

155. Agaricus (Collybia) dryophilus. *Bull.* "Wood Collybia."

Pileus somewhat fleshy, nearly plane, obtuse, rather depressed, even, smooth, turning pale; stem fistulose, smooth, reddish brown, or yellowish; gills sinuate, adnexed (at length with a decurrent tooth), nearly free, crowded, narrow, white or pallid.—*Fr. Epicr. p.* 92. *Bull. t.* 434. *Sow. t.* 127. *Schœff. t.* 255. *Price, f.* 12. *Huss.* i. *t.* 39. *Eng. Fl.* v. *p.* 47. *Badh.* i. *t.* 8, *f.* 2, ii. *t.* 7, *f.* 5.

Amongst leaves in woods. Very common. [United States.]

Pileus 1-2 in., whitish, pinkish, yellowish, or livid, plane, sometimes depressed, fleshy, thin, tender, easily injured, of a watery substance; gills free, white, or very pale flesh colour, soft, tender, entire, or serrate, numerous; stem 2-3 in. high, $\frac{1}{4}$-$\frac{1}{2}$ in. thick, shining, splitting, sometimes twisted, of the same colour as the pileus, summit generally darker and pinkish; the whole plant fragile, and the pileus easily detached from the stem.—*Grev.* Spores pip-shaped as in *Marasmius peronatus*, Fr.; length ·00025 in.—*W. G. S.*

156. Agaricus (Collybia) exsculptus. *Fr.* "Sulphur-gill Collybia."

Pileus somewhat fleshy, tough, convex, then expanded, umbilicate, unchangeable; stem fistulose, slender, incurved, short, smooth; gills almost free (with a decurrent tooth), arcuate, much crowded, narrow, sulphur coloured.—*Fr. Epicr. p.* 93. *B. & Br. Ann. N.H.* 1866, *no.* 1109.

On decayed oak and on turf.

Pileus 1-2 in.; allied to *A. dryophilus*, but tougher; the gills are sulphur coloured and transversely striate.

157. Agaricus (Collybia) tenacellus. *P.* "Delicate Collybia."

Pileus rather fleshy, nearly plane, sub-umbonate, smooth, even; stem scantily fistulose, tough, naked, tawny; root strigose; gills emarginate, adnexed, broad, loose, sub-distant, snowy white.—*Fr. Epicr. p.* 92. *Sow. t.* 206. *Pers. Ic. pict. t. f.* 3-4. *Eng. Fl.* v. *p.* 50. *A. griseus, Schæff. t.* 236.

On fir cones. [S. Carolina.]

Pileus 1 in. across, tinged with brown, when young conic, then convex and sub-hemispherical, at length expanded and nearly plane, sometimes slightly umbilicate, not striate, sub-carnose, smooth, dry, cinereous, inclining to yellowish, often altogether abortive; gills free, or often adnexed, ventricose, rather distant, shorter ones truncate behind, in general pure white, sometimes with a tinge of grey, under a powerful lens covered with variously hooked or conic papillæ; stem 2-4 in. long, scarcely 1 line thick, flexuous, filiform, attenuated very much towards the base, and somewhat strigose, hollow, pale above, below tawny, very minutely pubescent under a good lens, when young beautifully downy, and then not distinctly hollow, but with only a pale line down the centre. Taste pleasant.—*M. J. B.* Spores ·0002 × ·00013 in.

158. Agaricus (Collybia) esculentus. *Jacq.* "Nail Mushroom."

Pileus somewhat fleshy, nearly plane, obtuse, smooth; stem fistulose, equal, tough, straight, rooting, very smooth, clay coloured; gills adnate, lax, whitish.—*Fr. Epicr. p.* 92. *Jacq. Coll.* ii. *t.* 14, *f.* 4. *Tratt. Esb. t. F. Lenz. f.* 18. *Bull. t.* 422, *f.* 2. *Vaill. t.* 11, *f.* 16-18. *Cooke B.F. t.* 6, *f.* i. *Eng. Fl.* v. *p.* 50.

In pastures. Spring. Esculent. [United States.]

Pileus about 1 in. across, sometimes striate, and occasionally fuscous; gills broad, rather close; stem 2 in. high, 1 line thick, obsoletely fistulose; root generally smooth, sometimes 6 in. long, and downy when growing amongst leaves, either perpendicular or flexuous. Taste bitter, unpleasant.—*Eng. Fl.*

159. Agaricus (Collybia) clavus. *Bull.* "Bolton's Collybia."

Pileus rather fleshy, almost plane, obtuse, even; stem stuffed, thin, smooth, straight, white; gills free, crowded, white, separating slightly at the base.—*Fr. Epicr. p.* 94. *Bull. t.* 148, *A.C., t.* 569 *F. Bolt. t.* 39, *B. Vaill. t.* 11, *f.* 19-20.

On twigs, leaves, &c.

"This is a minute species, differing from *A. acicula* in its white stem and gills, but agreeing somewhat in the orange-red pileus. It is introduced on the faith of Bolton's figure and description, t. 39, B, which however, may possibly be *A. acicula*. The 'English Flora' plant is *A. acicula*."—*M. J. B.*

160. Agaricus (Collybia) ocellatus. *Fr.* "Ocellatė Collybia."

Pileus somewhat fleshy, nearly plane, even, disc depressed, darker, umbonate; stem minutely fistulose, filiform, smooth, brownish white; base rooting, fibrillose; gills adnexed, then separating, crowded, white.—*Fr. Epicr. p.* 94. *Bull. t.* 569, *f.* 1, *H.P. Eng. Fl.* v. *p.* 51.

On the ground, amongst leaves.

Pileus even, smooth, sometimes repand; disc yellow, brown, or rufous; gills close, narrow; stem obsoletely fistulose, 1-3 in. long, sub-filiform, paler above.—*Fries.*

Sect. 4. *Tephrophanæ*—dingy, hygrophanous.

161. Agaricus (Collybia) inolens. *Weinm.* "Scentless Collybia."

Inodorous. Pileus rather fleshy, campanulato-convex, then expanded, rigid, umbonate, smooth, hygrophanous, opaque; margin finely striate, stem stuffed, then hollow, rigid, undulated, whitish-strigose at the base, whitish-squamulose at the apex, gills adnexed, seceding, crowded, whitish, then grey.—*Weinm, no.* 183. *Fr. Epic. p.* 96.

In pine woods. Street.—*J. A. C.*

Livid, stem 2-3 in. long, 1-1½ lin. thick, but compressed, 3 lin. broad. Pileus 1-2 in. broad, repand, unequal, livid, when dry rather silky, pale tan colour.

162. Agaricus (Collybia) plexipes. *Fr.* "Twisted Collybia."

Inodorous. Pileus submembranaceous, campanulate, subrugose, somewhat striate, smooth; stem fistulose, equal, tough, sericeo-fibrous, with entangled fibres, base abruptly rooting; gills free, rather crowded, white, becoming glaucous.—*Fr. Epicr. p.* 96. *S. M.* i. *p.* 146. *Fl. Dan. t.* 2023, *f.* 2.

On trunks.

Pileus at first blackish, dirty white at the margin, then livid-fuliginous. Firm stem, scarcely rooting, about 3 in. long, 1-2 lines thick, dingy, fibrous, obsoletely striate. Pileus campanulate, 1-2 in. broad.—*Fries.* Spores ·00016 × ·00033 in.—*W. G. S.*

163. Agaricus (Collybia) laceratus. *Lasch.* "Torn Collybia."

Pileus between fleshy and membranaceous, campanulate, rather blunt, moist, streaked with brown; stem stuffed, then hollow, firm, twisted, fibroso-striate, floccoso-pruinose above, at length compressed; gills adnexed, distant, broad, thick, greyish white. —*Fr. Epicr. p.* 96. *Berk. Out. p.* 120.

In pine woods.

Pileus 1½ in. across, dingy, pallid when dry.

164. Agaricus (Collybia) protractus. *Fr.* "Protracted Collybia."

Pileus submembranaceous, convexo-plane, shining, disc fleshy, depressed, sub-papillate, darker; margin striate; stem obsoletely fistulose, even, smooth, grey; root long, fibrilloso-strigose; gills fixed, ventricose, very broad, grey, finely dusted with the white spores.—*Fr. Ep. p.* 97. *B. & Br. Ann. N.H.* (1866), *no.* 1110.

On the ground. Nov. Ascot.

Stem 3 in. and more, pileus grey-brown, scarcely an inch broad, gills obliquely ovate, 3 lines broad and more.—*E. F.*

165. Agaricus (Collybia) atratus. *Fr.* "Charcoal Collybia."

Pileus somewhat fleshy, plane, then depressed, umbilicate, smooth, shining, margin convex; stem stuffed, tough, even, smooth, short, brown without and within; gills adnate, rather broad, whitish-grey.—*Fr. Epicr. p.* 98. *Ann. N.H. no.* 671.

On burnt soil in woods.

Pileus 1 in. across, dark brown at first; stem 1 in. high, 1-2 lines thick. Spores ·00023 × ·00016 in.—*W. G. S.*

Sub.-Gen. 8. MYCENA. Fr. S. M. i. p. 140.

Pileus more or less membranaceous, generally striate, with the margin always straight, and at first pressed to the stem, never involute, expanded, campanulate, and generally umbonate (not depressed, as in *Omphalia*); stem externally cartilaginous, tubular, not stuffed when young, confluent with the hymenophore, but heterogeneous from it; gills never decurrent, though some species have a broad sinus near the stem.—(*Pl. II., fig.* 8.)

HAB. Mostly epiphytal.

Most of the species are small, beautiful, and inodorous, but some which have a strong alkaline odour are probably poisonous; none are known to be edible. They appear after rain in summer and autumn.

Sect. 1. *Calodontes*—margin of gills darkest.

166. Agaricus (Mycena) pelianthinus. *Fr.* "Purplish Mycena."

Pileus somewhat fleshy, convex, then expanded, obtuse, moist, hygrophanous; margin striate; stem firm, fibrilloso-striate above, equal, pallid; gills adnexed, emarginate, beautifully connected by veins, purplish, with a darker, toothed edge.—*Fr. Epicr. p.* 99. *Batt. t.* 19, *f. F. Bolt. t.* 4, *f.* 1. *Fl. Dan. t.* 1911, *f.* 1. *Berk. Outl. t.* 6. *f.* 1. *Eng. Fl.* v. *p.* 43. *Mag. Zool. & Bot. no.* 2.

Amongst dead leaves in woods.

Pileus 1-2 in. broad, when moist transparent, when dry whitish, tinged with purple, the disc fleshy, even, rather obtuse, flesh white; gills elegantly connected by a net-work of veins, distant, purple, when dry fuscous-umber; veil none; stem 2-3 in. high, 1½-2 lines thick, smooth, becoming pallid; spores white.—*Fries.* The gills are sprinkled over with short purple hairs, arranged in fascicles on the edge. Smell strong.—*M. J. B.*

167. Agaricus (Mycena) balaninus. *P.* "Beech-mast Mycena."

Pileus somewhat fleshy, convex, then plane, smooth when dry, striate when moist; stem striate, rooting, villous below, squamulose above; gills adnate, then seceding, connected by veins, somewhat reddish, with a purple edge.—*Fr. Epicr. p.* 99. *Berk. Mag. Zool. & Bot.* i. *t.* 15, *f.* 2.

Amongst leaves, beech-mast, &c. Rare.

Pileus 1½ in. broad, convex, sub-campanulate, obtusely umbonate, at length more or less expanded, ochraceous, with a slight tinge of umber, very minutely mealy, slightly rugulose, carnoso-membranaceous, margin scarcely striate; gills broad, rounded, quite free, with the exception of a connecting tooth, rather distant, pale, sprinkled, and fringed with dull purple spiculæ, interstices veiny. Spores white, elliptic; stem 2½ in. high, 1-2 lines thick, attenuated downwards, flexuous, rigid, white, and mealy within the pileus, deep sienna brown below, dark brown at the base, which is embedded more or less in a spongy mass, by which it adheres to the "mast," shining, quite smooth, fistulose.—*M. J. B.*

168. Agaricus (Mycena) marginellus. *Fr.* "Margined Mycena."

Pileus fleshy, campanulate, umbo darker, smooth, finely striate; stem smooth, gills slightly adnexed, distant, white, the edges darkened with minute particles.—*Epicr. p.* 100. *B. & Br. Ann. N.H.* 1865, *no.* 988.

On fir trunks, amongst *Hypnum.* Aug. Aboyne.

"Pileus 3 lines across, conical, striate, pallid grey, darker in the centre, minutely rivulose ; margin sub-crenulate ; stem short, slightly curved, shining, quite smooth, minutely fistulose ; gills distant, slightly adnexed, white, with a purple margin. Under a high magnifying power the pileus (especially the edge) and stem appear clothed with minute glandular particles, similar to those which colour the edge of the gills."—*B. & Br.*

169. Agaricus (Mycena) elegans. *P.* "Elegant Mycena."

Pileus submembranaceous, campanulate, striate, almost umbonate ; stem even, equal, rigid, floccoso-fibrillose at the base ; gills narrow, adnate, livid or whitish, edge yellow, entire.—*Fr. Epicr. p.* 100, *Fl. Dan. t.* 2024, *f.* 2. *Eng. Fl.* v. *p.* 59.

In woods. [S. Carolina.]

Pileus ½ in. or more across, greyish, or livid yellow, obtuse, striate, margin paler, gills rather broad, adnate, with a minute tooth, scarcely ventricose, the part nearest the pileus livid ; margin beautiful yellow ; stem 1-2 in. high, rather brittle, slender, minutely pilose, yellow above, brown below, fistulose, the base strigose, rather swollen, filled with watery juice.—*M. J. B.*

170. Agaricus (Mycena) rubromarginatus. *Fr.* "Red-bordered Mycena."

Pileus somewhat membranaceous, campanulate, obtuse, striate, hygrophanous ; stem rigid, even, without juice ; gills adnate, distant, whitish, edged with purple or purple-brown.—*Fr. Epicr. p.* 101. *Berk. Out. p.* 122.

On pine stumps. Nov.

Stem 1-2 in. long, scarcely exceeding 1 line thick, equal, livid, pallid. Pileus membranaceous, obtuse, about an inch across, hygrophanous, livid reddish or purplish-brown, becoming pale. Somewhat resembling *A. sanguinolentus* but distinguished at once by the absence of red juice in the stem.—*M. J. B.*

171. Agaricus (Mycena) strobilinus. *Pers.* "Fir-cone Mycena."

Scarlet. Pileus rather fleshy, campanulate, with an acute umbo, even ; margin striate ; stem rigid, without juice, even, clothed with white strigose hairs at the base ; gills adnate, edge of a dark blood-red colour.—*Fr. Epicr. p.* 101. *Fl. Dan. t.* 2025, *f.* 1. *Ag. coccineus, Sow. t.* 197. *Eng. Fl.* v. *p.* 59. *A. coccinellus, Fr. Mon. Hym.* ii. *p.* 200.

On fir cones. Rare.

Subgregarious, subfasciculate. Pileus 3-5 lines broad, campanulate, with a rather short, fleshy umbo, smooth, bright red, or red-orange, striate at the margin ; gills adnate, with a decurrent process, distant, whitish-red, edges dull and darker red ; stem 1-2 in. high, hollow, firm, smooth, pale red, strigose at the base and whitish, often with a long root.—*Grev.*

172. Agaricus (Mycena) rosellus. *Fr.* "Rosy Mycena."

Rose-coloured. Pileus membranaceous, hemispherical, obtuse, umbonate, striate : stem thin, soft, without juice, whitish fibrillose at the base ; gills adnate, with the edge darker.—*Fr. Epicr. p.* 101. *Fl. Dan. t.* 2025. *f.* 2. *Pers. Syn. t.* 5, *f.* 3.

Amongst fir leaves. Rare.

Smaller, thinner, softer, and paler, than *A. strobilinus*, which it otherwise somewhat resembles, although perfectly distinct.

Sect. 2. *Adonideæ*—stem not dilated at base, gills of one colour.

173. Agaricus (Mycena) purus. *P.* "Amethyst Mycena."

Strong scented. Pileus rather fleshy, campanulate, then expanded, obtuse, umbonate, smooth, turning pallid ; margin striate; stem rigid, even, nearly naked, villous at the base ; gills very broad, widely sinuate, adnexed, connected by veins, paler than the pileus.—*Fr. Epicr. p.* 102. *Huss.* ii. *t.* 49. *Eng. Fl.* v. *p.* 60. *Paul. t.* 119. *Fl. Dan. t.* 1612, 1673, *f.* 1. *Batsch. f.* 20. *Larbr. t.* 13, *f.* 4. *Bull. t.* 507. *Schæff. t.* 303.

Amongst leaves in woods. Common. [S. Carolina.]

Gregarious. Pileus ½-2 in. broad, sub-carnose, obtuse, convex, at length depressed, the margin thin, pellucid, sometimes marked with two or three concentric groves, amethyst, or rose-coloured, soon changing to a pale brown purple, at last nearly white ; gills broad, adnate, sometimes almost decurrent, at first whitish, then amethyst or rose, then subrufescent, connected by veins, margin uneven ; stem often twisted, more or less fibrillose, at length smooth, tough, hollow, lined with silky fibres, splitting easily upwards, the base often strigose. Always distinguishable by its taste, and odour like that of radishes. —*M. J. B.* Spores ·00023 × ·00013 in.

174. Agaricus (Mycena) Iris. *Berk.* "Blue Mycena."

Pileus hemispherical, obtuse, striate, sub-viscid, adorned with blue fibrillæ ; stem fasciculate, pilose ; gills almost free.—*Berk. Outl. t.* 6. *f.* 3. *Eng. Fl.* v. *p.* 56.

On fir stumps. Oct. Rare.

Fasciculate or scattered, brittle, when young the pileus and stem are bright sky-blue, and beautifully tomentose. Pileus ⅜-⅝ in. broad, membranaceous, hemispherical, obtuse, striate, umber, clothed with blue fibrillæ, which are glued down to the epidermis, scattered in the centre, thicker and more free on the margin, which is slightly denticulate ; gills free or slightly adnexed, linear, pale cinereous, the margin sometimes denticulate ; stem, 1½-3½ in. high, not 1 line broad, not rooting, blue below, above subrufescent, the tomentum below depressed and blue, above nearly white, minutely but distinctly fasciculato-pilose, in very elongated specimens obsolete.—*M. J. B.*

175. Agaricus (Mycena) Adonis. *Bull.* "Delicate Mycena."

Pileus membranaceous, conico-campanulate, smooth, nearly even; stem slender, even, smooth; gills adnexed, uncinate, narrow, white, or tinged with rose colour.—*Fr. Epicr. p.* 102. *Bull. t.* 560, *f.* 2. *Eng. Fl.* v. *p.* 60.

In woods. Rare. [S. Carolina.]

Pileus 3-4 lines high and broad, campanulate, rose-coloured, white, yellowish, or green; gills not decurrent; stem 2 in. or more high.—*Fries.*

176. Agaricus (Mycena) luteo-albus. *Bolt.* "Bolton's Mycena."

Pileus membranaceous, campanulate, umbonate, slightly striate; stem filiform, dry, shining, smooth, yellowish; gills adnate, subuncinate, broad, white.—*Fr. Epicr. p.* 103. *Bolt. t.* 38, *f.* 2. *Eng. Fl.* v. *p.* 60.

Amongst moss in woods. Rare.

Pileus 3-4 lines high and broad, dry; gills sub-ventricose; stem 1-2 in. high, filiform, sub-flexuous.—*Fries.*

177. Agaricus (Mycena) flavo-albus. *Fr.* "Yellow-white Mycena."

Pileus somewhat membranaceous, campanulate, or convex, smooth, almost even, then expanded and umbonate; stem slightly rigid, straight, white, pellucid, pruinose above; gills free, separating, at length plane, ventricose, white.—*Fr. Epicr. p.* 103. *B. & Br. Ann. N. H.* 1865, *no.* 989. *A. pumilus. Bull. t.* 260. *A. lacteus, Berk. Eng. Fl.* v. *p.* 60.

On moss at the base of trunks of trees. Formerly mixed up by Fries with *A. lacteus.*

Pileus variable, yellowish, or entirely white; sometimes difficult to distinguish from *A. lacteus*, 3-6 lin. broad, conico-campanulate, at length expanded, minutely umbonate, when dry pure white; flesh thin, margin transparent, more or less striate and crenulate; gills white, slightly ventricose, adnate or adnexed, connected by veins; stem 1-2 in. high, ½ line thick, sometimes rooting, pulverulent above, pulverulento-fibrillose below, with a little down at the base, not brittle.—*M. J. B.*

178. Agaricus (Mycena) lacteus. *P.* "Milk-white Mycena."

Pileus membranaceous, campanulate, sub-umbonate, when moist striate, even when dry; stem equal, filiform, rather tough, flexile, smooth; gills adnate, ascending, narrow, milk-white.—*Fr. Epicr. p.* 103. *Fl. Dan. t.* 1845, *f.* 1. *Bull. t.* 563, *f. N. O. Buxb.* iv., *t.* 31, *f.* 3.

In fir woods, on leaves, or naked soil. [S. Carolina.]

Stem 1 in. and more long, villous at the base. Pileus thin, papillate, even when dry, 3-5 lin. broad; gills scarcely ½ lin. broad. Spores ·0002 × ·00013 in.

Sect. 3. *Rigidipedes*—stem firm, rigid.

179. Agaricus (Mycena) proliferus. *Sow.* "Proliferous Mycena."

Pileus somewhat fleshy, campanulate, then expanded, dry, with a broad darker umbo; margin at length sulcate; stem firm, rigid, smooth, shining, minutely striate, rooting; gills adnexed, sub-distinct, white, then pallid.—*Fr. Epicr. p.* 105. *Sow. t.* 169.

On soil in gardens. Inodorous.

Densely cæspitose; stem frequently proliferous. Stem pallid above, but below tawny or bay; pileus pallid, disc darker and obtusely umbonate; margin somewhat striate, and at length cracked.

180. Agaricus (Mycena) rugosus. *Fr.* "Rugose Mycena."

Pileus somewhat fleshy, campanulate, then expanded, with unequal elevated wrinkles, cinereous; stem firm, tough, smooth, pallid, strigose below; gills arcuato-adnate, uncinate, connected by veins, sub-distant, whitish grey.—*Fr. Ep. p.* 106. *B. & Br. Ann. N.H.* 1865, *no.* 990. *Bull. t.* 518. *f.* K.M.

On a prostrate oak. Sep. Bodelwyddan.

"Pileus at first campanulate, then convex, sulcate up to the umbo, cinereous, as well as the short compressed stem, which is glabrous above; gills distant, cinereous, uncinato-adnate, connected by veins."—*B. & Br.*

181. Agaricus (Mycena) galericulatus. *Scop.* "Little-cap Mycena."

Pileus submembranaceous, conico-campanulate, then expanded, striate to the umbo, dry, smooth; stem rigid, polished, even, smooth, base rooting, fusiform; gills adnate, with a decurrent tooth, connected by veins, whitish, or flesh-coloured.—*Fr. Epicr. p.* 106. *Bull. t.* 518. *f. C.D.E. Hoffm. t.* 4, *f.* 1. *Paul. t.* 122, *f.* 7. *Eng. Fl.* v. *p.* 58. *Price f.* 55.

On trunks of trees. Very common. [United States.]

Often densely cæspitose, sometimes scattered. Pileus 3-9 lines broad, sometimes larger, campanulate or conical, often subumbonate, at length depressed, innato-fibrillose, striate, brownish-white, with sometimes tints of blue or yellow; gills rather distant, not so broadly adnate as in *A. alcalinus*, sometimes nearly free, often pinkish; stem variable in length, rigid, smooth, except at the base, which is densely strigose. Inodorous, insipid.—*M. J. B.*

182. Agaricus (Mycena) polygrammus. *Bull.* "Sulcate-stem Mycena."

Pileus submembranaceous, conico-campanulate, sub-umbonate, dry, striate; stem rigid, tough, sulcato-striate throughout its length, rooting, strigose at the base, shining; gills attenuated behind (free or uncinate), whitish or flesh-coloured.—*Fr. Epicr. p.* 107. *Bull. t.* 395. *Sow. t.* 222. *Fl. Dan. t.* 1615, *f.* 1, *t.* 1498. *Batsch. f.* 85 *(young). Linnæa.* v. *t.* 7, *f.* 1. *Eng. Fl.* v. *p.* 58.

On trunks of trees. Common. [S. Carolina.]

Pileus 1-1½ in. broad, at first cinereous, umber towards the margin, glandiform, pruinose, then livid brown, conico-campanulate, submembranaceous, rugose, with innate fibres, margin striate; gills rather distant, at first dirty white, then pinkish, ventricose, though sometimes almost linear, all but free, margin subserrulate; stem 3 in. high, 1 line or more thick, regularly and deeply striate, the interstices fibrillose, but occasionally the striæ are obsolete, silvery, rooting, fistulose, nearly the colour of the pileus, but paler, twisted, brittle; inodorous, insipid.—*M. J. B.* Spores ·00035 × ·00026 in. *(Pl. II., fig. 8, reduced.)*

183. Agaricus (Mycena) parabolicus. *A. & S.* "Fir-trunk Mycena."

Pileus submembranaceous, at first oval, then parabolic, obtuse, discoid, becoming pale, striate half way; margin entire, turning white; stem rigid, even, smooth, colour of the pileus, base strigose, swollen, abruptly rooting; gills simple, adnate, ascending, nearly distinct, whitish.—*Fr. Epicr. p.* 107. *Sow. t.* 165.

On trunks, especially of fir.

Stem 2-3 in. long, 1 lin. thick, incrassated at the base, below becoming pale, above dull violet, mealy when young. Pileus obtuse, moist, disc blackish, verging on violet, otherwise becoming pale and whitish.

Sect. 4. *Fragilipedes*—stem fragile.

184. Agaricus (Mycena) atro-albus. *Bull.* "Bi-coloured Mycena."

Rather firm; pileus somewhat fleshy, obtuse, campanulate, even, smooth, opaque, brown; whitish and striate about the margin; stem straight, shining, two-coloured; root swollen, bulbous, hairy; gills attenuated, almost free, ventricose, white.—*Fr. Epicr. p.* 108. *Bolt. t.* 137. *Eng. Fl.* v. *p.* 56.

Amongst moss, at the roots of trees.

Solitary, or gregarious, rather firm; pileus obtuse; stem 2-3 in. long, sometimes pruinose at the apex.—*Fries.*

185. Agaricus (Mycena) dissiliens. *Fr.* "Splitting Mycena."

Very fragile; pileus submembranaceous, conico-campanulate, obtuse, lineato-plicate to the middle; stem attenuated, somewhat incurved, minutely striate, cinereous, dark; base strigose; gills rounded, seceding, at length free, broad, soft, whitish, grey at the base.—*Fr. Epicr. p.* 108. *Bolt. t.* 154. *Mich. t.* 79, *f.* 5. *Paul. t.* 122, *f.* 8 ?

On trunks of trees. Strong scented.

Stem 2 in. long, strigose at the base, very fragile, 1-2 lin. thick, cinereous, compressed, splitting in revolute flaps. Pileus cinereous-brown, whitish at the margin, sulcate to the middle, dry.

186. Agaricus (Mycena) alcalinus. *Fr.* "Stump Mycena."

Rigid, but brittle, strong scented; pileus rather membranaceous, campanulate, obtuse, naked, deeply striate, moist, shining when dry; stem smooth, slightly sticky, shining, villous at the base; gills adnate, rather distant, white, then glaucescent.—*Fr. Epicr. p.* 109. *Schæff. t.* 31-32. *Eng. Fl.* v. *p.* 57. *Gard. Chron.* (1861), *p.* 1114.

On trunks of trees. Common. [S. Carolina.]

Solitary or cæspitose; pileus ½-2 in. broad, subcarnose, umbonate, sub-umbonate, or quite obtuse, even, with or without imbedded fibrillæ, at first conico-papillate, rugose, cinereous, or tinged with olive, sub-striate, when old expanded or depressed, but little changed in colour, though occasionally with a pink or yellow hue; gills adnate, with a tooth, distant when old, slightly ventricose, at first pale, then glaucous, pinkish, or yellowish, more or less connected by veins. Stem 3 in. high, 1-2 lines thick, fistulose, sub-fibrilloso-striate, attenuated upwards, downy at the base, the down sometimes tawny, sometimes firm and tenacious, sometimes very brittle, grey above, yellowish or reddish beneath when young, but when old sometimes changing above to a bright yellow; odour pungent, like fermented or putrid walnuts.—*M. J. B.* Spores ·0003 × ·0002 in.

187. Agaricus (Mycena) pauperculus. *Berk.* "Little-stump Mycena."

Strong scented; pileus obtusely conical or hemispherical, minutely innato-fibrillose, submembranaceous; stem smooth, rooting, villous at the base; gills at first free, then adnexed, white.—*Berk. Outl. p.* 125. *Eng. Fl.* v. *p.* 57.

Inside decayed stumps.

Minute, ochraceous-white. Pileus 1 line broad, fleshy, rather firm, scarcely membranaceous, obtusely conic or hemispherical, most minutely but decidedly innato-fibrillose, pale ochraceous-white, in age almost tawny, probably stained by the wood on which it grows. When moist the gills shine through, giving a striate appearance, but not always. Gills white, adnexed by reason of the growth of the pileus, when young free. Stem ½-1 in. high, ½ line thick, white, curved, rooting, the root villous, minutely stuffed, smooth, even under a high magnifying power, powdered at the top with the spores, generally thicker below; spores white, round; odour farinaceous.—*M. J. B.*

188. Agaricus (Mycena) vitreus. *Fr.* "Glassy Mycena."

Very fragile; pileus membranaceous, campanulate, everywhere lineato-striate, except the umbo or somewhat fleshy disc; stem slender, minutely striate, shining, base fibrillose; gills adnate, distinct, linear, whitish.—*Fr. Epicr. p.* 111. *B. & Br. Ann. N.H.* (1866), *no.* 1111.

In woods. Oct. Bryn Tyrch, Caernarvon.

Pileus livid brown, margin naked. Stem 2-4 in. long, ½ lin. thick, minutely striate, base fibrillose, insinuating itself amongst moss, falsely rooting (pseudo-radicate).

189. Agaricus (Mycena) tenuis. *Bolt.* "Slender Mycena."

Very brittle; pileus membranaceous, campanulate, then convex, obtuse, lineato-striate, margin crenate, appendiculate; stem membranaceous, pellucid, straight; gills adnate, distant, distinct, thin, watery, whitish.—*Fr. Epicr. p.* 111. *Bolt. t.* 37. *Price f.* 9.

In shady moist woods. Rare.

Delicate, very fragile and watery. Stem 3 in. or more long, scarcely 1 lin. thick; hyaline white, or yellowish, at the base. Pileus about ½ in. broad, hyaline, or tawny white. Spores ·00015 × ·0001 in.—*W. G. S.*

190. Agaricus (Mycena) tenellus. *Schum.* "Delicate Mycena."

Cæspitose. Pileus membranaceous, campanulate, then convex, obtuse, pellucid; margin striate; stem slender, soft, smooth; base villous; gills uncinate, very thin, crowded, white or flesh-coloured. —*Fr. Epicr. p.* 111. *Ray. Syn. t.* 1, *f.* 2.

On decayed trees.

Pileus ½ in. broad, entirely white, or tinged with rose-colour. Has not been found since the time of Ray, and it is very rare on the Continent.—*M. J. B.*

Sect. 3. *Filopedes*—stem filiform, flaccid.

191. Agaricus (Mycena) filopes. *Bull.* "Thready-stem Mycena."

Pileus membranaceous, obtuse, campanulate, then expanded, striate; stem filiform, flaccid, rather brittle, smooth; base pilose, rooting; gills free, lanceolate, crowded, white.—*Fr. Epicr. p.* 112. *Bull. t.* 320. *Hoffm. t.* 6. *f.* 1. *Batsch. f.* 2. *Eng. Fl.* v. *p.* 56.

In woods, amongst leaves. [United States.]

Pileus livid, brown, or umber, tinged with pink, ½ in. broad, convex, or conico-campanulate, striate; gills free, or minutely adnexed, slightly ventricose, white, or a dilute shade of the pileus; stem 2-3 in long, fistulose, juicy, smooth, except the rooting base, which is pilose, livid, dirty white, or brownish.—*M. J. B.*

192. Agaricus (Mycena) vitilis. *Fr.* "Flexile Mycena."

Pileus membranaceous, conical, then expanded, papillate, moist, deeply striate, becoming pale; stem filiform, straight, flexile, smooth, without juice, shining, rooting; gills attenuato-adnate, rather distant, greyish-white.—*Fr. Epicr. p.* 113. *Sow. t.* 385, *f.* 5. *Bull. t.* 518, *f. O.*

Amongst leaves.

Stem thin, hollow, 3-6 in. long, filiform, rooting; pileus papillate, 3-4 lin. broad, striate to the middle, dry, livid, or brown, becoming pale or whitish; gills linear, whitish, or grey, edge growing paler.

193. Agaricus (Mycena) speireus. *Fr.* "Opaque Mycena."

Pileus membranaceous, conico-convex, then plane, unpolished, striate; disc darker, at length depressed; stem filiform, tough, shining, fibrillose, rooting; gills plane, then decurrent, distant, white.—*Fr. Epicr. p.* 113. *Berk. Out. p.* 126.

On mossy trunks.

Stem 2 in. long, ½ lin. thick; pileus 2-3 lines broad, opaque, greyish brown, sometimes fibrillose or pruinose.

194. Agaricus (Mycena) acicula. *Schæff.* "Orange Mycena."

Pileus membranaceous, campanulate or convex, smooth, orange-red; margin striate, stem rooting, setaceous, tough, shining; gills rounded-adnexed, ventricose, distant, yellow, becoming whitish at the edge.—*Fr. Epicr. p.* 114. *Schæff. t.* 222. *Eng. Fl.* v. *p.* 52.

On leaves, twigs, &c., in woods.

Pileus ½-4 lines broad, campanulate, generally umbonate, margin striate, under a powerful lens, most minutely pilose, bright orange, the umbo darkest, sub-carnose, within deep orange; gills few, somewhat ventricose, adnexed or adnate, with shorter ones between them, white, tinged with yellow; stem about 1 in. long, quite filiform, flexuous, nearly equal, minutely pilose, like the pileus, pale yellow, with a line within.—*Eng. Fl.*

Sect. 4. *Lactipedes*—gills and stem milky.

195. Agaricus (Mycena) hæmatopus. *Pers.* "Bleeding Mycena."

Cæspitose; pileus fleshy, campanulate, obtuse, smooth, margin denticulate; stem rigid, pulverulent, yielding a dark-red juice; gills adnate, white.—*Pers. Obs.* ii. *p.* 56. *B. & Br. Ann. N.H.* 1865, *no.* 991.

On old dead trunks. Sept. Bodelwyddan. [United States.]

"Tufted; pileus moist, campanulate, then expanded, reddish, with a tinge of purple, ½-1 in. or more across, striate, very minutely rivulose; stem pale rufous, flesh-coloured, at first thickened at the base, then nearly equal, farinaceous; gills distant, adnato-sub-decurrent, white, edge red; interstices even; everywhere distilling when broken a dark-red juice. Far larger than any form of *A. sanguineolentus* or *A. cruentus*."—*B. & Br.*

196. Agaricus (Mycena) cruentus. *Fr.* "Red-juiced Mycena."

Pileus submembranaceous, conico-campanulate, striate, margin entire; stem rigid, glabrous, villous at the base, distilling a red juice; gills adnate, whitish.—*Fr. Sys. Myc.* i. *p.* 149. *B. & Br. Ann. N.H.* 1865, *no.* 992.

On fir cones. Bodelwyddan, Flintshire.

"Pileus conic, obtuse, striate, margin inflexed, entire; substance at first rather thick in proportion; stem rigid, smooth, full of red juice, strigose at the base; gills obtuse in front, shortly adnate, white; margin of the same colour."—*B. & Br.*

197. Agaricus (Mycena) sanguineolentus. *A. & S.* "Stinking Mycena."

Pileus membranaceous, campanulate or convex, striate; stem flaccid, smooth, yielding a red juice; gills adfixed, reddish, with a dark purplish edge.—*Fr. Epicr. p.* 115. *Bull. t.* 518, *f.* P. (*right*). *Eng. Fl.* v. *p.* 59.

Amongst leaves in woods. Sept. Oct.

Solitary or gregarious; pileus 1-2 lines broad, obtuse, margin striate, brownish purple, resembling that of the crust of port wine; gills paler, adnate, with a tooth, margin purple; stem straight, smooth, sometimes attenuate, upwards of the same colour as the pileus, darker below, fistulose, replete with pellucid juice of the same colour; when growing on fir cones strigose at the base; odour strong.—*M. J. B.* Spores large, irregular, approaching in shape some Hyporhodii ·00034 × ·0002 in.

198. Agaricus (Mycena) crocatus. *Schrad.* "The Stainer."

Pileus sub-membranaceous, campanulate, sub-striate; stem tall, attenuated, with a villous, rooting base, yielding a copious saffron-coloured juice; gills attenuated behind, adnexed, ventricose, white.—*Fr. Epicr. p.* 115. *Fl. Dan. t.* 1550, *f.* 1, 2024, *f.* 1. *Knapp. Journ. Nat. t.* 7. *Ann. N.H. no.* 672.

Amongst leaves.

Stem 3-5 in. long, about 1 lin. thick; pileus ½-1 in. broad, olive, greyish, or whitish, margin quite smooth.

199. Agaricus (Mycena) chelidonius. *Fr.* "Celandine Mycena."

Pileus membranaceous, campanulate, then convex, obtuse, nearly even; stem even, smooth, rooting, compressed, with a yellow juice; gills adnate, whitish, then yellowish.—*Fr. Epicr. p.* 115. *Sow. t.* 385, *f.* 4.

On stumps of beech.

Only found by Sowerby. Stem 1½-2 in. long, about 1 lin. thick, smooth, yellowish, with a sparing yellow juice, rooting; base villous; pileus ½-1 in. broad, pellucidly striate when moist, even and opaque when dry, yellowish, tinged with flesh colour.

200. Agaricus (Mycena) galopus. *Schrad.* "White milky Mycena."

Pileus membranaceous, campanulate, rather umbonate, striate; stem slender, fibrillose, and rooting base, filled with white milk; gills attenuated, adnexed, white, then glaucous.—*Fr. Epicr. p.* 115. *Berk. Outl. t.* 6, *f.* 2. *Fl. Dan. t.* 1550, *f.* 2. *Batt. t.* 28. *Q. Eng. Fl.* v. *p.* 58.

Amongst leaves, under trees. [S. Carolina.]

Pileus ½-1 in. broad, campanulate, or convex, ochraceous, the centre blackish, pellucid, striate; gills white, arcuato-adnate, or even decurrent; stem 2-3 in. high, about 1 line thick, pale umber, base somewhat rooting, fibrilloso-tomentose, or even strigose, fistulose, not brittle; milk mild, taste like that of radishes; variable, but known by its white milk.—*M. J. B.*

Sect 5. *Glutinipedes*—stem viscid, not milky.

201. Agaricus (Mycena) epipterygius. *Scop.* "Yellow-stem Mycena."

Pileus membranaceous, campanulate, then expanded, rather obtuse, striate, cuticle viscid, separable; stem elongated, tough rooting, smooth, viscid, yellowish; gills adnate, with a decurrent tooth, variable in colour.—*Fr. Epicr. p.* 116. *Sow. t.* 92. *Fl. Dan. t.* 2078, *f.* 2. *Eng. Fl.* v. *p.* 62. *Schæff. t.* 31.

Amongst fern leaves in woods. Aug.—Nov. Common. [United States.]

Pileus 1 in. or more broad and high, obtuse, sometimes umbilicate, cinereous yellow, occasionally white, bluish or rufous, sub-membranaceous, margin striate and toothed, cuticle viscid, when moist easily tearing off; gills arcuato-adnate, sub-decurrent, partaking of the colour of the pileus. Stem 3-4 in. high, about 1 line thick, full yellow, viscid, smooth, tomentose at the base.—*M. J. B.*

202. Agaricus (Mycena) pelliculosus. *Fr.* "Pelliculose Mycena."

Pileus membranaceous, campanulate, then convex, obtuse, lineato-striate, cuticle viscid, separable; stem short, smooth, viscid, livid; gills distant, glaucescent, joined behind and slightly decurrent.—*Fr. Epicr. p.* 116. *B. & Br. Ann. N.H. no.* 788, *no.* 1110*.

On heaths, on the ground. Hanham.

Pileus ½-1 in., grey. Stem rather thickened above, short, viscid, livid, or brownish; remarkable amongst its allies for the viscid separable cuticle.

203. Agaricus (Mycena) vulgaris. *P.* "Common Mycena."

Pileus somewhat membranaceous, convex, then depressed, papillate, viscid; stem tough, fibrillose at the base, rooting, cinereous; gills sub-decurrent, thin, white.—*Fr. Epicr. p.* 116. *Fl. Dan.* 1678, *f.* 2. *Berk. Outl. t.* 6, *f.* 4. *Mag. Zool. & Bot. no.* 46. *Pers. Ic. Pict. t.* 19, *f.* 3. *Berk. exs. no.* 133.

On plantations, especially of larch. Oct. [United States.]

Gregarious. Stem 1-2 in. long, about 1 lin. thick, greyish, rooting at the base, and whitish strigose. Pileus 3 lin. and more broad, slightly viscid, grey or tawny.

204. Agaricus (Mycena) citrinellus. *P.* "Lemon-coloured Mycena."

Pileus membranaceous, hemispherical, then plane, umbonate, striate, viscid, as well as the stem, which is villous at the base and lemon-coloured; gills uncinate, white.—*Fr. Ep. p.* 116. *Pers. Ic. Desc. t.* 11, *f.* 3. *Fl. Dan. t.* 1614, *f.* 1. *Batsch. f.* 88.

In fir woods, &c.

Small, delicate, becoming pale. Pileus 2-3 lin. broad, scarcely viscid, lemon-coloured, with the disc darker. Gills distant. Spores ·00033 × ·00028 in.

205. Agaricus (Mycena) roridus. *Fr.* "Dripping Mycena."

Very delicate; pileus very thin, convex, sub-umbilicate, sulcate, dry; stem thread-like, very glutinous; gills decurrent, distant, white.—*Fr. Epicr. p.* 117. *Eng. Fl.* v. *p.* 30*.

On dead bramble-twigs, &c.

Pileus ½ in. broad, or more, dirty ochraceous, at length umbilicate, and slightly depressed, striate or plicate, often rugose, very minutely scabrous under a high magnifier. Gills white, strongly decurrent, broad, their edge powdery; stem 1½ in. or more high, very slender, fistulose, at first tinged with violet above, at length dirty ochre, pulverulent within the pileus, below clothed with abundant white pellucid gluten, which almost drips from it; sometimes the whole plant is nearly white.—*M. J. B.*

Sect. 6. *Basipedes*—stem dry, dilated at the base into a little disc.

206. Agaricus (Mycena) stylobates. *P.* "Discoid Mycena."

Pileus membranaceous, campanulate, obtuse, striate, sub-pilose; stem filiform, smooth; base orbicular, plane, villous, striate; gills free, distinct, ventricose.—*Fr. Epicr. p.* 117. *Berk. Outl. t.* 6, *f.* 5. *Pers. Syn. t.* 5, *f.* 4. *Sturm. t.* 29. *Fl. Dan. t.* 2025, *f.* 3. *Eng. Fl.* v. *p.* 61.

On fern, twigs, &c. Aug. [S. Carolina.]

Pure white. Pileus 2 lines or more broad, campanulate or hemispherical, sometimes broadly and obtusely umbonate, striate, with a round mark in the centre caused by the insertion of the stem, minutely pilose, not granulose; gills unequal, rounded, free. Stem 1–2 in. high, ½ line thick, rather thicker at the base, flexuous, fistulose, downy or minutely pilose, though sometimes, as the pileus becomes quite smooth, fragile, adhering by a broad membranous, tomentose, radiato-striate disc.—*M. J. B.* Spores ·0001 × ·00005 in.

207. Agaricus (Mycena) tenerrimus. *Berk.* "Delicate Mycena."

White, very delicate; pileus convex, pruinose; stem pilose, adhering by a minute pubescent disc; gills free, ventricose.—*Berk. Outl. t.* 6, *f.* 6. *Eng. Fl.* v. *p.* 61.

On fir-cones, sticks, &c.

Gregarious, pure white. Pileus 1–1½ lines broad, very delicate, tender, and easily injured, not pilose, but frosted with minute granules; gills distant, unequal. Stem 1 in. high, scarce ½ line thick, flexuous, fistulose, adhering by a minute pubescent disc, which is not the least striate; spores white, round. —*M. J. B.*

208. Agaricus (Mycena) pterigenus. *Fr.* "Fern-stem Mycena."

Very delicate, rose-coloured ; pileus campanulate, obtuse, nearly even ; stem flexuose, thread-like, smooth ; base swollen into a little bulb, which is radiato-strigose ; gills adnate, broad, distant, entire.—*Fr. Epicr. p.* 118. *Pers. M.E. t.* 28, *f.* 6. *Berk. Outl. t.* 6, *f.* 7. *Eng. Fl.* v. *p.* 63. *Mag. Zool. & Bot. no.* 47. *Berk. exs. no.* 134.

On dead fern stems. Rare.

This species varies in different individuals from bright orange-red to rose-colour, occasionally the upper part of the stem is brown ; the gills are ornamented with a bright orange margin ; the pileus in the young state is oblong, oval, obtuse, minutely furfuraceous at the apex, marked with darker, slightly anastomosing veins, which at length, in consequence of the quicker growth of the subjacent stratum, and the collection of the veins themselves into bundles radiating from the centre, form striæ on the pileus. The stem under a high magnifier is often streaked with veins like the pileus.—*M. J. B.* A variety on oak leaves is described in "Eng. Fl."

Sect. 7. *Insititiæ*—stem slender, dry, growing on other plants, without root ; gills adnate, with decurrent tooth.

209. Agaricus (Mycena) corticola. *Schum.* "Bark Mycena."

Pileus thin, hemispherical, at length obsoletely umbilicate, sulcato-striate ; stem slender, short, incurved, furfuraceous ; gills broadly adnate, uncinate, broad, rather ovate, pallid.—*Fr. Epicr. p.* 118. *Mich. t.* 74, *f.* 8. *Bull. t.* 519, *f.* 1. *Eng. Fl.* v. *p.* 62. *Schn. Sturm t.* 2. *Sow. t.* 243.

Amongst moss on bark. [S. Carolina.]

Gregarious. Pileus 1-3 lines broad, hemispherical, in general obtuse, but sometimes slightly papillose, rarely umbilicate, umber, white, cinereous, lilac, flesh-coloured, rufous, bluish, &c., flesh rather thick in proportion ; gills variously adnato-uncinate or sub-decurrent, partaking more or less of the colour of the pileus ; stem ½-1 in. high, incurved, minutely pulverulent, stuffed, and not truly fistulose, minutely strigose, or tomentose at the base. The whole plant dries up in dry weather, but revives with the first shower. —*M. J. B.* Spores ·0003 × ·00015 in.—*W. G. S.*

210. Agaricus (Mycena) hiemalis. *Osbeck.* "Winter Mycena."

Pileus thin, campanulate, obsoletely umbonate, margin striate ; stem slender, ascending, downy below ; gills adnate, linear, whitish.—*Fr. Epicr. p.* 119. *B. & Br. Ann. N.H.*, 1865, *no.* 993. *Bull. t.* 519, *f.* i. *a.*

On trunks of trees. Nov. Apethorpe. North Badminston, Gloucestershire.

A more delicate species than *A. corticola*; stem longer, colour constantly paler, whitish, pinkish-red, &c.

211. Agaricus (Mycena) setosus. *Sow.* "Setose Mycena."

Pileus very delicate, hemispherical, obtuse, smooth; stem thread-like, covered with spreading hairs; gills distant, white. —*Fr. Epicr. p.* 119. *Sow. t.* 302. *Eng. Fl.* v. *p.* 64.

On dead leaves in woods.

Pileus not $\frac{1}{16}$ in. broad; stem $\frac{1}{2}$ in. long, finer than a hair, closely allied to *Ag. capillaris*, from which it is distinguishable by the spreading hairs of the stem.

212. Agaricus (Mycena) capillaris. *Schum.* "Capillary Mycena."

Very delicate, white; pileus campanulate, at length umbilicate, smooth; stem thread-like, smooth; gills adnate, ascending, rather distant.—*Fr. Epicr. p.* 119. *Fl. Dan. t.* 1670, *t.* 2142, *f.* 1. *Bull. t.* 601, *f.* 2 *C. Hoffm. t.* 5, *f.* 2. *Eng. Fl.* v. *p.* 64. *Mich. t.* 80, *f.* 10-11.

On dead leaves, in woods.

Pileus $\frac{1}{2}$-1 line broad, at first conic, like the head of a very small pin, grey, the margin rounded, the stem dark above, and minutely pulverulent, gradually the stem elongates extremely, becoming much finer, the pileus hemispherical, delicate, white, with a dimple in the centre; gills very few, two or three only, in general reaching the stem, in specimens 1 line broad, regularly ascending about 9, adnate, with two or three intermediate ones; stem flaccid, extremely slender, very minutely dilated at the base.—*M. J. B.* Spores very minute, oval, ·000018 in. long.

213. Agaricus (Mycena) juncicola. *Fr.* "Rush Mycena."

Very delicate; pileus convex, striate, smooth, rufescent; stem thread-like, smooth, brownish; gills adnate, distant, white.—*Fr. Epicr. p.* 19. *Mich. t.* 80, *f.* 9. *Paul. t.* 105, *f.* 11. *Bull. t.* 148, *f. D. Eng. Fl.* v. *p.* 63.

On dead rushes, in bogs. June. July. Rare.

Pileus 1 line broad, of a deep blood red, inclining to tawny, sometimes minutely umbonate, at length depressed, distinctly and broadly striate; stem 1 in. high, brown, paler above, smooth; gills few, yellowish white, at length detached, so as to form a collar round the stem.

Sub-Gen. 9. Omphalia. Fr. Epicr. p. 119.

Pileus generally from the first umbilicate, afterwards funnel-shaped, almost always membranaceous or sub-membranaceous and hygrophanous, margin incurved or straight; stem cartilaginous and tubular, when young often stuffed, confluent with the hymenophore, but heterogeneous from it; gills truly and considerably decurrent.

HAB. Generally epiphytal, and mostly peculiar to hilly regions, preferring a damp, woody situation, and a rainy climate.—*Pl. II. fig.* 9.

The species, though small, are many of them beautiful; their properties are not known, and they endure changes of temperature like the hygrophanous species of *Clitocybe*. *Omphalia* is naturally divided into two groups—one, *Collybariæ*, approaching *Collybia*, and the other, *Mycenariæ*, *Mycena*.

A. *Collybariæ.*

Sect. 1. *Pyxidatæ*—pileus depressed.

214. **Agaricus (Omphalia) pyxidatus.** *Bull.* "Variable Omphalia."

Pileus sub-membranaceous, umbilicate, then funnel-shaped, smooth, hygrophanous; margin striate; stem stuffed, then hollow, even; gills decurrent, rather distant, narrow, reddish grey. —*Fr. Epicr. p.* 122. *Bull. t.* 568, *f.* 2. *Ann. N.H. no.* 144. *Berk. Outl. t.* 6, *f.* 8. *Eng. Fl.* v. *p.* 65-30*. *Sow. t.* 210. *Berk. exs. no.* 14.

Amongst short grass, on lawns, &c. Nov.

Pileus smooth; disc sub-membranaceous; gills decurrent, rather distant, narrower than in any neighbouring species, dirty white, with a rufescent tinge, then of the same colour as the pileus; stem when young stuffed, then hollow, thickened at the base, and there clothed with whitish down, subattenuated upwards.—*Fries.* Variable in size and colour, flesh-coloured, brick red, dirty tawny, rufous, &c.

215. **Agaricus (Omphalia) hepaticus.** *Batsch.* "Liver-coloured Omphalia."

Tough, rigid; pileus smooth, rather shining, even; stem at length compressed, flesh-coloured, inclined to rufous; gills distant, connected by veins, and forked, rather thick, pallid.—*Fr. Epicr. p.* 122. *Batsch. f.* 211. *Berk. Outl. p.* 131.

On lawns.

Stem about 1 in. long, 1 lin. thick, flesh colour, inclining to brown, naked, rarely pruinose; pileus becoming funnel-shaped, $\frac{1}{2}$-$1\frac{1}{2}$ in. broad, even, red brown when moist, tawny or tan-coloured when dry.

216. Agaricus (Omphalia) affricatus. *Fr.* "Hairy Bog Omphalia."

Pileus sub-membranaceous, umbilicate, then infundibuliform, obscurely variegated with hair-like squamules; stem fistulose, glabrous, cinereous; gills decurrent, rather distant, broadest in the middle, greyish white.—*Fr. Epicr. p.* 123. *B. & Br. Ann. N.H.* 1865, *no.* 994.

On *Sphagnum.* Aug. Aboyne, Aberdeenshire.

"Pileus ¾ in. across, infundibuliform or deeply umbilicate, hygrophanous, brown, then mouse-coloured, minutely virgate; stem compressed, tomentose at the base; gills distinct, distant, ending abruptly, decurrent."—*B. & Br.*

217. Agaricus (Omphalia) sphagnicola. *Berk.* "Bog-moss Omphalia."

Tough; pileus infundibuliform, sub-carnose, minutely squamulose, moist; stem fistulose; gills narrow, dirty-ochraceous.—*Berk. Outl. p.* 131. *Eng. Fl.* v. *p.* 67.

On *Sphagnum.* June.

Whole plant tough and elastic; odour scarcely any; pileus 1-1½ in. broad, funnel-shaped from a very early stage of growth, faintly striate, and minutely squamulose, dirty ochraceous, becoming darker in age, moist, but not viscid; gills pale, decurrent, narrow, moderately distant, thick, so as to present in front a flat edge; stem 1-2 in. long, 1 line thick, hollow, somewhat cracked, smooth, except at first, when it is very minutely squamulose above; in age it is nearly pervious above.—*M. J. B.* Spores ·00025 × ·00017 in.

218. Agaricus (Omphalia) oniscus. *Fr.* "Bolton's Omphalia."

Pileus sub-membranaceous, convex, then plane or depressed, remotely radiato-striate, smooth, hygrophanous; stem sub-fistulose, firm, equal; gills adnate, decurrent, straight, somewhat distant, livid, or whitish, as well as the stem.—*Fr. Epicr. p.* 123. *Bolt. t.* 41, *f.* C. c.

In swamps.

Stem rather firm, about an inch long, and a line thick, straight or curved, grey. Pileus flaccid, irregular, scarcely 1 in. broad, smooth, dark cinereous, paler when dry. Spores ·00025 × ·00022 in.

Sect. 2. *Umbelliferæ*—parasol-like.

219. Agaricus (Omphalia) muralis. *Sow.* "Wall Omphalia."

Pileus sub-membranaceous, umbilicate, radiato-striate, smooth, margin crenulate; stem somewhat stuffed, short, tough, brownish rufous; gills decurrent, distant, paler.—*Fr. Epicr. p.* 124. *Sow. t.* 322. *Eng. Fl.* v. *p.* 65.

On old walls, banks, &c., amongst moss. [Cincinnati.]

Pileus at length funnel-shaped, ⅓-1 in. broad, convex, reddish brown; gills broad, pale, whitish-brown, distant, decurrent; stem ¼-½ in. high, thickish, usually sub-incurved, pale-brown, solid.—*Grev.*

220. Agaricus (Omphalia) umbelliferus. *L.* "Common Omphalia."

Pileus between fleshy and membranaceous, convexo-plane, obconic, brittle, radiato-striate, when dry becoming pallid, even, silky; margin at first inflexed, crenate; stem sub-fistulose, equal, base downy; gills decurrent, very distant, broad behind.—*Fr. Epicr. p.* 125. *Hed. Obs. t.* 3 *Holms.* ii. *t.* 34. *Fl. Dan. t.* 1015, *t.* 1672, *f.* 1. *Buxb.* ii. *t.* 50, *f.* 4. *Eng. Fl.* v. *p.* 65. *Berk. Ann. N.H. no.* 267.

In swamps, exposed pastures, &c. Common. [Cincinnati.]

Subgregarious. Pileus ½-1 in. broad, depressed in the centre, margin deflexed, and sometimes waved, striate, whitish, whitish-brown, or yellow, darker when moist; gills broad towards the stem, whitish, decurrent; stem ½-1 in. high, about 1 line thick, whitish or yellowish, paler below, and pubescent.—*Grev.* Spores ·0001 × ·00012 in.

221. Agaricus (Omphalia) rufulus. *B. & Br.* "Reddish Omphalia."

Pileus umbilicate, reddish-grey, growing pale, somewhat mealy; stem of the same colour, shining; gills decurrent, rather thick, forked, flesh-coloured.—*Ann. Nat. Hist. Oct.* 1848, *p.* 260, *no.* 325. *Berk. Outl. p.* 132.

On an exposed common, amongst *Polytrichum.* Hanham, near Bristol.

Pileus ½ in. across, at first convex, soon expanded, and umbilicate, subcarnose, reddish grey or buff, at length pale, minutely mealy, margin crenulate; stem ½ in. high, 1 line thick, flexuous, same colour as the pileus, smooth, shining, solid; gills decurrent, rather thick, flesh-coloured, especially towards the margin, forked, rather distant, interstices veiny; spores oblong, oblique, with somewhat the aspect of *A. laccatus.*—*M. J. B.*

222. Agaricus (Omphalia) stellatus. *Sow.* "Stellate Omphalia."

White. Pileus membranaceous, convex, umbilicate, smooth, silky, diaphanous; stem somewhat stuffed, equal, fragile, base floccoso-radiate; gills decurrent, thin, broad, very distant.—*Fr. Epicr. p.* 126. *Eng. Fl.* v. *p.* 64. *Sow. t.* 107. *Ann. N.H. no.* 268.

On sticks, decayed herbaceous stems, &c. Oct.

Gregarious. Pileus 4 lines broad, striated; gills thin; stem scarcely 1 in. high, stuffed, incurved, brittle.—*Fries.*

B. *Mycenariæ.*

Sect. 3. At first campanulate, margin straight.

223. Agaricus (Omphalia) campanella. *Batsch.* "Tawny Omphalia."

Pileus membranaceous, convex, umbilicate, striate, hygrophanous; stem fistulose, attenuated below, clothed with tawny, spongy down; gills decurrent, arcuate, connected by veins, yellow.—*Fr. Epicr. p.* 126. *Nees. f.* 191. *Schæff. t.* 230. *Eng. Fl.* v. *p.* 66.

In fir woods. [United States.]

Often cæspitose. Pileus ferruginous-yellow, 3-7 lines broad, tough; gills connected by veins; stem 2 in. long, rooting from below.—*Fries.*

var. β. **badipus.** Solitary or sub-cæspitose; stem stuffed, thickened at the base, clothed with ferruginous down.—*Eng. Fl.* v. *p.* 66. *A. caulicinalis. Sow. t.* 163.

Amongst leaves, &c. Oct.

Pileus 3-11 lines across, broadly campanulate, umbilicate, sometimes quite plane, of a beautiful yellow, inclining to ferruginous, edge slightly silky; gills yellow, arcuato, sub-decurrent, beautifully connected by veins; stem 1-2 in. high, ½-1 line thick, scarcely fistulose, yellow above, then rufescent, clothed with little yellow scales, thickest below, and there covered with a dense tawny tomentum.—*M. J. B.*

224. Agaricus (Omphalia) camptophyllus. *Berk.* "Berkeley's Omphalia."

Pileus convexo-plane, deeply striate; stem minutely pubescent, radiato-strigose at the base, minutely fistulose; gills white, ascending, then suddenly decurrent.—*Berk. Eng. Fl.* v. *p.* 62. *Outl. p.* 133.

On sticks, &c. Rare. Margate.

Solitary or sub-gregarious. Pileus ½ in. broad, dry, convex, obtuse, sub-hemispherical, smooth, brown, with a grey margin, gills rather distant, at first adnate, nearly plane, then ascending and suddenly decurrent. Stem 2 in. or more high, not a line thick, sub-flexuous, somewhat rigid, minutely fistulose, with a few white fibres, under a lens minutely but beautifully pubescent; base radiato-strigose, at first yellow, when full-grown pale above, pale rufescent below.—*M. J. B.*

225. Agaricus (Omphalia) griseus. *Fr.* "Grey Omphalia."

Pileus sub-membranaceous, campanulate, then convex, smooth, striate, hygrophanous; stem fistulose, rather firm, smooth, self-coloured; gills slightly decurrent, arcuate, rather thick, sub-distant, whitish-grey.—*Fr. Epicr. p.* 127. *Ann. N.H. no.* 141.

In pine woods.

Stem 3 in. long, 1 lin. thick, slightly thickened above, straight, smooth, whitish, cinereous. Pileus ½ in. broad, striate, hygrophanous, livid grey, becoming hoary.

226. Agaricus (Omphalia) helvelloides. *Bull.* "Delicate Omphalia."

Pileus obconic, umbonate, at length depressed, somewhat funnel-shaped, remotely radiato-sulcate; stem elongated; gills thick, forked, decurrent, broad in front.—*Bull. t.* 601, *f.* 3. *Berk. Outl. p.* 132. *Ann. N.H., no.* 324.

On the ground. Oct.

Far more graceful and delicate than any form of *A. umbelliferus.*

227. Agaricus (Omphalia) fibula. *Bull.* "Button Omphalia."

Pileus membranaceous, turbinate, expanded, then somewhat umbilicate, striate, becoming pale, dry, even; stem slender, nearly orange colour, as well as the pileus; gills strongly decurrent, distinct, paler.—*Fr. Epicr. p.* 127. *Bull. t.* 186, *t.* 550, *f.* 1. *Sow. t.* 45. *Fl. Dan. t.* 1071, *f.* 2. *var. Eng. Fl.* v. *p.* 65.

Amongst moss. Sept.—May. Common. [United States.]

Pileus 1-6 lines broad, at first hemispherical; margin inflexed, then plane, more or less depressed, yellow or tawny, with a dusky centre, obscurely striated, the whole minutely pilose; gills yellowish or white, distinct, not ventricose, decurrent; stem 1-1½ in. high, not a line thick, slender, yellow or tawny, with a violet-brown apex, the whole minutely pilose, like the pileus, and obsoletely fibrillose.—*M. J. B.* Spores ·00013 × ·00008 in.—*W. G. S.*

[*Pl. II., fig.* 9, *nat. size.*]

228. Agaricus (Omphalia) gracillimus. *Weinm.* "Delicate Omphalia."

Snow-white; pileus membranaceous, hemispherical, sub-flocculose, sulcate; stem filiform, slender, floccose at the base; gills decurrent, thin, alternately sub-dimidiate.—*Weinm. p.* 121. *Fr. Ep. p.* 128. *B. & Br. Ann. N.H.* (1866), *no.* 1112.

In marshy ground, on decaying stems of vegetables. Aug. King's Cliffe.

Pileus sometimes depressed, sometimes papillate, 2-3 lines broad; stem 3-6 lines long.

229. Agaricus (Omphalia) belliæ. *Johnst.* "Cup-like Omphalia."

Pileus dry, membranaceous, cup-shaped, of a pale wood-colour; stem thin, fistulose, cartilaginous, pale above, brownish below, adhering by a floccose base; gills thick, paler than the pileus, decurrent, interstices veiny.—*Ann. Nat. Hist. ser.* i, vol. vi., *t.* 10, *f.* 1. *Berk. Outl. p.* 134.

* Hymenophore distinct from the fleshy Stem.

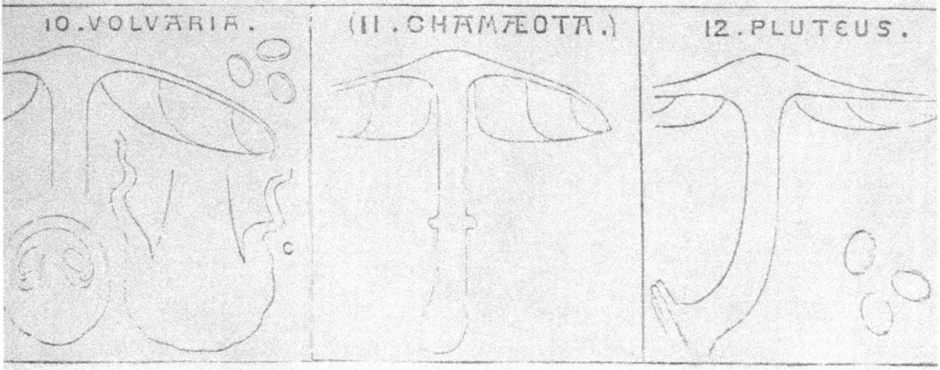

** Hymenophore confluent and homogeneous with the fleshy Stem.

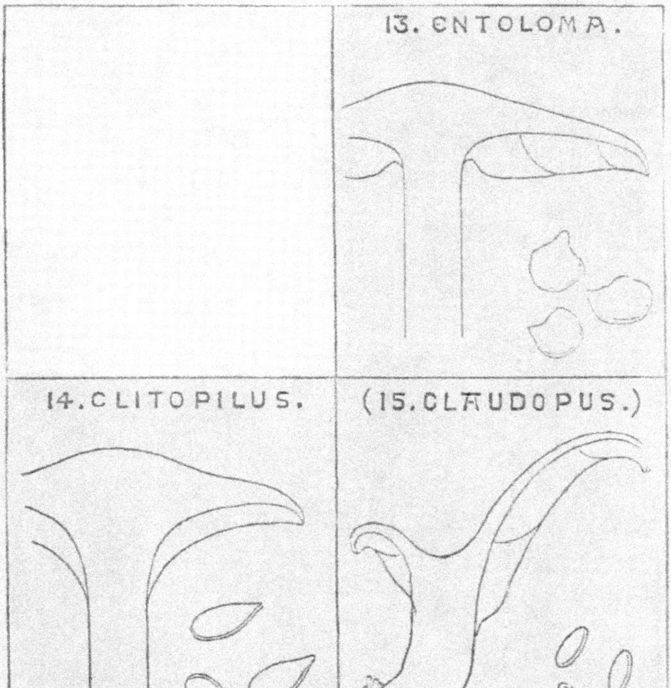

** Hymenophore confluent with, but heterogeneous from the cartilaginous Stem

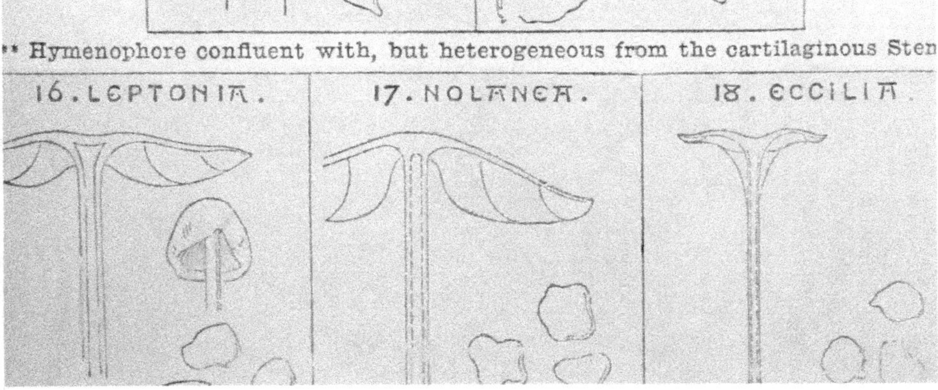

On dead stems of reed. Oct. Berwickshire.

Pileus membranaceous, inverted, deeply cyathiform, ½ in. broad, smooth, waved and furrowed at the edges, of a wood-brown hue, becoming paler when dry; gills adnato-decurrent, at least in the inverted pileus, 1 line broad, rather distant, thick, more or less undulated, wrinkled on the sides and in the interstices with flexuous veins, once or twice divided near the edge, of a dull chalky white. Spores oblong, colourless, pellucid. Stem 1½ in. high, about 1 line thick, fistulose, erect, stiff, and elastic, smooth, white, or very pale wood-brown above, towards the base of a dirty dark brown, becoming paler when dry, then apparently mealy; root slightly incrassated, bent, fixed by a dense cottony web.—*M. J. B.*

230. Agaricus (Omphalia) integrellus. *P.* "Little-white Omphalia."

White, fragile; pileus membranaceous, hemispherical, then expanded, pellucid; striate; stem very slender, short, pubescent below; gills decurrent, distant, slightly branched, edge acute.—*Fr. Epicr. p.* 128. *Pers. Ic. & Des. t.* 13, *f.* 5. *Eng. Fl.* v. *p.* 64. *Ann. N.H. no.* 142. *Ray. Syn. t.* i., *f.* 2, *a. a.*

On decayed sticks. Rare.

Cæspitose. Pileus 2-3 lines broad, at first hemispherical, obtuse, at length rather plane, substance thin, pellucid. Gills narrow, arcuate, decurrent, notwithstanding the form of the pileus, some branched, especially in younger specimens, with but few short ones. Stem 1 in. high, fistulose, sub-pulverulent, villous at the base.—*Pers.*

Series 2. **Hyporhodii,** Fr. Epicr. p. 138.—Spores pink or salmon-colour.

There is not one quarter so many Agarics bearing pink or salmon-coloured as white spores. The size of the spores varies greatly. A few are very small, others equally large (see Plate), whilst the majority are remarkably irregular, resembling the fragments of granite seen in the roads. Some of the species are edible, as in *Clitopilus* (analogous with the white-spored edible species of *Clitocybe*), whilst others are poisonous, as in *Entoloma*, reminding us of such dangerous species of *Tricholoma* as *A. sulfureus*, Bull, etc.—*W. G. S.*

Sub-Gen. 10. Volvaria, Fr. S. M. i. p. 277.

Spores regular in shape, oval or pip-shaped, pink or salmon-colour; veil universal, forming a perfect volva (c), distinct from the cuticle of pileus (a); stem distinct from the hymenophore; gills free, rounded behind, at first white, then pink, soft, liquescent.

Hab. Gardens and hot houses, and in woods and on manured ground, growing on rotten wood and damp ground; one species is parasitic on *Agaricus nebularis*.—(*Plate III., fig.* 10.)

The species of *Volvaria* are very closely allied; some appear in spring and early summer, others later in the year; they are almost tasteless, and none are known to be edible. *Volvaria* corresponds with *Amanita.—W. G. S.*

Sect. 1. Silky or fibrillose.

231. Agaricus (Volvaria) bombycinus. *Schæff.* "Silky Volvaria."

Pileus fleshy, soft, campanulate, then expanded, sub-umbonate, silky, fibrillose, self-coloured; stem solid, attenuated, smooth, volva very large; gills free, flesh-coloured.—*Fr. Epicr. p.* 138. *Schæff. t.* 98. *Krombh. t.* 23, *f.* 15-21. *Berk. Outl. t.* 7 *f.* 1. *Eng. Fl.* v. *p.* 104. *Barla. t.* 25, *f.* 1-5.

On decayed wood. Rare. [S. Carolina.]

Pileus 3-4 in., at first entirely enclosed in a slimy dark volva, at length protruded, campanulate, dirty white, silky, with yellowish white narrow silky scales, and marked frequently with a few dark blotches, the remains of the volva, flesh whitish, firm, elastic, margin involute; gills numerous, close, ventricose, quite free, not reaching the margin, at first white, then rose-coloured, with a tinge of yellow, at length deliquescent, tinged with umber. Stem 2½ in. high, ½ in. thick in the centre, firm, solid, thickest downwards, the tough volva remaining like a cup at the base.—*M. J. B.*

232. Agaricus (Volvaria) volvaceus. *Bull.* "Stove Volvaria."

Pileus fleshy, soft, campanulate, then expanded, obtuse, virgate, with adpressed black fibrils; stem solid, subequal; volva loose; gills free, flesh-coloured.—*Fr. Epicr. p.* 138. *Bull. t.* 262. *Fl. Dan. t.* 1731, *f.* 2. *Letell. t.* 623. *Sow. t.* 1. *Eng. Fl.* v. *p.* 104. *Barla. t.* 25, *f.* 6. 13. *Vent. t.* 22.

In stoves, by roadsides, &c. July. Aug. [S. Carolina.]

Pileus 3-4 in. broad, obtuse, pallid, cinereous, with cinereous and black streaks; gills obtuse behind, almost remote; stem 3-5 in. high, ½ in. thick, white; gills adhering, almost delinquescent as in *Coprinus.* Spores ·0002 × ·00013 in.—*W. G. S.* (*Pl. III., fig.* 10, *reduced.*)

233. Agaricus (Volvaria) Loveianus. *Berk.* "Parasitic Volvaria."

Pileus thin, fleshy, subtruncate, globose, then convex, obtuse, white, silky; stem solid, attenuated upwards; volva loose, lobed; gills free, rose-coloured.—*Berk. Outl. p* 140, *t.* 7, *f.* 2. *Fr. Epicr. p.* 139. *Smith. Seem. Jour. Dec.* 1867. *Eng. Fl.* v. *p.* 104.

Parasitic on *A. nebularis.* Rare.

Cæspitose. At first appearing like a small round *Bovista*, from the size of a pea upwards, then oblong, and the top of the pileus, which at that stage is flattish, bursts through the volva, which is ultimately split into three or four regular laciniæ, with a somewhat wrinkled surface, and the pileus from sub-truncato-globose, becomes convex, or slightly expanded, 2½ in. broad, moderately fleshy and beautifully silky, white, with a slight shade of pink or cinereous, margin involute; gills broad in front, quite free, sub-deliquescent, gradually with a pink tinge. Stem 2 in. high, 2-3 lines thick, white, closely fibrillose, juicy, solid, bulbous, volva pure white. Spores minute, elliptic, rosy, ·0001 in. long. Artificially developed by Mr. W. G. Smith, from specimens of *Ag. nebularis.*—(Seem. Journal.)

234. Agaricus (Volvaria) Taylori. *Berk.* "Taylor's Volvaria."

Pileus thin, conical, obtuse, livid, striato-rimose from the apex; stem pale, solid, nearly equal; volva lobed, brown, small; gills uneven, broad in front, attenuated behind, rose-coloured.—*Berk. Outl. p.* 140. *Ann. N.H. no.* 675.

On the ground. Jersey.

Pileus 1¾ in. high and broad, beautifully pencilled and cracked, margin lobed and sinuated; stem 2½ in. high, ¼ in. thick, slightly bulbous at the base; gills uneven. The dark volva, campanulate pileus, and uneven attenuated gills are marked characters.—*M. J. B.*

235. Agaricus (Volvaria) parvulus. *Weinm.* "Little Volvaria."

Pileus rather fleshy, conic, then expanded, umbonate, dry; stem stuffed, equal, silky; volva small, lobed; gills free, rose-coloured. *Fr. Epicr. p.* 139. *Bull. t.* 330. *Pers. Obs. t.* 4, *f.* 4-5. *Krombh. t.* 3, *f.* 20? *A. pusillus. Berk Out. p.* 140.

In pastures, after stormy weather. [S. Carolina.]

Abounds some years in autumn, in exposed rather rich pastures, and may be confounded by superficial observers with the true mushroom; but a glance at the volva, which is always present, and the attenuated stem, is sufficient to prevent mistakes—a point of some consequence, as the qualities of all the species in the sub-genus are, to say the least, doubtful.—*M. J. B.* Spores ·0002 × ·00014 in.

Sect. 2. Pileus smooth, sub-viscid.

236. Agaricus (Volvaria) speciosus. *Fr.* "Dunghill Volvaria."

Pileus fleshy, soft, campanulate, then expanded, obtuse, smooth, even, viscid, disc grey; stem solid, attenuated, rather bulbous; volva loose, villous, as well as the stem; gills free, rose-coloured. —*Fr. Epicr. p.* 139. *Fl. Dan. t.* 1737. *Krombh. t.* 26, *f.* 1-8. *Ann. N.H. no.* 902*.

On dunghills, roadsides, &c. [S. Carolina.]

Very closely allied to the next, but differing in the absence of a distinct umbo, and in the smooth margin of the pileus.

237. Agaricus (Volvaria) gloiocephalus. *Fr.* "Umbonate Volvaria."

Pileus fleshy, convex, then plane, umbonate, glutinous; margin striate; stem solid, equal, smooth; volva tuberose, sub-obliterated; gills free, white, then flesh-coloured.—*Fr. Epicr. p.* 140. *Letell. t.* 645, *f. H.* 1. *Gard. Chron.* 1860, *p.* 933, *fig. A. speciosus. Berk. Outl. t.* 7, *f.* 3. *Barla. t.* 26.

On the ground.

Pileus about 3 in. across, with a strong regular obtuse umbo in the centre, of a delicate mouse-grey, viscid when moist, but when dry shining, quite smooth, margin striate in consequence of the thinness of the flesh; stem 6 in. or more high, about ½ in. thick in the centre, attenuated upwards, bulbous at the base, clothed with a few slight fibres, easily splitting, solid, rather dingy, ringless. Volva loose, villous like the base of the stem, splitting into several unequal lobes; the gills are broad, especially in front, narrower behind, and quite free, so as to leave a space round the top of the stem, white, tinged with greyish pink; margin slightly toothed. Smell strong and unpleasant, and taste disagreeable.—*M. J. B.*

Sub-Gen. 11. CHAMÆOTA. *Smith. Seem. Journal,* 1870.
(*Psalliota*, Fr. partly.)

Spores pale rose; stem distinct from the hymenophore, furnished with a fugitive ring; gills free.

HAB. On the ground, or on decayed wood.—(*Pl. III., fig.* 11.)

Corresponds in structure with *Lepiota* and *Psalliota*. The species figured is *A. (Chamæota) xanthogrammus*, Ces. an Italian species.

238. Agaricus (Chamæota) cretaceus. *Fr.* "Chalky Chamæota."

Pileus fleshy, campanulate, then convexo-plane, naked, even, nearly smooth, or rivulose; stem hollow, equally attenuated, even, white; ring simple, reflexed, and again ascending; gills rather remote, broader in front, for a long time white.—*Fr. Epicr. p.* 213. *Sv. Bot. t.* 596, *f.* 2. *Krombh. t.* 26, *f.* 16, 17. *Berk. Outl. t.* 10, *f.* 5. *Ann. N.H. no.* 148.

In meadows and stoves.

Distinguished from *A. campestris* by its gills, which remain for a long time white, and are at length rose-coloured, and also by the spores, which are ·0001 × ·00015 in.

239. Agaricus (Chamæota) echinatus. *Roth.* "Bristling Chamæota."

Pileus rather fleshy, campanulate, then expanded, obtuse; at first pulverulent, then squamose; stem fistulose, equal, floccosopulverulent below the ring ; gills free, crowded, blood-red.—*Fr. Epicr. p.* 215. *Roth. Cat.* ii. *t.* 9, *f.* 1. *Ann. N.H. no.* 147. *Ag. hæmatophyllus. Mag. Zool. & Bot. no.* 38, *t.* xv. *f.* 1.

On peat beds in gardens. Rare. [S. Carolina.]

Solitary or gregarious, often fasciculate. Pileus 1-1½ in. broad, thin, brittle, chocolate, or olive brown, clothed with minute raised scales, and copious meal of the same colour ; flesh pale, not changing when cut ; gills varying greatly in breadth, rounded behind, quite free, but approximate, at first of a fine red, at length deep chocolate. Ring broad, fugacious, attached at first in ragged triangular laciniæ to the edge of the pileus, mealy externally, of a beautiful pink within ; stem 1½ in. high, 1-2 lines or more thick, chocolate-red when rubbed, clothed with meal, red within, stuffed, penetrating ; smell strong.—*M. J. B.*

Sub-Gen. 12. Pluteus. Fr. Epicr. p. 140.

Spores generally regular in shape, but in some species approaching the irregularity of *Hebeloma*, pink or salmon-colour, more or less bright, some approaching in colour the spores of genus 5, *Paxillus*, others sub-genus 19, *Flammula ;* veil none ; pileus of the same nature with the stem and gills, smooth, silky, or wrinkled ; stem ringless and without a volva, distinct from the hymenophore; gills free, at first white, then yellowish, afterwards pink, very crowded, almost cohering, sometimes subliquescent.

Hab. The species almost always grows on, or *close to*, the trunks of trees.—(*Pl. III., fig.* 12.)

The characters of this sub-genus agree with those of *Volvaria*, with the exception of the volva, which is absent in *Pluteus*. Fries thinks it doubtful whether the pellicle of the pileus, always fibrous, flocculose, or pruinose, should not be considered as a universal concrete veil, which would give an analogy with *Lepiota*. The species of *Pluteus* appear in spring, early summer, or late in the autumn. They are tasteless, and none edible.—*W. G. S.*

Sect. 1. Pileus with evanescent fibrils.

240. Agaricus (Pluteus) cervinus. *Schæff.* "Fawn Pluteus."

Pileus fleshy, campanulate, then expanded, nearly even, smooth, then clad with evanescent fibrillose scales ; margin naked ; stem solid, with black fibrils ; gills free, crowded, white, then flesh-coloured.—*Fr. Epicr. p.* 140. *Schæff. t.* 10. *Sow. t.* 108. *Batsch. f.* 76. *Krombh. t.* 2, *f.* 7-10. *Sturm t.* 28. *Fl. Dan. t.* 1067, *f.* 2.

On trunks of trees.

Pileus 3 in. and more broad, dingy, growing pale, sometimes tawny yellow. Spores very bright, orange pink. ·00023 × ·00018. in.
[*Pl. III., fig.* 12, *reduced.*]

241. Agaricus (Pluteus) umbrosus. *Pers.* "Brown Pluteus."

Pileus fleshy, campanulate, then expanded, lacunose, rugose, at first villous; margin ciliate or fimbriate; stem solid, villoso-squamulose; gills free (sub-fuliginous), margin fimbriate.—*Fr. Epicr. p.* 140. *Pers. Ic. & Desc. t.* 2, *f.* 5-6. *A. umbrinus. Berk. Outl. p.* 141.

On dead trunks.

Blackish umber. Pileus 3 in. broad.

Sect. 2. Pileus pruinate, sub-pulverulent.

242. Agaricus (Pluteus) nanus. *P.* "Mealy Pluteus."

Pileus somewhat fleshy, convexo-plane, rugulose, obtuse, sprinkled with dingy meal; stem solid, rigid, short, striate, white; gills free, white, then flesh-coloured.—*Fr. Epicr. p.* 141. *Ann. N.H. no.* 676. *Bull. t.* 547, *f.* 3.

On fallen sticks. Aug. [S. Carolina.]

Pileus umber, about 1 in. broad. Stem 1 in. long, 1-2 lin. thick. Spores irregular hexagons, &c., very pale rose, average diameter about ·00023 in.

Sect. 3. Pileus naked, smooth.

243. Agaricus (Pluteus) petasatus. *Fr.* "Broad-capped Pluteus."

Pileus fleshy, campanulate, then expanded, umbonate, very smooth, with a viscid cuticle, membranaceous to the middle, and at length striate; stem solid, tall, rigid, fibrilloso-striate, attenuated equally from the base; gills free, very broad, much crowded, drying up, white, then reddish.—*Fr Epicr. p.* 142. *Ann. Nat. Hist.*, xiii., *t.* 9, *f.* 2, *no.* 271. *Gonn. & Rabh.* iv. *t.* 4.

On sawdust. Jan. Hitchin.

Stem 6 in. long, firm, pallid, at length tawny. Pileus 5-6 in., with a separable cuticle, pale cinereous, rather bright brown, &c.

244. Agaricus (Pluteus) leoninus. *Schæff.* "Yellow Pluteus."

Pileus sub-membranaceous, campanulate, then expanded, smooth, naked; margin striate; stem solid, smooth, striate; gills free, yellowish, then flesh-coloured.—*Fr. Epicr. p.* 142. *Schæff. t.* 48. *Berk. Outl. t.* 7, *f.* 4. *Pers. Ic. & Des. t.* 1, *f.* 3-4. *Eng. Fl.* v. *p.* 78.

On wood. Sept. Oct. [S. Carolina.]

Solitary or sub-gregarious. Pileus 1-3 in. broad. tawny yellow, shaded with bright orange, or purplish brown, tinged with yellow, umbonate, flesh thick in the centre, margin thin, firm, covered with a smooth, wrinkled, glutinous cuticle, sometimes pitted round the umbo, margin more or less striate; gills rather broad, rounded behind and in front, flesh-coloured, moderately distant, perfectly free, edge at first yellowish. Stem 2-3 in. high, 2-6 lines thick, downy at the base, sometimes rooting, attenuated upwards, twisted and striate, yellow or ochraceous, shaded with orange, solid, at length imperfectly hollow. Spores rose-coloured, elliptic.—*M. J. B.*

245. Agaricus (Pluteus) chrysophæus. *Schæff.* "Dingy Pluteus."

Pileus sub-membranaceous, campanulate, then expanded, naked, nearly even, smooth or slightly virgate; margin striate; stem hollow, smooth; gills free, white, then flesh-coloured.—*Fr. Epicr. p.* 142. *Schæff. t.* 253. *Sow. t.* 174. *Grev. t.* 173. *Berk. Outl. t.* 7, *f.* 5.

On wood, hollow trees, &c. [United States.]

Somewhat gregarious, distinct, or two or three growing from the same base. Pileus 1-3 in. convex, at length nearly plane, undulated at the margin, nearly membranaceous; colour yellowish or ochraceous brown. Surface glabrous, rugose, with veins in the direction from the centre to the circumference. Gills rather numerous, broad, ventricose, free. Stem 2-4 in. long, 2-5 lines thick, somewhat fistulose, whitish, mostly twisted, equal, except at the base, which is often thickened and frequently incurved.—*Grev.*

246. Agaricus (Pluteus) phlebophorus. *Ditm.* "Veined Pluteus."

Pileus rather fleshy, convex, then expanded, veined, rugose; margin naked, without striæ; stem hollow, smooth, incurved, shining; gills free, white, then flesh-coloured.—*Fr Epicr. p.* 142. *Ditm. t.* 15. *Nees. f.* 202. *Eng. Fl.* v. *p.* 79. *Ann. N.H. no.* 676*.

On fallen sticks. Rare.

Pileus about 1 in. broad, convex, becoming nearly plane when mature, cuticle rugose, with prominent anastomosing veins, leaving deep pits between them, of a pleasant yellowish brown, or pale reddish orange, with the margin generally incurred. Gills broad, at first white, becoming flesh-coloured. Stem 2 in. high or more, hollow, incurved, ascending. A very beautiful species, distinguished at once by the rugose pileus; the pits are very deep, and the reticulations very distinct. Spores sub-globose, ·0003 in. long, ·0002 in. diameter.—*W. G. S.*

Sub-Gen. 13. Entoloma. Fr. Epicr. p. 143.

Spores extremely irregular in shape, salmon colour, pink, or more or less approaching bright-red or brown; veil "potential rather than definite;" pileus, margin at first incurved, never at first umbilicate, fleshy, or thin according to the species, viscid, smooth, hygrophanous, dry, silky, or flocculose; stem fleshy-fibrous, sometimes waxy, continuous with the hymenophore, and homogeneous with it; gills sinuated, as in *Tricholoma*, etc., almost free, or more or less adnate, sometimes parting from the stem.—*(Pl. III., fig.* 13.*)*

HAB. All are terrestrial.

Allied to *Tricholoma*, but, with few exceptions, the species of *Entoloma* are much thinner and often brittle. Many possess the odour of new flour, but none are edible, and some highly poisonous. They appear in summer after heavy rains. Besides corresponding with *Tricholoma*, *Entoloma* agrees in structure with *Hebeloma* and *Hypholoma*.—*W. G. S.*

Sect. 1. *Genuini*—pileus smooth, moist, or sub-viscid.

247. Agaricus (Entoloma) sinuatus. *Fr.* "Large-waved Entoloma."

Pileus fleshy, convex, then expanded, sub-repand, even, smooth; stem solid, compact, fibrillose, whitish; gills adnexed, very broad, crowded, pale, rufescent.—*Fr. Epicr. p.* 143. *Saund. & Sm. t.* 11. *A. fertilis. Pers. M.E.* 281. *Bull. t.* 547, *f.* 1, 590. *Smith P.M. f.* 14. *Eng. Fl.* v. *p.* 77.

In woods. Poisonous. [S. Carolina.]

Pileus 4 in. and upwards, expanded, obtuse, somewhat lobed, pulverulento-squamulose, fleshy, dry, pinkish-buff, with sometimes a tinge of yellow; gills rose-coloured, adnexed, nearly free; stem 3-6 in. high, ¾-1 in. thick, stuffed, firm, fibrillose, sub-squamulose, sub-compressed, somewhat bulbous at the base, paler than the pileus. Spores brownish salmon, very irregular, ·00035 in. diameter. Smell like that of fresh meal. *(Pl. III., fig.* 13, *reduced.)*

248. Agaricus (Entoloma) prunuloides. *Fr.* "Plum-like Entoloma."

Pileus fleshy, campanulate, then expanded, umbonate, even, smooth, sub-viscid; stem solid, unequal, smooth, sub-striate, white; gills free, ventricose, white, then flesh-coloured.—*Fr. Epicr. p.* 144. *Berk. Outl. p.* 142.

On the ground. Rare. Mossburnford.

Pileus white, yellowish, greyish, &c., at length longitudinally cracked; gills emarginate, rarely rounded, at first slightly adnexed.

249. Agaricus (Entoloma) placenta. *Batsch.* "Brown Entoloma."

Pileus fleshy, convex, then plane, umbonate, regular, smooth, brown; stem solid, equal, fibroso-striate, brown; gills emarginate, adnexed, crowded, rather thick, pallid flesh colour.—*Fr. Epicr. p.* 144. *Batsch. f.* 18. *Ann. N.H. no.* 789.

On the ground. Oct. Swanage, Dorset.

Solitary; stem 2-3 in. long, 2-3 lin. thick, brown; pileus $1\frac{1}{2}$in. broad, orbicular, smooth, brown; gills separating from the hymenophore.

250. **Agaricus (Entoloma) helodes.** *Fr.* "Moor Entoloma."

Pileus slightly fleshy, convexo-plane, sub-umbonate, moist, becoming smooth; stem hollow, pallid, fibrillose; base rather thickened; gills emarginate, adnexed, somewhat distant, white, then flesh-coloured.—*Fr. Epicr. p.* 144. *Ann. N.H. no.* 790.

On moors. Coed Coch.

Pileus purple, dingy, brown, &c., when old becoming pale, spotted, not hygrophanous, 2 in. or more broad; stem 2-3 in. long, 3 lin. thick, pale, cinereous; smell like that of fresh meal.

251. **Agaricus (Entoloma) repandus.** *Bull.* "Repand Entoloma."

Pileus fleshy, conical, umbonate, indistinctly silky; margin lobed; stem short, solid, minutely silky, white; gills dull rose-coloured, broad in front.—*Bull. t.* 423, *f.* 2. *Berk. Outl. p.* 143. *Eng. Fl.* v. *p.* 78. *Ann. N.H. no.* 676*.

Amongst grass. Rare.

Pileus 1-2 in. across, conic, obtuse, at length expanded, very fleshy, the margin incurved and lobed, pale whitish, ochraceous, with a few streaky shades, clothed with a very close, adpressed, indistinct silkiness; gills pale dull rose, broad in front; stem $1\frac{1}{2}$ in. high, 3 lines thick, white, beautifully adpresso-sericeous; spores rose-coloured, irregular, stellate; odour like that of fresh meal.—*M. J. B.*

252. **Agaricus (Entoloma) Bloxami.** *B. & Br.* "Blue Entoloma."

Pileus compact, campanulate, obtuse, somewhat lobed, moist, blackish-blue, somewhat silky; flesh white; stem slightly attenuated upwards, obtuse at the base; gills rather broad, attenuated, adnexed.—*Berk. Outl. p.* 143. *Ann. N.H. no.* 677. *Price, f.* 89.

In open exposed pastures.

Pileus 1 in. or more across, campanulate, very obtuse, moist, of a dark dingy blue or purple, or sometimes slate-coloured, tinged with lilac, slightly silky, inclined to be lobed below, flesh very thick in the centre, white, except near the edge, where it partakes of the hue of the pileus; stem $1\frac{1}{2}$ in. high, $\frac{1}{2}$ in. thick, attenuated upwards, of the same colour as the pileus, solid; gills moderately broad, pale pink, attenuated behind, or slightly adnexed.—*M. J. B.* Spores very irregular in shape, very brilliant pink orange, ·0003 in. diameter.—*W. G. S.*

253. Agaricus (Entoloma) ardosiacus. *Bull.* "Meadow Entoloma."

Fragile; pileus slightly fleshy, convex, then expanded and depressed, even, smooth, moist; stem hollow, elongated, steel blue, attenuated from the white base; gills nearly free, crowded, greyish, flesh-coloured.—*Fr. Epicr. p.* 145. *Bull. t.* 348. *Eng. Fl.* v. *p.* 78.

In moist meadows.

Introduced solely on the authority of Sibthorpe. Pileus 3 in. broad, fleshy, when young campanulate, margin sub-sinuate; gills 4 lines broad, rufescent; stem 4-5 in. long, 2-3 lines thick, attenuated, of the same colour as the pileus. —*Fries.*

254. Agaricus (Entoloma) frumentaceus. *Bull.* "Mealy Entoloma."

Pileus fleshy, firm, rather brittle, nearly plane, dry, finely streaked; stem streaked and slightly cracked, obtuse at the base; gills broad, emarginate, or rounded behind, cinereous, with a reddish yellow tinge.—*Bull. t.* 571, *f.* 1. *Ann. N.H. no.* 678. *Berk. Outl. p.* 144.

On the ground under a hedge. Rare.

Somewhat cæspitose; pileus 3½ in. across, plane, with the margin arched and sinuated, dry, buff, tinged with red, marked with fine streaks, which are sometimes slightly raised, fleshy, firm, rather brittle; stem 2 in. high, 1 in. thick, of the same colour as the pileus, streaked and slightly cracked, sometimes compressed, blunt at the base, with a little white down, stained with the spores; gills broad, moderately distant, sinuated and toothed, rounded behind, sometimes emarginate, adnate, cinereous, with a reddish-yellow tinge; spores elliptic, minute, ·0002 in. long, rose-coloured; taste agreeable; smell farinaceous.—*M. J. B.*

Fries places this species in *Tricholoma*, both in the "Epicrisis" and "Monograph." We retain it here in deference to the Rev. M. J. Berkeley's opinion.

255. Agaricus (Entoloma) ameides. *B. & Br.* "Scented Entoloma."

Pileus irregular, broadly campanulate, centre smooth; margin whitish flocculent, at length glabrous, with a silky lustre, undulated; stem stuffed, compressed, whitish, villous at the base, above striato-fibrillose, apex flocculent; gills distant, slightly adnexed, rugose.—*Ann. N. Hist.* 1865, *no.* 999.

In pastures. Sept. Bodelwyddan, Flintshire.

Pileus 1-2½ in. across, varying from hemispherical in smaller specimens to campanulate, thin, pale reddish grey; spores rose-coloured, irregular; large specimens at first sight closely resemble *Hygrophorus ovinus;* smell peculiar, resembling a mixture of orange flower water and starch. The whole plant acquires a reddish tint in drying.—*B. & Br.*

Sect. 2. *Leptonidei*—pileus flocculose, sub-squamose, dry.

256. Agaricus (Entoloma) jubatus. *Fr.* "Crested Entoloma."

Pileus fleshy, campanulate, at first acutely, then obscurely umbonate, clothed with fibres, glossy, not hygrophanous, gills slightly adnexed, inclined to ventricose; stem fleshy, glossy, striate, and shining, white at the base, stuffed or hollow, clothed with minute sooty fibres.—*Fr. Epicr. p.* 145. *Fr. S.M. p.* 196. *Trans. Woolhope Club* (1868), *p.* 246, *with plate.*

In mossy places. Merry Hill Common and Haywood Forest, near Hereford, 1868 (*W. G. S.*), Ascot (*M. J. B.*), near Goudhurst, Sussex (*F. C.*)

Grows in dense clusters. Young specimens acutely campanulate, full grown attain 5 or more in., with a diameter of 3 or 4 in. Spores extremely irregular ·00025 × ·0004 in.—*W. G. S.*

257. Agaricus (Entoloma) griseo-cyaneus. *Fr.* "Blue-Grey Entoloma."

Pileus sub-carnose, campanulato-convex, obtuse, floccoso-squamose; stem hollow, floccose or fibrillose, pallid, then bluish; gills adnexed, seceding, whitish, becoming flesh-coloured.—*Fr. Epicr. p.* 145. *B. & Br. Ann. N.H.* (1866) *no.* 1113.

On lawns. Oct. Coed Coch.

With the habit of a *Leptonia*, smaller, soft; stem fibrous, 2-3 lines thick, white when young. Pileus grey, or verging towards lilac.

258. Agaricus (Entoloma) sericellus. *Fr.* "Silky Entoloma."

Pileus rather fleshy, convex, then plane or depressed, silky, at length squamulose; stem sub-fistulose, fibrillose, white, then pallid, gills adnate, seceding, slightly distant, white, then flesh-coloured. —*Fr. Epicr. p.* 146. *Pers. Ic. t.* 6, *f.* 2. *Eng. Fl.* v. *p.* 76.

In woods. July—Sept.

Sub-gregarious. Pileus ¾ in. broad, white, sub-carnose, silky, slightly umbilicate, gills pale rose-colour, broad, adnate, nearly horizontal, sub-decurrent; stem 2 in. high or more, 1 line thick, thickest and downy at the base, sometimes sub-bulbous, solid, or closely stuffed, white, silky. Odour and taste like *A. campestris.*—*M. J. B.*

Sec. 3. *Nolanidei*—pileus thin, hygrophanous.

259. Agaricus (Entoloma) clypeatus. *L.* "Buckler Entoloma."

Pileus slightly fleshy, campanulate, then expanded, umbonate, smooth, hygrophanous; stem stuffed, attenuated, fibrillose, becoming pale; gills rounded, adnexed, seceding, serrulated, dirty flesh colour.—*Fr. Epicr. p.* 146. *Bull. t.* 534. *Huss.* ii. *t.* 42. *Berk. Outl. t.* 7, *f.* 6. *Bolt. t.* 69. *Buxb.* iv. *t.* 6.

In gardens, &c.

Pileus 4 in. or more across, gregarious, lurid, when dry grey and rather shining, virgate, and spotted.

260. Agaricus (Entoloma) rhodopolius. *Fr.* "Rosy Entoloma."

Pileus slightly fleshy, campanulate, then expanded, at length slightly depressed, hygrophanous; margin flexuose, broken; stem hollow, nearly equal, smooth, white, pruinose above; gills adnate, sinuate, white, then roseate.—*Fr. Epicr. p.* 147. *Bolt. t.* 6. *Fl. Dan. t.* 1736. *Krombh. t.* 55, *f.* 17-22.

In woods. Sept. [Cincinnati.]

Pileus about 3 in. across; pileus when young fibrillose, soon smooth, when moist livid or tawny; margin slightly striate, when dry shining, with a satiny lustre. Spores very irregular; average diameter ·00027 in.

261. Agaricus (Entoloma) majalis. *Fr.* "Cinnamon Entoloma."

Pileus between fleshy and membranaceous, campanulate or convex, umbonate, even, smooth, hygrophanous; margin expanded, repand; stem fistulose, twisted, striate, whitish, tomentose at the base; gills nearly free, crenate, pallid, then roseate.—*Fr. S. M. p.* 205. *B. & Br. Ann. N.H.* 1865, *no.* 998.

In woods. Coed Coch, Denbighshire.

Sub-cæspitose. Pileus cinnamon-colour, when dry ochraceous, 2-3 in. broad. Stem 3-4 in. long, 2-3 lines thick, twisted; gills free, ventricose.

262. Agaricus (Entoloma) costatus. *Fr.* "Costate Entoloma."

Pileus rather membranaceous, convexo-bullate, then nearly plane, sub-umbilicate, undulate, smooth, hygrophanous; stem hollow, short, deformed, sub-striate, grey, whitish-squamulose above; gills nearly free, entire, transversely ribbed, pallid.—*Fr. Epicr. p.* 147. *Ann. N.H. no.* 679.

In meadows. Oct. Common.

Pileus 2 in. or more, livid, tawny, or with a scorched appearance, shining; stem 2 in. long, 3-4 lines thick. Readily distinguished by the distant broad gills, which are rounded behind, and nearly free, traversed at length by waved ribs, and with their margin undulate, and not discoloured. Smell none; spores irregular, sub-globose, with a globular nucleus.—*M. J. B.*

263. Agaricus (Entoloma) sericeus. *Bull.* "Meadow Entoloma."

Pileus between fleshy and membranaceous, convex, then expanded, smooth, hygrophanous, when dry silky; margin inflexed, repand, rather striate; stem fistulose, short, fibrillose; gills emarginate, plane, rather distant, grey.—*Fr. Epicr. p.* 147. *Bull. t.* 413, *f.* 1. *A. pascuus, Eng. Fl.* (*in part.*) *Berk. Outl. p.* 145.

In meadows.

Gregarious. Stem hollow, 1-2 in. long, 1-2 lines thick, grey. Pileus 1 in. and more broad, umber, paler when dry, margin at first involute and striate. Odour strong of new meal.

264. Agaricus (Entoloma) nidorosus. *Fr.* "Strong-scented Entoloma."

Pileus between fleshy and membranaceous, convex, then expanded, rather depressed, smooth, hygrophanous; when dry silky, shining; stem stuffed, equal, smooth, white, then growing pallid; whitish pruinose above; gills emarginate, free, broad, rather distant, flexuose, pallid flesh-colour.—*Fr. Epicr. p.* 148. *A. rhodopolius, Eng. Fl.* v. *p.* 76.

In woods. Common.

Pileus 1½ to 3 in. broad, plano-expanded or sub-depressed, occasionally minutely umbonate, ochraceous, with a brownish tint, the margin sometimes darker and waved, in large specimens sub-carnose, smooth and shining, with a satiny lustre, most minutely silky under a lens, but the silkiness quite adpressed; gills very broad, thick, and adnate, more or less rounded behind, and separating from the stem; stem 2-4 in. high, 2 lines or more thick, hollow and stringy within, sub-flexuous, pulverulent at the apex, downy at the base, minutely fibrilloso-striate. Odour strong.—*M. J. B.* Spores somewhat irregular, ·00034 in. average length.

Sub-Gen. 14. CLITOPILUS. Fr. Epicr. p. 148.

Spores salmon colour, in some species very pale, almost white, pip-shaped, somewhat irregular spheres, or altogether irregular, as in *Entoloma*, fig. 12; pileus pruinose, dull white, cinereous, or brownish, generally fleshy; stem fleshy or fibrous, confluent with the hymenophore and homogeneous with it; gills decurrent, never sinuated.

HAB. All are terrestrial.—(*Pl. III., fig.* 14.)

With the exception of the gills, most of the characters correspond with *Entoloma*. The odour of the species is more or less mealy, some, however, are oily, some tasteless, others edible. *Clitopilus* is closely allied to *Clitocybe*, and differs from *Entoloma* precisely as *Clitocybe* differs from *Tricholoma*. *Clitopilus* agrees more or less with *Flammula*.—*W. G. S.*

265. Agaricus (Clitopilus) prunulus. *Scop.* "Plum Clitopilus."

Pileus fleshy, compact, at first convex, regular, at length depressed, repand, pruinose, dry; stem solid, ventricose, naked, striate: gills strongly decurrent, rather distant, white, then flesh-coloured.—*Fr. Epicr. p.* 148. *Trans. Woolh. Cl.* 1869, *plate. Berk. Outl. t.* 7, *f.* 7. *Huss.* ii. *t.* 47. *Schæff. t.* 78. *Sow. t.* 143. *Hogg & Johnst. t.* 20. *Lenz. t.* 26. *Kromb. t.* 55, *f.* 7-8. *Eng. Fl.* v. *p.* 76. *Smith E.M. f.* 15.

In woods. June—Oct. Esculent. [United States.]

Pileus fleshy, compact, at first convex, then expanded, becoming depressed in the centre, irregularly waved, slightly pruinose, 2-5 in. broad, surface dry, soft, white, or sometimes grey, flesh thick, white, unchangeable; stem white, solid, firm, slightly ventricose, 1 in. or more long, ½ in. thick, naked, often striate, and villous at the base; often excentric; gills crowded, deeply decurrent, white, then of a pale, dull, flesh colour, or yellowish brown; spores pale brown, oval, with an apiculus at one end, ·00045 × ·0002 in. Odour of new meal, strong.—*H. G. B.* (*Pl. III., fig.* 14, *reduced.*)

var. **Orcella.**—*Trans. Woolh. Cl.* 1869, *fig. Badh.* i. *t.* 13. ii. *t.* 11, *f.* 1-2. *Vent. t.* 14, *f.* 1-3.

In open places. June—Oct. Esculent.

Pileus thin, irregular, depressed in the centre, lobed, undulated, 2-3 in. broad, clear white, sometimes tinted with pale brown on its prominences, occasionally with a grey centre, or slightly zoned with grey; surface soft and smooth to the touch, except in wet weather, when it becomes soft and sticky; flesh soft, colourless, and unchangeable; stem smooth, white, solid, short, decreasing in size, central when young, becoming excentric from the pileus growing irregularly; gills crowded, decurrent, at first nearly white, then pinkish grey, at length with a light brown tint; spores pale brown, ·00035 × ·00018 in.; odour pleasant; smaller than the typical form, less fleshy, and grows in more open glades.—*H. G. B.*

266. Agaricus (Clitopilus) cretatus. *Berk.* "Chalky Clitopilus."

Small; pileus membranaceous, at length umbilicate, dead-white, shining, margin involute; stem very short, tomentose; gills decurrent, narrow, rosy.—*Ann. N.H. no.* 903.

On naked soil in woods and pastures.

Single or gregarious; pileus ¼-⅜ in. across, at first convex, then umbilicate, of a dead white, but shining, membranaceous, not striate, margin involute; stem a few lines high, 1 line thick, often curved at the base, and sometimes thickened, tomentose, especially below, white; gills pale pink, not broad, very decurrent; mycelium white, floccose.—*M. J. B.*

267. Agaricus (Clitopilus) mundulus. *Lasch.* "Delicate Clitopilus."

Pileus fleshy, thin, tough, plane, then depressed, unequal, unpolished, dry; stem stuffed, thin, flocculose, thickened at either end, at length black within; gills deeply decurrent, much crowded, narrow, pallid.—*Fr. Epicr. p.* 149. *Batsch.f.* 119. *Batt. t.* 16, *f. F.*

In woods. King's Cliffe. Scotland.

Whitish; from 1 in. to 2 in. broad, even or rivulose; stem about 1 in. long, at first floccoso-villose, then becoming smooth.

268. Agaricus (Clitopilus) popinalis. *Fr.* "Greyish Clitopilus."

Pileus somewhat fleshy, unequal, sub-repand, flaccid, smooth; stem stuffed, slender, equal, naked, rather flexuous; gills deeply decurrent, crowded, lanceolate, dark grey.—*Fr. Epicr. p.* 149. *B. & Br. Ann. N.H.* (1866) *no.* 1114.

On downs. Oct. Worthing. Near Bath.

A curious species, with a rank and strong odour; the pileus and flesh are of a greyish tint, the gills are strongly decurrent, and the spores pink; probably esculent. Spores irregular spheres, so pale as to be hardly distinguished from white; might easily be referred to *Clitocybe*, diameter ·00018 in.

269. Agaricus (Clitopilus) undatus. *Fr.* "Waved Clitopilus."

Pileus somewhat fleshy, deeply umbilicate, opaque when dry; stem hollow, short, unequal; gills very decurrent, thin, scarcely crowded, dark, cinereous.—*Epicr. p.* 149. *B. & Br. Ann. N.H.* 1865, *no.* 1000.

In open downs. Oct. Batheaston, &c.

Inodorous; stem soft, attenuated at the base; pileus 1½ in. wide, sooty grey, often infundibuliform and zoned.—*Fries.* Spores brilliant salmon-pink, very irregular, average diameter ·00025 in.—*W. G. S.*

270. Agaricus (Clitopilus) cancrinus. *Fr.* "Flesh-coloured Clitopilus."

Pileus between fleshy and membranaceous, umbilicate, then convex and expanded, unequal; without striæ, growing pale; stem stuffed, then fistulose, tough, short, smooth, white; gills decurrent, distant, arcuate, white, then pale flesh-colour.—*Fr. Epicr. p.* 150. *B. & Br. Ann. N.H.* (1866), *no.* 1115.

In a grass field. Aug. Apethorpe.

Pileus of a very pale flesh-colour, or whitish, at first umbilicate, gills distant, at first white.

Sub-Gen. 15. Claudopus. *Smith. Seem. Journal. Pleurotus* and *Crepidotus.* Fr. partly.

Spores pink, or pale lilac; stem lateral or none, when present confluent and homogeneous with the hymenophore; gills sinuate or decurrent.—(*Pl. III., fig.* 15.)

Hab. On wood or the ground.

Claudopus corresponds with *Pleurotus*, only differing in the colour of the spores.—*W. G. S.*

271. Agaricus (Claudopus) euosmus. *Berk.* "Tarragon Claudopus."

Imbricated, strong-scented. Pileus depressed, shining, and satiny when dry; stem short or obsolete, confluent; gills ventricose, very decurrent, dingy white; spores pinkish.—*Berk. Outl. p.* 135. *Huss.* i. *t.* 75. *Badh. t.* 11, *partly. Ann. N.H. no.* 326.

On elm posts, stumps, &c. Spring.

Pilei very much crowded, 2 in. or more across, deeply depressed, unequal, at first white, invested with a light blue varnish, at length of a light brown; stem distinct above, connate below; gills rather broad, running down to the bottom of the free portion of the stem. Spores oblong, narrow, oblique, whitish, tinged with purple. The whole plant smells when first gathered strongly of tarragon.—*M. J. B.* *(Plate III., f.* 15, *reduced.)*

272. Agaricus (Claudopus) variabilis. *P.* "Variable Claudopus."

Pileus sub-membranaceous, resupinate, then reflexed, silky with white down; gills radiating, rather crowded, white, then rusty-red, at length pale cinnamon.—*Fr. Epicr. p.* 211. *Pers. Obs.* ii. *t.* 5, *f.* 12. *Sow. t.* 97. *Bull. t.* 152, 581. *Fl. Dan. t.* 1556. *Eng. Fl.* v. *p.* 103.

On sticks, &c. Common. [S. Carolina.]

Pileus ½-1 in. broad, membranaceous, at first hemispherical, with a short stem, soon resupinate, and then again reflexed, the stem becoming quite obsolete, white, covered with silky down; sometimes there is no stem at first, but the pileus is resupinate from the earliest stage of growth. Spores elliptic, rusty-pink.—*M. J. B.* Spores ·0002 × ·00013 in.—*W. G. S.*

273. Agaricus (Claudopus) depluens. *Batsch.* "Ground Claudopus."

Pileus submembranaceous, resupinate, reflexed, somewhat conchate, clothed with white down behind; gills broad, crowded, grey, then reddish.—*Fr. Epicr. p.* 212. *Batsch. f.* 122. *Pers. M. E. t.* 24, *f.* 5. *Ann. N.H. no.* 73.

On the ground, in stoves, &c. Oct. [S. Carolina.]

Whitish when dry.

274. Agaricus (Claudopus) byssisedus. *P.* "Little Claudopus."

Pileus membranaceous, resupinate, then reflexed, nearly plane, pruinose with grey down; stem incurved; gills broad, whitish, then cinereous.—*Fr. Epicr. p.* 212. *Pers. Ic. Desc. t.* 14, *f.* 4. *Pers. Obs.* ii. *t.* 5, *f.* 8, 9. *Ann. N.H. no.* 686.

On the ground. Sept. Rare.

Sometimes with a distinct slender stem. Pileus ½-1 in. broad, grey; spores angulato-stellate, in this respect resembling the *Hyporhodii*, ·0004 in. long, ·00028 in. wide.

Sub-Gen. 16. Leptonia. Fr. S.M. i., p. 201.

Spores salmon colour, irregular in shape; pileus less campanulate than *Nolanea*, and never truly fleshy, cuticle always torn into scales, disk umbilicate, and often darker than margin, which is at first incurved (B); stem rigid, with a cartilaginous bark, often dark blue, confluent with the hymenophore, but heterogeneous from it; gills not decurrent, but often with a small tooth or sinus, separating from the stem, variable in colour, at first dirty white, yellowish, greenish-grey, or blue.—(*Pl. III., f.* 16.)

Hab. Dry hills, and sometimes marshy places, in July and August.

Most of the species grow in clusters, are small, and of an elegant colour; most common in rainy seasons. Structurally the same as *Collybia*, and bears the same relationship to *Clitopilus* as *Collybia* to *Clitocybe*.—*W. G. S.*

The small sketch, showing incurved margin of pileus, is *A. (Leptonia) chalybæus*, P.

275. Agaricus (Leptonia) lampropus. *Fr.* "Mouse-coloured Leptonia."

Pileus rather fleshy, obtuse, convex, then plane, not striate, at length depressed, squamulose, broken up into flocci; stem subfistulose, even, unspotted, steel-violet; gills adnate, ventricose, whitish.—*Fr. Epicr. p.* 152. *Bull. t.* 521, *f.* 1. *Ann. N.H. no.* 145.

In pastures.

Pileus 1½ in. across, opaque, not umbilicate, nor papillate, from mouse-colour to steel-grey.

276. Agaricus (Leptonia) serrulatus. *P.* Saw-gilled Leptonia."

Pileus between fleshy and membranaceous, hemispherical, then expanded, umbilicate, sub-squamose; stem fistulose, smooth, dotted above, black; gills adnate, seceding, broad, bluish, then greyish, flesh coloured, edge black, serrulated.—*Fr Epicr. p.* 153. *Holms.* ii. *t.* 38. *Bull. t.* 413, *f.* 1. *Ann. N.H. no.* 146.

In woods. Rare. Wothorpe.

Remarkable for its black margined, serrated gills; stem black, steel blue, glaucous, or grey. Pileus at first blackish blue.

277. Agaricus (Leptonia) euchrous. *P.* "Violet Leptonia."

Pileus rather fleshy, campanulate, then convex, obtuse, squamulose, or fibrillose; stem stuffed, smooth, violet; gills adnexed, ventricose, violet; edge darker, entire.—*Fr. Epicr. p.* 153. *Pers. Syn. p.* 343. *Ann. N.H. no.* 791.

On alder trunks.

Pileus violet, scarcely an inch broad; stem about 1½ in. long, 1 line thick, tough. The habitat as well as structure of this species is analogous with certain species of *Collybia.*

278. Agaricus (Leptonia) chalybœus. *P.* "Steel-blue Leptonia."

Pileus rather fleshy, convex, sub-umbonate, without striæ, at first flocculose, then squamulose; stem stuffed, smooth, blue; gills emarginate, adnexed, broad, ventricose, glaucous, dirty white, edge darker.—*Fr. Epicr. p.* 153. *Sow. t.* 161. *Krombh. t.* 2. *f.* 11, 16. *Eng. Fl.* v. *p.* 80.

In pastures. July—Sept.

Pileus ½-1 in. broad, convex, minutely umbonate, scaly, dark blue, or almost black, sub-carnose, slightly striate on the margin, flesh dark blue; gills at first pale, then clouded lightly, of the colour of the pileus. Stem 1½ in. high, 1 line thick, stuffed, at length hollow, indigo without, dark within, nearly smooth above, downy at the base. Spores rose-coloured, elliptic, with a globular nucleus.—*M. J. B.* (*Pl. III., f.* 16, *small fig.*)

279. Agaricus (Leptonia) incanus. *Fr.* "Hoary Leptonia."

Pileus submembranaceous, convexo-plane, umbilicate, smooth, with a silky lustre, or virgate, margin striate; stem fistulose, shining, smooth, brownish-green; gills adnate, seceding, broad, somewhat distant, white, then greenish.—*Fr. Epicr. p.* 154. *Sow. t.* 162. *A. Sowerbei. Eng. Fl.* v. *p.* 82.

In pastures.

Smell like that of mice; gregarious; pileus about 1 in. broad, variegated brown and greenish; stem 1-2 in. long, greenish or greenish brown. Spores very irregular, dull-yellowish, pink, average diameter ·00034 in.

(*Pl. III., f.* 16, *reduced.*)

280. Agaricus (Leptonia) asprellus. *Fr.* "Rough Leptonia."

Pileus somewhat membranaceous, convex, then expanded, striate, hygrophanous, with a darker umbilicus, squamuloso-fibrillose: stem fistulose, slender, smooth; gills adnate, seceding, rather distant, equally attenuated, whitish grey.—*Fr. Epicr. p.* 154. *Berk. Outl. p.* 147.

In open pastures. Bristol. Wansford.

Pileus at first dingy or mouse colour, soon plane and livid grey, usually smooth, except in the centre, 1-1½ in. broad; stem 1-2 in. long, scarcely 1 lin. thick, even, smooth, livid, greenish, or light blue.

Sub-Gen. 17. NOLANEA. Fr. S. M. i. p. 204.

Spores salmon colour: pileus submembranaceous (as in *Leptonia* and *Eccilia*), sub-campanulate, and papillose, not umbilicate, at first straight and pressed to the stem, not incurved as in *Leptonia;* stem cartilaginous, fistulose, sometimes stuffed, confluent with but heterogeneous from the hymenophore; gills not decurrent.

HAB. Generally terrestrial, growing on grassy hills, and in wet places in woods.—*Pl. III., fig.* 17.

The species are thin, slender, inodorous, and brittle (but some very tenacious), growing in summer and autumn. *Nolanea* corresponds with *Mycena, Galera, Psathyra,* and *Psathyrella.*—*W. G. S.*

281. Agaricus (Nolanea) pascuus. *P.* "Pasture Nolanea."

Pileus membranaceous, conical, then expanded, sub-umbonate, smooth, striate, hygrophanous, when dry shining like silk; stem fistulose, fragile, silky fibrous, striate; gills attenuated behind, nearly free, ventricose, crowded, dirty greyish.—*Fr. Epicr. p.* 155. *Schæff. t.* 229. *Buxb. iv. t.* 21, *f.* 1. *Batt. t.* 25, *E. Bolt. t.* 35. *Eng. Fl. v. p.* 81, *partly.*

In pastures. Inodorous. [United States.]

Stem soft, 2-3 in. long, 1-2 lin. thick, striate; pileus 2-3 in. broad, sometimes scarcely exceeding 1 in., dingy when moist, when dry hoary or pale fawn-colour. Spores irregular, rounded, pentagonal, hexagonal, &c., diameter from ·0003 to ·00042 in. (*Pl. III., f.* 17, *reduced.*)

282. Agaricus (Nolanea) rufo-carneus. *Berk.* "Red-brown Nolanea."

Pileus submembranaceous, hemispherical, umbilicate, indistinctly fibrilloso-squamulose, red brown; margin striate; stem elongated, pale rufous, rather incrassated at the base; gills adnate, ventricose, attenuated behind, slightly connected and traversed by veins.—*Eng. Fl.* v. *p.* 2, *p.* 82. *Berk. Outl. p.* 148.

On heaths. Sept.

Pileus 1 in. broad, umbilicate, membranaceous, indistinctly fibrilloso-squamulose, margin striate, dark red brown ; gills adnate, ventricose, waved, rose-coloured, slightly connected and traversed by veins ; stem 2½ in. high, 1 line thick, curved at the base, where it is slightly thickened, pale rufescent, nearly white above, fistulose, smooth, under a lens minutely fibrillose ; taste rather bitter.—*M.J.B.*

283. Agaricus (Nolanea) rubidus. *Berk.* "Ruddy Nolanea."

Pileus membranaceous, convex, at length umbilicate, finely silky ; stem short, thickest above, solid, minutely silky ; gills ventricose, adnate, attenuated behind, sometimes sub-decurrent, whitish, then rose-coloured.—*Mag. Zool. & Bot.* i. *t.* 2, *f.* 2. *Berk. Outl. p.* 155.

In stoves. March. Milton, Norths.

Pileus ⅓ in. across, convex, at length umbilicate, margin sometimes slightly wavy, membranaceous, finely silky, white or greyish, acquiring at length a pale, ruddy tinge ; gills broad, ventricose, adnate, with frequently a more or less distinct tooth, sometimes at length decurrent, rose-coloured, as well as the elliptic spores ; stem 1½-2 lines high, thickest above, white or greyish like the pileus, solid, minutely silky ; smell like new flour.—*M.J.B.* Spores ·00018 × ·00015 in.

284. Agaricus (Nolanea) Babingtonii. *Blox.* "Babington's Nolanea."

Pileus conico-campanulate, cinereous, shining like silk, adorned with dark brown sub-fasciculate fibres, which are free at one end ; stem equal, fistulose, clothed with dark brown down, sub-strigose ; gills ventricose, distant, cinereous, darker at the base, adnate, glittering with little points.—*Ann. Nat. Hist.* xiii. *Ser.* 2, *p.* 400, *pl.* xv. *f.* 1, *no.* 903*.

Rare. Twycross. Collyweston. [Pennsylvania, U. S.]

Pileus scarcely ½ in. across, conico-campanulate, cinereous, shining, with dark-brown silky sub-fasciculate hairs, the ends of which are free, disc sub-squamulose, margin straight ; stem about 1 in. high, not 1 lin. thick, equal, fistulose, spadiceo-tomentose, sub-strigose ; gills ventricose, distant, cinereous, darker behind, adnate, glittering ; spores oblong, ventricose on the outer side, rather irregular, sometimes with a distinct septum.—*M. J. B.*

285. Agaricus (Nolanea) junceus. *Fr.* "Rush-stemmed Nolanea."

Pileus membranaceous, conical, then expanded, radiato-striate, shining, hygrophanous, disc umbilicate, sub-squamulose ; stem fistulose, slender, smooth, brown ; gills adnexed, seceding, ascending, obovate, somewhat distant, grey-brown, then purplish. —*Fr. Ep. p.* 156. *B. & Br. Ann. N.H.* (1866), *no.* 1116.

In a wood. Oct. Caernarvonshire.

Stem slender, 3 in. long, smooth, brown, then livid-brown. Pileus very obtuse, about 1 in. broad, dingy when fresh, livid when dry.

Sub-Gen. 18. Eccilia. Fr. S. M., i. p. 207.

Spores salmon-colour; pileus generally umbilicate, disc homogeneous, margin at first incurved, as in *Leptonia*; stem hollow, confluent with but heterogeneous from the hymenophore; gills truly decurrent.—(*Pl. III., fig.* 18.)

Corresponds with *Omphalia*. The species figured is *Agaricus (Eccilia) Parkensis*, Fr., for specimens of which I am indebted to Mr. C. E. Broome. Averagesize of spores ·00027 in.—*W. G. S.*

286. Agaricus (Eccilia) carneo-griseus. *B. & Br.* "Flesh-grey Eccilia."

Pileus umbilicate, greyish-flesh colour, finely striate, margin darkened with micaceous particles; stem slender, shining, smooth, of the same colour, whitish tomentose at the base, hollow upwards; gills distant, adnato-decurrent, sub-undulate, rosy, margin irregularly darkened.— *B. & Br. Ann. N.H.* (1865), *no.* 1001, *pl.* xiii. *fig.* 1.

Amongst fir leaves. Aug. Aboyne, Aberdeenshire.

Spores irregular, rose-coloured. Its closest ally is *A. atrides*, from which it differs in the smooth stem, delicate colour, &c.—*B. & Br.*

287. Agaricus (Eccilia) Parkensis. *Fr.* "Umbilicate Eccilia."

Pileus membranaceous, plano-convex, strongly umbilicate, quite smooth, brown when moist, blackish when dry; stem fistulose, short, attenuated downwards, smooth, brown; gills decurrent, crowded, whitish, then dingy flesh colour.—*Fr. Monogr. p.* 301.

In grassy places. Elmhurst.

Pileus scarcely an inch broad, striate to the middle, not hygrophanous; stem short, scarcely 1 in. (*Pl. III., fig.* 18.)

288. Agaricus (Eccilia) rhodocylix. *Lasch.* "Roseate Eccilia."

Pileus membranaceous, rugulose, floccose, soft, umbilicate, then infundibuliform; stem stuffed, slender, incurved, even, smooth; gills strongly decurrent, distant, thick, whitish.—*Ann. Nat. Hist. no.* 94. *Fr. Epicr. p.* 160.

On rotten wood.

Stem stuffed, scarcely an inch long, ½ line thick, cinereous. Pileus ½ in. broad, hygrophanous, when moist remotely striate and brownish, when dry flocculose and grey. Just the habit of *A. umbelliferus*, its analogue amongst the *Leucospori*.

Series III. Dermini, Fr. Epicr. p. 160.

Spores various shades of reddish-brown, brown, red, or yellowish-brown.

In the *Dermini* there are no species with the hymenophore free from the stem, neither are any furnished with a volva, unless, indeed, a trace of such species is indicated in the genus *Cortinarius* (for *Cortinarius* is certainly allied to *Pholiota* and *Hebeloma*), where many of the species have an adnate volva and arachnoid ring.—*W. G. S.*

Sub-Gen. 19. Pholiota. Fr. S. M. i. p. 240. (*fig.* 19.)

Spores sepia-brown, bright yellowish-brown, or light red; stem confluent and homogeneous with the hymenophore, furnished with a ring, persistent, friable, fugacious.

Hab. All the British species grow on stumps except five, which grow on the ground, principally in damp, mossy places.—(*Pl. IV., fig.* 19.)

A few species are said to be edible, but they cannot be recommended. *Pholiota* is analogous to *Armillaria* and *Stropharia*. There is some danger of confusing *Pholiotæ* with *Cortinarii*, but attention must be paid to the spidery veil and the *rust-of-iron* tint of the spores in the latter.—*W. G. S.*

A. *Humigenei*—Terrestrial.

289. Agaricus (Pholiota) durus. *Bolt.* "Hard Pholiota"

Pileus sub-compact, convexo-plane, smooth, at length cracked; margin even; stem stuffed, hard, externally fibrous, rather thickened upwards and mealy; ring slightly torn; gills adnate (often with a tooth), ventricose, livid, then of a brown rust colour.—*Fr. Epicr. p.* 162. *Bolt. t.* 67, *f.* 1. *Krombh. t.* 28, *f.* 14, 22. *Ann. N. H. No.* 327.

In gardens. [Cincinnati.]

Pileus pale, tawny, or brownish tan, 3 in. or more broad, stem usually short, about ½ an in. thick; spores ·00035 × ·00024 in.

* Hymenophore distinct from the fleshy Stem.

** Hymenophore confluent and homogeneous with the fleshy Stem.

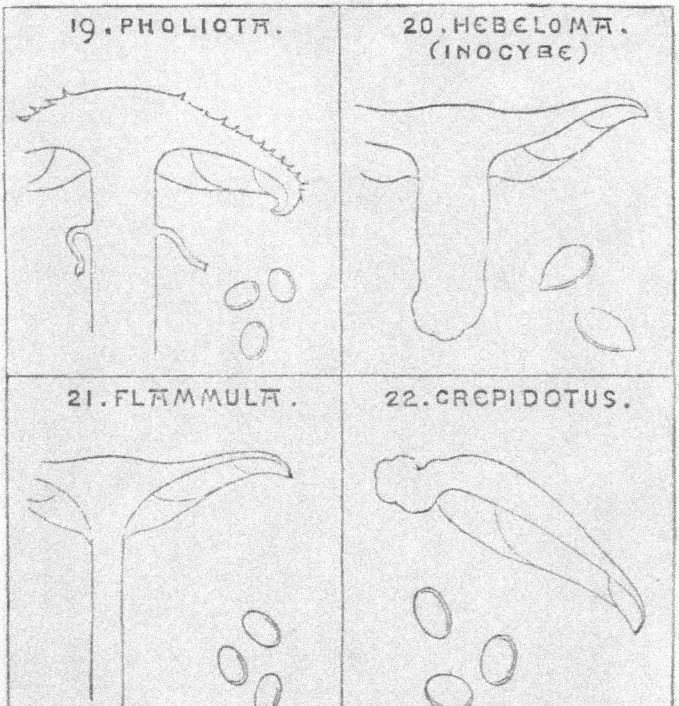

*** Hymenophore confluent with, but heterogeneous from the cartilaginous Ste

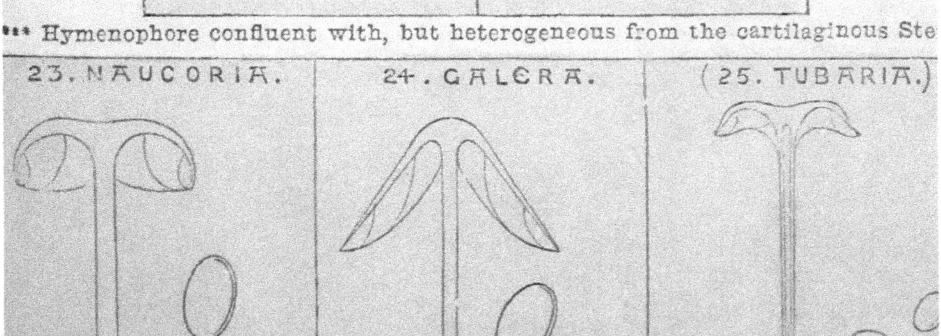

290. Agaricus (Pholiota) præcox. *P.* "Spring Pholiota."

Pileus fleshy, soft, convexo-plane, obtuse, at length smooth, even; stem stuffed, then hollow, cylindrical, pubescent or mealy, at length smooth, white as well as the ring; gills emarginate, adnexed, crowded, white, then brownish.—*Fr. Epicr. p.* 162. *Schæff. t.* 217. *Berk. Outl. t.* 8 *f.* 1. *Eng. Fl.* v. *p.* 107. *Krombh. t.* 55, *f.* 11-16. *Letell. t.* 608.

In gardens and pastures. Spring. [United States.]

Pileus about 2 in. across, very fleshy, flesh firm, white or pale buff, watery near the gills, cuticle when moist subviscid, when dry resembling white kid leather, retaining the impression of the fingers, somewhat tesselated, yellowish or pale tawny. Gills adnexed or subadnate, moderately broad, not ventricose, slightly hollowed out behind with a sub-decurrent tooth, pale brownish purple, edge white or yellowish; stem 1½-3 in. high, 2-3 lines thick, sub-flexuous, equal or sub-bulbous, solid, but sometimes decidedly hollow, juicy, white, or faintly shaded with buff, fibrillose, under a lens sub-pubescent, ring near the top deflexed and striate, or attached in fragments to the edge of the pileus; root strong, white, branched.—*M. J. B.* Spores ·00031 × ·0002, sometimes inclined to be irregular in shape as in some Hyporhodii.

B. *Truncigenei*—on wood, sub-cæspitose.

291. Agaricus (Pholiota) radicosus. *Bull.* "Rooting Pholiota."

Pileus fleshy, equal, obtuse, even, smooth, spotted; stem solid, rooting; above the distant ring mealy, below concentrically squamulose; gills free, ventricose, pallid, then reddish brown. *Fr. Epicr. p.* 163. *Bull. t.* 160. *Krombh. t.* 62 *f.* 6-10. *Eng. Fl.* v. *p.* 90.

In woods.

Pileus 3 in. or more broad, convex, fleshy, the whole covered at first with a slimy web which leaves behind broad adpressed scales on the stem and pileus, besides these there are many fine close silky scales, pallid ochre, margin downy, involute; gills incarnato-ferruginous, pale, adnate, nearly horizontal, minutely serrulate; stem 4 in. high, 1 in. thick, deeply rooting, firm, solid, white within, ring thick, sub-erect, beneath the slimy coat silky and furfuraceous, above the ring pruinose. Odour of prussic acid; taste soon disagreeable.—*M. J. B.* Spores ·00034 × ·00017 in., oval, with an apiculus at one end, somewhat irregular in shape.

292. Agaricus (Pholiota) pudicus. *Bull.* "Modest Pholiota."

Pileus fleshy, convex, then expanded, obtuse, even, dry, smooth; stem solid, sub-equal, even; ring spreading, persistent; gills rounded behind, adnate, ventricose, whitish, then tawny.—*Fr. Epicr. p.* 164. *Bull. t.* 597, *f.* 2. *R. S.* and *L. O. Huss.* ii. *t.* 31. *Batt. t.* 8, *A. Letell. t.* 664.

On elder trunks, &c., and on the ground. Esculent.

Pileus sometimes rivulose, dirty white, simple, or cæspitose. Stem excentric, curved at the base; spores ·0002 × ·00032 in.

293. Agaricus (Pholiota) leochromus. *Cooke.* "Tawny Pholiota."

Pileus fleshy, convexo-plane, at length depressed, soft, smooth, not shining; stem solid, nearly equal, even; ring persistent, tawny; gills rounded, adnate, slightly ventricose, pallid, then cinnamon-coloured; spores profuse.—*Seem. Journ. Bot. No.* 3 (1863), *t.* 3, *f.* 3. *Ann. N. H.* 1865.

On stumps, &c. Esculent.

Cæspitose; pileus 2-3 in., bright tawny, paler (whitish) at the margin, generally rivulose from the cracking of the cuticle; stem 3-4 in., slender, solid, fibrous, internally amber-brown at the base, externally paler, white above, nearly equal, smooth, shining. Allied to *A. pudicus* and *A. capistratus*, but differing in habit and structure from both. Found at Millfield-lane, Highgate, plentifully in the autumn of 1862 and 1863. Since met with by W. G. Smith in other localities. *(Pl. I., fig.* 2.*)*

294. Agaricus (Pholiota) capistratus. *Cooke.* "Ruffed Pholiota.'

Pileus fleshy, convex, somewhat viscid, margin involute, slightly striate; stem nearly equal, stuffed, thick, subsquamulose; ring spreading, persistent; gills decurrent, pallid, growing darker.—*Seem. Journ. Bot. No.* 3 (1863), *t.* 3, *f.* 4. *Ann. Nat. Hist.* (1865.)

On old stumps, elm, &c. Highgate.

Subcæspitose. Pileus 2-3 in., livid, tawny, rather viscid when moist, whitish when dry, margin folded inwards and obscurely striate; stem 3-4 in. thick, nearly equal; ring large and entire, spreading, and persistent; gills rather fleshy, crowded, decurrent, pallid. Taste rather unpleasant. Distinguished from *A. pudicus* and *A. cylindraceus* by its decurrent gills, its more robust habit, and the folding in of the margin of the pileus. *(Pl.* 1 *fig.* 1.*)* This species is stated to be edible by Mr. J. A. Clark, who found it at Street, Somerset; Mr. W. G. Smith, who has found it in several places, says the spores are the same in size and colour as the last.

295. Agaricus (Pholiota) heteroclitus. *Fr.* "Bulbous-stemmed Pholiota."

Compact. Pileus plano-convex, then expanded, very obtuse, rather excentric, marked with scattered, innate, adpressed scales; stem solid, short, bulbous at the base, fibrillose, white; gills rounded, adnexed, very broad, at first pallid, then ferruginous. —*Fr. Epicr. p.* 165. *Gard. Chron.* 1868, *p.* 1113.

On poplar. Bromley.

Odour strong and pungent. Pileus whitish or yellowish, broken up into scales, sometimes smooth if dry, viscid when moist, disc plano-truncate; stem within at the base of a rhubarb colour, ring fugacious, appendiculate.

296. Agaricus (Pholiota) comosus. *Fr.* "Hairy Pholiota."

Pileus fleshy, convex, obtuse, viscid, sprinkled with evanescent, superficial, floccose scales; stem solid, slightly bulbous, white, as well as the evanescent, floccose ring; gills rather decurrent, quite entire, white, becoming of a brownish clay colour.—*Fr. Epicr. p.* 165. *Bolt. t.* 42.

On trunks.

Pileus 3 in. broad, brownish, with the scales paler. Flesh compact, white.

297. Agaricus (Pholiota) squarrosus. *Müll.* "Scaly Pholiota."

Pileus fleshy, campanulate, convex, then expanded, dry; stem stuffed, attenuated at the base, squarrose, as well as the pileus, with crowded darker, innate, revolute scales; gills sub-decurrent, crowded, narrow, pallid, olivaceous, then ferruginous.—*Fr. Epicr. p.* 166. *Bull. t.* 266. *Schæff. t.* 61. *Sow. t.* 284. *Grev. t.* 2. *Huss.* i. *t.* 8. *Eng. Fl.* v. *p.* 91. var. *Mulleri.* *Saund. & Sm. t.* 18, *f.* 1.

On trunks of trees. Common. [S. Carolina.]

Cæspitose. Pileus 2-5 in. across, firm, convex, expanded, obtusely umbonate, tawny-yellow, clothed with rich brown scales, flesh yellow near the surface; gills at first yellowish, then pale-olive, changing to ferruginous, broad, rounded behind, and adnate or sub-decurrent. Stem 3-7 in. high, ½-1 in. thick, at first pale, then croceo-ferruginous, solid, pithy in the centre, equal, or attenuated at the base from the tufted mode of growth, fibrillose and squarrose, with reflexed scales, above the ring very pale yellow and smooth. Ring near the apex, radiato-floccose, rich brown, inclining to orange. Odour disagreeable.—*M. J. B.* Spores ·00022 × ·00017 in. *(Pl. IV., fig.* 19.)

298. Agaricus (Pholiota) aurivellus. *Batsch.* "Golden Pholiota."

Pileus fleshy, campanulate, then convex, gibbous, slightly viscid, variegated with darker, adpressed scales; stem stuffed, nearly equal, curved, clad with scattered, adpressed, floccose, ferruginous-brown scales; ring rather distant; gills sinuated behind, fixed, white, straw-coloured, then ferruginous-umber.—*Fr. Epicr. p.* 165. *Fl. Boruss. t.* 386. *Batsch. f.* 115. *Fl. Dan. t.* 2074. *Eng. Fl.* v. *p.* 91. *Ann. N.H. no.* 680*. *Saund. & Sm. t.* 9.

On trunks of trees. Rare. [S. Carolina.]

Generally solitary. Pileus tawny, 3 in. across, when young hemispherical, at length expanded; gills fixed, very broad, plane, pallid olive, at length ferruginous; stem hard, abrupt, various in length, incurved, sub-bulbous, whitish, within rhubarb-coloured at the base, veiled at the very apex.—*Fries.*

299. Agaricus (Pholiota) adiposus. *Fr.* "Pine-apple Pholiota."

Pileus compact, convex, then plane, obtuse, glutinous; stem stuffed, somewhat bulbous, yellow, squarrose as well as the pileus with superficial, evanescent, darker, concentric scales; gills adnate, broad, yellow, then ferruginous.—*Fr. Epicr. p.* 166. *Berk. Outl. t.* 8, *f.* 2. *Fl. Dan. t.* 2078. *Krombh. t.* 3, *f.* 1. *Batsch. f.* 31. *Eng. Fl.* v. *p.* 91.

On beech and ash trunks. [Cincinnati.]

Extremely beautiful, growing in large tufts, coloured like a ripe pine-apple. Pileus convex, firm, fleshy, margin thin, of a beautiful tawny, very viscid, smooth and shining, with a few superficial darker scales; remains of the woven ring attached to the margin. Gills broad, rounded behind, and adnate with a tooth, ferruginous, edge white. Stem equal, scarcely thickened at the base, solid, firm, brown below, yellowish above, with tawny, adpressed scales, near the apex whiter and more silky.—*M. J. B.* Spores ·00029 × ·00021 in.

300. Agaricus (Pholiota) spectabilis. *Fr.* "Orange Pholiota."

Pileus compact, convex, then plane, dry, cuticle torn into fibrous or silky scales; stem solid, ventricose, somewhat rooting; gills adnato-decurrent, crowded, narrow, yellow, then ferruginous.—*Fr. Epicr. p.* 166. *Bull. t.* 92. *Krombh. t.* 3, *f.* 3. *Ann. N. H. no.* 904*. *Sow. t.* 77. *Huss.* i. *t.* 71. *A. aureus*, *Eng. Fl.* v. *p.* 90. *Berk. Outl. p.* 140.

On dead stumps.

Subcæspitose. Pileus 4 in. or more broad, convexo-expanded, rich tawny, with broad, adpressed, silky scales in the centre, which towards the margin become mere streaks, fleshy; flesh pale yellow; gills at length tawny ferruginous, adnexed, rounded behind, or decurrent; stem 4 in. high, 1 in. or more thick, solid, tough, and spongy, the centre a little looser, thickened downwards and bulbous, with a small (sometimes rather large) deflexed, rather thick ring near the top, which is densely powdered with the spores, under the gills minutely squamulose, below fibrillose, the fibrillæ close, paler than the pileus, rhubarb-coloured within; root a few downy fibres; taste bitter.—*M. J. B.* Spores ·0003 × ·0002 in.

301. Agaricus (Pholiota) flammans. *Fr.* "Yellow scaly Pholiota."

Pileus fleshy, convex, then plane, somewhat umbonate, dry, clothed with superficial, hairy, paler scales; stem stuffed, then hollow, equal, rather flexuose, squamoso-squarrose, ring entire, yellow, as well as the fixed, crowded, quite entire gills.—*Fr. Epicr. p.* 167. *Eng. Fl.* v. *p.* 92.

In pine woods. Sept. Oct.

Taste bitter. Pileus 1½-3 in. broad, margin at first inflexed, then repand, scales concentric, yellow, scarcely innate; gills rather thin, close, adnate, without a tooth, at length ferruginous; stem 3 in. high, 2-3 lines thick, stuffed, at length hollow, yellow; ring entire, close to the gills.—*Fries.*

302. Agaricus (Pholiota) Junonius. *Fr.* "Beautiful Pholiota."

Pileus fleshy, convexo-plane, obtuse, when dry smooth; stem solid, equal, incurved, even, furfuraceous above the ring; gills adnate, crowded, yellow, then tawny.—*Fr. Epicr. p.* 167. *Sv. Bot. t.* 584. *Saund. & Sm. t.* 18, *f.* 2.

On trunks. Oct. Highgate.—*M.C.C.*

Single, or in small tufts, of a beautiful deep brownish-orange, minutely fibrillose when moist, smooth when dry; gills at first yellow, then of a deep cinnamon-brown; spores nearly ferruginous. Fries, to whom a drawing of our specimens was submitted, refers them without doubt to this species, which he describes as rare everywhere. Spores oval, or with an apiculus at one end, ·00027 × ·00017 in.

303. Agaricus (Pholiota) mutabilis. *Schæff.* "Changeable Pholiota."

Pileus fleshy, convex, then expanded, smooth, becoming pale; margin thin; stem stuffed, then hollow, rigid, rough with scales, dark-brown at the base; gills adnato-decurrent, crowded, pallid, then cinnamon colour.—*Fr. Epicr. p.* 169. *Schæff. t.* 9. *Lenz. f.* 20. *Krombh. t.* 73, *f.* 7-9*a*. *Bull. t.* 543, *O. P. R.* *Badh.* i. *t.* 16, *f.* 4*a*. *Gonn. & Rabh.* iv. *t.* 6. *Price, f.* 123. *Berk. Outl. t.* 8, *f.* 3. *Eng. Fl.* v. *p.* 92. *Huss.* ii. *t.* 27.

On trunks, especially lime stumps, or on the ground. Esculent. [United States.]

Cæspitose. Pileus expanded, obtuse, cinnamon, becoming pale when dry; centre of the pileus at length bright tawny, quite smooth, the margin thin transparent, flesh white; gills broad, rounded behind, or sub-decurrent, pale umber; stem slender, fistulose, dark-brown, smooth above, or minutely pulverulent, and pale, below squamulose, ring woven, sub-erect.—*M. J. B.* Spores ·00045 × ·00025 in.

304. Agaricus (Pholiota) marginatus. *Batsch.* "Marginate Pholiota."

Pileus rather fleshy, convex, then expanded, smooth, moist, hygrophanous; margin striate; stem fistulose, soft, not scaly, pruinose above the fugacious ring, base darker, clothed with whitish velvety down; gills adnate, crowded, watery-cinnamon coloured.—*Fr. Epicr. p.* 168. *Batsch. f.* 207 (208 *var.*) *Krombh. t.* 73, *f.* 5-6.

On the ground amongst firs.

Solitary or gregarious, rarely cæspitose. Stem about 2 in. long, 1-2 lines thick; pileus when moist honey-coloured, when dry tan-coloured, ring 1-2 lines distant from the apex of the stem.

C. *Muscigenei*—growing on moss, &c.

305. Agaricus (Pholiota) pumilus. *Fr.* "Little Pholiota."

Pileus somewhat fleshy, hemispherical, obtuse, even; stem fistulose, slender, sub-fibrillose; ring collar-like, rather fugacious; gills adnate, crowded, broad, pallid-yellowish.—*Fr. Epicr. p.* 170.

In woods. October. Rare.

Pileus only a few lines broad, yellowish; stem 1-1½ in. long; 1-1½ line thick.

306. Agaricus (Pholiota) mycenoides. *Fr.* "Delicate Pholiota."

Pileus membranaceous, campanulate, then convex, deeply striate, hygrophanous; stem fistulose, slender, ferruginous, smooth as well as the pileus; ring membranaceous, white; gills adnate, rather distant, ferruginous.—*Fr. Epicr. p.* 170. *A. mesodactylus. B. & Br. Ann. N.H. Ser.* 2, ii. *p.* 261, *t.* 9, *f.* 1, *p.* 400, *no.* 681.

On the ground, in damp dells. Oct. Rare.

"My plant has a white stem, but Fries considers it the same with his *A. mycenoides*. Pileus 1½ in. broad, obtusely conical, with the margin expanded, hygrophanous, pale tawny, slightly fleshy in the centre, margin striate; stem flexuous, 2½ in. high, 2 lines thick, white, nearly smooth above and below the ring, sometimes showing a vinous stain where bruised, nearly equal, fistulose. Ring central, expanded, quite entire, deeply striate within; gills moderately broad, slightly ventricose, ascending, affixed."—*M. J. B.*

307. Agaricus (Pholiota) Leveillianus. *D. & M.* "Leveille's Pholiota."

Hard, fleshy, thin, convex, umbonate, clothed with a glutinous, dark brown, opaque pellicle, at length wrinkled, and paler when dry; stem hollow, nearly equal, fibrilloso-squamose below the ring, white, with a reddish tinge; gills broad, adnate, decurrent, white, then pink, at length rufous.—*Berk. Outl. p.* 152. *A. jecorinus. B. & Br. Ann. N.H. Ser.* 2, ii. *p.* 260, *no.* 328.

On soil about beech trees. Aug. Rushton, Norths.

Fasciculate or gregarious. About 1½-2 in. across, hemispherical, at length expanded, quite smooth and even, at first clothed with a viscid pellicle, at length slightly wrinkled, somewhat fleshy, dark brown, paler when dry; stem 2½ in. high, ¼ in. thick, incrassated, below umber, dark brown at the base, fibrillose, stuffed, at length hollow. Ring near the top persistent, mostly deflexed; stem above the ring paler, fibrillose; gills umber, with a rosy tinge, adnate, with a decurrent tooth, rather distant; spores brownish. —*M. J. B.* Allied to *A. pudicus*, &c., but distinct in its very dark head, and umber adnato-decurrent gills. Taste like that of the common mushroom, with a slight acidity.

Sub-Gen. 20. HEBELOMA. Fr. S. M. i. p. 249.

(Including *Inocybe.* Fr. Mon. Hym.)

Spores for the most part clay-coloured, or in *Inocybe* ferruginous brown; veil of a different texture from the pellicle of the pileus, or in *Inocybe* homogeneous with the fibres of the pileus; pileus fleshy, pelliculose, damp, subviscid, or (in *Inocybe*) fibrous; stem confluent and homogeneous with the hymenophore, fleshy-fibrous, ringless; gills sinuato-adnate.

HAB. All terrestrial. (*Pl. IV., f.* 20.)

All the species are gregarious, and many so similar in appearance as to be with difficulty distinguished from each other. Some are scentless, several smell like rotten pears, and many have a disgusting odour and are poisonous; none are esculent. Fries, in his 'Monographia Hymenomycetum Sueciæ,' has introduced a new sub-genus after *Hebeloma*, which he names *Inocybe*, distinguished by the pileus being *silky-fibrous*, and having a few other unimportant characters; but such characters seeming insufficient, we have preferred to adhere to the views expressed in the 'Epicrisis,' and to retain *Inocybe* as a section of *Hebeloma*.—*W. G. S.*

A. HYMENOCYBE.

Sect. 1. Veiled, odour mild.

308. Agaricus (Hebeloma) punctatus. *Fr.* "Punctate Hebeloma."

Pileus fleshy, nearly plane, silky, becoming smooth, disc dotted with darker papillæ; stem hollow, equal, fibrillose, silky, growing pale, whitish-pruinose above; gills arcuate, fixed, narrow, pallid, ferruginous, or bay-coloured.—*Fr. Epicr. p.* 179. *Ann. Nat. Hist. no.* 906.

In pine woods. Sept. Near Gainsborough.

Pileus 1-2 in. broad, at first convex, soon becoming flattened, disc obtuse and swollen, umber about the centre, at length depressed; stem 2-4 in. high, 2-4 lines thick.

309. Agaricus (Hebeloma) versipellis. *Fr.* "Changeable Hebeloma."

Pileus fleshy, convexo-plane, disc viscid, with a tenacious gluten, beyond this silky-agglutinate, then smooth; stem fistulose, tough, whitish and silky, pruinose above; gills rounded, crowded, broad, whitish, flesh-coloured, then clay-coloured.—*Fr. Epicr. p.* 179. *Ann. N.H. no.* 907.

In grassy places, amongst fir leaves.

Silky, with an evanescent fibrillose veil, stem fibrilloso-striate, brownish internally; pileus thin, sub-punctate, regular, at length repand, dry, tan-coloured and opaque; odour faint, not unpleasant.

310. Agaricus (Hebeloma) mesophæus. *Pers.* "Pine Hebeloma."

Pileus rather fleshy, conical, convex, then plane, equal, even, with a viscid disc; stem sub-fistulose, equal, slender, fibrillose, white, then ferruginous, pruinose above; gills emarginate, crowded, thin, clay-coloured or ferruginous.—*Fr. Epicr. p.* 179. *Ann. N.H. no.* 908.

In pine woods.

Stem tough, 2-3 in. long, 2 lines thick, veil fugacious; pileus about 1 in., ash-coloured or pallid, rarely fibrillose at the margin; gills entire, and of one colour.

Sect. 2. Odour nauseous.

311. Agaricus (Hebeloma) sinapizans. *Fr.* "Clayey Hebeloma."

Pileus compact, convexo-plane, sub-repand, even, smooth, slightly viscid, stem nearly solid, stout, equal, fibrilloso-striate, whitish, apex squamose; gills deeply emarginate, broad, dry, crowded, quite entire, clay-coloured cinnamon.—*Fr. Epicr. p.* 180. *Paul. t.* 82. *Saund. & Sm. t.* 2.

In moist woods.

Pileus clay-coloured or grey, 3-5 in. or more broad; flesh white; stem 3-5 in. long, 1 in. thick.

312. Agaricus (Hebeloma) crustuliniformis. *Bull.* "Ring Hebeloma."

Pileus fleshy, convexo-plane, sub-repand, smooth, slightly viscid, stem stuffed, firm, rather bulbous, flocculoso-squamose, whitish; gills adnexed, crowded, thin, whitish, then watery cinnamon; edge crenulate, guttate.—*Fr. Epicr. p.* 180. *Bull. t.* 308, 546. *Batsch. f.* 195. *Batt. t.* 47. *Paul. t.* 52. *Berk. Outl. p.* 9, *f.* 1. *Krombh.* 62, *f.* 3-5. *Smith. P.M. f.* 24.

In woods. Common.

Forming large rings; pileus whitish, pallid, or tan-coloured, with the disc flesh-coloured or brick-red, variable in size and in length of the stem.—Spores pip-shaped, ·00035 × ·00023 in.

313. **Agaricus (Hebeloma) fastibilis.** *Fr.* "Ochrey Hebeloma."

Pileus compact, convexo-plane, repand, obtuse, viscid, smooth; stem solid, firm, sub-bulbous, white, fibroso-squamose; veil evident; gills emarginate, rather distant; pallid, whitish, then clay-coloured or cinnamon.—*Fr. Epicr. p.* 178. *Schæff. t.* 221. *Batt. t.* 15, *D.* *Paul. t.* 53, *f.* 2. *Eng. Fl.* v. *p.* 94 *(partly.)* *Ann. N.H. no.* 905.

In woods. July—Oct. Common. [United States.]

Densely gregarious or solitary; pileus 1-3 in. broad, viscid, moist, or dry, very fleshy, sometimes only sub-carnose, sub-hemispherical, sometimes rugoso-plicate, in large specimens ochraceous, with a rufous tinge, margin pale, involute and downy; gills broad, edges often lachrymose, ventricose, adnexed, emarginate or adnate, rather irregular, sub-argillaceous or cinnamon; stem 2-4½ in. high, 2 lines-1 in. thick, sub-bulbous, or nearly equal, somewhat rooting, clothed with scattered fibrillose scales, especially towards the apex, often twisted; at length hollow; odour disagreeable, somewhat resembling cherry-laurel flowers.—*M. J. B.* Spores pip-shaped ·0004 × ·0003 in. *(Pl. IV., f.* 20.*)*

314. **Agaricus (Hebeloma) testaceus.** *Batsch.* "Brick-red Hebeloma."

Pileus fleshy, campanulate, convex, obtuse, even, rather viscid; stem hollow, rather bulbous, flocculose or fibrillose, pallid, mealy above; gills attenuated, nearly free, lanceolate, crowded, ascending, pale, then ferruginous.—*Fr. Epicr. p.* 178. *Batsch. f.* 198.

In woods.

Pileus about 1½ in. broad, pale brick-red, ochraceous, or tan-coloured; stem 3 in. long, 3 lines thick, pallid, sprinkled above, with a whitish meal.

Sect. 3. Veil and odour none.

315. **Agaricus (Hebeloma) longicaudus.** *P.* "Long-stemmed Hebeloma."

Pileus fleshy, convex, then expanded, even, smooth, viscid; stem almost hollow, fragile, nearly equal, white, mealy above; gills emarginate, crowded, serrulated, dry, pale clay-coloured.—*Fr. Epicr. p.* 181. *Batt. t.* 21, *f. F.* *Berk. Outl. t.* 9, *f.* 2.

In woods.

Pileus pale 1½-2 in. broad; stem 4 in. long, 3-4 lines thick, white, farinaceous above; flesh soft, watery; odour faint, not unpleasant. Spores ·0004 × ·00025 in.

B. Inocybe.—Cuticle fibrous, dry.

Sect. 1. *Squarrosi*—pileus squarrose.

316. Agaricus (Hebeloma) relicinus. *Fr.* "Moss Hebeloma."

Pileus fleshy, thin, conical, then expanded, obtuse, squarrose, with tomentose scales, stem solid, soft, equal, floccoso-squamose; gills adnexed, crowded, yellow, then olivaceous.—*Fr. Epicr. p.* 171. *Eng. Fl. v. p.* 96.

In marshy fir woods, amongst *Sphagnum.*

Gregarious; pileus 1 in. across, at first conic obtuse, 4 lines high, then expanded; gills close, alternate, at length dingy-olive; stem 2 in. high, 2 lines thick.—*Fries.*

317. Agaricus (Hebeloma) flocculentus. *Poll.* "Woolly Hebeloma."

Pileus somewhat fleshy, hemispherical, then expanded, obtuse, floccoso-squamose, the scales of the disc erect, and sharp; stem solid, slender, squamoso-fibrillose, powdered with white dust above; gills seceding, thin, toothed, of a pallid clay colour.—*Fr. Mon. Hym.* i. *p.* 336. *Ag. lanuginosus. Fr. Epicr. p.* 171. *Eng. Fl. v. p.* 96. *Vaill. t.* 13, *f.* 4-6. *Pers. Ic. t.* 8, *f.* 4. *Bull. t.* 370.

On the ground.

Inodorous; pileus 1 in. or less broad, campanulato-convex, obtuse, then expanded, sub-umbonate, clothed with close squamuloso-squarrose down, which at length becomes obsolete, and leaves the pileus yellowish; flesh of the pileus and stem dirty white; gills broad, ventricose, close, pallid, at length brownish; stem 1½-2 in. high, 1-2 lines thick, equal, tough, covered with brown fibrillose down, apex minutely pruinose.—*Fries.*

318. Agaricus (Hebeloma) plumosus. *Bolt.* "Downy Hebeloma."

Pileus rather fleshy, convexo-plane, disc squarrose, with erect fasciculate flocci, margin fibrillose; stem stuffed, then hollow, slender, flexuose, floccoso-squamose, naked above; gills subadnate, scarcely crowded, ventricose, quite entire, dingy.—*Fr. Epicr. p.* 172. *Bolt. t.* 33. *Eng. Fl. v. p.* 96.

In moist pine woods. Aug.

Pileus 1½ in. broad, thickly covered with little downy tufts; stem 4 in. high, 1 line or more thick.

Sect. 2. *Laceri*—pileus torn.

319. **Agaricus (Hebeloma) pyriodorus.** *P.* Pear-scented Hebeloma."

Pileus fleshy, conical, then expanded, umbonate, clad with fibrous adpressed scales; stem stuffed, firm, equal, fibrillose, pruinose, and pale above; gills emarginate, rather distant, dirty white, then nearly cinnamon brown.—*Fr. Epicr. p.* 173. *Bull. t.* 532, *f.* 1. *Eng. Fl.* v. *p.* 96.

In woods. Sept. Oct. [Cincinnati.]

Pileus 2 in. across, broadly and strongly umbonate, the margin at length a little turned up, fibrilloso-squamulose, fleshy, pallid umber; gills adnexed, ventricose, pale; stem 2-3 in. high, 4 lines thick, fibrillose, white, when bruised somewhat of the same hue as the pileus; veil very fugacious; odour penetrating, like that of rotten pears.—*M. J. B.*

320. **Agaricus (Hebeloma) scaber.** *Müll.* "Rough Hebeloma."

Pileus fleshy, conical, then convex, obtusely gibbous, sprinkled with fibrous adpressed scales; stem solid, thick, equal, silky fibrillose, veiled; gills adnexed, crowded, dingy.—*Fr. Epicr. p.* 172. *Sow. t.* 207. *Eng. Fl.* v. *p.* 96.

In woods.

Pileus 1½ in. across, campanulate, subumbonate, dingy greyish-brown, scaly; gills pale dingy brown, rather numerous, nearly free; stem 1-1½ in. high, 2-3 lines thick, solid, whitish, fibrillose, furnished with a bark-like external coat; sometimes subgregarious.—*Grev.*

321. **Agaricus (Hebeloma) lacerus.** *Fr.* "Torn Hebeloma."

Pileus somewhat fleshy, convex, then expanded, obtuse, umbonate, squamoso-fibrillose; stem stuffed, slender, short, fibrillose, naked above, reddish within; gills adnexed, broad, ventricose, white, tinged with red, then mouse-coloured.—*Fr. Epicr. p.* 173. *Fl. Dan. t.* 1846, *f.* 1.

On the ground in woods.

Stem 1-2 in. long, equal, or attenuated at the base, tough, paler than the pileus; pileus about 1 in. broad, obtusely umbonate, at first closely fibrillose, then rimoso-squamose and squarrose, mouse-coloured, growing pale and yellowish.

322. **Agaricus (Hebeloma) obscurus.** *P.* "Violet Hebeloma."

Pileus somewhat fleshy, campanulate, then plane, umbonate, longitudinally fibrillose; disc squamose; stem stuffed, subflexuose, fibrillose, violet brown; gills uncinate, adnexed, crowded, ventricose, olivaceous, then brown.—*Fr.Epicr. p.* 173. *Ann. N.H. no.* 682.

On the naked ground. Nov.

Remarkable for its violet coloured stem or flesh, and its uncinate adnexed gills.—*M. J. B.* Spores pale brown, oval, or obovate, ·0003 × ·0002. in.

323. Agaricus (Hebeloma) flocculosus. *Berk.* "Flocculose Hebeloma."

Pileus subcarnose, convex, subcampanulate, umbonate, sericeo-squamulose; stem fibrillose, squamuloso-pulverulent above; gills pale, fawn-coloured, then obscurely ferruginous, ventricose, adnate.—*Eng. Fl.* v. *p.* 97. *Berk. Outl. p.* 154.

On naked soil, and amongst grass. Rare.

Pileus 1 in. broad, convex, subcampanulate, umbonate, sericeo-squamulose, brownish fawn colour, margin smoother, veil white, fibrillose, fugacious; gills at first pale fawn, at length dull ferruginous, ventricose, arched behind, and then adnate but not broadly so, margin white; stem 1½ in. high, 2 lines thick, fibrillose, pale fawn, beneath the fibrillæ brown, the apex minutely squamuloso-pulverulent. Odour like new meal.—*M. J. B.*

324. Agaricus (Hebeloma) Hookeri. *Klotsch.* "Hooker's Hebeloma."

Pileus submembranaceous, obtuse, umbonate, clothed with branny scales; stem shining, purple, pruinose with fawn-coloured meal; gills purple, at length cinnamon, adnexed.—*Eng. Fl.* v. *p.* 97. *Berk. Outl. p.* 154.

In garden pots. April—Oct. Glasgow.

Pileus 5-8 lines broad, fawn-coloured, centre umber; gills 1-1½ line broad, beautiful purple, at length cinnamon, veil floccoso-fibrillose, very fugacious; stem 1-1½ in. high, ½ line thick, fistulose, shining purple, pruinose with fawn-coloured meal.—*Klotsch.*

325. Agaricus (Hebeloma) deglubens. *Fr.* "Peeling Hebeloma."

Pileus somewhat fleshy, convexo-plane, obtuse, umbonate, torn into adpressed fibrils, disc somewhat scaly; stem solid, with adpressed fibrils, pallid, apex darker, mealy; gills adnate, ventricose, somewhat distant, dingy, then cinnamon.—*Fr. Epicr. p.* 173. *B. & Br. Ann. N.H.* 1866, *no.* 1117.

In woods. Aug. King's Cliffe.

Stature of *A. obscurus*, but colour and punctate apex of the stem (not white) very distinct. Pileus reddish bay, then yellowish, peeling off in darker fibrous scales; flesh white.

Sect. 3. *Rimosi*—pileus cracked.

326. Agaricus (Hebeloma) fibrosus. *Sow.* "Fibrous Hebeloma."

Pileus fleshy, thin, obtusely campanulate, silky, even, at length cracked; margin flexuous, broken; stem long, solid, striate, squamoso-flocculose above; gills free, crowded, linear-lanceolate, dirty-white.—*Sow. t.* 414. *Berk. Outl. p.* 155. *Eng. Fl.* v. *p.* 95.

In fir woods. July—Sept.

Pileus 3 in. broad, fleshy, especially in the disc, campanulate, irregular, longitudinally rimose, silky, dingy; gills semi-lanceolate, 2-3 lines broad, pallid. Stem 2 in. or more high, 3 lines thick, equal, striate, dirty-white, odour nauseous. *Fries.* Spores ·0004 × ·00025 in.

327. Agaricus (Hebeloma) fastigiatus. *Fr.* "Peaked Hebeloma."

Pileus fleshy, thin, conico-campanulate, longitudinally fibrous, and cracked; stem solid, stout, twisted, fibrously-silky; gills free, crowded, yellow, then brownish-olive (spores rough.)—*Fr. Epicr. p.* 174. *Berk. Outl. t.* 8, *f.* 4. *Sterb. t.* 22. D. E.

In woods. Rare.

Yellow-brown. Stem 3-4 in. long, but variable in stature, attenuated upwards. Spores rough, with little nodules.

328. Agaricus (Hebeloma) Curreyi. *Berk.* "Currey's Hebeloma."

Pileus convex, expanded, longitudinally fibrous, slightly cracked, not umbonate; stem straight, attenuated upwards, finely fibrillose; gills yellowish, then brownish-olive, free; spores perfectly even. —*Berk. Outl. p.* 155.

In woods. Aug.

Closely resembling *A. fastigiatus*, but by no means umbonate. The stem is dark, and the spores, which are subcymbiform, perfectly even.—*M. J. B.*

329. Agaricus (Hebeloma) euthelus. *B. & Br.* "Fir-leaf Hebeloma."

Pileus expanded, strongly umbonate, undulating, fawn-coloured, shining, silky, subsquamulose; stem nearly equal, pallid, striate, solid, fibrous; gills pallid, margin white, toothed, adnate.—*Ann. Nat. Hist.* 1865, *no.* 1004, *pl.* xiii. *fig.* 2.

On the ground amongst fir leaves. Aug. Aboyne, Aberdeenshire.

Smell farinaceous, rather disagreeable. Spores even, sub-elliptic, ·00029 in. long. It differs from *A. fastigiatus* in the adnate gills, smooth, not rough, spores; and from *A. Curreyi*, with which it agrees as to the spores, in its strongly umbonate pileus, nearly equal stem, and adnate gills.—*B. & Br.*

330. Agaricus (Hebeloma) rimosus. *Bull.* "Cracked Hebeloma."

Pileus fleshy, thin, campanulate, silky, fibrous, expanded longitudinally, cracked; stem solid, firm, nearly smooth, bulbous, whitish mealy above; gills free, subventricose, brownish clay-coloured.—*Fr. Epicr. p.* 174. *Eng. Fl.* v. *p.* 97. *Bull. t.* 388. *Berk. Outl. t.* 8, *f.* 5. *Sow. t.* 323. *Grev. t.* 128. *Batsch. f.* 107. *Krombh. t.* 44, *f.* 10-12. *Jungh. t.* 6, *f.* 6, *var. Gard. Chron.* (1861), *p.* 5, *fig.*

Woods and waste places. June—Sept. [United States.]

Subgregarious. Pileus 1-2 in. broad, shining, satiny, with adpressed fibrillæ, brown-yellow, at first campanulate, then nearly plane and umbonate, cracked in a radiate manner, the inner substance appearing through the cracks of a yellow hue, sometimes the cuticle cracks concentrically, and the lower edge of the cracked portions is reflected so as to present a squarrose appearance; gills ventricose, adnexed, at first mealy white, the margin opaque, then olivaceous, with the margin white and crenate. Stem 1½-2½ in. high, distinct from the pileus, sub-bulbous, nearly white, fibrillose at the base, clothed above with white mealy scales.—*M. J. B.* Spores ·0004 × ·00028 in.

331. Agaricus (Hebeloma) auricomus. *Batsch.* "Golden-haired Hebeloma."

Small, thin; pileus yellowish, margin striate, stem fistulose; gills fixed, ventricose, whitish, then brown.—*Fr. Epicr. p.* 175. *Batsch. f.* 21. *Berk. Outl. p.* 155.

In woods. [Cincinnati.]

Included by Fries as a variety of *Ag. descissus.* Pileus much cracked.

332. Agaricus (Hebeloma) trechisporus. *Berk.* "Rough-spored Hebeloma."

Pileus submembranaceous, convex, strongly umbonate, at first viscid, but soon dry and silky; stem slightly striate and mealy; gills ventricose, emarginate, scarcely adnate, pinkish-grey; spores rough.—*Berk. Outl. p.* 156, *t.* 8, *f.* 6. *Ann. N.H. no.* 71.

In woods, amongst fern. August.

Pileus 1 in. broad, convex, strongly umbonate; margin thin, viscid, but soon dry and satiny; umbo tawny, margin paler, with a slight livid tinge; gills ventricose, emarginate, pinkish grey, extreme margin denticulate. Spores bistre-brown, subreniform, covered with granules. Stem 2 in. high, 2 lines thick, white, slightly striate under a lens, and farinulent, nearly equal, except at the base, the outer coat of which is cottony.—*M. J. B.*

333. Agaricus (Hebeloma) hiulcus. *Fr.* "Red-flesh Hebeloma."

Pileus somewhat fleshy, conical, expanded, umbonate, fibrillose, rimoso-squamose; stem stuffed, rigid, elongated, silky-fibrillose, pruinose above, as well as the flesh, pale flesh-coloured; gills nearly free, scarcely crowded, broad, whitish flesh-colour, darker at the base, at length olivaceous.—*Fr. Ep. p.* 175. *Batt.* t. 18, c. *B. & Br. Ann. N.H.* (1866), *no.* 1118.

In woods. Sept. Fineshade.

Allied to *A. rimosus*, but the flesh turns everywhere reddish, when cut or bruised. Stem 2-3 in. long, 2-3 lines thick, closely fibrillose. Pileus 1-2 in. broad, closely fibrillose and scaly, cracked, brown or olive.

334. Agaricus (Hebeloma) lucifugus. *Fr.* "Strong-scented Hebeloma."

Pileus rather fleshy, convexo-plane, sub-umbonate, clad with adpressed fibrils or scales. Stem solid, firm, equal, smooth, sub-pruinose above; gills nearly free, crowded, plane, from yellowish-white changing to olive.—*Fr. Epicr. p.* 177. *Pers. Ic. Pict. t.* 15, *f.* 2. *Jungh. t.* 6, *f.* 4. *Ann. N.H. no.* 792.

On the ground in woods. Sept.

Pileus about an inch across, brownish, or olive. Stem 1½ in. long, 2 lines thick. Odour strong.

335. Agaricus (Hebeloma) sindonius. *Fr.* "Delicate Hebeloma."

Pileus fleshy, thin, conical, then convex, gibbous, obtuse, velvety-villose, veil sub-appendiculate; stem with a distinct medulla, at length hollow and smooth; gills attenuated, adnexed, lanceolate, whitish, then brown.—*Fr. Epicr. p.* 176. *Sow. t.* 365. *Batt. t.* 18, B.

In moist, shady places. Rare.

Pileus at length smooth, dirty white, becoming yellowish. Stem 2-3 in. long, white.

336. Agaricus (Hebeloma) geophyllus. *Sow.* "Wood Hebeloma."

Pileus somewhat fleshy, conical, then expanded, umbonate, even, silky-fibrillose; stem stuffed, equal, rather firm, white; veil fibrillose; gills adnexed, crowded, white, dingy, then earth-coloured.—*Fr. Epicr. p.* 176. *Sow. t.* 124. *Pers. Ic. t.* 14, *f.* 2. *Ic. & Des. t.* 1, *f.* 0. *Eng. Fl.* v. *p.* 98. *Bull. t.* 522, *f.* 2. *Fl. Boruss. t.* 388.

On the ground in woods. Common. [S. Carolina.]

Pileus 1 in. broad, umbonate, at length sub-inverted, white, lilac, brownish, yellowish, &c., satiny, often rimose. Gills adnate or adnexed, ventricose, earthy, not cinnamon, margin white, sub-dentate. Stem 1-3 in. high, 1-2 lines thick, flexuous, equal, or sub-bulbous, firm, very minutely farinaceous above, solid, less compact within. Odour strong and disagreeable.—*M. J. B.*

337. Agaricus (Hebeloma) vatricosus. *Fr.* "Little Hebeloma."

Pileus rather fleshy, convexo-plane, subumbonate, smooth, viscid, silky about the margin; stem fistulose, contorted, pulverulent; gills emarginate: ventricose, whitish, becoming brown.—*Fr. Epicr. p.* 177. *B. & Br. Ann. N.H.* (1865), *no.* 1005.

On dead stumps. Sept. Bodelwyddan, Flintshire.

Before the veil is ruptured it looks like a smooth *Lepiota.*—*B. & Br.*

Small, scarcely exceeding half an inch broad, viscid when young and moist, shining when dry, obsoletely silky at the margin. Inodorous.

Sub-Gen. 21. FLAMMULA, Fr. S. M. i. p. 250.

Spores in most species purely ferruginous, occasionally approaching yellow ochre, always bright in colour; veil filamentous, often obsolete; pileus fleshy, and, as the sub-genus is at present constituted, very variable. It may be,—1, covered with an inseparable fibrillose cuticle; 2, covered with a more or less viscid and *separable* cuticle; 3, pileus moist, and with *no separable* cuticle; 4, pileus neither pelliculose nor viscid, and broken up more or less into scale or fibrils; stem fleshy, fibrous, confluent, and homogeneous with the hymenophore; gills adnate, acutely adnate, or decurrent.

HAB. On the ground or on wood.—(*Pl. IV. fig.* 21.)

Fries says the natural affinity of *Flammula* is with *Pholiota*, but I consider all true *Flammulæ* should correspond with *Clitocybe* and *Clitopilus*. I suspect some of the species of *Flammula* that approach *Pholiota* in structure might with propriety be removed to that sub-genus, and *Flammula* proper be restricted to species with decurrent gills. Most of the species are tasteless or bitter, and none edible. They appear in late autumn or early winter. Some species of *Paxillus* may be mistaken for *Flammulæ*, but attention must be paid to the persistent gills, separating from the hymenophore and other characters in *Paxillus*.—*W. G. S.*

Sect. 1. *Heterogenei*—variable.

338. Agaricus (Flammula) helomorphus. *Secr.* "White Flammula."

White; pileus fleshy, convexo-plane, gibbous, unequal, viscid, when dry silky, becoming even; margin naked; stem solid, unequal, curved, even, nearly smooth; gills adnato-decurrent, crowded, white, then tan coloured.—*Fr. Epicr. p.* 184. *Secr. No.* 837.

In pine woods. (A. Jerdon.)

Stem about an inch long, 2-3 lines thick, rather attenuated downwards, above slightly silky. Pileus about 1 in. broad, sub-angular; gills 1 line broad.—*Fries.* Spores very small, ·0001 × ·00014 in.

339. Agaricus (Flammula) scambus. *Fr.* "Bow-legged Flammula."

Pileus somewhat fleshy, convexo-plane, then slightly depressed and floccoso-villose, viscid in moist weather; stem rather stuffed, short, incurved, flocculose, and veiled, white, attenuated below; gills subdecurrent, yellowish clay-coloured.—*Fr. Epicr. p.* 184. *Berk. Outl. p.* 157.

On larch.

Small, white, pileus scarcely exceeding an inch broad, at length dingy and clay-coloured, stem becoming somewhat ferruginous.

340. Agaricus (Flammula) floccifer. *B. and Br.* "Floccose Flammula."

Cæspitose, subcarnose; pileus convex, tawny, sprinkled with white fibrils; stem attenuated downwards, white, with silky scales, fistulose, umber within; gills rather broad, adnate, ferruginous.—*B. & Br. Ann. Nat. Hist. no.* 909. *t.* 14, *f.* 1.

On stumps of lime. Oct. Colleyweston.

Cæspitose; pileus 2 inches across, convex, expanded, tawny, somewhat zoned in drying, sprinkled with white fibrils, rather fleshy; flesh tawny at the edge and beneath the cuticle, elsewhere white; stem 1½ in. high, ¼ in. thick, attenuated downwards, furfuraceous within the pileus, white, with silky scales, hollow, umber within; gills moderately broad, rounded behind, adnate, scarcely ventricose, wrinkled transversely, ferruginous, edge white, spores ferruginous; ring none. The habit is that of *A. velutinus.*

Sect. 2. *Lubrici*—viscid.

341. Agaricus (Flammula) lentus. *Pers.* "Dusky Flammula."

Pileus fleshy, convexo-plane, even, viscid; stem rather stuffed, long, equal, squamose; gills adnate, whitish, then clay-coloured. —*Fr. Epicr. p.* 184. *Eng. Fl.* v. *p.* 95.

On stumps. [S. Carolina.]

Gregarious, subcæspitose; pileus 2-3 in. broad, plane, obtuse, very glutinous in wet weather, varying, with a yellowish, or pallid-livid (dirty-white) hue; stem 2-3 in. high, at length hollow.—*Fries.*

342. Agaricus (Flammula) gummosus. *Lasch.* "Viscid Flammula."

Pileus fleshy, plane, floccoso-squamulose, then even, viscid; stem stuffed, silky, fibrillose, red brown at the base; gills adnate, crowded, yellow, then cinnamon.—*Lasch. Linn.* (1827), *no.* 325. *Fr. Epicr. p.* 185. *B. & Br. Ann. N. H.* (1866), *no.* 1119. *Tratt. Aust. f.* 38.

On old stumps. Dec. Cambridge.

Pileus conical, then depressed, whitish, then olivaceous or greenish yellow, margin pallid, 1-2 in. broad. Flesh yellowish.

343. Agaricus (Flammula) spumosus. *Fr.* "Sulphury Flammula."

Pileus fleshy, thin, even, viscid; stem hollow, equal, slender, fibrillose, yellowish, then discoloured; gills adnate, yellow, at length ferruginous.—*Fr. Epicr. p.* 185. *S. M.* i. *p.* 252.

In woods. Epping Forest. [United States.]

Gregarious, yellow, flesh greenish-yellow; stem attenuated at the base, at length darker, slender, 2-4 in. long, 2 lines thick, obsoletely fibrillose; pileus rather fleshy, subumbonate, becoming plane, about 2 in. broad, disc darker.—*Fries.* Spores ·00023 × ·00015 in.

344. Agaricus (Flammula) carbonarius. *Fr.* "Viscid Charcoal Flammula."

Pileus fleshy, becoming plane, then even, viscid; stem narrowly fistulose, slender, rigid, squamulose, pallid; gills adnate, clay-coloured brown.—*Fr. Ep. p.* 186. *B. & Br. Ann. N. H.* (1866), *no.* 1120. *Seem. Jour.* 1868. *t.* 75, *f.* 5-8. *Cooke exs. no.* 401.

On charcoal and burnt earth. Nov. Dec. Ascot. Epping.

This species, remarkable for its viscid pileus, squamulose stem, and adnate clay-coloured gills, occurred in great quantities as above. It is a very late species; gregarious, tough, 1 in. or more high; pileus rather tawny, flesh yellow; spores ferruginous, with an apiculus at one end.

Sect. 3. *Udi*—moist.

345. Agaricus (Flammula) flavidus. *Schæff.* "Yellow Flammula."

Pileus fleshy, convexo-plane, equal, smooth, moist; stem somewhat hollow, fibrillose, yellow, then ferruginous; gills adnate, yellow, then ferruginous.—*Fr. Epicr. p.* 187. *Schæff. t.* 35. *Tratt. Austr. f.* 14 ? *Eng. Fl.* v. *p.* 94. *Ann. N.H. no.* 330, 792*.

On trunks of firs, lime, &c. Oct. [S. Carolina.]

Very various in size; pileus obtuse, 1-2 in. or more broad, never viscid, when moist dirty yellow; gills obtusely adnate; veil web-like, sometimes forming a ring. Stem stuffed, sometimes hollow, ferruginous at the base, sometimes attenuated.—*Fries.*

346. Agaricus (Flammula) inopus. *Fr.* "Bolton's Flammula."

Pileus fleshy, thin, convexo-plane, moist, smooth; stem fistulose, thin, flexuose, with adpressed fibrils, at length brick-red below; gills adnate, crowded, linear, pallid yellowish, white.—*Fr. Epicr. p.* 187. *Bolt. t.* 148. *Batt. t.* 22. *C. Eng. Fl.* v. *p.* 95.

On pine trunks.

Introduced on the authority of Fries' quotation of Bolton's figure. Pileus ½-2 in. broad; veil fugacious; stem 3 in. high, ¼ in. thick.—*Eng. Fl.*

Sect. 4. *Sapinei*—growing on firs.

347. Agaricus (Flammula) hybridus. *Fr.* "Hybrid Flammula."

Pileus fleshy, hemispherical, then expanded, obtuse, smooth, even, moist; stem stuffed, soft, attenuated upwards, tawny, with a whitish veil, which forms a ring; gills adnate, rather crowded, pale yellow, then tawny.—*Fr. Epicr. p.* 189.

On fir stumps. Gopsall.

Pileus regular, disc compact, at first tawny cinnamon, then brownish orange; flesh pallid.

348. Agaricus (Flammula) decipiens. *Smith.* "Charcoal Flammula."

Cæspitose; pileus convex, fleshy, minutely squamulose, dry, rich brown, becoming pallid; umbo almost white, stem often swollen, twisted, striate, attenuated downwards, rich tawny; gills crowded, moderately broad, decurrent, luminous brown, flesh within golden yellow, bright brown at base; spores bright tawny, ring none.—*Seem. Journ.* 1869, *p.* 249, *t.* 95, *f.* 5-8.

On burnt earth, charcoal, &c. June. Epping.

Pileus 1 in. across. Stem 2 in. high. Inclined to be fasciculate; mixed in growth with *A. (Flammula) carbonarius.* Fr. Though at a first glance it resembles the latter species, it differs greatly in the attachment of the gills, which are adnate in *A. carbonarius*, but truly decurrent in *A. decipiens.* Spores oval, or with an apiculus at one end, ·0003 × ·00017 in.—*W. G. S.*

349. Agaricus (Flammula) sapineus. *Fr.* "Bright-spored Flammula."

Pileus compact, convexo-plane, very obtuse, finely floccoso-squamulose, then cracked; stem rather stuffed, thick, sulcate, rooting, yellowish, without a ring; gills adnate, broad, golden yellow, then tawny cinnamon.—*Sys. Myc.* i. *p.* 239. *Eng. Fl.* v. *p.* 95. *B. & Br. Ann. N.H.* 1865, *no.* 1006. *Pers. Ic. & Descr. t.* 4, *f.* 7. *Trans. Woolhope Club*, 1868, *p.* 246.

On fallen branches of Scotch fir, and chips and sawdust about a saw-pit. Aboyne. Aug. On charcoal heaps in woods, round the Wrekin. [Cincinnati.]

This species is extremely variable especially as to the breadth and mode of attachment of the gills. It is remarkable for the bright colour of the spores.—*B. & Br.* Subcæspitose; stem usually short, solid, or hollow, often compressed, lacunose, &c. Pileus 1-4 in. broad, disc subopaque, margin paler, shining. Vestiges of the yellow veil scarcely manifest. Odour strong. Spores ·00032 × ·0002 in. *(Pl. IV., f.* 21.)

350. Agaricus (Flammula) picreus. *Fr.* "Delicate Flammula."

Pileus rather fleshy, convex, then expanded, even, smooth; stem fistulose, thin, almost umber, attenuated upwards, without a veil, at first pulverulent; gills adnate, subseceding, crowded, narrow, yellow, then ferruginous.—*Fr. Epicr. p.* 190. *Pers. Ic. Descr. t.* 4, *f.* 7. *Fr. Mon. Hym.* i. *p.* 362.

On old deal boards and pine stumps.—*W. G. S.*

Cæspitose, delicate. Stem 2-3 in. long, 1-2 lin. thick, slightly attenuated upwards, straight, when young pulverulent, umber. Pileus obtuse, regular, 1 in. broad, when young rufous or brownish cinnamon, when older becoming paler and tawny. Gills scarcely 1 line broad, normally adnate. Spores ·00023 × ·00015 in.

351. Agaricus (Flammula) filiceus. *Cooke.* "Fern-stem Flammula."

Pileus fleshy, convexo-plane, minutely squamuloso-fibrillose; stem stuffed, equal, slender; veil adhering to the stem and margin of pileus in reddish fugacious threads; gills crowded, adnate, sulphur yellow, at length tawny cinnamon.—*Seem. Journ.* (1863) *p.* 66, *t.* 3, *f.* 1.

On old tree-fern stems.

Pileus 1-2 in., obtusely convex, at length plane, golden yellow, minutely flocculoso-squamulose. Stem 1½-2½ in. high, yellowish, dark at the base; often tufted, sometimes solitary. Spores ·0003 × ·0002 in.

This species was first discovered in a conservatory at Highgate, on old tree-fern stems, originally from New Zealand. It has since been found by Mr. W. G. Smith, and is therefore included here as having equal claim with some other species to find a place in the British Flora.

Sub-Gen. 22. CREPIDOTUS. Fr. S. M. i. p. 272, in part.

Spores dark, or yellowish brown ; veil none ; pileus excentric, dimidiate, or resupinate ; flesh soft ; stem lateral, or wanting ; when present, confluent with and homogeneous with the hymenophore.

HAB. Most of the species grow on wood, a few on moss.— (*Pl. IV., f.* 22.)

The species are very irregular and variable. They mostly appear late in the autumn, and none are known to be edible. The pink-spored species, included by Fries in this sub-genus, are removed to Smith's new sub-genus *Claudopus*.

Sect. 1. *Eudermini.*

352. **Agaricus (Crepidotus) alveolus.** *Lasch.* "Ochrey Crepidotus."

Pileus fleshy, soft, lateral, obovate, then repand, opaque, contracted, and tomentose-villous behind ; gills determinate, crowded, broad, clay-brown.—*Fr. Epicr. p.* 210. *Pers. M.E. t.* 24, *f.* 3. *Ann. N.H. no.* 685.

On old stumps. Aug. Sept. Northamptonshire.

Closely allied to *A. mollis*, but not at all gelatinous. Spores ·0003 in. long. Pileus 2 in. and more broad, ochraceous brown, then olive at the margin, when dry becoming paler.

353. **Agaricus (Crepidotus) mollis.** *Schæff.* "Soft Crepidotus."

Pileus between subgelatinous and fleshy, flaccid, even, smooth, becoming pale ; stem obsolete ; gills crowded, linear, from whitish to watery cinnamon.—*Fr. Epicr. p.* 210. *Schæff. t.* 213. *Sow. t.* 98. *Batsch. f.* 38. *Berk. Outl. t.* 9, *f.* 6. *Huss.* i. t. 74. *Eng. Fl.* v. *p.* 102. *Letell. t.* 688. *Price, f.* 25. *Berk. exs. no.* 18.

On old stumps. July—Oct. Common. [United States.]

Solitary or imbricated. Pileus 1-2 in. broad, at first horizontal, subgelatinous, the base tomentose, or substrigose, margin transparent, minutely tomentose, then ascending, subfulvous, pallid when dry, margin waved, sometimes minutely squamulose, often stained with the elliptic ferruginous spores. Gills rounded behind, watery-umber, at first saturated with moisture, then dry and crisp.—*M. J. B.* Spores dark umber, ·00035 × ·00022 in. (*Pl. IV., fig.* 22.)

354. Agaricus (Crepidotus) haustellaris. *Fr.* "Kidney-shaped Crepidotus."

Pileus rather fleshy, reniform, even, slightly villous; stem lateral, attenuated upwards, villous, white; gills rounded, nearly free, brownish cinnamon.—*Fr. Epicr. p.* 211. *Berk. Outl. p.* 164. *Batsch. f.* 121.

On dead trunks. Rare.

Not observed since the time of Withering; gregarious, cæspitose, or imbricated. Stem distinct, attenuated upwards, 2-4 lines long, 1 line and more thick, at first ascending, then horizontal. Pileus lateral, kidney-shaped, ½-1 in. broad, pale red tan-colour, becoming pale. Flesh watery, pale yellowish.

355. Agaricus (Crepidotus) Rubi. *Berk.* "Bramble Crepidotus."

Pileus fleshy, clothed with very minute crystalline meal; stem short, incurved, solid, strigose at the base; gills adnato-decurrent, greyish, then umber, slightly ventricose.—*Berk. Outl. p.* 164, *t.* 9, *f.* 7. *Eng. Fl.* v. *p.* 102.

On dead bramble, &c. Aug. Rare.

Pileus ¼ in. or more broad, at first regular, with a short stem, gradually becoming excentric, and resupinate, of a yellowish, or livid-grey hue, pallid when old; gills rather distant, at first greyish, then umber, edge pulverulent. Stem very short, at first straight, then incurved, solid, externally mealy, adhering by a little fine down.—*M. J. B.*

356. Agaricus (Crepidotus) chimonophilus. *B. & Br.* "Downy Crepidotus."

White. Pileus convex, rather thick, villous; stem very short, or obsolete; gills distant, attenuated behind.—*Berk. Outl. p.* 164. *Ann. Nat. Hist. no.* 687.

On small dead branches of *Pyrus torminalis.* Benefield, Norths.

Pure white. Pileus ¼ in. across, convex, clothed with villous down, margin inflexed. Stem extremely short or obsolete. Gills few, distant. Spores very pale, yellow-brown, oblongo-elliptic, with a distinct lateral nucleus.—*M. J. B.*

357. Agaricus (Crepidotus) pezizoides. *Nees.* "Pezizæform Crepidotus."

Pileus sessile, thin, cup-shaped, then reflexed, mealy, subtomentose; gills meeting in the centre, somewhat distant, olivaceous-brown, then tawny.—*Fr. Epicr. p.* 212. *Nees. A.N. Cur.* ix. *t.* 6, *f.* 18. *Eng. Fl.* v. *p.* 103.

On rotten branches. Rare.

Gregarious, fleshy, subgelatinous, 1 line high and broad, fixed at the base by very delicate white fibres; gills about 12, thick, ventricose.—*Fries.* Gills white to stone-colour, margin sub-crenate, white, and somewhat cottony in young specimens.—*Purton.*

Sub-Gen. 23. NAUCORIA. Fr. S. M., i. p. 260.

Spores various shades of brown, dull or bright; veil absent, or attached to the edge of the pileus, in young plants in the form of minute flakes; pileus convex and inflexed, smooth, flocculent or squamulose; stem cartilaginous, confluent with but heterogeneous from the hymenophore.

HAB. Terrestrial or epiphytal. (*Pl. IV., f.* 23.)

No subgenus includes so many dissimilar species as this. In size, structure, the nature of the veil, and the colour of the spores, they differ exceedingly. *Naucoria* corresponds with *Collybia*, *Leptonia*, and *Psilocybe*.—*W.G.S.*

Sect. 1. *Gymnoti*—naked, spores rusty.

358. Agaricus (Naucoria) cucumis. *P.* "Cucumber Naucoria."

Pileus somewhat fleshy, broadly campanulate, smooth, growing pale; stem thin, firm, smooth, dark-brown, thickened at the apex, hollow, sub-pruinose; gills slightly adnexed, ventricose, pallid, saffron-yellow.—*Fr. Epicr. p.* 193. *Sow. t.* 344. *Eng. Fl.* v. *p.* 99.

Amongst sawdust.

Pileus 1-1½ in. broad, even, smooth, when moist bay-brown, with a purplish tinge, pale about the margin, when dry fawn-coloured or tan; gills very ventricose, close, distinct, dirty white, with somewhat of a saffron tint. Stem 1½-2 in. high, 1-1½ line thick, attenuated downwards, firm, smooth, hollow, pale at the apex. Odour exactly that of fresh cucumber.—*Fries.*

359. Agaricus (Naucoria) centunculus. *Fr.* "Lurid Naucoria."

Pileus somewhat fleshy, convexo-plane, obtuse, lurid-greenish, then yellowish, turning pale; stem fistulose, with whitish down at the base, pulverulent above; gills adnate, then seceding, thick, broad, cinereous yellow, as well as the stem.—*Fr. Epicr. p.* 193. *Ann. N.H. no.* 72.

On rotten wood. Oct. Rare.

Gregarious. Pileus 3-10 lines broad, olivaceous brown, becoming pale, even or slightly striate; gills emarginate or free, sometimes crowded, sometimes somewhat distant, crisped when old, the edge denticulate with greenish-yellow flocci.

360. Agaricus (Naucoria) horizontalis. *Bull.* "Horizontal Naucoria."

Pileus somewhat fleshy, plano-convex, obtuse, even, smooth; stem solid, very short, incurved, naked; gills rounded behind, free, broad, plane. The whole plant of a watery cinnamon colour. —*Fr. Epicr. p.* 194. *Bull. t.* 324. *Ann. N.H. no.* 331.

On elm trunks. Rare.

Pileus ½ in. broad, gills adnexed or nearly free; stem ½ in. long, 1 line thick.

361. Agaricus (Naucoria) melinoides. *Fr.* "Tawny Naucoria."

Pileus somewhat fleshy, convexo-plane, obtuse, umbonate, even, smooth, moist; stem hollow, slightly-thickened, pruinose above, base white; gills adnate, triangular, toothed, honey-coloured.— *Fr. Epicr. p.* 195. *Berk. Outl. t.* 9, *f.* 3. *Bull. t.* 560, *f.* 1. *Krombh. t.* 3, *f.* 14. *Eng. Fl.* v. *p.* 100.

On lawns. Oct. Common.

Pileus 2 lines to 1 in. broad, submembranaceous, umbonate, when moist tawny, margin pellucid, ochraceous or whitish when dry; gills very variable, adnexed, or broadly adnate, ventricose, at first paler than the pileus, at length cinnamon. Stem 1·2 in. high, scarce 1 line thick, fistulose, fibrillose above, subpruinose, thickened below and downy, changing colour. The gills remain bright.—*M. J. B.*

362. Agaricus (Naucoria) nuceus. *Bolt.* "Nut-like Naucoria."

Pileus submembranaceous, globoso-campanulate, umbilicate, punctulate; margin incurved, somewhat lobed; stem fistulose, slender, silky-fibrillose, white; gills attenuated, adnate, ascending, slightly lobed, cinnamon.—*Fr. Epicr. p.* 194. *Bolt. t.* 70.

On the ground amongst firs.

Slender, but tough. Stem 2-3 in. Pileus ½-1 in., pale chestnut colour; gills semi-circular, not sinuate, 3-4 lines broad. Spores, with an apiculus at one or both ends, ·00045 × ·00025 in.

363. Agaricus (Naucoria) sideroides. *Bull.* "Stellate Naucoria."

Pileus rather fleshy, campanulate, then expanded, umbonate, smooth, slightly viscid; stem stuffed, attenuated, even, pallid; gills with a decurrent tooth, uncinate, fixed, narrow, crowded, pallid, ochraceous, then cinnamon.—*Fr. Epicr. p.* 196. *Bull. t.* 588. *B. & Br. Ann. N.H.* 1865, *no.* 1007.

On the trunk of an ash tree. Nov. Apethorpe.

Probably common. Much thicker than *A. hypnorum*, which it somewhat resembles.—*B. & Br.* Pileus ochraceous and shining when dry, margin at first incurved, then striate, about ½ in. high and broad, when expanded 1 in. broad. Stem 3 in. long, pallid yellowish, at length becoming ferruginous.

Sect. 2. *Phæoti*—spores brown.

364. Agaricus (Naucoria) vervacti. *Fr.* "Meadow Naucoria."

Pileus fleshy, convexo-plane, umbonate, even, smooth, viscid; shining when dry; stem stuffed, then hollow, attenuated, smooth, rigid, rootless, whitish; gills adnate, with a decurrent tooth, crowded, then ventricose, pallid, then ferruginous-brown.—*Fr. Epicr. p.* 197. *Batt. t.* 13, *F.* *Batsch. f.* 108 (?) *Ann. N.H. no.* 273.

In meadows, gardens, &c. Bromley.

Stem short, about 1 in., rather thick. Pileus yellow, slightly viscid, soft, obtuse. Flesh white.

365. Agaricus (Naucoria) pediades. *Fr.* "Tan-coloured Naucoria."

Pileus somewhat fleshy, convexo-plane, obtuse or depressed, dry, at length opaque; stem medullate, rather flexuous, slightly silky, yellowish, base somewhat bulbous; gills adnexed, broad, subdistant, brownish, then dirty cinnamon.—*Fr. Epicr. p.* 197. *Paul. t.* 106, *f.* 2, 3. *Schæff. t.* 203. *Ann. N. H. no.* 683. *Letell. t.* 675.

In pastures. Nov. Cranford. Middlesex.

Stature variable, stem usually elongated; pileus about an inch broad, ochraceous, then tan-coloured.

366. Agaricus (Naucoria) semiorbicularis. *Bull.* "Half-round Naucoria."

Pileus rather fleshy, hemispherical, then expanded, even, smooth, rather viscid, at length rivulose; stem slender, tough, almost straight, pallid, ferruginous, shining, with a separable pith; gills adnate, very broad, crowded, pallid, then ferruginous.—*Fr. Epicr. p.* 197. *Bull. t.* 422. *Berk. Outl. t.* 9, *f.* 4. *Ann. N.H. no.* 274.

On lawns and pastures. Common.

Stem cartilaginous, tough, 3-4 in. long, scarcely exceeding 1 line thick, at length pale, ferruginous, darker at the base; pileus 1-2 in. broad, tawny, ferruginous, then ochrey; spores ·0005 × ·00032 in. *(Pl. IV., f.* 23.*)*

367. Agaricus (Naucoria) sobrius. *Fr.* "Sober Naucoria."

Pileus somewhat fleshy, convexo-plane, slightly viscid, sub-silky, disc darker, veil pruinose, fugacious; stem nearly fistulose, brownish at the base, clad with white flocci; gills adnate, crowded, broad, pallid, saffron yellow.—*Fr. Epicr. p.* 200. *Ann. N. H. no.* 912.

On the ground. Sept. King's Cliffe.

Pileus about an inch broad, yellowish, the edge of the gills becoming whitish; stem 1½ in. long, 1 line thick, pallid above, ferruginous brown below, here and there with whitish silky spots.

368. Agaricus (Naucoria) escharoides. *Fr.* "Campanulate Naucoria."

Pileus rather fleshy, conico-convex, then expanded, obtuse, squamuloso-furfuraceous, becoming pallid; stem fistulose, flexuous, with adpressed fibrils, at length smooth and pallid; gills fixed, lax, ventricose, pallid, clay-colour or cinnamon.—*Fr. Epicr. p.* 201. *B. & Br. Ann. N. H.* (1866), *no.* 1122. *Schæff. t.* 226.

On bare ground. Aug. Apethorpe.

Pileus campanulate, obtuse, slightly fleshy, umbonate or umbilicate, sometimes plane, hygrophanous, innato-squamulose, often venulose, tawny, at length pallid; veil white, evanescent; stem flexuous, nearly equal, clothed with white fibrils, pale, ringless, fistulose; gills broad, bright cinnamon, distant, fixed, acute behind, at length seceding; spores ·0006 × ·00065 in. long, of a pure ochre, not peroxidate, brittle.—*B. & Br.*

369. Agaricus (Naucoria) conspersus. *P.* "Sprinkled Naucoria."

Pileus rather fleshy, convexo-plane, obtuse, nearly even, at length mealy, and broken up into scales, hygrophanous; stem fibrillose, brownish cinnamon; gills adnate, rather receding, crowded, cinnamon colour.—*Fr. Epicr. p.* 201. *Pers. Ic. & Desc. t.* 12, *f.* 3. *Krombh. t.* 3, *f.* 12. *Ann. N. H. no.* 911.

In woods and moist places. Sept. Colleyweston.

Gregarious; pileus cinnamon-bay, ochrey when dry, ½-1 in. broad; gills linear or ventricose; stem 1-2 in. long, 1 line thick, fibrillose, cinnamon, mealy above.

370. Agaricus (Naucoria) erinaceus. *Fr.* "Hedgehog Naucoria."

Pileus rather fleshy, convex, subumbilicate, squamose with fasciculate hairs; stem slender, fistulose, short, incurved, hairy; gills adnate, rather crowded, quite entire.—*Fr. Epicr. p.* 201. *Sow. t.* 417. *Batt. t.* 28, *f. K. Eng. Fl.* v. *p.* 98.

On dead sticks. Rare.

Small, solitary, persistent; stem slightly fistulose, adnate, on the epidermis of branches, by a dilated base, clothed with white pubescence, incurved, equal, about 4 lines high, scarce 1 line thick, umber-ferruginous; pileus subcarnose, disc umbilicate, ½ in. broad, scaly with very dense fasciculate locks, umber-ferruginous, margin at first involute; gills rather broad, not close, adnate.—*Fries.*

371. Agaricus (Naucoria) siparius. *Fr.* "Veiled Naucoria."

Pileus rather fleshy, plane, obtuse; stem stuffed, pruinose above, clothed, as well as the pileus, with downy scales; gills adnate, broad, rather distant, floccose at the edge.—*Fr. Epicr. p.* 201. *Chev. t.* 6, *f.* 9. *Ann. N. H. no.* 684.

On soil, fern stems, &c.

Resembling *A. erinaceus*, but softer, and not so bright in colour, brownish rust-colour; stem ½-1 in. long; pileus 3-5 lin. broad, densely villoso-squamulose.

372. Agaricus (Naucoria) carpophilus. *Fr.* "Beech-mast Naucoria."

Pileus submembranaceous, convex, obtuse, mealy with shining atoms (not pilose, rarely squamulose); stem somewhat stuffed, short, slender, mealy, then naked, pallid; gills rounded behind, adnexed, nearly free, broad, rather distant, crenulate, ochraceous.—*Fr. Epicr. p.* 202. *Ann. N.H. no.* 910.

On the pericarps and leaves of beech. Sept. Colleyweston.

Small, pallid when dry; pileus 2-3 lines broad, hygrophanous, shining, with mealy atoms, tan-coloured when moist. Stem scarcely 1 in. long, filiform, pallid, at first mealy, then naked.

Sub-Gen. 24. GALERA. Fr. S. M. i. p. 264.

Spores ochraceo-ferruginous; veil often wanting, when present fibrous and fugacious; pileus more or less campanulate, margin straight, at first adpressed to the stem; stem cartilaginous, fistulose, confluent with but heterogeneous from the hymenophore; gills adnate, or with a decurrent tooth (exactly as in *Mycena*).

HAB. The greater number of species are terrestrial.

(*Pl. IV., f.* 24.)

The species are not numerous, and most are slender and brittle, appearing in the autumn. *Galera* corresponds with *Mycena*, *Nolanea*, *Psathyra*, and *Psathyrella*.—*W. G. S.*

Sect. 1. *Pluteotropi*—viscid.

373. Agaricus (Galera) reticulatus. *P.* "Reticulated Galera."

Pileus slightly fleshy, campanulate, then expanded, rugoso-reticulate, viscid; margin striate; stem fragile, fibrillose, white; gills free, ventricose, crowded, saffron yellow, to ferruginous.—*Fr. Epicr. p.* 203. *Pers. Ic. & Desc. t.* 4. *f.* 4-6. *Berk. Outl. t.* 9, *f.* 5. *Ann. N.H. no.* 70.

On dead wood. Rare.

In the young state the pileus is of a delicate bistre, and it is only in age that it assumes a violet tinge, apparently from the colour of the spores being partly seen through the flesh.—*M.J.B.* Stem 2 in. long, white, slightly mealy above. Pileus 2 in. broad, at first viscid, and reticulated with anastomosing veins, becoming smooth with age.

374. Agaricus (Galera) aleuriatus. *Fr.* "Striate Galera."

Pileus submembranaceous, conico-convex, then plane, viscid, not wrinkled, striate; stem slender, pulverulent, rather incurved, white; gills free, ventricose, ochraceous saffron-colour.—*Fr. Epicr. p.* 203. *B. & Br. Ann. N.H.* (1866), *no.* 1123.

On rotten sticks. Oct. Coed Coch.

An extremely pretty species. Smaller and more delicate than *A. reticulatus.* Pileus blue-grey, pallid, or roseate; spores pale saffron yellow. Stem about 1 in. long. Pileus about 1 in. broad, striate, but not rugose.

Sect. 2. *Polytropi.*

375. Agaricus (Galera) ovalis. *Fr.* "Oval Galera."

Pileus submembranaceous, oval, or campanulate, even, hygrophanous; stem straight, equal, slightly striate, nearly of the same colour; gills almost free, ventricose, very broad, ferruginous.—*Berk. Outl. p.* 163. *Bull. t.* 552. *f.* 1. *A. campanulatus. Fr. Epicr. p.* 205.

On dung. Rare.

Pileus dusky-ferruginous, larger than *A. tener.* Gills at length somewhat liquescent. Stem about 3 in. long, straight, of the same colour as the pileus. Pileus about 1 in. high and broad, ferruginous when moist, yellowish when dry.

Sect. 3. *Teneri*—slender.

376. Agaricus (Galera) lateritius. *Fr.* "Brick-red Galera."

Pileus submembranaceous, acorn-shaped, then conical, even, hygrophanous; stem tall, fragile, straight, attenuated upwards, frosted with white meal; gills nearly free, linear, very narrow, tawny, ferruginous.—*Fr. Epicr. p.* 204. *Fl. Dan. t.* 1846, *f.* 2. *Batt. t.* 28, *T.*

In rich pastures. Rare.

Stem white, 3 in. and more long; pileus pinkish ochre, about 1 in. high; when moist the margin is closely striate.

377. Agaricus (Galera) tener. *Schæff.* "Slender Galera."

Pileus submembranaceous, conico-campanulate, obtuse, hygrophanous; stem straight, fragile, rather shining, nearly of the same colour; gills adnate, crowded, ascending, rather broad, cinnamon.—*Fr. Epicr. p.* 204. *Schæff. t.* 70, *f.* 6-8. *Sow. t.* 33. *Bull. t.* 535. *Bolt. t.* 66, *f.* 2. *Eng. Fl.* v. *p.* 100.

Rich pastures, dungy ground, &c. Common.

[United States.]

Pileus 1 in. high and broad, subcarnose, campanulate, or conico-campanulate, smooth, shining, ochraceous when dry; gills pale ferruginous, ascending, more or less adnate, ventricose, or sublinear, margin white, subserrulate; stem 3-5 in. high, 1½ line thick, striate, pulverulento-fibrillose, not brittle, bulbous at the base.—*M.J.B.* Spores ·00054 × ·0003 in. (*Pl. IV., f.* 24.)

378. Agaricus (Galera) antipus. *Lasch.* "Little pale Galera."

Pileus campanulate, then convex, even, hygrophanous, when dry sprinkled with atoms, disc slightly fleshy; stem straight, short, striate, mealy; base bulbous, fusiform, rooting; gills almost free, crowded, lanceolate, yellowish ochre.—*Lasch. no.* 401. *Fr. Epicr. p.* 205. *Smith in Trans. Woolh. Cl.* (1870).

On mould in flower pots.

Simple, slightly rigid; stem 1 in., paler than the pileus. Pileus ½-1 in., not striate, when moist ochraceous, when dry paler, almost white. Spores and then the gills rubiginous.

379. Agaricus (Galera) confertus. *Bolt.* "Crowded Galera."

Pileus submembranaceous, acutely conico-campanulate, smooth, hygrophanous; stem slender, silky, shining, naked; base equal, deeply rooting; gills slightly adnexed, subdistant, white, then brownish-ochraceous.—*Fr. Epicr. p.* 206. *Bolt. t.* 18.

In stoves. Rare.

Densely crowded, very fragile; pileus brown, ochraceous when dry, "conical, terminating in an acute point, which point is tinged with yellowish brown, the rest white, the surface smooth, the substance light and cottony. In large specimens it is about 1 in. in diameter; in decay it withers, and becomes like soft paper."—*Bolton.*

380. Agaricus (Galera) sparteus. *Fr.* "Meadow Galera."

Pileus membranaceous, campanulate, convex, then expanded, obtuse, hygrophanous, dry, even, smooth; stem slender, rigid, flexible, smooth; gills adnate, crowded, plane, cinnamon coloured. —*Fr. Ep. p.* 206. *Bolt. t.* 51, *f.* 1.

Amongst moss in meadows. Rare.

Pileus 5 lines broad, cinnamon, striate and pellucid when moist, when dry tan-coloured. Stem 1-2 in. long, polished, smooth, base darker, of a brightish brown.

Sect. 4. *Hypnophilæ*—amongst moss.

381. Agaricus (Galera) embolus. *Fr.* "Heath Galera."

Pileus membranaceous, campanulate, obtuse, radiato-striate, hygrophanous; stem very smooth, shining, thickened upwards; gills adnate, triangular, thick, very distant, cinnamon.—*Fr. Epicr. p.* 207.

Amongst heath.

When moist shining, reddish tawny, when dry ochraceous. Stem 2 in. long, yellow, manifestly thickened upwards, smooth, naked. Pileus ½ in. broad, hygrophanous.

382. Agaricus (Galera) hypnorum. *Batsch.* "Moss-loving Galera."

Pileus membranaceous, campanulate, subpapillate, smooth, striate, hygrophanous; stem slender, flexuose, lax, of the same colour, apex pruinose; gills adnate, rather distant, broad, lax, at length plane, cinnamon-yellow.—*Fr. Epicr. p.* 207. *Batsch. f.* 96. *Sow. t.* 282. *Bull. t.* 560, *f.* i. *C.E.* *Eng. Fl.* v. *p.* 100.

Amongst moss. Common. [United States.]

Pileus 2-3 lines broad, conico-campanulate, of a beautiful tawny brown when moist, or sometimes reddish, the striate margin only when dry retaining its original hue, the rest pale, flesh thick in the centre, turning pale like the pileus. Gills ventricose, adnexed or adnate, tawny, rather broad. Stem 1 in. high, filiform, minutely fistulose, paler than the pileus, pruinose. —*M. J. B.*

383. Agaricus (Galera) sphagnorum. *Pers.* "Bog-moss Galera."

Pileus membranaceous, campanulate, smooth, striate, yellow-ochraceous, disc broad; stem long, slender, sub-fibrillose, tawny, gills adnate, subdistant, broad.—*Pers. Syn. p.* 385. *Bull. t.* 560, *f. H.* *B. & Br. Ann. N.H.* 1865, *no.* 1008.

On *Sphagnum*, on the borders of a pine wood. Aug. Aboyne.

Twice or three times larger than *A. hypnorum*, of which Fries considers it a variety.

Sect. 5. *Eriodermei*—squamulose.

384. Agaricus (Galera) mycenopsis. *Fr.* "White-scaled Galera."

Pileus submembranaceous, campanulate, then expanded, disc even, slightly striate to the middle, about the margin at first whitish-silky, and veiled; stem much attenuated, whitish-silky; gills adnexed, seceding, ventricose, rather distant, whitish, then pale ochre.—*Fr. Epicr. p.* 208. *B. & Br. Ann. N.H.* 1866, *no.* 1124.

In marshy ground amongst *Sphagnum*. Aug.—Oct.

The specimens hitherto found belong to the variety mentioned by Fries, with adnate gills. Pileus with the margin clothed, with little white scales, the remains of the veil; stem slightly furfuraceous above; gills adnate, not merely fixed by a tooth.—*B. & Br.*

385. Agaricus (Galera) paludosus. *Fr.* "Swamp Galera."

Pileus submembranaceous, campanulate, then convex, acutely umbonate, hygrophanous, silky everywhere with persistent white hairs; stem fistulose, twisted, encircled with the remains of the white veil; gills adnate, plane, ovate, pale honey colour. —*Fr. Epicr. p.* 209. *B. & Br. Ann. N.H.* 1866, *no.* 1125.

In marshy ground, amongst *Sphagnum*. Aug. King's Cliffe.

Stem $1\frac{1}{2}$-3 in. long, 1 line thick. Pileus $\frac{1}{2}$ in., when moist brownish honey colour, when dry tan-coloured.

Sub-Gen. 25. TUBARIA. *Smith. Seem. Journ.*, 1870.

Pileus generally depressed, at first with an incurved margin; stem cartilaginous, hollow, confluent with but heterogeneous from the hymenophore; gills decurrent. (*Pl. IV., fig.* 25.)

As in *Eccilia* there are very few known representatives of this sub-genus, either British or Foreign. It is analogous with *Omphalia*, *Eccilia*, and *Deconica*.—*W. G. S.*

386. Agaricus (Tubaria) inquilinus. *Fr.* "Little Tubaria."

Pileus submembranaceous, convexo-plane, smooth, slightly striate, hygrophanous, centre somewhat fleshy; stem fistulose, short, tough, dark brown, attenuated downwards; gills adnato-decurrent, triangular, convex, scarcely crowded, brownish ferruginous.—*Fr. Epicr. p.* 199. *Eng. Fl.* v. *p.* 99.

On chips in woods, gardens, &c.

Pileus a few lines across (3-6.) Stem 1 in. or more high, minutely fistulose, dark umber, with white fibrillæ and scales.—*M. J. B.* Analogous with *A. (Omphalia) sphagnicola.*—*W. G. S.*

387. Agaricus (Tubaria) furfuraceus. *P.* "Mealy Tubaria."

Pileus somewhat fleshy, convexo-plane, obtuse, then depressed, moist, hygrophanous, at first clothed with silky evanescent scales, then naked; stem fistulose, flocculose, rigid, pallid; gills adnato-decurrent, rather distant, cinnamon coloured.—*Fr. Epicr. p.* 200. *Bull. t.* 593, *f.* 3. *Batsch. f.* 98. *Eng. Fl.* v. *p.* 98.

On chips, &c. Common. [Cincinnati.]

Spores ·00022 in. long. Pileus ½-1 in. broad, subcarnose, at first convex, at length expanded, often umbilicate, rich umber, or cinnamon when moist; margin transparent, sprinkled, especially towards the margin, with white fibrillæ, or little branny scales, when dry white or reddish-tan; gills broad, subdecurrent, moderately distant, pale cinnamon. Stem 1-2 in. high, 1-2 lines thick, nearly equal, or slightly thickened at the base, flexuous, fistulose, fibrillose, or furfuraceous.—*M. J. B.*

388. Agaricus (Tubaria) autochthonus. *B. & Br.* "Ochrey-white Tubaria."

Pileus obtuse, hemispherical, ochrey-white, silky, margin flocculose; stem slender, flexuous, incrassated above and below, whitish, woolly; gills horizontal, with a distinct adnate tooth, honey-coloured.—*B. & Br. Ann. N.H.* (1866), *no.* 1121.

On the naked soil. Woodnewton, Norths.

Pileus ¼ in. across; stem ¾ in. high, not half a line thick in the centre. Spores paler than in *A. furfuraceus*, ·00019 inch long. It does not become pallid in drying, like that species, but is of an ochraceous white from the first. —*B. & Br.*

Series 4. **Pratellæ**, Fr. Epicr. p. 212.—Spores various shades of brownish purple, dark purple, or intense brown.

Sub-Gen. 26. Psalliota, Fr. Epicr. p. 212.

Spores dark brownish-purple, dead brown, reddish-purple, pale slate, or pinkish; veil universal, concrete with the cuticle

* Hymenophore distinct from the fleshy Stem.

26. PSALLIOTA.

27. PILOSACE.

NOT BRITISH.

** Hymenophore confluent and homogeneous with the fleshy Stem.

28. STROPHARIA

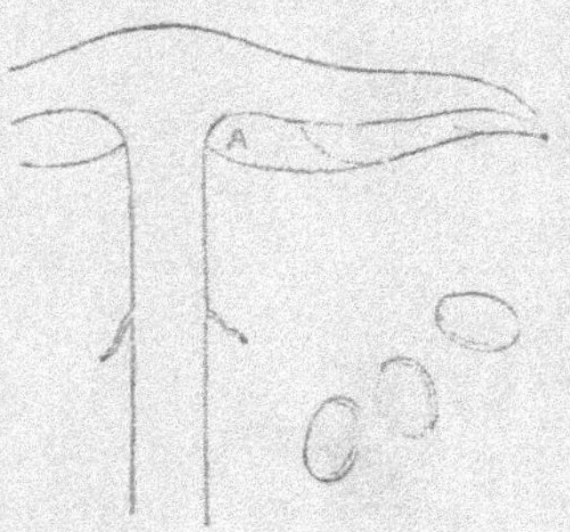

29. HYPHOLOMA.

** Hymenophore confluent with, but heterogeneous from the cartilaginous Stem

30. PSILOCYBE.

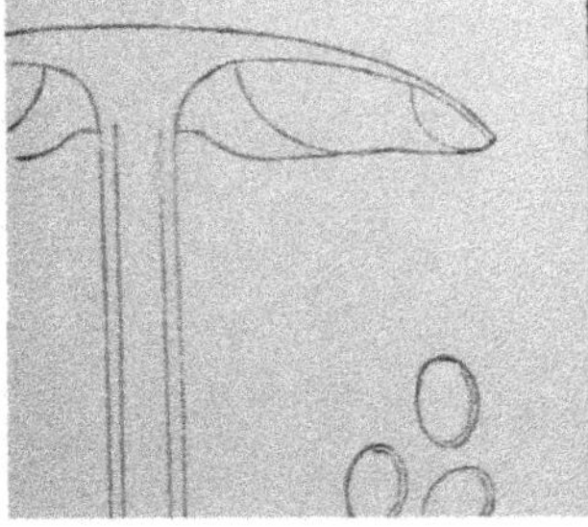

31. PSATHYRA.

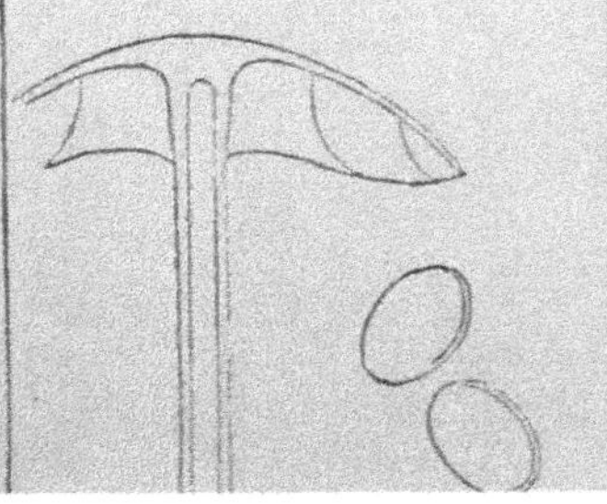

(32. DECONICA.)

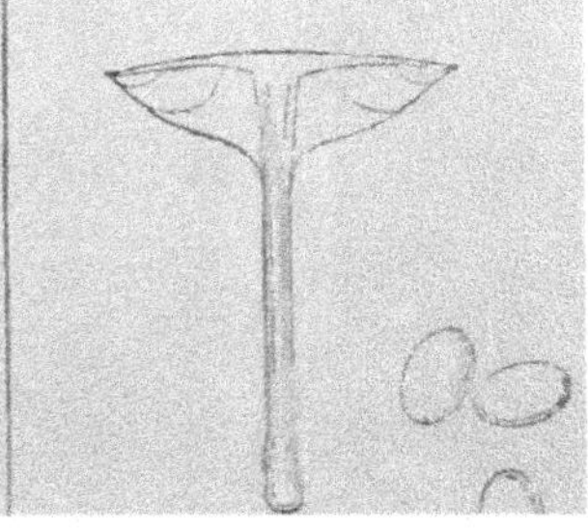

of the pileus, and fixed to the stem, forming a ring; pileus fleshy; stem distinct from the hymenophore, furnished with a ring; gills free, and rounded behind, at first white, then pink, afterwards intense purple-brown. (*Pl. V., f.* 26.)

HAB. All the species are terrestrial, mostly growing in rich pastures and on manured ground.

Most of the species appear in the autumn, and several are valued for their esculent properties. *Psalliota* corresponds with *Lepiota.*

389. Agaricus (Psalliota) arvensis. *Schæff.* "Horse Mushroom."

Pileus fleshy, conico-campanulate, then expanded, at first floccoso-farinose, then nearly smooth, even, or cracked; stem hollow, with a floccose pith; ring pendulous, broad, double, the outer split in rays; gills free, broader in front, dirty white, then reddish-brown.—*Fr. Epicr. p.* 213. *Schæff. t.* 310, 311. *Paul. t.* 134, *f.* 1-2. *Smith, E.M.* 9. *Hogg & Johnst, t.* 17. *Vent. t.* 15, *f.* 1-2. *Berk. Outl. t.* 10, *f.* 4. *Huss.* i. *t.* 76, 77. *Badh.* i. *t.* 6, *f.* 1. *A. Georgii, Sow t.* 304. *Eng. Fl.* v. *p.* 105. *A. edulis, Krombh. t.* 23, *f.* 11-14, *t.* 26, *f.* 9-13. *Tratt. essb. t. J.* *A. exquisitus, Vitt. Mang. t.* 20.

var. **villaticus.** *Brond.* Acquires a large size, and is very scaly.

In meadows, often in rings. Esculent. Suffolk.

Pileus 4-18 in. broad, white, stained with yellow, convex, very thick, firm and tough, quite smooth, or clothed with broad, tawny, more or less concentric, adpressed scales. flesh yellowish when cut, juice yellow; gills adnate, broad, numerous, white or very pale flesh colour, at length dark purplish brown. Stem 2-5 in. high, 1-2 in. thick, firm, the centre loose and web-like, when bruised yellow, especially below. Distinguished from *A. campestris* by the almost white gills (when young) and the yellow stains when bruised.—*M. J. B.* Spores variable in size, average ·0004 × ·00025 in.—*W. G. S.*

390. Agaricus (Psalliota) campestris. *L.* "Common Mushroom."

Pileus fleshy, convexo-plane, dry, silky, floccose or squamulose; stem stuffed, even, white, ring medial, somewhat torn; gills free, approximate, ventricose, sub-deliquescent, flesh-coloured, then brown.—*Fr. Epicr. p.* 213. *Berk. Outl. t.* 10, *f.* 2. *Huss.* 1, *t.* 90. *Hogg & Johnst. t.* 19. *Cooke, B.F. t.* 10. *Smith, E.M. f.* 5. *Schæff. t.* 33. *Vent. t.* 14, *f.* 4-7. *Paul. t.* 130. *Sow. t.* 305. *Grev. t.* 161. *Vitt. Mang. t.* 6-8. *Krombh. t.* 23, *f.* 1-8. *Tratt. essb. t. K.* *Eng. Fl.* v. *p.* 106. *Gonn. & Rabh.* iv. *t.* 1-2. *Barla, t.* 27. *Price, f.* 63. *Badh.* i. *t.* 4, 5, ii. *t.* 4. *f.* 3-5.

In rich pastures. Common. Esculent. [United States.]

var. **pratensis.** *Vitt.* Distinguished by the small rufous scales of the pileus, and the flesh having a slight pink tinge.

In pastures. Kings Cliffe. E. Bergholt.

var. **silvicola.** *Vitt.* Pileus smooth, shining; stem elongated, somewhat bulbous.—*Fr. Epicr. p.* 213. *Krombh. t.* 23, *f.* 8. *Paul. t.* 133.

In woods.

var. **hortensis.** *Auct.* Pileus fibrillose or squamulose, brownish. *var. elongatus, Gard. Chron.* 1860, *p.* 1061, *fig. var. Buchanani, Gard. Chron.* 1860, *p.* 1039, *fig.*

This is the cultivated form.

var. **vaporarius.** *Otto.* Pileus even, with a brown pilose coat, which also covers the stem and leaves transverse fragments thereon as it elongates.—*Krombh. t.* 26, *f.* 14, 15. *Paul. t.* 132. *Letell. t.* 659.

var. **rufescens.** *Berk.* A distinct variety, which is rufous, like *A. vaccinus*, and whose flesh turns of a bright red when bruised. The gills are at first perfectly white.—*Berk. Outl. t.* 10, *f.* 3.

Pileus 2-5 in. broad, at first convex, then plano-convex, white, silky, or clothed with reddish-brown, adpressed fibrillæ, collected into little fascicles, cuticle easily separating from the flesh, projecting beyond the gills and often curled back, fleshy; flesh firm, thick, white, more or less stained with reddish-brown, especially when bruised; gills very unequal, at first of a beautiful pink, free, obtuse, and sometimes forked behind, broad in the middle, at length dark, mottled with the brownish purple, minute, sub-elliptic spores, the edge white and minutely denticulate. Stem 2-3 in. high, ½-¾ in. thick, nearly equal or sub-bulbous, white, beautifully but minutely silky, furnished with a thick spongy ring, generally above the middle, firm, when quite young there is a fine silky universal veil.—*M. J. B.* Spores ·00032 × ·0002 in.—*W. G. S.* *(Pl. V., f. 26.)*

391. Agaricus (Psalliota) silvaticus. *Schæff.* "Wood Psalliota."

Pileus fleshy, thin, campanulate, then expanded, gibbous, fibrillose or squamulose; stem hollow, unequal, whitish; gills free, crowded, rather thin, dry, reddish, then brown.—*Fr. Epicr. p.* 214. *Schæff. t.* 242. *Krombh. t.* 23, *f.* 9, 10. *Berk. Outl. p.* 167.

In woods. [Cincinnati.]

Pileus brownish, smell strong. Stem longer and more slender than in *A. campestris*, 3 in. and more long, ½ in. thick. Ring distant, variable. Pileus 3 in. broad, floccose, scaly, disc at length smooth, sub-ferruginous, scales rufescent or tawny; margin cracked. Spores ·00017 × ·00025 in.

392. Agaricus (Psalliota) elvensis. *B. & Br.* "Tufted Psalliota."

Cæspitose. Pileus from sub-globose to hemispherical, fibrillose, broken up into large persistent brown scales, areolate in the centre, margin thick, covered with pyramidal warts; stem fibrillose below, ring very large, areolato-verrucose beneath; gills free, brownish flesh colour.—*B. & Br. Ann. N.H.* 1865, *no.* 1009.

Under oak trees. Sept. Bodelwyddan.

Pileus at first sub-globose, then hemispherical, 6 in. or more across, margin very obtuse; stem at first nearly equal, at length swollen in the centre, and attenuated at the base, 4 in. high, 2 in. thick in the centre, fibrillose and areolate below, nearly smooth within the pileus, solid, stuffed with delicate threads; ring thick, very large, deflexed, broken here and there; gills ½ in. broad, free, of a brownish-flesh colour; flesh of pileus ¾ in. thick in centre, turning red when cut. Taste and smell excellent.—*B. & Br.*

Sub-Gen. 27. Pilosace, Fr.

Agrees in structure with *Pluteus*, and has the hymenophore distinct from the ringless stem. There are no British representatives. *(Pl. V., fig 27.)*

Sub-Gen. 28. Stropharia, Fr. Monog. Hymen. i. p. 409.

Spores intense bright purple-brown, brown or slate-colour; veil, if present, universal, superficial, scaly, or viscid; stem confluent behind, and homogeneous with the hymenophore; gills not free, and rounded.

Hab. Terrestrial or epiphytal. *(Pl. V., f. 28.)*

Formerly included under *Psalliota*; but now separated by Fries on account of the different habit, different attachment of the gills, and other characters; the species, of which none are edible, have various habits, but most are epiphytal, as are the analogues. *Stropharia* corresponds with *Armillaria* and *Pholiota*.—*W. G. S.*

393. Agaricus (Stropharia) Jerdoni. *Berk.* "Jerdon's Stropharia."

Pileus campanulate, obtuse, umbonate, fleshy, ochraceous, dry, adorned with superficial white evanescent scales, cuticle not separating; stem silky or squamulose, hollow; ring superior; gills pallid, then brown, transversely striate.—*B. & Br. Ann. N.H. no.* 913, *t.* xiv. *f.* 2.

On fir stumps. Nov. Mossburnford.

Pileus 2 in., ochraceous (brown when dry), campanulate, obtuse, with a broad umbo, fleshy, minutely rivulose, adorned with superficial evanescent snow-white scales, cuticle not peeling off; stem 3 in., 2-3 lin. thick, cylindrical, snow-white, pulverulent above, brownish with silky transverse scales below; ring superior, deflexed; gills adnate, sending a line down the stem, but not truly decurrent, pallid, then brown, transversely striate. Spores dark brown.—*M. J. B.*

394. Agaricus (Stropharia) versicolor. *With.* "Withering's Stropharia."

Pileus fleshy, convexo-plane, squamose, scales of the disc crowded; stem spongy, stuffed, bulbous, whitish, then brownish, ring persistent; gills decurrent, pallid, then reddish-brown.—*Fr. Epicr. p.* 218. *Berk. Outl. p.* 167. *Eng. Fl.* v. *p.* 109.

Pileus greenish brown. Not been found since the time of Withering. "Pileus 1-4 in. broad, scurfy especially in the centre, convex, at length flat, but the edge much curled in; gills decurrent; stem 2 in. high, as thick as a swan's quill, thickest downwards."—*With.*

395. Agaricus (Stropharia) æruginosus. *Curt.* "Livid Green Stropharia."

Pileus fleshy, convexo-plane, subumbonate, clothed with green evanescent slime, becoming paler; stem hollow, equal, fibrillose or squamose below the ring, tinted with blue; gills adnate, soft, brown, tinged with purple.—*Fr. Epicr. p.* 218. *Curt. Fl. Lond. t.* 309. *Sow. t.* 261. *Krombh. t.* 3, *f.* 27, 28, *t.* 62, *f.* 11, 14. *Schæff. t.* 1. *Batsch. f.* 218. *Fl. Dan. t.* 1248. *Huss.* i. *t.* 35. *Eng. Fl.* v. *p.* 109. *Smith, P. M. f.* 25. *Price, f.* 121.

In meadows, &c. Common. [S. Carolina.]

Gregarious; pileus 1-4 in. broad, convex, thin, expanded, fleshy, dull yellow, but covered with blue gluten, above this, but not always, clothed with pure white scales; gills purple brown, or sometimes umber, plane, or very slightly ventricose, adnate with a small tooth, margin white, pulverulent; stem 2-3 in. high, 3-6 lines thick, penetrating into the soil by strong branched white fibres, straight or flexuous, sometimes bulbous, scaly; scales reflexed, at length more or less smooth, with various tints of blue, green, or yellow, at first stuffed, then hollow, various in stature, sometimes very short and thick, mottled longitudinally with blue within, the centre white; ring in general fugacious, smell disagreeable.—*M. J. B.* Spores ·00028 × ·0002 in. There is a variety of this species with the pileus perfectly white from the first. *(Pl. V., fig.* 28.)

396. Agaricus (Stropharia) albo-cyaneus. *Desm.* "Blue and White Stropharia."

Pileus fleshy, thin, umbonate, even, viscid, greenish, then whitish; stem hollow, thin, flexuose, even, whitish; ring incomplete; gills attenuated, fixed, whitish flesh-colour, then brownish purple.—*Fr. Epicr. p.* 219. *Pers. M. E. t.* 29, *f.* 2, 3. *Ann. N.H. no.* 793.

In meadows and on dung. Oct. Nov.

Resembling *A. æruginosus*, but more delicate and softer. Both sometimes occur together. It may possibly be only a variety. Stem about 2 in. long. Spores a different shade of colour from the last; ·00027 × ·00017 in.

397. Agaricus (Stropharia) obturatus. *Fr.* "Compact Stropharia."

Pileus rather compact, convex, then plane, obtuse, somewhat dry, at length cracked or squamulose; stem stuffed, short, somewhat attenuated downwards, white, as well as the tumid ring; gills adnate, plane, white, becoming purplish-umber.—*Fr. S. M. p.* 285. *Epicr. p.* 219. *Mon. Hym.* i. *p.* 412. *Paul. t.* 104. *f.* 6. *bis.*

On the ground. Gomshall. [W. G. S., etc.]

Stem firm, short, 1-1½ in. long, 3 lin. and more thick, even, not squamose, white; ring superior, deflexed, white. Pileus fleshy, slightly viscid, usually dry, yellow; flesh compact, white; gills crowded.

398. Agaricus (Stropharia) melaspermus. *Bull.* "Black Spored Stropharia."

Pileus fleshy, convexo-plane, obtuse, soft, even, smooth, rather viscid; stem hollow, equal, smooth, white, as also the membranaceous ring; gills slightly adnexed, ventricose, crowded, pallid, then violet-black.—*Fr. Epicr. p.* 219. *Bull. t.* 540, *f.* 1. *Schæff. t.* 51. *Berk. Outl. p.* 168.

In meadows and woods. Rare.

Somewhat resembling *A. præcox*, but with different coloured spores and gills.—*M. J. B.*

399. Agaricus (Stropharia) squamosus. *Fr.* "Scaly Stropharia."

Pileus fleshy, thin, convexo-plane, subviscid, sprinkled with superficial concentric scales; stem subfistulose, slender, below the distant ring villoso-squamose; gills adnate, crowded, blackish, with a whitish edge.—*Fr. Epicr. p.* 220. *Fl. Dan. t.* 2077, *f.* 1, 2. *Berk. Outl. t.* 10, *f.* 6. *Eng. Fl.* v. *p.* 31*.

In woods.

Pileus 1 in. or more broad, at length nearly plane, obtuse, slightly viscid, shining when dry, ochre tinged with red-lead, cloth d with concentric, yellowish, scattered scales; gills broad, clouded with olive-black or purplish-brown; stem 3 in. or more high, 2 lines thick, with a white pith, at length hollow, furnished half-way up with a sub-erect ring, above which it is white and pulverulent, below ferruginous and villoso-squamose, strigose at the slightly incrassated base.—*M. J. B.* Spores ·00042 × ·00027 in. There is a variety of this species with a chestnut-brown pileus, which is smooth from the first.

400. Agaricus (Stropharia) stercorarius. *Fr.* "Dung Stropharia."

Pileus rather fleshy, hemispherical, then expanded, even, smooth, discoid; stem stuffed, elongated, at first flocculose below the distant ring, with a distinct pith, subviscid; gills adnate, broad, white, umber, then olive-black.—*Fr. Epicr. p.* 220. *Ann. N. H. no.* 688. *Bull. t.* 566, *f.* 4. *(not Eng. Fl.* v. *p.* 111.*)*

On dung.

Distinguished from *A. semiglobatus* by the distinct medullary substance with which the stem is stuffed; stem 3 in. and more long, 2-3 lin. thick, yellow; pileus about an inch broad, yellowish; spores unusually large, even for a dung-born agaric, ·00067 × ·00053 in.

401. Agaricus (Stropharia) semiglobatus. *Batsch.* "Semiglobose Stropharia."

Pileus somewhat fleshy, hemispherical, even; stem fistulose, slender, straight, smooth, glutinous, yellowish; veil abrupt; gills adnate, broad, plane, clouded with black.—*Fr. Epicr. p.* 220. *Batsch. f.* 110. *Grev. t.* 344. *Huss.* i. *t.* 39. *Eng. Fl.* v. *p.* 108.

On dung. Common. [United States.]

Pileus ½-1 in. or more broad, hemispherical, yellow, or slightly mottled from the shining through of the gills, viscid when moist, shining and smooth when dry, obtuse, fleshy, flesh white beneath the cuticle, umber near the gills; gills very broad, adnate with a little tooth, ventricose or plane, mottled with the purple-brown spores, with at length a cinereous, sometimes a yellow tinge; stem 2-3 in. high, 1-1½ line thick, very viscid, shining when dry with a closely glued silkiness, fistulose; ring more or less perfect, deflexed.—*M. J. B.* Spores ·00054 × ·00034 in.

Sub-Gen. 29. Hypholoma, Fr. S. M. i. p. 287.

Spores brownish-purple, sometimes intense purple, almost black; veil woven into a spidery fugacious web which adheres to the margin of the pileus, B. (not properly ring-shaped round the stem); pileus with an inseparable pellicle; stem confluent and homogeneous with the hymenophore.

Hab. Generally stumps. *(Pl. V., fig. 29.)*

Most of the species are gregarious and not edible. *Hypholoma* corresponds with *Tricholoma*, *Entoloma*, and *Hebeloma*.

A. *Fasciculares.*

402. Agaricus (Hypholoma) sublateritius. *Fr.* "Brick-red Hypholoma."

Pileus fleshy, convexo-plane, obtuse, discoid, dry, at length smooth; flesh compact, whitish; stem stuffed, fibrillose, attenuated downwards, ferruginous; gills adnate, crowded, white, then dingy-olive.—*Fr. Epicr. p.* 221. *Schæff. t.* 49, *f.* 6, 7. *Krombh. t.* 44, *f.* 1-3. *Hedn. Cryp. t.* 38. *Huss.* i. *t.* 60. *Ag. lateritius. Eng. Fl.* v. *p.* 110. *Smith. P. M. f.* 22.

On old stumps. Common. [United States.]

Gregarious, cæspitose; pileus 2-3 in. or more broad, fleshy, always very obtuse, not conic, at length expanded, ochraceous, tawny in the centre, paler at the margin, where it is slightly silky, when young it is silky all over. Veil stained with the spores, adhering in fragments to the margin; gills rounded behind, adnate with a tooth, scarcely green, clouded with the spores, margin uneven; stem 3 in. or more high, 2-3 lines thick, often thickest below, stuffed, yellow, with a more or less rufescent tinge, silky when young, distinctly squamulose, or fibrillose, firm, at length fistulose; spores elliptic, brown-purple, but not with a ferruginous tint; taste bitter and nauseous; sometimes rather difficult to distinguish from *A. fascicularis.*—*M. J. B.* Spores ·0002 × ·00012 in.

403. Agaricus (Hypholoma) capnoides. *Fr.* "Fir Wood Hypholoma."

Pileus fleshy, convexo-plane, obtuse, dry, very smooth; flesh thin, white; stem nearly hollow, equal, even, silky, pallid; gills adnate, scarcely crowded, broad, dry, smoky-grey, then purplish.—*Fr. Epicr. p.* 222. *B. & Br. Ann. N. H. no.* 913*.

In fir woods. April. Apethorpe.

Odour and taste mild; pileus of one colour, usually yellowish, 1-3 in. broad; stem 2-3 in. long, 2-4 lin. thick, equal, curved and flexuous, pallid, whitish above.

404. Agaricus (Hypholoma) epixanthus. *Fr.* "Grey-gilled Hypholoma."

Pileus fleshy, thin, convexo-plane, somewhat gibbous, even, silky, at length smooth, flesh yellow; stem hollow, subequal, floccoso-fibrillose, whitish, pruinose at the apex, brownish at the base; gills adnate, crowded, whitish-yellow, at length cinereous.—*Fr. Epicr. p.* 222. *Paul. t.* 107. *Batt. t.* 23, *D.?*

On old fir stumps. Mossburnford. Lea.

Easily known by the absence of the bitter taste and cinereous tint of the gills; stem about 3 in. long, 3-4 lin. thick, pale, ferruginous, or tawny at the base, pruinose above; pileus 2-3 in. broad, yellow or pallid, the disc usually darker.

405. Agaricus (Hypholoma) fascicularis. *Hud.* "Tufted yellow Hypholoma."

Pileus fleshy, thin, subumbonate, smooth ; stem hollow, thin, fibrillose, flexuose, flesh yellow; gills adnate, much crowded, linear, subdeliquescent, sulphur-coloured, then greenish.—*Fr. Epicr. p.* 222. *Bolt. t.* 29. *Sow. t.* 225. *Fl. Dan. t.* 2075. *Krombh. t.* 44, *f.* 4-5. *Paul. t.* 107. *Vent. t.* 58, *f.* 3. *Berk. Outl. t.* 11, *f.* 1. *Huss.* ii. *t.* 15. *Eng. Fl.* v. *p.* 111. *Smith. P.M.* i. *Gard. Chron.* 1860, *p.* 337, *fig.*

On old stumps, &c. Common. [United States.]

Gregarious, densely cæspitose. Pileus 2-in. broad, at first conic, then expanded, more or less irregular from the tufted mode of growth, subcarnose, thick in the centre, tawny, margin thin, yellow, with portions of the veil adhering to it, often stained with the ferruginous-purple spores. Gills green, clouded, adnate with a subdecurrent tooth. Stem 2-9 in. high, 2 lines thick, curved and unequal, hollow, fibrillose or squamulose, yellow-greenish above. Ring stained with the spores. Taste bitter and nauseous.—*M. J. B.* Gills separating from the hymenophore. Spores ·00025 × ·00016 in.

406. Agaricus (Hypholoma) dispersus. *Fr.* "Dispersed Hypholoma."

Pileus somewhat fleshy, campanulate, then expanded, obtuse, even, margin silky from the veil; stem subfistulose, thin, tough, fibrillose or silky, base brownish ; gills adnate, thin, subventricose, crowded, pallid straw colour, then clouded.—*Fr. Epicr. p.* 222. *Ann. N.H. no.* 794.

On stumps, and on the ground, in pine woods.

Either scattered or fasciculate. Pileus 1¼ in. broad, honey-brown. Stem straight, 2-3 in. long, sometimes 6-7 in., for the greater part ferruginous, the apex pale.

B. *Velutini.*

407. Agaricus (Hypholoma) lacrymabundus. *Fr.* "Weeping Hypholoma."

Pileus fleshy, campanulate, then convex, spotted with innate pilose scales ; flesh white ; stem hollow, fibrilloso-squamose, rather thickened at the base, white ; gills adnate, seceding, white, then brown purple.—*Fr. Epicr. p.* 223. *Bull. t.* 194.

On trunks and on the ground. July—Nov.

Pileus not hygrophanous, 2-4 in. broad, at first somewhat campanulate, at length expanded, fleshy, margin thin, with a few fragments of the veil attached, firm, pale reddish brown, darker in the centre, fibrilloso-squamulose ; flesh pale umber ; gills at first pale, then reddish brown, sub-ventricose towards the base, slightly attached. Stem 2-3 in. high, 3 lines or more thick, pale umber towards the base, whitish above, subincrassated below, subflexuous, fibrillose or squamuloso-fibrillose from the remains of the floccose ring, above squamuloso-pubescent, truly fistulose, the inside downy, firm, elastic, pale umber within. Odour disagreeable.—*M. J. B.* Spores almost black, ·0003 × ·0002 in. (*Pl. V., f.* 29.)

408. Agaricus (Hypholoma) velutinus. *P.* "Velvety Hypholoma."

Pileus rather fleshy, ovate, then expanded, gibbous, fibrillose or velvety, becoming smooth, hygrophanous, flesh yellowish; stem hollow, equal, fibrilloso-striate, mealy above, yellowish; gills truncato-adnexed, ventricose, scarcely crowded, brown, then umber, studded with drops of moisture.—*Fr. Epicr. p.* 224. *Bull. t.* 525. *f.* 3. *Holms.* ii. *t.* 35. *Berk. Outl. t.* 11, *f.* 2. *Paul. t.* 55. *f.* 1. *Schæff. t.* 84, *var.*

On stumps. Common.

var. β. **leiocephalus.** *B. & Br.*

Pileus hygrophanous, rugged, smooth, except at the margin, where it is fibrillose, pallid, as is the stem, whose apex is farinose.—*B. & Br. Ann. N.H.* 1865, *no.* 1009*.

On old stumps. Sept. Bodelwyddan.

Densely cæspitose, much smaller than the common form, but apparently a mere variety, though a very striking one, from its smooth, but very rugged disc.—*M. J. B.*

C. *Appendiculati.*

409. Agaricus (Hypholoma) Candollianus. *Fr.* "Candolle's Hypholoma."

Pileus somewhat fleshy, campanulate or convex, then expanded, obtuse, smooth, hygrophanous; stem hollow, fragile, subfibrillose, white, apex striate; gills rounded behind, adnexed, crowded, violet, then brownish cinnamon.—*Fr. Epicr. p.* 224. *Fl. Dan. t.* 774. *Eng. Fl.* v. *p.* 113.

On dead stumps. Rare.

Pileus whitish, ochraceous in the centre, 2-4 in. broad. Stem 3 in. long, 2-4 lines thick, solid at the base.

410. Agaricus (Hypholoma) lanaripes. *Cooke.* "Woolly-stemmed Hypholoma."

Pileus somewhat fleshy, campanulate, then expanded, hygrophanous, squamose with superficial scales arising from the breaking up of the cuticle, pallid; veil attached in fugacious patches; stem hollow, fragile, subfibrillose, white, tomentose at the base; gills crowded, reaching the stem, whitish, then purplish brown.—*Seem. Journ.* (1863), *p.* 66, *t.* 3, *f.* 2.

On the soil in conservatories.

Subcæspitose. Pileus 1½-3 in., rather fleshy, margin thin, pallid, disc often tawny or brownish, margin purplish, with a shade of pink derived from the dark gills beneath, the whole plant becoming dark brown on decay. Stem 2-3 in., white, with radiating white hairs at the base. Gills reaching the stem, not ventricose. (*Pl. I., fig.* 3.)

411. Agaricus (Hypholoma) appendiculatus. *Bull.* "Appendiculate Hypholoma."

Pileus between fleshy and membranaceous, ovate, then expanded; when dry rugose, and sprinked with atoms; stem fistulose, equal, smooth, white, pruinose above; gills subadnate, crowded, dry, whitish, then rosy brown.—*Fr. Epicr. p.* 224. *Bull. t.* 392. *Sow. t.* 324. *Berk. Outl. t.* 11, *f.* 3-4.

On dead stumps. Common.

Pileus tawny or pale ochre, 2-3 in. broad. Veil attached in patches to the margin. Stem 3 in. long, 2-3 lin. thick. Spores ·00015 × ·0002 in.

412. Agaricus (Hypholoma) egenulus. *Berk.* "White Hypholoma."

Solitary. Pileus hemispherical, then expanded, whitish, then snowy-white, umbonate, appendiculate; stem minutely adpresso-squamulose, fistulose; gills adnate with a tooth, purplish-umber.—*B. & Br. Ann. N.H. no.* 915.

On the ground, amongst grass. May. Apethorpe.

Solitary. Pileus 1½ in. across, hemispherical, expanded, umbonate, but not decidedly rugose or atomate, of a watery white, when dry snow-white, quite smooth as if delicately gummed, even, except towards the edge, margin finely striate, appendiculate; stem 2 in. high, 1½ line thick, attenuated upwards, or nearly equal, minutely adpresso-squamose, fistulose; gills purplish-umber, with a white edge, moderately distant, slightly ventricose, adnate with a tooth. Spores brown-purple.

413. Agaricus (Hypholoma) hydrophilus. *Bull.* "Watery Hypholoma."

Pileus fleshy-membranaceous, convex, then expanded, subrepand, smooth, hygrophanous, rugose, disc even, margin rather broken; stem fistulose, curved, closely fibrillose, growing pale; gills adnexed, ventricose, crowded, dripping, pallid, then brownish-cinnamon or bay.—*Bull. t.* 511. *Paul. t.* 110, *f.* 1. *Fr. Epicr. p.* 225. *B. & Br. Ann. N.H.* (1866), *no.* 1126. *A. stipatus. Eng. Fl.* v. *p.* 113, *partly.*

In woods. Oct.

The veil, though fugacious, at once distinguishes it from other species, with which it might easily be confounded. Pileus when fresh usually bay, when dry tawny, about 1½ in. broad, flesh whitish. Stem 2 in. long, 1-2 lin. thick, at first white, then becoming ferruginous, slightly mealy above.

Sub-Gen. 30. PSILOCYBE, Fr. S. M. i. p. 289.

Spores purple, purple-brown, or slate-colour; veil obsolete (or in a few species fugacious, when present not forming a ring); pileus glabrous, at first incurved; stem cartilaginous, ringless, confluent with but heterogeneous from the hymenophore.

HAB. All grow on the ground. *(Pl. V., f. 30.)*

The species are almost all gregarious, cæspitose, inodorous, with fugitive colouring, and not edible. Fries divides the sub-genus into two groups, the *tenacious* and the *fragile*. *Psilocybe* corresponds with *Collybia*, *Leptonia*, and *Naucoria*.

A. *Tenaces*—pileus pelliculose.

414. Agaricus (Psilocybe) areolatus. *Klotsch.* "Patchy Psilocybe."

Pileus somewhat fleshy, convex, clothed with minute fibrils; cuticle cracking into nearly square patches; stem fistulose, fibrillose, dirty white; gills adnate, umber, at length black; edge white.—*Berk. Outl. p.* 172, *no.* 336. *Eng. Fl.* v. *p.* 112.

In gardens. May—Oct. Glasgow.

Pileus ochraceous or brown, 1½-3 in. broad, convex, veil between fibrous and membranaceous, fugacious; gills 2-3 lines broad, the edge white, and beaded with drops of moisture. Stem 2-3 in. high, 3 lines thick, generally thickened at the base, fibrillose, dirty white.—*Klotsch.* Spores ·00055 × ·00034 in.

415. Agaricus (Psilocybe) comptulus. *B. & Br.* "Sprinkled Psilocybe."

Pileus between conic and campanulate, at length expanded, pallid, then pallid ochraceous, striate; margin sub-crenulate; stem flexuose, shining, silky, smooth; gills distant, ventricose, adnate, and rosy-umber.—*B. & Br. Ann. N.H. no.* 917, *t.* 14, *f.* 4.

In woods, amongst grass. Oct. Collyweston.

Pileus 1-1½ in., between conical and campanulate, at length expanded, pallid, acquiring a pallid ochraceous tint as it loses its moisture, sprinkled with shining particles, scarcely rugulose, striate; margin somewhat crenulate, at first inflexed; stem 2 in. high, 1-1½ line thick, flexuose, undulate, smooth, but with a shining, silky aspect, not striate above, below acquiring a very pale rufous tinge; gills distant, ventricose, broad, adnate, umber, with a rosy tinge. Spores umber-brown.—*B. & Br.*

416. Agaricus (Psilocybe) ericæus. *Pers.* "Heath Psilocybe."

Pileus fleshy, tough, conical, then convex, at length plane, even, smooth, rather viscid when moist, shining when dry; stem somewhat hollow, elongated, tough, pallid; gills adnate, broad, plane, pallid, then black.—*Pers. Syn. p.* 413. *Fr. Epicr. p.* 228. *Berk. Ann. N.H. no.* 149.

In exposed pastures, after rain. July—Oct.

Stem firm, 3-4 in. long, yellowish, or pallid. Pileus scarcely umbonate, 1 in. and more across. Gills rather distant, margin becoming whitish.—*Fries.*

Omitted from Berkeley's "Outlines" by oversight.

417. Agaricus (Psilocybe) semilanceatus. *Fr.* "Liberty-cap Psilocybe."

Pileus submembranaceous, acutely conical, almost cuspidate, moist, viscid, slightly striate; stem medullate, tough, flexuose, smooth, pallid; gills adnexed, ascending, purple-black.—*Fr. Epicr. p.* 231. *Sow. t.* 240, *f.* 1-3. *A. callosus. Eng. Fl.* v. *p.* 111.

In rich pastures. Common. Poisonous.

Pileus ⅜ in. broad, ⅓ high, conico-campanulate, apiculato-umbonate, viscid when moist, shining when dry, pale ochraceous, the margin darker from its transparency, flesh thick in the centre; gills ventricose, adnate, chocolate-coloured, extreme margin white. Stem 4 in. high, slender, flexuous, nearly equal, thickened at the very base, subrufescent, fibrillose below, pulverulento-squamulose above, fistulose, base sometimes clothed with blue down.—*M.J.B.* Spores ·0005 × ·0003 in.

B. *Fragiles.*

418. Agaricus (Psilocybe) spadiceus. *Schæff.* "Bay Psilocybe."

Rigid; pileus fleshy, convexo-plane, obtuse, even, moist, hygrophanous; stem hollow, tough, pallid, apex even; gills rounded behind, adnexed, dry, crowded, whitish, then rosy-brown.—*Fr. Epicr. p.* 226. *Schæff. t.* 60, *f.* 4, 6. *Buxb.* iv. *t.* 29, *f.* 2, *var. A. stipalus. Eng. Fl.* v. *p.* 113, *partly.*

On dead stumps, ground, &c., in woods. Common.

Subcæspitose. Usually of a bright bay-brown, paler when dry. Stem 3-4 in. long, whitish. Pileus 3-4 in. broad, even, smooth. Spores ·0003 × ·0002 in. [*Pl.* V., *f.* 30.]

419. Agaricus (Psilocybe) cernuus. *Müll.* "Nodding Psilocybe."

Pileus somewhat fleshy, campanulate, convex, then expanded, smooth, hygrophanous, wrinkled when dry; stem fistulose, flexuose, smooth, white, apex even, pruinose; gills adnate, subventricose, scarcely crowded, whitish-cinereous, then brownish-black.—*Fr. Epicr. p.* 226. *Schæff. t.* 205. *Paul. t.* 110, *f.* 3. *Fl. Dan. t.* 1008 (*not Eng. Fl.* v. *p.* 114).

On chips, decayed wood, &c. Dec. Apethorpe.

Pileus pallid, 1-2½ in. broad, veil absent. Stem hollow, 2 in. and more long, about 2 lines thick, whitish. Spores ·0003 × ·0002 in.

420. Agaricus (Psilocybe) clivensis. *Berk.* "Pallid Psilocybe."

Pileus subhemispherical, pallid brown, then whitish ochre, even, atomate, margin striate; stem equal, somewhat silky; gills adnate, broadly emarginate, horizontal, umber.—*B. & Br. Ann. N.H. no.* 916, *t.* xiv. *f.* 3.

On the ground. Oct. King's Cliffe.

Pileus 1 in. across, subhemispherical, at first pallid brown, then pallid ochre inclining to white, even, sprinkled with shining particles; margin striated, not straight; stem 1½ in. high, 1 line thick, fistulose, nearly equal, except at the very base, where it is slightly clavate, somewhat silky; gills broad, adnate, widely emarginate, ventricose in front, rather distant, umber, margin white. Spores umber.—*B. & Br.*

421. Agaricus (Psilocybe) fœnisecii. *P.* "Brown Psilocybe."

Pileus somewhat fleshy, campanulate, then expanded, obtuse, dry, becoming dry; stem fistulose, not rooting, pallid-rufous, even, smooth; gills adnate, ventricose (as if broadly emarginate), scarcely crowded, brownish umber.—*Fr. Epicr. p.* 227. *Pers. Ic. & Des. t.* 11. *f.* 1. *Buxb.* iv. *t.* 28, *f.* 1. *Berk. Outl. t.* 11. *f.* 5. *Huss.* i. *t.* 39. *Eng. Fl.* v. *p.* 112.

Amongst grass in fields and gardens. Common.
[United States.]

Gregarious. Pileus 1-2 in. broad, hemispherical, or campanulate, brown umber, margin transparent, and minutely rugose, banded with various tints when losing its moisture; in decay it has a burnt appearance, and at length dries up and is black. Gills distant, broad, ventricose, attached, umber, mottled, extreme margin white. Stem 2-3 in. high. 1½ line thick, subflexuous, fistulose, at first slightly pulverulent, umber, apex striate, base cottony.—*M. J. B.* Spores with an obscure apiculus at one end, ·0004 × ·00025 in.

Sub-Gen. 31. Psathyra. Fr. Epicr. p. 231.

Spores dark purple-brown, approaching slate-colour; veil universal, fibrous, or absent, not forming a ring; pileus submembranaceous, conical or campanulate, margin at first straight and adpressed to the stem; stem fistulose, ringless, cartilaginous, fragile, confluent with but heterogeneous from the hymenophore.

HAB. On the ground or rotten wood. (*Pl. V., f.* 31.)

All are slender and hygrophanous, with fugitive colouring, and closely allied to the *fragile* species of the last subgenus. *Psathyra* agrees with *Mycena, Nolanea, Galera, Psathyrella.*

Sect. 1. *Conopili.*

422. Agaricus (Psathyra) conopilus. *P.* "Silvery Psathyra."

Pileus submembranaceous, campanulate, even, smooth, growing pale; stem tall, attenuated upwards, smooth, silvery-shining; gills slightly adnexed, crowded, brownish purple.—*Fr. Epicr. p.* 231. *Jungh. Linn.* v. *t.* 6, *f.* 11.

In gardens. Rare.

Stem 4-6 in. long, 1-2 lines thick. Pileus dirty white at first, 2 in. broad.

423. Agaricus (Psathyra) mastiger. *Berk. & Br.* "Peaked Psathyra."

Pileus conico-campanulate, repand, dark brown, then tan-coloured; stem straight, attenuated upwards; gills ascending, fixed, umber.—*B. & Br. Ann. N.H. no.* 921, *t.* xiv, *f.* 6.

On the roadside, amongst grass. Sept. Apethorpe.

Pileus about 1 in. across, at first nearly cylindrical, obtuse, then conico-campanulate, with a strong mammiform umbo, repand, dark rich brown when moist, umber tan when dry, somewhat fleshy, not striate; margin straight; stem 3 in. or more high, 1½-2 lines thick, attenuated upwards, white, smooth, or fibrillose and furfuraceous, fistulose, pale umber within, and as the plant dries, acquiring the tint of the pileus, but pale; veil none; gills umber, paler on the edge, rather narrow, affixed, ascending.—*B. & Br.*

424. Agaricus (Psathyra) corrugis. *P.* "Wrinkled Psathyra."

Pileus submembranaceous, campanulate, umbonate, somewhat wrinkled, smooth, growing pale; stem elongated, equal, smooth, white; gills sinuate, fixed, ventricose, violet, black.—*Fr. Epicr. p.* 231. *Holms.* ii. *t.* 32. *Eng. Fl.* v. *p.* 115.

In pastures.

var. β. **gracilis.** Fr.—*Bull. t.* 561, *f.* 1. *B. & Br. Ann. N.H.* (1866), *no.* 1126*.

On the ground. Aug. Woodnewton.

Pileus 1in. or more broad, turning pale, when dry corrugated; gills broad; stem 2-4 in. high, 1-2 lines thick, smooth, hairy at the base.—*Fries.* Spores ·0005 × ·0003 in. (*Pl. V. fig.* 31.)

425. Agaricus (Psathyra) bifrons. *Berk.* "Changing Psathyra."

Pileus submembranaceous, campanulate, obtuse, ochraceous brown, tinged with red, turning pale-tan; stem straight, naked; gills pinkish-cinereous, adnate; margin white.—*Berk. Eng. Fl.* v. *p.* 114. *Berk. Outl. p.* 173.

In ditches. Sept. Rare.

Pileus ¾ in. broad, furnished at first with a minute fibrillose, very evanescent veil, rugulose, ochraceous-brown, more or less tinged with red, margin thin, transparent; gills adnate, moderately broad, cinereous, shaded with pink, margin white, composed of minute wavy teeth; stem 2½ in. high, 1 line thick, filiform, thickest at the base, beautifully but very minutely satiny, not pulverulent, very brittle.—*M. J. B.*

Sect. 2. *Obtusati.*

426. Agaricus (Psathyra) spadiceo-griseus. *Schæff.* "Bay-grey Psathyra."

Pileus submembranaceous, conical, then campanulate, expanded, sub-umbonate, smooth, striate to the middle, hygrophanous; stem firm, attenuated upwards, shining, white, striate at the apex; gills adnexed, rather crowded, brown.—*Fr. Epicr. p.* 232. *Schæff. t.* 237. *Fl. Dan. t.* 1673, *f.* 2. *A. stipatus, Eng. Fl.* v. *p.* 113. *partly.*

On chips, &c.

Subcæspitose. Pileus bright brown, 2 in. and more broad. Gills pale umber at first. Stem umber within, about 3 in. long, whitish and shining, striate above.

427. Agaricus (Psathyra) obtusatus. *Fr.* "Obtuse Psathyra."

Pileus submembranaceous, conical, campanulate, then expanded, obtuse, smooth, wrinkled, hygrophanous, rather shining; stem somewhat rigid, equal, even, nearly naked, pallid; incurved at the base; gills adnate, sub-ventricose, pallid, then umber.—*Fr. Epicr. p.* 232. *Schæff. t.* 60, *f.* 1-3. *Vaill. t.* 12, *f.* 5, 6. *Ann. N.H. no.* 918.

On oak trunks and on the ground.

Solitary or cæspitose. Stem rooting, 2-3 in. long, 1-2 lines thick. Pileus umber, paler at the margin, 1 in. and more broad.

428. Agaricus (Psathyra) fibrillosus. *P.* "Fibrillose Psathyra."

Pileus sub-membranaceous, campanulato-convex, then expanded, slightly striate, at first fibrillose; stem elongated, very fragile, white, fibrilloso-squamose; gills aduate, plane, very broad behind, purplish-black.—*Fr. Epicr. p.* 232. *Eng. Fl.* v. *p.* 113.

On the ground, in woods. Rare.

Pileus when moist livid, sub-striate; when dry white, not striate, often fibrilloso-squamose; stem 3 in. high, 2-3 lines thick, beset with villous fasciculated scales.—*Fries.*

429. Agaricus (Psathyra) urticæcola. *Berk. & Br.* "Nettle-root Psathyra."

Pileus campanulate, margin striate; stem fistulose, attenuated upwards, flocculent from the first, white; gills ventricose in front, attenuated behind, white, then chocolate colour.—*B. & Br. Ann. N.H. no.* 919.

On nettle roots. Aug. King's Cliffe.

Pileus 2 lines across, campanulate, flocculent, white; margin at length straight, striate; stem short, slender, attenuated upwards, flocculent, fistulose, springing immediately from the matrix; gills ventricose in front, attenuated behind, adnexed, at first white, then of a rich chocolate.—*B. & Br.*

430. Agaricus (Psathyra) pennatus. *Fr.* "Scaly Psathyra."

Pileus submembranaceous, campanulate, obtuse, even, at first clad with white scales, then naked; stem villous, silvery, pulverulent above; gills adnexed, crowded, broad, livid, then brownish-black.—*Fr. Epicr. p.* 234. *Sys. Myc.* i. *p.* 297. *B. & Br. Ann. N.H.* (1865), *no.* 1010.

On naked soil in gardens. King's Cliffe, occasionally, but never in any abundance.

Stem 1-1½ in. long, 1-2 lin. thick, equal, villous, at the apex sprinkled with whitish meal, silvery. Pileus ½ in. high and broad, at length expanded to an inch in breadth, not striate, at first densely clothed with whitish scales, at length naked.

431. Agaricus (Psathyra) gossypinus. *Fr.* "Cottony Psathyra."

Pileus submembranaceous, campanulate, then expanded, tomentose, becoming smooth; margin striate; stem tomentose, whitish;

gills adnexed, ventricose, white, then brownish-black.—*Fr. Epicr. p.* 234. *Bolt. t.* 71, *f.* 1.

In woods on the ground. Rare.

Subcæspitose, fragile, pale ochraceous; gills livid, then brown.

432. Agaricus (Psathyra) semivestitus. *Berk. & Br.* "Half-clothed Psathyra."

Pileus ovate, obtuse, brown, growing pale, even, sprinkled with short snowy fibrils; stem fibrillose, silky, white: gills ascending, adnate, umber.—*B. & Br. Ann. N.H. no.* 920, *t.* xiv., *f.* 5.

Amongst grass in rich pastures. Oct. King's Cliffe.

Pileus about ½ in. across, ovate, obtuse, dark brown, turning pale, sprinkled with little fibrils more than half-way up; not striate; stem nearly straight, 2 in. high, 1½ line thick, fibrilloso-silky, rather strong, white, with a pale under tinge of brown, fistulose, the walls within white with down; gills ascending, broad behind, adnate, umber-brown, tinged with the dark spores. —*B. & Br.*

433. Agaricus (Psathyra) Gordoni. *Berk.* "Gordon's Psathyra."

Cæspitose; pileus campanulate, pallid cinereous, then whitish, more or less floccoso-squamulose, sulcato-striate; stem flexuose, floccose, becoming smooth, whitish pruinose above; gills ascending, narrowly adnate, distant, cinereous.—*B. & Br. Ann. N.H. no.* 922, *t.* xv. *f.* 7.

On old stumps. Oct. Overton Longueville.

Densely cæspitose. Pileus 1½ in. across, campanulate, membranaceous, at first pale cinereous, then white, sprinkled with white floccose scales, sulcato-striate; stem 2 in. high, 1½ line thick, transversely undulated, pruinose above, floccose below, but becoming at length smooth and shining, brittle, fistulose; gills ascending, narrowly adnate, distant, moderately broad, scarcely ventricose, cinereous. Smell faint, nauseous. When young wholly covered with white flocci.—*B & Br.*

Sub-Gen. 32. DECONICA, Smith. Seem. Jour. 1870.

(*Psilocybe*, Fr. Epicr. partly.)

Pileus thin, plane, at first incurved, veil obsolete, or adhering to the margin of the pileus, not forming a ring; stem cartilaginous, hollow, confluent with, but heterogeneous from, the hymenophore; gills decurrent. (*Pl. V., fig.* 32.)

This sub-genus is analogous with *Omphalia*, *Eccilia*, and *Tubaria.*

434. Agaricus (Deconica) coprophilus. *Bull.* "Dung Deconica."

Pileus somewhat fleshy, hemispherical, then expanded, umbonate, even; stem subfistulose, attenuated above, pruinose, becoming smooth; gills arcuate, sub-decurrent, broad, livid-brown. *Fr. Epicr. p.* 229. *Bull. t.* 566, *f.* 3. *Ann. N.H. no.* 689.

On dung. Rare.

Pileus when very young white and downy, sub-hemispherical, clothed with little white superficial scales, brown, at length smooth and pale umber, darker at the obtuse apex, slightly fleshy. Stem flexuous, slightly attenuated upwards, whitish, shining, at first scaly, like the pileus, within which it is pruinose. Gills nearly plane, ventricose, adnato-arcuate or sub-decurrent, umber brown.—*M. J. B.*

435. Agaricus (Deconica) bullaceus. *Bull.* "Mottled-gilled Deconica."

Pileus somewhat fleshy, hemispherical, then expanded, smooth, at length umbonate, striate to the middle; stem fistulose, short, equal, fibrillose; gills adnate, triangular, plane, crowded, ferruginous-brown.—*Fr. Epicr. p.* 229 *(not Eng. Fl.* v. *p.* 114). *Bull. t.* 566. *f.* 2. *A. stercorarius. Eng. Fl.* v. *p.* 111. *Krombh. t.* 3, *f.* 33, 34.

On horse dung.

Pileus ½-1 in. broad, sub-carnose, sub-umbonate, umber, almost tawny, slightly viscid, moist, shining, quite smooth, even; in infancy flat, then hemispherical, when old quite plane, the margin transparent, slightly notched; when dry pale. Gills umber, mottled with the brown-purple spores, broad, plane, with a decurrent tooth, or ventricose and emarginate. Stem 1½-2 in. high, 1 line thick, umber, tough, flexuous, below squamuloso-fibrillose, with a little down at the base, above shining, but minutely pubescent, striate with the decurrent teeth of the gills, fistulose, but with a few fibrils within, flesh dark umber; when young there is a narrow ring.—*M. J. B.* Spores with an obscure apiculus at both ends, ·0004 × ·00028 in.—*W. G. S.*

436. Agaricus (Deconica) physaloides. *Bull.* "Dung Deconica."

Pileus somewhat fleshy, campanulate, then expanded, even, rather viscid; stem fistulose, flexile, closely fibrillose, bright brown at the base; gills decurrent, crowded, sub-ferruginous.—*Fr. Epicr. p.* 229. *Bull. t.* 366, *f.* 1. *Paul. t.* 122, *f.* 5. *var. Gard. Chron. Sept.* 25, 1852. *Ann. N.H. no.* 690.

On dung, in mossy places, &c.

Spores ·0005 in. long, ·0003 in. broad. Pileus 3-4 lin. broad, purplish-brown, paler about the margin, at length umbonate, and depressed round the umbo. Spores ·00034 × ·0002 in. [*Pl. V., f.* 32.]

* Hymenophore distinct from the fleshy Stem.

** Hymenophore confluent and homogeneous with the fleshy Stem.

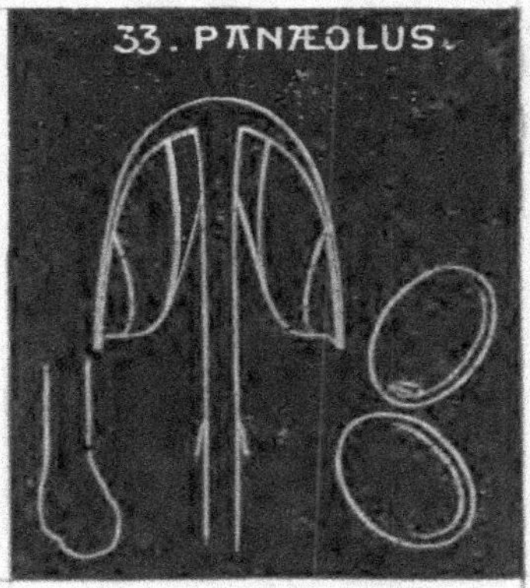

** Hymenophore confluent with, but heterogeneous from the cartilaginous Stem

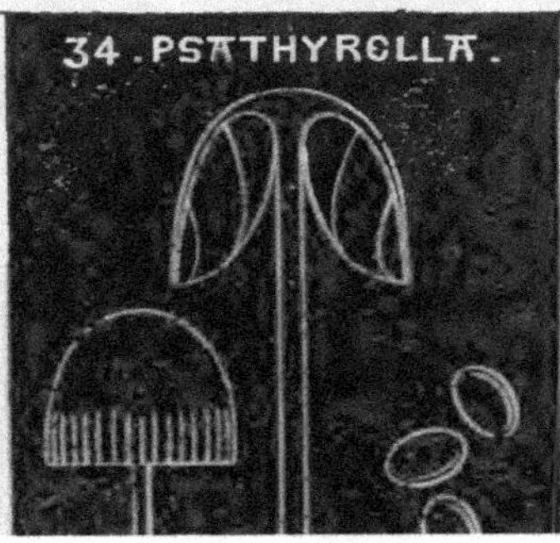

Series V. **Coprinarii.** Fr. Epicr. p. 234. Spores black.

Psathyrella is very close to *Coprinus*, more so than *Panæolus*. In the *Coprinarii* the unrepresented spaces are very numerous.

Sub-Gen. 33. PANÆOLUS, Fr. Epicr. 234.

Veil, when present, interwoven, sometimes wanting; spores black, oval, smooth lemon-shaped, or echinulate; pileus somewhat fleshy, viscid when moist, shining when dry, *never striated*, the *margin exceeding the variegated gills*; gills clouded, never becoming purple or brown.

HAB. Almost all grow on dung, often near towns, in summer and autumn. *(Pl. VI., fig. 33.)*

This and the following subgenus differ from all the preceding in their *black spores*, and occupy an intermediate position between *Agaricus* and *Coprinus*, agreeing with the latter in the colour of the spores, but joined more properly to the genuine Agarics by the *gills not deliquescing*. Although the veil may be entirely absent in some species, yet they are so allied that they cannot be well separated.—*W. G. S.*

Sect. 1. Pileus viscid, shining when dry.

437. Agaricus (Panæolus) separatus. *L.* "Ochrey Panæolus."

Pileus somewhat fleshy, campanulate, obtuse, even, viscid; stem straight, shining, white, thickened downwards, ring distant; gills fixed, cinereous-black.—*Fr. Epicr. p.* 234. *Bolt. t.* 53. *Berk. Outl. t.* 11, *f.* 7. *Bull t.* 84. *A. semiovatus. Sow. t.* 131. *Eng. Fl.* v. *p.* 116. *Price. f.* 39.

On dung. Common.

Pileus 1½ in. broad, semiovate, very obtuse, at first ochraceous, then dirty white, shining, smooth, slightly viscid, wrinkled when old, subcarnose but watery, gills subdeliquescent, broad, ventricose, adnate by a small portion, clouded, cinereous, margin white; stem 5 in high, or more, 2 lines thick, at first fibrillose, beneath the ring squamuloso-pulverulent, above dotted, as is the ring, with the large, black, elliptic spores.—*M. J. B.* Spores ·0006 × ·0004 in. *(Pl. VI., f. 33.)*

438. Agaricus (Panæolus) leucophanes. *B. & Br.* "Shiny-white Panæolus."

Pileus campanulate, obtuse, viscid, shining when dry, innate-silky white, here and there with an ochraceous tinge; margin appendiculate; stem attenuated upwards, white, fibrillose, with scattered farinaceous particles, transversely subundulate, fistulose; gills adnate, pale flesh-tinted grey, then black.—*B. & Br. Ann. N. H.* (1866) *no.* 1127, *t.* 11, *f.* 1.

In grass fields. Aug. King's Cliffe.

A very pretty species, allied to *A. separatus*; pileus ¾ in. across; stem 2 in. high, about 1 line thick in the centre; spores ·00037 in. long, somewhat cymbiform.

439. Agaricus (Panæolus) fimiputris. *Bull.* "Dark-grey Panæolus."

Pileus submembranaceous, conical, then expanded, somewhat gibbous, even, viscid; stem slender, equal, smooth, pallid; annular zone marked; gills fixed, livid-black.—*Fr. Epicr. p.* 235. *Bull. t.* 66. *Bolt. t.* 57. *Batt. t.* 28, *P. Berk. Outl. t.* 11, *f.* 6. *Eng. Fl.* v. *p.* 116.

On dung and in pastures. Common. [Cincinnati.]

Pileus 1-2 inches broad and high, at first obtuse, conic, reticulato-rugulose, at length campanulate, dark cinereous, livid when dry; the ring broken into triangular loops or laciniæ, fringing the margin, which is minutely downy and frequently split; gills adnate, ascending, mottled, cinereous-black, sub deliquescent; stem 2-6 in. high, squamuloso-tomentose, pulverulent, often beaded with little drops, striate above, nearly white, at length rufescent, zoned within.—*M. J. B.* Spores ·00027 × ·00034 in.

440. Agaricus (Panæolus) phalænarum. *Fr.* "Ruddy-stemmed Panæolus."

Pileus rather fleshy, campanulato-convex, obtuse, even, smooth, viscid; veil appendiculate, fugacious; stem equal, rather firm, almost naked, pallid, rufescent; gills adnexed, broad, cinereous black.—*Fr. Epicr. p.* 235. *Bull. t.* 58. *Paul. t.* 121, *f.* 1. *Ann. N.H. no.* 796.

On dung. Sept. Apethorpe.

Allied closely to *A. papilionaceus*, but larger, pileus viscid, clay colour.

Sect. 2. Pileus opaque when moist. When dry subflocculose.

441. Agaricus (Panæolus) retirugis. *Batsch.* "Ribbed Panæolus."

Pileus somewhat fleshy, globose, then hemispherical, subumbonate, reticulated, with raised ribs, sprinkled with opaque atoms; veil torn, appendiculate; stem equal, pruinose, pinkish purple; gills fixed, ascending, cinereous black.—*Fr. Epicr. p.* 235. *Batsch. f.* 91.

On dung. Coed Coch.

Pileus pinkish tan-colour, distinguished from *A. corrugis* by its black pores. Spores with a distinct apiculus at both ends, ·0003 × ·0004 in.

Sect. 3. Pileus dry, smooth, shining, without zone.

442. Agaricus (Panæolus) campanulatus. *L.* "Campanulate Panæolus."

Pileus somewhat fleshy, campanulate, dry, even, smooth, somewhat shining; stem equal, straight, rufous, striate above, powdered with black; gills fixed, ascending, variegated with grey and black.—*Fr. Epicr. p.* 236. *Bull. t.* 561, *f.* 2, *L. Buxb.* iv. *t.* 13. *Fl. Dan. t.* 1959. *Batsch, f.* 6.

On rich soil, &c. Common. [Cincinnati.]

Pileus brownish tinged with rufous, ½-1 in high and broad, rather shining. Stem straight, commonly 3 in. long, 1-2 lin. thick, rufescent.

443. Agaricus (Panæolus) papilionaceus. *Bull.* "Butterfly Panæolus."

Pileus somewhat fleshy, hemispherical, smooth, when dry rimoso-squamose; stem equal, even, whitish, powdered with white above; gills broadly adnate, very wide, at length plane, blackish.—*Fr. Epicr. p.* 236. *Bull. t.* 561, *f.* 2, *N.M. Eng. Fl.* v. *p.* 116. *Vent. t.* 58, *f.* 4-5.

On rich soil, dung, &c. Common. [United States.]

Pileus ½-1 in. broad, at length convex, when dry subrufescent, even, never viscid; gills ascending, close, quite entire; veil very fugacious; stem 3 in. high, 1-2 lines thick, rufescent.—*Fries.*

Sect. 4. Pileus dry, smooth, zoned at the margin.

444. Agaricus (Panæolus) cinctulus. *Bolt.* "Ringed Panæolus."

Pileus somewhat fleshy, campanulate, then expanded, even, smooth, margin with a broad, brown zone; stem rather firm, equal, brownish, gills free (?), ventricose, olivaceous black.—*Fr. Epicr. p.* 237. *Bolt. t.* 152.

On dung. Halifax.

Inserted on the authority of Bolton's figure. Distinguished by the broad brown zone at the margin of the pileus.

445. Agaricus (Panæolus) subbalteatus. *Berk. & Br.* "Zoned Panæolus."

Pileus convex, fleshy, hygrophanous, fawn-coloured, pallid when dry, zoned, rugulose; stem fragile, with white fibrils; gills brownish, adnate, subventricose.—*B. & Br. Ann. N.H. no.* 923.

In a tare field. Sept. Apethorpe.

Cæspitose. Pileus 1½-2 in. across, at first convex, with the margin slightly incurved, then expanded, obtuse, or slightly umbonate, irregular, rather fleshy, hygrophanous, of a dull deep fawn colour, pallid when dry, slightly rugose, and marked near the margin with a dark narrow zone; veil none; stem 2-2½ in. high, 2 lines thick, fistulose, red brown, brittle, stringy, splitting longitudinally, marked with short white fibrils; gills brownish, slightly ventricose, adnate, margin white, slightly toothed. Spores black. Closely allied to *A. cinctulus*, Bolt, but differing in habit, &c.—*B. & Br.*

446. Agaricus (Panæolus) fimicola. *Fr.* "Dung Panæolus."

Pileus somewhat fleshy, campanulato-convex, obtuse, smooth, opaque; marked near the margin with a narrow brown zone; stem fragile, elongated, equal, pallid, pruinose above; gills adnate, broad, variegated with grey and brown.—*Fr. Epicr. p.* 237. *Buxb.* iv. *t.* 28, *f.* 4. *Bolt. t.* 66, *f.* 1.

On dung, rich pastures, &c. [United States.]

Not gathered since Bolton's time. Stem 3-4 in. long, 1 line thick, dingy. Pileus obtuse, even, smooth, dingy grey when moist, clay-coloured when dry. Flesh greyish white.

Sub-Gen. 34. PSATHYRELLA. Fr. Epicr. 237.

Spores black, oval, smooth, or echinulate; veil inconspicuous, not interwoven, generally absent; pileus membranaceous, striated, margin straight, adpressed to the stem, *not exceeding the gills;* stem confluent with but heterogeneous from the hymenophore; gills adnate or free. (*Pl. VI., f.* 34.)

The species are all very slender, and the only other subgenus with black spores (*Panæolus*), is readily distinguished by the characters of the pileus; it agrees in every point with *Psathyra*, except the colour of the gills being never brown or purple, and the spores black. It also agrees, more or less, in structure with *Mycena*, *Nolanea*, and *Galera*, and also appears to be allied to BOLBITIUS, which, however, is at once distinguished by its coloured spores.—*W. G. S.*

Sect. 1. Stem straight, smooth.

447. Agaricus (Psathyrella) gracilis. *Fr.* "Slender Psathyrella."

Pileus submembranaceous, conical, slightly striate when moist, hygrophanous; stem slender, straight, naked, pallid;

gills broadly adnate, subdistant, cinereous black, edge pale rose. —*Fr. Epicr. p.* 238. *Berk. Outl. p.* 176.

On hedge borders. Common.

Gregarious. Pileus brownish, at length often tinged with pink, ½-1 in. broad. Stem 3 in. and more long, naked, whitish. Spores ·00024 × ·00049 in.

448. Agaricus (Psathyrella) hiascens. *Fr.* "Fissured Psathyrella."

Pileus membranaceous, campanulate, smooth, fisso-sulcate, disc even; stem straight, rigid, brittle, smooth, white; gills adnate, linear, sub-distant, acute in front, pallid, then black.—*Fr. Epicr. p.* 238. *Bull. t.* 552, *f.* 2, F. G. *Berk. Outl. p.* 176.

Under hedges.

Pileus 1 in. high, 1½ in. across, sulcate up to the disc, pale dirty-ochraceous. —*M. J. B.*

449. Agaricus (Psathyrella) aratus. *Berk.* "Sulcate Psathyrella."

Pileus membranaceous, campanulato-conic, rather acute, deeply sulcate: stem tall, thickened at the base, white, smooth, fistulose; gills lanceolate, quite free, purplish-black.—*Berk. Outl. p.* 176.

Under hedges. Woodnewton.

Pileus 1 in. high, ⅓ in. across, bright brown; flesh of the disc of the same colour. Stem 5 in. high.

Sect. 2. Stem flexuose, pruinose above.

450. Agaricus (Psathyrella) pronus. *Fr.* "Stooping Psathyrella."

Pileus membranaceous, hemispherical, obtuse, striate, hygrophanous, dry, opaque, slightly silky, atomate; stem very slender, equal, flexuose, sub-pellucid; gills adnate, ventricose, sub-distant, livid sooty-black.—*Fr. Epicr. p.* 239. *Ann. N. H. no.* 924.

Amongst grass. Sept. Apethorpe.

Stem filiform, fragile, 1½ in. long. Pileus 4-6 lines broad, dingy.

451. Agaricus (Psathyrella) atomatus. *Fr.* "Sprinkled Psathyrella."

Pileus submembranaceous, campanulate, obtuse, slightly striate, hygrophanous, dry, rugulose, entire, furfuraceous with shining atoms; stem lax, fragile, white, mealy at the apex, gills adnate, broad, cinereous-black.—*Fr. Epicr. p.* 239. *Eng. Fl.* v. *p.* 115.

About hedge borders. Common.

Pileus $1\frac{1}{2}$ in. broad, at first obtusely conic, then sub-hemispherical, at length plano-expanded, with a fine evanescent arachnoid veil, ochraceous, inclining to pale rufous, at length cream-coloured, or nearly white, sometimes purplish, or rose-coloured; gills broad, ventricose, rather distant, at first pale ochraceous, then brown purple, or cinereous-black. Stem 2-3 in. high, 1-2 lines thick, somewhat rooting, fistulose, brittle, striate above, and slightly pulverulent, base thickest, and more or less cottony, never quite smooth.—*M. J. B.* Spores ·0005 × ·00035 in.

452. Agaricus (Psathyrella) disseminatus. *Fr.* "Clustered Psathyrella."

Pileus membranaceous, ovato-campanulate, furfuraceous, then naked, sulcato-plicate, entire, discoloured; stem lax, subflexuose, fragile, at first mealy, then smooth; gills adnate, broadly linear, whitish, cinereous, then black.—*Fr. Epicr. p.* 240. *Sow. t.* 166. *Paul. t.* 123. *f.* 6. *Fl. Dan. t.* 1848. *Schæff. t.* 308. *Batsch. f.* 3. *Buxb.* ii., *t.* 50, *f.* 5. *Eng. Fl.* v. *p.* 118. *Batt. t.* 27, C. *Vent. t.* 35, *f.* 3-4.

About trunks of trees, and on the ground. Common.
[United States.]

Gregarious, cæspitose. Pileus 3 lines broad, campanulato-conic, minutely pubescent, strongly striate, submembranaceous, tender, fragile, ochraceous, at length white, with a pearly tint towards the margin; gills broadly adnate, pink, inclining to cinereous. Stem 1 in. high, $\frac{1}{2}$ line thick, fistulose, curved, white, pubescent, attenuated upwards, downy at the base.—*M. J. B.* Spores ·0003 × ·0002 in. (*Pl. VI. fig.* 34.)

Genus **2.** **COPRINUS,** Fr. Epicr. p. 241.

Fig. 38.

Spores black; pileus: margin of pileus straight, at first adpressed to the stem; stem confluent with or distinct from the hymenophore; gills free, at first coherent, and sprinkled with a micaceous scurf, soon deliquescing into a black fluid, trama none.

Hab. Fat and rank places, often on dung, but sometimes on decaying wood. (*Figs.* 38, 39.)

Readily distinguished by its deliquescent habit.

Sect. 1. *Pelliculosi.*—pileus rather fleshy.

* *Comati.*

453. **Coprinus comatus.** *Fr.* "Shaggy Coprinus."

Pileus rather fleshy, cylindrical, then expanded, even, soon torn into broad, adpressed, scattered scales; stem hollow, fibrillose, bulb solid, rooting; ring moveable; gills free, linear, white, then purplish.—*Fr. Epicr. p.* 242. *Batt.* 26, B. *Fl. Dan. t.* 831. *Schæff. t.* 46, 47. *Sow. t.* 189. *Grev. t.* 119. *Paul. t.* 127. *Krombh. t.* 3, *f.* 35, *t.* 30, *f.* 15-21. *Cooke, B. F. t.* 11. *Smith, E.M. f.* 13. *Badh.* i. *t.* 10, *f.* 2, ii. *t.* 7, *f.* 1-3. *Price, f.* 49. *Gard. Chron.* (1860), *p.* 73, *fig. Trans. Woolh. Cl.* 1868, *t.* 13. *Curt. Fl. L. t.* 93. (*Bolt. t.* 142, *var.?*) *Eng. Fl.* v. *p.* 118. *Fl. Boruss. t.* 389. *Hogg. & Johnst. t.* 3.

Sides of roads, pastures, &c. Common. Esculent.
[S. Carolina.]

Pileus 3-4 in. high, 2 in. broad, campanulato-cylindrical, cuticle white, breaking up into broad fibrillose, sub-fuscous scales; beneath this coating the pileus is finely plicate, often split, and of a pinky-brown, flesh scarcely any on the margin, rather thick in the centre; gills very numerous and close, beautifully varied with pink and brown-black, margin white, or pinkish, minutely downy, slightly undulated, quite free, so as to leave a sort of collar round the stem. Stem 5 in. or more high, ¾ in. thick at the base, hollow, filled with arachnoid fibres, bulbous, fibrillose, and sub-adpresso-squamose, sometimes tinged with pink, brittle, but tolerably firm; ring thick and moveable.—*M. J. B.* Spores with an apiculus at one end, or on one side, ·00058 × ·00032 in.—*W. G. S.*

454. **Coprinus ovatus.** *Fr.* "Ovate Coprinus."

Pileus submembranaceous, ovate, then expanded, striate; at first woven into densely imbricated, thick, concentric scales; stem bulbous, rooting, flocculose, hollow above, ring deciduous; gills remote, lanceolate, white, then brownish-black.—*Fr. Epicr. p.* 242. *Schæff. t.* 7. *Ray. Syn. no.* 22, *p.* 5. *Ann. N.H. no.* 925.

In pastures. Woodnewton.

Similar to *C. comatus*, but smaller, and more delicate; pileus whitish; the gills are less deliquescent. Stem 3-4 in. long.

455. **Coprinus sterquilinus.** *Fr.* "Sulcate-dung Coprinus."

Pileus membranaceous, conical, then expanded, sulcate, at first villous or silky, disc rather fleshy, squarroso-squamose; stem attenuated; fibrillose, base solid, not rooting, annulate; gills free, ventricose, purplish.—*Fr. Epicr. p.* 242. *Mich. t.* 83. *f.* 3. *Eng. Fl.* v. *p.* 119. *Ann. N. H. no.* 150.

On dung. Rare. King's Cliffe.

Pileus 1½ in. broad, dingy; stem 5 in. long, hollow, solid at the base.

** *Atramentarii.*

456. Coprinus atramentarius. *Fr.* "Inky Coprinus."

Pileus slightly fleshy, ovate, then expanded, repand, spotted at the top with innate squamules; stem hollow, firm, zoned within; ring abrupt, fugacious; gills free, ventricose, white, then purplish-black.—*Fr. Epicr. p.* 243. *Fl. Dan. t.* 1370. *Fl. Boruss. t.* 390. *Price. f.* 40. *Sow. t.* 188. *Vaill. t.* 12, *f.* 10-11. *Bull. t.* 164. *Berk. Outl. t.* 12, *f.* 1. *Cooke. B. F. t.* 12. *Eng. Fl.* v. *p.* 119. *Badh.* i. *t.* 10, *f.* 1. ii. *t.* 9, *f.* 1-2.

About old stumps and on naked soil. Common. Esculent. [United States.]

Gregarious, cæspitose; pileus 3½ in. or more high, subcarnose, campanulate, obtuse, edge uneven, dirty-grey, at length brownish, innato-fibrillose, more or less furfuraceous and corrugated, apex often scaly; gills very broad and close, ventricose, umber, margin white, rounded behind, quite free; stem 3½ in. high, ½ in. thick, fistulose, juicy, fibrillose, attenuated upwards, brittle, the substance banded concentrically.—*M. J. B.* Spores ·00035 × ·00021 in.

[COPRINUS LURIDUS. *Fr.* (Bolton. t. 25.) has only been found by Bolton, at Halifax, and is probably a variety of the above.]

457. Coprinus fuscescens. *Fr.* "Brownish Coprinus."

Pileus submembranaceous, ovate, then expanded, unpolished; disc rather fleshy, even or cracked, scaly; stem hollow, fragile, incurved, subfibrillose, scarcely annulate; gills fixed, umber-black.—*Fr. Epicr. p.* 244. *Schæff. t.* 17. *Paul. t.* 125, *f.* 1.

On dead stumps. Rare. Kilmory. [Cincinnati.]

More delicate than *C. atramentarius*, smaller and more fragile; pileus brownish-grey, 2, rarely 3 in. broad; the disc becoming brown, not sprinkled with micaceous particles, but at first covered with an opaque mealiness; stem 3 in. long, 2-3 lin. thick; spores with an oblique apiculus, ·0004 × ·00023 in. *(Fig. 38, reduced.)*

*** *Picacei.*

458. Coprinus picaceus. *Fr.* "Magpie Coprinus."

Pileus membranaceous, ovato-campanulate, striate, variegated with broad, white, superficial scales; stem hollow, bulbous, not rooting, fragile, smooth; gills free, ventricose, cinereous-black.—*Fr. Epicr. p.* 244. *Bull. t.* 206. *Sow. t.* 170. *Fl. Dan. t.* 144. *Smith. P.M. f.* 9. *Eng. Fl.* v. *p.* 119.

On roadsides. Rare.

Pileus 2 in. broad and high, campanulate, glutinous, closely grooved, brown with a tinge of red above; margin cinereous, dimpled at the apex; cuticle cracking into large pale fawn-coloured subconic scales, flesh very thin; gills broad, ventricose, narrow in front, black, the extreme margin, except when deliquescent, white, quite free; stem 6 in. high, ½ in. thick at the base, beautifully satiny with adpressed fibrillæ, attenuated above, where it is subtomentose and stained with the spores, sub-bulbous below, hollow.—*M. J. B.* Spores ·00055 × ·00036 in.

459. Coprinus aphthosus. *Fr.* "Scaly Coprinus."

Pileus membranaceous, ovato-campanulate, without striæ, sprinkled with superficial floccose scales, then naked; stem hollow, equal, twisted, fibrillose; gills adnate, linear, white, then black.—*Fr. Epicr. p.* 245. *Bolt. t.* 26.

In hollow trees, cellars, etc.

Pileus about an inch high, livid, not striate; stem 2 in. long, 2 lines thick, soft, white.

460. Coprinus similis. *B. & Br.* "Striate Coprinus."

Pileus ovato-campanulate, lineato-striate, pallid, centre obscurely hygrophanous, clothed with acute brown warts; stem hollow, white, largest at the base; gills adnate, attenuated behind, sublinear, brownish near the margin.—*B. & Br. Ann. N. H.* 1865, *no.* 1011.

On trunks of dead trees. Sept. Bodelwyddan.

Resembling *C. aphthosus*, but differing in the striate pileus, &c.

461. Coprinus flocculosus. *D. C.* "Flocculose Coprinus."

Pileus membranaceous, globose, then expanded, striate, discoid; clothed with evanescent floccose scales, at length smooth; stem hollow, equal, smooth, naked; gills remote, ventricose, violaceous, then brownish-black.—*Fr. Epicr. p.* 245. *Batt. t.* 25, *f. A. Ann. N. H. no.* 926.

In pastures. Aug. King's Cliffe.

Pileus 2½ in. across, ovate, at length expanded, dirty-white, striate, splitting in the direction of the gills, covered with innate scales, thus resembling *C. picaceus*; stem 3 in. high, attenuated upwards, white, slightly swollen at the base, smooth, or rather finely silky under a lens; gills free, generally solitary.—*B. & Br.*

** Tomentosi.

462. Coprinus extinctorius. *Fr.* "Extinguisher Coprinus."

Pileus submembranaceous, clavate, then campanulate, straight, margin striate, at first clothed with evanescent floccose scales; stem hollow, attenuated from the rooting base, smooth; gills reaching the stem, lanceolate, white, then brown-black.—*Fr. Epicr. p.* 245. *Paul. t.* 124, *f.* 7. *Bull. t.* 437, *f.* 1. *Bolt. t.* 24.

On the ground.

Stem hollow, attenuated from the rooting base, 4-5 in. long, 3 lin. thick; pileus about 3 in. broad, becoming pale; disc darker, somewhat livid.

463. Coprinus fimetarius. *Fr.* "Shaggy dung Coprinus."

Pileus submembranaceous, clavate, then conical, at length torn and revolute, at first rough with white floccose scales, then naked, longitudinally rimoso-sulcate, even at the apex; stem squamulose, thickened at the base, solid; gills free, lanceolate, then linear and flexuose, black.—*Fr. Epicr. p.* 245. *Bull. t.* 88.

On dung heaps. Mar. Apr. Common.

Variable; sometimes there is a root as long as the stem; subcæspitose; stem about 2-3 in. long, 2-3 lin. thick; spores ·00056 × ·00035 in.

464. Coprinus tomentosus. *Fr.* "Downy Coprinus."

Pileus submembranaceous, cylindrical, then conical, striate, floccoso-tomentose, then longitudinally cracked; stem hollow, rather short, equal, velvety; gills free, linear, brownish-black. *Fr. Epicr. p.* 246. *Bull. t.* 138. *Bolt. t.* 136. *Mich. t.* 75, *f.* 3.

On dung and in rich pastures.

The coating sometimes peels off in broad patches. Pileus narrowly pyramidical, tomentum subpersistent, whitish grey, sometimes furfuraceous; 1½ in. high. Stem 2-3 in. long, 2-3 lines thick.

465. Coprinus niveus. *Fr.* "Snowy Coprinus."

Pileus submembranaceous, oval, then campanulate, and expanded, floccoso-squamulose, with dense white down, and nearly persistently furfuraceous; stem fistulose, equal, villous, white; gills subadnate, narrow, blackish.—*Fr. Epicr. p.* 246. *Eng. Fl.* v. *p.* 121. *Fl. Dan. t.* 1671. *Paul. t.* 125, *f.* 2. *Sow. t.* 262?

On horse dung. Common. [United States.]

Pileus ½-1 in. broad, campanulate, at length expanded and depressed, margin rolled back, clothed with dense scaly meal, margin striate, very thin and delicate; gills narrow, free, subventricose, black, stem 2 in. or more high, 1 line thick, thickest at the base, sericeo-squamulose, hollow, fragile, splitting longitudinally.—*M. J. B.* Spores ·0004 × ·00047 in.

***** *Micacei.*

466. Coprinus micaceus. *Fr.* "Glistening Coprinus."

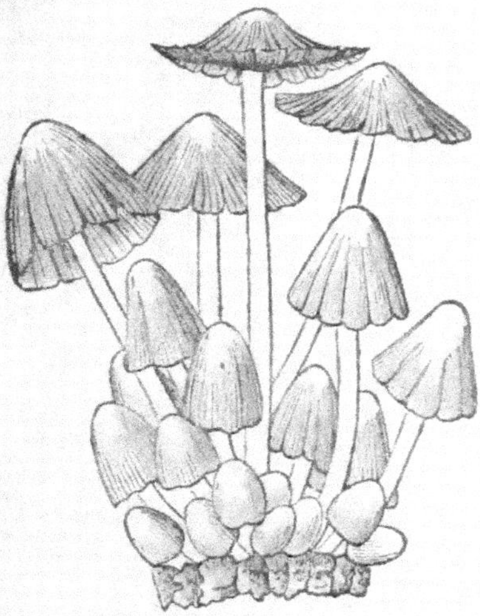

Fig. 39.

Pileus submembranaceous, oval, then campanulate, subrepand, striate, discoid, sprinkled with fugacious micaceous granules, at length naked, rimoso-sulcate; stem hollow, silky, or even, whitish; gills adnexed, lanceolate, whitish, brown to the middle, then blackish.—*Fr. Epicr. p.* 247. *Fl. Dan. t.* 1193. *Bolt. t.* 54. *Bull.* 246, 565. *Schæff. t.* 66, *f.* 4-6. *Sow. t.* 261. *Grev. t.* 76. *Paul. t.* 126. *Eng. Fl.* v. *p.* 120. *Fl. Boruss. t.* 376. *Corda. Sturm. t.* 2.

About old stumps. Common. [S. Carolina.]

Cæspitose. Pileus ¾-1 in. broad, or more, half ovate, often more or less irregular from the dense mode of growth, sprinkled with glittering meal, strongly striate, almost plicate, rufous, the umbo darkest, margin cinereous, very thin, veil very fugacious; gills attenuated in front, broad behind, ascending, attached above, umber, mottled with the spores, which appear black when viewed in a mass, but are really brown purple. Stem 2-3 in. high, 2 lines thick, hollow, brittle, squamulose, pulverulent, cuticle often cracked into little scales, very faintly tinged with red, attenuated upwards, base downy.—*M. J. B.* Spores with an oblique apiculus, ·0003 × ·00026 in. (*Fig.* 39, *reduced.*)

467. Coprinus aratus. *Berk. & Br.* "Umber Coprinus."

Solitary. Tall. Pileus campanulate, umber, deeply sulcate, micaceous; disc rugose; stem attenuated upwards, sub-bulbous at the base, minutely silky, snow white; gills narrow, bright brown, free.—*Ann. N.H. no.* 927.

In a hollow tree. May. King's Cliffe.

Pileus campanulate, 3 in. across, umber, deeply sulcate up to the darker wrinkled disc, sprinkled with large micaceous particles, revolute in decay; stem 5 in. high, 2½ lines thick, attenuated upwards, slightly bulbous at the base, straight, smooth, or rather minutely silky, snow-white, fistulose, umber within; gills narrow, attenuated at either end, free, deep rich brown, then black.—*B. & Br.*

468. Coprinus radians. *Fr.* "Radiating Coprinus."

Pileus membranaceous, ovato-campanulate, micaceous, disc granuloso-squamose, margin striate; stem equal, naked, short, fibrilloso-radiating at the base; gills reaching the stem, sublinear, white, then violaceous-black.—*Fr. Epicr. p.* 248. *Ann. Sc. Nat.* xiii. *t.* 10, *f.* 1. *Sow. t.* 145. *Eng. Fl.* v. *p.* 121.

On plaster walls.

Pileus 2 in. broad, gills free, numerous, at first white. Stem 1½ in. high, 2 lines thick, cylindric, fistulose, almost equal, curved in consequence of its vertical place of growth, naked, smooth, furnished with a radiating base 2 in. broad.—*Desm.* Spores ·00033 × ·00027 in.—*W. G. S.*

*** *Glabrati.*

469. Coprinus deliquescens. *Fr.* "Deliquescent Coprinus."

Pileus submembranaceous, ovato-campanulate, then expanded, subrepand, broadly striate, smooth, top studded with innate papillæ; stem hollow, smooth; gills at length remote, linear, lurid black.—*Fr. Epicr. p.* 249. *Fl. Dan. t.* 1070. *Bull. t.* 558, *f.* 1. *Fl. Boruss. t.* 375.

On old stumps.

Sometimes confounded with *C. atramentarius.* Pileus 3-4 in. broad, livid, never floccose. Gills at length very narrow.

Sect. 2. *Veliformes.* Pileus plicato-sulcate.

* *Cyclodei*—stem annulate or volvate.

470. Coprinus Hendersonii. *Fr.* "Henderson's Coprinus."

Pileus very delicate, oval, campanulate, smooth, striate to the middle; stem filiform, becoming smooth, with a small erect entire ring (at length evanescent); gills black.—*Fr. Epicr. p.* 250. *Berk. Hook. Journ. t.* 26, *f.* 1. *Berk. Outl. t.* 24, *f.* 8. *Price, f.* 114.

On hot beds and on dung in fields. Rare. Milton, &c., Norths.

Looks like a small annulate *A. disseminatus*. Pileus finely granulated under a lens.

** *Lanatuli*—pileus superficially floccose, veil evanescent.

471. **Coprinus macrocephalus.** *Berk.* "Stunted Coprinus."

Pileus at first cylindrical, then cylindrico-campanulate, sprinkled with pointed scales; stem dirty white, fistulose, clothed with short cottony down and loose fibres, strigose at the base; gills linear, perfectly free.—*Berk. Outl. p.* 180. *Eng. Fl.* v. *p.* 122.

On putrid dung. Cotterstock, Norths.

Pileus ⅜ in. broad, ¾ in. high, linear when young, then cylindrico-campanulate, margin slightly spread out, adorned with elegant, adpressed, or patent scales, the remains of the veil; apex brown, shaded off into slate-colour on the margin, scarcely at all pubescent; gills linear, perfectly free, at length black. Stem 1-2 in. high, 2 lines thick, ascending, dirty white, fistulose, clothed with short cottony down, and with longer, sometimes deflexed loose fibres, strigose at the base, somewhat attenuated upwards, and stained with the black elliptic spores.—*M. J. B.*

472. **Coprinus lagopus.** *Fr.* "Hare's-foot Coprinus."

Pileus very thin, cylindrical, then campanulate, clothed with white flocci, at length split, radiato-sulcate, somewhat revolute; stem very fragile, on all parts woolly, white; gills free, linear, black.—*Fr. Epicr. p.* 250. *Saund. & Sm. t.* 19.

On dung.

Remarkable for the dense cottony coat of the stem, which is 5 in. long or more. Pileus about 1 in. broad, whitish; disc livid.

473. **Coprinus nycthemerus.** *Fr.* "Thin-capped Coprinus."

Pileus very thin, soon rimose, expanded, flocculoso-furfuraceous, discoid, then naked, furcato-striate; stem equal, flaccid, smooth, whitish; gills free, narrow, blackish, at first crowded, then distant, remote.—*Fr. Epicr. p.* 251. *Bull. t.* 542, *f. D.I.*

On dung. King's Cliffe. Norths. [Cincinnati.]

Pileus grey, a few lines across, from 4 lines to ½ in. or more high; disc brown; stem whitish.

474. Coprinus radiatus. *Fr.* "Delicate Coprinus."

Very delicate; pileus clavate, then campanulate, tomentose, soon splitting, expanded, naked, discoid, plicato-radiate; stem filiform, unpolished; gills free, distant, few.—*Fr. Epicr. p.* 251. *Bull. t.* 542, *f. L. & E.H. Eng. Fl.* v. *p.* 123.

On dung. Common. [United States.]

Very tender, so that a breath destroys it. Pileus 1-2 lines broad, at first digitaliform, yellowish, apex obtuse, darker, striate and downy, when full grown pale brown, or nearly colourless, centre sometimes dimpled, strongly furrowed, edge notched, and often split in a radiated manner, so as to appear like the spokes of a wheel. Gills about ten, with minute smaller ones in the interstices. Stem 1-3 in. high, very slender, quite filiform, smooth, but sometimes fibrillose and tomentose, dusky or colourless, a little thickened at the base, which is slightly downy.—*M. J. B.* Spores ·0003 × ·0002 in.

*** *Furfurelli*—pileus mealy or micaceous.

475. Coprinus domesticus. *Fr.* "Domestic Coprinus."

Pileus thin, ovate, campanulate, obtuse, splitting, undulato-sulcate, furfuraceo-squamulose; stem attenuated, silky, white; gills fixed, crowded, linear, white with reddish, then brown-black. —*Fr. Epicr. p.* 251. *Huss. t. Eng. Fl.* v. *p.* 121.

On damp carpets, &c. [United States.]

Very brittle, often cæspitose. Pileus 2 in. broad, membranaceous, campanulate, apex nearly smooth, reddish brown; gills white when young, then ruddy, at length brown-black; stem 2-3 in. high, 3 lines thick, even, attenuated upwards.—*Fries.*

476. Coprinus ephemerus. *Fr.* "Ephemeral Coprinus."

Pileus very thin, ovali-clavate, then campanulate, splitting, radiato-sulcate, sub-furfuraceous; disc elevated, even; stem slender, equal, pellucid, smooth; gills reaching the stem, distant, whitish, then brown and black.—*Fr. Epicr. p.* 252. *Fl. Dan. t.* 832. *f.* 2. *Bull. t.* 128. *Batt. t.* 27, *B. Eng. Fl.* v. *p.* 123.

On dung hills. Common. [United States.]

Extremely fugacious. Pileus $\frac{1}{4}$-$\frac{3}{4}$ in. broad, ovate or campanulate, at length deflexed, margin finally splitting and curling back; apex umber, shaded gradually into a delicate bluish-grey, striate, scaly when young; gills at length black, linear, edge downy, white; stem 1-2 in. high, 1 line thick, dirty white, with a few fibrillæ, at length naked.—*M. J. B.*

477. Coprinus plicatilis. *Fr.* "Plaited Coprinus."

Pileus very thin, ovali-cylindrical, then expanded, splitting, sulcato-plicate, somewhat smooth; disc broad, at length depressed, even; stem equal, smooth, white; gills adnate to a distinct collar, distant, greyish black.—*Fr. Epicr. p.* 252. *Curt. Fl. Lond. t.* 200. *Sow. t.* 364. *Fl. Dan. t.* 1134. *Batt. t.* 28, *A. B. Bull. t.* 552, *f.* 2 *(partly)*. *Eng. Fl.* v. *p.* 122. *Price, f.* 33.

In pastures. Common. [United States.]

Extremely fugacious; pileus ½-1 in. broad, cylindrical, furfuraceous, at length plane, nearly naked, umbilicate, grey, yellowish-brown in the centre, beautifully plicate, membranaceous, pellucid; gills free, dark-grey, subdistant, very narrow, tender; stem 1-3 in. high, very slender, fragile, smooth, grey, tinged with brown, sometimes white, hollow.—*Grev.*

478. Coprinus Spraguei. *B. & C.* "Garden Coprinus."

Very delicate; pileus campanulate, then conical, tomentose, plicate; stem fistulose, pale cinnamon, gills few, narrow.—*Ann. Nat. Hist. Oct.* 1859. *Berk. Outl. p.* 182.

In gardens. July. King's Cliffe. [New England.]

Spores narrow, subcymbiform, ·0004 in. long. The difference between it and *C. plicatilis*, as regards the spores, is very striking.—*M. J. B.*

**** *Hemerobii*—pileus always smooth.

479. Coprinus hemerobius. *Fr.* "Collared Coprinus."

Pileus very thin, ovate, nearly even, then expanded, campanulate, splitting, sulcate, smooth, apex subpruinose; stem elongated, attenuated, smooth, pallid; gills linear, pallid, then black, adnexed to an obscure collar.—*Fr. Epicr. p.* 253. *Bolt. t.* 31. *Fl. Dan. t.* 1960, *f.* 2.

On roadsides. Rare.

With the habit of *C. plicatilis*, but the stem longer, 4-5 in., and very fragile, pileus persistently campanulate, disc bright brown, never the least depressed; gills 1-1½ lines broad.

480. Coprinus filiformis. *Berk. & Br.* "Filiform Coprinus."

Very minute; pileus cylindrical, striate, grey, with white micaceous particles; stem capillary, white, very minutely pilose. —*Ann. N. H. no.* 928, *t.* 15, *f.* 8.

On the ground, in woods. Sept. Colleyweston.

Pileus not a line high, cylindrical, striate, grey, shining with white mealy particles; stem half-an-inch high, extremely fine, white, sprinkled with a few short delicate hairs; not larger than *Mucor caninus.*—*B. & Br.*

Gen. 3. **BOLBITIUS**, Fr. Epicr. p. 253.

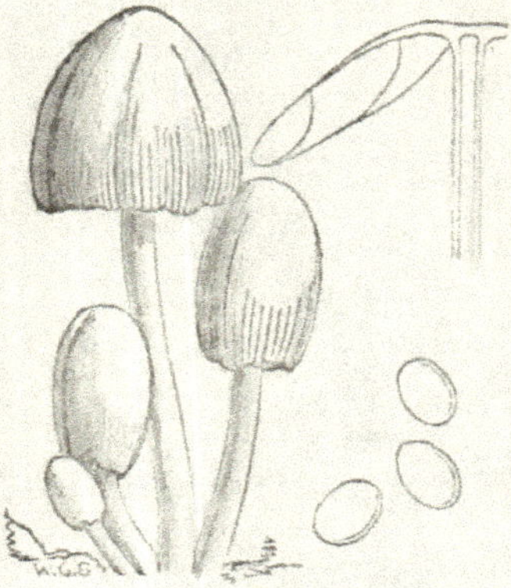

Fig. 40.

Spores coloured; pileus yellow, becoming moist; stem hollow, confluent with the hymenophore; gills becoming moist, but not deliquescent, at length losing their colour and becoming powdery.

HAB. Dung or rank earth near to towns. (*Fig* 40.)

A very natural but small genus, intermediate between *Agaricus* and *Coprinus* on one side, and *Coprinus* and *Cortinarius* on the other; it resembles *Coprinus* in its mode of growth, and ephemeral existence. The species have no known use.—*W. G. S.*

481. Bolbitius Boltoni. *Fr.* "Bolton's Bolbitius."

Pileus somewhat fleshy, viscid, at first smooth, then the membranaceous margin is sulcate; disc darker, subdepressed; stem attenuated, yellowish, ring fugacious, at first flocculose; gills sub-adnate, livid yellow, then brown.—*Fr. Epicr. p.* 254. *Bolt. t.* 149. *Ag. Boltonii. Eng. Fl.* v. *p.* 117.

On dung. June—Sept.

Pileus at first conical, 2 in. broad, yellow, turning pale; stem 3 in. high. Spores brownish.

482. Bolbitius fragilis. *Fr.* "Fragile Bolbitius."

Pileus sub-membranaceous, viscid, pellucid, margin striate, disc sub-umbonate; stem attenuated, naked, smooth, yellow; gills attenuated, adnexed, yellowish, then pale cinnamon.—*Fr. Epicr. p.* 254. *Bolt. t.* 65. *Sow. t.* 96.

On dung. Common.

Pileus yellow, then whitish, more delicate and fragile than *B. Boltoni.* Spores rusty brown. Stem 3 in. long.

Ag. vitellinus, Eng. Fl. v. p. 311, is probably this species.

(*fig.* 40.)

483. Bolbitius titubans. *Fr.* "Wavering Bolbitius."

Pileus membranaceous, expanded, pellucid, discoid, striate to the middle; stem slender, straight, shining, yellowish; gills slightly adnexed, pallid, then fleshy-brown (salmon coloured. B.)—*Fr. Epicr. p.* 254. *Bull. t.* 425, *f.* 1. *Sow. t.* 128. *Eng. Fl.* v. *p.* 117.

Amongst grass. May—Oct. Common.

Pileus 1 in. broad, campanulato-convex, yellow, viscid, shining, margin notched, plicate and striate, pale cinnamon, submembranaceous, very delicate and tender, smooth, at length almost deliquescent, shining, and subochraceous; gills narrow, slightly ventricose, very minutely adnexed, cinnamon. Stem 4-5 in. high, 1-1½ line thick, striate above, pulverulento-squamulose, pale yellow, fistulose, very tender and delicate.—*M. J. B.* Spores salmon colour, ·00032 × ·00017 in.

484. Bolbitius apicalis. *Smith.* "Two-coloured Bolbitius."

Pileus membranaceous, brown, striate from the first, then plicate, liable to split; disc ochraceous, somewhat fleshy, obscurely umbonate, the difference in colour between the two parts defined by a distinct line; stem hollow, striate, white, minutely pruinose under a lens; gills somewhat broad, ventricose, free, at first pressed to the stem, brown.—*W. G. Smith, in litt.*

In pastures. Early summer. Staplehurst.

Spores brown, ·00035 × ·00025 in. Stem about 2 in. long. Pileus ¾ in. high. —*W. G. S.*

485. Bolbitius tener. *B.* "Delicate Bolbitius."

Very delicate; pileus white, moist, conical, elongated; stem white, bulbous at the base; gills attenuated behind, nearly free, salmon coloured.—*Berk. Outl. p.* 183, *t.* 12, *f.* 2. *B. albipes, Fr. Mon. Hym.*

Amongst short grass. Apethorpe.

At first looking like a dry specimen of *Ag. tener.*

Gen. 4. CORTINARIUS, Fr. Epicr. p. 255.

Spores rusty-ochre, resembling in colour peroxide of iron; veil universal, of a different texture to the pileus, and consisting of arachnoid threads; a similar veil is found in *Agaricus*, but it is there either partial, or continuous with the cuticle of pileus; stem confluent with the hymenophore; gills adnate, membranaceous, persistent, cinnamon-coloured and powdery; trama floccose.

HAB. Woods and fields.

This genus, the most natural amongst the *Agaricini*, is readily distinguished by its peculiar habit, but is badly defined by artificial characters; the species are variable in size and changeable in colour; when old they present a different appearance to their young state, and are very different when dry to when fresh.—*W. G. S.*

Sub-Gen. 1. PHLEGMACIUM, Fr. Epicr. p. 256.

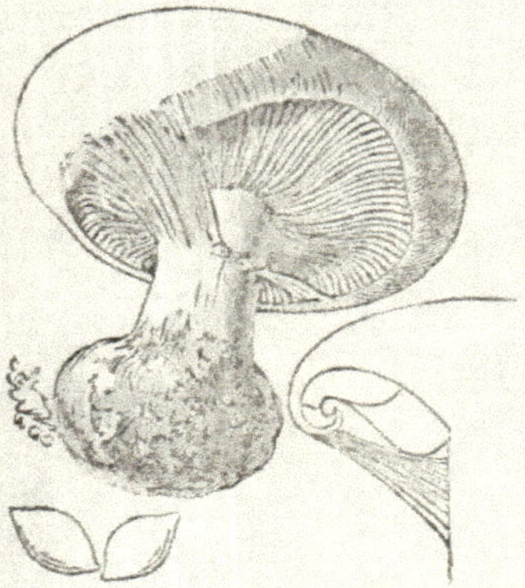

Fig. 41.

Pileus with a continuous pellicle, viscid when moist; veil (and consequently the stem) dry, not glutinous. (*Fig.* 41, *reduced.*)

486. Cortinarius (Phlegmacium) caperatus. *Fr.* "Wrinkled Cortinarius."

Pileus fleshy, ovate, then expanded, obtuse, moist, incrusted with superficial white flocci; stem stout, smooth, white, squamulose at the apex, from the broken, reflexed, membranaceous ring; gills fixed, seceding, serrate, crowded, clay-coloured.—*Fr. Epicr. p.* 256. *Fl. Dan. t.* 1675. *Krombh. t.* 73, *f.* 10-12. *Bot. E. Bord. t.* 9. *Ann. N.H. no.* 691.

In woods. Sept. Berwickshire. Lancashire.

Pileus, ring, and stem presenting deeper or lighter shades of ferruginous orange, dusted with pulverulent particles, which consist of obovate pedicellate cells, the sides of which are sometimes proliferous. Spores bright ferruginous, ·0004 in. long.—*M. J. B.*

487. Cortinarius (Phlegmacium) varius. *Fr.* "Variable Cortinarius."

Pileus compact, hemispherical, then expanded, even, viscid, discoid; margin smooth; flesh white; stem solid, short, with conical adpressed flocci, whitish; gills emarginate, crowded, quite entire, purplish, at length clay-coloured or cinnamon.—*Fr. Epicr. p.* 258. *Schæff. t.* 42. *Eng. Fl.* v. *p.* 87.

In woods. Sept.—Nov. [Cincinnati.]

Very variable in size, but nearly constant in colour, never having a blue tint on the stem; gills when young pale (purplish, margin yellow), at length dilute, of a clay colour, inclining to cinnamon. Stem short or elongated, marginato-bulbous, or nearly equal, even or scaly.—*Fries.*

488. Cortinarius (Phlegmacium) cyanipes. *Fr.* "Blue-stemmed Cortinarius."

Pileus fleshy, hemispherical, then expanded, even, viscid; margin thin, smooth, of the same colour; flesh whitish; stem solid, violaceous then whitish, naked above the thin veil; bulb depressed, oblique; gills adnate, then emarginate, broad, rather crowded, violaceous, then pallid.—*Mon. Hym.* ii. *p.* 8. *Fr. Epicr. p.* 258. *Sow. t.* 223. *C. cyanopus, Berk. Outl. p.* 184.

In woods.

Pileus 2½ in. broad, at first livid brown, then opaque tan-colour; stem 2-3 in. long, ½ in. thick, naked, white, violet upwards; gills 3-4 lines broad, at first adnate, at length emarginate.

489. Cortinarius (Phlegmacium) russus. *Fr.* "Ruddy Cortinarius."

Pileus fleshy, convexo-plane, viscid, margin innately silky-fibrillose; stem somewhat hollow, soft, attenuated, closely fibrillose, pallid, nearly white, veil fugacious; gills adnate, broad, crowded, connected by veins, reddish-ferruginous.—*Fr. Epicr. p.* 261. *Trans. Woolh. Cl.* 1870, *t.* 1.

In moist woods. Autumn.

Pileus 4 in. broad, fleshy, convex, then flattened, obtuse, viscid, glabrous at the disc, fibrous at the margin, brittle, uniformly red. Veil tender, fugacious. Gills obtusely adnate, scarcely perceptibly rounded, or with a slight decurrent tooth, crowded, veined, of a red peroxide of iron colour, similar to the pileus. Stem stuffed, then hollow, not bulbous, often curvato-ascending, soft, streaked with fine silky fibres, somewhat pruinose at the apex. Flavour not bitter but nauseous. Spores brown, ·00032 × ·0002 in.—*W. G. S.*

490. Cortinarius (Phlegmacium) anfractus. *Fr.* "Bent Cortinarius."

Pileus fleshy, unequal, plicate, at length undulato-repand, rather viscid, shining when dry; stem stuffed, unequal, closely fibrillose; apex violaceous and veiled; gills arcuato-adfixed, crisped, somewhat distant, dingy olive, then cinnamon.—*Fr. Epicr. p.* 262. *Ann. N.H. no.* 692.

In woods. Rare. King's Cliffe.

Pileus covered completely by a close white volva when young.—*M. J. B.* Stem clavate, immarginate, 2 in. long, ½ in. or more thick; pileus 2-3 in. broad, even, dark olive, then dingy tawny. Gills emarginate, distant, 3-4 lines broad.

491. Cortinarius (Phlegmacium) multiformis. *Fr.* Multiform Cortinarius."

Pileus fleshy, convex, then expanded, equal, smooth, viscid; flesh and fugacious veil white; stem solid, attenuated, closely fibrillose, naked, white, then yellowish; bulb submarginate; gills emarginate, crowded, serrated, white, then clay-coloured cinnamon.—*Fr. Epicr. p.* 263. *Sow. t.* 102.

In woods. Rare.

Stem solid, 2-4 in. long, about ½ in. thick, equal or attenuated, naked, white, then yellowish. Pileus yellow, clayey yellow, tawny, &c. Flesh white, at first compact, then soft. Spores ochraceous.

492. Cortinarius (Phlegmacium) glaucopus. *Fr.* "Brown-zoned Cortinarius."

Pileus compact, torn, expanded, subrepand, viscid, then floccoso-squamose or fibrillose, flesh at length yellowish; stem solid, stout, striate, bluish, then pale yellowish, margined at the base; gills emarginate, broad, bluish, then clay-coloured cinnamon.—*Fr. Epicr. p.* 264. *Schæff. t.* 53. *Batsch. f.* 73. *Huss. t. Mag. Zool. & Bot. no.* 4.

In pine woods. [S. Carolina.]

Stem solid, very thick, at first bulbous, 3 in. long, bulb evanescent, but the base marginate, pale blue, without and within base yellowish Pileus rather viscid, rarely even, commonly floccoso-squamose, dingy yellow, tan-coloured, tawny, or clay colour.

493. Cortinarius (Phlegmacium) callochrous. *Fr.* "Tawny-viscid Cortinarius."

Pileus fleshy, convex, then expanded, smooth, viscid, unchangeable; flesh compact, white; stem solid, equal, fibrillose, white, then yellowish; bulb distinct, margined; gills emarginate, crowded, serrated, bright blue, then purplish.—*Fr. Epicr. p.* 265. *Berk. Outl. t.* 12, *f.* 3. *Eng. Fl.* v. *p.* 86.

In woods. [S. Carolina.]

Pileus 3-4 in. broad, truly carnose, viscid when moist, nearly smooth, with a satiny lustre, olivaceous tawny when young, tawny when full grown; flesh tinged with yellow, and when young very dilute violet. Veil arachnoid. Gills close, thin, emarginate, serrulate, at first bright violet, then ferruginous, with a dilute violet tinge, not at all olivaceous. Stem 1-3 in. high, 1 in. thick, fibrillose, the fibrillæ above copiously dusted with the spores, bulbous, violet towards the gills, the rest whitish, when young very shaggy at the base.—*M. J. B.*

494. Cortinarius (Phlegmacium) cœrulescens. *Fr.* "Azure-blue Cortinarius."

Pileus fleshy, convex, then expanded, even, viscid; flesh soft; stem solid, attenuated, naked, bluish, then whitish; bulb marginate; gills adnexed, crowded, quite entire, at first of a pure dark blue.—*Fr. Epicr. p.* 265. *Schæff. t.* 34, *f.* 5. *Letell. t.* 651. *Ann. N.H., no.* 68. *Vent. t.* 32, *f.* 1-3.

In woods. Sept. Oct. [Cincinnati.]

Pileus 2½-3 in. broad, at length nearly plane, with the margin repand, of a beautiful azure blue; at first viscid, when dry marked with a few innate indistinct squamiform patches, fleshy, flesh rather firm, not changing to violet when bruised. Gills rather distant, adnate, subdecurrent, obscurely emarginate, violet, at length stained with the spores. Stem 3 in. high, ½-¾ in. thick, solid, bulbous, of the same colour as the pileus, fibrillose. Smell like that of radishes.—*M. J. B.*

495. Cortinarius (Phlegmacium) purpurascens. *Fr.* "Purplish Cortinarius."

Pileus compact, dilated, subrepand, grained, viscid; flesh blue; stem solid, blunt, fibrillose; bulb marginate, vanishing; gills broadly emarginate, crowded, bluish, then clay-coloured cinnamon, purplish when rubbed.—*Fr. Epicr. p.* 265.

In woods. Common.

Pileus obtuse, disc compact, 4-5 in broad, bay or bright brown, then tawny olive, with an elevated brown zone. Stem solid, thick, bulbous, pale blue. Gills 3 lines and more broad.

496. Cortinarius (Phlegmacium) dibaphus. *Fr.* "Spotted Cortinarius."

Pileus fleshy, plano-depressed, smooth, viscid, variegated; flesh yellow, under the cuticle violet; stem stuffed, fibrillose, shining, yellow, purplish above; bulb marginate; gills adnate, somewhat crowded, quite entire, ferruginous purple.—*Fr. Epicr. p.* 266. *Saund. & Sm.* i. *t.* 10.

In woods.

Stem 3 in. high, ½ in. thick. Pileus 3-4 in. broad, purplish, disc yellow, at length spotted with lilac and repand.—*Fries.* Spores, with an apiculus at both ends, ·0004 × ·0003 in.

497. Cortinarius (Phlegmacium) turbinatus. *Fr.* "Top-shaped Cortinarius."

Pileus fleshy, plane, then depressed, even, viscid, of one colour, smooth, growing pale; flesh white, soft; stem stuffed, sub-equal, shining, whitish; bulb marginate; gills attenuated, isabelline, then ferruginous.—*Fr. Epicr. p.* 266. *Bull. t.* 110. *Eng. Fl.* v. *p.* 31*.

In woods. King's Cliffe. [S. Carolina.]

Pileus 2-3 in. broad, convex, scarcely umbonate, at length often depressed, viscid when moist, at length shining, very even, yellow tawny, carnose, cuticle easily peeling off. Gills numerous, yellowish, then cinnamon, acutely adnate. Stem 2-3 in. high, ½ in. or more thick, bulbous at the base, and often marginate, solid, not the least violet.—*M. J. B.*

498. Cortinarius (Phlegmacium) fulgens. *Fr.* "Shining Cortinarius."

Pileus fleshy, plane, equal, silky-fibrillose, viscid, flesh at length spongy, tan coloured; stem stout, bulb depressed, marginate, yellow, woolly, filamentose, at length pulverulent, ferruginous; gills emarginate, somewhat tawny.—*Fr. Epicr. p.* 267. *B. & Br. Ann. N.H.* 1865, *no.* 1012. *Saund. &. Sm. t.* 12.

In pine woods, &c. Sept. Bathford Down.

Stem woolly, when young moist, viscid. Gills somewhat crowded, quite entire, at first yellowish, then ferruginous. Pileus 2-3 in. broad, sometimes squamulose. Spores with an apiculus at both ends, ·00036 × ·0002 in. (*fig.* 41, *reduced.*)

499. Cortinarius (Phlegmacium) scaurus. *Fr.* "Club-footed Cortinarius."

Pileus fleshy, equal, smooth, tiger-spotted, viscid, becoming pale, margin thin, at length somewhat striate; stem solid, spongy at the base, then marginato-bulbose, attenuated, striate, growing pale; gills attenuated, adnate, rather thin, crowded, purplish, then olivaceous.—*Fr. Epicr. p.* 268. *Berk. Outl. p.* 186. *Eng. Fl.* v. *p.* 86.

In woods. King's Cliffe. [S. Carolina.]

Soft, insipid. Pileus 2-3 in. broad, sometimes depressed; gills rather thin, at length cinnamon. Stem about 3 in. high, fibrillose, sometimes marginato-bulbous, when growing amongst moss nearly equal.—*Fries.*

500. Cortinarius (Phlegmacium) prasinus. *Fr.* "Leek-green Cortinarius."

Pileus compact, equal, viscid, variegated with scale-like spots; stem solid, short, firm, base marginato-bulbose, pallid greenish, as well as the veil; gills rounded, rather distant, yellow-olive.—*Fr. Epicr. p.* 268. *Schæff. t.* 218. *Vent. t.* 23, *f.* 1-3.

In beech woods.

Stem short, solid, very thick, pale greenish, not violet, flesh greenish-white. Pileus very obtuse, regular, viscid, spotted, sometimes bluish-green, sometimes dingy brown, margin regularly involute; flesh dirty white; gills emarginate, not crowded, yellowish olive or olivaceous, base darker, cinereous-olive.

Sub-Gen. 2. Myxacium, Fr. Epicr. p. 273.

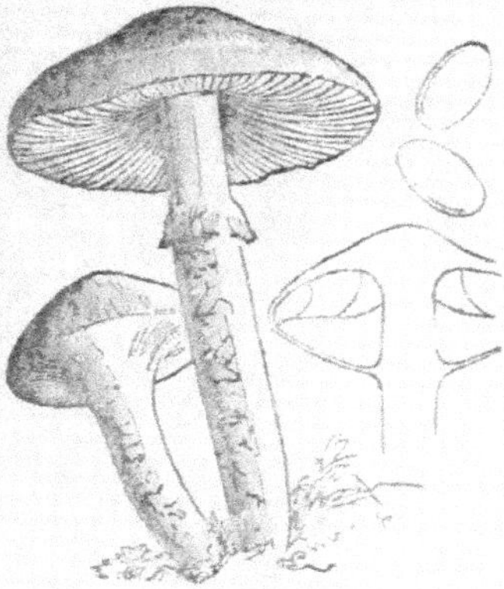

Fig. 42.

Pileus glutinous; veil (and consequently the stem) viscid, polished when dry.
(*Fig.* 42, *reduced.*)

501. Cortinarius (Myxacium) collinitus. *Fr.* "Smeared Cortinarius."

Pileus fleshy, convex, then expanded, obtuse, even, glutinous, shining; stem firm, cylindrical, transversely squamose from the breaking up of the glutinous floccose veil; gills adnate, clay-coloured, or grey, then cinnamon.—*Fr. Epicr. p.* 274. *Sow. t.* 9. *Bull. t.* 549, 596. *Buxb.* iv. *t.* 9. *Batsch. f.* 197, C. *var. Eng. Fl.* v. *p.* 93. *Vent. t.* 32, *f.* 4-6.

In woods. Common. [S. Carolina.]

Gills and stem sometimes purplish, sometimes without any purple tint, except when very young. Pileus 3 in. broad, expanded, very slimy, shining when dry, tawny-ochraceous, margin thin; gills broad, ventricose, rounded behind and adnate with a tooth, connected by veins, distant; stem 4 in. high, ¾ in. thick, solid, white within, except at the base, which is rhubarb-coloured without, covered below with a white silky, slimy coat, broken transversely into scales, beneath which it is rhubarb-coloured; fibrillose above the obsolete ring.—*M. J. B.* Spores ·00038 × ·00022 in. (*Fig.* 42, *reduced.*)

502. Cortinarius (Myxacium) elatior. *Fr.* "Tall Cortinarius."

Pileus cylindrical, then expanded, viscid, disc rather fleshy, even, otherwise membranaceous, and plicato-rugose; stem elongated, soft, stout, attenuated at either end, squamose from the torn veil; gills adnate, broad, connected by veins, and rugose, brownish-ferruginous.—*Fr. Epicr. p.* 274. *Berk. Outl. p.* 186.

In woods. Common.

Stem solid, soft, 5-7 in. long, ½ in. and more thick, commonly attenuated, longitudinally fibrous; pileus about 3-4 in. broad, when moist livid yellow, when dry dingy ochre, but variable in colour, whitish, tan colour, bright brown, violet-brown, &c.; gills sub-distant, at first 3 lines broad, afterwards broader.

503. Cortinarius (Myxacium) stillatitius. *Fr.* "Dripping Cortinarius."

Pileus thin, convexo-plane, subumbonate, even; stem hollow, very soft, equally attenuated, at first covered with a blue gluten; gills emarginate, somewhat distant, broad, ferruginous, cinnamon.—*Fr. Epicr. p.* 277. *Saund. & Sm. t.* 3.

In mossy places.

Stem 2, scarcely 3 in. long, 3-4 lines thick. Pileus slightly fleshy, scarcely 2 in. broad, even, smooth, covered with a blue gluten, afterwards livid brown, and at length greyish-white. Flesh soft, watery, hygrophanous.

504. Cortinarius (Myxacium) livido-ochraceus. *B.* "Livid ochrey Cortinarius."

Pileus plane, submembranaceous, viscid, margin not striate; stem attenuated at either end, subsquamose, striate above the fugitive veil, stuffed with cottony fibres; gills cinnamon, sub-adnexed, broad in front.—*Berk Outl. p.* 187. *Eng. Fl.* v. *p.* 89.

In woods. King's Cliffe. Coed Coch.

Pileus 1 in. across, quite smooth, shining, covered with a thick sub-cartilaginous skin, the margin very thin but not striate, plane, livid-ochraceous; edge with a few indistinct fragments of the veil; gills cinnamon, the extreme margin pale, moderately distant, broad in front, appearing as if adnexed; stem 1 in. high, ⅜ thick in the middle, where it is swollen, attenuated below, silky, beautiful violet, ochraceous at the base; sub-squamose, portion above the obsolete ring striate, stuffed with cottony fibres. Inodorous.—*M. J. B.*

Sub-Gen. 3. Inoloma. Fr. Epicr. p. 278.

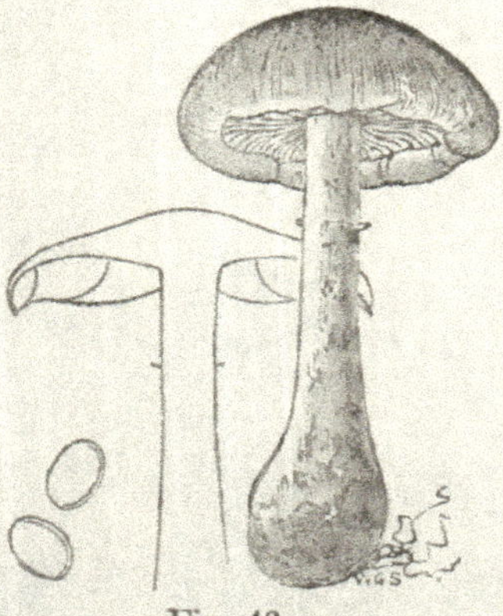

Fig. 43.

Pileus fleshy, subcompact, perfectly dry, with no viscid pellicle, silky with scales, or innate fibres, not hygrophanous; stem bulbous.

The species are handsome and easily distinguished. (*Fig.* 43.)

505. Cortinarius (Inoloma) violaceus. *Fr.* "Violet Cortinarius."

Dark violet; pileus fleshy, obtuse, villoso-squamose; stem bulbous, spongy, villous, internally cinereous violet; gills fixed, broad, thick, distant, darker.—*Fr. Epicr. p.* 279. *Eng. Fl.* v. *p.* 85. *Huss.* i. *t.* 12. *Sv. Bot. t.* 288. *Hedw. obs. t.* 4. *Bull t.* 250. *Smith, E.M. f.* 12. *Hogg & Johnst. t.* 6. *Vent. t.* 38, *f.* 1-3.

In woods. Esculent. [United States.]

Pileus 4 in. or more across, obtuse, expanded, gills when young deep violet, almost black, stem 4 in. high, when young subtomentose.—*Fries.*

506. Cortinarius (Inoloma) camphoratus. *Fr.* "Strong-scented Cortinarius."

Pileus fleshy, obtuse, lilac, silky, then smooth and discoloured; stem bulbous, dry; base white within, becoming bluish as well as the veil; gills thin, crowded, bright cœrulean, then purplish.—*Fr. Ep. p.* 280. *B. & Br. Ann. N. H.* (1866), *no.* 1128.

On the ground in woods. Sept. Fineshade.

Stem solid, soft, bulbous or obclavate, 3-5 inches long, ½-1 in. thick, woolly when young, violet, white within at the base. Pileus 2-3 in. broad, at first silky, lilac, then smooth and discoloured (whitish, yellowish, &c.), not hygrophanous; flesh blue, gills decurrent or emarginate. Odour strong and fœtid.

507. Cortinarius (Inoloma) callisteus. *Fr.* "Stout Cortinarius."

Yellowish tawny; pileus fleshy, convex, then plane, rather smooth, even, and innato-squamulose; margin rather silky; flesh yellowish-white; stem elongated, bulbous, tawny fibrillose; gills adnate, floccose, connected behind.—*Fr. Epicr. p.* 281. *A. validus B. Eng. Fl.* v. *p.* 84. *Saund. & Sm. t.* 3.

In woods. Rare.

Pileus 4 in. broad, fleshy, margin thin, deep tawny inclining to ferruginous, at first convex, flatly hemispherical, or sub-campanulate, very obtuse, at length expanded, plano-convex, clothed with very minute reflexed scales; flesh whitish, partaking very slightly of the colour of the pileus; margin at first subinvolute. Gills ⅜th in. broad, brittle, undulate, nearly horizontal, adnate, soon starting from the stem, and connected with it by a few fibres, very minutely emarginate, pale tawny, clouded with the spores. Stem 4 in. high, nearly 1 in. thick in the centre, 1¼ at the base, bulbous, fibrillose from the remains of the fugacious veil, which forms in the very young plant a slight extremely evanescent ring, which is coloured by the spores, solid, tawny like the pileus. At the base are a few strong roots There is not the slightest tinge of purple or violet in any stage of growth.—*M.J.B.* Spores ·0003 × ·00022 in. *(Fig. 43, reduced.)*

508. Cortinarius (Inoloma) Bulliardi. *Fr.* "Red-rooted Cortinarius."

Pileus fleshy, campanulato-convex, sub-gibbous, even or squamulose, rufescent; stem bulbous, short, firm, vermilion below, with fibrils of the same colour, apex whitish; gills adnexed, broad, purplish, then ferruginous.—*Fr. Epicr. p.* 282. *Bull t.* 431, *f.* 3. *B. & Br. Ann. N.H. no.* 693, 1128 *.

In woods. Sept. Fineshade, Bristol.

Remarkable for its bright red mycelium. Stem solid, 2-3 in. long, ½ in. thick. Pileus obtuse, 2-3 in. broad, dry, dark rufescent or sanguineous brown. Gills 3 lin. broad, rather crowded, purplish then ferruginous, edge crenulate (whitish). Flesh pallid.

509. Cortinarius (Inoloma) bolaris. *Fr.* "Collared Cortinarius."

Pileus fleshy, obsoletely umbonate, growing pale, variegated with saffron-red, adpressed, innate, pilose scales; stem stuffed, then hollow, nearly equal, squamose, of the same colour; gills subdecurrent, crowded, watery cinnamon.—*Fr. Epicr. p.* 282. *Pers. Ic. pict. t.* 14, *f.* 1. *Berk. Outl. t.* 19, *f.* 1. *Ann. N. H. no.* 69.

In Beech woods. Sept. and Oct. Rare. King's Cliffe. Argyllshire.

Stem hard, equal, 2-3 in. long, 3-5 lines thick, straight, curved, or flexuose. Pileus 1-2 in. broad and upwards, reddish yellow, growing paler; variegated with red maculæform adpressed scales. Flesh firm white.

510. Cortinarius (Inoloma) pholideus. *Fr.* "Scaly Cortinarius."

Pileus fleshy, expanded, obtuse, umbonate, fawn coloured, densely squamulose with innate, blackish, fasciculated hairs; stem attenuated, transversely squarrose with sooty-brown scales, even and violet above the veil; gills sub-emarginate, crowded, violet then clay-coloured cinnamon.—*Fr. Epicr. p.* 283. *A. & S. t.* 12, *f.* 1. *Ann. N.H. no.* 272.

In woods. King's Cliffe. [United States.]

Stem solid, 3-4 in. long, 3-6 lin. thick, attenuated upwards. Pileus 2-4 in. broad, sub-umbonate, depressed about the umbo, fawn coloured, growing pale. Flesh pallid. Gills 2-4 lin. broad.

511. Cortinarius (Inoloma) sublanatus. *Fr.* "Woolly Cortinarius."

Pileus fleshy, campanulate, then expanded, umbonate, tan coloured, inclining to brown, clothed with innate, pilose scales;

stem bulbous, attenuated, smooth above, pallid, squamose below with brownish down; gills sub-adnate, scarcely crowded, yellowish-olivaceous.—*Fr. Epicr. p.* 283. *Sow. t.* 224. *Huss.* ii. *t.* 22. *Eng. Fl.* v. *p.* 84.

In woods. Oct. Rare.

Smell like that of radishes. Pileus 3 in. broad, at length broadly and obtusely umbonate, colour variable, scales brownish or white, sometimes silky, adpressed; gills adnate or emarginate. Stem 3 in. high, yellowish-pallid, sometimes violet above.—*Fries.*

512. Cortinarius (Inoloma) arenatus. *P.* "Sandy Cortinarius."

Pileus fleshy, convex, at first gibbous, granulated with floccose scales, light red, then brownish; stem clavato-attenuated, beyond the middle clad with brown scales, apex even, pallid; gills emarginate, ventricose, rather crowded, yellowish-cinnamon.—*Fr. Epicr. p.* 283. *Bull. t.* 586. *Huss.* i. *t.* 72.

In woods. Coed Coch.

This cannot be distinguished safely from *C. pholideus* except when the specimens are young, in which case the colour of the gills is distinctive.—*M. J. B.*

Sub-Gen. 4. Dermocybe, Fr. Epicr. p. 283.

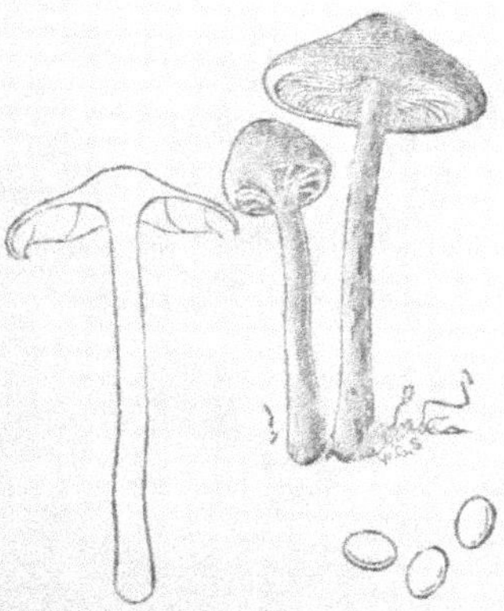

Fig. 44.

Pileus thin, but fleshy, with no viscid pellicle, entirely dry, not hygrophanous, at first clothed with a superficial down, then glabrous; stem thin, somewhat stuffed, equal or attenuated, not bulbous; gills changeable in colour.

The species are polymorphous and defined with difficulty, in consequence of the changeable colour of the gills. (*Fig.* 44.)

513. Cortinarius (Dermocybe) ochroleucus. *Fr.* "Pallid Cortinarius."

Pileus fleshy, convex, gibbous, then obtuse, even, nearly smooth, pallid-white; stem solid, firm, ventricose, white, fibrillose above, veiled; gills adnexed, nearly free, crowded, whitish, clay-coloured ochre.—*Fr. Epicr. p.* 284. *Schæff. t.* 54.

In woods. Rare. Mossburnford. [United States.]

Stem solid, 3 in. long, ½ in. thick, naked, white, apex and veil fibrillose. Pileus 2 in. broad, minutely silky, then smooth, pallid, at length nearly white. Flesh firm, white.

514. Cortinarius (Dermocybe) tabularis. *Fr.* "Flat Cortinarius."

Pileus fleshy, equal, soon plane, flocculose, then smooth, brownish clay-coloured, becoming pale; stem stuffed, tough, elastic, white, closely fibrilloso-squamose or smooth; gills emarginate, crowded, whitish, then clay-coloured.—*Fr. Epicr. p.* 284. *Bull. t.* 431, *f.* 5.

In woods. Common.

Stem stuffed, at length hollow, tough, elastic, attenuated at the base or equal, 2-3 in. long, 3 lin. and more thick, erect; veil whitish, fugacious; pileus 3 in. or more broad, clay-coloured, then brownish clay colour, growing pale. Gills 3 lin. broad. Flesh white.

515. Cortinarius (Dermocybe) diabolicus. *Fr.* "Tawny Cortinarius."

Pileus fleshy, thin, hemispherical, obtuse, then gibbous, brownish, clothed with grey threads, at length smooth, yellowish tawny; stem stuffed, rather thin, smooth, growing pale, bluish-grey above; gills sub-emarginate, adnexed, crowded, pallid (whitish or fugacious blue-grey), then clay-coloured.—*Fr. Epicr. p.* 285.

In woods.

Stem 3 in. long, usually slender, 2 lin. thick, sometimes twice that thickness. Pileus 1 in. broad and more, dry, fragile, soon rimose; gills adnate, 2 lines and more broad, firm.

516. Cortinarius (Dermocybe) caninus. *Fr.* "Rufous Cortinarius."

Pileus fleshy, convexo-plane, obtuse, becoming smooth, bright-rufous, changing colour; stem clavato-bulbose, elastic, closely fibrillose, pallid, violaceous above; gills emarginate, broad, rather distant, purplish, then cinnamon.—*Fr. Epicr. p.* 285. *Bull. t.* 544. *f.* i. *Boxb.* iv. *t.* 22. *Saund. and Sm. t.* 15.

In woods. King's Cliffe.

Stem stuffed, spongy within, at length hollow, 3 in. and upwards long, ½ in. thick, thickened at the base, somewhat bulbous. Veil in the perfect state double. Pileus 3-4 in. broad, firm, colour variable, tawny, brown, or brick red. Flesh white, at length somewhat yellowish.

517. Cortinarius (Dermocybe) anomalus. *Fr.* "Thin-capped Cortinarius."

Pileus fleshy, thin, convex, obtuse, then gibbous, dingy-rufous, discoloured with evanescent fibrils; stem somewhat stuffed, thin, attenuated, fibrillose, rather scaly, pallid-violaceous; gills crowded, with a decurrent tooth, bluish-purple, then cinnamon.—*Fr. Epicr. p.* 286. *Bull. t.* 431, *f.* 3. *Letell. t.* 634. *Berk. Outl. t.* 12, *f.* 4. *Eng. Fl.* v. *p.* 86.

In woods. Common. [United States.]

Pileus 1-2 in. broad, very obtuse, sometimes broadly, but very flatly umbonate, tinged at first with violet, minutely silky, so as to present a white satiny appearance, gradually changing to ochraceous or slightly tawny, flesh thick, except at the extreme margin, which has often traces of the arachnoid veil dusted with the spores; gills close, rounded behind, at first violet, at length pale ferruginous; stem 2½ in. high, ⅜ in. thick, in the middle subbulbous, more or less tinged with violet, solid, fibrillose, with more or less distinct, transverse, closely pressed, brownish scales, which originate in the veil, the top adorned with the descending fibres of the veil, which form a spurious ring; beneath this there is sometimes another red circle, which is the true ring.—*M. J. B.*

518. Cortinarius (Dermocybe) spilomeus. *Fr.* "Scaly-stemmed Cortinarius."

Pileus slightly fleshy, gibbous, dry, becoming smooth, brownish, changing colour; stem nearly hollow, thin, white or lilac, variegated with rufous or tawny scales; gills emarginate, crowded, narrow, bluish-lilac, pallid, at length cinnamon.—*Fr. Epicr. p.* 287. *Eng. Fl.* v. *p.* 85. *Sow. t.* 384, *f.* 1?

In woods. King's Cliffe, Bristol. [United States.]

Pileus 1 in. broad, slightly fleshy, colour various, when young whitish, then ferruginous, tinged with fuscous, yellowish when dry. Gills violet, then lilac, at length cinnamon. Stem 2-4 in. high, 2-3 lines thick, white, tinged with violet.—*Fries.*

519. Cortinarius (Dermocybe) sanguineus. *Fr.* "Blood-red Cortinarius."

Pileus fleshy, thin, obtuse, innate, silky, or squamulose; stem stuffed, then hollow, thin, equal, as well as the veil, dark blood-red; gills crowded, rather broad, darker.—*Fr. Epicr. p.* 288. *Jacq. Coll.* ii. *t.* 15, *f.* 3. *Sow. t.* 43. *Bolt. t.* 56. *Eng. Fl.* v. *p.* 87. *Krombh. t.* 2, *f.* 28, 30. *Fl. Boruss. t.* 385.

In woods.

Pileus about 1 in. across, convex, blood-red; gills sometimes adnate, sometimes emarginate; stem stuffed, then hollow.—*Fries.* Dried specimens retain their colour many years. Spores ·00025 × ·00017 in.

520. Cortinarius (Dermocybe) cinnamomeus. *Fr.* "Cinnamon Cortinarius."

Pileus fleshy, thin, obtuse, umbonate, cinnamon-brown, silky with innate yellowish fibrils, or squamulose, at length becoming smooth; stem stuffed, then hollow, thin, equal; flesh and veil yellowish; gills adnate, broad, crowded, shining.—*Fr. Epicr. p.* 288. *Krombh. t.* 71, *f.* 12-15. *Letell. t.* 652. *Bolt. t.* 156. *Sow. t.* 205. *Vars. Eng. Fl.* v. *p.* 88. *Mag. Zool. & Bot. no.* 49.

In woods. [United States.]

Pileus 1-2½ in. broad, convex, or even obtusely conical when young, becoming nearly plane, obtusely umbonate, deep reddish-cinnamon, often cracking at the margin, which is thin and sometimes fibrillose, smooth, somewhat fleshy; flesh yellowish; gills numerous, adnate, yellow cinnamon, broad, margin often notched; stem 2-3 in. high, 2-4 lines thick, equal, fibrillose, yellow, solid, hollow in old plants.—*Grev.*

(Fig. 44, reduced.)

521. Cortinarius (Dermocybe) uliginosus. *Berk.* "Bog Cortinarius."

Pileus campanulato-conical, then expanded, bright red brown, very strongly umbonate, silky, sometimes streaked, flesh yellow-olive, then cinnamon; stem flexuous, paler than the pileus; gills distant, adnate with a tooth, yellow, then olive, then cinnamon. —*Berk Outl. p.* 191.

In boggy woods amongst *Sphagnum.* King's Cliffe.

Pileus not exceeding 2 in. in diameter, of a beautiful red brown (almost brick-red), and remarkable for its very strong but scarcely acute umbo.—*M. J. B.*

522. Cortinarius (Dermocybe) raphanoides. *Fr.* "Olive Cortinarius."

Olivaceous, then discoloured; pileus fleshy, campanulate, then expanded, gibbous, silky with innate fibrils; stem stuffed, firm, fibrillose, opaque, and veil paler; gills adnato-ventricose, rather crowded, olivaceous then cinnamon.—*Fr. Epicr. p.* 290. *Mich. t.* 75, *f.* 2? *Eng. Fl.* v. *p.* 88.

In beech and fir woods. Scotch Highlands.

Pileus 2 in. broad, when moist brownish-olive, when dry yellowish-olive, convex at first, then expanded. Gills broad, darker, adnate, or emarginate; stem 3 in. high, 4 lines thick, subascending, fibrillose, villous at the base.—*Fries.*

Sub-Gen. 5. TELAMONIA. Fr. Epicr. p. 291.

Fig. 45.

Pileus moist, hygrophanous, at first glabrous or sprinkled with the arachnoid superficial fibres of the veil, thin or moderately compact in the disc; stem peronate, and annulate from an inferior veil. Mostly large and handsome. (*Fig.* 45.)

523. Cortinarius (Telamonia) bulbosus. *Fr.* "Bulbous Cortinarius."

Pileus somewhat fleshy, campanulate, then expanded, smooth, bright brown; disc fleshy, subgibbous; stem stout, bulbous, pallid, or paler than the pileus, veil white, peronate, subannulate; gills adnate, rather distant, opaque, cinnamon.—*Fr. Epicr. p.* 292. *Sow. t.* 130. *Eng. Fl.* v. *p.* 84.

In woods. Rare.

Pileus 2-3 in. broad, fibrillose under a lens, brittle, margin thin; gills rounded, subadnate, distinct, 3-5 lines broad. Stem 3-4 in. high, subfibrillose, in full grown specimens ferruginous at the base. Smell like that of radishes.—*Fries.*

524. Cortinarius (Telamonia) torvus. *Fr.* "Crabby Cortinarius."

Pileus fleshy, convex, then expanded, obtuse, pale-red brown, whitish with fibrils or scales, at length pierced, smooth; stem stout, sheathed with the white persistent veil, annulate, veil violaceous at the apex; gills thick, distant, very broad, purplish-umber then cinnamon.—*Fr. Epicr. p.* 293. *Bull. t.* 600, *f. Q. R. S. Krombh. t.* 73, *f.* 19-21? *Eng. Fl.* v. *p.* 82.

In woods.

Pileus 3 in. or more broad; stem 3-5 in. high, ½-1 in. thick, violet, but clothed below with the white veil.

525. Cortinarius (Telamonia) evernius. *Fr.* "Tufted Cortinarius."

Pileus between fleshy and membranaceous, conico-campanulate, then expanded, smooth, purplish-bay, reddish-white, at length fibrillose and torn; stem stout, cylindrical, soft, violaceous, scaly from the remains of the white veil; gills adnate, very broad, distant, purplish-violet.—*Fr. Epicr. p.* 294. *Sow. t.* 125. *Eng. Fl.* v. *p.* 83.

In woods.

Tufted or subgregarious. Pileus 1-2 in. broad, purple brown, shining with a satiny lustre, umbonate, the umbo generally subumbilicate; flesh moderately thick in the centre. Gills very broad, at length subferruginous, distant, adnate for half their breadth. Stem 2½-4 in. high, ⅜ in. thick, undulated, silky, much paler than the pileus, with a few slight traces of the veil. —*M. J. B.*

526. Cortinarius (Telamonia) armillatus. *Fr.* "Red-zoned Cortinarius."

Pileus fleshy, campanulate, then expanded, soon innato-fibrillose and scaly, torn, bright red brown, margin thin; stem solid, elongated, bulbous, fibrillose, rufescent, circled by a red zone; gills fixed, very broad, distant, pallid, then dark cinnamon.—*Fr. Epicr. p.* 295. *Bull. t.* 527, *f.* 1. *Huss.* i. *t.* 19.

In woods.

Stem solid, firm, 3-6 in. long, ½ in. thick, remarkable for its blood-red zone. Pileus 3-5 in. broad, dry, brick red, at first smooth, soon innato-fibrillose or squamulose. Odour of radishes.

527. Cortinarius (Telamonia) limonius. *Fr.* "Lemon Cortinarius."

Pileus fleshy, convexo-plane, obtuse, smooth, tawny (ochraceous yellow), at length rivuloso-squamulose; stem solid, firm, equal; veil floccoso-squamose, of the same colour; gills adnate, emarginate, rather distant, yellow, then tawny-cinnamon. *Fr. Epicr. p.* 296. *Holms.* ii. *t.* 40. *Eng. Fl.* v. *p.* 84.

In pine woods.

Pileus 2-4 in. broad, when dry ochrey-yellow, subsquarrose; gills sometimes adnate, sometimes emarginate, veil rarely forming a perfect ring. Stem 2-4 in. high, ½ in. thick, firm, fibrillose, dull yellow, sometimes saffron-red.—*Fries.*

528. Cortinarius (Telamonia) hinnuleus. *Fr.* "Fawn Cortinarius."

Pileus between fleshy and membranaceous, conico-campanulate, then expanded, sub-umbonate, smooth, pallid, tawny cinnamon, at length pierced; stem stuffed, rigid, tawny, attenuated downwards, girt above by the white silky veil; gills sub-emarginate, distant, broad, thin, quite entire, tawny-cinnamon.—*Fr. Epicr. p.* 296. *Sow.* t. 173.

In woods. Common.

Stem sometimes short, about 1 in. sometimes 2 in. long, 2-3 lines thick, and sometimes 3-4 in. long and flexuous. Pileus obtuse or obtusely umbonate, pale tawny cinnamon, growing paler, shining when dry. Flesh of the same colour. (*Fig.* 45, *reduced.*)

529. Cortinarius (Telamonia) gentilis. *Fr.* "Delicate Cortinarius."

Pileus rather fleshy, conical, then expanded, acutely umbonate, even, smooth, at length cracked; stem slender, equal, squamose, with tawny-cinnamon (yellowish) scales, and oblique; ring yellow; gills adnate, thick, very distant, quite entire, tawny-cinnamon, of one colour.—*Fr. Epicr. p.* 297. *Br. Bath. Trans.* 1870, *p.* 72. *Fr. Mon. Hym.* ii. *p.* 87.

In pine woods. Box. Hanham.

Gregarious, tawny-cinnamon. Stem 2 lines thick, nearly straight, usually attenuated at the base. Pileus ½-1 in., rarely more, frequently squamulose, of the same colour as the stem, hygrophanous, when dry bright yellow and silky.

530. Cortinarius (Telamonia) helvelloides. *Fr.* "Thick-gilled Cortinarius."

Pileus rather fleshy, thin, sub-convex, obsoletely umbonate, ferruginous, at length rimose. Stem fistulose, slender, undulate, silky-fibrillose, as well as the veil yellowish, gills adnate, very distant, violaceous-umber then cinnamon, edge whitish-floccose.—*Fr. Epicr. p.* 297. *Ann. N.H. no.* 929.

In woods.

Stem fistulose, 2-3 in. long, 1-2 lin. thick, equal, veil yellowish, about the margin of the pileus silky. Pileus ½-1 in. broad, striate, when mature rimose and squarrose, tawny when dry. Gills adnate, very thick and distant.

531. Cortinarius (Telamonia) periscelis. *Weinm.* "Lilac and White Cortinarius."

Pileus campanulate, then convex, lilac and white. silky, umbo fleshy, elsewhere membranaceous; stem equal, fibrillose, of the same colour; veil woven, brownish, sub-annulate; gills adnate, crowded, narrow pallid, then obscurely ferruginous.—*Fr. Epicr. p.* 300. *Ann. N.H. no.* 694.

In bogs or under beech. Bowood.

Stem 3-4 in. long, 2-3 lines thick, straight, brownish when dry, whitish villous at the base. Pileus 2 in. broad, hygrophanous.—*Fries*.

532. Cortinarius (Telamonia) psammocephalus. *Fr.* "Little Tawny Cortinarius."

Tawny cinnamon; pileus rather fleshy, convex then expanded, at length umbonate, furfuraceo-squamulose, stem stuffed, attenuated, squamulose, sheathed with the contiguous veil; gills adnate, arcuate, crowded.—*Fr. Epicr. p.* 301. *Bull. t.* 531, *f.* 2. *Ann. N.H. no.* 695.

In woods. King's Cliffe.

Pileus about an inch across. Stem one inch long, gills darker than the pileus, flesh of the same colour, not white.

533. Cortinarius (Telamonia) ileopodius. *Fr.* "Tan-coloured Cortinarius."

Pileus rather fleshy, convex, subumbonate, at first with silky-white threads, becoming smooth, light reddish-yellow (tan coloured), at length even and rimose; stem equal, thin, tawny (without and within), sheathed with a pallid veil, naked upwards, fibrilloso-striate; gills adnate, somewhat crowded, thin, inclining to cinnamon.—*Fr. Epicr. p.* 301. *Bull. t.* 586, *f.* 2, *A. B. Eng. Fl.* v. *p.* 88.

In woods. July—Nov. [United States.]

Pileus ¾ in. broad, at first conic, with the silky veil attached to the margin, then convex, rather acutely umbonate, the umbo cinnamon, then brownish, changing to ochraceous, sub-carnose, silky, especially on the margin, which is pellucid when moist; gills at first pale, changing to dark cinnamon. Stem 2 in. or more high, scarce 1 line thick, rufescent, pruinose, or sericeo-squamulose, moderately tough, at length hollow.—*M. J. B.*

534. Cortinarius (Telamonia) hemitrichus. *Fr.* "Fringed Cortinarius."

Pileus somewhat fleshy, convexo-plane, umbonate, brown (tan coloured), margin fringed or silky with dense white superficial fibrils; stem hollow, nearly equal, pallid, brown, floccoso-squamose from the white veil, and annulate; gills adnate, crowded, clay coloured, then cinnamon.—*Fr. Epicr. p.* 302. *Ann. N.H. no.* 930.

In woods. Sept. Lea. [S. Carolina.]

Stem 1½-2½ in. long, thick, firm; pileus acute or obtuse, 1-3 in. broad, with the margin fringed, or altogether covered with superficial erect white fibrils, becoming smooth, colour dark brown, tan coloured when dry.

Sub-Gen. 6. HYGROCYBE. Fr. Epicr. p. 303.

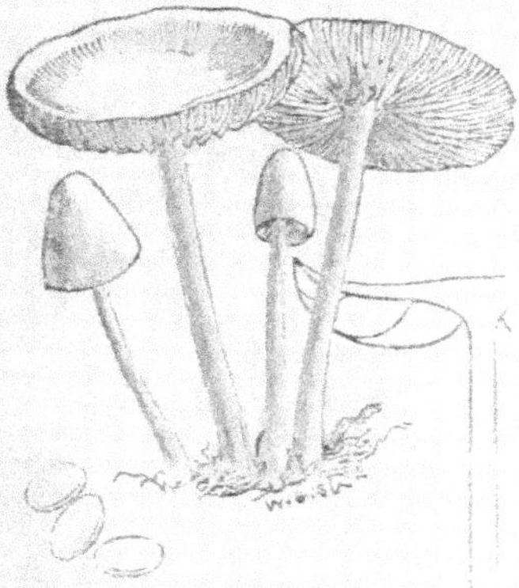

Pileus generally thin, glabrous, hygrophanous, but not viscid, cuticle rigid, not fibrolacerate; stem rigid, subcartilaginous without, never annulated or scaly.

(*Fig.* 46.)

Fig. 46.

535. Cortinarius (Hygrocybe) Armeniacus. *Fr.* "Peach Cortinarius."

Pileus somewhat fleshy, convexo-plane, gibbous, even, smooth, tawny-cinnamon (at length tan coloured), shining; stem stuffed, conical, attenuated, rigid, soft within, as well as the sub-peronate veil white; gills adnate, crowded, pallid, then tawny cinnamon.—*Fr. Epicr, p.* 304. *Schæff. t.* 81. *Eng. Fl.* v. *p.* 88. *Ann. N.H. no.* 696.

In pine woods. [United States.]

Pileus 2-4 in. broad, campanulate, soon convex, expanded, sometimes acutely umbonate, margin thin, patent, moist, not viscid, when dry tan, inclining to light red; gills distinct, 2-3 lines broad, when young watery-cinnamon; stem 2-3 in. high, 2 lines-2 in. thick, rather soft, sometimes violet above, conic or sub-equal, veil rather woven.—*Fries.*

536. Cortinarius (Hygrocybe) dilutus. *Fr.* "Bolton's Cortinarius."

Pileus somewhat fleshy, convexo-plane, sub-umbonate, smooth, even, opaque, light red; stem stuffed, then hollow, soft, pallid, thickened at the base, veil fibrillose; gills emarginate, adnexed, broad, crowded, pallid cinnamon.—*Fr. Epicr. p.* 305. *Bolt. t.* 10.

In woods. Halifax.

Not found since the time of Bolton. Stem 2-3 in. long, 2-4 lines thick, whitish, at first silky, then becoming smooth. Pileus about 2 in. broad; when moist of a brick-red, tan-coloured when dry, but variable, in either state opaque. Gills deeply emarginate, very ventricose, 3-4 lin. broad, crowded.

537. Cortinarius (Hygrocybe) castaneus. *Fr.* "Chestnut Cortinarius."

Pileus somewhat fleshy, firm, campanulate or convex, then expanded or gibbous, even, chestnut (shining); stem cartilaginous, stuffed, then hollow, even, violaceous, or pallid-rufescent; veil white, fibrillose; gills fixed, ventricose, rather crowded, violet, then ferruginous.—*Fr. Epicr. p.* 307. *Bull. t.* 268. *Eng. Fl.* v. *p.* 89.

In woods and gardens. Common. Esculent.

[United States.]

Gregarious. Pileus 1 in. or more broad, sub-carnose, at first obtuse, with a delicate fibrillose veil, which makes the margin appear silvery, dark bay or dirty violet, sometimes with a tawny tint, soon expanded, broadly umbonate; umbo more or less obtuse; gills of the colour of the pileus, or purplish umber, at length sub-ferruginous, ventricose, adnate. Stem 1½ in. high, 2 lines thick, beautifully fibrillose, and white from the veil beneath, much paler than the pileus, but with more or less of the same tint, sometimes tinged with violet. Odour none; taste like *Marasmius oreades*.—*M. J. B.*

538. Cortinarius (Hygrocybe) Reedii. *Berk.* "Reed's Cortinarius."

Pileus conical, then expanded and strongly umbonate, smooth, shining, persistently brown, disc areolate, margin splitting; stem white, solid, fibrilloso-striate, slightly bulbous; veil fibrillose, evanescent; gills broad, ventricose, ascending, attenuated behind, free, white or pallid, then cinnamon.—*Berk. Outl. p.* 194. *Huss.* ii. *t.* 45.

Amongst moss and beech mast. May. Hayes. Surrey.

Stem 1½-2 in. high. Flesh pallid. Tasteless and scentless.

539. Cortinarius (Hygrocybe) rigens. *Fr.* "Rigid Cortinarius."

Pileus somewhat fleshy, conical, soon convex, obtuse, even, smooth, opaque, clay-coloured; stem cartilaginous, rigid, rooting, smooth, naked, white, somewhat attenuated upwards; gills adnate, sub-decurrent, broad, distant, clay-coloured, then dark cinnamon.—*Fr. Epicr. p.* 311. *Ann. N.H. no.* 931.

In woods. Mossburnford.

Stem elastic, rigid, and tough, pallid when moist, white when dry, 2-4 in. long, 2-5 lin. thick. Veil scarcely manifest. Pileus 1-2 in. or more broad. Flesh rather firm, white.

540. Cortinarius (Hygrocybe) leucopus. *Fr.* "White-stemmed Cortinarius."

Pileus rather fleshy, conical, then expanded, at length umbonate, even, smooth, light red, shining; stem stuffed, then hollow, equal, white; gills sub-adnexed, ventricose, crowded, pallid, then cinnamon.—*Fr. Epicr. p.* 311. *Bull. t.* 533, *f.* 2.

In woods.

Stem 1-2 in. long, 2-4 lin. thick, soft, white. Pileus scarcely an inch broad, moist, but not viscid, light red, tan-coloured when dry. Gills adnexed, seceding, crowded, ventricose, pallid, then cinnamon, edge quite entire and of the same colour. (*Fig.* 46, *reduced.*)

541. Cortinarius (Hygrocybe) decipiens. *Fr.* "Deceptive Cortinarius."

Pileus submembranaceous, conical, smooth, shining, bay-brown (brick-red), at length depressed around the somewhat fleshy, prominent, darker umbo; stem sub-fistulose, equal, slender, covered with a pallid, separable cuticle, internally rather bright brown; gills adnate, thin, somewhat crowded, ferruginous brown. *Fr. Ep. p.* 312. *Pers. Syn. p.* 289. *B. & Br. Ann. N.H.* (1866), *no.* 1129.

In woods. Sept. King's Cliffe. [United States.]

Stem 2-4 in. long 1-2 lines thick, straight or flexuose, pale rufous, or spotted with brick-red. Pileus about an inch broad, smooth, shining, bay, umbo darker, margin when mature finely striate.

542. Cortinarius (Hygrocybe) acutus. *Fr.* "Acute Cortinarius."

Pileus membranaceous, conical, acutely umbonate, striate, light reddish-brown (at length tan-coloured and even); stem fistulose, equal, slender, flexuose, growing pale, veil fugacious, white; gills adnate, rather crowded, thin, narrow, quite entire, ochraceous.—*Fr. Epicr. p.* 314. *Ann. N.H. no.* 797.

On moist spots in fir woods. [United States.]

Cæspitose, with the habit of a *Galera*. Stem slender, 3 in or more long, 1-2 lines thick. Veil adhering to the margin, fibrillose, white.

543. Cortinarius (Hygrocybe) Junghuhnii. *Fr.* "Junghuhn's Cortinarius."

Pileus rather fleshy, thin, conical, then expanded, papillate, clothed with innate, white, thin fibrils, persistently rather velvety, shining cinnamon; stem stuffed, equal, sub-flexuous, pale red-brown, with shining, closely-pressed, brown fibrils; gills adnate, thin, ventricose, saffron yellow, then red brown.—*Fr. Ep. p.* 314. *B. & Br. Ann. N.H.* (1866) *no.* 1130.

In woods. Aug. King's Cliffe.

Stem 2-3 in. high, 2 lines thick, internally darker, base whitish. Veil obsolete. Pileus 1 in., striate to the middle when moist. Gills 2 lines broad, veined at the base. Spores ·0003 in. long.

Gen. **5.** **LEPISTA.** Smith. Seem. Journ. 1870.

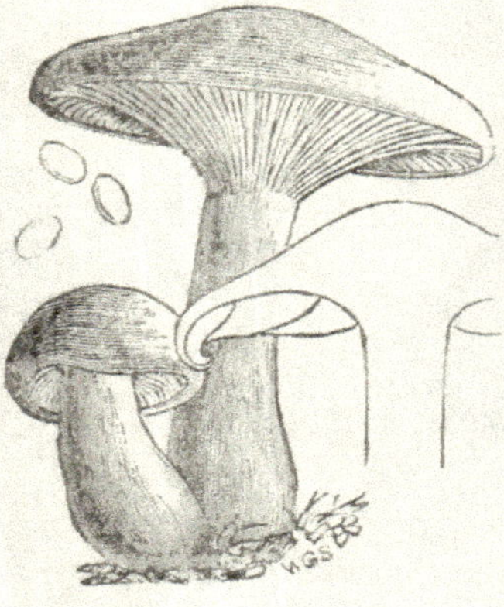

Fig 47.

Spores (as well as the whole plant) dirty white; pileus with an involute margin gradually increasing indefinitely; stem continuous with the horny hymenophore; gills fragile, persistent, decurrent, anastomosing behind or branching, membranaceous, entire, with a sharp edge, supported by a horny trama. (*Fig.* 47.)

HAB. All the species are terrestrial.

The character of the spores, the presence of a trama, and the habitat of the section of *Lepista* of *Paxillus*, as established by Fries, appear to me to be so important that I have given it a generic position.—*W. G. S.*

544. **Lepista nuda.** *Bull.* "Amethyst Lepista."

Pileus fleshy, rather thin, convex, then expanded and depressed, obtuse, smooth, moist, changing colour; margin inflexed, thin, naked; stem stuffed, elastic, equal, rather mealy; gills rounded behind, or slightly decurrent, crowded, narrow, violet, stained when old with reddish-brown.—*Bull. t.* 439. *Fr. Epicr. p.* 48. *Krombh. t.* 71, *f.* 27-29. *Price. f.* 35. *Paul. t.* 78, *f.* 3. *Berk. Outl. t.* 4, *f.* 7. *Eng. Fl.* v. *p.* 20.

In plantations, woods, &c., especially among pines.

[United States.]

Smaller than *L. personata*, and more brightly coloured. Pileus 2 in. broad, thin, obtuse, plane or sub-depressed, at first amethyst-coloured, but changing to a pinky rufous, margin involute. Gills of the same colour as the pileus, rounded behind, sometimes adnate-decurrent, connected and traversed by veins. Stem 2 in. high, 3-4 lines thick, stuffed, sub-equal, at first fibrillose, at length nearly smooth, more or less of the colour of the pileus.—*M. J. B.* Spores dirty white, ·0002 × ·00013 in. (*Fig.* 47, *reduced.*)

545. **Lepista cinerascens.** *Bull.* "Cinereous Lepista."

Pileus fleshy, convex, then expanded, obtuse, smooth, even; margin thin, naked, striate; stem stuffed, elastic, sub-equal, smooth; gills rounded behind, crowded, rather undulated, veined at the base, easily separating from the pileus, white, then reddish-grey, at length yellowish.—*Bull. t.* 428, *f.* 2. *Fr. Epicr. p.* 50. *Ann. N.H. no.* 787.

In woods. Aug.

Cæspitose. Pileus 2-3 in. across, convex, of a dirty pale ochre, slightly streaked with watery lines, firm but not brittle, clothed with very obscure matted down, flesh thin, white. Stem curved, slightly streaked, tinged like the pileus, paler above, and slightly pulverulent, solid, stringy. Gills moderately distant, at first attenuated behind, at length rounded and easily separating, white, or very slightly ochraceous, stained like the pileus when old and bruised, very slightly anastomosing behind. Spores certainly not cinereous, but white. Smell rather disagreeable, pungent.—*M. J. B.*

546. **Lepista personata.** *Fr.* "Purple-stemmed Lepista."

Pileus at first compact, then soft, convex, then plane, obtuse, even, smooth, moist; margin at first involute, villoso-pruinose; stem solid, blunt, somewhat bulbous, villous, stained with lilac; gills rounded behind, then free, crowded, broad, dirty white.—*Fr. Epicr. p.* 48. *Berk. Outl. t.* 5, *f.* 1. *Smith. E.M.* 18. *Huss.* ii. *t.* 40. *Fl. Dan. t.* 1133. *Cooke, B.F. t.* 4, *f.* 1. *Eng. Fl.* v. *p.* 19. *Gard. Chron.* (1861), *p.* 696, *fig. Badh.* i. *t.* 8, *f.* 1, ii. *t.* 1, *f.* 2.

In pastures. Common. Esculent. [United States.]

Gregarious, frequently in large rings. Pileus 2-6 in. broad, fleshy, firm, pale bistre or purple lilac, occasionally violet, convex, obtuse, very smooth and shining as if oiled, but not viscid; margin involute, pulverulento-tomentose; gills rounded, free, not distant, narrow in front, paler than the pileus, sometimes violet, turning to a dirty flesh colour, especially when bruised. Stem 1-3 in. high, $\frac{3}{4}$ in. thick, firm, bulbous, solid, mottled within towards the apex with watery spots, clothed more or less with villous fibrils, tinged with violet. Odour rather overpowering, taste pleasant.—*M. J. B.* Spores ·00024 × ·00016 in.

The three British species included in this new genus were formerly classed by Fries with the sub-genus *Tricholoma*, but removed by him, in his latest work, to *Lepista*, as a sub-genus of *Paxillus*. We have followed Mr. W G. Smith in his arrangement recently proposed in "Seemann's Journal of Botany," but not without some hesitation, in separating *Lepista* from *Paxillus*, and giving it a generic position.—*M. C. C.*

Gen. **6. PAXILLUS,** Fr. Gen. Hymen. p. 8, *ex parte.*

Fig. 48.

Spores (as well as the whole plant) ferruginous; pileus with an involute margin, and gradually increasing indefinitely; stem continuous with the hymenophore; gills tough, soft, persistent, decurrent, anastomosing behind, or branching, membranaceous, entire, with a sharp edge, separating from the horny or furrowed hymenophore; trama absent.

HAB. Some on the ground, others on trunks of trees, sawdust, &c. (*Fig.* 48.)

547. Paxillus involutus. *Fr.* "Involute Paxillus."

Pileus compact, convexo-plane, then depressed, moist, becoming smooth, margin involute and tomentose; stem fleshy, solid, firm, naked, thickened upwards, paler; gills branched, broad, porous and anastomosing behind, paler, besmeared and spotted.—*Fr. Epicr. p.* 317. *Batsch. f.* 61. *Sow. t.* 98. *Schæff. t.* 72. *Bull. t.* 240, 576, *f.* 2. *Krombh. t.* 71, *f.* 24-26. *Paul. t.* 61? 62, 63, *f.* 1. *Buxb.* iv. *t.* 26. *Schæff t.* 71, *var. Berk. Outl. t.* 12, *f.* 5. *Ag. involutus, Eng. Fl.* v. *p.* 101. *Fl. Boruss. t.* 391. *Vent. t.* 42, *f.* 6-7.

On the ground. Common. [United States.]

Pileus 3-5 in. broad, wavy, tawny or yellow-ferruginous when moist, slimy, uneven; margin involute and downy, the extreme edge striate from the pressure of the gills; flesh thick, firm, at first pale, changing to dirty umber on exposure to the air, as does every part of the plant when bruised, black when dried; gills pale yellow ferruginous, wavy forked, decurrent, poriform behind, easily separating from the pileus; stem 2-3 in. high, ½-1 in. or more thick, blunt, sometimes attenuated below, tomentoso-squamulose, firm, solid.—*M. J. B.* Spores ·00026 × ·0002 in. (*Fig.* 48, *reduced.*)

548. Paxillus atro-tomentosus. *Fr.* "Dark-downy Paxillus."

Pileus fleshy, convexo-plane, then depressed or infundibuliform, granulose, rivulose; margin thin, involute; stem between spongiose and solid, firm, velvety; gills crowded, straight, branched behind.—*Fr. Epicr. p.* 317. *Batsch. f.* 32. *Nees. f.* 175. *Paul. t.* 33, *f.* 2-3. *Ann. N.H. no.* 697.

On pine stumps. Wilts.

Stem solid, elastic, 2-3 in. long, ½-1 in. thick, curved, ascending, rooting, clad with a dense, velvety, soft, blackish umber down; pileus compact, excentric, 2-4 in. or more broad, dry, ferruginous; gills adnate or decurrent, branched at the base and somewhat anastomosing, yellowish.

549. Paxillus panuoides. *Fr.* "Pale Paxillus."

Pileus fleshy, dimidiate, conchate, at length smooth, dirty yellow, elongated behind, sessile or stipitate; gills decurrent, crowded, branched, crisped, yellow.—*Fr. Epicr. p.* 318. *Buxb.* ii. *t.* 49, *f.* 2. *Sow. t.* 403. *Berk. Outl. t.* 12, *f.* 6. *Letell. t.* 665. *Eng. Fl.* v. *p.* 102.

In cellars, on sawdust, &c. Coed Coch, &c.

Pileus 1-4 in. broad, white, often tinged with violet, very soft to the touch in consequence of the fine-matted silky pubescence with which it is clothed, either perfectly sessile, or furnished with a spurious stem which is silky like the pileus and most beautifully tinged with violet; gills variously anastomosing and wrinkled, yellow with abundant oval ferruginous spores.—*M. J. B.* Spores ·00018 × ·00013 in.

Gen. **7. HYGROPHORUS,** Fr. Epicr. p. 320.

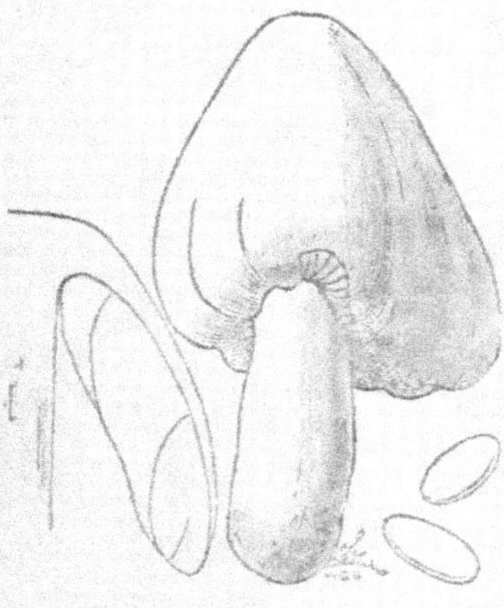

Fig. 49.

Spores white; veil, when present, universal; stem confluent with the hymenophore; gills sharp-edged; trama similar in substance to that of the pileus. (*Fig.* 49.)

Hab. On the ground, mostly late in the autumn, some in the summer.

Most of the species are handsome and easily recognized. From *Agaricus* this genus differs by the manifest trama, the substance of which is similar to that of the pileus; from *Lactarius* and *Russula* by the trama not being vesicular, but subfloccose, and intermixed with granules; and from its nearest ally, *Cantharellus*, by the sharp-edged gills. In *Cortinarius, Paxillus*, and *Gomphidius*, the spores are coloured, and the gills lose their colour.

This genus is distinguished by the hymenophore being changed into a waxy mass, and at length detached from the trama. Many species are sapid and edible.—*W. G. S.*

Sect. 1. *Limacium.*

550. Hygrophorus chrysodon. *Fr.* "Yellow-downy Hygrophorus."

White; pileus fleshy, convexo-plane, viscid, margin involute; stem stuffed, subequal, squamulose (yellowish), floccose above;

gills rather thin, distant, at length crisped.—*Fr. Epicr.* 320. *Batsch. f.* 212. *Fl. Dan. t. Ann. N.H. no.* 258.

In woods. [S. Carolina.]

Resembles closely, in many respects, *H. eburneus*, but is beautifully distinguished by the golden yellow pubescence, which is sprinkled here and there over the plant, but principally on the stem and margin of the pileus. Sometimes the gills are elegantly edged with yellow flocci. Smell strong.

551. Hygrophorus eburenus. *Fr.* "Ivory Hygrophorus."

White; pileus fleshy, even, smooth, margin entire; stem stuffed, then hollow, unequal, punctate above with glandular scales; gills firm, distant, straight.—*Fr. Epicr. p.* 321. *Bull. t.* 551, *f.* 2. *Lenz. f.* 8. *Schæff. t.* 39. *Buxb.* iv. *t.* 30, *f.* 2. *Berk. Outl. t.* 15, *f.* 1. *Eng. Fl.* v. *p.* 13. *Price, f.* 19. *Krombh. t.* 61, *f.* 11-14.

In woods. Oct. Nov. Esculent. [S. Carolina.]

Pileus 2-3 in. broad, shining when dry; stem at length hollow, very various in stature, flexuous in elongated specimens.—*Fries.* Spores ·00017 × ·00022 in.

552. Hygrophorus cossus. *Fr.* "Goat-moth Hygrophorus."

White; pileus fleshy, even, smooth, viscid, inclining to yellowish, margin naked; stem stuffed, subequal, furfuraceous above; gills thin, distant, straight.—*Fr. Epicr. p.* 321. *Sow. t.* 121. *Eng. Fl.* v. *p.* 13. *Mag. Zool. & Bot. no.* 40. *Berk. exs. no.* 2.

In woods. Oct. Strong scented.

Pileus 1½ in. broad, pure white, slimy, shining when dry, stained here and there with yellowish, the disc sometimes sub-ochraceous. Gills broad, thick, distant, adnato-decurrent, connected by veins, and themselves slightly veined. Spores white, elliptic. Stem 2½ in high, 1-3 lines thick, nearly equal, here and there yellow when bruised. Smell like that of the larva of the goat-moth.—*M. J. B.*

553. Hygrophorus cerasinus. *B.* "Waxy Hygrophorus."

Pileus fleshy, convex, broadly umbonate, pale umber, then grey, viscid, margin minutely tomentose; stem white, solid, attenuated below, punctato-squamulose above; gills broad, decurrent, white, tinged with pink, sometimes forked, very distant.—*Berk. Outl. p.* 197. *Eng. Fl.* v. *p.* 12.

In fir plantations. Oct. Rare. Winkbourn, Notts.

Subgregarious, sometimes three from the same root. Pileus 1½ to 2½ in. broad, pale umber, or ochraceous-bistre, inclining to grey when old, fleshy, convex, broadly umbonate, often more or less wavy, at length sometimes somewhat depressed, viscid, shining when dry; margin clothed with minute white down, divided into little linear heaps by the pressure of the gills in the early stage of growth; gills broad, decurrent, white, with a slight tinge of ochre or flesh colour, thick, very distant, some of them forked. Stem 1-2 in. high, 2-6 lines thick, white, solid, generally attenuated below, punctato-squamulose above. Odour pleasant, like cherry laurel leaves.—*M. J. B.*

554. Hygrophorus aromaticus. *B.* "Aromatic Hygrophorus."

Very tender; pileus fleshy, smooth, cinnamon, glutinous; stem stuffed, then hollow, reticulated; gills pinkish, decurrent when young.—*Berk. Outl. p.* 198. *Sow. t.* 144. *Eng. Fl.* v. *p.* 14.

Smell agreeable, spicy. Not found since the time of Sowerby.

Pileus 2-3½ in. broad, fleshy, generally covered with a thick glutinous skin, which becomes corrugated in drying, cinnamon, blackish, like the rest of the plant when bruised; gills pinkish. Stem 1½-3 in. long, 3-5 lines thick, hollow, and pithy. Whole plant when fresh so tender that it is difficult to gather. Odour agreeable, spicy. Taste watery, with a peppermint-like coolness in the mouth, and a lasting roughness in the throat.—*Sow.*

555. Hygrophorus mesotephrus. *B. & Br.* "Brown-disc Hygrophorus."

Pileus convex, subhemispherical, hygrophanous, white, with a brown disc, striate, viscid, as well as the slender stuffed stem, which is floccoso-granulated above; gills decurrent, pure white. —*Ann. N.H. ser.* ii. xiii. *t.* 15, *f.* 2. *Berk. Outl. p.* 198.

In woods. Rare. Bowood.

Pileus about 1 in. across, convex, subhemispherical, white, with the disc brown, viscid, striate, the extreme margin often remaining quite even; flesh white, hygrophanous; stem about 2 in. high, 2 lines thick, flexuous, attenuated at the base, white, viscid, floccoso-granulated at the apex, stuffed with a fibrillose pith. Gills pure white, moderately broad, rather distant, ventricose, shortly decurrent. Spores ·00035 in. long. In age the lower part of the stem slightly stained.—*B. & Br.*

556. Hygrophorus arbustivus. *Fr.* "Wood Hygrophorus."

Pileus fleshy, convexo-plane, obtuse, viscid, innato-virgate, becoming tawny; stem solid, naked, equal, elastic, incurved, smooth, white, mealy above; gills adnate, distant, thick, firm, white.—*Fr. Epicr. p.* 323. *B. & Br. Ann. N.H.* (1865), *no.* 932, 1013.

In woods, under birch, &c. Dec. Wiltshire.

Pileus 2 in., brick-red or red-brown, margin paler. Stem 1½ in. and upwards. Gills scarcely decurrent. Odour and taste not unpleasant.

557. Hygrophorus hypothejus. *Fr.* "Pine-wood Hygrophorus."

Pileus fleshy, clothed with thin olive evanescent gluten, somewhat virgate; stem stuffed, equal, somewhat spotted, viscid; gills distant, yellowish.—*Fr. Epicr. p.* 324. *Krombh. t.* 72, *f.* 24-25. *Sow. t.* 8. *A. & S. t.* 10, *f.* 3. *Buxb.* iv. *t.* 2. *Eng. Fl.* v. *p.* 14.

In pine woods, on sandy soil.

Pileus 1-4 in. broad, fleshy, at first conic, obtuse, at length expanded, and depressed round the umbo or even infundibuliform, covered with a thick dark gluten, yellow towards the margin and beneath the gluten, the extreme margin turned in. Flesh yellow, deeper towards the margin. Gills adnato-decurrent, yellow, sometimes varying to a flesh-coloured tint, distinct, distant. Stem 1½-3 in. high, 2-9 lines thick, flexuous, stuffed above, fibrillose below, slimy, submaculate, yellow. Odour fungoid, rather disagreeable.—*M. J. B.* Spores ·00049 × ·00017 in.

558. Hygrophorus olivaceo-albus. *Fr.* "Olive Hygrophorus."

Pileus fleshy, even, clothed with evanescent olivaceous gluten, umbo brown; stem solid, equal, at first with a floccose ring, spotted with dark scales, viscid, even above; gills white.—*Fr. Epicr. p.* 324. *Schæff. t.* 312. *Eng. Fl.* v. *p.* 13.

In woods and woodland pastures.

Pileus 2-3 in. broad, at first conic, then expanded, and broadly umbonate, livid olive brown, varied with tints of yellow and umber, very viscid; flesh thin on the margin, which is turned in, minutely downy, sometimes slightly grooved or striate. Gills adnate, scarcely decurrent, white, in decay greenish yellow, sometimes ventricose, veiny. Spores white, elliptic with a distinct border. Stem 1½-2½ in. high, ¼-½ in. thick, generally curved, fibrous within, above granulato-fibrillose, pitted, covered with milky drops. Ring in general indistinct; sometimes the margin of the viscid veil which clothes the rest of the stem, marking it with irregular dark blotches, is visible; base of stem yellow.—*M. J. B.* Spores ·00018 × ·00027 in.

Sect. 2. *Camarophyllus.*

559. Hygrophorus leporinus. *Fr.* "Hare-coloured Hygrophorus."

Pileus equally fleshy, convex, gibbous, equal, fibrilloso-floccose, opaque; stem stuffed, short, firm, attenuated, fibrillose, pallid; gills decurrent, reddish-grey.—*Fr. Epicr. p.* 326. *Batt. Bt.* 9. *Schæff. t.* 313. *Ann. N. H. no.* 700.

On downs. Sept. Durdham Downs. Kent.

Stem rigid, 2 in. long. Pileus 1-2 in. broad, cuticle splitting into flocci, colour tawny, reddish yellow, &c. The spores have a pale umber tint, nearly globose, and about ·0002 in. diameter.

560. Hygrophorus pratensis. *Fr.* "Pasture Hygrophorus."

Pileus convexo-plane, then turbinate, smooth, moist, disc compact, gibbous, margin thin ; stem stuffed, even, attenuated downwards ; gills deeply decurrent, arcuate, distant, thick.—*Fr. Epicr. p.* 327. *Fl. Dan. t.* 1735, *f.* 1. *Grev. t.* 91. *Krombh. t.* 43, *f.* 7-10. *Bull. t.* 587, *f.* 1. *Sow. t.* 141. *Bolt. t.* 56. *Huss.* ii. *t.* 40. *Eng. Fl.* v. *p.* 39. *Gard. Chron.* (1861), *p.* 289. *Berk. exs. no.* 123.

On downs and short pastures. Aug.—Nov. Esculent.

Pileus 1-2 in. broad, at length spreading towards the margin, but leaving the centre more or less convex, as if umbonate, glabrous, margin often cracked, frequently contracted or lobed, buffish-reddish, or brownish ; flesh whitish, thick in the centre, thin at the margin ; gills thick, distant, decurrent, connected by veins, separable from the flesh of the pileus. Stem 1-2 in. high, 3-8 lines thick, whitish, attenuated towards the base.—*Grev.* Spores ·00023 × ·00015 in.

561. Hygrophorus virgineus. *Fr.* "Satin-white Hygrophorus."

Pileus fleshy, convexo-plane, obtuse, moist, at length areolato-rimose ; stem stuffed, firm, short, attenuated at the base ; gills decurrent, distant, rather thickened.—*Fr. Epicr. p.* 327. *Grev. t.* 166. *Jacq. Misc.* ii. *t.* 15, *f.* 1. *Sow. t.* 32. *Bull. t.* 188. *Batt. t.* 19, *H. Price. f.* 41. *Batsch. f.* 200. *var. Eng. Fl.* v. *p.* 39. *Krombh. t.* 25, *f.* 1-3. *Smith, E. M. f.* 23.

On downs and short pastures. Common. Esculent.

Pileus 1 in. or more broad, slightly viscid when moist, and shining as if oiled, with a satiny lustre when dry, white, sometimes with a tinge of yellow or pink, various in shape, sometimes umbonate, often quite plane or depressed, frequently obconic, margin more or less thin and transparent. Gills broad, distant, with very prominent connecting veins, adnato-decurrent, sometimes forked above. Stem 2 in. long, 1-2 lines thick, under a lens fibrillose, sometimes pulverulento-squamulose at the apex, stuffed, the centre fibrous, at length more or less hollow, white, with sometimes a tinge of pink at the base. Taste like *Marasmius oreades.*—*M. J. B.*

562. Hygrophorus niveus. *Fr.* "Snow-white Hygrophorus."

Tough. Pileus submembranaceous, campanulato-convex, then umbilicate, smooth, moist, striate, viscid ; stem fistulose, thin, equal ; gills decurrent, thin, arcuate, distant.—*Fr. Epicr. p.* 327. *Schæff. t.* 232. *Krombh. t.* 25, *f.* 1-3.

In mossy pastures. Common.

Stem equal, 2 in. long, 1-2 lines thick, even, smooth, straight. Pileus scarcely an inch broad, striate and viscid when moist, not rimose when dry. Flesh of the pileus thin, everywhere equal, white, hygrophanous. Gills distant, thin, scarcely connected by veins, arcuate, quite entire.

563. Hygrophorus russo-coriaceus. *B. & Mill.* "Russian-leather Hygrophorus."

Sweet scented. Pileus very white, slightly viscid, convex, fleshy; stem slender, smooth, solid; gills broad, thick, arched, decurrent, very few, and distant.—*Berk. Outl. p.* 200. *Ann. N.H. no.* 332.

In exposed pastures. Rare.

Pileus about ½ in. broad, convex, fleshy, slightly viscid, ivory white. Stem ¾-1 in. high, not a line thick, incrassated upwards, smooth, solid, pure white; gills thick, broad arched, decurrent, very few and distant, with a few shorter ones intermixed. The whole plant exhales a strong musky smell like that of Russian leather.—*M. J. B.*

564. Hygrophorus distans. *Berk.* "Distant-gilled Hygrophorus."

Pileus somewhat fleshy, plane or depressed, viscid, white, with a silky lustre, here and there stained with brown; stem white above, cinereous below, and attenuated, not spotted; gills few, very distant, subventricose, decurrent, pure white at first, then tinged with cinereous, interstices obscurely rugose.—*Berk. Outl. p.* 200, *t.* 13, *f.* 1. *Price. f.* 5. *H. clivalis, Fr. Mon. Hym.* ii. *p.* 134.

In woods. Rare.

About 2 in. across, often umbilicate, remarkable for the few and distant gills.

565. Hygrophorus ovinus. *Fr.* "Sheep Hygrophorus."

Pileus fleshy, thin, conico-convex, then expanded, gibbous, viscid, then squamulose, brown; stem slightly stuffed, smooth, somewhat shining, thickened at either end; gills arcuato-decurrent, connected by veins, white, then dingy, edge thin.—*Fr. Epicr. p.* 328. *Bull. t.* 580. *Huss.* ii. *t.* 50. *Ann. N.H. no.* 262. *A. compressus. Sow. t.* 66. *?*

In pastures.

Stem about 2 in. long, 3 lin. thick, sub-equal, or slightly thickened at either end, curved or twisted, compressed, smooth, pallid, or blackish-brown; pileus 2 in. broad, at length revolute, undulate. Gills 3 lin. broad.

566. Hygrophorus Colemannianus. *Blox.* "Coleman's Hygrophorus."

Pileus sub-carnose, umbonate, umber, turning pale except in the centre, even, striate when moist, and slightly viscid. Stem nearly equal, somewhat silky, whitish; gills rather broad, of the same colour as the pileus, distant, deeply decurrent, interstices venoso-rugose.—*Berk. Outl. p.* 200. *Ann. N.H. no.* 701. *Batsch. f.* 215 ?

In grassy pastures. Twycross.

Pileus 1-2 in. broad, at first sub-campanulate, at length expanded, strongly umbonate, reddish umber, paler when dry, except in the centre, when moist striate, and very obscurely viscid. Stem 1 in. or more high, 1-2 lines thick, brittle, fibrous, nearly equal, white, very slightly tinged with umber, somewhat silky; gills umber, but paler than the pileus, strongly decurrent, broad, distant, interstices strongly veined and rugose.—Spores ·00025 × ·0003 in. long, obovate.

Sect. 3. *Hygrocybe.*

567. Hygrophorus lætus. *Fr.* "Shining Hygrophorus."

Pileus thin, convexo-plane, nearly even, viscid, somewhat shining, tawny; stem tough, equal, tawny; gills sub-decurrent, thin, distant, paler.—*Fr. Epicr. p.* 330. *Ann. N.H. no.* 702.

On open pastures.

Stem hollow, 2-3 in. long, slender, 2 lin. thick, equal, tough, even, quite smooth. Pileus about an inch broad, slightly fleshy, margin membranaceous, obtuse, even, or slightly striate at the margin. Spores ·0003 in. long, nearly globose.

568. Hygrophorus ceraceus. *Fr.* "Wax-like Hygrophorus."

Brittle. Pileus thin, convexo-plane, obtuse, slightly striate, viscid, waxy, as well as the fistulose, unequal, shining stem; gills adnate, sub-decurrent, distant, yellow.—*Fr. Epicr. p.* 330. *Jacq. Coll.* ii. *t.* 15, *f.* 2. *Sow. t.* 20. *Eng. Fl.* v. *p.* 40.

In pastures. Common. [Cincinnati, United States.]

Pileus 1 in. broad, convexo-plane, occasionally sub-umbonate, viscid, subcarnose, margin sub-striate; gills very broad (¼ of an inch), ventricose, connected by veins. Stem 2-3½ in. long, 2 lines or more thick, flexuous, equal, or slightly unequal, sometimes compressed, yellow, occasionally orange at the base.—*M. J. B.* Spores ·00026 × ·00018 in.

569. Hygrophorus coccineus. *Fr.* "Carmine Hygrophorus."

Fragile. Pileus thin, convex, obtuse, viscid, scarlet, growing pale, smooth; stem hollow, compressed, yellowish; gills adnate, with a decurrent tooth, connected by veins, variously shaded.—*Fr. Epicr. p.* 330. *Schæff. t.* 302. *Bull. t.* 570. *f.* 2, *S. Y. X. Huss.* i. *t.* 61. *Fl. Dan. t.* 7, 5. *Sow. t.* 381 (*partly*). *Batt. t.* 19, *B. Eng. Fl.* v. *p.* 40. *Price, f.* 57. *Vent. t.* 52, *f.* 1-5.

In open pastures. Sept. Oct. Common.

Pileus 1-2 in. broad, at first obtuse, conico-campanulate, at length inverted, sometimes strongly umbonate, splitting from the centre, yellow, orange or scarlet, viscid when moist, when dry pallid, appearing to the eye fibrillose, but not really so, margin thin, more or less wavy. Gills broad, ventricose, wrinkled, thick, connected by veins, retaining their colour longer than the pileus, adnate, with a decurrent tooth in depressed specimens. Stem 1½ in. long, ⅓ in. thick, more or less hollow, sub-flexuous, smooth, though apparently sub-fibrillose, tough, but easily splitting.—*M. J. B.* Spores ·00016 × ·00027 in.

570. Hygrophorus miniatus. *Fr.* "Vermilion Hygrophorus."

Fragile. Pileus thin, convex, thin, umbilicate, vermilion, soon dry, changing colour, opaque, and squamulose; stem somewhat stuffed, equal, polished, scarlet; gills adnate, distant, yellow, or yellowish vermilion.—*Fr. Epicr. p.* 330. *Fl. Dan. t.* 1009, *f.* 2. *Krombh. t.* 1, *f.* 29. *Bull. t.* 570, *fig.* 2 (*smaller figs*). *Eng. Fl.* v. *p.* 41.

In moist places, on heaths, &c. July. Aug. Common.

Pileus ½-1 in. broad, obtuse, even, moist but not viscid, turning pale; gills not decurrent nor connected by veins, distant, broad, plane, yellow, with a tinge of scarlet, or dull yellow; stem 2 in. high, 1 line thick, brittle, even, shining, at length hollow at the apex.—*Fries.* Spores ·00023 × ·00034 in.

571. Hygrophorus puniceus. *Fr.* "Blood-red Hygrophorus."

Fragile; pileus fleshy, thin, campanulate, obtuse, repand, even, viscid, blood-scarlet, then becoming pale; stem hollow, thick, ventricose, striate, white at the base; gills adnexed, thick, distant, yellow.—*Fr. Epicr. p.* 331. *Fl. Dan. t.* 883, *f.* 1. *Bull. t.* 202. *Bolt. t.* 67, *f.* 2. *Paul. t.* 120, *f.* 1, 2, 6. *Tourn. t.* 327, *f.* A. B. *Eng. Fl.* v. *p.* 40.

In meadows. July—Aug.

Pileus 2-4 in. broad, at first campanulate, then plano-convex, broadly and obtusely umbonate, even, undulated and lobed, irregular, when moist subviscid, blood-coloured, when dry the centre becoming pale; gills ventricose, 2-4 lines broad, at length connected by veins, altogether adnate, but, because of the form of the pileus, appearing free, yellow, varying to whitish-yellow, and purplish at the base; stem 3 in. long, ½-1 in. thick, attenuated at both ends, dry, striate, often squamulose at the apex, stuffed when young, then hollow, yellowish, or of the colour of the pileus.—*Fries.*

572. Hygrophorus obrusseus. *Fr.* "Golden Yellow Hygrophorus."

Fragile, bright golden yellow; pileus fleshy, thin, conico-convex, obtuse, flexuose, rather dry; stem hollow, sub-compressed, smooth, even; gills adnate, ventricose, thick, distant.—*Fr. Epicr. p.* 331. *Batt. t.* 19, *D. Bolt. t.* 68. *Ann. N. H. no.* 798.

In woods. Oct. Rare. Mossburnford.

Remarkable for its bright gold-coloured pileus, and adnate ventricose gills. —*B. & Br.*

Pileus 2-3 in. broad, flexuous, sub-lobate; stem thick, ascending, compressed, 3 in. long, ½ in. thick, or broader when compressed, sulphur-coloured, tawny at the base.

573. Hygrophorus conicus. *Fr.* "Conical Hygrophorus."

Fragile; pileus submembranaceous, conical, acute, smooth, somewhat lobed, at length expanded, and rimose; stem hollow, cylindrical, fibroso-striate; gills attenuated, free, ventricose, thin, rather crowded.—*Fr. Epicr. p.* 331. *Schæff. t.* 2. *Sow. t.* 381. *Batsch. f.* 28. *Bull. t.* 50, 524, *f.* 3. *Eng. Fl.* v. *p.* 40. *Smith. P.M. f.* 2.

In pastures. Common. [Low. and Mid. Carolina.]

Pileus 1-2 inches high, acutely conic, variously waved and lobed, fibrillose, viscid when moist or young, juicy, turning black, as does the whole plant when broken or bruised, orange, yellow, scarlet, brown, dusky, &c., various colours often blended together; gills thick, fleshy, ventricose, attenuated behind, free or adnexed, yellowish with frequently a cinereous tinge; stem 3-4 in. long, 2-4 lines thick, often splitting, fibrilloso-striate, coloured like the pileus.—*M. J. B.* Spores ·0004 × ·00025 in. *(Fig. 49.)*

574. Hygrophorus chlorophanus. *Fr.* "Sulphury Hygrophorus."

Fragile; pileus submembranaceous, convex, obtuse, somewhat lobed, striate; stem hollow, equal, even, viscid; gills adnexed, ventricose, thin, rather distant, becoming whitish.—*Fr. Epicr. p.* 332. *B. & Br. Ann. N.H. no.* 933. *Krombh. t.* 3, *f.* 6, 7.

Amongst grass and moss. King's Cliffe.

Stem hollow, equal, rarely compressed, 2-3 in. long, 2-3 lin. thick, smooth, viscid when moist, shining when dry, yellow; pileus about 1 in., usually bright sulphur-yellow, sometimes red, viscid; gills emarginate, adnexed, with a small decurrent tooth.

575. Hygrophorus psittacinus. *Fr.* "Parrot Hygrophorus."

Pileus thin, campanulate, then expanded, umbonate, somewhat striate, clothed with green evanescent gluten, as well as the hollow, tough, even stem; gills adnate, ventricose, thick, distant, greenish.—*Fr. Epicr. p.* 332. *Schæff. t.* 301. *Grev. t.* 74. *Bull. t.* 545, *f.* 1. *Batt. t.* 21, E. *Sow. t.* 82. *Huss* i. *t.* 41. *Eng. Fl.* v. *p.* 39. *Gard. Chron.* 1860, *p.* 240. *Vent. t.* 42, *f.* 1-3.

In fields, &c. Common [Mid. Carolina.]

Pileus 1 in. broad, conical, at length spreading, sometimes concave from the margin turning up, smooth, glutinous, green at first, partly changing to yellow of various intensity, often cracking; gills slightly adnate, bright yellow, often shaded with green, sub-distant, thick, broad in the centre; stem 2-3 in. high, about 2 lines thick, hollow, splitting, green, yellow at the base, very slimy. – *Grev.* Spores ·0002 × ·00028 in.

576. Hygrophorus calyptræformis. *B. & Br.* "Hood-like Hygrophorus."

Pileus thin, acutely conical, lobed below, minutely innato-fibrillose; stem white, smooth, slightly striate, hollow; gills rose-coloured, at length pallid, very narrow, acutely attenuated behind.—*Berk. Outl p.* 202. *Mag. Zool. & Bot. no.* 63. *Trans. Woolh. Cl.* 1861, *t.* 21, *f.* 4-6.

On the borders of woods and open pastures. Oct.

Pileus acutely conic, lobed below, about 1 in. high, ¾ in. broad at the base, in unexpanded specimens moist, striate under a lens, with innate, but raised fibrillæ, rose-coloured, gradually turning pallid; flesh rather thin; gills rose-coloured, at length pallid like the pileus, very narrow, and often almost evanescent behind, though properly adnate, distinct; stem 1 in. or more high, pure white, except within the pileus, where it has a slight roseate tinge, brittle, often splitting longitudinally, remarkably smooth, slightly striate, hollow, the walls fibrous within; the young pileus has a great resemblance to the internal bractœa of an artichoke just before expansion.—*M. J. B.* Spores ·0001 × ·00015 in.

577. Hygrophorus unguinosus. *Fr.* "Dingy Hygrophorus."

Fragile. Pileus thin, campanulate, then convex, obtuse, even, clothed with dingy gluten, as well as the hollow, unequal, sub-compressed stem; gills adnate, ventricose, plane, thick, white, becoming glaucous.—*Fr. Epicr. p.* 332. *Mag. Zool. & Bot. no.* 62.

In woods and pastures. Oct.

Stem hollow, 2 in. long, 3 lin. thick, commonly attenuated towards either end; pileus smooth or at length cracked, about 2 in. broad; gills thick, distant, connected by veins, broad. Inodorous.

578. Hygrophorus murinaceus. *Fr.* "Mouse-coloured Hygrophorus."

Fragile, strong scented. Pileus thin, campanulate, then expanded, irregular, viscid, soon dry, rimuloso-squamulose; stem nearly hollow, unequal, sub-compressed, even; gills adnate, seceding, broad, distant, somewhat waved, white, then glaucous.—*Fr. Epicr. p.* 333. *Bull. t.* 520. *Sow. t.* 106. *Krombh. t.* 72. *Batt. t.* 19, *f.* A.

In pastures.

Stem twisted, equal but compressed, fragile, 2-3 in. long, 3-5 lin. thick, polished, whitish; pileus 2 in. broad, at first rather viscid, then squamulose, growing pale; gills broadly emarginate, very broad, connected by veins.

Gen. 8. **GOMPHIDIUS,** Fr. Epicr. p. 319.

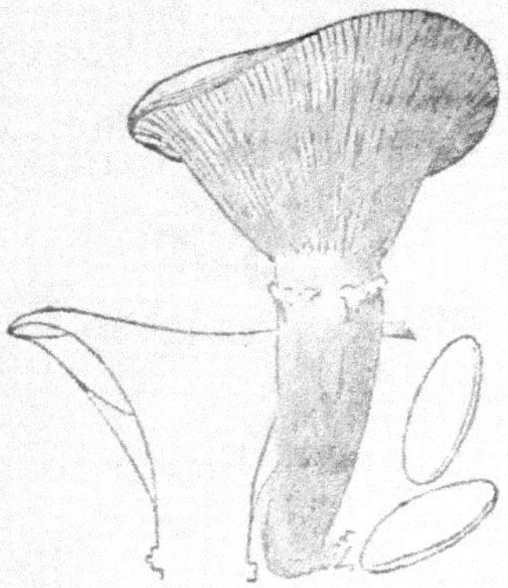

Fig. 50.

Spores large, greenish-grey, becoming black, fusiform (often spuriously uniseptate, according to Fries); veil universal, glutinous, terminated on the stem by a floccose annulus; pileus continuous with the stem, fleshy, convex, at length top-shaped; stem with a floccose annulus, confluent with the hymenophore; gills strongly decurrent, somewhat branched, soft, mucilaginous, often spreading in a continuous membrane.

HAB. Growing on the ground, chiefly in pine woods, solitary, sub-persistent. (*Fig.* 50.)

Principally distinguished by the mucilaginous nature of the gills. Nearly allied to *Cortinarius*, but at once distinguished by the nature and colour of the spores, and from all the dark purple and black-spored Agarics by the compact pileus, etc. Properties unknown; none edible.—*W. G. S.*

579. Gomphidius glutinosus. *Fr.* "Glutinous Gomphidius."

Pileus obtuse, glutinous, purplish-brown; gills whitish, then cinereous, shortly adnexed; trama none.—*Fr. Epicr. p.* 319. *Sow. t.* 7. *Fl. Dan. t.* 1247. *Schæff. t.* 36. *Letell. t.* 647. *Krombh. t.* 4. *f.* 3,4, *t.* 62, *f.* 15-20. *Eng. Fl.* v. *p.* 124. *Corda. Sturm. t.* 51.

In fir woods.

Pileus 2-5 in. broad; gills truly branched; stem 2-3 in. high, or more, ½ in. thick, dirty white, the base thickened and yellow, sometimes adorned with black scales.—*Fries.* Spores ·0006 × ·00025 in.

var. β. **roseus.** Smaller, base of stem and pileus rose-red.—*Krombh. t.* 63, *f.* 13-17. *Saund & Sm. t.* 8. *Eng. Fl.* v. *p.* 124.

Spores larger than the typical form. (*Fig.* 50, *reduced.*)

580. Gomphidius viscidus. *Fr.* "Viscid Gomphidius."

Pileus at length umbonate, viscid, brownish-red; gills purplish-umber, truly branched; trama similar to the pileus.—*Fr. Epicr. p.* 319. *Schæff. t.* 55. *Letell. t.* 603. *Krombh. t.* 4, *f.* 5-7. *Pers. Ic. & Desc. t.* 13, *f.* 1-3. *Sow. t.* 105. *Ag. rutilus, Eng. Fl.* v. *p.* 124.

Under Scotch firs. Aug.—Oct. [Low. Carolina.]

Pileus 2-3 in. broad, top-shaped, umbonate, yellow in the centre, the margin liver-coloured, shining; gills decurrent, somewhat branched, firm, elastic, thick, entire, purple-brown, the shorter connected with the longer; spores dark, fusiform. Stem 2-3 in. high, ½-¾ in. thick, rhubarb-coloured without and within, fibrillose, attenuated below, firm, solid, slimy from the remains of the veil, which form an obsolete filamentous ring.—*M. J. B.* Spores ·00063 × ·00025 in.

581. Gomphidius stillatus. *Strauss.* "Slender Gomphidius."

Pileus conico-hemispherical, clothed with dingy gluten, at length spotted with black; gills of a watery, dingy white, forked; stem slender, sprinkled with minute scales above, virgate below. *Str. Sturm. t.* 2. *G. gracilis, Berk. Outl. t.* 12, *f.* 7. *Ann. N.H. no.* 698.

In fir woods. Llanberris. Lea.

Pileus 1 in. across, conico-subhemispherical, of a pale vinous brown, when dry clothed with dirty fuliginous slime, which dries, especially round the margin, into black spots, or forms a narrow, irregular black border. Stem 2 in. high, 1½ line thick, flexuous, pale, especially above, where it is sprinkled with minute white scales, virgate below, with the remains of the slime, yellow at the base; gills arched, decurrent, forked, thick, obtuse, clothed under a lens with short tomentose hairs, of a washy bistre. Spores oblong, elliptic, ·0009 in. long, ·0003 in. wide, with a nucleus at either end. Distinguished from every other species by its slender stem and delicate habit.—*M. J. B.*

Gen. **9.** **LACTARIUS,** Fr. Epicr. p. 333.

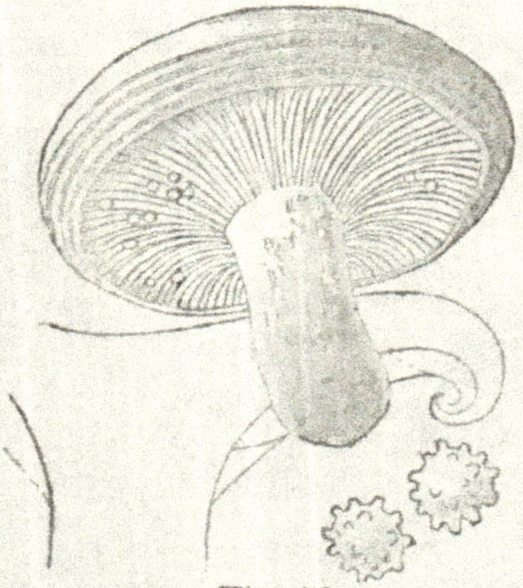

Fig. 51.

Spores white or very pale yellow, generally echinulate; veil none, but in some species the margin of pileus is bearded or pubescent; pileus fleshy, of a floccose or vesiculose (not fibrous) texture, at length depressed in the middle, margin at first involute; stem fleshy, not corticate, often hollow when old, confluent with the hymenophore: gills milky, in nearly all the species at first white, often changing to sulphur colour, red, or violet on exposure to the air, subdecurrent, unequal, with an acute edge; trama subvesiculose.

Hab. All grow on the ground. (*Fig.* 51.)

The species are easily recognised by the milky gills. The genus is nearly allied to *Russula*, but easily distinguished by its milky juice. They vary greatly in taste, being mild, aromatic, bitter, or acrid and burning. *Lactarius* therefore includes delicate and excessively poisonous species.

A. *Piperites*—milk at first white, acrid.

Sect. 1. *Torminosi.*

582. **Lactarius torminosus.** *Fr.* "Woolly Lactarius."

Pileus fleshy, depressed, subzonate, pallid; stem stuffed, soon hollow, equal (rarely spotted), pallid; margin involute, bearded; gills thin, whitish, milk persistently white, acrid.—*Fr. Epicr. p.* 334. *Schæff. t.* 12. *Fl. Dan. t.* 1068. *Fr. Fung. Esc. t.* 38. *Krombh. t.* 13, *f.* 15-23. *Bull. t.* 529, *f.* 2. *Smith. P.M. f.* 11. *Sow. t.* 103. *Eng. Fl.* v. *p.* 24. *Barla. t.* 18, *f.* 7-10. *Vent. t.* 30, *f.* 2.

In woods, fields, &c. June—Oct. Local. [S. Carolina.]

Pileus 2-5 in. broad, smooth, or nearly so, except the involute margin, which is most copiously shaggy, depressed, more or less zoned, of a beautiful ochre or strawberry colour, at first viscid, milk white, very acrid, not changeable; gills rather narrow, nearly of the same colour as the pileus, but yellower and paler, slightly forked; stem 1½-2 in. long, ½ in. thick, sometimes shining, obtuse, paler than the pileus, at length hollow, clothed with minute adpressed down. Very acrid.—*M. J. B.* Spores echinulate, ·00035 × ·00025 in.

583. **Lactarius cilicioides.** *Fr.* "Tomentose Lactarius."

Pileus fleshy, soft, depressed, tomentose, not zoned, turning pallid; margin fibrillose or woolly; stem stuffed, even, pruinose, silky, spotless, pallid; gills crowded, branched, white, then yellowish, as well as the milk.—*Fr. Epicr. p.* 334. *Schæff. t.* 228. (*Krombh. t.* 40, *f.* 17-19 ?) *Eng. Fl.* v. *p.* 24.

In pine woods. Rare.

Pileus 2-4 in. broad, depressed, margin rounded, involute, reddish-buff, sometimes glutinous, very downy, becoming fibrillose at the margin; gills yellowish, irregular and often branching, apparently decurrent from the expansion of the stripes into the substance of the pileus. Flesh yellowish white, darker towards the surface. Stem about 2 in. high, nearly 1 in. thick, dingy white, yellow or brown. There is no juice, but a considerable moisture on the surface of the pileus, which seems to originate from the plant.—*Grev.*

584. **Lactarius turpis.** *Fr.* "Dirty Lactarius."

Pileus compact, plane, olivaceous-umber, zoneless; margin at first yellowish-downy; stem stuffed, short, viscid, attenuated downwards, olivaceous; gills thin, pallid; milk white, acrid.—*Fr. Epicr. p.* 335. *Fl. Dan. t.* 1913. *Krombh. t.* 69, *f.* 1-6. *Ann. N. H. no.* 703.

In fir woods. Coed Coch. East Bergholt. [Mid. Carolina.]

Growing to a large size, and remarkable for its yellow, olive, or umber hue. Stem 1½-3 in. long, ½-1 in. and more thick, viscid or dry, not spotted, pale or dark olive, apex becoming ochraceous. Pileus fleshy, rigid, olive, verging on umber; margin at first involute and villous, with a yellowish olive down, then more or less expanded, at length closely sulcate.

585. Lactarius controversus. *Pers.* "Stained Lactarius."

Pileus compact, rather fragile, umbilicate, infundibuliform, floccose, then smooth, viscid, variegated with blood-red spots; margin at first involute, villous; stem solid, blunt, unequal; gills thin, much crowded, simple, flesh-coloured; milk white, acrid.—*Fr. Epicr. p.* 335. *Vitt. Mang. t.* 27. *Fr. Fung. Esc. t.* 39. *Trans. Woolhope Club,* 1868, *p.* 245, *plate. Bull. t.* 538. *Batsch. f.* 201. *Paul. t.* 68, *f.* 1. *Vent. t.* 51. *Barla. t.* 18, *f.* 1, 2?

Under poplars. Abergavenny. Breinton, etc.

Stem stout, swollen, 1-2 in. long, sometimes excentric, pruinose at the top, never marked with pits or depressions; gills decurrent, with an obscure tooth; pileus fleshy, compact, rigid, convex, then depressed and subinfundibuliform; at first dry, but after rain viscid in all its parts; margin at first involute and villous; stem and pileus more or less covered with blood-red spots and smears; flesh very firm, like *L. piperatus.* Fr. Milk very acrid, white, plentiful; odour faint, but pleasant; taste exceedingly acrid. "Feels and looks soapy." Spores echinulate, ·0003 × ·00025 in.—*W. G. S.*

586. Lactarius pubescens. *Schrad.* "Pubescent Lactarius."

Pileus fleshy, firm, plano-umbilicate, whitish, disc glabrous, shining; margin whitish-fibrillose (or tomentose); stem stuffed, then hollow, very short, attenuated downwards; gills somewhat crowded, flesh-coloured; milk acrid, white.—*Schrad. Spic. p.* 122.

var. **margine-tomentoso.** *B. & Br. Ann. N.H.* 1865, *no.* 1015. *Krombh. t.* 13, *f.* 1-12.

In pastures. Aug. Aboyne.

Pileus 2 in. across, depressed, clothed with fine matted down; margin involute, tomentose; flesh firm; stem nearly equal, 1¼ in. high, about 5 lines thick, smooth, pale flesh-coloured; gills thin, scarcely branched; milk extremely acrid, white, not changeable; odour pungent.—*B. & Br.*

Sect. 2. *Limacini.*

587. Lactarius insulsus. *Fr.* "Unsavoury Lactarius."

Pileus fleshy, umbilicate, then infundibuliform, viscid, somewhat zoned, yellowish, margin naked; stem stuffed, then hollow, firm, pallid; gills crowded, forked, pallid; milk white, acrid.—*Fr. Epicr. p.* 336. *Krombh. t.* 12, *f.* 1-6. *Huss.* i. *t.* 59. *Berk. Outl. t.* 13, *f.* 2. *Gard. Chron.* 1860, *p.* 752.

In woods and on their borders. Common. [Mid. Carolina.]

Stem 1½ in. long, 1 in. thick, rarely protracted to 3 in. and then equal. Pileus 3-4 in. broad, zoned, chiefly about the margin, smooth, yellowish brick red, viscid, cuticle slightly separating, margin naked. Flesh firm, pallid; gills decurrent, forked at the base, whitish, becoming pallid.

588. Lactarius zonarius. *Fr.* "Zoned Lactarius."

Pileus compact, umbilicate, even, viscid, with yellowish zones; margin involute, naked; stem solid, short, elastic, even, yellowish; gills crowded, thin, whitish; milk white, acrid, unchangeable.—*Fr. Epicr. p.* 336. *Bull. t.* 104. *Vaill. t.* 12, *f.* 7. *Eng. Fl.* v. *p.* 25. *Vent. t.* 34, *f.* 4-5.

On the borders of woods. Aug.—Oct. Rare.

[Cincinnati, U.S.]

Pileus 2-3 in. broad, nearly plane, rufescent from cinereous with brown zones, milk at first white. Stem 1½ in. high, pale.—*Fries.* Spores minutely echinulate, almost globular, diameter ·00027 in.

(*Fig.* 51, *reduced.*)

589. Lactarius blennius. *Fr.* "Slimy Lactarius."

Pileus fleshy, depressed, glutinous, often concentrically guttate, greenish-grey; margin from the first slightly pubescent; stem stuffed, then hollow, viscid, of the same colour; gills crowded, white, as well as the acrid milk.—*Fr. Epicr. p.* 337. *Kromb. t.* 69, *f.* 7-9. *Krapf. t.* 4, *f.* 11, 13. *Sterb. t.* 5, *E. Fl. Dan. t.* 1961, *f.* 1. *Eng. Fl.* v. *p.* 26. *Berk. exs. no.* 3.

In woods. Common.

Pileus 2-4 in. broad, fleshy, rarely subzonate, convex, the margin generally involute and adpresso-tomentose, at length more or less depressed, dull cinereous green, at first viscid; more or less pitted. Milk white, not changeable; gills rather narrow, pale ochraceous, scarcely forked, not connected by veins. Stem 1 in. long, ¼-½ in. thick, paler than the pileus, attenuated downwards, obtuse, smooth, at length hollow, sometimes pitted; very acrid.—*M. J. B.* Spores sparingly echinulate, ·0002 × ·0003 in.

590. Lactarius hysginus. *Fr.* "Reddish viscid Lactarius."

Pileus fleshy, rigid, umbilicate, even, viscid, fleshy-red, growing pale; margin thin, inflexed; stem stuffed, then hollow, smooth, rather spotted; gills crowded, white, as well as the acrid milk.—*Fr. Epicr. p.* 337. *Krombh. t.* 14, *f.* 15, 16. *Eng. Fl.* v. *p.* 26.

In woods. Aug.—Oct.

Pileus 4-5 in. broad, pinky or brownish-white, viscid; gills white, yellowish with age; stem 3-4 in. high, ½ in. thick, solid (then hollow), white, with a pinky tinge; juice dilutely milky, very acrid.—*With.*

591. Lactarius trivialis. *Fr.* "Large lurid Lactarius."

Pileus fleshy, depressed, viscid, zoneless, lurid, becoming pale, cuticle inflexed at the margin; stem hollow, stout; gills thin, crowded, white, as well as the acrid milk.—*Fr. Epicr. p.* 337. *Krombh. t.* 14, *f.* 17-18. *Ann. N.H. no.* 934.

In pine woods. Sept.

Stem 1-6 in. long, 1 in. or more thick, paler than the pileus, smooth, unspotted. Pileus 4-7 in. broad, depressed, at length funnel-shaped. Margin at first involute, then expanded, dark lurid, becoming pale, or flesh-coloured tan. Flesh white. Gills sub-decurrent, 2-4 lin. broad, rather thin, whitish becoming pallid.

592. Lactarius circellatus. *Fr.* "Dingy-zoned Lactarius."

Pileus fleshy, convex, then plane, repand, viscid, zoned with ferruginous, disc from the first umbilicate, darker; stem solid, firm, attenuated downwards; gills crowded, whitish; milk white, acrid.—*Fr. Epicr. p.* 338. *Batt. t.* 13, *D. Sow. t.* 203.

In woods. Rare.

Stem 1½-2 in. long, ½ in. and more thick, even, smooth, growing pale. Pileus depressed-convex, then expanded and depressed in the centre, 2-3 in. broad, when young and moist viscid, rufous-brown, variegated with darker zones. Gills horizontal, with a subdecurrent tooth, very thin and crowded, narrow.

593. Lactarius uvidus. *Fr.* "Moist Lactarius."

Pileus fleshy, thin, convex, then depressed, zoneless, viscid, dingy; margin at first involute, naked; stem soon hollow, viscid, pallid; gills thin, crowded, white, when wounded becoming lilac; milk white, then lilac.—*Fr. Epicr. p.* 338. *Batsch. f.* 202. *Eng. Fl.* v. *p.* 25. *Krombh. t.* 57, *f.* 14-16.

In woods. July—Sept.

Pileus 2-2½ in. broad, fleshy, depressed, sometimes obsoletely zoned, viscid, pale, dirty rufescent, or cinereous with a shade of lilac, speckled with small watery spots, which originate beneath the epidermis; gills paler, adnato-decurrent, the shorter ones very obtuse, and truncate behind, connected by veins; milk white, acrid; stem 2 in. high, ½ in. thick, spongy, at length hollow, marked with little longitudinal pits, strigose at the base, the whole plant white when cut, turning to a beautiful lilac.—*M. J. B.*

Sect. 3. *Piperati*—pileus dry.

594. Lactarius pyrogalus. *Fr.* "Pear-scented Lactarius."

Pileus fleshy, plane, then depressed, subzonate, smooth, even, rather moist, livid, cinereous; stem stuffed, then hollow, pallid, attenuated downwards; gills thin, rather distant, yellowish;

milk very acrid, copious, white.—*Fr. Epicr. p.* 339. *Bull. t.* 529, *f.* 1. *Krombh. t.* 14, *f.* 1-9. *Paul t.* 72, *f.* 1-2? *Larbr. t.* 18, *f.* 3. *Eng. Fl.* v. *p.* 29. *Smith. P.M.f.* 18. *Ann. N.H. no.* 798*.

In woods and meadows. Aug.

Pileus 2-3 in. broad, firm, at length dirty yellowish, in shady places almost zoneless. Milk abundant, extremely acrid. Stem 1½ in. long, 3-5 lines thick, stuffed, soon hollow, often attenuated, smooth or scrobiculate. —*Fries.* Spores sparingly echinulate, white, or with a suggestion of ochre, almost globular, ·00026 in. diameter.—*W. G. S.*

595. Lactarius plumbeus. *Fr.* "Lead-coloured Lactarius."

Pileus compact, convex, at length infundibuliform, dry, unpolished, dingy, then blackish brown; stem solid, equal, blunt; gills crowded, white then yellowish; milk acrid, white, unchangeable.—*Fr. Epicr. p.* 339. *Bull. t.* 282, 559, *f.* 2. *Krapf. t.* 4, *f.* 1-3. *Sow. t.* 245. *Eng. Fl.* v. *p.* 29. *Barla. t.* 21, *f.* 1-5.

In woods. Rare.

Pileus 3-5 in. broad, large, convex, becoming depressed, firm, never zoned or glutinous; margin mostly involute, dark, fuliginous-grey or brown; flesh compact, white; gills numerous, yellowish, varying with different shades; stem 2-3 in. high, firm, thick, brownish, or dingy-olive.—*Grev.*

596. Lactarius acris. *Fr.* "Acrid Lactarius."

Pileus fleshy, irregular, at length infundibuliform, viscid, dusky cinereous; stem stuffed, then hollow, somewhat excentric, pallid, attenuated downwards; gills rather crowded, pallid, yellow, turning red; milk acrid, white, then reddish.—*Fr. Epicr. p.* 342. *Bolt. t.* 60. *Batsch. f.* 68. *Batt. t.* 13, E. *Eng. Fl.* v. *p.* 25. *Smith. P.M.f.* 28.

In woods. Aug.—Nov. Rare. [S. Carolina.]

Gills distant; pileus almost black, extremely acrid and bitter.—*W. G. S.*

Pileus almost always excentric, emarginate, unequal, livid brown; gills rather distant; stem attenuated downwards, short, pallid; milk extremely acrid, dirty white, then rose-coloured, then yellowish, seldom unchangeable. —*Fries.* Spores echinulate, yellow, ·00026 × ·00034 in.

597. Lactarius chrysorrhæus. *Fr.* "Yellow-juiced Lactarius."

Pileus rather fleshy, umbilicate, then infundibuliform, yellowish flesh-coloured, marked with darker zones or spots; stem stuffed, then hollow, equal, even, white; gills decurrent, thin, crowded, yellowish; milk white, then golden yellow, very acrid. —*Fr. Epicr. p.* 342. *Price, f.* 71. *Bolt. t.* 144. *Krombh. t.* 12, *f.* 7-14. *Ann. N.H. no.* 705. *A. theiogalus, Eng. Fl.* v. *p.* 28.

In woods. Common. [United States.]

Pileus 1-3 in. broad, buff, sometimes slightly tinged with tawny, at first hemispherical, dimpled, at length depressed, more or less zoned; margin wavy, involute, and minutely downy when young; flesh firm, crisp; gills very slightly decurrent, connected by veins, distant, by no means rigid, salmon-coloured, slightly forked, about as broad as the flesh of the pileus; milk white, rather acrid, with a peculiar taste, changing instantly on exposure to a delicate but beautiful yellow; stem 1½ in. high, ½-1 in. thick, at first nearly white obese, paler than the pileus, downy at the base, more or less hollow.—*M. J. B.*

598. Lactarius piperatus. *Fr.* "Peppery Lactarius."

White. Pileus compact, umbilicate, then infundibuliform, rather regular, not zoned, even, smooth; stem solid, thick, very short, white; gills decurrent, arcuate, crowded, narrow, dichotomous, white; milk copious, acrid, white.—*Fr. Epicr. p.* 340. *Fl. Dan. t.* 1132. *Krombh. t.* 56, *f.* 1-4. *Bull. t.* 200. *Paul. t.* 68, *f.* 3-4. *Smith. P.M. f.* 15. *Eng. Fl.* v. *p.* 30. *Barla. t.* 22, *f.* 1-5. *Berk. exs. no.* 61.

In woods. July—Sept. Common. Poisonous. [United States.]

Pileus 3-7 in. broad, slightly rugulose, quite smooth, white, a little clouded with yellow or stained with umber where scratched or bruised, convex, more or less depressed, often quite infundibuliform, more or less waved, fleshy, thick, firm but brittle; margin involute at first, sometimes excentric; milk white, hot; gills generally very narrow, $\frac{1}{20}$ in. broad, but sometimes much broader, cream-coloured, repeatedly dichotomous, very close "like the teeth of an ivory comb," decurrent from the shape of the pileus, when bruised changing to umber; stem 1-3 in. high, 1½-2 in. thick, often compressed, minutely pruinose, solid but spongy within, the substance breaking up into transverse cavities.—*M. J. B.* Spores not echinulate, generally with an apiculus, ·0002 × ·00024 in.

599. Lactarius vellereus. *Fr.* "Woolly-white Lactarius."

White. Pileus compact, umbilicate or convex, tomentose, zoneless; margin reflexed; stem solid, blunt, pubescent; gills distant, arcuate, whitish; milk scanty, acrid, white.—*Fr. Epicr. p.* 340. *Krombh. t.* 57, *f.* 10-13. *Sow. t.* 204. *Bull. t.* 538, *f.* G.H.N. *Schæff. t.* 225. *Eng. Fl.* v. *p.* 31. *Barla. t.* 22, *f.* 6-8. *Berk. exs. no.* 122.

In woods. Common. [Cincinnati, United States.]

Pileus 4-7 in. broad, more or less infundibuliform, the whole surface minutely but densely tomentose, white, firm, fleshy; margin at first involute; milk white, acrid; gills white, narrow (occasionally broad and brittle), distant forked, connected by veins, at length slightly buff or yellowish, rufescent after being bruised; stem 1 in. high, 2 in. thick, blunt, rather less downy than the pileus, solid.—*M. J. B.* Spores hardly echinulate, ·00019 × ·00034 in.

var. **exsuccus** *Otto.* is a very different looking plant from *L. vellereus, Fr.*; it is destitute of milk, and is like a *Tricholoma* or

Clitocybe, not rigid as in *L. vellereus*, *Fr.* The gills are pale lemon colour with a shade of green; stem short; spores covered with spines almost globular, ·00035 in. diameter.—*W. G. S.*

B. *Dapetes*—Stem central; gills naked and milk aromatic, at first acrid, then mild; gills becoming pallid.

600. Lactarius deliciosus. *Fr.* "Delicious Lactarius."

Pileus fleshy, umbilicate, viscid, zoned, smooth, rufous-orange, growing pale; margin smooth; stem stuffed, then hollow, rather spotted; gills and milk at first saffron-red, then greenish.—*Fr. Epicr. p.* 341. *Fl. Dan. t.* 1151. *Schæff. t.* 11. *Krombh. t.* 11. *Lenz. f.* 9. *Letell t.* 633. *Vitt. Mang. t.* 42. *Cooke B.F. t.* 13. *Sow. t.* 202. *Huss.* i. *t.* 67. *Smith E.M. f.* 11. *Eng. Fl.* v. *p.* 26. *Vent. t.* 29, *f.* 3-4, *t.* 30, *f.* 1. *Hogg & Johnst. t.* 5. *Trans. Woolh. Cl.* 1867, *t.* 11. *Badh.* i. *t.* 6, *f.* 2-ii. *t.* 5, *f.* 4. *Barla. t.* 19.

In fir woods. Sept. Oct. Esculent. [United States.]

Gregarious, sometimes subcæspitose. Pileus 4 in. or more broad, zoned, orange rufous, dull, as if there were the remains of a minute, very closely pressed, dirty white web; hemispherical when young, in which state the margin is decidedly involute and tomentose, at length expanded, depressed, fleshy. The whole plant abounding with orange milk, and when bruised or old, stained with green; gills decurrent, from the first of the same colour as the pileus, forked at the base, rather broad and distant; stem 3 in. high, curved, stuffed, more or less hollow, scrobiculate, strigose at the base. Odour and taste agreeable, but slightly acrid.—*M. J. B.* Spores echinulate, almost round, ·00025 in. diameter.

C *Russulares*—Gills discoloured, milk at first white.

Sect. 1. Pileus at first viscid.

601. Lactarius pallidus. *Fr.* "Pallid Lactarius."

Pileus fleshy, obtuse, depressed, smooth, viscid, zoneless, pallid; stem stuffed, then hollow, pruinose, white, then pallid; milk sweet, white.—*Fr. Epicr. p.* 343. *Krombh. t.* 56, *f.* 10-14. *Paul. t.* 80? *Ann. N.H. no.* 705. *Saund. & Sm. t.* 16.

In woods. Bowood. [Mid. Carolina.]

Stem 2 in. and more long, $\frac{3}{4}$ in. thick, even, smooth. Pileus 3-6 in. broad, pallid, pinkish, pale clay-coloured, or tan-coloured. Margin broadly, and for a long time involute. Flesh pallid. Gills subdecurrent, arcuate, broad ($1\frac{1}{2}$-2 lin.), rather thin, crowded, somewhat branched, whitish, at length of the colour of the pileus. Spores echinulate, almost round, diameter ·0003 in.

602. Lactarius quietus. *Fr.* "Mild reddish Lactarius."

Pileus fleshy, depressed, obtuse, viscid at first, soon dry, growing pale, somewhat zoned, opaque, rufescent; stem stuffed, smooth, of the same colour; gills white, then reddish; milk mild, white.—*Fr. Epicr. p.* 343. *Kromb. t.* 40, *f.* 1-9. *Eng. Fl.* v. *p.* 27.

In woods. Sept.—Nov.

Pileus 2 in. or more broad, opaque, rufescent, often slightly zoned, at first deep liver-coloured, obtuse, at length depressed, smooth; the margin incurved, and delicately downy; flesh firm, thick; milk white, but sometimes of a decided pale yellow; gills pale rufescent, gradually becoming darker, decurrent, forked at the base, rather numerous, and narrow; stem 2 in. long, ¼-½ in. thick, thickest upwards, of the same texture and colour as the pileus; flesh firm, bearing a strong pressure without breaking, when old less firm, but not hollow. Mild; odour oily and somewhat like that of bugs.—*M. J. B.* Spores papillose, ·00034 × ·00024 in.

603. Lactarius theiogalus. *Fr.* "Sulphur-juiced Lactarius."

Pileus fleshy, convex, then depressed, viscid, smooth, reddish-tawny; stem stuffed, even, of the same colour; gills thin, crowded, reddish-yellow; milk white, then sulphur-coloured, at length acrid.—*Fr. Epicr. p.* 342. *Bull. t.* 567, *f.* 2. *Krombh. t.* 2, *f.* 23, 24. *Bolt. t.* 9. *Paul. t.* 71. *Ann. N. H. no.* 704. *Barla. t.* 20, *f.* 14-16. *Smith. P. M. f.* 20.

In woods. [United States.]

Stem 1-2 in. long, 2-4 lin. thick, even, of the same colour as the pileus. Pileus 1½-2½ in. broad. Margin more or less thin, viscid, shining when dry, reddish-tawny. Gills adnato-decurrent, about 1 lin. broad, thin, crowded. The milk does not assume so bright a yellow tint as in *L. chrysorrhœus.*

604. Lactarius cyathula. *Fr.* "Cup-like Lactarius."

Pileus fleshy, convexo-plane, umbonate, at length depressed, zoned, viscid, flesh-coloured, when dry rivulose, pallid, opaque; stem stuffed, equal, pallid; gills linear, narrow, crowded, white, then yellowish-flesh colour; milk acrid, white, unchangeable.—*Syst. Myc. p.* 66. *B. & Br. Ann. N. Hist.* 1865, *no.* 1016. *Krapf. t.* 8, *f.* 8, 9.

In woods. Aug. Aboyne.

Pileus plane, at length depressed or infundibuliform, 1½-2 in. across, opaque, slightly viscid, obtuse or obscurely umbonate, somewhat zoned, of a pallid flesh colour; stem spongy, stuffed, 1½-2 in. high, ⅓ in. thick, nearly equal, at length compressed, shining, with a silky aspect; gills narrow, crowded, of a yellowish-flesh colour, sub-decurrent; milk white, not changeable, at length acrid; smell somewhat like that of bugs.—*B. & Br.*

Sect. 2. Pileus dry.

605. Lactarius rufus. *Fr.* "Red Lactarius."

Pileus fleshy, umbonate, at length infundibuliform, dry, flocculose, then becoming smooth, shining, zoneless, dark-rufous; stem stuffed, rufescent; gills crowded, ochraceous then rufous, milk white, very acrid.—*Fr. Epicr. p.* 347. *Lenz. f.* 11. *Krombh. t.* 39, *f.* 12-15. *Paul. t.* 69, *bis. Huss.* i. *t.* 15. *Eng. Fl.* v. *p.* 28. *Smith. P.M. f.* 12.

In fir woods. Sept.

Pileus 3 in. broad, plano-convex, slightly or strongly umbonate, with a depression round the umbo as the plant advances, deep rufescent, adpresso-tomentose, the margin slightly turned in and sub-striate, fleshy, firm, not very brittle nor zoned; milk white, insupportably acrid, not changeable; gills at first pale, then slightly rufescent, decurrent, here and there forked. Stem 2½ in. high, ½ in. thick, nearly equal, obtuse, firm, bearing a strong pressure, rufescent, but hoary or mealy, turning brown when bruised, somewhat stuffed, at length partly hollow, base downy.—*M. J. B.* Spores scarcely echinulate, almost round, diameter ·00024 in.

606. Lactarius glyciosmus. *Fr.* "Scented Lactarius."

Pileus fleshy, thin, convexo-plane, somewhat umbonate, dry, squamulose, lurid, opaque; stem stuffed, thin, pubescent, pallid; gills crowded, yellowish-ochre; milk acrid, white.—*Fr. Epicr. p.* 348. *Eng. Fl.* v. *p.* 29. *Krombh. t.* 39, *f.* 16-18.

In fir woods. Sept. Oct.

Pileus 1-3 in. broad, more or less plane, often umbonate, various in colour, lurid-brown, brick-red, flesh-colour, or rufous, known by its peculiar scent, brittle. Gills narrow, opaque, pale when young; milk white, at length acrid. Stem 1½ in. long, 3-4 lines broad.—*Eng. Fl.*

607. Lactarius serifluus. *Fr.* "Thin-juiced Lactarius."

Pileus fleshy, plane, then depressed, sub-flexuose, dry, smooth, zoneless, brownish-tawny; margin inflexed; stem solid, equal, rather incurved, paler, turning yellowish, as well as the crowded gills; milk sparing, colour of serum.—*Fr. Epicr. p.* 345. *Krombh. t.* 40, *f.* 15, 16. *Berk. Outl. t.* 13, *f.* 4.

In woods. Common.

Milk of a watery white.

Sect. 3. Pileus at first velvety.

608. Lactarius fuliginosus. *Fr.* "Dingy Lactarius."

Pileus fleshy, soft, depressed, obtuse, very dry, zoneless, at first clouded with a dingy bloom, then naked, cinereous tan-coloured;

stem stuffed, spongy, of the same colour; gills crowded, tan-coloured, flesh and milk acrid, white, then saffron coloured.—*Fr. Epicr. p.* 348. *Krombh. t.* 14, *f.* 10-12. *Bull. t.* 567, *f.* 3. *Eng. Fl.* v. *p.* 29. *Barla. t.* 21, *f.* 6, 7.

In woods. Aug.—Nov. Common. [Low. Carolina.]

Pileus 1-3 in. broad, not viscid, minutely pitted, plane, slightly depressed, of a dull grey buff, or umber, with a minute bloom; not zoned; margin not the least involute; flesh when cut soon changing to salmon colour; milk white, not changeable; gills slightly forked at the base, not connected by veins, ochraceous, sub-decurrent, mealy with the yellow spores, which are round and echinulate; stem 1½-3 in. long, 4-5 lines thick, solid, but the inner substance less dense, obese, much paler than the pileus, with a minute bloom. The colour of the pileus is exactly that of coffee and milk.—*M. J. B.* Spores yellow, echinulate, almost globular, diameter ·00028 in.

Sect. 4. Pileus smooth, polished.

609. Lactarius volemum. *Fr.* "Orange-brown Lactarius."

Pileus compact, rigid, plane, then depressed, obtuse, dry, golden tawny, at length rimoso-rivulose; stem solid, hard, blunt, pruinose; gills crowded, white, then yellowish; milk copious, sweet, white.—*Fr. Epicr. p.* 344. *Letell. t.* 624. *Lenz. t.* 3, *f.* 12. *Huss.* i. *t.* 87. *Eng. Fl.* v. *p.* 27. *Krombh. t.* 39, *f.* 1-4. *Barla. t.* 20, *f.* 1-3. *Smith. E.M. f.* 26.

In woods. King's Cliffe. Esculent. [S. Carolina.]

Pileus 4 in. broad, flesh thickish, moderately firm, obtuse, minutely umbonate, though the umbo at length vanishes, subdepressed, sometimes very faintly zoned, with a few minute wrinkles towards the margin, dry, at length cracked, of a rich orange brown, darker in the centre, the whole rather dull than shining; margin not the least involute, though when young the edge of the pileus is regularly incurved; milk white, abundant, quite mild; gills pale ochraceous, becoming fuscous on being touched, not very close, scarcely decurrent, even in depressed specimens, sometimes slightly forked; stem 2½-3½ in. high, above 1 in. thick, obese, minutely attenuated downwards, sculptured longitudinally, paler than the centre of the pileus, spongy in the centre, outer flesh reddish.—*M. J. B.*

610. Lactarius mitissimus. *Fr.* "Mild Lactarius."

Pileus fleshy, thin, convex, then depressed, papillate, dry, zoneless, even, orange; stem stuffed, then hollow, smooth, of the same colour; gills crowded, paler; milk white.—*Fr. Epicr. p.* 345. *Krombh. t.* 39, *f.* 19, 20. *Ann. N.H. no.* 799.

In woods and hedgebanks.

Stem 1-3 in. long, ⅓-½ lin. thick, even, smooth. Pileus thin, rather rigid, depressed, with evanescent papillæ, 1-3 in. broad, brightly coloured. Flesh pallid; gills adnato-decurrent, at first somewhat arcuate, then straight, thin, crowded, 1-1½ lin. or more broad.

611. **Lactarius subdulcis.** *Fr.* "Sweet Lactarius."

Pileus fleshy, thin, papillate, at length depressed, polished, even, zoneless, rufous-cinnamon; stem stuffed, then hollow, equal, somewhat pruinose, becoming rufous, as well as the crowded, fragile gills; milk rather mild, white.—*Fr. Epicr. p.* 346. *Bull. t.* 222, *A.B.* *Sow. t.* 204. *Krombh. t.* 40, *f.* 13, 14. *Lenz. f.* 11. *Bolt. t.* 3. *Schæff. t.* 73, *partly*. *Eng. Fl.* v. *p.* 28. *Barla. t.* 20, *f.* 4-10.

In woods. Sept. Oct. Common. [S. Carolina.]

Pileus 1-4 in. broad, dark chocolate, sometimes slightly viscid when young; milk white, acrid when the plant is old; gills at length deep brown, scarcely at all forked; stem 1-2 in. high, $\frac{1}{4}$-$\frac{1}{2}$ in. thick, substance looser than in *L. quietus*, at length hollow.—*M. J. B.* Spores between papillose and echinulate, diameter ·00028 in.

612. **Lactarius camphoratus.** *Fr.* "Camphory Lactarius."

Pileus fleshy, thin, depressed, dry, somewhat zoned, smooth, brownish-red; stem stuffed, sub-undulate, of the same colour; gills crowded, yellowish-red; milk mild, white.—*Fr. Epicr. p.* 346. *Bull. t.* 567, *f.* 1. *Krombh. t.* 39, *f.* 21-24. *Ann. N.H. no.* 706.

In woods. [Low. Carolina.]

Known by its powerful smell of melilot, which it retains for a long time in the herbarium. Pileus 1½ in. across.—*M. J. B.*

Gen. 10. **RUSSULA**, Fr. Gen. Hymen.

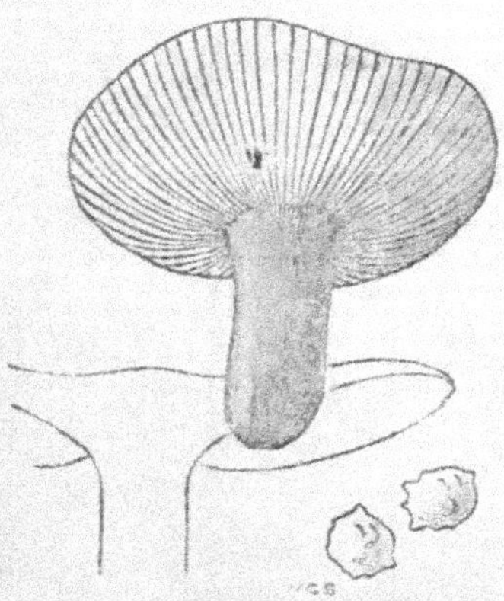

Fig. 52.

Spores white or very pale yellow, generally echinulate; veil entirely obsolete; pileus fleshy, convex, then expanded, and at length depressed; stem stout, polished, not corticate, generally spongy within, confluent with the hymenophore; gills nearly equal, milkless, rigid, brittle, with an acute edge, sometimes dropping water; trama vesiculose.

HAB. On the ground in late summer and autumn. (*Fig.* 52.)

This genus agrees with *Lactarius* in size, and some other characters, but differs in the absence of milk, and the gills being nearly equal. Odour none, or unpleasant. A few species are edible, but most are noxious.—*W. G. S.*

Sect. 1. *Compactæ.*

613. Russula nigricans. *Fr.* "Blackish Russula."

Pileus equally fleshy, compact, umbilicate, depressed, dingy-olive; margin inflexed, without striæ; stem solid, blunt, at length charry-black; gills rounded thick, distant, unequal.—*Fr. Epicr. p.* 350. *Bull. t.* 579, *f.* 2. *Krombh. t.* 70, *f.* 14, 15. *Sow. t.* 36. *Huss. t.* 73. *Ann. N.H. no.* 799*. *A. adustus*, *Eng. Fl.* v. *p.* 23.

In woods. Common.

Pileus 2½-3½ in. broad, white, smooth, or clothed with a very minute pubescence or meal, which when touched turns black, plano-depressed, at length infundibuliform, flesh thick, firm, crisp, turning red when cut, when old the whole plant is black. Margin not involute; gills narrow, pale yellowish, thick, distant, forked, decurrent; stem 3 in. high, nearly 1 in. thick, subincrassated below, very obtuse, substance and surface like that of the pileus. —*M. J. B.* Known from its coarse habit, and becoming red when bruised. Spores papillose, diameter ·0003 in.

614. Russula adusta. *Fr.* "Scorched Russula."

Pileus equally fleshy, compact, depressed, nearly infundibuliform; margin at first inflexed and smooth, then erect and without striæ; stem solid, blunt, dingy-cinereous; gills adnate, then decurrent, thin, crowded, unequal.—*Fr. Epicr. p.* 350. *Krombh. t.* 70, *f.* 7-11. *Batt. t.* 13, *C. Barla. t.* 17. *Ann. N.H. no.* 800.

In woods. Sept. Oct. [United States.]

Commonly smaller then *R. nigricans*, pileus at length infundibuliform; gills decurrent, thin, crowded; colour when young pallid or whitish, when old as if scorched, sooty-grey.—*Fries.* Well distinguished by its comparatively thin, crowded gills, and other points.—*B. & Br.*

615. Russula delica. *Fr.* "Whitish Russula."

Pileus equally fleshy, firm, umbilicate, even, shining; margin involute, smooth, without striæ; stem solid, compact, white; gills decurrent, thin, distant, white.—*Fr. Epicr. p.* 350. *Batt. t.* 17, *A. Paul. t.* 73, *f.* 1. *Krombh. t.* 70, *f.* 12, 13. *Vent. t.* 48, *f.* 3, 4.

In woods.

Stem solid, short, 1-2 in., ½ in. and more thick, even, smooth, white. Pileus everywhere fleshy, 3-5 in. broad, firm, umbilicate, then infundibuliform, regular, even, smooth; margin involute, without striæ. Flesh firm, dry, white.

Sect. 2. Furcatæ.

616. **Russula furcata.** *Fr.* "Forked Russula."

Mild, at length bitter. Pileus fleshy, rigid, plane, then depressed and infundibuliform, even, somewhat shining, with a silky lustre, at length smooth; margin even, acute; stem stout, firm, even, attenuated downwards; gills adnato-decurrent, rather thick, somewhat distant, forked, white, as well as the stem.—*Fr. Epicr. p.* 352. *Krombh. t.* 62, *f.* 1, 2, *t.* 69, *f.* 18-22. *Bull. t.* 26. *Schæff. t.* 94, *f.* 1. *Paul. t.* 74, *f.* 1. *Buxb.* v. *t.* 47, *f.* 2. *Eng. Fl.* v. *p.* 22. *Barla. t.* 16, *f.* 1-9.

In woods. Sept. Common. [United States.]

Stem stuffed, moderately firm, white. Pileus when young plane, the margin deflexed, then subinfundibuliform, green. Taste acrid.—*Fries.*

617. **Russula sanguinea.** *Fr.* "Blood-red Russula."

Acrid. Pileus fleshy, firm, convex, then gibbo-depressed and infundibuliform, at length even, moist; margin thin, acute, even; stem spongy or solid, slightly striate, white or reddish; gills decurrent, thin, very crowded, somewhat forked, connected, white. —*Fr. Epicr. p.* 351. *Bull. t.* 42. *Roq. t.* 12, *f.* 1. *Smith, P.M. f.* 17.

In woods.

Stem stout. Pileus fleshy, firm, obtuse, then depressed and infundibuliform, polished, 2-3 in. broad, blood-red, or growing pale about the margin. Flesh firm, cheesy, white. Gills very narrow, and much crowded. Taste acrid and peppery.

618. **Russula rosacea.** *Fr.* "Rosy Russula."

At length acrid. Pileus compact, convexo-plane, unequal, viscid, then dry, variegated with spots; margin acute, even; stem spongy or solid, even, white, or reddish; gills adnate, rather crowded, plane, unequal, white, divided behind.—*Fr. Epicr. p.* 351. *Bull. t.* 509, *f. Z.*

In woods. [United States.]

Stem solid, firm, at length spongy within, even, smooth, about 2 in. long. Pileus fleshy, convex, expanded, obtuse, but never depressed, 2-4 in. broad, cuticle when young and moist viscid and separable. Gills in all states adnate, crowded, fragile, forked behind, always persistently white. Spores papillose, almost globular, diameter ·00026 in. *(Fig. 52, reduced.)*

L 2

619. Russula sardonia. *Fr.* "Changeable Russula."

Pileus fleshy, firm, convexo-plane, then depressed, smooth; cuticle thin, adnate, viscid, changing colour; margin even; stem spongy or solid, short, white, or reddish; gills adnate, much crowded, somewhat forked, white, then yellowish.—*Fr. Epicr. p.* 353. *Schæff. t.* 16, *f.* 5, 6. *Krombh. t.* 68, *f.* 1-4.

Near paths in fir woods.

A robust and firm, but not large species. Stem solid, 1½-2 in. long, 1 in. thick, even, white, or reddish. Pileus 2-3 in. broad, reddish, pallid yellow, dirty yellow, opaque.

620. Russula depallens. *Fr.* "Bleached Russula."

Mild. Pileus fleshy, firm, undulate or irregular, even, opaque; cuticle thin, viscid, adnate, turning pale; margin even, at length slightly striate; stem firm, attenuated downwards, white, becoming cinereous; gills adnexed, crowded, fragile, furcate behind, whitish.—*Fr. Epicr. p.* 353. *Krombh. t.* 66, *f.* 12-13.

In pastures. [United States.]

Stem solid, about 1½ in. long. Pileus rarely depressed, but often undulate, at first pale-reddish or brownish, then whitish or yellowish, in all states opaque. Flesh white, mild. Gills forked at the base with shorter ones intermixed.

Sect. 3. *Rigidæ.*

621. Russula lactea. *Fr.* "Milk-white Russula."

Mild, milk-white. Pileus fleshy, compact, unpolished, then rivulose; margin straight, thin, obtuse, even; stem solid, compact, obese; gills free, thick, distant, rigid, slightly forked.—*Fr. Epicr. p.* 355. *B. & Br. Ann. N.H.* (1866) *no.* 1133. *Paul. t.* 74, *f.* 2.

On the ground. Aug. King's Cliffe. Esculent. [Mid. Carolina.]

The thick, distant gills, and milk-white pileus characterise this fine species. Stem 1½-2 in. long, 1½ in. thick. Pileus 2 in. broad, at first white, even, then whitish-tan coloured, when dry slightly cracked.

622. Russula virescens. *Fr.* "Greenish Russula."

Mild; pileus fleshy, firm, globose, then expanded and umbilicate, innato-flocculose, or areolate and warted; margin straight, obtuse, even; stem spongy or solid, stout, sub-rivulose, whitish;

gills free, rather crowded, unequal, and forked.—*Fr. Epicr. p.* 355. *Schæff. t.* 94 (*not f.* i.) *Vitt. t.* 3. *Sturm. t.* 31. *Larb. t.* 19, *f.* 3, *t.* 20, *f.* 5. *Krombh. t.* 67, *f.* 1-10. *Berk. Outl. t.* 13, *f.* 6. *Huss.* ii. *t.* 11. *Eng. Fl.* v. *p.* 23. *Barla. t.* 16. *f.* 10-12. *Vent. t.* 17, *f.* 1-2.

In woods. July—Sept. Esculent. [Mid. Carolina.]

Pileus 4 in. broad, convex, at length slightly depressed and irregular, of various livid hues, yellow, purple and green, fleshy, rugulose, very slightly viscid; margin even. The edge of the pileus sometimes hangs down in a singular manner. Gills white, forked, sometimes anastomosing at the base, rather close, moderately rigid, elastic. Stem 1-2 in. high, ½ in. or more thick, obtuse at the base, various in form, slightly reticulated with raised lines. Taste and odour mild.—*M. J. B.* Spores scarcely echinulate, almost globular, ·00025 in. diameter.

623. Russula lepida. *Fr.* "Scaly Russula."

Mild. Pileus fleshy, compact, convex, then depressed, unpolished, silky, rimoso-squamose, becoming pale; margin patent, obtuse, even; stem solid, compact, even, white or rosy; gills rounded, rather thick, somewhat crowded, many of them forked, white.—*Fr. Epicr. p.* 355. *Batsch. f.* 12. *Huss.* ii. *t.* 32. *Krombh. t.* 64, *f.* 19, 20. *Hogg. & Johnst. t.* 4.

In woods. Esculent. [Low. Carolina.]

Stem 3 in. long. 1 in. thick, even, white or roseate. Pileus 3 in. broad, opaque, unpolished, somewhat silky, at length rimoso-squamulose and discoloured; colour beautifully rosy-red, the disc especially becoming whitish.

624. Russula rubra. *Fr.* "Red Russula."

Acrid. Pileus fleshy, rigid, convex, then plane or depressed, dry, polished, becoming even; margin patent, obtuse, without striæ; stem solid, hard, stout, white, or red; gills obtusely adnate, rather crowded, whitish, often forked and dimidiate.—*Fr. Epicr. p.* 354. *Larbr. t.* 18. *f.* 7. *Roq. t.* 5, *f.* 2. *Krombh. t.* 65. *Vitt. Mang. t.* 38, *f.* 2. *Schæff. t.* 15, *f.* 4-6. *Eng. Fl.* v. *p.* 22.

In woods. Aug. [United States.]

Pileus compact, dry, even, scarcely brittle, of a cellular texture; gills close; stem 2 in. high, firm, often tinged with rose; very bitter, like gall, extremely acrid.—*Fries.*

Sect. 4. *Heterophyllæ.*

625. Russula vesca. *Fr.* "Edible Russula."

Mild, sweet-tasted. Pileus fleshy, firm, umbilicato-convex, then plane and infundibuliform, venoso-rugose, and streaked; flesh under the viscid cuticle reddish; margin even, or remotely striate; stem firm, unequal, rivuloso-rugose; gills adnate, rather crowded, unequal, and forked, white, as well as the stem.—*Fr. Epicr. p.* 352. *Krombh. t.* 67, *f.* 12-19. *Vitt. t.* 27. *Bolt. t.* 1. *Paul. t.* 76, *f.* 2, 3. *Huss.* i. *t.* 89.

In woods. Esculent.

Of medium size. Stem solid, peculiarly reticulated, attenuated at the base. Pileus flesh-red, disc darker, margin at length patent.

626. Russula cyanoxantha. *Fr.* "Blue and Yellow Russula."

Mild. Pileus compact, convex, then expanded and depressed, or infundibuliform, even, rugose or virgate; margin remotely and faintly striate; stem spongy, stuffed but firm, when old cavernose, equal, smooth, even, white; gills rounded behind, connected by veins, broad, little crowded, furcate, mixed with shorter, white.—*Fr. Hym. Suec.* ii. *p.* 194. *B. & Br. Ann. N.H.* (1866), *no.* 1131. *Schæff. t.* 93. *R. vesca, var. b. Fr. Ep. p.* 353.

In woods. Sept. Fineshade. [United States.]

Colour of the pileus variable, in the typical form lilac or purplish, or greenish olive, disc growing pale and yellowish; margin bluish or livid-purple; flesh firm, of a cheesy consistency, white, under the separable cuticle commonly reddish; pileus 2-3 in. broad or more; stem 2-3 in. long.

627. Russula heterophylla. *Fr.* "Variable Russula."

Mild. Pileus fleshy, firm, convexo-plane, then depressed, even, polished, cuticle very thin, evanescent; margin thin, even, or densely striate; flesh white; stem solid, firm, nearly equal, even, white; gills attenuated, nearly free, thin, much crowded, forked and dimidiate, white.—*Fr. Epicr. p.* 352. *Fl. Dan. t.* 1909, *f.* 1. *Paul. t.* 75, *f.* 1-5. *Badh.* i. *t.* 10, *f.* 3, ii. *t.* 3, *f.* 3, 4. *Price. f.* 37. *Smith E.M. f.* 3. *Hogg. & Johnst. t.* 9. *Berk. Outl. t.* 13, *f.* 5. *Huss.* i. *t.* 84. *Cooke. B.F. t.* 4.

In woods. Common. Esculent.

Always mild. Stem firm, solid; pileus never reddish or purple; gills very narrow, much crowded, white. Spores echinulate, ·00021 × ·00026 in.

628. Russula fœtens. *Fr.* "Fœtid Russula."

Acrid, fœtid. Pileus bullate, then expanded and depressed, rigid, cuticle adnate, viscid; disc fleshy; margin widely membranaceous, tuberculoso-sulcate; stem stout, stuffed, then hollow; gills adnexed, very unequal, and forked, anastomosing by veins, whitish, at first guttate.—*Fr. Epicr. p.* 359. *Krombh. t.* 70, *f.* 1-6. *Bull. t.* 292. *Sow. t.* 415. *Eng. Fl.* v. *p.* 22. *Smith. P.M. f.* 16.

In woods. July—Sept. Common. [United States.]

Generally rancid and stinking, but at times fragrant; it is not uncommon to find it as sweet smelling as *Ag. odorus*, Bull.—*W. G. S.*

Gregarious. Pileus 4-5 in. broad, at first convex; the margin broadly folded inwards, convex, at length more or less depressed, with the margin somewhat vaulted, fleshy in the centre; margin thin, furrowed and tubercled, the striæ appearing as if a glutinous membrane were stretched over them, dirty yellow, rather brittle. Gills forked, dirty white or yellowish, moderately broad, connected by veins. Stem 3-4 in. high, above 1 in. thick, obtuse, incrassated at the base, ruggedly hollow within, as if eaten by snails, white or with a dirty yellow tinge, depresso-tomentose, beneath the gills minutely pitted longitudinally, flesh rather yellow. Highly acrid, odour very strong and penetrating, empyreumatic, somewhat resembling that of prussic acid, but exceedingly disagreeable.—*M. J. B.* Spores minutely echinulate, almost globular, diameter ·00032 in.

Sect. 5. Fragiles.

629. Russula emetica. *Fr.* "Emetic Russula."

Acrid. Pileus fleshy, expanded or depressed, polished, shining; margin patent, at length sulcate; flesh white beneath the reddish separable cuticle; stem spongy-solid, firm, elastic, even, white or reddish; gills free, equal, broad, somewhat distant, white.—*Fr. Epicr. p.* 357. *Lenz. f.* 15. *Buxb.* v. *t.* 47, *f.* 1. *Ann. N.H. no.* 333. *Krombh. t.* 66, *f.* 4-7? *Cooke B.F. t.* 22. *Eng. Fl.* v. *p.* 21. *Barla. t.* 14, *f.* 4-9. *Smith P.M. f.* 21.

In woods. July—Dec. Poisonous. [United States.]

Pileus 2-5 in. broad, glutinous when young, smooth, hemispherical, at length plane, depressed in the centre; margin thin, striato-sulcate, purple, rose-red, bluish, fuscous, yellow, or even white; gills rather distant, broad, rigid, thickish, connected by veins, equal, with a very few smaller interspersed, always white; stem 2-3 in. high, longitudinally rugulose, firm, solid, white, or tinged with the colour of the pileus, very acrid and poisonous.—*Eng. Fl.* Known by its very acrid taste and free gills, between which and the stem is a distinct channel.—*M. J. B.* Spores echinulate, almost globular, diameter ·00028 in.

630. Russula ochroleuca. *Fr.* "Ochrey Russula."

Acrid. Pileus fleshy, expanded or depressed, polished, cuticle adnate, turning pale; margin patent, becoming even; stem spongy-stuffed, firm, reticulato-rugulose, white then cinereous; gills rounded behind, connected, broad, subequal, white then pallid.—*Fr. Epicr. p.* 358. *Krombh. t.* 64, *f.* 7-9. *Larbr. t.* 19. *f.* 1. *Buxb.* v. *t.* 45, *f.* 2. *Ann. N.H. no.* 707.

In fir woods. Sept. [United States.]

Pileus always yellowish, turning pale, about the same size as *R. emetica*, from which it differs in the finely reticulated rugose stem, which is white then greyish, and the adnate cuticle of the pileus. Spores papillose, diameter ·00029 in.

631. **Russula fragilis.** *Fr.* "Fragile Russula."

Very acrid; pileus lax, fleshy, thin, plane, depressed, unequal, polished, cuticle thin, becoming pale, opaque, slightly viscid; margin tuberculoso-striate; stem stuffed, then hollow, shining; gills fixed, thin, crowded, ventricose, white.—*Fr. Epicr. p.* 359. *Krombh. t.* 64, *f.* 12-18. *Bull. t.* 509, *f. T. U. Vent. t.* 33, *f.* 4, 5. *Corda. Sturm. t.* 53. *Barla. t.* 14, *f.* 10-12.

In woods. Common. [S. Carolina.]

Stem 1½-2 in. long, always finely striate, white. Pileus 1-1½ in. broad, rarely more, colour variable, always opaque.

632. **Russula integra.** *Fr.* "Entire Russula."

Mild. Pileus fleshy, expanded or depressed, with a viscid cuticle, growing pale; margin thin, at length sulcate and tuberculose; flesh white; stem spongy, stuffed, even, ventricose, white; gills nearly free, very broad, equal, distant, white, then pallid, powdered with yellow.—*Fr. Epicr. p.* 360. *Schæff. t.* 92. *Vitt. t.* 21. *Krombh. t.* 64, *f.* 4-6, *t.* 66, *f.* 14, 15. *Batt. t.* 16, c. *Ann. N.H. no.* 334. *Harz. t.* 59.

In woods. Aug. Bristol.

Distinguished by its mild taste, its at length sulcate and tuberculated margin, its white stem, and its gills, which gradually assume a pale dirty yellow hue.—*M. J. B.*

633. **Russula decolorans.** *Fr.* "Discolored Russula."

Mild. Pileus fleshy, firm, spherical, then expanded or depressed, polished, thin, cuticle becoming pale; margin thin, even; stem spongy, solid, elongated, cylindrical, rugoso-striate, white then cinereous; gills adnexed, forked behind, thin, crowded, white, then yellowish.—*Fr. Epicr. p.* 361. *Mag. Zool. & Bot. no.* 60.

In woods. Sept. Esculent.

Distinguished from *R. alutaceus* by its pale spores, in consequence of which the gills remain much longer white. The inside of the stem, which is thick and spongy, acquires in general a cinereous tinge.—*M. J. B.*

634. **Russula aurata.** *Fr.* "Golden Russula."

Becoming acrid. Pileus fleshy, rigid, convexo-plane, shining; margin at length striate; flesh under the viscid cuticle lemon-coloured; stem spongy or compact, rather striate, white or lemon-coloured; gills rounded behind, free, broad, equal, shining, edge lemon-yellow.—*Fr. Epicr. p.* 360. *Krapf. t.* 5. *Schæff. t.* 15, *f.* 1-3. *Krombh. t.* 66, *f.* 8-11. *Ann. N.H. no.* 335.

In woods. Aug. Bristol.

A most splendid species, distinguished by its golden yellow shining pileus, and yellow-margined gills.—*M. J. B.*

Stem firm, 2-3 in. long, cylindrical, obsoletely striate. Pileus 2-3 in. broad. Flesh lemon-coloured beneath the adnate cuticle.

635. Russula veternosa. *Fr.* "Sleepy Russula."

Acrid. Pileus loosely fleshy, plane, then depressed, polished, cuticle thin, adnate, becoming pale; margin membranaceous, even; stem spongy, then hollow, soft, equal, even, fragile, white; gills adnate, narrow, broader behind, unequal, straw-coloured.—*Fr. Epicr. p.* 354. *Paul. t.* 74, *f.* 3. *B.& Br. Ann. N.H.* (1866), *no.* 1132. *Krombh. t.* 66, *f.* 18, 19.

On the ground. Chatteris.

Flesh white, spongy. Pileus 2-3 in. broad, rose-coloured or flesh-coloured, soon with the disc whitish or yellowish.

636. Russula nitida. *Fr.* "Shining Russula."

Nauseous, rather fœtid. Pileus somewhat fleshy, becoming rigid, convexo-plane then depressed, shining, discoid; margin thin, from the first striate and tuberculose; flesh white; stem stuffed, soft, white, growing pallid; gills adnexed, seceding, then crowded, shining, white, then yellow, naked.—*Fr. Epicr. p.* 362. *Schæff. t.* 254. *Krombh. t.* 66, *f.* 1-3. *Berk. Outl. t.* 13, *f.* 7. *Eng. Fl.* v. *p.* 21.

In woods. King's Cliffe. [United States.]

Pileus 1-2 in. broad, convex, becoming nearly plane or depressed, viscid when moist; margin very thin, at first even, afterwards furrowed and tubercled, mostly yellow, but occasionally tinged with purple; gills buff, connected by veins, all equal, free; spores pale yellow; stem 1-2 in. long, ½ in. thick, spongy, at length hollow, white or yellowish, covered with minute white meal.—*M. J. B.*

637. Russula alutacea. *Fr.* "Tan-coloured Russula."

Mild. Pileus fleshy, expanded or depressed, with a viscid cuticle, growing pale; margin thin, at length striate, tuberculose; flesh white; stem spongy, solid, stout, white or reddish, even; gills at first free, thick, equal, somewhat distant, yellow, then ochraceous tan-coloured, naked.—*Fr. Epicr. p.* 362. *Vitt. t.* 34. *Roq. t.* 10, *f.* 4. *Krombh. t.* 1, *f.* 21, 22, *t.* 64, *f.* 1-3. *Berk. Outl. t.* 13, *f.* 8. *Hogg & Johnst. t.* 15. *Eng. Fl.* v. *p.* 21. *Price, f.* 36. *Barla. t.* 14, *f.* 1-3. *Smith. E.M. f.* 6.

In woods. Common. Esculent. [United States.]

Pileus 3 in. broad, fleshy, smooth, viscid when moist, depressed; margin at first even, more or less furrowed and tubercled when old, pink, livid, olive, &c.; gills broad, equal, sometimes slightly forked, ventricose, free, connected by veins; spores yellow; stem 1½ in. long, 1 in. thick, blunt, surface longitudinally wrinkled or grooved, solid, spongy within, smooth, white, sometimes yellow. Taste mild, pleasant; acrid when old.—*M. J. B.*

638. **Russula lutea.** *Fr.* "Yellow Russula."

Mild. Pileus rather firm, plano-depressed, with a viscid cuticle, becoming pale; flesh white; margin even; stem stuffed, then hollow, soft, white; gills free, crowded, connected by veins, egg-yellow.—*Fr. Epicr. p.* 366. *Eng. Fl.* v. *p.* 21.

In woods. Scotland. [United States.]

Pileus 1-2 in. broad, plano-depressed, rather viscid, yellow, becoming pale, rarely white; gills connected by veins; stem more or less hollow, slender; taste mild; brittle.—*Fries.* Spores yellow, echinulate, diameter ·00032 in.

639. **Russula vitellina.** *Fr.* "Egg-yellow Russula."

Strong-scented, mild. Pileus submembranaceous, at length tuberculoso-striate, self-coloured; disc minute, rather fleshy; stem thin; gills free, seceding, equal, saffron-yellow.—*Fr. Epicr. p.* 363. *Batsch. f.* 72.

In fir woods.

Stem equal, scarcely exceeding an inch long, 2 lin. thick. Pileus about an inch broad, yellow, then becoming pale. Gills distant, rather thick, connected by veins.—*Fries.*

640. **Russula chamæleontina.** *Fr.* "Chameleon Russula."

Mild, fragile. Pileus fleshy, plane or depressed, pellicle thin, discoloured, viscid; margin smooth, then striate; stem hollow, white; gills much crowded, even, furcate, yellow.—*Fr. Obs.* i., *no.* 89. *B. & Br. Ann. N.H.* (1865), *no.* 1014.

In woods. King's Cliffe. Sept. 30, 1863.

Pileus rosy-red, purplish-lilac, &c., ultimately wholly or partially yellowish, adnexed or free, narrow.—*Fries.*

Gen. **11.** **CANTHARELLUS,** Adams. Fung. Ord. V.

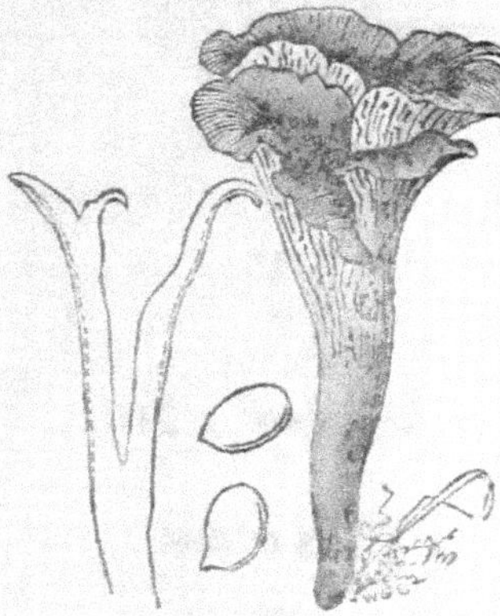

Fig. 53.

Spores white ; veil entirely absent; pileus fleshy or membranaceous ; stem confluent with the hymenophore, or absent ; gills decurrent, folded, more or less thick and swollen, branched ; trama floccose. (*Fig* 53.)

HAB. Growing on the ground, or on rotten wood, moss, etc.

This genus holds an intermediate place between *Agaricus* and *Craterellus*, some species being close to one, some to the other genus. Some are said to be poisonous, others edible.—*W. G. S.*

Sect. 1. *Mesopodes.*

641. Cantharellus cibarius. *Fr.* "Edible Chantarelle."

Egg-yellow. Pileus fleshy, at first repand, smooth, at length turbinate ; stem solid, attenuated downwards ; gills thick, distant, of the same colour.—*Fr. Epicr. p.* 365. *Grev. t.* 258. *Hogg & Johnst. t.* 16. *Lenz. f.* 27. *Krombh. t.* 45, *f.* 1-11. *Vitt. t.* 25, *f.* 1. *Sow. t.* 46. *Batsch. f.* 120. *Paul. t.* 36. *Cooke B.F. t.* 13, *f.* 1. *Smith E.M. f.* 8. *Gard. Chron.* (1860), *p.* 312. *Badh.* i. *t.* 9, *f.* 2, ii. *t.* 8, *f.* 1. *Price f.* 94. *Barla. t.* 28, *f.* 7-15. *Eng. Fl.* v. *p.* 125. *Vent. t.* 39, *f.* 3, 4.

In woods. Common. Esculent. [United States.]

Subgregarious. Pileus 1-4 in. broad, fleshy, firm, variously lobed, depressed, the margin vaulted, smooth, shining, of a rich yolk of egg yellow, paler when dry, flesh white or yellowish. Folds much sinuated, but evidently forked, thick, fleshy, decurrent; stem 1-2 in. high, ⅓-½ in. thick, attenuated downwards, smooth, tough, yellow, diffused into the pileus. Smell very agreeable like that of ripe apricots, taste agreeable, but pungent.—*M. J. B.* Spores ·0003 × ·0002 in.

642. Cantharellus aurantiacus. *Fr.* "False Chantarelle."

Nearly orange-colour. Pileus fleshy, soft, depressed, tomentose ; stem stuffed, unequal ; gills crowded, straight, darker than the pileus.—*Fr. Epicr. p.* 365. *Jacq. Coll.* ii. *t.* 14, *f.* 3. *Batsch. f.* 37. *Sow. t.* 413. *Schæff. t.* 206. *Berk. Outl. p.* 14, *f.* 1. *Krombh. t.* 46, *f.* 3-6. *Smith P.M. f.* 19.

In fir woods and on heaths. Common. [S. Carolina.]

Stem at length hollow, 2 in. long, somewhat curved and unequal, ochraceous. Pileus soft, depressed, 2-3 in. broad, sub-tomentose, ochraceous-orange. Margin involute. Gills repeatedly dichotomous and crowded, dark-orange.

643. Cantharellus Brownii. *B. & Br.* "Brown's Chantarelle."

Ochraceous-white, or cream-coloured. Pileus thin, convex, subumbonate; stem slender, tough, stuffed; folds rather distant, linear, extremely narrow, sometimes forked, obtusely decurrent. *B. & Br. Ann. N.H. ser.* ii., *vol.* ii., *p.* 262. *Berk. Outl. p* 216.

Amongst grass. Oct. Hitchin.

Whole plant of a pale ochraceous cream colour. Pileus orbicular, thin, convex, subumbonate, ½ in. across, sometimes rather larger, obscurely silky. Stem slender, 1½-2 in. high, scarce 1 line thick, nearly equal, subfurfuraceous, furnished with a little white fibrillose mycelium at the base, which sometimes forms a small earthy ball, rather tough, stuffed. Folds linear, very narrow, sometimes slightly forked, obtusely decurrent, insterstices smooth, occasionally quite obsolete, except towards the margin. Hymenium nearly white.—*B. & Br.*

644. Cantharellus umbonatus. *P.* "Umbonate Chantarelle."

Pileus fleshy, thin, umbonate, then depressed, flocculose, blackish-cinereous; stem stuffed, equal, paler; gills straight, crowded, white.—*Fr. Epicr. p.* 365. *Jacq. Coll.* ii. *t.* 16, *f.* 1. *Ann. N.H. no.* 701.

Amongst moss. Mossburnford. [United States.]

Stem 3 in. long, about 4 lines thick, elastic, villous at the base, cinereous. Pileus 1 in. and more broad, even, dry, between flocculose and silky dry. Flesh soft, white, reddish when wounded.

645. Cantharellus tubæformis. *Fr.* "Tubæform Chantarelle."

Pileus between fleshy and membranaceous, infundibuliform, repand, and lobed, flocculose, brownish, turning pale; stem hollow, smooth, orange-tawny, at length compressed, lacunose; gills thick, distant, multifid-branching, yellow or dingy, naked.—*Fr. Epicr. p.* 366. *Fl. Dan. t.* 2080, *f.* 1. *Pers. Ic. & Desc. t.* 6. *f.* 1. *Sturm. t.* 30. *Batt. t.* 23, *f.* 1. *Eng. Fl.* v. *p.* 125. *Ann. N. H. no.* 74. *Krombh. t.* 4, *f.* 8-10, *t.* 46, *f.* 7-9. *Berk. exs. no.* 140.

In woods. Aug.—Oct. [United States.]

Gregarious. Pileus 2 in. broad, thin, at first convex, at length much undulated, depressed, and very deeply umbilicate, occasionally pervious, scrobiculato-squamose, brownish-yellow. Folds straight, forked, slightly anastomosing, cinereous-yellow, frosted with a white bloom. Stem 2 in. high,

½ in. thick, hollow, compressed, thickest downwards, smooth, slightly downy at the base, saffron-coloured, brownish yellow above. Spores round, white.—*M. J. B.* Spores ·0003 × ·00018 in.

CANTHARELLUS LUTESCENS (Bull. t. 473, f. 3) has a paler yellow stem, and the gills less divided; the pileus, moreover, is merely umbilicate. It is scarcely to be deemed a distinct species, and occurs in the same localities with the above.—*M. J. B.*

646. Cantharellus infundibuliformis. *Fr.* "Funnel-shaped Chantarelle."

Pileus somewhat membranaceous, umbilicate, then infundibuliform, floccoso-rugose, dingy yellow, growing pale; stem fistulose, even, smooth, yellow; gills thick, distant, dichotomous, yellow or cinereous, at length pruinose.—*Fr. Epicr. p.* 366. *Sow. t.* 47. *Krombh. t.* 4, *f.* 8-10. *Fl. Dan. t.* 1617. *Vaill. t.* 12, *f.* 9, 10. *Cooke exs. no.* 226.

In woods.

Stem 2-3 in. long, about 2 lin. thick, somewhat thickened at the base, even, smooth, always yellow. Pileus 1-2 in. broad, at length funnel-shaped, ordinarily pervious to the base, when moist yellowish-cinereous or dingy, paler when dry, margin at length waved.

647. Cantharellus radicosus. *B. & Br.* "Rooting Chantarelle."

Small. Pileus deeply umbilicate, floccose, black; stem pallid, rooting; hymenium white; gills narrow.—*B. & Br. Ann. N.H.* (1860), *no.* 1134. *Saund. & Sm. t.* i. *C. carbonarius, A. & S. no.* 1129.

On charcoal heaps, &c. Sept.—Nov.

Pileus ¾-1 in. across, deeply umbilicate, dark brown or black, rough, with radiating flocci; stem rooting, deeply pallid; gills narrow, white. Two or three pilei often grow from the same obconical root, which is white and spongy.—*B. & Br.* Spores ·0035 × ·0002 in.—*W. G. S.* Apparently not the *Cantharellus carbonarius* of Fries.

648. Cantharellus cinereus. *Fr.* "Grey Chantarelle."

Pileus submembranaceous, infundibuliform, pervious to the base, villoso-squamulose, dingy black; stem hollow, of the same colour; gills thick, distant, cinereous.—*Fr. Epicr. p.* 366. *Krombh. t.* 45, *f.* 12. *Bull. t.* 465, *f.* 2. *Bolt. t.* 34. *B. & Br. Ann. N.H.* 1865, *no.* 1016*-1139*. *Eng. Fl.* v. *p.* 126. *Letell. t.* 684.

In woods. Rare. Halifax. Near Worcester (*E.L.*) Burnham Beeches. [United States.]

Spores ·00035 × ·00022 in. Sporophores obtuse. (*Fig.* 53, *reduced.*)

Sect. 2. *Pleuropus.*

649. Cantharellus muscigenus. *Fr.* "Moss Chanterelle."

Pileus submembranaceous, spathulate, horizontal, smooth, zoned, brown, then whitish-cinereous; stem lateral, short, villous at the base; gills swollen, distant, branched, of the same colour. —*Fr. Epicr. p.* 368. *Bull. t.* 288, 498. *f.* 1. *Nees. f.* 236. *Eng. Fl.* v. *p.* 127. *Schn. Sturm. t.* 3.

On the larger mosses. Berwick. Bristol. [S. Carolina.]

Pileus membranaceous, tough, nearly semicircular, somewhat zoned, slightly undulated, dirty-white, cinereous, or dingy. Folds somewhat tumid, divergent, scarcely anastomosing, confluent behind; stem villous at the base, sometimes obsolete.—*Fries.*

Sect. 3. *Resupinati.*

650. Cantharellus lobatus. *Fr.* "Lobed Chantarelle."

Membranaceous, sessile, horizontal, lobed, brown; gills fold-like, distinct, branched, divergent.—*Fr. Epicr. p.* 369. *Fl. Dan. t.* 1077. *Bolt. t.* 177. *Eng. Fl.* v. *p.* 127.

On mosses, in swamps.

Pileus 2 lines, $1\frac{1}{2}$ in. broad, membranaceous, horizontal, often at length vertical, attached laterally by a few byssoid fibres, which sometimes run down the moss for some distance, pale, cinereous umber; margin nearly white, under a lens most minutely scabrous, as if it were innato-fibrillose, occasionally there are two or three faint zones. Hymenium paler, consisting of radiating, more or less anastomosing wrinkles, with many connecting reticulate veins. Spores round, rather large. When old often very much lobed and crisped, and then the wrinkles, especially at the base, are reticulate, though towards the margin they continue distinct.—*M. J. B.*

651. Cantharellus retirugus. *Fr.* "Furrowed Chantarelle."

Membranaceous, expanded, repand, lobed, whitish cinereous, fixed behind with little threads; gills radiating from the centre, very thin, reticulated.—*Fr. Epicr. p.* 369. *Bull. t.* 498, *f.* 1. *Sow. t.* 348. *Berk. Outl. t.* 14, *f.* 2.

On mosses, in swamps. King's Cliffe.

Similar to *C. lobatus*, but the gills are thinner and reticulated. Pileus membranaceous, sub-rotund, 3-5 lin. broad, margin at first entire, then split, cinereous-white above, darker beneath.

Gen. 12. NYCTALIS, Fr. Gen. Hymen.

Fig. 54.

Veil universal, floccoso-pruinose; pileus in the British species fleshy and pruinose or pulverulent; stem confluent with the hymenophore; gills broad, simple, unequal, thick, fleshy, juicy, or subgelatinous, edge obtuse, not descending on the stem.

(Fig. 54.)

HAB. The British species are small and parasitic on other Agarics.

This genus consists of fleshy putrescent Fungi. Some species grow in subterranean passages.

652. Nyctalis asterophora. *Fr.* "Star-bearing Nyctalis."

Pileus somewhat fleshy, conical, then hemispherical, cuticle flocculoso-pruinose, breaking up into a fawn-coloured stratum; stem stuffed, pruinose, then brownish, twisted; gills adnate, distant, rather forked, straight, dingy.—*Fr. Epicr. p.* 371. *Bull. t.* 516, *f.* 1. *Sturm. t.* 26.

On dead *Russula nigricans.* Common. [Mid. & Up. Carolina.]

Stem scarcely exceeding ½ an in., ½-1 lin. thick, equal, twisted, at first whitish and pruinose, then brownish. Pileus white when young, papillate, then cracking, pulverulent and fawn-coloured. Gills thick. The powder of the pileus consists of the stellate bodies, constituting the spores in the genus *Alsterophora.* Diameter ·00055 in. Spores ·0001 × ·00005 in.

(Fig. 54, natural size.)

653. Nyctalis parasitica. *Fr.* "Parasitic Nyctalis."

Pileus somewhat fleshy, conical, then expanded, unequal, cuticle persistent, grey, pruinose; stem minutely fistulose, flocculoso-villous, whitish; gills adnate, thick, distant, at length contorted and anastomosing, brownish.—*Fr. Epicr. p.* 372. *Bull. t.* 574, *f.* 2. *Sow. t.* 543. *Berk. Outl. t.* 19, *f.* 2. *Eng. Fl.* v. *p.* 52. *Berk. exs. no.* 130.

On *Russula adusta* and *R. fœtens.*

Pileus ⅓ in. broad, conico-campanulate, silky, sub-carnose, somewhat irregular, grey, with a slight tinge of umber at the apex, flesh dark; gills darker than the pileus, paler at the edges, thick, distant, somewhat forked and anastomosing, connected by veins, broader towards the apex, slightly adnate, ventricose; stem 1-2 in. high, 1 line thick, thickest downwards, very silky, especially at the base, crisp, dark within. Odour like *Polyporus squamosus.*—*M. J. B.*

Gen. 13. MARASMIUS, Fr.

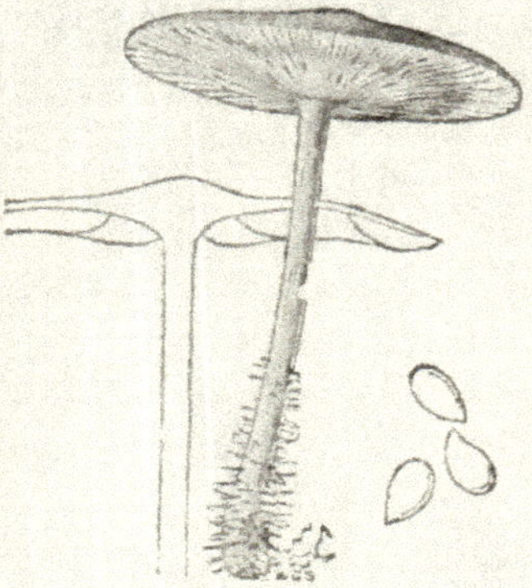

Fig. 55.

Spores white, sub-elliptical; pileus tough, fleshy, or membranaceous; stem central (in one species it is absent), confluent with the hymenophore, but of a different texture; gills thick, tough, and coriaceous, confluent at the base, generally distant, and rarely decurrent, with a sharp entire edge. *(Fig. 55.)*

HAB. Epiphytal, or growing on decayed leaves, or the roots of grasses.

This genus, closely allied to *Collybia*, commences the series of Agarics that are not putrescent, but which dry up with drought, and come to life with rain. This biological character is of great importance; by its neglect species nearly related have been widely separated. The texture of all the species is tough, distinguishing them from the preceding. The species are mostly small and slender. Some are edible, others have an offensive, fœtid, or alliaceous smell.—*W. G. S.*

Sect. 1. *Collybiæ.*

654. Marasmius urens. *Fr.* "Stinging Marasmius."

Acrid. Pileus between fleshy and coriaceous, convex, then plane, smooth, even, at length wrinkled or rivulose; stem fibrous, solid, rigid, pallid, mealy with white fibrils, and clothed with white down at the base; gills free, joined behind, pallid, somewhat yellowish, becoming brownish, at length remote, distant, firm.—*Fr. Epicr. p.* 373. *Bull t.* 528, *f.* 1. *Fl. Dan. t.* 2018, *f.* 1. *Berk. Outl. t.* 14, *f.* 3. *Ann. N.H. no.* 275. *Price, f.* 13. *Smith. P.M. f.* 30.

In woods.

Gregarious, cæspitose. Stem 2-3 in. long, 3 lin. thick, equal, clothed everywhere with white flocci, pallid, villous at the base. Pileus 2-3 in. broad, pinkish-tawny; margin thin, involute. Taste acrid, stinging. Spores ·0001 × ·00012 in.

655. Marasmius peronatus. *Fr.* "Masked Marasmius."

Acrid. Pileus between coriaceous and membranaceous, convexo-plane, opaque, at length lacunose; margin striate; stem fibrous, stuffed, outer coat villous, yellow, then rufescent, base peronate and strigose; gills adnexed, seceding, rather thin and crowded, pallid, then rufescent.—*Fr. Epicr. p.* 373. *Bolt. t.* 58. *Sow. t.* 37. *Fl. Dan. t.* 2018, *f.* 2. *Berk. Outl. t.* 14, *f.* 4. *Eng. Fl.* v. *p.* 47. *Cooke, B.F. t.* 14, *f.* 2. *Berk. exs. no.* 125.

In woods, amongst leaves. Common.

Pileus 1-2½ in. broad, convex or campanulate, at length expanded, sometimes umbonate, carnoso-coriaceous, subrufescent or yellowish, pallid when dry, clothed with a minute matted silkiness. Gills of the colour of the pileus, with a yellowish margin, distant, rounded behind, almost free. Stem 2-3 in. high, 2 lines thick, solid above and downy, hollow below, and there covered with dense yellow strigæ. Taste acrid.—*M. J. B.* Spores pip-shaped, ·00028 × ·00015 in. (*Fig.* 55, *reduced.*)

656. Marasmius porreus. *Fr.* "Garlic Marasmius."

Strong scented. Pileus between coriaceous and membranaceous, convex, then expanded, striate, floccid, disc of the same colour, even; stem stuffed, then hollow, tough, without juice, incrassated at either end, reddish-brown, pubescent; gills free, seceding, distant, firm, yellowish, becoming pallid.—*Fr. Epicr. p.* 374. *Sow. t.* 81. *Bull. t.* 158. *Eng. Fl.* v. *p.* 48.

In woods, amongst leaves. Sept.—Nov.

Smell strong of garlic, persistent sometimes for years in dried specimens. Pileus ½-1 in. broad, plane, slightly depressed, dirty white, with a brownish shade, paler on the margin, which is membranaceous, and regularly striate. Gills nearly free, paler than the pileus, slightly connected by veins. Stem 2-3 in. high, 2-3 lines thick, velvety, albido-pulverulent, rufescent, tomentose below, pale above, fistulose.—*M. J. B.* Spores pip-shaped, ·00015 × ·00025 in.

657. Marasmius oreades. *Fr.* "Fairy-ring Champignon."

Pileus fleshy, tough, convexo-plane, then somewhat umbonate, smooth, growing pale; stem solid, equal, naked, with a villous interwoven coat, pallid, base naked; gills free, broad, distant, cream-coloured.—*Fr. Epicr. p.* 375. *Bolt. t.* 151. *Grev. t.* 323. *Vitt. t.* 10, *f.* 1. *Krombh. t.* 43, *f.* 11-16. *Sow. t.* 247. *Schæff. t.* 77. *Bull. t.* 144, 528, *f.* 2. *Paul. t.* 103, *f.* 1-4. *Price f.* 11. *Cooke, B.F. t.* 14, *f.* 1. *Berk. Outl. t.* 14, *f.* 5. *Eng. Fl.* v. *p.* 48. *Gard. Chron.* (1860), *p.* 190. *Trans. Woolh. Cl.* (1867), *t.* xii. *Smith. E.M. f.* 28. *Badh.* i. *t.* 8, *f.* 3, ii. *t.* 7. *f.* 4.

In exposed pastures, forming rings. Common. Esculent. [Mid. Carolina.]

Gregarious. Pileus ½-1½ in. broad, smooth, fleshy, convex, at length nearly plane, more or less umbonate, generally more or less compressed and sinuate, tough, coriaceous, elastic, wrinkled, and sometimes cracked, watery brown, as it becomes dry cream-coloured, margin pale; flesh white, quite distinct from that of the stem. Gills free, pale, distant, slightly ventricose. Stem 1-2 in. high, 2-3 lines thick, equal, solid, very tough, the outer coat squamuloso-fibrous, base downy, somewhat rooting, and attached to the roots of grass. Taste and odour strong but agreeable.—*M. J. B.*

658. Marasmius fusco-purpureus. *Fr.* "Purple-brown Marasmius."

Inodorous. Pileus rather fleshy, convexo-plane, sub-umbilicate, growing pale; stem fistulose, smooth, without juice, brown-purple, base rubiginous, strigose; gills annulato-adnexed, at length free, distant, rufescent.—*Fr. Epicr. p.* 377. *Pers. Ic. & Desc. t.* 4, *f.* 1-3. *Eng. Fl.* v. *p.* 49. *Mag. Zool. & Bot. no.* 41. *Berk. exs. no.* 127.

In woods, amongst leaves. Common.

Stem short, scarcely exceeding 1 in. long, 1-2 lin. thick, smooth, at first pallid, then rufous or blackish purple, with a strigose, rubiginous, woolly base. Pileus ½-1 in. broad, brownish purple, growing pale, tan-coloured and rugulose.

659. Marasmius Wynnei. *B. & Br.* "Wynne's Marasmius."

Inodorous, cæspitose. Pileus fleshy, convexo-plane, subumbonate, lilac brown, tardily changing colour; stem fistulose, of the same colour, furfuraceous; gills thick, distant, adnexed, bright coloured.—*Berk. Outl. p.* 220, *t.* 19. *f.* 3. *Ann. N.H. no.* 802.

Amongst leaves, twigs, &c. Coed Coch.

Gregarious or cæspitose. Pileus 1-1½ in. across, variously tinged with brown and lilac, not rapidly changing colour, umbonate, slightly fleshy. Stem 2 in. high, 1½ line thick, rather paler than the pileus, fistulose, furfuraceous, springing from a white mycelium, but by no means strigose or tawny at the base. Gills distant, thick, moderately broad, adnexed, beautifully tinged with lilac; interstices even.—*B. & Br.*

660. Marasmius erythropus. *Fr.* "Pallid Marasmius."

Inodorous. Pileus rather fleshy, convexo-plane, then obtuse, even, turning pale, at length rugose; stem fistulose, striate, smooth, dark-red, somewhat pruinose when dry, base whitish, strigose; gills free, seceding, broad, lax, connected by veins, quite entire, whitish.—*Fr. Epicr. p.* 378. *Kromb. t.* 3, *f.* 8. *Ann. N.H. no.* 65.

Amongst leaves, near stumps. [Cincinnati.]

Stem tough, 2-3 in. and more long, 2 lin. thick, at length compressed, blackish-red, smooth above, paler from the first, base strigose. Pileus about an inch broad, pallid, with a pinkish tinge. Gills broad, lax.

661. Marasmius terginus. *Fr.* "Clustered Marasmius."

Inodorous. Pileus somewhat fleshy, convexo-plane, obtuse, shining, whitish ; stem fistulose, smooth above, shining, pallid, reddish below, whitish-villous, rooting ; gills seceding, free, scarcely crowded, narrow, pallid.—*Fr. Epicr. p.* 377. *B. & Br. Ann. N.H.* 1866, *p.* 55. *M. Stephensii, B. & Br. Ann. N.H. ser.* ii. *vol.* xiii. *p.* 403, *no.* 708.

Amongst dead beech leaves. Dursley.

Fasciculated. Pileus ½-1 in. across, depressed and wrinkled in the centre, opaque, tough, cream-coloured, stained with vinous red, especially when bruised; flesh white, thin; stem 1-2 in. high, hollow, twisted, white and mealy above, quite smooth and shining below, of a rich light nut-brown; gills few and distant, rather broad, of the same colour as the pileus. Taste and smell like that of *M. oreades.—B. & Br.*

662. Marasmius impudicus. *Fr.* "Strong-scented Marasmius."

Fœtid. Pileus rather fleshy, tough, convexo-plane, then depressed; margin at length striate and plicate, growing pale; stem fistulose, equal, purplish, when dry everywhere velvety-white, base naked, rooting; gills nearly free, ventricose, flesh-colour, then whitish.—*Fr. Epicr. p.* 377. *Br. Bath. Trans.* 1870, *p.* 77. *Fr. Mon. Hym.* ii. *p.* 222.

On and about pine trunks. Hanham.

Small, gregarious. Stem easily compressed, 2 in. long, 1 line thick, varying from rufous, rufous-brown, to violet. Pileus ½-1 in. broad, bay-brown or rufous, growing pale; margin membranaceous, paler.

663. Marasmius archyropus. *Fr.* "Tan-coloured Marasmius."

Inodorous. Pileus rather fleshy, convexo-plane or depressed, smooth, growing pale; stem stuffed, then hollow, rigid, straight, pallid, rufous beneath the white tomentose bark, base similar; gills adnexed, seceding, crowded, linear, pallid.—*Fr. Epicr. p.* 378. *Pers. M.E. t.* 25, *f.* 4. *Ann. N.H. no.* 276.

Amongst leaves. Rare. Bristol. [Mid. & Up. Carolina.]

Fasciculate. Pileus about an inch across, tan-coloured. Stem scarcely 1 lin. thick.

664. Marasmius scorodonius. *Fr.* "Strong-scented Marasmius."

Strong-scented. Pileus somewhat fleshy, tough, even, soon plane, rugulose, and crisped ; stem fistulose, equal, quite smooth, shining, rufous; gills adnate, crisp, whitish.—*Fr. Epicr. p.* 379.

Sv. Bot. t. 175. *Schæff. t.* 99. *Paul. t.* 104, *f.* 10, 11. *Lenz. f.* 17. *Eng. Fl.* v. *p.* 49.

Heaths and dry pastures. Rare. Esculent.
[S. Carolina.]

Pileus ½ in. or more broad, plane, rugulose; gills connected by veins, seceding. Stem 1 in. or more high, nearly 1 line thick, scarcely rooting, with a strong alliaceous odour.—*Fries.*

665. Marasmius Vaillantii. *Fr.* "Vaillant's Marasmius."

Inodorous. Pileus submembranaceous, tough, soon expanded, depressed, plicato-rugose, turning whitish; stem stuffed, smooth, bright brown, thickened above and paler; gills broad, adnate, thick, distant, white.—*Fr. Epicr. p.* 380. *Vaill. t.* 11, *f.* 21-23. *Buxb.* iv. *t.* 36, *f.* 2. *Mich. t.* 74, *f.* 4. *Eng. Fl.* v. *p.* 53. *Ann. N. H. no.* 66.

On dead wood. Sept. [Low. & Mid. Carolina.]

Pileus ½ in. broad, plane, now and then depressed, striato-rugose; gills distinct, simple, triangular, and thence apparently decurrent; stem 1 in. high, very tough, yellowish when young, base smooth, black, even and shining, the middle bay, the apex whitish, most minutely pruinose.—*Fries.*

666. Marasmius angulatus. *Pers.* "Angular Marasmius."

Gregarious, small. Pileus between fleshy and membranaceous, at first hemispherical, then becoming plane, at length angularly plicate, whitish tawny; gills distant, paler; stem slender, fistulose, greyish-rufescent.—*B. & Br. Ann. N. H.* (1865) *no.* 1018. *Agaricus angulatus, Pers. Myc. Eur.* iii., *p.* 155, *tab.* 26, *f.* 3-4. *Mich. t.* 74, *f.* 4.

On grass. Cefn, Denbighshire, just above the Bone cave.

Very different from *M. Vaillantii*, to which Fries refers it.—*M. J. B.*

Stem dry, rigid, slightly thickened towards either extremity, slightly hairy at the base; gills white when young, brownish when mature, equal; pileus dry, mutable in form, at first globose, then flattened or concave; margin angularly crenulate.—*Pers.*

667. Marasmius languidus. *Fr.* "Languid Marasmius."

Inodorous, whitish. Pileus somewhat fleshy, convex, gibbous, or umbilicate, flocculose, rugoso-sulcate; stem stuffed, incrassated upwards, pallid, naked, brownish downwards; gills adnate then decurrent, distant, broad, connected by veins.—*Fr. Epicr. p.* 379. *Pers. Myc. Eur.* iii. *t.* 26, *f.* 6. *B. & Br. Ann. N. H.* (1865) *no.* 1017. *Batt. t.* 27, *f.* O.

On dead leaves of grass. Coed Coch.

Small, gregarious, tough, inodorous. Stem scarcely an inch long, ½-1 lin. thick, brownish below, usually villous. Pileus at first convex, margin involute, ½ in. broad, white, with a pinkish or yellowish tinge.

668. Marasmius fœtidus. *Fr.* "Fœtid Marasmius."

Fœtid. Pileus submembranaceous, tough, convex, then expanded and umbilicate, striato-plicate, turning pale when dry, subpruinose; stem fistulose, velvety or pruinose, bright brown, base flocculose; gills annulato-adnexed, distant, rufous-yellow. —*Fr. Epicr. p.* 380. *Sow. t.* 21. *Eng. Fl.* v. *p.* 54.

On decayed twigs. Rare.

Pileus ¼-¾ in. broad, convex, rarely quite plane, plicate, reddish-brown, thin, glabrous; gills adnate, yellow, narrow, distant; stem 1 in. high, thin, dark brown, minutely velvety or hairy.—*Grev.* At the base is a small radiated membrane. Scent like that of garlic.

669. Marasmius amadelphus. *Fr.* "Pallid-branch Marasmius."

Inodorous. Pileus between fleshy and membranaceous, obtuse, convex, then plane and depressed, discoid, subpruinose; margin at length striate; stem stuffed, short, pallid, bright brown below, rather mealy; gills broadly adnate, distant, broad, pallid.—*Fr. Epicr. p.* 380. *Bull. t.* 550, *f.* 3. *Ann. N.H. no.* 277.

On dead branches. Rare. Bristol. Bath.

Gregarious, dry. Stem short, about ½ in. long, scarcely 1 lin. thick, somewhat mealy, pallid. Pileus 3-4 lin. broad, always obtuse, at length with the darker disc depressed, pinkish-tawny, becoming pallid, sometimes nearly white.

670. Marasmius ramealis. *Fr.* "Twig Marasmius."

Inodorous. Pileus somewhat fleshy, plane or depressed, obtuse, without striæ, rugulose, opaque; stem stuffed, short, mealy, white, rufous below; gills adnate, rather distant, narrow, white. —*Fr. Epicr. p.* 381. *Bull. t.* 336. *Mich. t.* 74, *f.* 7. *Eng. Fl.* v. *p.* 52. *Berk. exs. no.* 10.

On dry dead branches. Common. [United States.]

Gregarious. Pileus 3-4 lines broad, plano-convex, at length wrinkled and depressed, pale rufescent, the centre darker, under a lens clothed with minute matted silkiness. Gills distant, adnate, sometimes broad behind, whitish or subrufescent. Margin denticulate. Stem ½-¾ in. high, ½ line thick, curved, fibrillose, with furfuraceous scales, the base minutely dilated, whitish or subrufescent.—*M. J. B.*

Sect. 2. Mycena.

671. Marasmius alliaceus. *Fr.* "Onion-scented Marasmius."

Strong-scented. Pileus submembranaceous, campanulate, then expanded, subumbonate, at first even, then sulcate, growing pale; stem horny, tall, rigid, velvety or pruinose, black; base rooting, naked; gills free, brownish white.—*Fr. Epicr. p.* 383. *Jacq. Aus. t.* 82. *Fl. Dan. t.* 1251. *Mich. t.* 78, *f.* 4. *Paul. t.* 122, *f.* 1. *Eng. Fl.* v. *p.* 55.

In woods. Rare. [Low. & Mid. Carolina.]

Garlic-scented. Pileus 1 in. or more broad, at length plane, subumbonate, even, or obsoletely striate, becoming pallid. Stem long, attenuated upwards, rigid, rather horny, incurved at the base and rooting.—*Fries.* Root crooked, thick, knotty, sunk about an inch into the earth, and always attached to rotten wood.—*With.*

672. Marasmius caulicinalis. *Fr.* "Mealy-stemmed Marasmius."

Pileus membranaceous, campanulato-convex, obtuse, smooth, even, then striato-sulcate; stem fistulose, flocculose, bay, attenuated above and paler, farinose; gills adnato-decurrent, connected by veins, yellow.—*Fr. Epicr. p.* 383. *B. & Br. Ann. N.H.* (1866) *no.* 1136. *Eng. Fl.* v. *p.* 54?

On the ground, amongst leaves. Nov. Ascot.

Pileus smooth, white tinged with ochre, at length sulcato-striate.

673. Marasmius rotula. *Fr.* "Collared Marasmius."

Pileus membranaceous, slightly convex, umbilicate, plicate; stem horny, fistulose, shining, quite smooth, blackish; gills few, broad, distant, attached to a free collar behind, pallid, white.—*Fr. Epicr. p.* 385. *Sow. t.* 95. *Bull. t.* 64, 569, *f.* 3. *Fl. Dan. t.* 1134. *Mich. t.* 74, *f.* 5. *Berk. Outl. t.* 14, *f.* 7. *Eng. Fl.* v. *p.* 53. *Cooke exs. no.* 302. *Berk. exs. no.* 62.

On fallen twigs, &c. Common. [United States.]

Pileus 1-3 lines broad, hemispherical, umbilicate and minutely umbonate, plaited, smooth; margin crenate, white, or pale buff, with a dark umbilicus. Gills broad, distant, equal, or occasionally with a few short ones, colour of the pileus, connate behind, and separating from the stem, so as to present the appearance of being fixed to a free collar surrounding the stem. Stem setiform, slightly flexuous, white above, then tawny, deep shining brown at the base, striate, fistulose, frequently branched and sarmentose, with or without abortive pilei.—*M. J. B.*

674. Marasmius graminum. *B. & Br.* "Grass Marasmius."

Pileus nearly plane, umbonate, sulcate, very pale rufous, the furrows paler, umbo brown; stem quite smooth, shining, black, white above; gills few, sub-ventricose, cream-coloured, attached to a free collar.—*Berk. Outl. t.* 14, *f.* 8. *Agaricus graminum, Lib. Ex. no.* 119.

On leaves of grass. Aug. [Low. Carolina.]

Scarcely exceeding 3 lines in breadth. Gills even, with veiny interstices.

675. Marasmius androsaceus. *Fr.* "Black-stemmed Marasmius."

Pileus membranaceous, slightly convex, sub-umbilicate, striate, smooth; stem horny, fistulose, quite smooth, black; gills adnate, distinct, simple, whitish.—*Fr. Epicr. p.* 385. *Fl. Dan. t.* 1551, *f.* 1. *Bolt. t.* 32. *Sow. t.* 94. *Bull. t.* 569, *f.* 2. *Bocc. t.* 104. *Eng. Fl.* v. *p.* 53. *Berk. exs. no.* 131.

On leaves, &c., in woods. Common. [United States.]

Pileus 3-6 lines broad, convex, with a slight depression, pale rufescent, darker in the centre, grooved and notched, under a lens clothed with a minute matted silkiness. Gills adnate, sometimes quite simple (about 15), with shorter ones between, and no rugæ, occasionally forked, with wrinkles in the interstices. Stem 1-2 in. high, filiform, quite smooth, shining-black, twisted when dry, often branched, and sarmentose at the base.—*M. J. B.*

676. Marasmius perforans. *Fr.* "Fir-leaf Marasmius."

Fœtid. Pileus sub-membranaceous, becoming nearly plane, without striæ, rugulose, smooth; stem fistulose, equal, velvety, dark-bay, inserted at the base; gills adnate, simple, whitish, frequently dimidiate.—*Fr. Epicr. p.* 385. *Hoff. t.* 4, *f.* 2. *Schæff. t.* 239. *Batsch. f.* 10.

On fir leaves. Scotland. [United States.]

Stem tough, about an inch high, equal, velvety, bay, then black. Pileus 4 lin. broad, rarely depressed, not umbilicate, without striæ, at length rugulose, whitish, then pale reddish. Gills numerous, simple, unequal.

677. Marasmius insititius. *Fr.* "Horny-stemmed Marasmius."

Inodorous. Pileus membranaceous, tough, convexo-plane, sub-umbilicate, unpolished, at length plicato-sulcate; stem horny, fistulose, floccose or mealy, reddish-brown, attenuated downwards to the simple inserted base; gills broadly adnate, attenuated in front, distant, simple, unequal, pallid, white.—*Fr. Epicr. p.* 386. *Berk. Outl. t.* 14, *f.* 6. *Ag. calopus, Ann. N.H. no.* 266.

On leaves, decayed grass, &c. [Up. Carolina.]

Gregarious, dry, scentless. Stem scarcely an inch long. Pileus unpolished, ⅛ in. broad, even when young, then plicato-sulcate, white. With the habit of *M. Vaillantii.*

678. Marasmius Hudsoni. *Fr.* "Hudson's Marasmius."

Inodorous. Pileus membranaceous, hemispherical, rugulose; stem horny, filiform, dark purple, beset—as well as the pileus—with scattered purple hairs; gills adnexed, narrow, simple, white, alternately dimidiate.—*Fr. Epicr. p.* 386. *Sow. t.* 164. *Desm. exs. no.* 669. *Eng. Fl.* v. *p.* 55. *Ann. N.H. no.* 708, *t.* xv. *f.* 3. *A. pilosus, Hud. Fl. Ang.*

On fallen holly leaves. Winter.

Pileus 3 lines broad, convex, almost hemispherical, white, clothed with red, erect, subrigid hairs. Gills dirty white. Stem 1-2 in. high, filiform, whitish, red-brown, or reddish, somewhat hairy at the base.—*Hudson.*

The whole of the outer surface of the pileus is clothed with echinulate processes, and the spores are fusiform, ·0004 in. long, with a central nucleus. —*B. & Br.*

679. Marasmius epiphyllus. *Fr.* "Leaf Marasmius."

Pileus membranaceous, nearly plane, at length umbilicate, smooth, plicato-rugose; stem rather horny, fistulose, finely velvety; bright brown below, inserted; gills adnate, few, distant, entire, veined, white.—*Fr. Epicr. p.* 386. *Trat. Aus. f.* 22. *Fl. Dan. t.* 1194, *f.* 1. *Sow. t.* 93. *Batt. t.* 28, *f. D. Batsch. f.* 84. *Pers. Ic. & Desc. t.* 9, *f.* 7, 8. *Eng. Fl.* v. *p.* 55. *Berk. exs. no.* 11.

On fallen leaves, twigs, &c. Common. [United States.]

Pileus 3 lines broad, plane, at length umbilicate, cream-coloured, rugose; gills veiny, branched, adnate, broad at the base; in large specimens they are seen to form a close collar round the stem, which is evident when the gills are almost obsolete; margin of the collar cream coloured; stem 1-2 in. high, filiform, brown or blackish below, paler upwards, minutely velvety.—*M. J. B.*

680. Marasmius saccharinus. *Fr.* "Granular Marasmius."

Pileus membranaceous, convex, sub-papillate, smooth, sulcate and plicate; stem very thin, flocculose, becoming smooth, inserted obliquely, reddish; gills broadly adnate, narrow, thick, very distant, connected by veins, whitish.—*Fr. Epicr. p.* 386. *Batsch. f.* 83.

On dead twigs. Rare. King's Cliffe.

Differs from *M. epiphyllus* in the pileus being at first papillate, and the stem flocculose, then smooth; the gills united in a reticulated manner.

Sect. 3. *Stemless.*

681. Marasmius spodoleucus. *B. & Br.* "Stemless Marasmius."

Conchiform, resupinate, margin at length free, cinereous above, pulverulent or slightly furfuraceous; stem wanting; gills few, white; interstices even.—*B. & Br. Ann. N.H., May,* 1859. *Berk. Outl. p.* 224. *Ann. N.H. no.* 803.

On dead elm twigs. Batheaston.

About 2 lines across, resupinate, altogether stemless, conchiform; margin free, arched, above cinereous, pulverulent, or slightly furfuraceous. Hymenium white, very even. Gills few, narrow, entire, so short as to leave a naked space at the base.—*B. & Br.* Spores very small, ·00008 × ·00006 in.

Gen. **14. LENTINUS,** Fr. Ep. 45.

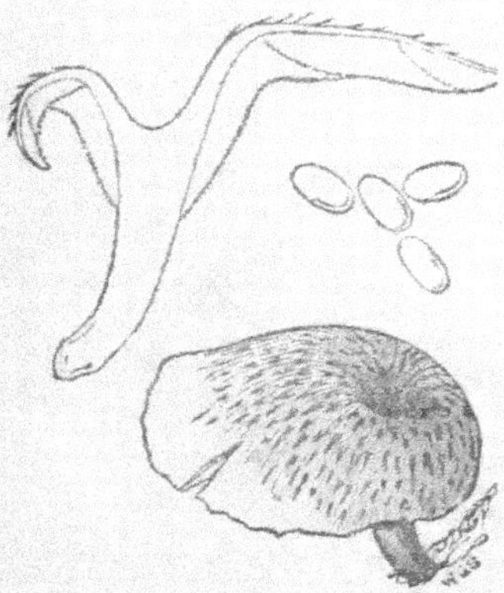

Fig. 56.

Spores white; pileus fleshy, coriaceous, tough, hard, and dry; stem hard and often obsolete, when present continuous, and the same with the hymenophore; gills tough, simple, unequal, thin, edge acute, generally toothed; trama none.

Hab. On stumps, rarely on the ground. (*Fig.* 56.)

A natural but very polymorphic genus, distinguished by its tough and fleshy substance.

682. Lentinus tigrinus. *Fr.* "Tiger-spot Lentinus."

Pileus fleshy-coriaceous, thin, orbicular, umbilicate, whitish, clothed with innate black scales; stem thin, without striæ, squamulose, with a decided veil; gills attenuated, decurrent, very narrow, white then yellowish.—*Fr. Epicr. p.* 389. *Bull. t.* 70. *Sow. t.* 68. *Batt. t.* 12, *f. B.D.* *Eng. Fl.* v. *p.* 69. *Vent. t.* 45, *f.* 6, 7.

On old stumps. Rare. [S. Carolina.]

Pileus 2 in. broad, thin, margin at length split; stem 1-2 in. long, dirty-white.—*Fries.* When fresh very tender and easily lacerated, when dry coriaceous, and the stem of a very firm and solid texture.—*Sow.* Spores ·00013 × ·00026 in. (*Fig.* 56, *reduced.*)

683. Lentinus Dunalii. *Fr.* "Dunal's Lentinus."

Pileus fleshy-coriaceous, thin, umbilicate, irregular, pallid; clothed with adpressed spot-like scales; stem short, somewhat silky; gills decurrent, crowded, pallid.—*Fr. Epicr. p.* 390. *Bull. t.* 36. *Batt. t.* 12, *A. Berk. Outl. t.* 15, *f.* 2. *Eng. Fl.* v. *p.* 68.

On ash trees. Rare.

Cæspitose. Pileus 2 in. broad, more or less unequal, carnoso-coriaceous, umbilicate; margin deflexed, sometimes variously split and sinuated, yellow-white, with brownish rather close scales; margin nearly smooth; gills dichotomous, crenate, sinuated, subdecurrent; stem 1 in. high, 3 lines thick, tough, the lower part clothed with dark, nearly square, adpressed scales, the upper half not scaly, white, resembling the under side of white kid leather. Odour sub-acid, farinaceous.—*M. J. B.*

684. Lentinus lepideus. *Fr.* "Scaly Lentinus."

Pileus fleshy, compact, tough, convex, then depressed, unequal, pallid-ochraceous, broken up into darker spot-like scales; stem stout, rooting, tomentose or scaly; gills sinuate, decurrent, broad, torn, transversely striate, whitish.—*Fr. Epicr. p.* 390. *Schæff. t.* 29, 30. *Buxb.* iv. *t.* 25. *Sow. t.* 382. *Eng. Fl.* v. *p.* 69.

On stumps of firs. Rare. [United States.]

Pileus 2-4 in. broad, convex or depressed, central or lateral; stem short, hard, very tender when fresh; monstrous forms occur in dark situations, with or without a pileus.—*M. J. B.* Spores ·0004 × ·00023 in.

685. Lentinus adhærens. *Fr.* "Pine-wood Lentinus."

Pileus somewhat fleshy, tough, irregular, lacunose, subpulverulent, dingy, pallid, glutinous, laccate, as well as the nearly hollow-rooting stem; gills decurrent, forming lines on the stem, very thin, torn, white.—*Fr. Epicr. p.* 391. *With.* iv. *p.* 160.

In pine-woods. Doubtful.

Small, unequal, taste at length astringent. Pileus convex, then somewhat umbonate, at length depressed and infundibuliform.

686. Lentinus cochleatus. *Fr.* "Shell Lentinus."

Annual, tough, flaccid. Pileus fleshy, but tough, irregular, somewhat lobed or contorted, rufescent, as well as the solid, firm, sulcate, smooth stem; gills crowded, serrated, pinkish-white.—*Fr. Epicr. p.* 394. *Sow. t.* 168. *Berk. Outl. t.* 19, *f.* 4. *Eng. Fl.* v. *p.* 69. *Price, f.* 125.

On trunks and the ground. Rare. [United States.]

Very much tufted; several stems confluent, surface rough with prominent minute ribs or prickles, pale rufescent, often powdered with the white spores, 1-1½ in. broad. Sometimes the surface is more even, but still somewhat sculptured, so as to be rough with raised lines. Stem compound, strongly ribbed and sulcate, the ribs being continuations of the serrated paler decurrent gills. At first the pileus and gills are tender; stem firm and leathery. Odour agreeable.—*M. J. B.* Spores almost globular, diameter ·00015 in.

687. Lentinus vulpinus. *Fr.* "Strong-scented Lentinus."

Sessile, imbricated. Pileus fleshy, but tough, conchate, connate behind, longitudinally rough, costate, corrugate or floccose, tan-coloured; margin incurved, entire; gills torn, white.—*Fr. Epicr. p.* 395. *Sow. t.* 361. *Eng. Fl.* v. *p.* 72. *Krombh. t.* 3, *f.* 16.

On stumps. Rare. [Cincinnati, U. S.]

Pileus 1-2 in. long, ascending, obovato-spathulate; margin involute, fleshy, tough, the outer surface cartilaginous, longitudinally lacunose and echinulate, reddish-buff, hoary with the round white spores, and within the flesh is a line of the same substance parallel with the surface; gills pale, more or less notched and sinuate, broad, not forked. Stem obsolete. Smell very strong and overpowering, somewhat resembling that of field mint.—*M. J. B.* Spores almost globular, very small, ·00006 in. diameter.

688. Lentinus fimbriatus. *Curr.* "Fringed Lentinus."

Pileus subdimidiate, subcoriaceous, depressed, fawn coloured, covered with darker floccose scales; margin slightly involute; stem lateral, squamulose; gills serrated and torn, descending (not decurrent), pale brown.—*Linn. Trans.* xxiv. *p.* 152. *t.* 25. *f.* 2.

On a stump standing in a pond. Lewes. Sept., 1862.

Pileus subdimidiate, subcoriaceous, thin (not fleshy) depressed, sometimes very much so, and almost cyathiform, ½ to 1 in. wide, fawn coloured, covered with floccose scales of a darker brown; margin slightly involute, almost strigose; stem lateral, from ⅛ to ¼ in. long, rough with somewhat reflexed scales of the same colour as the gills, or rather paler; gills pale brown, irregularly serrate and lacerated at the margin, descending, but not decurrent. In young specimens a delicate white fimbriate collar or fringe (the remains of the ruptured veil) separates the gills from the stem. Pilei 2 or 3 together, one above another in an imbricated manner. Some of the pilei tinged here and there with pink stains.

689. Lentinus flabelliformis. *Fr.* "Fan-like Lentinus."

Subsessile. Pileus thin, tough, kidney-shaped, plane, smooth, fawn coloured; margin crenato-fimbriate; gills broad, torn, pallid.—*Fr. Epicr. p.* 395. *Bolt. t.* 157. *Eng. Fl.* v. *p.* 72.

On stumps. Doubtful.

Inserted on the faith of Bolton's figure, which "may be only *Agaricus salignus.*" Pileus 2-3 in. broad; gills rather broad.

Gen. **15.** **PANUS,** Fr. Epicr. p. 396.

Fig. 57.

Spores white; pileus unequal-sided or lateral, tough, fleshy, at length coriaceous, but not woody, drying up, but reviving with moisture; stem the same with the hymenophore; gills thinner than in the last genus, tough, at length coriaceous, unequal, with an entire acute edge; trama floccose.

HAB. On stumps. (*Fig.* 57.)

All the species are tough (at first softer), never woody, drying up in decay.

690. **Panus torulosus.** *Fr.* "Twisted Panus."

Pileus fleshy, then tough, coriaceous, plane, then infundibuliform or dimidiate, even, flesh-coloured or ochraceous; stem short, oblique, clothed with grey down; gills decurrent, rather distant, distinct behind, ruddy, then tan-coloured.—*Fr. Epicr. p.* 397. *Batsch. f.* 33. *Paul. t.* 26, *f.* 3, 4. *Nees. f.* 176. *Krombh. t.* 42, *f.* 3-5. *Bolt. t.* 146.

On old stumps. [Mid. & Up. Carolina].

Stem solid, seldom exceeding an in. long, grey, covered with a violaceous down. Pileus entire, 2-3 in. broad, smooth. Flesh pale. Variable in colour, sometimes shaded very slightly, if at all, with pink. Spores ·0002 × ·00013 in. (*Fig.* 57, *reduced.*)

691. **Panus conchatus.** *Fr.* "Shell Panus."

Pileus fleshy, tough, thin, unequal, excentric and dimidiate, cinnamon, becoming pale, at length squamulose; stem short, unequal, pubescent at the base; gills forming decurring lines on the stem, somewhat branched, whitish, flesh-coloured, then ochraceous.—*Fr. Epicr. p.* 398. *Krombh. t.* 42, *f.* 1-2. *Schæff. t.* 43, 44. *Bull. t.* 298, 517, *f. O.P.* *Eng. Fl.* v. *p.* 71. *Ann. N.H. no.* 67.

On trunks. Rare. Margate. Apethorpe. [Cincinnati, U. S.]

Pileus flaccid, even; gills not anastomosing at the base, rather thick and close; stem not 1 in. high, sometimes obsolete.—*Fries.*

Always known by its conchate form and tougher substance from similar species of the genus *Agaricus.*—*M. J. B.*

692. Panus stypticus. *Fr.* "Styptic Panus."

Pileus coriaceous, reniform, cinnamon, growing pale, cuticle breaking up into mealy scales; stem lateral, short, dilated above; gills determinate, thin, crowded, connected by veins, cinnamon. —*Fr. Epicr. p.* 399. *Bull. t.* 140, 557, *f.* 1. *Schæff. t.* 208. *Sow. t.* 109. *Fl. Dan. t.* 832, *f.* 1. *t.* 1292, *f.* 1. *Tratt. Aus. t.* 2. *Krombh. t.* 44, *f.* 13-17. *Buxb.* v. *t.* 10, *f.* 1. *Eng. Fl.* v. *p.* 73. *Smith. P.M. f.* 6. *Berk. exs.no.* 136.

On stumps, dead trees, &c. Common. [S. Carolina.]

Gregarious or cæspitose. Pileus 1-1½ in. broad, semiorbicular, the margin entire or lobed, surface nearly even, pruinose or furfuraceous, often zoned, varying in depth of colour; margin involute; gills often branched, beautifully connected by veins, pale cinnamon. Stem about ½ in. high, ascending, dilated above, pruinose.—*M. J. B.* Spores ·0001 × ·00018 in.

Gen. **16. XEROTUS,** Fr. Ep. p. 48.

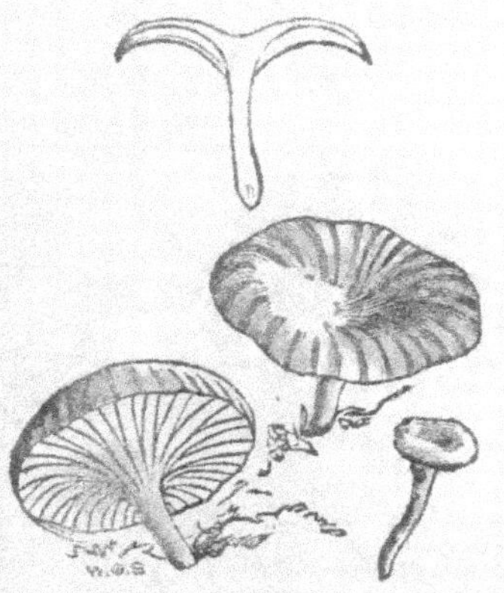

Fig. 58.

Spores white; pileus membranaceous; stem confluent with the hymenophore, which descends into and forms a trama; gills dichotomous, fold-like, coriaceous, adnato-decurrent, with an obtuse entire edge; in the single British species branched and very distant. (*Fig.* 58.)

HAB. The British plant grows in peat-mosses.

This genus, which is chiefly tropical, resembles a coriaceo-membranaceous *Cantharellus*, with narrow gills.

693. Xerotus degener. *Fr.* "Moss Xerotus."

Pallid. Pileus between coriaceous and membranaceous, plano-depressed, flocculose, hygrophanous, striate when moist; stem solid, thin, velvety; gills plicate, branched, distant, pallid.—*Fr. Epicr. p.* 400. *Schæff. t.* 243. *Sow. t.* 210.

In peat mosses. Very rare.

Pileus somewhat zoned, grey, thin, but tough. (*Fig.* 58.)

Gen. 16. TROGIA, Fr. Mon. Hym.

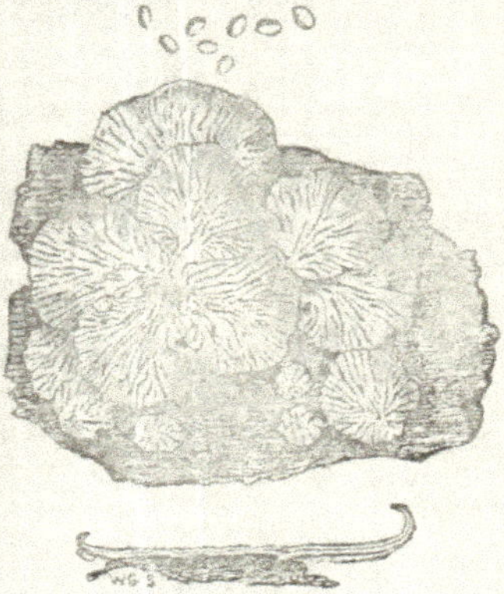

Fig. 59.

Pileus submembranaceous, soft, tough, flaccid, but very dry, flexible, reviving; gills venose, fold-like, forked, edge longitudinally channelled or crisped; texture fibrillose; spores white. *(Fig. 59.)*

In the only British species the edge of the gills is not channelled but obtuse, but it has the habit, form, and texture of *Trogia*, and is referred to that genus without doubt; although the edges of the gills are not channelled they are nevertheless crisped.

694. **Trogia crispa.** *Fr.* "Crisped Trogia."

Tough, cup-shaped, reflexed, lobed, villous, reddish-yellow; gills plaited, dichotomous, crisped, whitish or grey.—*Fr. Epicr. p.* 369. *Fl. Dan. t.* 1739. *Pers. Ic. & Desc. t.* 8, *f.* 7. *Buxb.* v. *t.* 7, *f.* 2. *B. & Br. Ann. N.H. no.* 1135.

On twigs of beech, birch, &c. Jedburgh. [United States.]

The colour of the pileus varies from a yellowish brown to white, sessile, lobed, ½-1 in. broad, finely villous, reddish-yellow behind. Margin whitish. Gills narrow, veinlike, crisped, with the edge obtuse, not channelled. *(Fig. 59, nat. size.)*

Gen. 17. SCHIZOPHYLLUM, Fr. Obs. i. p. 103.

Fig. 60.

Spores white; pileus not fleshy, dry, sessile; gills coriaceous, branched, split longitudinally at the edge, with the two divisions revolute or spreading, joined to the pileus by a tomentose pellicle.

HAB. Rotten wood.

An easily recognized but very aberrant genus of *Agaricini*. *(Fig. 60.)*

695. Schizophyllum commune. *Fr.* "Common Schizophyllum."

Pileus adnate behind, somewhat extended, simple, and lobed; gills grey, then brownish, purple, villous, edge revolute.—*Fr. Epicr. p.* 403. *Grev. t.* 61. *Krombh. t.* 4, *f.* 14-16. *Batsch. f.* 126. *Bull. t.* 346, 581, *f.* 1. *Sow. t.* 183. *Buxb.* v. *t.* 7, *f.* 1. *Eng. Fl.* v. *p.* 130. *Gard. Chron.* 1860, *p.* 1151.

On dead wood. [New Orleans, U. S., &c.]

Pileus 1-1½ in. broad, sessile or with a short lateral stem, sometimes resupinate, and supported by a stem-like process arising from the centre of the pileus, white or greyish, zoned, tomentose; margin even or variously lobed and split; gills reddish-brown or whitish, flabelliform, apparently but not truly forked, the inner barren face villous with the flocci, of which the substance of the pileus is composed, the outer surface alone bearing spores. Cosmopolitan.—*M. J. B.* Spores very small, almost globular, ·0001 in. diameter. *(Fig. 60, nat. size.)*

Gen. 18. LENZITES, Fr. Gen. Hymen.

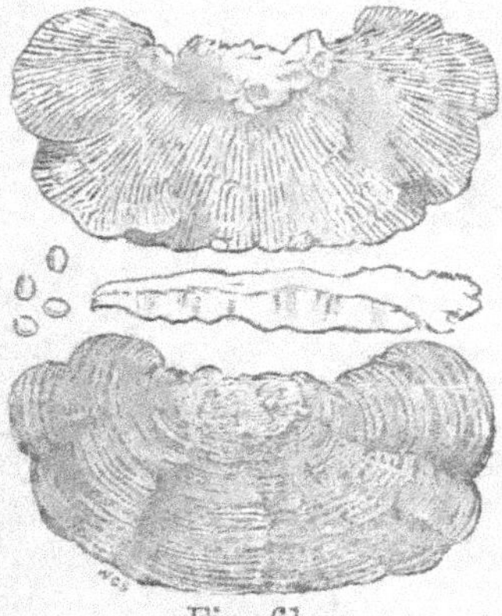

Fig. 61.

Spores white; pileus coriaceous, dimidiate, sessile; gills coriaceous, firm, unequal, simple, or branched, and anastomosing behind, edge obtuse or acute; trama floccose; often spuriously porous. (*Fig.* 61.)

Hab. On stumps, rails, etc.

Chiefly tropical, where the species become woody, with us they are only coriaceous. Allied to *Trametes* and *Dædalea*, amongst the *Polyporei*.

696. Lenzites betulina. *Fr.* "Birch Lenzites."

Pileus between corky and coriaceous, firm, obsoletely zoned, tomentose, pallid; margin of the same colour; gills straight, somewhat branched, anastomosing, pallid.—*Fr. Epicr. p.* 405. *Fl. Dan. t.* 1555. *Sow. t.* 182. *Berk. Outl. t.* 15, *f.* 3. *Dædalea betulina, Eng. Fl.* v. *p.* 131.

On stumps, &c. Common. [Cincinnati, U. S.]

Perennial. Pileus 2-4 in. broad, coriaceous, sessile, dimidiate, deeply grooved concentrically, and clothed with dense pubescence or coarse velvety down, greyish or pale, often green with minute *Algæ*. Gills straight, tan-coloured, not much branched or anastomosing, their margin at length torn. —*M. J. B.* *(Fig. 61, reduced.)*

697. **Lenzites flaccida.** *Fr.* "Flaccid Lenzites."

Pileus coriaceous, thin, flaccid, unequal, hairy, zoned, pallid; margin of the same colour; gills broad, crowded, straight, unequal and branched, white, becoming pallid.—*Fr. Epicr. p.* 406. *Bull. t.* 394. *Bolt. t.* 158.

On stumps.

Running by almost imperceptible gradations into *L. betulina.* Pileus thin (scarcely 1 lin. thick), hairy, strigose, at first whitish, then dingy, with zones of the same colour. Gills never anastomosing.

698. **Lenzites sepiaria.** *Fr.* "Chocolate Lenzites."

Pileus coriaceous, hard, zoned, strigoso-tomentose, rough, bright-brown; margin yellowish; gills rather thick, branched, anastomosing, yellowish.—*Fr. Epicr. p.* 407. *Ann. N.H. no.* 337. *Sow. t.* 418. *Schæff. t.* 76. *Buxb.* v. *t.* 6. *Vaill. t.* 1, *f.* 1-3. *Dædalea sepiaria, Eng. Fl. p.* 132.

On fir wood. [United States.]

Pileus 2-3 in. broad, dimidiate, elongated, often confluent, deeply zoned, strigoso-lacunose, of a rich deep-chocolate; margin paler, sometimes white, substance coriaceous, fibrous, of a fine ochre or rhubarb colour, occasionally entirely resupinate. Hymenium composed of brownish plates, tolerably regular, but here and there slightly branched, or interrupted so as to form pores.—*M. J. B.*

699. **Lenzites abietina.** *Fr.* "Larch Lenzites."

Pileus coriaceous, thin, effuso-reflexed, clothed with umber down, at length becoming smooth and whitish; gills decurrent, simple, unequal, pruinose or glaucescent, brownish.—*Fr. Epicr. p.* 407. *Bull t.* 442, *f.* 2, *t.* 541, *f.* 1. *Eng. Fl.* v. *p.* 132. *Vent. t.* 60, *f.* 3-5.

On deals. Glasgow. [United States.]

Perennial. Pileus umber and in age becomes quite smooth, and the gills nearly simple, of a pruinose cinereous hue. Pileus 1½-4 in. broad.—*M. J. B.* Thinner than *L. sepiaria.*

Order II. POLYPOREI.

Hymenium lining the cavity of tubes or pores, which are sometimes broken up into teeth or concentric plates.—*Fr. Berk. Outl. p.* 229.

Hymenium inferior, lining the cavity of tubes or pores, which are at first sinuous. Pores sometimes broken up into wavy or labyrinthiform, concentric (not radiating) laminæ, or teeth; when young, and the hymenium is sinuous, pores are present in the margin.

Hymenium lining tubes, *regular*—
 Trama none.
  Tubes separating from the hymenophore and from each other, terrestrial . . . . BOLETUS.
  Tubes adhering to the hymenophore and to each other, terrestrial. . STROBILOMYCES.
 Trama present.
  Trama dissimilar in substance (and often in colour) from the hymenophore, generally epiphytal . . . POLYPORUS.
  Trama the same in substance and colour with the hymenophore, epiphytal . . . . TRAMETES.
Hymenium lining tubes, *irregular*—
 Tubes forming deep labyrinthiform depressions—plant woody . . . . DÆDALEA.
 Tubes incomplete, reduced to shallow sinuous folds; plant waxy . . . . MERULIUS.
Hymenium at first papillose, papillæ at length elongating and forming tubes—
 Plant submembranaceous and resupinate . . . POROTHELIUM.
 Plant fleshy . . . . FISTULINA.

Gen. 18. BOLETUS, Fr.

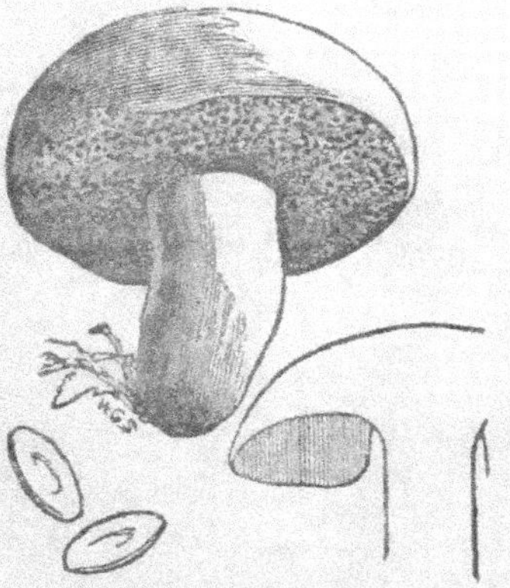

Fig. 62.

Hymenium quite distinct from the smooth hymenophore; trama none, the tubes easily separating from the hymenophore, and from each other; fleshy, putrescent, terrestrial fungi, having central stems. (*Fig.* 62.)

A clearly defined genus, with many handsome species, including some that are poisonous, and many that are esculent.

A. *Ochrospori*—spores ochraceous.

Sect. 1. *Viscipellis.*

700. **Boletus luteus.** *L.* "Brown-yellow Boletus."

Pileus gibbous, then pulvinate, smeared with brown evanescent gluten; stem equal, firm, whitish, above the ring punctato-scabrous; ring ample, membranaceous, white or brownish; tubes adnate, minute, simple, yellow.—*Fr. Epicr. p.* 409. *Schæff. t.* 114. *Lenz. f.* 30. *Fl. Dan. t.* 1135. *Krombh. t.* 33, *f.* 1-12. *Buxb.* v. *t.* 14. *Eng. Fl.* v. *p.* 147. *Price, f.* 1, 29. *Fl. Boruss, t.* 377.

In fir woods. Common. [S. Carolina.]

Pileus 3-4 in. broad, dingy yellow, convex, covered at first with thick brown gluten, which is soon washed off, but the pileus remains slightly viscid and clothed with very minute matted silkiness. Flesh at first firm, whitish, not changing. Tubes adnate, dull yellow, nearly simple, their orifices round, or slightly waved. Spores ochraceous, ferruginous. Stem 4 in. high, or more, ½ in. thick, straight or flexuous, at first white, but soon sordid, hoary beneath the white persistent ring, glandular above. sometimes the whole surface is glandular.—*M. J. B.* Spores spindle-shaped, yellowish-brown, ·0003 × ·00013 in.

701. **Boletus elegans.** *Schum.* "Elegant Boletus."

Pileus convex, then plane, viscid, golden yellow, and slightly ferruginous; stem firm, unequal, golden yellow, then rufous, punctate above the fugacious, white, then yellowish ring; tubes decurrent, minute, simple, golden, or sulphur-yellow.—*Fr. Epicr. p.* 409. *Grev. t.* 183. *Gard. Chron.* (1860), *p.* 529, *fig.* ?. *Price, f.* 110. *Krombh. t.* 34, *f.* 1-10. *Huss.* ii. *t.* 12.

In mixed woods. May—Oct. [Low. Carolina.]

From its nearest allies it is distinguished by its brilliant golden yellow or ferruginous tint, its neat form, its firm equal stem, which is at first coloured like the cap, and then acquires a rufous tint, but especially by its being marked with little dots, but not reticulate, above the fugacious ring, which is at first whitish, and then acquires a yellow tinge, and its decurrent, minute, simple, golden yellow pores, inclining to sulphur. The flesh, moreover, is of a decided, though pale yellow.—*M. J. B.*

702. **Boletus flavus.** *With.* "Bright-yellow Boletus."

Firm. Pileus yellow, with a tawny, evanescent gluten; stem yellow, then brownish, apex reticulated with the decurrent tubes; tubes rather large, angular, yellow.—*Fr. Epicr. p.* 410. *Bolt. t.* 169. *Sow. t.* 265. *B. Grevillei, Eng. Fl.* v. *p.* 148.

In woods. Common.

Fries regards this as a variety of *B. elegans*; it requires to be carefully distinguished from *B. luteus*. Pileus 2-5 in. broad, compact, in moist shady places glutinous and bright-yellow, in exposed situations dry and brown; flesh pale yellow, not changing; tubes unequal, of a golden sulphur, wavy, sometimes with their orifices ruddy. Ring dirty-yellow, membranaceous. Stem 2-3 in. high, 6-9 lines thick, yellow spotted with purple, thickened at the base, reticulated above the ring.—*Klotsch.* Spores spindle-shaped, yellowish-brown, ·0003 × ·00016 in.

703. Boletus laricinus. *Berk.* "Larch Boletus."

Pileus dirty white, with livid stains, covered at first with dirty yellow or brownish evanescent slime, subsquamose; stem cribrose above the ring, scrobiculate below, dirty white; tubes adnate, subdecurrent, compound, at first nearly white.—*Berk. Outl. p.* 230. *Huss.* i. *t.* 25. *Eng. Fl.* v. *p.* 148.

Amongst larch. Sept. Common.

Pileus 2-3 in. broad, dirty white, with livid stains, and sometimes adpressed, dirty yellow fascicles of filaments, the remains of the slimy ring; often deeply scrobiculate, covered with dirty yellow or brownish slime, which gradually disappears. Flesh white, very slightly tinged with yellow, not changeable. Tubes adnate or subdecurrent, compound, each consisting of two or three cells, their orifices angular, at first nearly white, with a tinge of yellow, at length brownish from the spores. Stem 2 in. or more high, ½-⅔ in. thick, nearly equal, reticulated above the ring, and frequently much scrobiculated below, dirty white like the pileus, stained with the spores, somewhat downy at the base. Spores oblong, brownish clay-coloured.—*M. J. B.* Spores spindle-shaped, pale brown, ·00042 × ·00017 in.—*W. G. S.*

704. Boletus granulatus. *L.* "Granulated Boletus."

Pileus convex, expanded, yellowish, with a brownish, ferruginous, evanescent gluten; stem without a ring, yellowish, punctato-granulose above; tubes adnate, short, simple, yellow; orifice granulated.—*Fr. Epicr. p.* 410. *Schæff. t.* 123. *Barla. t.* 31, *f.* 4-12. *Lenz. f.* 31. *Letell. t.* 604. *Krombh. t.* 34, *f.* 11-14. *Eng. Fl.* v. *p.* 149. *Vent. t.* 50, *f.* 3. *B. lactifluus*, *Sow. t.* 420.

In grass, amongst firs. Aug. Sept. Esculent. [Carolina.]

Gregarious, cæspitose. Pileus 2 in. or more broad, hemispherical, at first covered with a thick rufous brown slime, afterwards dirty rufous or yellowish; flesh thick, white or yellowish, not changeable; margin at first inflexed and downy. Pores at first whitish, then lemon-coloured, compound, the margin distilling a pale watery milk, which when dried gives them a granulated appearance, at length dirty yellow, adnate. Spores ochraceo-ferruginous; stem 1 in. or more high, ½ in. thick, generally short, but variable, obtuse at the base, rooting, more watery than the pileus, pale yellow above, white below, minutely tomentose and granulated, at first covered with milky drops.—*M. J. B.*—Spores spindle-shaped, yellowish orange, ·0003 × ·00013 in.

A very variable species, but the very glutinous pileus always the same colour, viz., a rich chestnut brown; tubes and stem sulphur colour, tubes exuding a thin gummy juice, which soon dries in the form of sugary granules. Stem rough, scabrous, as if covered with moist sugar.—*W. G. S.*

705. Boletus bovinus. *L.* "Shallow-pored Boletus."

Pileus nearly plane, smooth, viscid, reddish-grey; stem equal, even, self-coloured; tubes subdecurrent, angular, compound, greyish-yellow, then ferruginous.—*Fr. Epicr. p.* 411. *Lenz. f.* 38. *Krombh. t.* 75, *f.* 1-6. *Fl. Dan. t.* 1018. *Huss.* i. *t.* 34. *Eng. Fl.* v. *p.* 149. *Fl. Boruss. t.* 378.

Heathy fir woods. Sept. [United States.]

Gregarious, fasciculate. Pileus 1-2½ in. broad; when young hemispherical, margin white and tomentose, disc and top of the stem purplish, base rhubarb-coloured; when full-grown convex, expanded; margin still turned in, very glutinous, dull orange-yellow, or deep buff; flesh tinged with the colour of the pileus, not changeable. Tubes resembling the pores of *Merulius lachrymans*, very shallow (⅙ of an inch), compound, dirty yellow, not easily separating from the pileus. Stem 2-3 in. high, ½-¾ in. thick, subtomentose, not diffused gradually but rather abruptly into the pileus, of the same colour, but streaked with watery lines, attenuated below, or subequal; bulbous when very young. Spores elliptic. Smell strong, like *Marasmius oreades*.—*M. J. B.* Spores spindle-shaped, dingy green ochre, ·0003 × ·00015 in.

706. Boletus badius. *Fr.* "Bay Boletus."

Pileus pulvinate, soft, viscid, bay-tawny; stem solid, nearly equal, even, paler, brownish pruinose; tubes adnate, sinuate or depressed, rather large, angular, dingy, yellowish-white, then greenish.—*Fr. Epicr. p.* 411. *Lenz. f.* 35. *Krombh. t.* 36, *f.* 12-18. *Ann. N. H. no.* 804. *Fl. Boruss. t.* 379.

In pine woods. Rare.

Pileus viscid in wet, shining in dry weather, flesh turning partially blue.

707. Boletus sanguineus. *With.* "Blood-red Boletus."

Pileus convexo-plane, even, smooth, viscid, blood-red; stem equal, even, variegated with yellow and red; tubes adnate, broad, unequal, orange-yellow.—*Fr. Epicr. p.* 412. *Sow. t.* 225. *B. subtomentosus, var.* β. *Eng. Fl.* v. *p.* 150.

In woods. Rare.

Pileus crimson, semiglobular, ¾-1¼ over; when old rich brown, nearly 3 in. over, and the edge turning up. Flesh white, a little tinged with crimson next to the skin, changing slowly to a bluish cast when wounded. Stem blotches or streaks of dilute crimson on a yellow ground, apparently twisted, 1-2½ in. high, near ⅜ in. diameter. In the larger specimens the base is bulbous.—*With.*

708. Boletus piperatus. *Bull.* "Peppery Boletus."

Pileus convexo-plane, smooth, slightly viscid, yellow, inclining to reddish-grey; stem slender, even, fragile, yellow within, and at the base; tubes subdecurrent, large, angular, ferruginous.—*Fr. Epicr. p.* 412. *Bull. t.* 451, *f.* 2. *Batsch. f.* 28. *Sow. t.* 34. *Fl. Dan. t.* 1850. *Krombh. t.* 37, *f.* 16-20. *Eng. Fl.* v. *p.* 150. *Corda. Sturm. t.* 60. *Barla. t.* 32, *f.* 5-10. *Smith, P.M. f.* 26.

In woods. Autumn. [Carolina, U. S.]

Pileus 1-3 in. broad. at length plane, moist, or even glutinous, reddish-yellow or brownish. Flesh yellow, not changing colour. Tubes large, subdecurrent, angular, reddish-yellow or ferruginous. Stem 1-2 in. high, 3-4 lines thick, more or less deep yellow. Taste remarkably acrid and pungent. —*Grev.* Spores oval, brown, ·0003 × ·00015 in.

Sect. 2. *Subtomentosi.*

709. Boletus rubinus. *Smith.* "Red-tubed Boletus."

Pileus yellow-brown, gibbous, pulvinate, then plane, dry, subtomentose, slightly cracked; tubes wholly carmine, subdecurrent, compound, of a medium size; stem yellow, smeared with crimson, irregular; flesh vivid-yellow, perfectly unchangeable; spores pale-umber, ovate.—*Seem. Journ.* 1868, *p.* 33, *t.* 75, *f.* 1-4.

Under trees by the roadside. Sept. Near Dunstable.

It differs from all other British species in the wholly carmine tubes, together with the vivid-yellow, wholly unchangeable flesh. Pileus 2-3 in. broad, stem 2-3 in. high. Spores oval, almost round, pale warm brown, ·00025 × ·0002 in.

710. Boletus parasiticus. *Bull.* "Parasitic Boletus."

Pileus hemispherical, smooth, viscid, soon cracked and tesselated: stem thin, incurved, rigid, diffracto-rimose, yellow without and within; tubes decurrent, middle-sized, rounded, simple, golden-yellow.—*Fr. Epicr. p.* 412. *Bull. t.* 431, *f.* 1. *Berk. Outl. t.* 15, *f.* 4. *Ann. N.H. no.* 338.

On species of *Scleroderma.* Rare. Clifton. Kew. Coombe wood.

Pileus silky, dirty-yellow as well as the incurved, rigid, slightly silky stem; flesh of a pale-reddish hue; tubes decurrent, labyrinthiform, reddish. It is certainly not viscid in any stage of growth.—*B. & Br.*

We have met with it several times, but there has not been any reddish tint in the tubes of our specimens. Hence they may vary in colour. Tubes at first sulphur colour, yellow, then reddish-orange. Spores spindle-shaped, elongated, pale brown, very different from the last, ·0005 × ·00015 in.

711. Boletus variegatus. *Fr.* "Variegated Boletus."

Pileus convexo-plane, obtuse, moist, tawny-yellow, with scattered superficial, fasciculato-pilose scales; margin acute, at first flocculose; stem without ring, firm, equal, even; tubes adnate, unequal, minute, brownish cinnamon, then pallid.—*Fr. Epicr. p.* 413. *Lenz. f.* 39. *Krombh. t.* 34, *f.* 15-18, *t.* 75, *f.* 7-14. *Schæff. t.* 115? *Eng. Fl.* v. *p.* 150.

In pine woods. Aug. Sept. [Mid. Carolina.]

Pileus 3 in. or more broad, convex, fasciculato-squamose; scales small, tawny-yellow; flesh changing to blue when cut; margin tomentose, subinvolute; tubes very narrow, dull-yellow, blue when bruised, adnate, resembling somewhat those of *B. bovinus*; stem 3 in. high, ¾ in. thick, granulato-pulverulent, very neat, firm, yellow, obtuse. Smell unpleasant, taste not so.—*M. J. B.* Spores oval, very small, greenish ochre, ·0001 × ·00017 in.

712. Boletus striæpes. *Sec.* "Striate Boletus."

Pileus convex, then plane, soft, silky, olivaceous; cuticle ferruginous within; stem firm, curved, yellow, with blackish-brown striæ; base brownish-rufous; tubes minute, angular, greenish, orifice yellow.—*Fr. Epicr. p.* 415. *Batt. t.* 29 c.

In woods. Rare. Coed Coch.

Stem dirty-yellow, dotted under a lens with broad bay lines. Flesh white, red near the cuticle, sparingly changing to blue.—*M. J. B.*

713. Boletus chrysenteron. *Fr.* "Red-cracked Boletus."

Pileus convexo-plane, soft, floccoso-squamose, brownish, inclining to brick-red; flesh yellow, red beneath the cuticle; stem nearly equal, rigid, fibroso-striate, scarlet or yellow; tubes subadnate, rather large, angular, unequal, greenish-yellow.—*Fr. Epicr. p.* 415. *Bull. t.* 490, *f.* 3. *Krombh. t.* 76. *Ann. N.H. no.* 339. *Corda. Sturm. t.* 1. *Batt. t.* 30. *E. Hss.* i. *t.* 5. *B. subtomentosus, Eng. Fl.* v. *p.* 150, *in part.*

In meadows, woods, &c. Common. [Mid. and Up. Carolina.]

When the pileus is cracked, the cracks are red. Pileus 2-3 in. or more broad, variable, of some shade of red, olive, or yellow, pulvinate, minutely downy; cuticle often cracked, interstices reddish; flesh white or yellowish, changing slightly to blue; stem 3 in. high, ¼-½ in. thick, yellowish, more or less streaked with red, often crooked. Spores spindle-shaped, pale warm brown, ·0005 × ·00017 in.

714. Boletus subtomentosus. *L.* "Yellow-cracked Boletus."

Pileus pulvinate, expanded, soft, dry, villoso-tomentose, somewhat olive, not discoloured under the cuticle; stem stout, unequal, sulcate and ribbed, rough, punctate, yellow; tubes adnate, broad, angular, of the same colour.—*Fr. Epicr. p.* 415. *Nees. f.* 206. *Lenz. f.* 36, 37. *Schæff. t.* 112. *Krombh. t.* 37, *f.* 8-11, *t.* 48, *f.* 1-6. *Fl. Dan. t.* 1074. *Price, f.* 2. *Batt. t.* 30. F. *Eng. Fl.* v. *p.* 150, *in part.*

In woods. [United States.]

When the pileus is cracked, the cracks are yellow. Size and habit very much resembling *B. chrysenteron*, but less common. Often growing on beech nuts. Spores oval, yellowish brown, ·0005 × ·00021 in.

var. **radicans.** *Krombh. t.* 48, *f.* 1-6. Whole plant pale ochre or stone colour. Spores spindle-shaped, very pale ochre, almost white, ·00026 × ·00012 in., has the appearance of being distinct. Epping Forest. Staplehurst, &c.—*W. G. S.*

715. Boletus variecolor. *B. & Br.* "Varicolored Boletus."

Pileus convex, subtomentose, olive, margin involute, flesh under the cuticle dark-purple, stem bulbous, attenuated upwards, reticulated at the apex, yellowish below, rufescent above and finely pubescent; tubes minute, free, yellow.—*Ann. N.H.* 1865, *no.* 1020, *t.* xiii. *f.* 3.

In woods, &c. Aug. Deeside.

The flesh of the pileus and stem is pale, here and there inclining to yellow, and partially marbled. It approaches *B. subtomentosus* in habit, but with the bulbous reticulated stem of the section *Calopodes* of Fries.

Sect. 3. *Calopodes.*

716. Boletus calopus. *Fr.* "Scarlet-stemmed Boletus."

Pileus globose, then pulvinate, unpolished, somewhat tomentose, olivaceous; stem firm, conical, then nearly equal, reticulated entirely, or at the apex, scarlet; tubes adnate, minute, angular, yellow.—*Fr. Epicr. p.* 416. *Krombh. t.* 37. *f.* 1-7. *Schæff. t.* 315. *Bolt. t.* 84. *Eng. Fl.* v. *p.* 151. *Saund. & Smith, t.* 13.

In mixed woods. Aug. King's Cliffe. Epping Forest. [Mid. Carolina.]

Differs from *B. subtomentosus* in the red, thicker, reticulated stem and narrower tubes. Flesh more or less changing to blue.—*Fries.* Spores spindle-shaped, yellowish brown, ·0003×·00014 in.

717. Boletus olivaceus. *Schæff.* "Olive Boletus."

Pileus convex, even, at length smooth, olive-brown, margin at first inflexed, stem firm, clavato-bulbous, reticulate, punctate, blood-red, yellowish above; tubes adnate, short, minute, unequal, olive-yellow.—*Fr. Epicr. p.* 416. *Schæff. t.* 105. *B. pachypus, var. b. Eng. Fl.* v. *p.* 151. *Purt. no.* 988.

In woods. Rare. Oct.

Pileus olive brown; tubes bright yellow; stem brown below, yellow above. —*Part.* Pileus from 1½-2 in. in diameter, seldom more; stem rather short.

718. **Boletus pachypus.** *Fr.* "Thick-stemmed Boletus."

Pileus pulvinate, dry, subtomentose, brownish, then pallid tan; stem thick, firm, reticulated, variegated yellow and red; tubes somewhat elongated, shortened near the stem, almost free, rounded, yellow; orifice of the same colour.—*Fr. Epicr. p.* 417. *Letell. Supp. t.* 641. *Kromb. t.* 35. *f.* 13-15. *Eng. Fl.* v. *p.* 151. *Saund. & Sm. t.* 17.

In woods. July—Sept. Epping Forest. [Low. Carolina.]

Pileus 6-7 in. broad, dry, pulvinate, subtomentose, pale reddish brown, very thick and fleshy, when young firm, when full grown very soft; flesh white, not changeable; tubes free, at first lemon-coloured, afterwards dirty yellow, simple; stem 3-4 in. high, 2½ in. thick, bulbous, often swollen from the top, rarely equal, reticulated, yellowish when young, subrufescent when old, sometimes two or three springing from the same root.—*M. J. B.* This species sometimes changes very sparingly to blue. Taste not unpleasant. Spores large, oval, yellowish ochre, ·0005 × ·00022 in.

Sect. 4. *Edules.*

719. **Boletus edulis.** *Bull.* "Edible Boletus."

Pileus pulvinate, smooth, moist, brownish; stem stout, reticulated, pallid brown; tubes nearly free, elongated, minute, at first white, then yellow and greenish.—*Fr. Epicr. p.* 420. *Bull. t.* 60, 494. *Sow. t.* 111. *Sv. Bot. t.* 197. *Lenz. f.* 34. *Tratt. aus. f.* 34. *Krombh. t.* 31. *Vitt. t.* 22. *Letell. S. t.* 614. *Schæff. t.* 134, 135. *Paul. t.* 167, 168. *Berk. Outl. t.* 15. *f.* 6. *Huss.* i. *t.* 81. *Cooke, B.F. t.* 15. *Smith, E.M. f.* 2. *Eng. Fl.* v. *p.* 153. *Badh.* i. *t.* 3, ii. *t.* 3, *f.* 1, 2. *Price, f.* 63. *Barla. t.* 311. *Vent. t.* 8. *Hogg. & Johnst. t.* 11.

In woods. Common. Esculent. [Mid. Carolina.]

Pileus 6 in. or more broad, pulvinate, at length convexo-expanded, smooth, shining, often rugose, and much cracked, dark umber, pale towards the margin, slightly viscid, extreme margin white, scarcely downy. Flesh turning a little reddish near the epidermis. Tubes nearly free, at first white, then lemon-coloured, at length dull yellow, simple, their orifices angular. Spores large, greenish ochre. Stem 4 in. high or more, 2 in. thick, fawn coloured, incrassated above and below, reticulated.—*M. J. B.*

var. β. **elephantinus,** changes to blue when cut or bruised. Banstead Downs, Surrey.—*Schæff. t.* 277.

720. **Boletus fragrans.** *Vitt.* "Fragrant Boletus."

Pileus pulvinate, repand, sub-tomentose, umber-brown; margin inflexed; stem stout, even, variegated with red and yellow; tubes semi-free, minute, round, greenish-yellow.—*Fr. Epicr. p.* 421. *Vitt. F. Mang. t.* 19. *Smith. Seem. Journ.* 1868, *p.* 33. *B. xanthophorus, Krombh. t.* 75, *f.* 15-21.

In woods, under oaks, &c. Sept. Oct. Esculent.

The pileus is bronze-brown, pulvinate, and scabrous; tubes minute, and of a beautiful shade of subdued yellow-green; the stem, which is thickened downwards, is brown and also scabrous, and the flesh is pure white, which changes here and there to the slightest imaginable shade of cobalt on being cut or broken; the spores are pale yellowish-green, ovate, with an apiculus at one end, ·00045 in. long, ·00017 in. broad.—*W. G. S.*

721. **Boletus impolitus.** *Fr.* "Unpolished Boletus."

Pileus pulvinate, dilated, flocculose, dingy, pallid, at length granulose or cracked; margin obtuse; stem short, stout, compact, even, pallid; tubes nearly free, very long, rather large, yellowish.—*Fr. Epicr. p.* 421. *Krombh. t.* 74, *f.* 8, 9. *Schæff. t.* 108. *Letell. t.* 614.

On woodsides. Esculent.

Attains a diameter of four or more inches. Stem about 2 in. Flesh more or less changing to blue when cut. Often very large. Spores oval, or spindle-shaped, pale greenish brown, ·0005 × ·00022 in.

722. **Boletus æstivalis.** *Fr.* "Early Boletus."

Pileus pulvinate, silky, soft, then rivulose, minutely granulated and silky, opaque, pallid tan; stem stout, firm, sub-conical, even, pallid, white; tubes elongated, minute, equal, of the same colour.—*Fr. Epicr. p.* 422. *Paul. t.* 170. *Huss.* ii. 25. *Hogg & Johnst. t.* 13.

In woodland pastures. Esculent.

One of the largest of the genus, sometimes 6-8 in. in diameter; stem 2 in. thick. Pileus pale tan or grey silky, granulated when old, cracking into somewhat hexagonal or irregular patches. Flesh not turning blue. Spores elongated oval, greenish-brown, rather dark, ·00048 × ·00018 in.

Sect. 5. *Luridi.*

723. **Boletus Satanas.** *Lenz.* "Satanic Boletus."

Pileus pulvinate, smooth, somewhat viscid, brownish tan colour, then whitish, stem blunt, ovato-ventricose, reticulated above, blood red; tubes free, minute, yellow; orifice from the first blood red.—*Fr. Epicr. p.* 417. *Lenz. f.* 33. *Roq. t.* 6. *Krombh. t.* 38. *f.* 1-6. *Huss.* i. *t.* 7. *Ann. N.H. no.* 510. *Smith. P.M. f.* 27.

In woods. Poisonous. [Mid. Carolina.]

Pileus sometimes 8 in. across, commonly less, pulvinate, soft to the touch, naked, dry, smooth, whitish, leather-buff or greenish, often shading into a red tinge; flesh solid, becoming soft, tender, and juicy, white, turning reddish, then blue; stem 2-3 in. high, thick, finely reticulated above, the reticulations purple-crimson, often vanishing in age, the stem growing streaked below. Spores rich brown, oval, or spindle-shaped, ·00047×·00022 in.

724. Boletus luridus. *Fr.* "Lurid Boletus."

Pileus pulvinate, tomentose, olive-umber, then subviscid, dingy; stem stout, vermilion-red, reticulated, or punctate, with darker markings; tubes free, rounded, yellow, then greenish; orifice from vermilion to orange.—*Fr. Epicr. p.* 418. *Schæff. t.* 107. *Tratt. Aust. f.* 17. *Grev. t.* 121. *Letell. f.* 32. *Krombh. t.* 38. *f.* 11-17. *Bull. t.* 100. *Bolt. t.* 85. *var. Berk. Outl. t.* 15. *f.* 5. *Eng. Fl.* v. *p.* 152. *Gard. Chron.* (1860) *p.* 385. *Harz. t.* 56. *Badh. t.* 7. *f.* 12. ii. *t.* 6. *f.* 3-5. *Smith P.M. f.* 10. *Barla, t.* 33. *f.* 1-5.

In woods and woodland pastures. Common. Poisonous. [Mid. Carolina.]

Pileus 2-6 in. broad, convex, expanded, minutely tomentose, olive, brick-red, pinkish, cream-coloured, or ferruginous brown; flesh more or less yellow, changing to blue. Tubes free, yellow or greenish, their orifices of a beautiful red or bright orange, quite simple, round. Spores olivaceous-ochre. Stem variable in length, bulbous, tomentose, sometimes quite smooth, red, with ferruginous or the brightest yellow shades, solid, generally more or less marked or reticulated with crimson-red.—*M. J. B.* Spores very large, oval, greenish slate colour, ·0006×·00035 in.

725. Boletus erythropus. *P.* "Dotted-stem Boletus."

Pileus tomentose, almost velvety, tawny; stem elongated, equal, not reticulated, dotted with red, squamuloso-punctate, reddish within at the base; tubes free.—*Fr. Epicr. p.* 418. *Fl. Dan. t.* 1962. *Letell. t.* 612. *Barla. t.* 33, *f.* 6, 7.

In woods. King's Cliffe.

Included by Fries with *B. luridus* as a variety, smaller, but more beautiful. Flesh yellow here and there, blue when cut, but partially red, with a more slender, punctato-squamulose, and not reticulated stem.

726. Boletus purpureus. *Fr.* "Purple Boletus."

Pileus pulvinate, somewhat velvety, opaque, dry, purplish-red; stem stout, yellow, variegated with purple veins and dots; tubes almost free, minute, greenish yellow, orifice purple-orange.—*Fr. Epicr. p.* 418. *Krombh. t.* 37, 12-15. *Ann. N. H. no.* 341. *Letell. t.* 678. *Barla. t.* 33, *f.* 8-10.

In woods. Rare. King's Cliffe. Staplehurst.

[Mid. Carolina.]

Rev. M. J. Berkeley states that he has found all these four species together in the same wood, which consisted chiefly of lime trees. Spores somewhat spindle-shaped, green sepia-brown, ·0004 × ·0002 in. (*Fig.* 62, *reduced.*)

B. Dermini—spores subferruginous.

727. **Boletus viscidus.** *L.* "Viscid Boletus."

Pileus pulvinate, soft, smooth, viscid, dingy-yellowish; veil subannulate, torn, white, appendiculate; stem torn, reticulated above; tubes wide, adnate, unequal, livid.—*Fr. Epicr. p.* 423. *Ann. N. H. no.* 278.

In woods. Rare.

The rather large and angular tubes will distinguish this from the rest of the species with rusty spores. Spores very small, spindle-shaped, elongated, brownish green, ·00038 × ·00012 in.

728. **Boletus versipellis.** *Fr.* "Orange-cap Boletus."

Pileus pulvinate, dry, at first closely tomentose, then scaly and smooth between; veil membranaceous, annular, inflexed, appendiculate; stem solid, attenuated above, rugoso-squamose; tubes free, plane, minute, dingy-white, orifice greyish.—*Fr. Epicr. p.* 424. *Batt. t.* 50, *f. A.* *Schæff. t.* 103. *Sow. t.* 110. *Krombh. t.* 32.

In woods. [Mid. Carolina.]

Pileus of a beautiful orange, closely allied to *Boletus scaber*, but apparently not so common. Spores spindle-shaped, pale, ochraceous, ·00056 × ·00021 in.

729. **Boletus scaber.** *Fr.* "Shaggy Boletus."

Pileus pulvinate, smooth, viscid when moist, at length rugulose or rivulose; margin veiled; stem solid, attenuated, rough with fibrous scales; tubes free, convex, round, minute, white, then dingy.—*Fr. Epicr. p.* 424. *Lenz. f.* 32. *Vitt. t.* 28. *Bull. t.* 132, 489, *f.* 1, 2. *Fl. Dan. t.* 833, *f.* 3. *Eng. Fl.* v. *p.* 153. *Badh.* i. *t.* 7, *f.* 1, ii. *t.* 6, *f.* 1, 2. *Barla. t.* 35. *Vent. t.* 9, 10. *Sow. t.* 175. *Krombh. t.* 32, *f.* 1-10, *t.* 35, *f.* 1-6. *Schæff. t.* 104. *Huss.* i. *t.* 57. *Hogg. & Johnst. t.* 22.

In woods. Common. Esculent. [Carolina, U. S.]

Pileus 3-7 in. or more broad, pulvinate, viscid when moist, very variable in colour, white, cinereous, brown olive, deep orange, or vermilion, smooth or minutely downy, the down sometimes collected into minute fasciculate scales; flesh very thick, soft, not changeable in young specimens, in older ones reddish-grey when bruised, and sometimes black; tubes white, pulvinate, stained with the yellow-brown spores, their orifices often ferruginous before the expansion of the pileus, minute, round; stem 6 in. or more high, attenuated upwards, squarrose with black or orange scales, sometimes marked with coarse-raised lines. At first the stem is ovate and the pileus very narrow. There are frequent traces of a floccose veil.—*M. J. B.* Spores spindle-shaped, pale brown, ·00055 × ·00022 in. I have found a variety at Staplehurst, with the pileus snow-white.—*W. G. S.*

C. Hyporrhodii—spores roseate.

730. Boletus alutarius. *Fr.* "Tan-coloured Boletus."

Pileus pulvinate, expanded, soft, velvety, then smooth, brownish-tan; flesh white; stem solid, bulbous, nearly even, white; apex pitted; tubes depressed about the stem, short, plane, round, white, brown when bruised.—*Fr. Epicr. p.* 425. *Krombh. t.* 74, *f.* 8, 9. *Ann. N.H. no.* 342.

In woodland pastures. Rare.

731. Boletus felleus. *Bull.* "Bitter Boletus."

Pileus pulvinate, soft, smooth, even, brownish or reddish-grey; stem solid, attenuated upwards, reticulated; tubes adnate, convex, elongated, angular, white then flesh-coloured, as well as the substance of the pileus when broken.—*Fr. Epicr. p.* 425. *Bull. t.* 379. *Krombh. t.* 74, *f.* 1-7. *Ann. N.H. no.* 79. *Smith, P.M. f.* 29.

In woods, &c. Rare. King's Cliffe.

[Low. and Mid. Carolina.]

Spores spindle-shaped, salmon colour, ·00064 × ·0002 in.

D. Leucospori—spores white.

732. Boletus cyanescens. *Bull.* "Sibthorp's Boletus."

Pileus convexo-expanded, closely tomentose or floccoso-squamose, opaque, tan-coloured, becoming brownish; flesh compact, white, dark-blue when broken; stem stuffed, then hollow, ventricose, villoso-pruinose, of the same colour, constricted above, even, white; tubes free, minute round, white, then yellow.—*Fr. Epicr. p.* 426. *Bull. t.* 369. *Letell. t.* 654. *Krombh. t.* 35, *f.* 7-9. *Seem. Journ. t.* 30, *f.* 7, 8. *Roq. t.* 8, *f.* 1. *Eng. Fl.* v. *p.* 154. *Barla. t.* 37, *f.* 1-7.

In woods. Oxford, Neatishead, &c.

"Pileus 2-5 in. broad, rigid, pale, straw-coloured, subfuliginous, the margin acute; flesh white, when broken changing instantly to the most beautiful azure blue, and when squeezed distilling a blue juice; tubes short, when young scarcely a line long, white or lemon-coloured; stem distinct from the pileus, the apex contracted, brittle, never reticulated, but villoso-pruinose."—*Fries.*

Tubes very pale lemon colour. Spores white, or with a suggestion of sulphur, spindle-shaped, ·0006 in. long. It has now been recorded in Oxfordshire, Norfolk, Herts, Surrey, Devon, and Beds (Abbot).

733. Boletus castaneus. *Bull.* "Chestnut Boletus."

Pileus convex, expanded or depressed, firm, opaque, velvety, cinnamon; stem stuffed, then hollow, attenuated from the somewhat bulbous base, cinnamon; flesh white, unchangeable; tubes free, short, round, white, then dirty-yellow.—*Fr. Epicr. p.* 426. *Bull. t.* 328. *Huss.* ii. *t.* 17. *Eng. Fl.* v. *p.* 152. *Barla. t.* 32, *f.* 11-15.

In woods. Rare. Highgate. [Mid. Carolina.]

Pileus 3 in. broad, depressed when old, but broadly pulvinate in the centre, subtomentose, the down raised up into little flat scales, beautiful dark-rufous tan; flesh thick, mottled, stained beneath the cuticle with the colour of the pileus, not changing colour, viscid, insipid or subacid; tubes vivid yellow, half-free, not reaching to the extreme margin; spores yellow; stem sometimes short, swelling in the centre, attenuated below, hollow, sometimes long and equal, beautifully tinged with yellow and rufous.—*M. J. B.*

Gen. **19. STROBILOMYCES,** Berk.

Fig. 63.

Hymenophore quite distinct from the hymenium. Pileus fleshy, at length tough. Spores globose, or broadly elliptic, minutely rough.—*M. J. B.*
(*Fig.* 63.)

734. Strobilomyces strobilaceus. *Berk.* "Cone-like Boletus."

Blackish umber. Pileus pulvinate, rough with thick floccose scales; stem equal, veiled, sulcate above; tubes adnate, white, angular, whitish-brown.—*Berk. Outl. p.* 236. *Dicks.* i. *t.* 3, *f.* 2. *Pers. M.E. t.* 19. *B. strobilaceus, Fr. Epicr. p.* 422. *Krombh. t.* 4, *f.* 28-30, *t.* 74, *f.* 12-13. *Eng. Fl.* v. *p.* 154.

In fir woods. Rare. Ludlow. Haywood Forest, Hereford. [Carolina. Canada.]

Spores very dark. Pileus 2 in. broad, tesselated or cracked, like the cone of the Scotch fir; pores very white; stem 3-4 in. high, thick, solid.—*M. J. B.* (*Fig.* 63.)

Pileus 2-4 in. broad, tough, pulvinate, brown, broken up into large, thick projecting scales (like the cone of the Scotch fir), merging into a thick floccose, ragged and pendulous, white veil at margin; stem solid, equal, coarsely, fibrillose, 3-6 in. long, ½ in. or more thick, brown at the base, and white at the deeply sulcato-reticulated apex, which runs gradually into the tubes; tubes white, very large, adnate, or with a decurrent tooth anastomosing; spores oval, nearly globose, stalked, blackish-brown, ·00038 × ·00053 in. The whole plant turns deep sienna-red when cut or bruised.—*W. G. S.*

Gen. **20.** **POLYPORUS,** Fr. Gen. Hym.

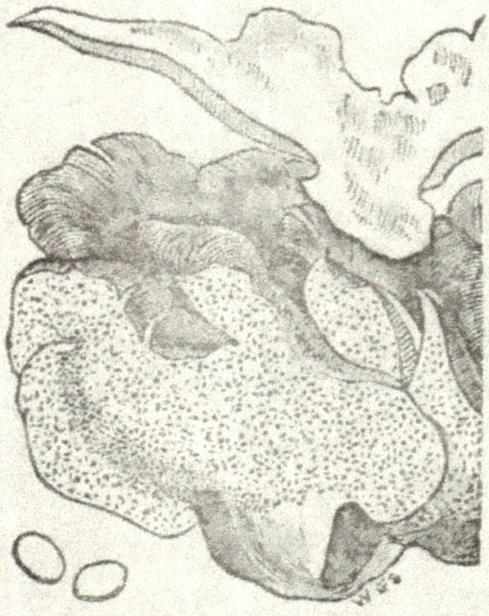

Fig. 64.

Hymenophore descending into the trama of the pores, which are not easily, if at all, separable, and changed with them into a distinct substance. (*Fig.* 64.)

Hymenophore descending into the trama of the pores, which are confluent with the substance of the pileus, and not easily, if at all, separable from each other, or from the hymenophore; the trama, with the pores, when full grown, being different from the hymenophore in substance and often in colour. Pores at first clearly formed by the perforation of the substance of the pileus, very minute, imperfect, or entirely absent, then rounded, angular, or lacerated.

Fungi of various forms, at first of an acid odour, not preformed like *Boletus*, but growing indefinitely. *Polyporus* is the central genus of the *Polyporei*, more or less approaching in character to all the other genera, as *Agaricus* does to the genera of the *Agaricini*. The sections of *Polyporus* are founded on structural characters, but the genus might be divided according to the colour of the spores, like *Agaricus*.—*W. G. S.*

Sect. 1. *Mesopus*—pileus entire, stem distinct.

735. **Polyporus brumalis.** *Fr.* "Winter Polyporus."

Pileus between fleshy and coriaceous, subumbilicate, zoneless, in the first season dingy villous, in the second squamulose, becoming smooth, pallid; stem thin, hirsuto-squamulose, pallid; pores oblong, angular, slender, acute, denticulate, white.—*Fr. Epicr. p.* 430. *Batsch. f.* 42. *Fl. Dan. t.* 1297. *Rostk. t.* 8. *Eng. Fl.* v. *p.* 135. *Ann. N.H. no.* 343. *Krombh. t.* 4. *f.* 19-21. *Fl. ex. no.* 204. *Fckl. exs.* 1396.

On dead trunks and branches. Rare. [Low. and Mid. Carolina.]

Pileus 1-4 in. broad, nearly plane, depressed in the centre, dingy, clothed with minute scales, at length fawn-coloured, and nearly smooth. Pores very slightly angular, white, the dissepiments rather thick. Stem ¾-2 in. high, 2-4 lin. thick, central, velvety, hirsute or squamulose.—*M. J. B.*

736. **Polyporus fuscidulus.** *Fr.* "Yellow-brown Polyporus."

Pileus fleshy, tough, subcoriaceous, convexo-plane, zoneless, even, yellowish-brown; stem rather slender, equal, smooth, pallid; pores adnate, somewhat rounded or angular, obtuse, quite entire, yellowish.—*Fr. Epicr. p.* 431. *Bolt. t.* 170.

Amongst chips, &c. Rare.

Stem 1-2 in. long, 2 lin. thick, nearly straight, equal, or thickened towards each extremity, tawny or yellowish. Pileus 1-2 in. broad; flesh tough, yellowish white.

737. **Polyporus leptocephalus.** *Fr.* "White-pored Polyporus."

Pileus tough, coriaceous, convexo-plane, thin, smooth, zoneless, even, pallid, then fawn-coloured; stem short, smooth, pallid; pores adnate, minute, subrotund, obtuse, whitish.—*Fr. Epicr. p.* 432. *Jacq. Misc.* i. *t.* 12. *Paul. t.* 164. *f.* 1. *Mich. t.* 70. *f.* 1. *Eng. Fl.* v. p. 135.

On trunks. Rare.

Pileus 1 in. broad, tawny-bay, flat, thin, leather-like; pores white, very short; stem pale or reddish-brown, thick as a crow quill, and about half an inch high.—*With.*

738. **Polyporus lentus.** *Berk.* "Tough Polyporus."

Pileus fleshy, but tough, umbilicate, minutely scaly, especially at first; stem hispid, furfuraceous, rather slender, incurved, central or excentric; pores irregular, decurrent, white.—*Berk. Outl. p.* 237. *t.* 16, *f.* 1. *Eng. Fl.* v. *p.* 134.

On old furze stems. Northamptonshire and Notts.

Pileus 1½ in. broad, convex or slightly depressed, at first furfuraceo-squamulose, reddish-brown, at length nearly smooth, ochraceous; the margin fibrilloso-squamose, of a tough, fleshy substance; pores large, rather deep, decurrent, roundish or subquadrate, at first white; edges slightly toothed, and powdered with the white oblong spores; stem ½-1 in. high, ⅜ in. thick, central, covered with pores to the very base, only the lower ones abortive, and their interstices pilose, or distinctly furfuraceous, nearly of the colour of the pileus.—*M. J. B.*

739. Polyporus Schweinitzii. *Fr.* "Schweinitz's Polyporus."

Pileus thick, spongy, then corky, strigoso-tomentose, rough, bright brown; stem thick, very short or obsolete, ferruginous; pores large, variable, and torn, greenish-sulphur.—*Fr. Epicr. p.* 433. *Sv. Bot. t.* 720. *Mich. t.* 70. *f,* 1. *Ann. N.H. no.* 805. *Corda.* v. *t.* 10. *f.* 88. *Kl. ex. no.* 513.

Amongst roots of pines. Rare. [Mid. Carolina.]

It occurs with a central stem, and also imbricated, and varies in the thickness of the tomentose coat.—*B. & Br.* Spores oval, white or transparent, ·00014 × ·00031 in.

740. Polyporus rufescens. *Fr.* "Rufescent Polyporus."

Flesh-coloured. Pileus between spongy and corky, soft, unequal, hairy; stem short, irregular; pores large, sinuose and lacerated, white or flesh-coloured.—*Fr. Epicr. p.* 433. *Sow. t.* 190.

On the ground, about stumps. [United States.]

Smaller than *P. Schweinitzii*, softer, and of a different colour.

741. Polyporus perennis. *Fr.* "Perennial Polyporus."

Cinnamon, then bright brown. Pileus coriaceous, thin, plane, then infundibuliform, velvety, becoming smooth, zoned; stem rather firm, thickened below, velvety; pores minute, angular, acute, at first veiled, then naked and torn.—*Fr. Epicr. p.* 434. *Rostk. t.* 6. *Bolt. t.* 87. *Sow. t.* 192. *Fl. Dan. t.* 1075, *f.* 1. *Bull. t.* 449, *f.* 2. *Schæff. t.* 125. *Kl. exs. no.* 31. *Fckl. exs.* 1400. *Paul. t.* 164, *f.* 5, 6. *Huss.* i. *t.* 51. *Eng. Fl.* v. *p.* 136. *Price, f.* 86. *Vent. t.* 61, *f.* 1. *Bisch. f.* 3257.

On the ground and stumps. [United States.]

Pileus 1½-2 in. broad, varying in depth of colour, cup-shaped when young, nearly plane when old; often confluent, zoned, soft and velvety, and marked with little raised, radiating lines, giving it a striated appearance; margin fimbriate or laciniated; pores small, roundish or angular, at length torn, decurrent. Stem 1 in. high, variable in thickness, very tough, velvety, bulbous at the base.—*M. J. B.* Spores oval, white, ·0001 × ·00018 in. A beautiful variety occurs on charcoal heaps in woods, with a zoned pileus, dark rich chestnut brown, sometimes almost jet black.

Sect. 2. *Pleuropus*—pileus horizontal, stem lateral or excentric.

742. Polyporus squamosus. *Fr.* "Scaly Polyporus."

Pileus fleshy, tough, flabelliform, expanded, sub-ochraceous, variegated, with broad, adpressed, spot-like, centrifugal, darker scales; stem excentric and lateral, blunt, reticulated above, blackened at the base; pores thin, variable, at first minute, then broad, angular and torn, pallid.—*Fr. Epicr. p.* 438. *Grev. t.* 207. *Rostk. t.* 2. *Schæff. t.* 101,102. *Fl. Dan. t.* 983, 1196. *Bolt. t.* 77. *Paul. t.* 16. *Sterb. t.* 13. 14. *Huss.* i. *t.* 51. *Cooke, B.F. t.* 19. *Vent. t.* 37. *Price. f.* 115. *Kl. exs. no.* 30. *Harz. t.* 32. *Gard. Chron.* (1860), *p.* 975. *Eng. Fl.* v. *p.* 134. *Fckl. exs.* 1328.

On trunks, especially ash. Common.

Solitary or imbricated. From a globose, or turgid, scaly, blackish knob, arise one or more stems, which are at first slightly compressed, flat, and hollowed out above where they are furfuraceous; gradually the depressed surface expands, and the hymenium is formed beneath the small scales of the upper part of the stem. Pileus, when fully expanded, pallid ochraceous, with scattered, brown, adpressed scales; spores oblong, white. In vaults and hollow trees it sometimes assumes the form of a *Clavaria*, but in this case seldom produces a pileus.—*M. J. B.* Spores oval, white, very large, ·0005 × ·000025 in.

743. Polyporus Rostkovii. *Fr.* "Rostkovius's Polyporus."

Pileus fleshy, tough, dimidiate, somewhat infundibuliform, smooth, even, dingy; stem long, excentric, reticulated, abruptly black, base thickened; pores decurrent, broad, pentagonal, acute, toothed, white, then dirty yellow.—*Fr. Epicr. p.* 439. *Rostk. t.* 17. *Ann. N.H. no.* 709. *Bisch. f.* 3305.

On stumps. Rare.

Thin, flaccid, 6 in. across, infundibuliform, but often lateral, smooth, even, pale ochraceous, mottled below with darker spots and virgate, dark brown at the base; margin lobed, involute. Flesh white, tough. Stem connate, black, tough, reticulate from the decurrent pores. Pores large, 2 lines or more long, elongated, edge obtuse, or very thin and torn. Spores with two nuclei, ·0005 in. long, ·0002 in. broad.—*B. & Br.*

744. Polyporus picipes. *Fr.* "Pied-stem Polyporus."

Pileus fleshy, coriaceous, rigid, tough, even, smooth, depressed behind or in the centre; stem excentric and lateral, equal, firm, at first velvety, then naked, punctate, with black dots; pores decurrent, rounded, small, tender, white, at length reddish-grey. —*Fr. Epicr. p.* 440. *Grev. t.* 202. *Pers. Ic. Pict. t.* 4, *f.* 1, 2. *Rostk. t.* 20. *Fckl. exs.* 1397.

On trunks.

Imbricated, flesh white. Pileus depressed behind, commonly emarginate. Colour usually livid, with a chestnut coloured disc.

745. Polyporus varius. *Fr.* "Variable Polyporus."

Pileus fleshy, tough, thin, soon woody, smooth, sub-virgate, irregular, depressed behind or in the centre ; stem excentric and lateral, even, smooth, gradually blackish-cinereous downwards ; pores decurrent, minute, short, rounded, unequal, whitish, or watery cinnamon.—*Fr. Epicr. p.* 440. *Batsch. f.* 129. *Bull. t.* 360, 445, *f.* 2. *Buxb.* v. *t.* 15, *f.* 2. *Bolt. t.* 168. *Eng. Fl.* v. *p.* 136. *Kl. exs. no.* 223.

On trunks. [Mid. & Up. Carolina.]

Variable in size, ½-4 in. broad. Pileus hard, lateral, excentric or regular, infundibuliform or convex, deep red brown or dirty white, smooth and even. Pores decurrent, very minute and shallow. Stem, when present, generally either altogether or abruptly jet black at the base. Occasionally the stem is altogether pale.—*M. J. B.*

746. Polyporus elegans. *Fr.* "Elegant Polyporus."

Pileus equally fleshy, soon indurated, woody, expanded, even, smooth, self-coloured ; stem excentric or lateral, even, smooth, pallid, base from the first abruptly black, rooting ; pores plane, minute, sub-rotund, pallid, yellowish-white.—*Fr. Epicr. p.* 440. *Bull t.* 46. *Fl. Dan. t.* 1075, *f.* 1. *Rostk. t.* 11. *Bolt. t.* 83. *Fckl. exs.* 1395.

On trunks. [Up. Carolina.]

var. β. **nummularius,** smaller, thinner, sub-regular ; stem equal, excentric.—*Rostk. t.* 12. *Bull. t.* 124.

On trunks.

Pileus 2-4 in. broad, pale ochre or orange, shining, not infundibuliform, scarcely depressed. In the variety the pileus does not exceed 1 in.

747. Polyporus quercinus. *Fr.* "Oak Polyporus."

Pileus corky, soft, tongue-shaped, very thick, convexo-plane, even, at first flocculoso-granulose, pallid tan, narrowed behind into the thick horizontal stem ; pores short, minute, whitish.—*Fr. Epicr. p.* 441. *Krombh. t.* 5, *f.* 3-5, *t.* 48, *f.* 11-13. *Paul. t.* 18, *f.* 1-4. *Huss.* i. *t.* 52. *Ann. N. H. no.* 344.

On old oaks. Rare. Apethorpe, Kent.

A very distinct species, having somewhat the form of *Fistulina hepatica*. It is of a beautiful yellow-brown with rather shallow pores.—*B. & Br.*

748. Polyporus lucidus. *Fr.* "Shining Polyporus."

Pileus corky or woody, flabelliform, sulcate, rugose, yellow, then reddish-chestnut, varnished and shining, as well as the lateral, equal stem; pores determinate, long, minute, white, then cinnamon.—*Fr. Epicr. p.* 442. *Grev. t.* 245. *Rostk. t.* 13. *Krombh. t.* 4, *f.* 22-24. *Sow. t.* 134. *Paul. t.* 10, *f.* 1-2. (*Batt. t.* 36. *t.* 35, *D. var.*) *Berk. Outl. t.* 15, *f.* 2. *Eng. Fl.* v. *p.* 136. *Vent. t.* 49, *f.* 1, 2. *Roq. t.* 2, *f.* 1.

On the ground about stumps. [United States.]

Pileus 2-6 in. broad, generally more or less oblique, very variable in thickness, rugose, often marked with concentric grooves or ridges chocolate brown, the edge often tawny or bright chestnut, shining as if varnished, with occasionally a vitreous appearance. Pores very minute, sub-rotund, pale, equal, at length cinnamon. Stem 6-10 in. high, 1 in. or more thick, rugose, marked occasionally with transverse lines of growth, shining like the pileus, sometimes chocolate. Both the pileus and stem occasionally marked with minute wavy wrinkles.—*M. J. B.*

Sect. 3. *Merisma*—divided into numerous pileoli.

749. Polyporus intybaceus. *Fr.* "Grey-branched Polyporus."

Very much branched, fleshy, somewhat brittle, pileoli very numerous, dimidiate, expanded, sinuate, at length spathulate, nearly even, greyish-brown; stems united into a very short trunk; pores firm, obtuse, white, then brownish.—*Fr. Epicr. p.* 446. *Fl. Dan. t.* 1793. *Paul. t.* 30. *Huss.* i. *t.* 6. *Sow. t.* 87. *P. frondosus*, *Eng. Fl.* v. *p.* 137.

On trunks. Rare. Esculent.

Pilei very numerous, dimidiate, condensed into a convex tuft, ½-1 foot broad, imbricated, variously confluent, irregular, at first downy, dusky, then smooth, livid grey, disc depressed, dilated above, ½-1 in. broad, convex, the base confluent with the compound stem. Smell like that of mice.—*Fries.* Spores oval, white, ·0002 × ·00014 in.

750. Polyporus cristatus. *Fr.* "Crested Polyporus."

Branched, firmly fleshy, fragile, pileoli entire and dimidiate, imbricated, depressed, somewhat pulverulent or villous, then rimoso-squamose, greenish-brown; stems connate, irregular, white; pores minute, angular and torn, whitish.—*Fr. Epicr. p.* 447. *Rostk. t.* 16. *Schæff. t.* 113? *Eng. Fl.* v. *p.* 138. *Krombh. t.* 48, *f.* 15, 16. *Barla. t.* 29, *f.* 4-7. *Bisch. f.* 3297. *Fckl. exs.* 1394.

In beech woods. Rare. [Mid. Carolina.]

Stem lateral, irregular, pruinose, white, at length brown. Pilei subcarnose, irregular, confluent in an involute manner, villoso-pulverulent, about 3 in. broad, yellow-green. Pores unequal, dirty-white, when torn more or less of a green hue.—*Fries.*

751. Polyporus giganteus. *Fr.* "Large-branched Polyporus."

Imbricated, fleshy, tough, somewhat coriaceous; pilei dimidiate, very broad, flaccid, somewhat zoned, rivulose, bright-brown, depressed behind; stem branched, connate from a common tuber; pores minute, nearly round, pallid, at length torn.—*Fr. Epicr. p.* 448. *Rostk. t.* 19. *Schæff. t.* 267. *Bolt. t.* 76. *Huss.* i. *t.* 82. *Holms. t.* 13, *var. Eng. Fl.* v. *p.* 137. *Bisch. f.* 3324. *Fl. Dan. t.* 1793. *Fckl. exs. no.* 1897.

On trunks. Rare. [Low. and Mid. Carolina.]

Forming large tufts, 1-2 feet or more broad, branched in an imbricated manner. Pilei sublateral, flaccid, various in form, the surface granulated with minute brown flocci, rigid, when dry squamoso-fibrillose, at first pale, then brownish-yellow, disc depressed, at length black. Pores minute, dirty brown when bruised, at length torn.—*Eng. Fl.* (*Fig.* 64, *reduced.*)

752. Polyporus sulfureus. *Fr.* "Sulphury Polyporus."

Fig. 65.

Cæspitose, of a cheesy consistence, soon growing pale, cracking; pileoli very broad, imbricated, undulated, nearly smooth, reddish-yellow; pores minute, plane, sulphur-coloured, at length torn.—*Fr. Epicr. p.* 450. *Grev. t.* 113. *Bisch. f.* 3287. *Kl. exs. no.* 1005. *Rostk. t.* 20. *Bull. t.* 429. *Sow. t.* 135. *Huss.* i. *t.* 46. *Berk. Outl. t.* 16, *f.* 3. *Eng. Fl.* v. *p.* 138. *Letell. t.* 626. *Price. f.* 116. *Fckl. exs.* 1392.

On trunks. Common. [United States.]

Pilei imbricated, forming a large, compact, somewhat branched mass, sometimes 2-3 feet broad. Pores minute, often formed of inflexed or incurved portions of the mass. Spores white. Dry specimens are often incrusted with crystals of binoxalate of potash.—*Eng. Fl.* Spores oval, white, minutely papillose, ·0003 × ·00023 in. (*Fig.* 65, *reduced.*)

753. Polyporus alligatus. *Fr.* "Connected Polyporus."

Cæspitose, fibrous or of a cheesy consistence, rigid, but brittle; pileoli imbricated, unequal, without zones, villous, isabelline or tan-coloured; pores minute, soft, white, easily obliterated with flocci.—*Fr. Epicr. p.* 450. *Sow. t.* 422.

At the base of trunks. Rare.

754. Polyporus heteroclitus. *Fr.* "Ground Polyporus."

Cæspitose, coriaceous; pileoli sessile, expanded everywhere from a common, radical tubercle, lobed, villous, without zones, orange; pores irregular and elongated, golden-yellow.—*Fr. Epicr. p.* 451. *Bolt. t.* 164. *Eng. Fl.* v. *p.* 135.

On the ground, under oaks.

Pileus 2½ in. broad. It shoots out several flat pieces from a hard and coriaceous root, which is white within, lying on the surface of the earth in a horizontal direction. Pores very variable in size and form.—*Purton.*

755. Polyporus salignus. *Fr.* "Willow Polyporus."

Imbricate, cæspitose, coriaceous, soft, elastic; pileoli dimidiate, dilated, reniform, incrusted with adpressed, whitish down, tumid, sublobate, somewhat sulcate and depressed about the margin; pores thin, crowded, elongated, flexuose, intricate, white.—*Fr. Epicr. p.* 452. *Bolt. t.* 78. *Batt. t.* 38, E. *P. salicinus, Grev., Rostk. t.* 2.

On willows.

Sect. 4. *Apus*—Sessile.

A. *Anodermei.*

756. Polyporus epileucus. *Fr.* "Grey-elm Polyporus."

Pileus of a cheesy consistence, firm, pulvinate, villoso-scrupose, unequally grey, internally white-zoned; pores round and elongated, obtuse, entire, white.—*Fr. Epicr. p.* 452. *Rostk. t.* 26. *Smith. Seem. Journ.* 1868, *p.* 34. *P. spumeus, Fl. Dan. t.* 1794.

On elm trunks. Nov. Holloway. London. [United States.]

It is a very large and handsome species, stemless, of a rich but subdued yellow colour, and somewhat corky consistence; the tubes are very minute, and about ¾ of an inch long; the pileus is tough, shaggy, and dingy-white.—*W. G. S.*

757. Polyporus chioneus. *Fr.* "Soft white Polyporus."

White. Pileus fleshy, soft, without zones, somewhat even and smooth, rather expanded behind; margin acute, inflexed; pores short, small, rounded, equal, quite entire.—*Fr. Epicr. p.* 453. *Pers. M.E.* ii., *t.* 15. *f.* 2. *Ann. N.H. no.* 806.

On trunks.

Always soft, fragile, hyaline white when moist, whitish when dry, about 1 in. broad. Spores white, oval, ·0008 × ·00013 in.

758. Polyporus fragilis. *Fr.* "Fragile Polyporus."

Whitish, spotted with brown when touched; pileus between fleshy and fibrous, fragile, plano-depressed, or versiform, fibroso-rugose, convex below; pores slender, elongated, flexuose, intricate.—*Fr. Epicr. p.* 454. *Ann. N.H. no.* 710.

On fir. Cornwall.

759. Polyporus cæsius. *Fr.* "Blue-grey Polyporus."

White, here and there tinged with blue; pileus fleshy, soft, tough, unequal, silky; pores small, unequal, elongated, flexuose, dentate, and torn.—*Fr. Epicr. p.* 454. *Sow. t.* 226. *Eng. Fl.* v. *p.* 139. *Fl. Dan. t.* 1963. *f.* 2.

On fallen sticks. [Mid. Carolina.]

A small species, ½-3 in. broad, variously imbricated and laciniated, sometimes stipitate, very delicate, changing when touched to bluish; flesh thin; pores of various lengths, sometimes oblique, and deeper than the flesh of the pileus.—*M. J. B.* Spores pale blue, oval, ·0001 × ·0005 in.

760. Polyporus destructor. *Fr.* "Destructive Polyporus."

Pileus fleshy, watery, fragile, effused or reflexed, rugose, whitish, tinged with brown, zoned within; pores long, rounded, toothed, and torn, whitish.—*Fr. Epicr. p.* 454. *Krombh. t.* 3, *f.* 3. *Rostk. t.* 27. *Bisch. f.* 3422. *Kl. exs. no.* 225.

On larch and Scotch fir, and on the ground. [Mid. Carolina.]

Waved and incrusting, broad, wholly resupinate.

761. Polyporus nidulans. *Fr.* "Nestling Polyporus."

Pileus fleshy, tough, very soft, subpulvinate, villous, becoming even, not zoned, reddish-grey, within of the same colour; pores long, medium sized, unequal, angular, tawny, inclining to brick-red.—*Fr. Epicr. p.* 455. *Schæff. t.* 136? *Ann. N.H. no.* 345. *Kl. exs. no.* 809, 1914.

On fallen sticks.

Fragrant when dry; colour of the pileus rufescent or yellowish; margin spreading, somewhat obtuse.

762. Polyporus rutilans. *Fr.* "Reddish Polyporus."

Pileus fleshy, tough, thin, soft, at first villous, then smooth, not zoned, tawny cinnamon, growing pale, of the same colour within; pores short, minute, thin, equal, acute, cinnamon.—*Fr. Epicr. p.* 455. *Pers. Ic. & Desc. t.* 6, *f.* 4. *Ann. N.H. no.* 346.

On fallen branches. July.

When fresh very soft, of a beautiful reddish grey, and with a powerful but pleasant odour, like that of aniseed.—*B. & Br.*

763. Polyporus fumosus. *Fr.* "Smoky Polyporus."

Pileus fleshy, corky, firm, without zones, silky, becoming smooth, undulated, dingy pale umber, dilated and adnate behind, fibrous within and somewhat zoned; pores short, round, minute, whitish or dingy, darker when bruised.—*Fr. Epicr. p.* 456. *Tratt. Aust. t.* 3. *f.* 5. *Fl. Dan. t.* 1963. *f.* 2. *Fl. Boruss. t.* 392. *Bail. t.* 31. *Fckl. exs.* 1391.

On stumps.

Cæspitose or imbricated, thick, of a smoky hue.

764. Polyporus adustus. *Fr.* "Scorched Polyporus."

Pileus fleshy, tough, firm, thin, villous, pallid cinereous, margin straight, blackish, effuso-reflexed behind; pores short, minute, round, obtuse, whitish pruinose, soon cinereous brown.—*Fr. Epicr. p.* 456. *Fl. Dan. t.* 1850, *f.* 1. *Batsch, f.* 226. *Sow. t.* 231. *Eng. Fl.* v. *p.* 139. *Kl. exs. no.* 620. ii. 412. *Fckl. exs.* 1390.

On stumps. [United States.]

Pores very small and grey, even in younger specimens always leaving a whitish margin on the under side, which will readily distinguish it.—*Sow.*

765. Polyporus crispus. *Fr.* "Crisped Polyporus."

Pileus fleshy, tough, coriaceous, rugose, blackish-cinereous, effuso-reflexed behind; margin thin, crisped, at length black; pores rather large, unequal, at length labyrinthiform, silvery-grey.—*Fr. Epicr. p.* 457. *Batsch, f.* 227.

On stumps. [Mid. and Up. Carolina.]

Smaller than *P. adustus.* Pileus when young dingy black, floccoso-rugose, without zones; margin white, when mature thinner, becoming pale-grey, with a brown marginal zone.

766. Polyporus adiposus. *B. & Br.* "Foxy-white Polyporus."

White, here and there acquiring a foxy tinge; pileus soft, waxy, shortly reflexed, obscurely tomentose, hymenium rather thick; pores small, edge obtuse.—*Berk. Outl. p.* 243. *Ann. N.H. no.* 711.

On the ground.

Very variable in form, sometimes fixed by the apex, sometimes resupinate, white, waxy, thickish when fresh, but losing much of its substance in age, here and there acquiring a foxy tinge; substance not zoned within; pores when horizontal with the edges even, but often elongated and irregular, not stratose; surface scarcely tomentose, uneven. Turning brownish in drying. —*B. & Br.*

767. Polyporus amorphus. *Fr.* "Amorphous Polyporus."

Pileus fleshy, tough, thin, generally effuso-reflexed, pores minute, unequal, golden-yellow, at first dusted with white.—*Fr. Epicr. p.* 457. *Sow. t.* 423. *Nees. f.* 223. *Eng. Fl.* v. *p.* 139. *Fckl. exs.* 1372.

On the ground amongst pine leaves.

Resupinate with the upper margin reflexed or dimidiate, imbricated, somewhat zoned, white and silky; pores minute, short, yellowish, or rich tawny, pruinose when young.—*M. J. B.*

768. Polyporus hispidus. *Fr.* "Hispid Polyporus."

Pileus compact, spongy, fleshy, dimidiate, pulvinate, hispid, sub-ferruginous, divergently fibrous within; pores minute, round, inclined to separate, fringed, paler.—*Fr. Epicr. p.* 458. *Grev. t.* 14. *Bolt. t.* 161. *Sow. t.* 345. *Bull. t.* 210, 493. *Krombh. t.* 48, *f.* 7-10. *Huss.* i. *t.* 29, 31. *Eng. Fl.* v. *p.* 138. *Kl. exs. no.* 1913. *Fckl. exs.* 1389.

On trunks of living trees. Common. [United States.]

Spores yellowish. Pileus a foot or more across, 4 in. thick, dimidiate, with occasionally an obsolete, knob-like stem, generally very hispid, but sometimes almost smooth and cracked, substance fleshy but fibrous, marked with concentric lines, which seem to indicate different intervals in which vegetation has been more or less dormant, brown, blackish, yellowish, or reddish-brown, below pale yellow or rich sienna brown, margin paler.—*M. J. B.*

769. Polyporus cuticularis. *Fr.* "Hairy Polyporus."

Pileus very thin, spongioso-carnose, then dry, plane, hairy-tomentose, ferruginous, then blackish-brown; margin fibroso-fimbriate, internally loose and parallel, fibrous; pores long, minute, pallid, then ferruginous.—*Fr. Epicr. p.* 458. *B. & Br. Ann. N. H.* (1866), *no.* 1137. *Bull. t.* 462. *Kl. exs. no.* 33.

On trunks. Burnham Beeches.

The hairs are curiously trifid at the apex, the spores yellow. Pores longer than the thickness of the flesh. Spores copious, ochraceous.

770. **Polyporus spumeus.** *Fr.* "Oozing Polyporus."

Whitish. Pileus fleshy, spongy, compact, pulvinate, gibbous, rugose, hispid; base stem-like; margin incurved; pores seceding, minute, round, acute, entire.—*Fr. Epicr. p.* 459. *Sow. t.* 211. *Berk. Outl. t.* 16, *f.* 4. *Eng. Fl.* v. *p.* 139. *Ann. N.H. no.* 78. *Fckl. exs. no.* 1384.

On trunks.

Plant 3-4 in. across, thick, oozing out from the tree in a very soft mass, which hardens in a day, and if it dries favourably the pileus becomes hispid. —*Eng. Fl.*

B. *Placodermei.*

771. **Polyporus dryadeus.** *Fr.* "Dripping Polyporus."

Pileus spongy, fleshy, then corky, thick, pulvinate, sub-ferruginous, turning brown; cuticle thin, soft, pitted, then even and smooth; flesh fibrous, somewhat zoned, ferruginous; pores very long, slender, round, soft, ferruginous, orifice at first paler.—*Fr. Epicr. p.* 460. *Bull. t.* 458. *Huss.* i. *t.* 21. *Eng. Fl.* v. *p.* 143. *Rostk. t.* 9.

At the foot of old oaks.

Pileus 7 in. or more broad, 2½ in. thick, obtuse, pulvinate, grossly tuberculated, minutely pitted towards the edge, and when fresh distilling drops of moisture, which is sometimes glutinous. When young cinnamon, when old cinereous or whitish, and the white surface when bruised changes to red-brown. Mass of spores nearly plane, pores minute red-brown within, their orifices whitish or sub-cinereous; substance silky; smell strong, subacid.—*M. J. B.*

772. **Polyporus betulinus.** *Fr.* "Birch Polyporus."

Pileus fleshy, then corky, ungulate, obtuse, smooth, without zones; cuticle even, evanescent, brownish, vertex oblique, umbonately expanded, adnate; pores short, minute, round, unequal, white, at length seceding.—*Fr. Epicr. p.* 461. *Grev. t.* 246. *Rostk. t.* 22. *Bull. t.* 312. *Fl. Dan. t.* 1254. *Eng. Fl.* v. *p.* 140. *Bisch. f.* 3296. *Kl. exs. no.* 32. *Fckl. exs. no.* 1387.

On birch trees.

Pileus 4-6 in. across, smooth, pale reddish-brown when mature, often mottled, roundish, or somewhat reniform; flesh white, very thick; pores white or tinged with brown, narrow, the orifices toothed, separable from the pileus when fresh, but really concrete with it. Spores white.—*Grev.* Taste and smell acid.

773. Polyporus pallescens. *Fr.* "Pallid Polyporus."

Pileus fleshy, spongy, then corky, thin, zoneless, even, smooth, yellowish; margin acute, of the same colour; pores short, minute, roundish, yellowish white.—*Fr. Epicr. p.* 463. *Sow. t.* 230. *Eng. Fl.* v. *p.* 141. *Fckl. exs. no.* 1379.

On old stumps. [Mid. & Up. Carolina.]

Thin, imbricated, 2-3 in. or more broad, with scarcely any trace of zones, more or less tuberculated, pores minute, many quite superficial, but towards the base a line or more deep, with a pulverulent appearance, arising from a very minute down.—*M. J. B.*

774. Polyporus vegetus. *Fr.* "Lime Polyporus."

Pileus broad, dilated, smooth, opaque, brown, annual zone broad, concentrically sulcate, substance floccose, lax, very thin; cuticle of the second season thick, separable; pores minute, seceding, umber, each annual stratum separated by a distinct floccose layer.—*Fr. Epicr. p.* 464. *Ray. Syn.* ii. *app.* 335.

On lime trees.

775. Polyporus applanatus. *Fr.* "Flattened Polyporus."

Pileus expanded, tuberculose, obsoletely zoned, pulverulent, or smooth, cinnamon, becoming whitish, cuticle crustaceous, rigid, at length fragile, within very soft, loosely floccose; margin tumid, white, then cinnamon; pores very small, sub-ferruginous, orifice whitish, brownish when bruised.—*Fr. Epicr. p.* 465. *Batsch. f.* 130. *Bull. t.* 454, *f. C. Fl. Boruss. t.* 393. *Fckl. exs. no.* 1388.

On trunks. [Mid. & Up. Carolina.]

776. Polyporus fomentarius. *Fr.* "Dingy-hoof Polyporus."

Pileus ungulate, dilated, thick, smooth, remotely and concentrically zoned, smooth, opaque, dingy, becoming whitish, soft within, floccose, tawny-ferruginous, cuticle thick, very hard, persistent; margin, and very long minute pores, distinctly stratose, at first pruinose, then ferruginous.—*Fr. Epicr. p.* 465. *Lenz. f.* 48. *Sow. t.* 133. *Batt. t.* 37, *f. E. Eng. Fl.* v. *p.* 144. *Kl. exs. no.* 222. *Schnz. t.* 16, *f.* 28. *Fckl. exs. no.* 1386.

On trunks. Common. [United States.]

Pileus 4-5 in. broad, subtriangular, obsoletely zoned, nodulose, brownish-grey, resembling coffee slightly tinged with milk, sometimes in age, especially when growing on birch, nearly white, occasionally tinged with bright yellow; margin in general sub-acute, but sometimes very obtuse, substance reddish-brown, varying in density. Pores very minute, stratified, whitish, glaucous, or yellowish-grey, at length ferruginous, the mass of them generally concave.—*M. J. B.*

777. Polyporus nigricans. *Fr.* "Black-hoof Polyporus."

Pileus pulvinate, very thick, densely and concentrically sulcate, smooth, shining, black, cuticle very hard, crustaceous, varnished, persistent, internally very hard, ferruginous; margin very obtuse, ferruginous; pores very small, plane, confluent, stratose, naked, of the same colour.—*Fr. Epicr. p.* 466. *Eng. Fl.* v. *p.* 144. *Bisch. f.* 3426.

On birch.

Similar in form to *P. fomentarius*, but manifestly distinct.

778. Polyporus igniarius. *Fr.* "Rusty-hoof Polyporus."

Pileus at first tuberculoso-globose (immarginate), even, with a thin flocculent crust which becomes white, then ungulate ferruginous, becoming blackish-brown, opaque; cuticle concrete, pitted unequally, very hard, as well as the zoned, ferruginous flesh; margin rounded; pores very small, convex, stratose, cinnamon, at first whitish.—*Fr. Epicr. p.* 466. *Lenz. f.* 47. *Fckl. exs. no.* 1383 (?) *Sow. t.* 182. *Mich. t.* 62. *Eng. Fl.* v. *p.* 144. *Vent. t.* 61, *f.* 4. *Kl. exs. no.* 363.

On willows, poplars, plums, &c. Common. [United States.]

The pileus is narrower and much thicker than in *P. fomentarius*, resembling a horse's hoof; margin obtuse, and the mass of tubes in general plane or very convex. Occasionally the pileus is imperfectly developed.—*M. J. B.*

779. Polyporus fulvus. *Fr.* "Tawny-hoof Polyporus."

Pileus between woody and corky, very hard, globoso-tuberculose, then triangular, subimbricate, at first hairy or villous, pale tawny; margin rounded, internally of the same colour, radiating and zoned; pores short, round, rather minute, cinnamon, at first covered with a cinereous-yellow dust.—*Fr. Epicr. p.* 466. *Rostk. t.* 31. *Tratt. Aust. t.* 5, *f.* 9. *Batt. t.* 37, H. *B. & Br. Ann. N.H.* (1866), *no.* 1138. *Br. Bath. Trans.* 1870, *p.* 83.

On decayed trunks. Batheaston.

Distinct from *P. igniarius*, to which it is allied.

780. Polyporus ribis. *Fr.* "Currant-bush Polyporus."

Pileus corky, coriaceous, rather soft, somewhat plane, velvety, nearly even, ferruginous, then umber; margin acute; pores short, small, naked, tawny, as well as the margin and flesh.—*Fr. Epicr. p.* 467. *Fl. Dan. t.* 1790, *f.* 2. *Desm. exs. no.* 314. *Eng. Fl.* v. *p.* 145. *Corda. Sturm. t.* 62. *Kl. exs. no.* 118. *Fckl. exs. no.* 1381.

At the base of currant and gooseberry bushes. Common.

Imbricated, 3 in. or more broad, thin, zoned, and velvety, of a rather rich tawny-brown; margin paler and brighter; substance soft, silky; pores short, larger than in *P. igniarius*, brownish-grey.—*M. J. B.*

781. Polyporus conchatus. *Fr.* "Shell-shaped Polyporus."

Pileus corky or woody, thin, effuse, sub-conchiform, reflexed, concentrically sulcate, tomentose, bright-brown; margin acute; pores short, small, cinnamon.—*Fr. Epicr. p.* 467. *Eng. Fl.* v. *p.* 145. *Fckl. exs. no.* 1382.

On trunks. [Low. and Mid. Carolina.]

The principal distinction between this and *P. ribis* appears to reside in the harder substance, and smoother pileus. It varies in the degree in which its surface is grooved.—*M. J. B.*

782. Polyporus salicinus. *Fr.* "Scented-willow Polyporus."

Pileus woody, very hard, undulate, smooth, in great part resupinate; margin short, obtuse, patent, cinnamon, then brown; pores very small, round, ferruginous, cinnamon.—*Fr. Epic r. p.* 467. *Eng. Fl.* v. *p.* 140. *Ann. N. H. no.* 346, B.

On willows. Common. [United States.]

Hard when dry. Scent very strong, like that of aniseed in the fresh plant.

783. Polyporus ulmarius. *Fr.* "Elm Polyporus."

Pileus corky or woody, undulated, tuberculose, crustaceous, smooth, white without and within; pores decurrent, minute, round, stratose, yellowish.—*Fr. Epicr. p.* 469. *Sow. t.* 88. *Batt. t.* 36, *f.* C. *Huss.* i. *t.* 64. *Berk. Outl. t.* 16, *f.* 5. *Eng. Fl.* v. *p.* 142. *Kl. exs.* ii. *no.* 616.

On old elms. Common.

Effused with an obtuse, occasionally free margin, forming a new stratum every year, so that a section gives several distinct layers of pores and flesh, alternating with each other; flesh white; pores minutely tawny; substance, when dry, hard and corky.—*M. J. B.*

784. Polyporus fraxineus. *Fr.* "Ash Polyporus."

Pileus corky or woody, smooth, flattened, zoneless, white, then rubiginous and brown; at first even, then concentrically sulcato-plicate, pallid within; pores minute, short, rufous, at first clothed with white sebaceous down, as well as the margin.—*Fr. Epicr. p.* 470. *Bull. t.* 433. *Eng. Fl.* v. *p.* 142.

At the base of ash trees.

Solitary or imbricated, thick, rugged, somewhat zoned, dark red-brown; substance corky, pale. Pores minute, pale, of the same colour as the pileus within. Smell strong and penetrating.—*M. J. B.*

785. **Polyporus cytisinus.** *Berk.* "Laburnum Polyporus."

Large, imbricated; pileus coarsely tuberculated, hard, woody; margin subacute; substance nearly white, as well as the minute pores.—*Berk. Outl. p.* 247. *Sow. t.* 288. *Eng. Fl.* v. *p.* 142.

At the foot of a laburnum. London.

A foot or more across. Imbricated, dimidiate, quite smooth, at least when dry, but coarsely tuberculated; substance slightly zoned, very thick and close, pale, evidently composed of two or three successive layers.—*M. J. B.*

786. **Polyporus variegatus.** *Fr.* "Variegated Polyporus."

Pileus between corky and woody, smooth, flattened, even, zoneless, shining, variegated with orange and bay, pallid within; pores round, minute, short, unequal, and torn, yellowish.—*Fr. Epicr. p.* 470. *Sow. t.* 368.

On trunks.

787. **Polyporus cervinus.** *Pers.* "Fawn-coloured Polyporus."

Effused, very broad; pileus somewhat reflexed, zoned, cinereous-umber, clothed with spongy down; pores large, variable, greyish; dissepiments rigid.—*Pers. M. E.* ii. *p.* 87. *Ann. N. H. no.* 347.

On fallen branches of beech. [Mid. Carolina.]

Remarkable for its large pores and rigid dissepiments, especially when young.—*B. & Br.*

788. **Polyporus annosus.** *Fr.* "Imbricated Polyporus."

Pileus woody, convex, expanded, rugoso-tuberculose, in the first season silky, in the second, and after, covered with a rigid, smooth, blackish crust, white within; margin obtuse, whitish, as well as the medium-sized, obtuse pores.—*Fr. Epicr. p.* 471. *Schæff. t.* 138. *f.* 1-3. *P. Scoticus, Eng. Fl.* v. *p.* 142.

On stumps of larch. [United States.]

Forming masses 3-18 in. wide of imbricated, rugged, or radiato-striate, brown pilei, occasionally tawny towards the margin, marked with strong, vaulted zones, which arise from each annual layer projecting beyond that of the preceding year; substance white, hard, and woody; pores middle-sized, white, or with a pale reddish-brown tint, margined above as well as below, so that each layer appears resupinate.—*M. J. B.*

789. Polyporus connatus. *Fr.* "Connate Polyporus."

Pileus between corky and woody, effuso-reflexed, imbricated, subzonate, confluent, velvety, white without and within; pores minute, roundish, white.—*Fr. Epicr. p.* 472. *Batt. t.* 37. *G.*

On old trunks of crab trees, &c., "running up them for one or two feet, often amongst moss."

c. *Inodermei.*

790. Polyporus radiatus. *Fr.* "Hazel Polyporus."

Pileus corky, coriaceous, rigid, radiato-rugose, at first velvety, tawny, then smooth, ferruginous brown; margin patent, repand; pores minute, pallid, silvery-shining, at length ferruginous.—*Fr. Epicr. p.* 474. *Sow. t.* 190. *Batt. t.* 39. *C. Eng. Fl.* v. *p.* 143.

On hazel stems. [Up. Carolina.]

Tawny specimens of *P. versicolor* sometimes occur very much resembling this species, which is, however, altogether distinct.

791. Polyporus fibula. *Fr.* "Button Polyporus."

White; pileus coriaceous, tough, soft, hairy, substrigose, zoneless; margin entire, acute; pores rather small, round, acute, at length pallid.—*Fr. Epicr. p.* 475. *Sow. t.* 387.

On the door of a wine cellar.

Variable in form; pileus adnate behind. The usually recorded habitat is "branches of oak," &c.

792. Polyporus hirsutus. *Fr.* "Bristly Polyporus."

Pileus corky, coriaceous, convexo-plane, hairy with rigid bristles, zoned with concentric furrows, of one colour, whitish; pores round, obtuse, whitish, then brownish.—*Fr. Epicr. p.* 477. *B. & Br. Ann. N.H.* (1866) *no.* 1139. *Kl. exs. no.* 810. *Fckl. exs. no.* 1378.

On dead trunks. Near Twycross. [United States.]

793. Polyporus velutinus. *Fr.* "Velvety Polyporus."

Pileus corky, coriaceous, plane, velvety, slightly zoned, white, at length yellowish; margin extenuated, acute; pores round, minute, slender, white.—*Fr. S. M.* i. *p.* 368. *Eng. Fl.* v. *p.* 141. *Kl. exs.* ii. *no.* 701. *Rabh. F.E. no.* 15. *Fckl. exs. no.* 1377.

On branches. [Mid. Carolina.]

More or less imbricated. Pileus 2-3 in. broad, velvety, undulated, obscurely zoned, between corky and leathery; margin thinner than in *P. versicolor*, shrinking, and curling inwards when dried, colour various, whitish, with a cottony margin, yellowish fuscous, or brownish grey, the latter most common; pores whitish or yellowish, minute, round, very short, often disappearing towards the margin.—*Grev.*

794. Polyporus versicolor. *Fr.* "Common Zoned Polyporus."

Pileus coriaceous, thin, rigid, plane, depressed behind, velvety, nearly even and shining, variegated with coloured zones; pores minute, round, acute, and torn, white, then pallid.—*Fr. Epicr. p.* 478. *Sterb. t.* 27, *K. Batt. t.* 35. *A. Schæff. t.* 268. *Huss.* i. *t.* 24. *Eng. Fl.* v. *p.* 141. *Price, f.* 127. *Cooke exs. no.* 303. *Kl. exs. no.* 120. ii. *no.* 209. *Corda Anl. H.f.* 75. *Fckl. exs. no.* 1375.

On stumps, branches, &c. Common. [United States.]

Variable, sometimes quite resupinate, or with the margin reflexed, more generally dimidiate and densely imbricated, occasionally spuriously stipitate, more or less lobed, villous, marked with regular, concentric, smooth, shining zones of various colours, sometimes entirely white, and not unfrequently the whole surface is villous, and the zones mere depressions.—*M.J.B.*

795. Polyporus abietinus. *Fr.* "Whitish Fir Polyporus."

Pileus coriaceous, thin, effuso-reflexed, villous, obsoletely zoned, cinereous-white; pores unequal, torn, violaceous, then growing pallid.—*Fr. Epicr. p.* 479. *Grev. t.* 526. *Fl. Dan. t.* 2079. *f.* 1. *t.* 1298. *Eng. Fl.* v. *p.* 141.

On trunks of Coniferæ. [United States.]

Pileus 1-2 in. across, sometimes entirely resupinate, with the exception of the extreme margin, and spreading over several inches, more generally effuso-reflexed, thin, coriaceous, zoned, whitish, often stained with minute green Algæ, more or less villous; pores very regular, laciniated, sometimes resembling hydnoid teeth, more or less of a violet hue, which fades when past maturity.—*M. J. B.*

796. Polyporus Wynnei. *B. & Br.* "Wynne's Polyporus."

Confluent, various in form; pileus adnate behind, effuso-reflexed, then tan-coloured, marked with silky-raised lines; pores small, angular, white.—*Berk. Outl. p.* 249. *Ann. N.H. no.* 807.

Running over twigs, grass, &c. Rare.

Thin, incrusting various substances, with the margin more or less broadly reflected, tan-coloured, sericeous, and marked with raised lines; pores $\frac{1}{96}$ in. across, angular, white, acquiring a slight tint like that of the pileus in drying.—*B. & Br.*

Sect. 5. *Resupinatus*—Absolutely resupinate.

797. Polyporus contiguus. *Fr.* "Contiguous Polyporus."

Effused, firm, at first obscurely cinnamon, circumference villous or fibrous, then smooth, ferruginous; pores medium-sized, equal, obtuse, entire.—*Fr. Epicr. p.* 483. *P.cellaris, Ann. N.H. no.* 348. *Rostk. t.* 8. *Kl. exs. no.* 1007. *Desm. no.* 72.

On rotten wood and sticks. [United States.]

798. Polyporus ferruginosus. *Fr.* "Rusty Polyporus."

Effused, firm, brown, when old bright brown, ferruginous, circumference sterile; pores elongated, nearly round, medium-sized, cinnamon.—*Fr. Epicr. p.* 483. *Grev. t.* 155, *f.* 1. *Rostk. t.* 6. *Eng. Fl.* v. *p.* 146.

On gate posts, &c. Common. [United States.]

At first appearing under the form of a confervoid stratum, which gradually thickens and acquires pores in the centre; generally wholly resupinate, but occasionally slightly reflexed, in which case it is roughish and tomentose. Pores minute, roundish, unequal; specimens sometimes occur many inches in length, and in parts ½ in. thick, from several individuals having become confluent.—*M. J. B.*

799. Polyporus nitidus. *Fr.* "Yellow Polyporus."

Effused, thin, yellow, circumference of the interwoven mycelium paler; pores minute, nearly round, short, saffron-yellow. —*Fr. Epicr. p.* 483. *Pers. Obs.* ii. *t.* 4, *f.* 1. *Ann. N.H. no.* 349.

On dead wood. Rare. [Low. Carolina?]

Crust-like, adnate.

800. Polyporus Armeniacus. *Berk.* "Buff Fir Polyporus."

Suborbicular, confluent, extremely thin, circumference minutely downy; pores at first white, then deep buff.—*Berk. Outl. p.* 250. *Eng. Fl.* v. *p.* 147.

On the bark of firs. Appin.

Forming broadly effused patches, composed evidently of many confluent orbicular individuals, circumference minutely downy. Pores shallow, minute, nearly round, at first white, then bright buff, often confined to the centre, the marginal portion being of a byssoid structure under a lens.—*M. J. B.*

801. Polyporus bombycinus. *Fr.* "Silky Polyporus."

Effused, membranaceous, of a silky texture, dingy-yellowish, circumference byssoid, arachnoid, velvety below; pores large, angular.—*Fr. Epicr. p.* 482. *Sow. t.* 387, *f.* 5. *Ann. N.H. no.* 350.

On dead wood.

802. Polyporus incarnatus. *Fr.* "Flesh-coloured Polyporus."

Effused, coriaceous, firm, smooth, flesh-coloured, pores rather long, unequal.—*Fr. Epicr. p.* 484. *Pers. M.E. t.* 16, *f.* 4. *Eng. Fl.* v. *p.* 146.

On decaying trunks of firs. Rare. [United States.]

Effused, irregular, thin, coriaceous, marginate, or immarginate; margin white, cottony, rather thick, as if there was a tendency to become reflexed. Pores minute, very short, round, sub-equal, straight or oblique, or of a fine flesh colour, approaching in some cases to orange. Sometimes small cottony protuberances occur amongst the pores, which have the appearance of small pilei, with tubes underneath.—*Grev.*

803. Polyporus violaceus. *Fr.* "Violet Polyporus."

Effused, determinate, agglutinate, thin, dark blood-red or violet; pores very short, cellulose, nearly round, obtuse, quite entire.—*Fr. Epicr. p.* 484. *Sys. Myc.* i. *p.* 379. *B. & Br. Ann. N.H.* 1865, *no.* 1021. *Fl. exs. no.* 715, ii. 502.

On prostrate fir-poles. Scotland.

Allied to *Merulius*, for which a young specimen might easily be taken.

804. Polyporus purpureus. *Fr.* "Purple Polyporus."

Broadly and widely effused, mycelium mucedinous, flocculose, white, creeping on the surface of the wood; pores short, minute, unequal, obtuse, interruptedly scattered or conglomerate, purple lilac.—*Fr. Epicr. p.* 484. *Rostk. t.* 3.

On decayed willow. Rare. [Mid. Carolina.]

805. Polyporus cinctus. *Berk.* "Banded Polyporus."

White, turning pallid, forming little scattered patches, each surrounded by radiating strigose fibres; pores extremely minute, angular; dissepiments extremely thin, edge ragged.—*Mag. Zool. & Bot.* i. *t.* 2, *f.* 3. *Berk. Outl. p.* 250.

On old deal boards. Rare. King's Cliffe.

At first this curious species consists of small erect scattered tufts of radiating strigose fibres. Many of these remain barren. Under favourable circumstances a distinct hymenium, 1½ line think, with a free, even, abrupt, vertical circumference, is formed in the centre of each tuft. Numbers of these at length become confluent. Pores so minute as to be scarce visible to the naked eye. The colour of the whole is pale ochraceous, more or less tawny when dry.—*M. J. B.*

806. Polyporous medulla-panis. *Fr.* "Crumb of Bread Polyporus.

Effused, determinate, sub-undulate, firm, smooth, white, circumference naked, sub-marginate, wholly composed of middle-sized, rather long, entire pores.—*Fr. Epicr. p.* 485. *Sow. t.* 387, *f.* 7. *Jacq. Misc.* i. *t.* 11. *Fl. Dan. t.* 2028, *f.* 1. *Letell. t.* 690, *f.* 1. *Bolt. t.* 166, *f.* 2 ? *Eng. Fl.* v. *p.* 146. *Fckl. exs. no.* 1369.

On decaying wood. [United States.]

Effused, white, becoming yellowish in age, roundish, tolerably defined, dry, thickish, following in some degree the inequalities of the wood. Pores elongated, roundish, straight, or oblique, according to situation. Flesh almost none.—*Grev.*

807. Polyporus vitreus. *Fr.* "Glassy Polyporus."

Effused, sub-undulated, indeterminate, whitish, subhyaline, mycelium thin, separable, matted together; pores very small, round, long, obtuse, entire.—*Fr. Epicr. p.* 485. *Ann. N. H. no.* 351.

On decayed wood. Rare.

Distinguished by its distinct xylostromatoid sub-stratum, which separates easily from the matrix.—*B. & Br.*

808. Polyporus obducens. *Fr.* "Incrusting Polyporus."

Effused, incrusting, innate, firm, white, wholly composed of very small, crowded, equal pores, distinctly stratose, annual strata pallid tan colour.—*Fr. Epicr. p.* 485. *Ann. N. H. no.* 352. *Bisch. f.* 3294.

On rotten trunks. Bristol.

This species forms thick strata consisting of several layers, the growth of as many years.—*B. & Br.*

809. Polyporus vulgaris. *Fr.* "Common-effused Polyporus."

Broadly effused, thin, dry, closely adnate, even, white, circumference soon smooth, wholly composed of firm, crowded, small, round, nearly equal pores.—*Fr. Epicr. p.* 485. *Berk. Outl. t.* 16, *f.* 6. *Eng. Fl.* v. *p.* 146. *Fl. exs. no.* 619. *Fckl. exs. no.* 1366.

On dead wood and fallen branches. [United States.]

Effused, sometimes to the breadth of one foot, smooth, not a line thick, nor to be separated from the wood without destroying it; margin when young very slightly pubescent. Pores straight or oblique, roundish.—*M. J. B.*

810. Polyporus viridans. *Berk. & Br.* "Greenish Polyporus."

Resupinate, effused, at first white, when dry pallid green; border pulverulento-tomentose, very thin; pores minute, angular; dissepiments thin.—*Ann. N.H. no.* 347.

On very rotten wood. Sept.

This pretty species has the habit of *P. vulgaris.*

811. Polyporus sanguinolentus. *Fr.* "Bleeding Polyporus."

Nodulose, soon confluent, effused, soft, whitish, blood-stained when touched; circumference byssoid, evanescent; pores small, subrotund, unequal, at length torn.—*Fr. Epicr. p.* 486. *Seem. Journ. Bot.* vii. *p.* 61.

On rotten wood. [Low. Carolina.]

812. Polyporus molluscus. *Fr.* "Thin-pored Polyporus."

Effused, thin, soft, white; circumference byssoid, fibrilloso-radiate; pores in the centre, or here and there collected in patches, small, thin, round, unequal, and torn, growing pale. —*Fr. Epicr. p.* 486. *Fl. Dan. t.* 1299. *Sow. t.* 387. *f.* 9. *Eng. Fl.* v. *p.* 147.

On dead wood. Rare. [Low. Carolina.]

At first forming a mere fringed byssoid membrane, which gradually acquires moderate, rigid, subrotund, and angular pores, the partitions of which are so thin that they very generally become lacerated.—*M. J. B.*

813. Polyporus Gordoniensis. *B. & Br.* "Gordon's Fir Polyporus."

Effused, superficial, membranaceous, very thin, but separable, persistently white; margin shortly fimbriate; pores minute, unequal, angular; dissepiments very thin, fimbriato-dentate.—*Ann. N.H.* 1865, *no.* 1023.

On fir poles. Aboyne Castle.

An extremely delicate species, and not in the slightest degree innate. The margin remains snow-white, and the pores themselves change colour only very slightly in drying.—*M. J. B.*

814. Polyporus terrestris. *Fr.* "Ground Polyporus."

Effused, arachnoid, byssoid, delicate, fugaceous, white; pores central, very small, white, then rufescent.—*Fr. Epicr. p.* 486. *Pers. Ic. Pict. t.* 16. *f.* 1. *Ann. N.H. no.* 355.

On naked soil or rotten wood. Rare.

815. Polyporus vaporarius. *Fr.* "Creeping Polyporus."

Effused, innate ; mycelium creeping over the wood, floccose, white ; pores large, angular, white, growing pallid, crowded into a close, firm, persistent stratum.—*Fr.Epicr. p.* 487. *Ann. N.H. no.* 354. *Cooke exs. no.* 305.

On fallen branches. Common. [United States.]

var. β. Separable, white, honey colour when dry.—*Ann. Nat. Hist.* 1865. *no.* 1022*.

A remarkable variety occurred with *Hydnum niveum* at Ascot, creeping over fir leaves and heath twigs quite shaded from the light, and differing from the common form in being of a pure white when fresh, changing when dry to honey yellow. The subiculum is filmy and separable.—*M. J. B.*

816. Polyporus aneirinus. *Fr.* "Waxy Polyporus."

Effused, thin, sub-innate ; circumference byssoid, white ; pores large, cellular, waxy, angular, smooth, white, becoming tawny.—*Fr. Epicr. p.* 487. *Ann. N.H. no.* 353.

On fallen twigs. Rare. [Low. Carolina.]

Distinguished by its large pores, the hymenium of which has a peculiar, smooth, waxy aspect.—*B. & Br.*

817. Polyporus corticola. *Fr.* "Changeable Polyporus."

Much effused, thin, circumference byssoid, thin, whitish ; pores various, angular, shining, whitish, then brownish-yellow. —*Fr. Epicr. p.* 488. *P. subfuscus-flavidus, Rostk. Sturm. no.* 27, *t.* 11. *B. & Br. Ann. N.H.* 1865, *no.* 1022.

On oak planks in the roof of King's Cliffe Church.. [S. Carolina, U.S.]

The pores appear, when viewed one way, of a greyish-brown, and the other white. Fries (Mon. Hym.) quotes the figure of Rostkovius, to which Berk. & Br. referred their specimens, under *Polyporus corticola*, Fr.

818. Polyporus Stephensii. *B. & Br.* "Stephens' Polyporus."

Orbicular, white, at length confluent ; margin sometimes slightly reflexed, tomentose ; pores broad, nearly equal, angular, dissepiments rather thick, edge villous.—*Ann. N.H. no.* 356. *Rabh. F.E. no.* 117.

On twigs of privet. Oct. West of England. [Low. & Up. Carolina.]

Forming scattered orbicular white, or at length confluent resupinate patches about half an inch in diameter, which are sometimes slightly reflected with the free surface tomentose. Pores rather large, 1-20th in. broad, nearly equal, angular, sometimes sub-hexagonal; edge even, tomentose.—*B. & Br.* Spores very large, oval, white, ·00055 × ·00025 in.

819. Polyporus Vaillantii. *Fr.* "Vaillant's Polyporus."

White, thin, mycelium free, forming strings, or united in a membrane; pores here and there conglomerated, short, rather large, thin, unequal.—*Fr. Epicr. p.* 487. *Sow. t.* 326. *Eng. Fl.* v. *p.* 147. *Vaill. t.* 8, *f.* 1.

On dead wood. Rare. Glasgow. [Up Carolina.]

Forming a thin, white, or slightly rufescent, byssoid, broadly effused, close membrane, here and there traversed by rooting ribs.—*Fries.*

820. Polyporus hybridus. *B. & Br.* "Dry-rot Polyporus."

White, mycelium thick, forming a dense membrane or creeping branched strings, hymenium breaking up into areæ; pores long, slender, minute.—*Berk. Outl.* xvii. *Boletus hybridus, Sow. t.* 289, 387, *f.* 6.

On oak in ships, &c. The dry rot of our oak-built vessels.

Gen. 21. TRAMETES, Fr.

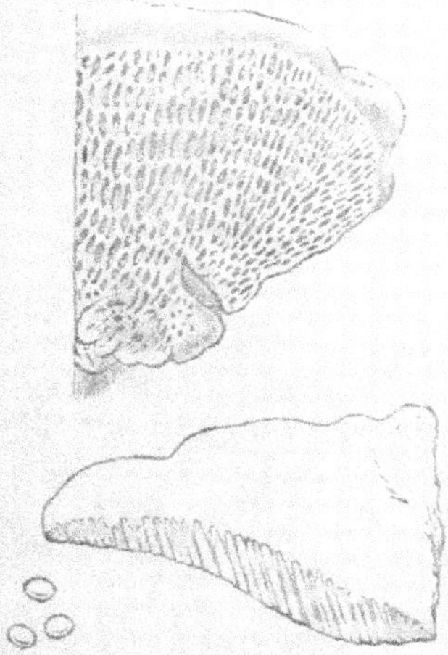

Fig. 66.

Hymenophore descending into the trama of the pores without any change, which are permanently concrete with the pileus. Pores entire. (*Fig.* 66.)

Hymenophore descending unchanged into the trama of the pores, which is permanently similar to the substance of the pileus. Pores concrete with the pileus, at first very small, then open, obtuse, entire, equal, round or linear, not labyrinthiform, or lacerated. Corky or woody fungi, arboreal, always dimidiate, at first generally fragrant, and never acid.

821. Trametes pini. *Fr.* "Fir-trunk Trametes."

Pileus corky or woody, pulvinate, concentrically sulcate, cracked and pitted, rough, ferruginous brown, then blackish, tawny ferruginous within ; pores large, nearly round or oblong, yellow or reddish brown.—*Fr. Epicr. p.* 489. *Fl. Boruss. t.* 380. *Corda. Anl. t. H. f.* 75, *no.* 36, 37. *Kl. exs.* ii. *no.* 118. *Bail. t.* 31.

On pine trunks. Rare. [Low. Carolina.]

Odour faint ; perennial.

822. Trametes suaveolens. *Fr.* "Sweet-scented Trametes."

Pileus corky, rather soft, pulvinate, villous, zoneless, white ; pores round, rather large, obtuse, brownish-white.—*Fr. Epicr. p.* 491. *Krombh. t.* 4, *f.* 25. *Fl. Dan. t.* 1849. *Tratt. Austr. f.* 4. *Fckl. exs. no.* 1365. *Bot. Zeit.* (1859), *t.* 11, *f.* 29. *Sow. t.* 228. *Sterb. t.* 27, *D. Dædalea suaveolens, Eng. Fl.* v. *p.* 133.

On willows, limes, &c.

Easily distinguished by its odour (when young), which resembles aniseed. White at first, then rufescent, zoned and scabrous, within dingy straw colour. —*Fries.* Spores white, oval, or pip-shaped, ·00035 × ·00018 in.

823. Trametes odora. *Fr.* "Small-pored Trametes."

Pileus corky, elastic, uneven, becoming smooth, zoneless, pallid ; pores minute, round, equal, whitish-ochre.—*Fr. Epicr. p.* 491. *Bolt. t.* 162.

On willows. Rare.

Very nearly related to *T. suaveolens.* It has the same smell. Spores white, oval, or pip-shaped, ·00012 × ·00022 in.

824. Trametes gibbosa. *Fr.* "Gibbous Trametes."

Dirty white. Pileus corky, villous, obsoletely zoned, expanded behind, gibbous ; pores linear, straight, equal.—*Fr. Epicr. p.* 492. *Bisch. f.* 3425. *Fckl. exs. no.* 1364. *Fl. Dan. t.* 1964. *Sow. t.* 194. *Huss.* ii. *t.* 4. *Dædalea gibbosa, Eng. Fl.* v. *p.* 133. *Strauss. Sturm. t.* 5.

On gate posts, &c. Sept. Rare.

Sessile, dimidiate, zoned, corky, hard, elastic, zones convex and tuberculated, dirty white, beautifully velvety, when old cinereous, and green from minute *Algæ*, the edge obtuse or subacute, often projecting at the base and very gibbous, but not invariably so, substance white, pores linear, mostly straight, except at the base, where they are roundish or irregular, very narrow, pale tan.—*M. J. B.*

(*Fig.* 66, *reduced, with section and spores.*)

Gen. 22. DÆDALEA, Fr. Epicr.

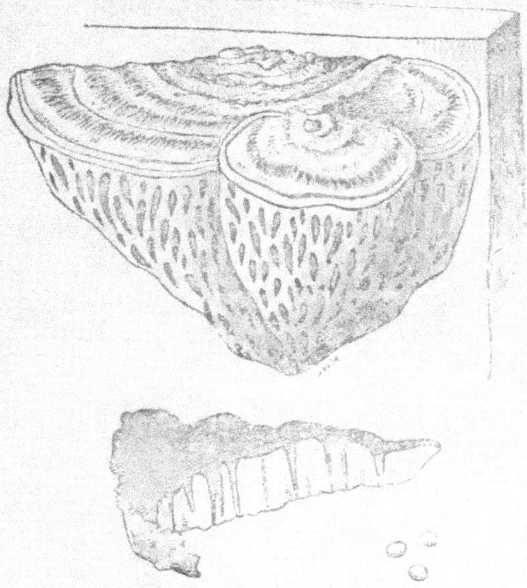

Fig. 67.

Hymenophore descending into the trama without any change; pores, when fully formed, torn, toothed, or labyrinthiform. (*Fig.* 67.)

Hymenophore descending unchanged into the trama, which is firmer than in *Trametes*. Pores, when fully formed, labyrinthiform, lacerated, and toothed. In habit the species resemble *Trametes*, but they are inodorous, and must not be confounded with the species of *Polyporus* that have elongated curved pores.—*W. G. S.*

825. Dædalea quercina. *P.* "Oak Dædalea."

Pallid wood colour. Pileus corky, rugulose, uneven, zoneless, becoming smooth, of the same colour within; hymenium first porous, then broken into contorted or gill-like labyrinthiform sinuses; edge obtuse.—*Fr. Epicr. p.* 492. *Lenz. f.* 28, 29. *Sow. t.* 181. *Bolt. t.* 73. *Bull. t.* 352. *Berk. Outl. t.* 19. *f.* 5. *Eng. Fl.* v. *p.* 131. *Bail. t.* 31. *Fckl. exs. no.* 1362. *Gard. Chron.* (1860) *p.* 576, *fig. Bisch. f.* 3329. *Kromb. t.* 5, *f.* 1, 2. *Price, f.* 20. *Vent. t.* 60. *f.* 1, 2. *Grev. t.* 238.

On oak stumps, &c. Common.

Perennial. Pileus 5-6 in. broad, sessile, dimidiate, of a pale, woody appearance, smooth, marked with concentric, raised, or depressed zones and little, radiating wrinkles, the margin in well-grown specimens thin, but in ill-developed individuals swollen and blunt; gills of the same colour as the pileus, with sometimes a slight shade of pink, woody, thick, sinuous, branched, and anastomosing, so as to form long, wavy pores, a line or more broad. Sometimes the whole plant is resupinate or decurrent, and the partitions elongated into tooth-like processes.—*M. J. B.*

(*Fig.* 67, *reduced, with section and spores.*)

826. Dædalea confragosa. *P.* "Willow Dædalea."

Pileus corky, coriaceous, rather convex, rough, subzonate, self-coloured, reddish-brown, somewhat ferruginous within; hymenium porous, then narrowly labyrinthiform and torn, pruinose, cinereous, then reddish brown.—*Fr. Epicr. p.* 493. *Bolt. t.* 160. *Bull. t.* 491. *Sow. t.* 193. *Eng. Fl.* v. *p.* 132. *Ann. N.H. no.* 279. 711*.

On willows, service, &c. Rare.

827. Dædalea unicolor. *Fr.* "One-coloured Dædalea."

Pileus corky, coriaceous, villoso-strigose, cinereous, with zones of the same colour; sinuses labyrinthiform, flexuose, intricate, acute, at length torn and toothed.—*Fr. Epicr. p.* 494. *Sow. t.* 325. *Eng. Fl.* v. *p.* 133. *Fckl. exs. no.* 1363. *Kl. exs. no.* 28. ii. *no.* 614. *Fl. Dan. t.* 2271. *f.* 1.

On stumps, &c. Common. [United States.?]

Imbricated. Pileus 2-4 in. broad, coriaceous, zoned, densely villous, often green from minute *Algæ;* pores narrow, small, irregular, unequal, subflexuous.—*M. J. B.*

828. Dædalea latissima. *Fr.* "Effused Dædalea."

Effused, between corky and woody, thick, undulated, rufescent or pallid wood colour; pores thin, distant, very obtuse, somewhat rounded and elongated, flexuose.—*Fr. Epicr. p.* 495. *Sow. t.* 424. *Eng. Fl.* v. *p.* 133.

On dead branches on the ground. Rare.

Gen. 22. MERULIUS. Fr. Syst. Myc.

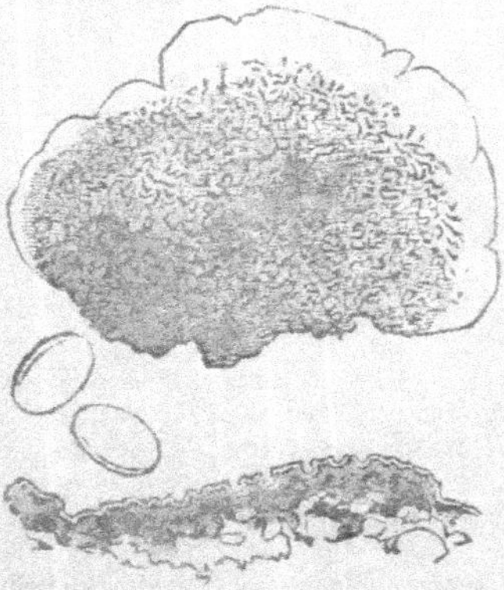

Fig. 68.

Hymenium soft, waxy, forming porous, reticulate, or sinuous, toothed folds. (*Fig.* 68.)

Hymenophore covered with the soft, waxy hymenium, which is incompletely porous, or arranged in reticulate, sinuous, dentate folds. Epixylous fungi, at first resupinate, expanded; the hymenophore springing from a mucous mycelium.

A. *Leptospori*—spores white.

829. **Merulius tremellosus.** *Schrad.* "Tremellose Merulius."

Resupinate, then free or reflexed, fleshy, tremelloid, tomentose, white; margin dentato-radiate; folds porous, variable pinkish.—*Fr. Epicr. p.* 500. *Fl. Dan. t.* 1553, 776. *f.* 1. *Ann. N.H. no.* 77. *Huss.* i. *t.* 10. *Fckl. exs. no.* 1358. *Ann. Sc. Nat.* 1837. viii. *t.* 10. *f.* 22. *Bail. t.* 30. *Kl. exs.* ii. *no.* 7. *Boletus arboreus, Sow. t.* 346. *Bisch. f.* 3447.

At the base of decayed trees. Rare. Oct. [United States.]

"Sometimes the edge is beautifully tinged with pink."

830. **Merulius corium.** *Fr.* "Leathery Merulius."

Resupinate, effused, soft, somewhat papyraceous, circumference at length free, reflexed, white, and villous below; hymenium reticulato-porose, flesh-coloured, or pallid tan-colour.—*Fr. Epicr. p.* 500. *Grev. t.* 147. *Bull. t.* 402. *Sow. t.* 349. *Eng. Fl.* v. *p.* 128. *Fckl. exs. no.* 1359. *Berk. exs. no.* 19. *Kl. exs. no.* 1916.

On dead trunks. Common. [United States.]

Plant 2-3 in. broad, sometimes completely effused with a white byssoid margin, but not unfrequently the margin, or even the whole pileus, is regularly reflexed, often imbricated, white, pubescent, and zoned above, below pale buff or lilac, variously sinuato-rugose or reticulato-porous, very various in thickness, being sometimes a mere pellicle, while on the contrary individuals occur as thick as *Stereum hirsutum.*—*M. J.B.* Spores oval, vivid orange, ·00018×·00023 in.

831. **Merulius himantoides.** *Fr.* "Fibrous Merulius."

Effused, silky, very soft, fibrous, silky beneath, lilac; circumference byssoid; folds porous, then gyrose, dirty yellow, at length inclining to olive.—*Fr. Epicr. p.* 501. *Pers. M.E. t.* 13. *f.* 3, 4. *Sow. t.* 346. *Br. Bath. Trans.* 1870. *p.* 84.

On fir wood, and on club mosses in a conservatory.

Similar to *M. lacrymans*, but thinner.

832. **Merulius aurantiacus.** *Klotsch.* "Orange Merulius."

Pileus tough, carnoso-coriaceous, effuso-reflexed, zoned, tomentose, between yellow and dirty white, here and there cinereous; folds minute, subporiform, dull orange.—*Berk. Outl. p.* 256. *Eng. Fl.* v. *p.* 128.

On dead beech. May. Rare. Scotland.

Pileus 1 in. broad; zones obsolete, hirsuto-tomentose. Nearly allied to *M. corium.*—*M. J.B.*

833. **Merulius molluscus.** *Fr.* "Thin Merulius."

Effused, thin, soft, membranaceous; margin byssoid, white; folds poroso-gyrose, flesh-coloured.—*Fr. Epicr. p.* 501. *Pers. M.E. t.* 14. *f.* 1, 2. *Ann. N.H. no.* 712.

On dead wood. Rare. Penzance. [Mid. Carolina.]

Hymenium dark brown when old; sometimes shortly reflexed, and then the hymenium not reticulated, but from the first gyrose and toothed.

834. **Merulius porinoides.** *Fr.* "Porose Merulius."

Crustaceous, adnate, thin, circumference byssoid, white, folds poriform, distant, dirty yellow.—*Fr. Epicr. p.* 501. *Pers. M.E. t.* 14, *f.* 7. *Ann. N.H. no.* 358.

On dead wood, chips, &c. Rare. [United States.]

835. **Merulius rufus.** *P.* "Rufous Merulius."

Crustaceous, adnate, smooth, flesh-red, circumference almost naked, hymenium equally porous, of the same colour.—*Fr. Epicr. p.* 502. *Pers. M.E. t.* 16, *f.* 1, 2. *Ann. N.H. no.* 357.

On fallen oak boughs. [Mid. Carolina.]

"This has a very Polyporus-like appearance, and I am not certain that it is anything more than a state of *Dædalea confragosa*, of which I believe *Trametes rubescens* is a synonym."—*M. J. B.*

836. **Merulius serpens.** *Fr.* "Creeping Merulius."

Crustaceous, adnate, thin, becoming smooth, pallid, then reddish, circumference byssoid, white, folds at first wrinkled, then porous, angular, entire.—*Fr. Epicr. p.* 502. *Fckl. exs. no.* 2096. *Kl. exs. no.* 1006, ii. *no.* 6.

On dead wood. Rare. Twycross. [Low. & Mid. Carolina.]

Not separable like *M. corium.*

837. **Merulius pallens.** *Berk.* "Pallid Merulius."

Adnate, thin, inseparable, pale-reddish, fleshy, subgelatinous, folds poriform, minute; margin indeterminate.—*Ann. N. Hist. ser.* i. *vol.* vi. *p.* 358, *no.* 151. *Berk. Outl. p.* 256.

On fir wood. Rare.

838. **Merulius Carmichaelianus.** *Berk.* "Carmichael's Merulius."

White, extremely thin, forming effused, entirely resupinate, irregular, interrupted, confluent patches; folds forming regular angular reticulations, dull brown when dry.—*Berk. Outl. p.* 256. *Grev. t.* 224. *Eng. Fl.* v. *p.* 130.

On bark. Rare. Appin.

This minute species forms a mere pellicle, in its dry state of a uniform dull brown, scarcely distinguishable from the bark on which it grows, but when examined with a moderate magnifying power the regular, often hexagonal reticulations, exhibit a very elegant appearance, like the cells of a honey-comb, but quite superficial.—*M. J. B.*

B. *Coniophori*—spores ferruginous.

839. Merulius lacrymans. *Fr.* "Dry-rot Merulius."

Large, fleshy, spongy, moist, ferruginous yellow, arachnoid and velvety beneath; margin tumid, tomentose, white; folds broad, porous, and gyroso-dentate.—*Fr. Epicr. p.* 502. *Fl. Dan. t.* 2026. *Krombh. t.* 46, *f.* 1-2. *Sow. t.* 113. *Jacq. Misc. t.* 8. *f.* 2. *Berk. Outl. t.* 2, *f.* 1. *Huss.* i. *t.* 3. *Eng. Fl.* v. *p.* 129. *Strauss. Sturm. t.* 4. *Price, f.* 30. *Fckl. exs. no.* 1361. *Payen. f.* 484. *Kl. exs. no.* 228.

In cellars, hollow trees, &c. Common. [Mid. Carolina.]

Whole plant generally resupinate, soft, tender, at first very light, cottony and white; when the veins appear they are of a fine yellow-orange, or reddish-brown, forming irregular folds, most frequently so arranged as to have the appearance of pores, but never anything like tubes, distilling, when perfect, drops of water. Sometimes the pileus, or substance of the plant, from its situation, produces pendant processes like inverted cones.—*Grev.* Spores ferruginous. Spores oval, rich, orange-brown, ·00035 × ·00023 in. (*Fig.* 68.)

Gen. **26. POROTHELIUM**, Fr. Obs.

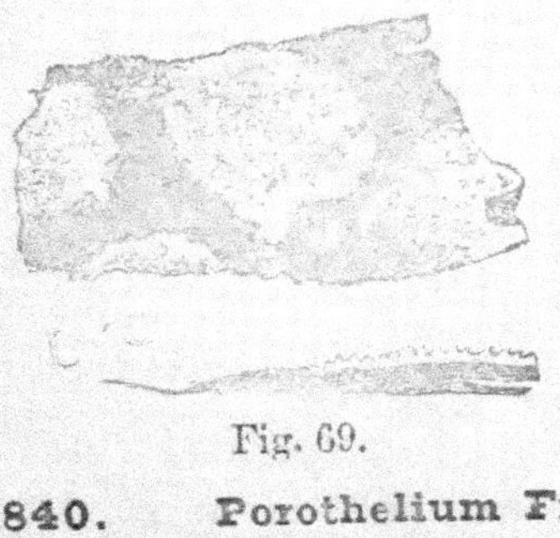

Fig. 69.

Hymenophore arachnoid, covered with distinct papillæ, at first closed, then open like pores. (*Fig.* 69.)

Hymenophore mycelioid, covered with papillæ, which are at first distinct and closed, soon opening into pores, which become elongated and tubular. Submembranaceous, resupinate fungi.

840. Porothelium Friesii. *Mont.* "Fries' Porothelium."

Effused, confluent, flocculoso-membranaceous, white, inclined to tan colour, circumference simple, papillæ immersed, yellowish, at length open and urceolate.—*Fr. Epicr. p.* 504. *Ann. des. Sc. Nat.* (1836), *vol.* v. *p.* 339. *Ann. N.H. no.* 359.

On pine wood. Rare.

Pores often crowned with a pellucid drop. (*Fig.* 69.)

Gen. 27. FISTULINA, Bull. Champ.

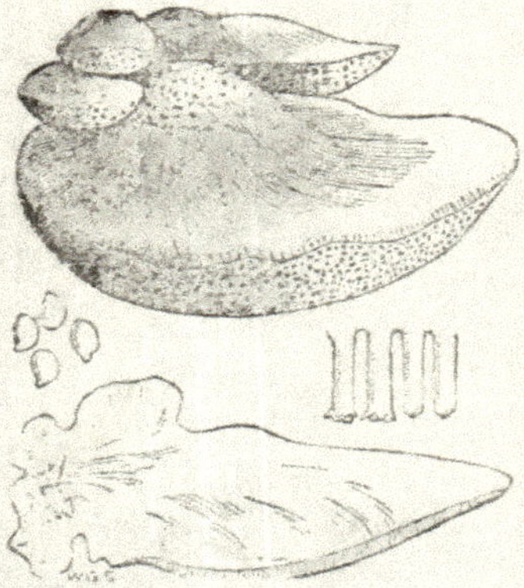

Fig. 70.

Hymenophore fleshy. Hymenium inferior, at first papillose; the papillæ at length elongated, and forming distinct tubes. (*Fig.* 70.)

Epixylous fungi, intermediate between *Polyporei* and *Hydnei*.

841. Fistulina hepatica. " Liver Fistulina."

Fleshy, juicy, rootless; pileus undivided, blood-red; tubes yellowish.—*Fr. Epicr. p.* 504. *Schaff. t.* 116-120. *Sow. t.* 58. *Roq. t.* 2. *f.* 4. *Bail. t.* 29. *Kl. exs. no.* 1404. *Fl. Dan. t.* 1039. *Grev. t.* 270. *Lenz. f.* 40. *Krombh. t.* 5. *f.* 9, 10. *t.* 47. *f.* 1-12. *Vitt. t.* 36. *Paul. t.* 12. *Cooke B.F. t.* 18. *Badh.* i. *t.* 12. *f.* 4. ii. *t.* 12. *f.* 2. *Berk. Outl. t.* 17. *f.* 1. *Huss.* i. *t.* 65. *Smith E.M. f.* 21. *Price, f.* 22. *Eng. Fl.* v. *p.* 154. *Gard. Chron.* (1861) *p.* 121. *Trans. Woolh. Cl.* 1869. *Hogg. & Johnst. t.* 7. *Barla. t.* 30. *f.* 4-7. *Vent. t.* 36. *f.* 1, 2. *Fckl. exs. no.* 1357.

On trunks of old oaks. Common. Esculent. [Up. Carolina.]

Pileus roundish, dimidiate, or subspathulate, in general more or less concave, studded with minute, stellate, furfuraceous tufts, the rudiments of tubes, rich red-brown, tinged with vermilion, sometimes substipitate; margin obtuse, substance thick and juicy, marbled like beet-root, distilling a red pellucid juice from different parts of the plant; hymenium convex, elegantly tinted with shades of red or vermilion, dotted with rose-like somewhat remote, radiated warts, which form a veil to the young tubes; as the pileus expands the tubes elongate and become approximate, and are jagged at their orifices. Taste rather acid. It attains sometimes an enormous size, even nearly 30 pounds in weight.—*Eng. Fl.* Spores salmon colour, nearly round, with an oblique apiculus, diameter ·00013 in. (*Fig.* 70, *reduced.*)

Order III. HYDNEI.

Hymenium inferior, or amphigenous, at first definitely protuberant, spread over persistent spines, bristles, teeth, tubercles, or papillæ.—*Fr. Epicr. p.* 504.

Hymenium of awl-shaped spines, distinct at the base . . *Hydnum.*
Hymenium of gill-like teeth –
Irregularly distributed, distinct from pileus . *Sistotrema.*
Disposed in rows, concrete with pileus . . . *Irpex.*
Hymenium waxy—
Of irregular tubercles . . . . *Radulum.*
Of crest-like wrinkles or veins . . . . . . *Phlebia.*
Of obtuse equal granules . . . . *Grandinia.*
Subiculum fibrous, with crested, papillose, or spiny warts . . . . *Odontia.*

Gen. 28. **HYDNUM,** Linn.

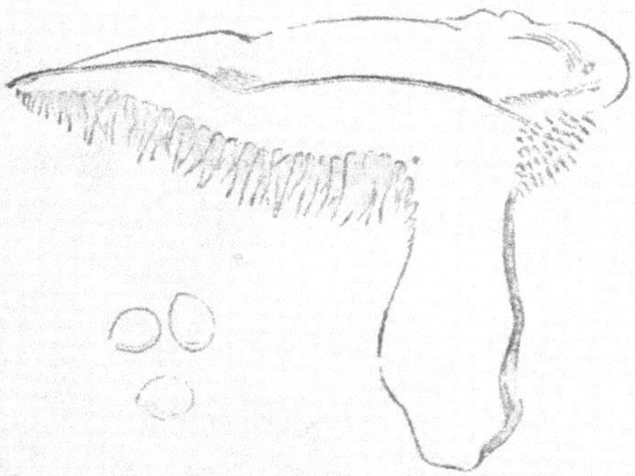

Fig. 71.

Hymenium inferior, aculeate; spines at first papillæform, awl-shaped, or compressed, distinct at the base.—*Fr. Epicr. p.* 505. (*Fig.* 71.)

Sect. 1. *Mesopus*—entire, simple; stem central. Terrestrial.

A. *Carnosa*—pileus fleshy, subfragile. Edible.

* Spines coloured.

842. Hydnum imbricatum. *L.* "Imbricated Hydnum."

Pileus fleshy, nearly plane, sub-umbilicate, tessulato-squamose, floccose, not zoned, umber; stem short, even; spines decurrent, whitish cinereous.—*Fr. Epicr. p.* 505. *Schæff. t.* 140. *Fl. Dan. t.* 176, 1500. *Krombh. t.* 49. *f.* 1-6. *Lenz. f.* 50. *Grev. t.* 71. *Cooke B. F. t.* 16, *f.* 1. *Kl. exs. no.* 127. *Eng. Fl.* v. *p.* 155. *Nees, f.* 240. *Barla. t.* 38. *f.* 1-4. *Harz. t.* 3. *b. Bisch. f.* 3244. *Bail. t.* 29.

On the ground, in pine woods. Esculent.
[Mid. & Up. Carolina.]

Pileus 2-5 in. broad, thick and fleshy, plane, or slightly convex, and rounded at the margin, at length somewhat hollowed in the centre, varying from reddish to mouse-brown, scaly; scales imbricated, numerous, the central ones being often mere cracked portions of the pileus, which render that part tesselated; flesh pale-buffish or reddish; spines entire, numerous, very short, of nearly equal length, greyish-white; stem 1-2 in. thick, firm, irregular, whitish.—*Grev.* Spores round, tuberculated, pale yellowish, brown, ·00025×·0002 in.

843. Hydnum fragile. *Fr.* "Fragile Hydnum."

Pileus fleshy, fragile, sub-repand, undulate and lobed, at first pubescent, then nearly smooth, commonly even, but sometimes minutely squamulose, at first pallid, then cinereous or brick-red; margin and flesh grey, somewhat zoned; stem unequal, short and thick, or elongated: spines scarcely decurrent, much elongated, slender, very fragile, whitish, then grey.—*Fr. Mon. H.S.* ii. *p.* 275. *Bergeret.* i. *t.* 13. *B. & Br. Ann. N.H.* 1865, *no.* 1024.

Amongst heath. Ascot.

This fine species, which attains a diameter of several inches, was included in Fr. Sys. Myc. under *H. lævigatum*, from which it is now very properly separated.—*M. J. B.*

** Spines immutable, whitish.

844. Hydnum repandum. *L.* "Spreading Hydnum."

Pileus fleshy, compact, subrepand, nearly smooth, pallid; stem deformed, pallid; spines unequal, of the same colour.—*Fr. Epicr. p.* 506. *Fl. Dan. t.* 310. *Roq. t.* 2, *f.* 2. *Harz. t.* 23. *Bisch. f.* 3430. *Sow. t.* 176. *Schæff. t.* 318. *Krombh. t.* 50, *f.* 1-9. *Vitt. Mang. t.* 25, *f.* 2. *Paul. t.* 35. *Cooke, B.F.* t. 16, *f.* 2. *Berk. Outl. t.* 17, *f.* 2. *Badh.* i. *t.* 12, *f.* 3, ii. *t.* 8, *f.* 3, 4. *Vent. t.* 27, *f.* 4-6, *t.* 28, *f.* 1, 2. *Smith, E.M. f.* 22. *Huss.* i. *t.* 16. *Eng. Fl.* v. *p.* 155. *Grev. t.* 44. *Bull. t.* 172. *Berk. exs. no.* 141. *Gard. Chron.* (1860), *p.* 121, *fig. Trans. Woolh. Cl.* 1869. *Barla. t.* 32, *f.* 1-9.

var. **rufescens.** Fr. Entire plant reddish.—*Fr. Epicr. p.* 506. *Bolt. t.* 89. *Schæff. t.* 141.

On the ground, in woods. Common. [United States.]

Subgregarious; pileus 2-4 in. broad, the margin more or less arched, very irregular in form, often excentric, or even laterally stipitate, more or less lobed or undulated, buffish or subrufescent, smooth, or frequently decidedly tomentose; spines unequal, conical, entire, or sometimes bifid or laciniated, and even compresed and lamellated, sometimes forming spurious pores.

Stem 1½-3 in. high, 1 in. thick, solid, paler than the pileus, sometimes clothed with white down, and at the apex with abortive spines.—*M. J. B.* Spores white, or with a suggestion of yellow, round, with an obtuse apiculus at one end. Diameter ·00022 in. (*Fig.* 71, *reduced.*)

B. *Lignosa*—pileus corky or coriaceous.

* Spines discoloured; spores brownish.

845. Hydnum compactum. *Fr.* "Compact Hydnum."

Pileus corky, compact, undulato-tuberculose, without zones, olivaceo-cinereous or brownish, commonly involved in whitish down, internally variegated with blue; stem very short, deformed, tawny-brown; spines brownish, pallid at the tips.—*Fr. Epicr. p.* 507. *Krombh. t.* 50, *f.* 12. *Str. Sturm. t.* 7. *Batsch. f.* 221. *Eng. Fl.* v. *p.* 156. *Rabh. F.E. no.* 803. *Vent. t.* 28, *f.* 3, 4.

On the ground, on heaths, and fir woods. Rare.
[Low. & Mid. Carolina.]

Irregular, confluent inodorous, resembling a thick, shapeless crust. Pileus 1-6 in. broad, thick. readily imbibing moisture, clotted with down of the same colour, or dirty white. Spines equal, chestnut; stem corky, obsolete or very thick.—*Fries.*

** Spines discoloured; spores ferruginous.

846. Hydnum zonatum. *Batsch.* "Zoned Hydnum."

Ferruginous; pileus equally coriaceous, thin, expanded, subinfundibuliform, zoned, becoming smooth, radiato-rugose; margin paler, sterile; stem slender, nearly equal, floccose, tuberous at the base; spines slender, pallid, then of the same colour as the pileus.—*Fr. Epicr. p.* 509. *Kl. exs. no.* 1715. *Batsch. f.* 224. *Nees. f.* 242. *Ann. N.H. no.* 360.

In woods. Rare. [United States.]

A small variety has been found at Ascot, remarkable for an appearance in the spines like that of shot silk. Spores ferruginous.—*B. & Br. Ann. N.H.* 1865, *no.* 1025.

*** Spines immutable; spores whitish.

847. Hydnum nigrum. *Fr.* "Black Hydnum."

Pileus corky, rigid, tomentose, zoneless, blue-black, within and the stout stem black; margin and spines white.—*Fr. Epicr. p.* 509. *Mich. t.* 72, *f.* 5. *Batsch. f.* 223. *Seem. Jour.* 1868, *p.* 334. *Fr. Icones. t.* 5. *Br. Bath. Trans.* 1870, *p.* 86.

In pine woods, &c. Street, Somerset.

Inodorous, woody. Pileus unequal, flattened or depressed, with a whitish margin. Spines slender, equal, becoming cinereous. Very distinct, and easily recognised by its black, zoneless flesh. Spores white, round, papillose, diameter ·00017 in. In my specimens of this species the pileus is distinctly zoned, as it is in Fries' own figure in his recently published Icones.—*W. G. S.*

848. Hydnum graveolens. *Del.* "Strong-scented Hydnum."

Pileus coriaceous, thin, soft, not zoned, rugose, dark-brown, brown within; margin becoming whitish; stem slender; spines short, grey.—*Fr. Epicr. p.* 509. *Ann. N.H. no.* 280. *Rabh. F.E. no.* 1004. *Fr. Icon. t.* 6, *f.* 1.

In woods. Rare. [United States.]

When fresh it is extremely beautiful, being dark in the centre with a white border. The spines are pale, and the spores evidently white. The whole plant smells extremely strong of melilot, and after it has been dried three or four years the scent is as strong as ever.—*B. & Br.*

849. Hydnum tomentosum. *L.* "Tomentose Hydnum."

Pileus coriaceous, thin, plano-infundibuliform, zoned, pale cinereous; stem slender, of the same colour; disc tomentose; margin and spines white.—*Fr. Epicr. p.* 510. *Schæff. t.* 139. *Kl. exs. no.* 123. *Fl. Dan. t.* 1020, *f.* 2. *B. & Br. Ann. N.H.* 1865, *no.* 1025. *Seem. Jour.* 1868, *t.* 76. *Harz. t.* 3. *a.*

In fir woods. Ascot. [Mid. Carolina.]

They have a strong smell of melilot, but differ from *H. graveolens* in the strongly zoned pileus, more coriaceous substance, and in the white (not grey) spines. The spores are thrown down in abundance on any subjacent objects. Spores white, globular, rough, or papillated, diameter ·00013 in.

Sect. 2. *Pleuropus*—sub-dimidiate; stem lateral.

850. Hydnum auriscalpium. *L.* "Fir-cone Hydnum."

Pileus dimidiate, coriaceous, reniform, hairy, bright brown, inclining to black: stem slender, rooting, hairy, of the same colour; spines tough, bright brown.—*Fr. Epicr. p.* 511. *Schæff. t.* 143. *Fl. Dan. t.* 1020, *f.* 1. *Grev. t.* 196. *Krombh. t.* 50, *f.* 15-17. *Eng. Fl.* v. *p.* 156. *Bull. t.* 481, *f.* 3. *Sow. t.* 267. *Cooke exs. no.* 306. *Bisch. f.* 3284. *Schnzl. t.* 16, *f.* 33-35. *Kl. exs. no.* 126.

On fir cones. Common.

Pileus ½-1 in. broad, subrotund, thin, coriaceous, often somewhat lobed, the margin of the lobes entire, more or less zoned, tomentose, purplish, or reddish-brown, sometimes pale; spines subcinereous, or a dilute shade of the pileus, the tips often darker, but not always so, more or less hoary from the spores. Stem buried to some depth amongst fir-leaves, 2-3 in. high, often confluent, slender, dark brown tomentose, attached by a shaggy or spongy base.—*M. J. B.*

Sect. 3. *Merisma*—much branched or tuberculiform, immarginate.

* Much branched or palmate.

851. Hydnum coralloides. *Scop.* "Coral-like Hydnum."

Very much branched, white, at length yellowish, broken up into intricate attenuated branches; spines unilateral, subulate, entire. —*Fr. Epicr. p.* 511. *Schæff. t.* 142. *Sow. t.* 252. *Lenz. f.* 53. *Krombh. t.* 51, *f.* 4-7. *Eng. Fl. v. p.* 157. *Bull. t.* 390. *Bisch. f.* 3393. *Kl. exs. no.* 125.

On decayed fir, beech, ash, &c. Rare. Esculent. [United States.]

Young plant, according to Persoon, resembling a cauliflower; when old it forms tufts, a foot or more in length, with flexuous, angular branches, beset with incurved ramuli bearing spines on the under side.

** Tuberculiform, immarginate.

852. Hydnum erinaceus. *Bull.* "Hedgehog Hydnum."

Fleshy, tough, elastic, pendulous, tuberculose, immarginate, white, then yellowish, torn into fibrils above; spines very long, straight, equal, pendulous.—*Fr. Epicr. p.* 512. *Bull. t.* 34. *Vitt. t.* 26. *Krombh. t.* 51, *f.* 1-3. *Eng. Fl. v. p.* 157. *Tratt. Essb. t.* Y.

On trunks of oak, beech, &c. Rare. [United States.]

Pileus a span or more broad, the base projecting, soft, torn into subfasciculate fibrillæ (abortive spines); margin obtuse, gradually giving out true spines, often imbricated with smaller pilei; spines 1½-2½ in. long, pendulous, thick set, very regular, soft, equally attenuated, connected two or three together at their bases, fastigiate; substance thick, tough, fleshy, very soft, elastic, white, not changing colour.—*Fries.* Spores white, plain, ·00019 × ·00023 in.

853. Hydnum caput-medusæ. *Bull.* "Medusa-head Hydnum."

Fleshy, tuberculiform, substipitate, white, then cinereous; upper spines distorted, lower spines fertile, long, straight.—*Fr. Epicr. p.* 512. *Bull. t.* 412.

On trunks of trees. Rare. Esculent. [United States.]

Large and fleshy, at first snowy-white, then dingy-cinereous; stem dilated into the pileus; all the spines at first straight, slender, long, the upper ones at length bent and contorted.

Sect. 4. *Apus*—pileus marginate, dimidiate, sessile, commonly effuso-reflexed. On trunks.

* Pileus gelatinous.

854. Hydnum gelatinosum. *Scop.* "Gelatinous Hydnum."

Pileus gelatinous, tremulous, dimidiate, substipitate, papillate, glaucous, turning brown; spines soft, pyramidal, glaucous.—*Fr. Epicr. p.* 512. *Schæff. t.* 144. *Jacq. Austr. t.* 239. *Fl. Dan. t.* 717. *Krombh. t.* 50, *f.* 18-22. *Jacq. Misc.* i. *t.* 9. *Gard. Chron.* (1860), *p.* 1080, *fig. Ann. N.H. no.* 808. *Curr. Linn. Journ.* v. *p.* 181.

On trunks of firs. Rare. [United States.]

Of a soft gelatinous consistence approaching that of a *Tremella.* Pileus fan-shaped, or rounded in front, attenuated behind so as to make a short spurious stem. In an early stage it is decurrent at the point of attachment. The surface is of a bistre brown, uneven with frequent depressions, and rough at first with little points, but at length nearly smooth. The hymenium is either pure white or shaded with a delicate blue tint, the spines straight, of moderate length, and very delicate. The plant shrinks much in drying.—*M. J. B.* Translucent like opal, gelatinous, soft, flaccid; spines white; pileus frosted with shining particles; taste pleasant. Spores round, somewhat irregular, white, diameter ·00027 in.—*W. G. S.*

** Pileus corky or coriaceous.

855. Hydnum ochraceum. *P.* "Ochrey Hydnum."

Pileus effuso-reflexed, coriaceous, thin, zonate, ochraceous; spines minute, pinkish-ochre.—*Fr. Epicr. p.* 514. *Sow. t.* 15. *Eng. Fl.* v. *p.* 158.

On fallen sticks, &c. Common. [United States.]

Small, at first entirely resupinate, gradually reflexed, and somewhat repand, at first sparingly clothed with dirty-white down, at length rugose, 1-3 in. broad. Spines short, acute, entire, becoming pale.—*Fries.*

Sect. 5. *Resupinatus*—pileus resupinate.

* Spines brown or ferruginous.

856. Hydnum squalinum. *Fr.* "Coarse Hydnum."

Subiculum, coriaceous, firm, adnate, wood-coloured; spines crowded, long, stout, compressed, entire, at length brownish.—*Fr. Epicr. p.* 515. *Ray. Syn. t.* i. *f.* 5. *Bolt. t.* 74.

On trunks of trees, especially beech.

Admitted on the authority of the figures of Ray and Bolton.

857. Hydnum membranaceum. *Bull.* "Membranaceous Hydnum."

Subiculum, effuse, waxy-membranaceous, agglutinate, smooth, tawny-ferruginous; spines subulate, crowded, equal, acute, of the same colour.—*Fr. Epicr. p.* 515. *Bull. t.* 481. *f.* 1. *Sow. t.* 327. *Eng. Fl.* v. *p.* 158. *Berk. exs. no.* 142. *Corda. Anl. t.* G., *f.* 74, *no.* 10, 11.

On fallen sticks. [United States.]

The spines are often collected in little fascicles, pallid when young, at length brownish.

858. Hydnum Weinmanni. *Fr.* "Weinmann's Hydnum."

Subiculum, effused, waxy, membranaceous, agglutinate, smooth, greyish, fawn-coloured; spines minute, acute, rather distant, equal.—*Fr. Epicr. p.* 516. *Pers. M.E. t.* 22, *f.* 2. *Ann. N.H. no.* 713.

On fallen branches. Bristol.

According to Fries this species occurs chiefly on poplar branches, and when dry acquires a cinereous tinge.

859. Hydnum fuscum. *P.* "Brown Hydnum."

Effused, rufous-brown; circumference paler, coarsely byssoid; spines long, quite entire, close, very acute, shining as if varnished.—*Pers. M.E.* ii. *t.* 17, *f.* 3. *Eng. Fl.* v. *p.* 158.

On dead wood. Rare.

In its dry state it is rather thicker than other effused species, and is remarkable for the long, dark, rufous-brown spines, which shine as if varnished.—*M. J. B.*

860. Hydnum ferruginosum. *Fr.* "Rusty Hydnum."

Subiculum effused, tomentose, tawny-ferruginous; spines crowded, conico-subulate, acute, of the same colour.—*Fr. Epicr. p.* 516. *Schrad. Spic. t.* 4. *f.* 2. *Nees. f.* 248. *Eng. Fl.* v. *p.* 158. *Purt. t.* 15.

On decaying wood. [United States.]

The whole plant consists of densely woven down, forming an effused, indeterminate mass, the hymenium composed of erect or oblique spines, which are villous and frequently abortive, so as easily to be taken for some species of the order *Hyphomycetes.* The colour varies from ferruginous to brownish. —*M. J. B.*

861. Hydnum variecolor. *P.* "Varicoloured Hydnum."

Subiculum effuse, adnate, furfuraceo-crustaceous, white; spines crowded, conical, short, unequal, minute, brownish.—*Fr. Epicr. p.* 516.

On dead stumps. Rare.

Somewhat similar to *Hyd. farinaceum*. The spines are usually adpressed.

** Spines yellowish or greenish.

862. Hydnum alutaceum. *Fr.* "Tan-coloured Hydnum."

Subiculum longitudinally effuse, crustaceous, adnate, smooth, pallid ochraceous, circumference naked; spines minute, crowded, equal, acute.—*Fr. Epicr. p.* 516. *Ann. N.H. no.* 714.

On dead wood. Rare. [Mid. Carolina.]

It has the colour and appearance, at first, of *Grandinia granulosa*, from which, however, it is quite distinct.

863. Hydnum spathulatum. *Fr.* "Spoon-shaped Hydnum."

Subiculum effused, membranaceous, seceding, whitish or yellowish, circumference fimbriate; spines spathulate, oblique, orange.—*Fr. Epicr. p.* 517. *Ann. N.H. no.* 281.

On decaying wood. Rare. [Mid. Carolina, U.S.]

The whole plant separates easily from the wood, and the teeth are broad and spathulate, by which characters it is readily distinguished.—*B. & Br.*

*** Spines flesh-coloured, lilac, or rufescent.

864. Hydnum udum. *Fr.* "Moist Hydnum."

Subiculum effused, thin, subgelatinous, agglutinate, smooth, flesh-coloured, then watery yellow; spines crowded, unequal, forked and fimbriate, of the same colour.—*Fr. Epicr. p.* 517. *Berk. Outl. t.* 17. *f.* 3. *Eng. Fl.* v. *p.* 160.

On fallen branches. [Low and Mid. Carolina.]

Forming elongated patches 4-5 in. long. When dry yellowish towards the margin, the more central parts being of a pale fawn-colour.—*M. J. B.*

**** Spines white.

865. Hydnum niveum. *P.* "Snowy Hydnum."

White; subiculum effused, thin, membranaceous, adnate, circumference byssoid; spines crowded, short, equal, smooth.—

Fr. Epicr. p. 518. *Pers. Disp. t.* 4. *f.* 6, 7. *Nees. f.* 246. *Ann. N.H. no.* 361.

On dead wood, leaves, &c. Rare. Bristol.

var. **Persistenter niveum.** Teeth compressed.

Running over shaded twigs of heath near the ground, in little membranaceous films. Ascot.

This does not become so yellow in drying as specimens from other localities. The patches are only a few lines across.

866. **Hydnum farinaceum.** *P.* "Mealy Hydnum."

White; subiculum effused, indeterminate, farinoso-crustaceous; circumference somewhat flocculose; spines slender, subdistant, very acute and entire.—*Fr. Epicr. p.* 519. *Fl. Dan. t.* 1375. *Eng. Fl.* v. *p.* 158. *Kl. exs. no.* 623.

On decayed wood. [United States.]

Forming thin, effused patches, resembling scattered meal, beset with distant, acute spines.

867. **Hydnum argutum.** *Fr.* "Spongy Hydnum."

White; subiculum effused, spreading, tomentose, interwoven, adnate; spines acute, subulate, unequal, serrate or toothed.—*Fr. Epicr. p.* 519. *Roth. Ust. Ann.* i. *t.* i. *f.* 5. *B. & Br. Ann. N.H.* 1865, *no.* 1026.

On wood and bark. Sept. Bodelwyddan. Twycross.

The distinctive character seems to reside in the spongy subiculum, which consists of rather strong perpendicular threads. The spores are large and subglobose.

868. **Hydnum plumosum.** *Duby.* "Feathered Hydnum."

Snow-white, downy; subiculum very delicate; spines divided, feathered at the apex.—*Duby. Bot. Gall.* ii. *p.* 778. *Berk. Outl. p.* 261.

On dead wood. Rare. Lambley, Notts. [Low. Carolina.]

Distinguished by the peculiar feathered apex of the spines. An anomalous species referred to this genus by Duby with doubt.

Gen. 29. SISTOTREMA, Fr. Sys. Myc.

Fig. 72.

Hymenium spread over gill-like, somewhat waxy teeth, irregularly distributed, distinct from the pileus, and easily separable.—*Fr. S. M. p.* 426. *Epicr. p.* 520. (*Fig.* 72.)

Fleshy or membranaceous fungi, either with a stem or sessile.

869. Sistotrema confluens. *Pers.* "Confluent Sistotrema."

Simple, confluent, white; pileus fleshy, irregular, horizontal, villous; stem somewhat excentric; teeth flexuose (entire or jagged).—*Fr. Epicr. p.* 520. *Bull. t.* 453, *f.* 1. *Grev. t.* 248. *Sow. t.* 112. *Eng. Fl.* v. *p.* 160.

On the ground. [Mid. Carolina.]

Gregarious, often anastomosing, or two or three growing into each other, scentless, brittle, whitish, at length yellowish, or tinged with brown; stem attenuated below, central or lateral, about an inch high; pileus about 1 in. broad, somewhat depressed. Tooth-like plates of the hymenium entire or jagged.—*Grev.* (*Fig.* 72.)

Gen. 30. IRPEX, Fr. El. p. 142.

Fig. 73.

Teeth formed at an early stage of the growth of the subiculum, concrete with it, and disposed in rows, or like network, and connected together. (*Fig.* 73.)

Hymenium inferior, at first toothed. Teeth variable, firm, somewhat coriaceous, acute, entirely concrete with the pileus, placed in rows, or netted and connected at the base into lamellæ, or porous folds. Lignatile fungi, rather coriaceous, approaching *Lenzites* and *Dædalea*, but the hymenium is toothed from the first, the teeth not lacerated.—*Fr. Epicr. p.* 521.

870. Irpex pendulus. *Fr.* "Pendulous Irpex."

Pileus membranaceous, plicate, clothed with adpressed, pilose scales, yellow; extended behind, pendulous; margin white; teeth seriate, large, incised, white.—*Fr. Epicr. p.* 521. *All. & Sch. t.* 6, *f.* 7. *Eng. Fl.* v. *p.* 160. *Bisch. f.* 3411. *Rabh. F.E. no.* 19.

On pine wood. Rare. Scotland. [Low. Carolina.]

Pilei 1 in. or more broad, very thin, somewhat resembling paper, capable of being folded up or stretched, concrete or infundibuliform, from a stem-like base, clothed with long, even, pilose scales, so closely pressed that the whole surface appears slightly rugulose; spines distinct, chiefly seated on the produced base, which is at length brownish, various in form, generally disposed in rows.—*Fries.*

871. Irpex Johnstoni. *Berk.* "Johnston's Irpex."

Pure white, coriaceo-membranaceous, separable from the matrix; circumference naked; teeth compressed, unequal, disposed in rows.—*Berk. Outl. p.* 262. *Irpex lacteus, Eng. Fl.* v. *p.* 161.

On dead branches of beech.

Two inches long, effused, with the margin reflexed all round, and the teeth exactly resembling those of many true species of *Hydnum*, but on minute inspection they will be found to be seated upon fine folds, and disposed in rows.—*M. J. B.*

872. Irpex obliquus. *Fr.* "Oblique Irpex."

Effuse, crustuso-adnate, white, then pallid, circumference byssoid, teeth springing from a porous base, compressed, unequal, incised, oblique.—*Fr. Epicr. p.* 523. *Bolt. t.* 167, *f.* 1. *Kl. exs. no.* 121.

On fallen branches. Berwick. Linlithgowshire. [Low. and Mid. Carolina.]

"This spreads in irregular patches on the surface of decaying wood. The pores for a small space round the margin are round and distinct, but towards the centre greatly lengthened out, lying one upon another in an imbricated manner. The colour is white at first, when old it changes to a yellow brown, and at last to a dirty, fuscous black."—*Bolton.* (*Fig.* 73.)

873. Irpex fusco-violaceus. *Fr.* "Violet Irpex."

Pileus effused, reflexed, coriaceous, silky, zoned, greyish white; teeth lamelloso-seriate, brownish violet, incised at the tips.—*Fr. Epicr. p.* 521. *Willd. Bot. Mag.* iv. *t.* 2. *f.* 5. *Fckl. exs. no.* 1337. *Br. Bath. Trans.* 1870. *p.* 87.

On pine trunks. Leigh Woods. [Mid. Carolina.]

Gen. 31. RADULUM, Fr. El. p. 148.

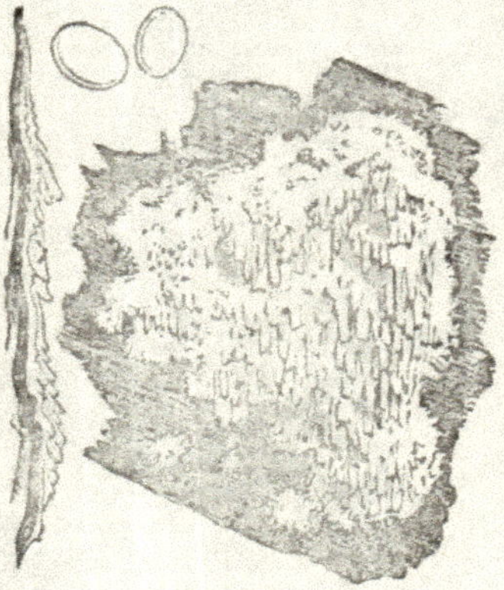

Fig. 74.

Tubercles rude, irregular, commonly elongated and cylindrical, obtuse, waxy. (*Fig.* 74.)

Hymenium amphigenous, tubercular. Tubercles rough, irregular, generally elongated and cylindrical, obtuse, waxy or fleshy, scattered or fasciculate. A very natural genus of epixylous fungi, resupinate, extended, usually breaking through the bark.—*Fr. Epicr. p.* 524.

874. Radulum orbiculare. *Fr.* "Orbicular Radulum."

In the autumn—effused, orbicular, confluent, white, then yellowish; circumference byssoid; tubercles elongated, irregular, roundish, scattered or fasciculate; in the spring—waxy or fleshy, smooth, flesh-coloured; tubercles broader and shorter.—*Fr. Epicr. p.* 524. *Grev. t.* 278. *Eng. Fl.* v. *p.* 161. *Bail. t.* 29.

On dead branches of birch.

Very variable, generally originating beneath the epidermis, 2-3 in. broad, quite membranaceous, or above 2 lines thick, margin byssoid, occasionally showing a disposition to become reflexed; hymenium consisting of irregularly disposed, oblique, or erect, tooth-like, obtuse, entire, or laciniated, often fasciculate tubercles, the apices sometimes somewhat tomentose. Occasionally they are much scattered and almost resemble spines.—*M. J. B.*

875. Radulum quercinum. *Fr.* "Oak Radulum."

Somewhat rounded, then broadly confluent, innate, crustaceous, becoming smooth, white, then pallid; tubercles rounded, elongated, stout, obtuse, scattered, or fasciculate, irregular, floccoso-villose at the apex.—*Fr. Epicr. p.* 525. *Ray. Syn. t.* 1. *f.* 4. *Ann. N. H. no.* 362. *Hydnum Barba-Jovis, Sow. t.* 328. *Eng. Fl.* v. *p.* 159.

On branches of oak. Rare.

Adnate, persistent, 2-3 in. long, according to Fries, but Eng. Fl. states—"Sometimes a foot or more broad, white when young, then yellowish rufous, membranaceous, composed of the finest down, margin byssoid, pure white." (*Fig.* 74.)

876. Radulum fagineum. *Fr.* " Beech Radulum."

Innate, decorticating, smooth, white, becoming pallid; tubercles elongated, terete, obtuse, entire.—*Fr. El. p.* 152. *Fr. Epicr. p.* 525.

On prostrate beeches. Feb. Mar. Epping Forest. *W.G.S.* [Mid. Carolina.]

This species was found in abundance in Epping Forest in 1869, but has not been met with since.

Gen. **32. PHLEBIA,** Fr. S. M. p. 426.

Fig. 75.

Hymenium soft and waxy (subgelatinous), spread over persistent crest-like wrinkles or veins, whose edge is entire. (*Fig.* 75.)

Hymenium amphigenous, of a soft, waxy texture, glabrous, continuous, from the first corrugated, spread over crowded, interrupted, and persistent wrinkles or veins, whose edge is entire. Resupinate, spreading fungi, when moist gelatinous and waxy, when dry cartilaginous.—*Fr. Epicr. p.* 526.

877. Phlebia merismoides. *Fr.* " Straight-folded Phlebia."

Effuse, even or encrusting, flesh-coloured, then livid, white and villous beneath, circumference orange, strigose; wrinkles simple, straight, crowded.—*Fr. Epicr. p.* 526. *Grev. t.* 280. *Huss.* ii. *t.* 44. *Eng. F.* v. *p.* 162. *Bail. t.* 29.

On old stumps and decayed branches. Rare. [United States.]

" Plant 2-3 in. across, folds nearly straight when growing on a smooth surface, passing into prominent papillæ in individuals incrusting mosses." Thin, almost tremelloid when fresh. (*Fig.* 75.)

878. Phlebia radiata. *Fr.* " Radiating Phlebia."

Subrotund, equal, smooth on both sides, fleshy-red, circumference radiato-dentate, folds straight, radiating in rows.—*Fr. Epicr. p.* 526. *Sow. t.* 291. *Eng. Fl.* v. *p.* 162.

On bark. Very rare. Appin. [United States.]

Between fleshy and membranaceous, tough, at first orbicular, then dilated, confluent, 1-3 inches broad; margin free, smooth, but beautifully fibroso-radiated; folds radiating from the centre, short, interwoven, very close.—*Fries.* Thicker than *P. merismoides*, and bright in colour, almost orange.—*M. J. B.*

879. **Phlebia contorta.** *Fr.* "Contorted Phlebia."

Effuse, rather firm, rufous, then brown, smooth on both sides, circumference indeterminate, folds here and there conglomerate, or ramulose, somewhat flexuose, irregularly disposed.—*Fr. Epicr. p.* 526. *Pers. M.E. t.* 18. *f.* 5.

On decayed wood. Rare.

Effused and contorted, substance firmer than in the last, folds not radiating, but sometimes scattered and sometimes conglomerated.

880. **Phlebia vaga.** *Fr.* "Rambling Phlebia."

Effuse, adnate; circumference byssoid or fibrillose, dirty-yellowish; hymenium yellowish-grey; veins creeping, intricate, at length coalescing, and granuloso-papillose.—*Fr. Epicr. p.* 527. *Ann. N.H. no.* 51. *Loudon, f.* 16126.

On decayed wood. Common. [Low. & Mid. Carolina.]

Arachnoid at first, then traversed with intricate fructifying veins, rather than wrinkles, which multiply rapidly and form an intricate mass.—*M. J. B.*

Gen. 33. **GRANDINIA,** Fr. Gen. Hym.

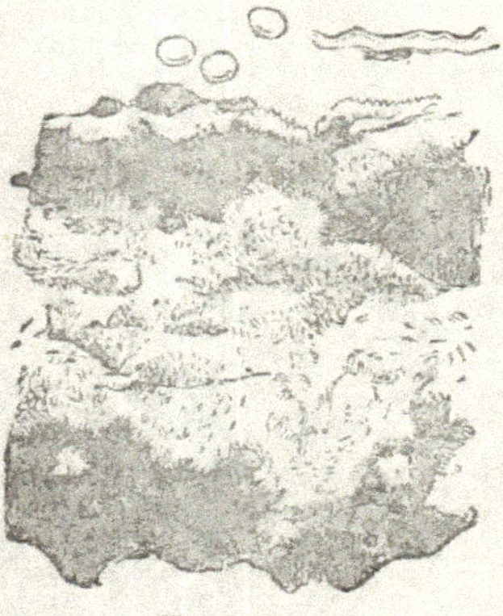

Fig. 76.

Hymenium waxy, granulated; granules obtuse, entire, equal, crowded, smooth, persistent. (*Fig.* 76.)

Hymenium amphigenous, continuous, waxy, papillose, warty, or granulose; the granules globular or hemispherical, entire, obtuse, crowded, regular, glabrous, persistent. Incrusting, spreading, soft fungi.—*Fr. Epicr. p.* 527.

881. **Grandinia papillosa.** *Fr.* "Papillose Grandinia."

Membranaceous, subrotund, entire, seceding, milk white, smooth and yellowish beneath; circumference furfuraceous; hymenium very much cracked; granules minute, crowded, equal, subspherical.—*Fr. Epicr. p.* 528. *Berk. Ann. N.H. no.* 282. *Libert. exs. no.* 21.

On sticks. Wiltshire. *C. E. B.*

The plant found by Mr. Broome in Wiltshire is exactly like that of Madame Libert; it was probably omitted from Berkeley's Outlines from a doubt whether it was really the species intended by Fries.

882. Grandinia granulosa. *Fr.* "Granular Grandinia."

Waxy, broadly effused, agglutinate, tan-coloured; circumference determinate, smooth; hymenium equal; granules hemispherical, equal, crowded.—*Fr. Epicr. p.* 527. *Thelephora granulosa, Eng. Fl.* v. *p.* 171. *Berk. exs. no.* 299.

On fallen branches. Common. [United States.]

Forming a thin, adnate, whitish, or sub-ochraceous stratum, following the irregularities of the wood, with scarcely any definite circumference, beset with crowded, rather sharp granules.—*M. J. B.* (*Fig.* 76.)

883. Grandinia ocellata. *Fr.* "Ocellate Grandinia."

Waxy, broadly effused, agglutinate, livid; circumference indeterminate, sterile; hymenium unequal; granules crowded, somewhat conical, obtuse, equal, of the same colour.—*B. & Br. Ann. N.H. no.* 1027. *Fr. Epicr. p.* 527.

On dead prostrate trunks. Aug. Sept. Bodelwyddan. Coed Coch.

Gen. 34. ODONTIA, Fr. Gen. Hym.

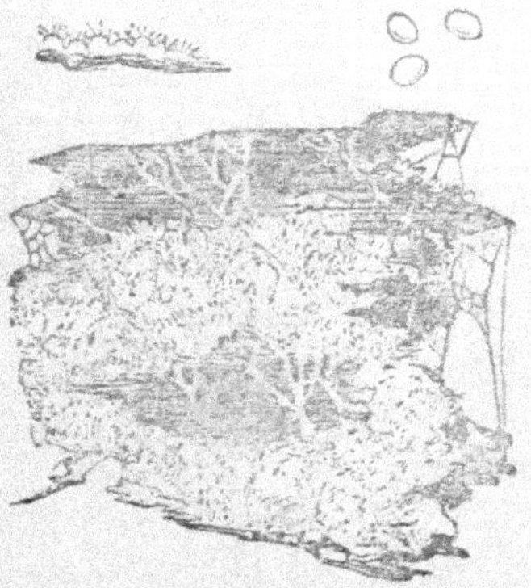

Fig. 77.

Subiculum formed of interwoven fibres, clothed with papillose or spine-shaped warts, which are crested at the apex. (*Fig.* 77.)

Hymenium inferior, formed of fibres interwoven into papillose warts, rarely awl or brittle-like, furnished at the apex with a multifid crest. Resupinate, spreading fungi, dry, not waxy, approaching more to *Hydnum*. —*Fr. Epicr. p.* 528.

884. Odontia fimbriata. *Fr.* "Fringed Odontia."

Effuse, membranaceous, separating, traversed by rhizomorphoid threads, pallid; circumference fibrilloso-fimbriate; warts minute, granuliform, apex multifid, rufescent.—*Fr. Epicr. p.* 529. *Pers. M.E.t.* 6, *f.* 5, 6. *Berk. exs. no.* 143. *Hydnum fimbriatum, Eng. Fl.* v. *p.* 159.

On fallen branches. [United States.]

In young perfect specimens the membrane is furnished with branched ribs, which adhere less firmly to the matrix. Margin most elegantly radiato-fibrillose, white. Dry specimens are of a uniform fawn-colour. Sometimes the fimbriated margin is entirely absent. Warts at first granular, minute, at length elongated.—*M. J. B.* (*Fig.* 77.)

Order IV. AURICULARINI.

Hymenium confluent with the hymenophore, at first even, or rarely veined, and commonly remaining even.

Fleshy—
- Hymenium distinct, even or rugose, putrescent when old . . . . *Craterellus.*
- Hymenium fleshy, tough, at length rigid, striate, veined, or papillose . . . . *Thelephora.*
- Hymenium coriaceous, even, without bristles *Stereum.*
  - Beset with short stiff bristles . . . *Hymenochæte.*
- Hymenium gelatinous when moist, folded . . *Auricularia.*
- Hymenium fleshy, collapsing when dry, even . *Corticium.*

Cup-shaped, submembranaceous—
- Hymenium inferior . . . . *Cyphella.*

Cylindrical, tubular . . . . *Solenia.*

Hymenium homogeneous, closely floccose, beset with rigid, fasciculate bristles . . . . *Kneiffia.*

Gen. 35. KNEIFFIA, Fr. Gen. Hym.

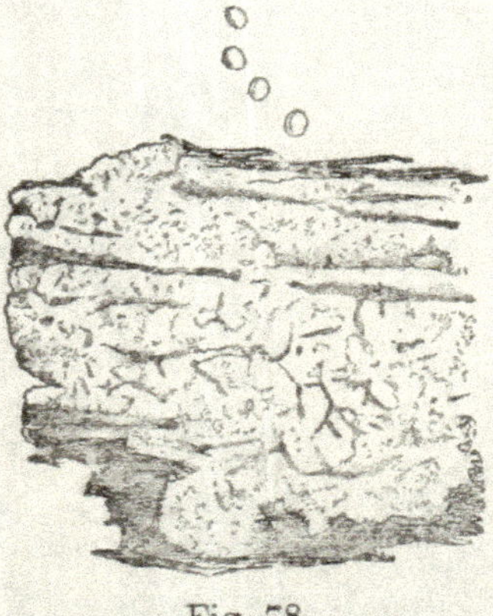

Fig. 78.

Soft, loosely fleshy, flocculose and collapsing when dry; hymenium rough with rigid, scattered, and fasciculate bristles. (*Fig.* 78.)

Hymenium amphigenous, continuous, destitute of granules or warts, rough with stiff bristles scattered or fasciculate. Fleshy, soft fungi protruding in various forms from the clefts of bark, in their most perfect form hemispherical; collapsing into flocci when dry.—*Fr. Epicr. p.* 529.

885. Kneiffia setigera. *Fr.* "Bristly Kneiffia."

White, irregularly effused, thickish, fleshy, undulate, flocculose within, silky beneath, bristles scattered, hyaline.—*Fr. Epicr. p.* 529. *Fr. El. p.* 208. *Ann. N.H. no.* 363.

On fallen branches. Wraxall. [United States.]

White, somewhat resembling *Grandinia granulosa* in general appearance.—*M. J. B.* (*Fig.* 78.)

Gen. **36. CRATERELLUS,** Fr. Gen. Hym.

Fig. 79.

Fleshy. Hymenium unchangeable, carnoso-membranaceous, distinct, smooth, even, or at length rugose. Putrescent when old. (*Fig.* 79.)

886. Craterellus lutescens. *Fr.* "Yellowish Craterellus."

Pileus submembranaceous, tubæform, soon pervious, undulated, brown, flocculose; stem hollow, yellow; hymenium remotely costate, even, then rough with interwoven veins.—*Fr. Epicr. p.* 532. *Pers. M.E. t.* 13, *f.* 1. *Schæff. t.* 157. *Kl. exs.* ii., *no.* 208. *Bolt. t.* 105, *f.* 2. *Batsch. f.* 36. *Cantharellus lutescens, Eng. Fl.* v. *p.* 126.

In woods. Rare. Edinburgh. [Low. Carolina.]

Single or gregarious. Pileus 1-3 in. broad, depressed, at length infundibuliform, yellowish livid-brown; veins decurrent, anastomosing, flexuous, yellow or flesh colour; stem 2-3 in. high, 2-3 lines thick, yellow, hollow, unequal.—*Grev.*

887. Craterellus cornucopioides. *Fr.* "Horn-like Craterellus."

Pileus submembranaceous, tubæform, pervious, squamulose, dingy-black; stem hollow, black; hymenium even, then rugulose, cinereous.—*Fr. Epicr. p.* 532. *Bisch. f.* 3304. *Fl. Dan. t.* 384, 1260. *Kl. exs. no.* 626. *Schæff. t.* 165, 166. *Sow. t.* 74.

Krombh. t. 45, *f.* 18, *t.* 46, *f.* 10-13. *Mich. t.* 82, *f.* 5, 6. *Berk. Outl. t.* 19, *f.* 6. *Huss.* ii. *t.* 37. *B. & Br. Ann. N. H.* 1866, *p.* 55. *Cantharellus cornucopioides*, *Eng. Fl.* v. *p.* 126. *Schnitz. Sturm. t.* 5.

In woods, on the ground. [United States.]

Spores ·0006 × ·00035 in. Sporophores forked above, the spicules long and often less than four in number. More or less tufted. Pileus 3 in. or more broad, dark brown-black, perforated, trumpet-shaped, somewhat lobed and split, tough, elastic, rugoso-squamulose, confluent with the subobsolete black stem. Hymenium decurrent, cinereous, either very slightly rugulose, or disinctly wrinkled.—*M. J. B.* (*Fig.* 79.)

888. Craterellus sinuosus. *Fr.* "Waved Craterellus."

Pileus rather fleshy, infundibuliform, undulated, flocculoso-villous, brownish-grey; stem stuffed; hymenium at length implexo-rugose, pallid cinereous, as well as the stem.—*Fr. Epicr. p.* 533. *Vaill. t.* 11, *f.* 11-13. *Cantharellus sinuosus*, *Eng. Fl.* v. *p.* 127. *Kl. exs. no.* 625. *Berk. exs. no.* 280.

In woods. Scotland.

Distinguished from every state of the preceding by the colour, and the different nature of the stem.—*M. J. B.* Spores cream colour, ·00021 × ·00035 in.

889. Craterellus crispus. *Fr.* "Crisped Craterellus."

Pileus somewhat pervious, crisped, dingy, inclined to tawny; stem stuffed below; hymenium nearly even.—*Fr. Epicr. p.* 533. *Bull. t.* 465. *Sow. t.* 75. *Cooke exs. no.* 225.

In woods.

Hymenium sometimes white, sometimes dingy. Fries appears to consider it a variety of *C. sinuosus.*

Gen. **37. THELEPHORA,** Fr. Gen. Hym.

Fig. 80.

Pileus destitute of cuticle, consisting of interwoven fibres. Hymenium costato-striate or papillose, of a tough, fleshy consistence, at length rigid, and finally collapsing and flocculent. (*Fig.* 80.)

Sect. 1. *Mesopus.*

890. Thelephora Sowerbei. *Berk.* "Sowerby's Thelephora."

White, infundibuliform, at length discoloured, rough and aculeate above, hymenium not setulose.—*B. & Br. Ann. N.H.* 1865, *no.* 1027*. *Berk. Outl. p.* 266. *Sow. t.* 155.

On the ground in woods. Rare. Burnham Beeches.

When fresh of a pure white, when exposed to the weather it assumes a dingy yellow tinge here and there. The hymenium is not in the slightest degree setulose. The pileus is rough, with radiating processes projecting from the surface. Sowerby's figure was evidently taken from discoloured specimens, but is very faithful.—*M. J. B.*

891. Thelephora multizonata. *B. & Br.* "Many-zoned Thelephora."

Pileus multiplex, infundibuliform, originating from the variable confluent lobes and stems, above of a beautiful fleshy-red, and much zoned; margin lobato-crenulate, hymenium finely ribbed, paler, smooth.—*Ann. N.H.* 1865, *no.* 1028, *t.* xiii. *f.* 4. *T. pannosa, Eng. Fl.* v. *p.* 163. *T. Sowerbei, Berk. Outl. in part.*

On the ground. Cotterstock.

Forming a dense mass, of a beautiful reddish tint; flesh and stem zoned within. Perfectly distinct from Sowerby's plant, with which it is confounded in Eng. Fl. and Berk. Outl.

892. Thelephora tuberosa. *Grev.* "Tuberous Thelephora."

Subcoriaceous, smooth, pallid, becoming rufous; pileus cut down to the bulbous stem into compressed branches, disposed in an infundibuliform manner, hymenium inferior, smooth.—*Fr. Epicr. p.* 535. *Grev. t.* 178. *Eng. Fl.* v. *p.* 164.

On the ground. Rare. Edinburgh. [Mid. Carolina.]

Scattered, subcoriaceous, about 1 in. high; pileus about two-thirds of the height of the entire plant, variously divided into compressed, acute, or obtuse branches. The main branches are given off from the same point, and are disposed in a circular manner, leaving the centre free, and somewhat infundibuliform; stem nearly cylindrical, obscurely furrowed, or lacunose, bulbous at the base. Hymenium covering the whole plant except the stem. Spores oval, numerous.—*Grev.*

893. Thelephora anthocephala. *Fr.* "Flower-headed Thelephora."

Coriaceous, soft, subferruginous; pileus divided to the simple, equal, villous stem, into sub-erect laciniæ, which are dilated upwards, and fimbriate, becoming whitish; hymenium inferior, even.—*Fr. Epicr. p.* 536. *Bull. t.* 452, *f.* 1. *Berk. Outl. t.* 17, *f.* 4. *Sow. t.* 156. *Berk. exs. no.* 244. *T. coralloides, Eng. Fl.* v. *p.* 163.

On the ground in woods. [United States.]

From the same point spring many erect, often confluent, pale branches, spreading upwards into greyish or purplish brown, strongly streaked branchlets, dispersed frequently like the petals of a pink, their apices dilated, pale, and generally fimbriated. Smell scarcely any.—*M. J. B.*

894. Thelephora caryophyllea. *Fr.* "Clove-coloured Thelephora."

Subcoriaceous, purplish brown; pileus depressed, fibroso-lacerate; margin sometimes incised, sometimes divided into a few linear branches, hymenium nearly even, smooth.—*Fr. Epicr. p.* 536. *Ann. N. H. no.* 283. *Berk. exs. no.* 241. *Cooke. exs. no.* 219. *Corda. Icon.* v. *f.* 72. *Schnitz. Sturm. t.* 6.

On the ground in woods. Rare. Bungay. [United States.]

It assumes every form, from that of a perfect cup with a central stem to a much and irregularly branched frond.—*M. J. B.*

Sect. 2. *Merisma.*

895. Thelephora palmata. *Fr.* "Palmate Thelephora."

Coriaceous, soft, erect, very much branched, pubescent, purplish-brown, base simple and stem-like, branches flat, even; dilated above, palmate, sub-fastigiate, tips fimbriate, whitish.—*Fr. Epicr. p.* 537. *Grev. t.* 46. *Krombh. t.* 54, *f.* 24, 25. *Holms.* i. *t.* 10. *Bisch. f.* 3311. *Nees. f.* 151. *Eng. Fl.* v. *p.* 163. *Smith, P.M. f.* 4. *Rabh. F.E. no.* 119.

On the ground. Very fœtid. [United States.]

Smell very bad a few minutes after gathering, varying from ½ in. to more than 4 in. in height, and from a single stem to a dense mass, 2 or 3 in. in thickness.—*Grev.*

896. Thelephora terrestris. *Fr.* "Ground Thelephora."

Cæspitose, soft, brown, at length blackish; pileoli imbricated, plane, fibroso-strigose, zoneless, elongated into a somewhat lateral stem; margin similar; hymenium inferior, radiato-rugose. *Fr. Epicr. p.* 538. *Nees. f.* 251. *Batsch. f.* 121. *Eng. Fl.* v. *p.* 165. *Bail. t.* 28. *Ann. de. Sc. Nat.* (1837) viii. *t.* 8. *f.* 12, *t.* 11, *f.* 29.

On the ground. [Mid. & Up. Carolina.]

Pileus 1-2 in. across, somewhat zoned, papillæ scattered.—*Eng. Fl.*

Sect. 3. Apus.

897. **Thelephora cristata.** *Fr.* "Crested Thelephora."

Incrusting, rather tough, pallid, passing into branches, or ascending cæspitose laciniæ, apices subulate, fimbriate; hymenium papillose, on even spaces, or the sides of the branches.—*Fr. Epicr. p.* 539. *Desm. exs. no.* 362. *Bull. t.* 415, *f.* 1. *Sow. t.* 158. *Linnæa.* v. *t.* 7, *f.* 2. *Eng. Fl.* v. *p.* 164. *Bisch. f.* 3290. *Ann. N.H. no.* 284. *Berk. exs. no.* 243. *Fl. Dan. t.* 2272, *f.* 3.

On moss, &c.

Whitish, greyish, or purplish brown; at first quite resupinate, gradually extending, and acquiring a branched appearance, the apices compressed, expanded, and beautifully fringed or laciniated.—*Eng. Fl.*

898. **Thelephora mollissima.** *P.* "Soft Thelephora."

Fleshy, soft, incrusting: pileus effuso-reflexed, laciniate, subtomentose, whitish, hymenium inferior, smooth, even, purplish-brown.—*Fr. Epicr. p.* 540. *Berk. Outl. t.* 17, *f.* 5. *Ann. N.H. no.* 286. *Berk. exs. no.* 245. *Desm. exs. no.* 362.

On the ground in woods.

Extremely variable, sometimes quite effused, sometimes assuming the form of *T. palmata.*—*M. J. B.* Often incrusting the stems of grasses, as in the figure quoted above.

899. **Thelephora laciniata.** *P.* "Torn Thelephora."

Coriaceous, soft, incrusting, ferruginous brown; pilei subimbricated, effuso-reflexed, fibroso-squamose, margin fibrous, fimbriated, at first whitish; hymenium inferior, papillose, flocculose.—*Fr. Epicr. p.* 540. *Bolt. t.* 173. *Sow. t.* 213. *Fl. Dan. t.* 1198, 949. *Eng. Fl.* v. *p.* 165. *Berk. exs. no.* 242. *Cooke exs. no.* 220.

On branches, heathy ground, &c. Common.

[United States.]

Larger, paler, and not so strigose as *T. terrestris*, the fibres being adnate forming little ridges, rather than scales; margin fringed and laciniated; papillæ closer.—*M. J. B.* (*Fig.* 80.)

900. **Thelephora biennis.** *Fr.* "Biennial Thelephora."

Coriaceous, soft, broadly incrusting, cinereous-brown; pilei at length reflexed, narrow, tomentose; circumference fimbriated; hymenium subresupinate, smooth, subsetulose, plicate at the base.—*Fr. Epicr. p.* 540. *Bull. t.* 436. *Ann. N.H. no.* 364.

On the ground, incrusting stones, &c. Rare. Kew and Bowood. [Mid. and Up. Carolina.]

901. Thelephora fastidiosa. *Fr.* "Stinking Thelephora."

Effused, soft, amorphous, incrusting, white, passing into laminose branches; hymenium inferior, at length rufous, papillose.—*Fr. Epicr. p.* 540. *Ann. N.H. no.* 285.

On the ground. Fœtid.

Distinguishable at once by its abominable odour, which remains for a long time in dried specimens.—*M. J. B.*

902. Thelephora byssoides. *P.* "Byssoid Thelephora."

Irregularly effused, at first byssoid, ochraceous-white, then in a compact, fleshy disc, pulverulent, yellowish, circumference byssoid, whitish.—*Fr. Epicr. p.* 542. *Eng. Fl.* v. *p.* 168. *Berk. exs. no.* 20. *Fl. Dan. t.* 2276. *f.* 2.

On the ground amongst fir leaves, &c.

Patches 1 ft. or more broad, at first white, very thin, soft and cottony, but not radiating, with a slight ochraceous tinge in the centre, gradually thickening, and becoming more or less tuberculated; at length of a more or less intense yellow-brown from the ejection of the oval, obtuse spores.—*M. J. B.*

Sect. 4. *Resupinatus.*

903. Thelephora cæsia. *P.* "Ash-grey Thelephora."

Effused, determinate, soft, continuous, ashy-grey; hymenium nearly even; setæ quaternate.—*Fr. Epicr. p.* 541. *Nees. f.* 254. *Pers. Obs.* i. *t.* 3. *f.* 6. *Ann. N.H. no.* 365. *Berk. Outl. p.* 269.

On the ground in woods.

The surface is sometimes quite smooth, sometimes distinctly papillose.—*M. J. B.*

904. Thelephora sebacea. *Fr.* "Waxy Thelephora."

Effused, fleshy, waxy, becoming hard, incrusting, variable, tuberculose or stalactitic, whitish, circumference similar; hymenium flocculose, pruinose, or evanescent.—*Fr. Epicr. p.* 542. *Pers. Comm. t.* 4. *f.* 4. *Fl. Dan. t.* 1302. *Letell. t.* 607. *f.* 3. *Berk. Outl. t.* 17. *f.* 6. *Bon. t.* 12. *f.* 253. *Kl. exs. no.* 1811.

On grass, &c. Common. [United States.]

905. Thelephora puteana. *Schum.* "Cellar Thelephora."

Roundish and effused, fleshy, rather thick, fragile, pallid-yellowish; circumference mucedinous, white; hymenium sub-undulated.—*Fr. Epicr. p.* 542. *Fl. Dan. t.* 2035. *f.* 1. *Ann. N.H. no.* 7.

On stumps, wood in cellars, &c.

Varying from almost perfect evenness to considerable inequality of surface, with various tints of olive, tawny, ferruginous, cinereous, &c., in the same patch. When rubbed it has a disagreeable fishy odour.—*M.J.B.*

906. Thelephora laxa. *Fr.* "Loose Thelephora."

Membranaceous, soft, loosely adherent, beneath arachnoid, tomentose; circumference byssoid, white; hymenium papillose, pallid, then olive-ferruginous, powdered with ferruginous spores.—*Fr. Epicr. p.* 543. *Ann. N.H. no.* 366.

On lichens, moss, &c. Rare.

Analogous to *Thelephora puteana.*

907. Thelephora arida. *Fr.* "Dry Thelephora."

Membranaceous, effused, adnate, continuous, circumference whitish; hymenium even, sulphureous tan colour, then setulose, powdery, ferruginous-umber.—*Ann. N.H. no.* 8. *Fr. El.* i. *p.* 197. *Berk. exs. no.* 148.

On decayed pine-wood. Common. [Low. Carolina.]

Not so thick as *Thelephora puteana.*

908. Thelephora olivacea. *Fr.* "Olive Thelephora."

Membranaceous, effused, adnate, circumference fimbriated, whitish; hymenium dull olive, setulose, tomentose.—*Fr. Epicr. p.* 543. *Berk. Outl. p.* 269.

On pine wood.

909. Thelephora anthochroa. *P.* "Bright-coloured Thelephora."

Effused, sub-adnate, circumference byssoid, paler; hymenium even, brownish-rose, then pallid, floccose, velvety.—*Fr. Epicr. p.* 544.

var. **versicolor.** Variously tinted with fugitive shades of lilac and brown.—*Berk. Outl. p.* 270. *Ann. N.H. no.* 809.

On sycamore twigs. Rare. [Mid. Carolina.]

The young plant of the above variety is not at all brick-coloured, but variously tinted with fugitive shades of lilac and brown.—*B. & Br.*

Gen. 38. **STEREUM,** Fr.

Fig. 81.

Hymenium coriaceous, rather thick, concrete with the intermediate stratum of the pileus, which has a cuticle, always even and veinless, unchangeable, not beset with bristles. *(Fig.* 81.*)*

910. Stereum purpureum. *Fr.* "Purple Stereum."

Coriaceous, soft; pileus effuso-reflexed, obsoletely zoned, villoso-tomentose, pallid or whitish; hymenium naked, even, smooth, purplish.—*Fr. Epicr. p.* 548. *Sow. t.* 388, *f.* 1. *Bull. t.* 483, *f.* 1. *Desm. exs. no.* 117, 414. *Mich. t.* 66, *f.* 4. *Huss.* i. *t.* 20. (*Batsch. f.* 131. *var.*) *Thelephora purpurea, Eng. Fl.* v. *p.* 166. *Berk. exs. no.* 147.

On fallen trunks, especially poplar. Common.
[United States.]

Perennial. In general densely imbricated, soft but coriaceous, very rigid when dry, deeply zoned, strigose, but not so much as in the next species; margin much waved, and almost plicate, varying greatly in colour, whitish, yellowish-pallid lilac, and with frequently a black zone near the margin. Hymenium smooth, in general of a fine purple or lilac, at length cinereous, sometimes dark brown.—*M. J. B*

911. Stereum hirsutum. *Fr.* "Hairy Stereum."

Coriaceous; pileus effused and reflexed, strigose, hairy, somewhat zoned, becoming pallid; margin rather obtuse, yellow; hymenium even, smooth, naked, juiceless, yellowish, unchanged when bruised.—*Fr. Epicr. p.* 549. *Sow. t.* 27. *Grev. t.* 256. *Fl. Dan. t.* 1199 (1738 *f.* 1. *var.*) *Bull. t.* 274 (483, *f.* 2, 4, *var.*) *Desm. exs. no.* 116. *Price, f.* 8. *Mich. t.* 66, *f.* 2. *Berk. Outl. t.* 17, *f.* 7. *Huss.* i. *t.* 58. *Thelephora hirsuta, Eng. Fl.* v. *p.* 166. *Cooke, exs. no.* 307. *Rabh. F.E. no.* 1109. *Berk. exs. no.* 146.

On stumps, &c. Common everywhere. [United States.]

Perennial. Variable. At first resupinate, at length generally reflexed, often imbricated, more or less zoned, strigose, tough and leathery, but not rigid, buff, yellowish, or greyish, often acquiring a greenish tinge from the presence of minute *Algæ*. Hymenium smooth, even, buff, sometimes cinereous; margin entire, more or less lobed.—*M. J. B.* (*Fig.* 81.)

912. Stereum spadiceum. *Fr.* "Bright-brown Stereum."

Coriaceous; pilei effuso-reflexed, villous, sub-ferruginous; margin rather obtuse, white, even beneath, smooth and brownish, bleeding when bruised.—*Fr. Epicr. p.* 549. *Fl. Dan. t.* 1619, *f.* 1. *Bull. t.* 483, *f.* 5. *Sow. t.* 25. *Ann. N.H. no.* 50. *Berk. exs. no.* 144. *Cooke, exs. no.* 304.

On sticks, especially ash. Common. [United States.]

Easily known from every state of *Stereum purpureum* by its becoming blood-stained when scratched. Spores copious, pure white, oblong-elliptic.—*M. J. B.*

913. Stereum sanguinolentum. *Fr.* "Bleeding Stereum."

Coriaceous, thin: pileus effuso-reflexed, closely silky, somewhat striate, pallid; margin acute, white; hymenium even, smooth, brownish-cinereous, bleeding when wounded, when old pruinose.—*Fr. Epicr. p.* 549. *Bail. t.* 28. *Grev. t.* 225. *Fl. Boruss. t.* 381. *Thelephora sanguinolenta, Eng. Fl.* v. *p.* 167.

On wood of firs. Common. [Low. and Mid. Carolina.]

Densely gregarious, at first resupinate and circular, at length dimidiate, or with the margin more or less reflexed all round, silky or almost strigose, zoned, the zones darker; hymenium rough, from the inequalities of the matrix, otherwise smooth, pale greyish-brown, when scratched or bruised becoming instantly blood-red.—*M. J. B.*

914. Stereum rugosum. *Fr.* "Rugose Stereum."

Corky, rigid; pileus effused, and shortly reflexed, obtusely marginate, at length smooth, bright-brown; hymenium unpolished, pruinose, somewhat blood-stained when bruised.—*Fr. Epicr. p.* 552. *T. Lauro-cerasi, Eng. Fl. var. Thelephora rugosa, Eng. Fl.* v. *p.* 166. *Berk. exs. no.* 145.

On stumps, especially hazel. Common.
[Mid. & Up. Carolina.]

Assuming a blood-red colour when scratched. Sometimes surviving one or more seasons, and then thick and zoned within.

915. Stereum acerinum. *Fr.* "Maple Stereum."

Crustaceous, adnate, even, smooth, white.—*Fr. Epicr. p.* 553.

Thelephora acerina, Eng. Fl. v. *p.* 172. *Moug. exs. no.* 991. *Berk. exs. no.* 65.

On living maple trunks. Common. [United States.]

Spreading in small detached patches over the whole trunk, and resembling the barren-white crust of a lichen; distinguished from *C. sambuci* by its thicker substance, and not changing colour at all when dry. It is of a somewhat farinaceous texture, and cracks very slightly in drying.—*M. J. B.*

Gen. **39.** **HYMENOCHÆTE,** Lev.

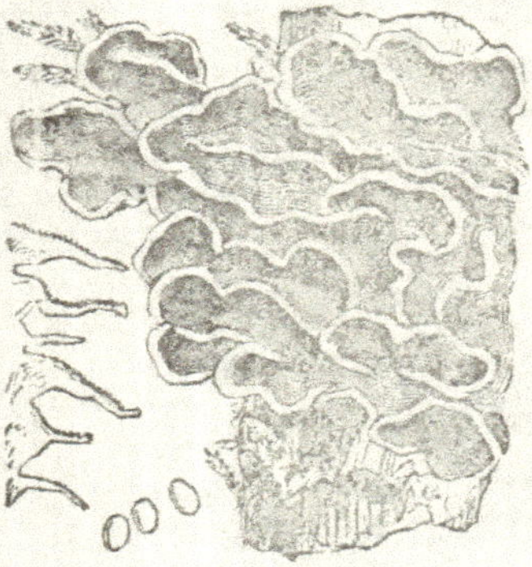

Fig 82.

Coriaceous, dry. Hymenium even, beset with short, stiff, coloured bristles. (*Fig.* 82.)

916. **Hymenochæte rubiginosa.** *Lev.* "Rubiginous Hymenochæte."

Coriaceous, rigid; pileus effuso-reflexed, somewhat fasciated, velvety, rubiginous, then becoming smooth and bright-brown, intermediate stratum tawny-ferruginous; hymenium ferruginous, velvety.—*Fr. Epicr. p.* 550. *Fl. Dan. t.* 1619, *f.* 2. *Berk. exs. no.* 247. *Moug. exs. no.* 394. *Desm. exs. no.* 413. *Sow. t.* 26. *Thelephora rubiginosa, Eng. Fl.* v. *p.* 165.

On gate posts. Common. [United States.]

Perennial. At first resupinate, at length reflexed, the lower margin generally adhering firmly, very rigid and brittle, often so deeply grooved as to cause corresponding ridges in the hymenium, which is velvety and coarsely, but sparingly, papillose. Margin paler and minutely tomentose.—*M. J. B.* (*Fig.* 82.)

917. **Hymenochæte tabacina.** *Lev.* "Flaccid Hymenochæte."

Coriaceous, thin, flaccid; pileus effused, reflexed, silky, at length smooth, somewhat ferruginous; margin and intermediate filamentose stratum golden-yellow; hymenium paler, pubescent. —*Fr. Epicr. p.* 550. *Bolt. t.* 174. *Berk. exs. no.* 248. *Desm. exs. no.* 415. *Thel. tabacina, Eng. Fl.* v. *p.* 165. *Ann. N.H. no.* 152.

On fallen branches. Rare. [Mid. & Up. Carolina.]

Differs from the foregoing in not being rigid, and in consequence shrivelling when dry, and losing all its beauty; margin in general reflexed all round —*M. J. B.*

918. Hymenochæte corrugata. *Berk.* "Cracked Hymenochæte."

Effused, closely adnate, indeterminate, cinnamon, cracked when dry.—*Berk. Outl. p.* 272. *Grev. t.* 234. *Berk. exs. no.* 298, 249. *Thelephora corrugata, Eng. Fl.* v. *p.* 172.

On sticks in woods. Common. [United States.]

Ferruginous brown, with sometimes a slight purplish tinge and a grey bloom, as if covered with a thin coat of white body-colour; bristles under the microscope jointed.—*Grev.*

Gen. **40. AURICULARIA,** Fr.

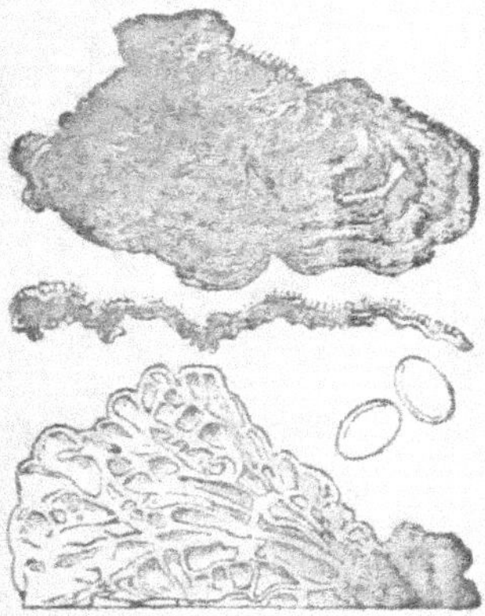

Fig. 83.

Hymenium irregularly and distantly folded, gelatinous when wet, different in substance from the pileus. *(Fig.* 83.*)*

919. Auricularia mesenterica. *Bull.* "Entire Auricularia."

Pilei resupinate, then reflexed, entire, villous, zoned and fasciate, brownish-cinereous; hymenium costato-plicate, brownish-violet.—*Fr. Epicr. p.* 555. *Bull. t.* 290. *Sow. t.* 290. *Bolt. t.* 172. *Moug. exs. no.* 492. *Desm. exs. no.* 221. *Mich. t.* 66, *f.* 4. *Huss.* ii. *t.* 6. *Phlebia mesenterica, Eng. Fl.* v. *p.* 162. *Cooke, exs. no.* 308. *Rabh. F.E. no.* 1215. *Price, f.* 27.

On stems of trees. [Mid. Carolina.]

At first effused, and quite resupinate, at length more or less reflexed, often dimidiate, occasionally infundibuliform, 2-3 in. broad, gelatinous in wet weather, hard and cartilaginous when dry, the upper surface tomentose, more or less zoned or fasciated; hymenium purplish-violet or light-brown, quite smooth or wrinkled, especially when dry, powdered with a beautiful bloom.—*M. J. B.* Spores white, ·00027 × ·00018 in. *(Fig.* 83.*)*

920. Auricularia lobata. *Somm.* " Lobed Auricularia."

Pileus effuso-reflexed, lobed, variegated with strigose or tomentose, velvety or smooth zones, brownish-white ; hymenium livid-tawny; folds distant, reticulated.—*Fr. Epicr. p.* 555. *Berk. Outl. t.* 18, *f.* 1.

On bark of trees. Staunton.

Very nearly allied to *Auricularia mesenterica.*

Gen. **41.** **CORTICIUM,** Fr.

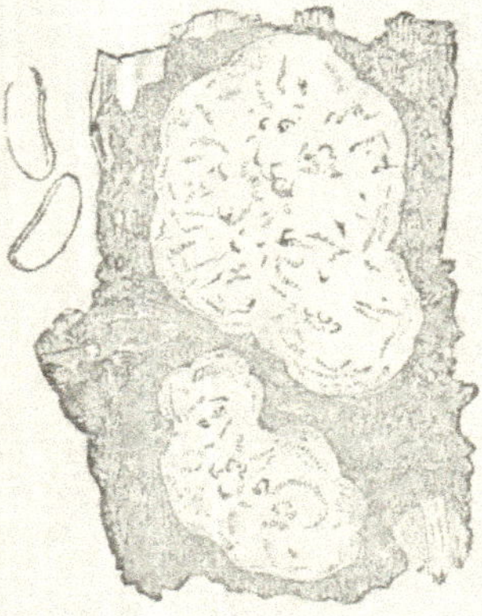

Fig. 84.

Hymenium soft and fleshy, swollen when moist, collapsing and becoming even when dry, often rimose. (*Fig.* 84.)

Sect. 1. *Apus.*

921. Corticium evolvens. *Fr.* " Unfolding Corticium."

Soft, resupinate, submarginate, floccose with pallid down; hymenium zoneless, naked, smooth, somewhat rugose, brown, becoming pale, cracked when dry.—*Fr. Epicr. p.* 557. *Ann. N.H. no.* 1029. *Schnitz. Sturm. t.* 7. *Fr. Obs.* i. *t.* 4, *f.* 5. *Fl. Dan. t.* 840, *f.* 1.

On dead cherry. Jan. King's Cliffe.

[Low. & Mid. Carolina.]

Sect. 2. *Himantia.*

922. Corticium giganteum. *Fr.* " Large Corticium."

Broadly effused, swelling when moist, waxy, hyaline, white, cartilaginous or papery when dry, free, milk-white; circumference strigoso-radiate; hymenium even, continuous.—*Fr. Epicr.*

p. 560. *Moug. exs. no.* 778. *Desm. exs. no.* 417. *Thelephora gigantea, Eng. Fl.* v. *p.* 170.

On pine stems. Common. [United States.]

Circumference very broad and almost byssoid, with here and there a tendency to become strigoso-radiate.

923. Corticium lacteum. *Fr.* "Milk-white Corticium."

Effused, membranaceous, milk white beneath, and circumference loosely fibrillose; hymenium waxy, darker, cracked when dry.—*Fr. Epicr. p.* 560. *Rabh. F.E. no.* 1212. *Berk. exs. no.* 250. *Thel. lactea, Ann. N.H. no.* 81.

On trunks.

Easily known by its smooth, white hymenium, covering a stratum consisting of thick fibrillæ.—*M. J. B.*

924. Corticium arachnoideum. *Berk.* "Web-like Corticium."

Effused, delicately byssoid, as also the circumference; hymenium white, very thin, patchy.—*Berk. Outl. p.* 273. *Ann. N.H. no.* 287. *t.* 9. *f.* 3.

In woods. [United States.]

Running over lichens, &c., the mycelium as delicate as a spider's web.
Forming delicate, effused, arachnoid patches of a snowy white; threads by no means forming fibres, but spreading like a delicate web, and often remaining barren, but under favourable circumstances giving rise to a smooth, even hymenium, consisting of elliptic sporophores arranged in little bunches.—*M. J. B.*

925. Corticium læve. *Fr.* "Even Corticium."

Effused, membranaceous, seceding, villoso-fibrillose beneath; circumference byssoid, not radiating; hymenium even, smooth, flesh-coloured and livid.—*Fr. Epicr. p.* 560. *Rabh. F.E. no.* 120. *Berk. exs. no.* 246. *Letell. t.* 630. *f.* 1. *Thel. lævis, Ann. N.H. no.* 80.

On decayed wood, sticks, &c. Common. [United States.]

This is the commonest of all the species, and assumes a variety of forms. Sometimes it remains closely attached, sometimes the margin is broadly reflexed. The hymenium varies also in colour, being sometimes pure white. The circumference is occasionally almost naked.—*M. J. B.*

926. Corticium roseum. *P.* "Rosy Corticium."

Effused, adnate, rosy; circumference fringed, whitish; hymenium pruinose, growing pale, at length much cracked and corrugated, indurated.—*Fr. Epicr. p.* 560. *Kl. exs. no.* 1516. *Thelephora rosea, Eng. Fl.* v. *p.* 168.

On poplar, &c. [Mid. Carolina.]

At first forming small scattered patches, which at length become more or less confluent, the cobweb-like fringe gradually obsolete.—*M. J. B.*

927. Corticium velutinum. *Fr.* "Velvety Corticium."

Effused, adnate, flesh-coloured; circumference with straight, strigose, diverging fibres, of the same colour; hymenium thick, fleshy, soft, even, densely velvety with bristles.—*Fr. Epicr. p.* 561. *Ann. N.H. no.* 288.

On logs. [Carolina, U.S.]

A very elegant species, of a pale pink, remarkable for its floccose mycelium, and the delicate frill with which the whole of the hymenium is clothed, giving it a velvety appearance.—*M. J. B.*

928. Corticium sanguineum. *Fr.* "Blood-red Corticium."

Effused, loosely adhering, arachnoid beneath, blood-colour; circumference loosely fibrillose, flesh-coloured, as well as the even, smooth hymenium.—*Fr. Epicr. p.* 561. *C. miniatum, Berk. exs. no.* 251.

On dead larch. Rare.

929. Corticium sulfureum. *Fr.* "Sulphury Corticium."

Effused, fibrillose or byssoid, bright sulphur-coloured; hymenium (when perfect) thick, waxy, soft, somewhat tawny, rimose when dry.—*Fr. Epicr. p.* 561. *Letell. t.* 630. *f.* 4. *Thelephora sulphurea, Eng. Fl.* v. *p.* 169.

On fallen sticks. [Mid. and Up. Carolina.]

At first consisting of loose, distinct, byssoid fibres, in which state it frequently remains without producing a true hymenium, next forming a thin, resupinate, silky, subpulverulent stratum, with a beautiful byssoid margin, at length furnished with a true hymenium, and beset with minute white bristles. The loose fibrillæ of a beautiful saffron yellow, the more advanced stage paler, with a yellowish or cinereous tinge in the centre, the byssoid margin nearly white.—*Eng. Fl.*

930. Corticium cœruleum. *Fr.* "Blue Corticium."

Roundish, then effused, adnate, at first tomentose, bright blue; circumference byssoid, of the same colour or whitish; hymenium waxy, soft, papillose or setulose, becoming smooth.—*Fr. Epicr. p.* 562. *Letell. t.* 630. *f.* 2. *Sow. t.* 350. *Cooke, exs. no.* 221. *Roth. Cat.* ii. *t.* 9. *f.* 2. *Desm. exs. no.* 396. *Thelephora cœrulea, Eng. Fl.* v. 168. *Rabh. F.E. no.* 1005.

On rails, &c. Common. [United States.]

At first byssoid, but when fully developed forming a close membrane, following the undulations of the wood on which it grows, of a beautiful dark satiny blue, the margin whitish.—*M. J. B.* Said to be phosphorescent.

931. Corticium atrovirens. *Fr.* "Black-green Corticium."

Irregularly effused, black-green, beneath and circumference tomentose, of the same colour; hymenium (?).—*Fr. Epicr. p.* 562.

On sticks in woods. Rare. [Mid. Carolina.]

Mr. Berkeley states that, like Fries, he has never found this species with a perfect hymenium.

932. Corticium lactescens. *Berk.* "Juicy Corticium."

Agglutinate, soft, waxy, undulated, flesh coloured, milky; margin shortly byssoid, at length cracked, interstices silky; hymenium flesh coloured, or pale salmon colour.—*Berk. Outl. p.* 274. *Thelephora lactescens, Eng. Fl.* v. *p.* 169. *Ann. N.H. no.* 153. *Berk. exs. no.* 21.

On decayed wood of willows, &c.

Thin, spreading for a considerable distance over the bark, and following all its inequalities, with a scarcely byssoid border, inner substance variegated with bands of different shades running parallel with the surface. When broken it gives out a milky juice which in taste and smell resembles exactly that of *Lactarius quietus.*—*M. J. B.*

Sect. 3. *Leiostroma.*

933. Corticium calceum. *Fr.* "Chalky Corticium."

Effused, agglutinate, waxy, quite smooth, white, circumference similar, hymenium even, smooth, cracked when dry.—*Fr. Epicr. p.* 562. *Thelephora calcea, Eng. Fl.* v. *p.* 170. *Kl. exs. no.* 325.

On pine wood. Common. [United States.]

Unequal in thickness, effused, hard, extending over several inches; hymenium white, discoloured in age, much cracked, papillose, sometimes quite plane and smooth.—*Grev.*

934. Corticium lividum. *P.* "Livid Corticium."

Effused, agglutinate, waxy, soft, smooth, changing colour, circumference similar, hymenium even, naked, rather viscid, cracked when dry.—*Fr. Epicr. p.* 563. *Berk. Outl. p.* 275. *Thelephora livida, Eng. Fl.* v. *p.* 171.

On wood. Appin.

In the same individuals the colour will be livid-blue and purplish-brown.

935. Corticium ochraceum. *Fr.* "Ochraceous Corticium."

Effused, agglutinate, waxy, soft, at length smooth, circumference white, somewhat radiating, evanescent; hymenium pallid, then ochraceous, sprinkled with gold-coloured, micaceous atoms, at length naked, tuberculose or papillose.—*Fr. Epicr. p.* 563. *Berk. Outl. p.* 275. *Thelephora ochracea, Eng. Fl.* v. *p.* 170.

On pine wood. [Mid. Carolina.]

Covering a large surface, being often a foot or more broad, mostly resupinate, but sometimes slightly reflexed or rather detached at the margin, adhering close to the wood; margin entire in old plants, villous when young; hymenium smooth ochraceous, sometimes with a faint purplish tinge, papillæ rather large, irregular, and spurious, being produced by the asperities of the wood.—*Grev.*

936. Corticium quercinum. *P.* "Oak Corticium."

Membranaceous, waxy, at first agglutinate, indeterminate, then fixed at the centre; border free and involute, blackish and smooth beneath; hymenium continuous, flesh-coloured.—*Fr. Epicr. p.* 563. *Nees. f.* 253. *Gard. Chron.* (1860), *p.* 481, *fig. Grev. t.* 142. *Bull. t.* 436, *f.* 1. *Cooke, exs. no.* 222. *Thelephora quercina, Eng. Fl.* v. *p.* 167. *Rabh. F.E. no.* 1211.

On oak branches. Common. [Mid. & Up. Carolina.]

Roundish, resupinate, the margin reflexed all round and involute; pileus smooth, black; hymenium flesh coloured, generally cracked, more or less tuberculated and wrinkled.—*M. J. B.*

937. Corticium cinereum. *Fr.* "Cinereous Corticium."

Waxy, at length rigid, confluent, agglutinate, lurid; hymenium cinereous, with a very delicate bloom.—*Fr. Epicr. p.* 563. *Desm. exs. no.* 119, 666. *Moug. exs. no.* 681. *Berk. exs. no.* 63, 64. *Rabh. F.E. no.* 20. *Thelephora cinerea, Eng. Fl.* v. *p.* 172.

On dead wood, sticks, &c. Common. [United States.]

The principal distinctive mark of this species is its dingy colour, which varies from brown to cinereous, or almost black.—*M. J. B.*

938. Corticium incarnatum. *Fr.* "Bright-coloured Corticium."

Waxy, becoming rigid, confluent, agglutinate, circumference radiating; hymenium persistently bright coloured (red or orange), covered with a delicate flesh-coloured bloom.—*Fr. Epicr. p.* 564. *Fl. Dan. t.* 2035, *f.* 2. *Berk. Outl. p.* 275. *Thelephora incarnata, Eng. Fl.* v. *p.* 171.

On timber, rails, &c. Common. [United States.]

Extremely variable, forming a thin, variously, but brightly coloured stratum.

939. Corticium nudum. *Fr.* "Naked Corticium."

Waxy, becoming rigid, agglutinate, flesh-coloured, growing pallid; circumference determinate, smooth; hymenium covered with a fugacious, whitish bloom.—*Fr. Epicr. p.* 564. *Ann. N.H. no.* 715. *Thelephora nuda, Eng. Fl.* v. *p.* 172.

On twigs in woods.

Distinguished from the last by its dull colour when dry. On the same branch individuals occur very thin, quite smooth, and effused, while others are thicker, more cinereous, and tuberculate. Spores oblong, slightly curved, ·0005 in. long, ·00015 in. broad.—*B. & Br.*

940. Corticium confluens. *Fr.* "Confluent Corticium."

Membranaceous, waxy, agglutinate; circumference radiating; hymenium naked, hyaline, then brightly coloured, somewhat shining.—*Fr. Epicr. p.* 564. *Ann. N.H. no.* 716.

On ash twigs, &c.

Distinguished from *C. nudum* more especially by its white, tomentose margin. Spores oblong, ·0008 in. long, ·0004 in. broad. The more perfect specimens have a few scattered papillæ.—*B. & Br.*

941. Corticium polygonium. *P.* "Patchy Corticium."

Determinate, adnate, soon grumoso-cartilaginous, hard, flesh-coloured; circumference similar; hymenium continuous, red, pruinose.—*Fr. Epicr. p.* 564. *Berk. Outl. p.* 276.

On poplar branches. [Mid. Carolina.]

Growing in little round detached patches from the ostiola of *Sphæriæ*.

942. Corticium comedens. *Fr.* "Erumpent Corticium."

Effused, exposed by the splitting of the epidermis of the matrix, thin, innate, flesh-coloured, then pallid; hymenium even, smooth.—*Fr. Epicr. p.* 565. *Nees, f.* 255. *Berk. Outl. p.* 276. *Berk. exs. no.* 22. *Thelephora comedens, Eng. Fl.* v. *p.* 171.

On branches. Common.

Distinguished at once by its peculiar mode of growth. It originates beneath the bark, which peels off and leaves it naked, forming a margin round it.—*M. J. B.*

943. Corticium Sambuci. *P.* "Elder Corticium."

Effused, subinnate, variously incrusting, white, continuous when growing, when dry cracked or flocculose and collapsing.—

Fr. Epicr. p. 565. *Grev. t.* 242. *Moug. exs. no.* 779. *Desm. exs. no.* 220. *Thelephora Sambuci, Eng. Fl.* v. *p.* 170.

On elder stumps. Common. [Mid. Carolina.]

Apparently papillose, but the papillæ arise from the inequalities of the bark or wood on which it grows.

944. Corticium aurora. *B. & Br.* "Rosy Corticium."

Very thin, effused, agglutinate, rose-coloured, turning pallid; circumference indeterminate.—*Berk. Outl. p.* 276.

On dead leaves of *Carices.* Batheaston.

Gen. 42. CYPHELLA, Fr.

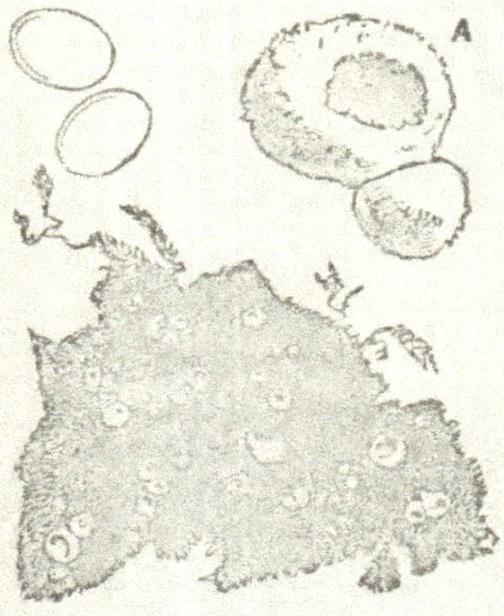

Fig. 85.

Submembranaceous, cup-shaped, elongated behind and frequently pendulous; hymenium distinctly inferior, completely confluent with the pileus. *(Fig. 85.)*

945. Cyphella griseo-pallida. *Fr.* "Pale-grey Cyphella."

Submembranaceus, globose, then campanulate, sessile, pallid, grey, floccose without; hymenium even, smooth.—*Fr. Epicr. p.* 567. *Ann. N.H. no.* 289.

On dead *Carex paniculata.* Spye Park.

Whole plant one-third of a line in diameter, at first granuliform, then regularly cup-shaped, with a short stem, and attached by a few radiating, white, strigose, short threads, at length dependent, mostly entire, clothed with white villous down. Hymenium even, pale reddish-grey, border slightly undulated. —*M. J. B.*

946. Cyphella muscigena. *Fr.* "Whitish Moss Cyphella."

Membranaceous, soft, subsessile, dimidiate, plane, white, silky without; hymenium rugulose.—*Fr. Epicr. p.* 567. *Pers. M.E. t.* 7, *f.* 6. *Ann. N.H. no.* 717. *Price, f.* 45.

On mosses. Hanham, near Bristol.

White, with a slight ochraceous tinge. At first flabelliform, fixed by a little down, at length laterally confluent, downy above, often spathulate. Hymenium slightly corrugated.—*B. & Br.*

947. Cyphella galeata. *Fr.* "Hooded Cyphella."

Membranaceous, soft, subsessile, cup-shaped, then dimidiate, helmet-shaped, even, whitish; margin quite entire; hymenium at length somewhat rufous, rugulose.—*Fr. Epicr. p.* 569. *Fl. Dan. t.* 2027, *f.* 1. *Ann. N.H. no.* 718. *Cantharellus lævis, Eng. Fl.* v. *p.* 127.

On mosses.

Pileus 2 lines or more broad, at first subglobose, then expanded, minutely tomentose, somewhat lobed, very thin, dirty-white. Hymenium rather uneven.—*Eng. Fl.* Differs from *C. muscigena* in its dingy hue, and bullate pileus. —*M. J. B.* Spores ·00038 × ·0003 in.

948. Cyphella ochroleuca. *B. & Br.* "Whitish-ochre Cyphella."

Membranaceous, cup-shaped, villous, and whitish ochre above: margin at length split; hymenium even, pale ochre, brighter than the pileus.—*Berk. Outl. p.* 277. *Ann. N.H. no.* 719.

On decayed bramble twigs. Batheaston.

One line or more broad, at first cup-shaped, but mostly irregular, then lobed or fissured, villous above, white tinged with yellow. Hymenium even, ochraceous, brighter than the pileus.—*B. & Br.*

949. Cyphella muscicola. *Fr.* "Greyish Moss Cyphella."

Membranaceous, subsessile, persistently cup-shaped, cinereous, pallid-whitish, fibrilloso-striate without; margin slightly downy, repand, torn; hymenium even.—*Fr. Epicr. p.* 568. *Fl. Dan. t.* 2083, *f.* 2. *Kl. exs. no.* 824.

On mosses. Apethorpe.

950. Cyphella lacera. *Fr.* "Torn Cyphella."

Membranaceous, cup-shaped, pendulous, then multifid, torn, vertex extended, stem-shaped, striate above with dense black fibrils; hymenium rugulose, white.—*Fr. Epicr. p.* 568. *A. & S. t.* 1, *f.* 5. *Bisch. f.* 3351.

On dead twigs, &c. Apethorpe. [Mid. Carolina.]

951. **Cyphella capula.** *Fr.* "Stalked Cyphella."

Membranaceous, obliquely campanulate, extended into a curved stem, smooth, whitish; margin irregular, sinuated; hymenium even.—*Fr. Epicr. p.* 568. *Holms.* ii. *t.* 22. *Fl. Dan. t.* 1970, *f.* 3. *Cooke exs. no.* 275.

On dead stems. [United States.]

Looks very much like a *Peziza*. It is sometimes yellow.

952. **Cyphella Goldbachii.** *Fr.* "Villous Cyphella."

Membranaceous, cup-shaped, urceolato-concave, sessile, externally villous, white; hymenium even, pallid.—*Fr. Epicr. p.* 569. *Sturm. t.* 63. *Ann. N.H. no.* 720.

On dead leaves of *Aira cæspitosa.* Spye Park, Wilts.

Differs from *C. cuticulosa* in its villous coat.

953. **Cyphella Curreyi.** *Berk.* "Currey's Cyphella."

Gregarious, sometimes slightly crowded, pezizæform, white, externally villous.—*B. & Br. Ann. N. Hist. no.* 935.

On twigs of broom, furze, elm, &c.

This resembles very closely *Peziza albo-violascens*, but has the true fruit of a *Cyphella*. It is probably the incomplete state of some *Peziza*.

954. **Cyphella fulva.** *B. & Rav.* "Tawny Cyphella."

Membranaceous, cup-shaped, the mouth more or less directed downwards, tawny, externally tomentose. Spores ovate, ·0006 in. long.—*B. & Rav. Ann. N.H. no.* 936.

On dead bark. [S. Carolina, U. S.]

The American specimens are generally fasciculate.

955. **Cyphella cuticulosa.** *Fr.* "Dickson's Cyphella."

Membranaceous, white, diaphanous, at first oblong, then cup-shaped, elongated into a stem, smooth externally.—*Dicks.* iii. *t.* 9. *f.* 11. *Fr. S.M.* ii. *p.* 201. *Berk. Outl. p.* 278. *Eng. Fl.* v. *p.* 215.

On dried grass stems. Oct.—Feb.

Not found since the time of Dickson.

Gen. 43. SOLENIA, Pers.

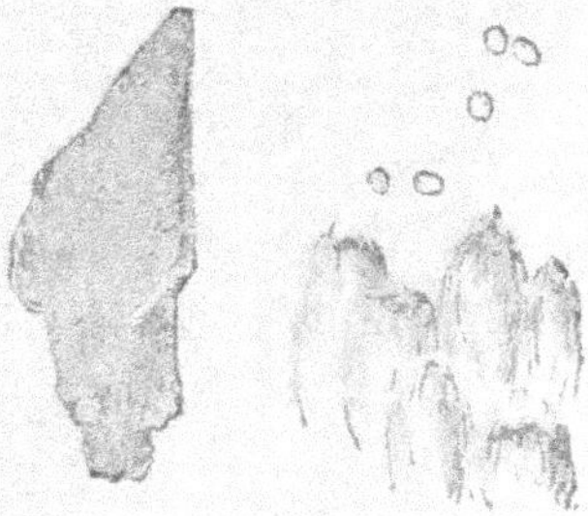

Fig. 86.

Cups tubular, cylindrical; mouth narrowed, inferior, or turned downwards. (*Fig.* 86.)

This genus has been placed amongst the Discomycetes from neglect of its mode of fruiting; the spores are produced as in *Cyphella.*—*C. E. B.*

956. Solenia candida. *Hoffm.* "White Solenia."

Scattered, cylindrical, smooth, whitish.—*Hoffm. Dent. Fl. t.* 8. *f.* 1. *Br. Bath. Trans.* 1870, *p.* 90. *Bisch. f.* 3391. *Kl. exs. no.* 922.

On rotten beech. Jan. Batheaston. [Low. Carolina.]

957. Solenia ochracea. *Hoffm.* "Ochrey Solenia."

Scattered, clavato-cylindrical, subtomentose, ochraceous.—*Hoffm. Dent. Fl. t.* 8. *f.* 2. *Sow. t.* 369. *f.* 3. *Br. Bath. Trans.* 1870, *p.* 90. *Bisch. f.* 3392. *Kl. exs.* ii. *no.* 232. *Fckl. exs. no.* 1144. *Peziza anomala, Eng. Fl.* v. *p.* 199. *Berk. exs. no.* 260. *Trichia faginea, Johnst. F. B.* ii. *p.* 191.

On dead trees. [Low. & Mid. Carolina.]

Spores subglobose, ·00025 × ·0003 in.

Order V. CLAVARIEI.

Hymenium scarcely distinct from the hymenophore, vertical, amphigenous, reaching to the very apex, even, or at length wrinkled. Never incrusting or coriaceous.—*Fr. Epicr. p.* 570.

Fleshy, frondose, and laciniate . . . . *Sparassis.*
Stem not distinct—
Fleshy, hymenium dry . . . . *Clavaria.*
Gelatinous, then horny; hymenium viscid . . . *Calocera.*
Stem more or less distinct—
Flaccid, stem thread-like, hymenium waxy. . . *Typhula.*
Waxy, then horny, cellular (sometimes fibrous) . *Pistillaria.*

Gen. **44.** **SPARASSIS,** Fr. S.M., p. 464.

Fig. 87.

Fleshy, frondose; branches laciniate.—*Fr. Epicr. p.* 570. (*Fig.* 87.)

Only one British species, which is rare.

958. **Sparassis crispa.** *Fr.* "Crisped Sparassis."

Very much branched, fragile, whitish; branches intricate; tips recurved, not zoned, serrate.—*Fr. Epicr. p.* 570. *Berk. Intell. Obs. no.* 25. *t.* 1. *Lenz. f.* 56. *Jacq. Misc.* ii. *t.* 14. *f.* 1. *Schæff. t.* 163. *Hogg. & Johnst. t.* 24. *Ann. N.H.* 1866. 1139*. *Bail. t.* 27 *Kl. exs. no.* 517.

Amongst heath. Sept. South-east Berkshire. Didlington, near Brandon. Esculent. [Up. Carolina.]

Pale ruddy yellow, forming a rounded mass attaining a diameter of 18 in. The laminæ rounded and leaf-like, though curled and folded, and variously lobed and laciniate, with a crest-like margin, and springing from a well-marked, thick, rooting stem, the greater part of which is sunk in the soil. Hymenium more or less uneven, and rather wrinkled or rough, with wart-like elevations. In decay the margin becomes soft, acquiring first a yellow, then a brownish tinge, and finally the whole forms a loathsome mass.—*M. J. B.*

Gen. **45.** **CLAVARIA,** L.

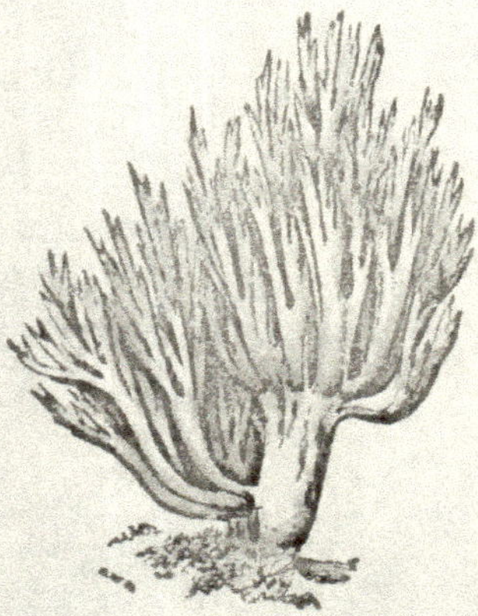

Fig. 88.

Fleshy, branched, or simple, without any stem of a distinct substance. Hymenium dry. — *Berk. Outl. p.* 278. (*Fig.* 88.)

Sect. 1. *Ramaria*—branched.

A. *Leucosporæ*—white spored.

959. Clavaria botrytis. *P.* "Red-tipped Clavaria."

Fragile, trunk thick, fleshy, unequal, very much branched; branches swollen, unequal, sub-rugose, tips red.—*Fr. Epicr. p.* 571. *Fl. Dan. t.* 1303. *Krombh. t.* 53.*f.* 1-3. *Schæff. t.* 176. *Ann. N.H. no.* 721. *Bisch. f.* 3390. *Badh.* i. *t.* 16. *f.* 2. ii. *t.* 5. *f.* 3. *Price, f.* 76. *Barla, t.* 40. *f.* 1-3. *Harz. t.* 67. *Corda. Ic.* v. *f.* 75.

In woods. Rare. Inverary. Bowood. [United States.]

960. Clavaria amethystina. *Bull.* "Amethyst Clavaria."

Fragile, very much branched, violet; branches round, even, obtuse.—*Fr. Epicr. p.* 571. *Bull. t.* 496. *f.* 2. *Holm.* i. *p.* 110. *Nees. f.* 151. *Schæff. t.* 172. *Cooke, B. F. t.* 17. *f.* 2. *Eng. Fl.* v. *p.* 174. *Vent. S. M. f.* 113.

In mossy places. Rare. Esculent.

Very variable in size. Sometimes 3 in. or more high, and very much branched, sometimes a few lines and nearly simple.—*M. J. B.*

961. Clavaria fastigiata. *D.C.* "Fastigiate Clavaria."

Tough, cæspitose, yellow, slender-stemmed, very much branched; branches short, divaricate; branchlets fastigiate.—*Fr. Epicr. p.* 571. *Bull. t.* 358. *f. D. F.* *Holms.* i. *p.* 90. *with fig. Fl. Dan. t.* 836, *f.* 2. *Pers. Com. t.* 4. *f.* 5. *Vaill. t.* 8. *f.* 4. *Ray. Syn. t.* 24. *f.* 5. *Clav. pratensis, Eng. Fl.* v. *p.* 174.

In pastures. Common. [Mid. Carolina.]

Sometimes the apices are yellow and at others brown. Slightly fragrant. Spores not truly white, pale buff, irregular; diameter ·00027 in.

962. Clavaria muscoides. *L.* "Forked Yellow Clavaria."

Rather tough, graceful, yellow, slender-stemmed, twice or thrice forked; branchlets lunate, acute.—*Fr. Epicr. p.* 571. *Fl. Dan. t.* 775. *f.* 3. *Holm.* i. *p.* 87. *with fig.* *Schæff. t.* 173. *Krombh. t.* 53. *f.* 22, 23. *Kl. exs. no.* 1123. *Bull. t.* 496. *f. O. Q.* *Clav. corniculata, Eng. Fl.* v. *p.* 174.

In pastures. [Mid. Carolina.]

Taller than the last, solitary, less branched, dry, very smooth, except the base, which is tomentose, bright yellow, resembling somewhat the yolk of an egg; branchlets elongated, attenuated, subcompressed, acute, or obtuse.—*Eng. Fl.*

963. Clavaria coralloides. *L.* "White coral Clavaria."

Rather fragile, white, hollow within; stem slightly thickened, repeatedly and irregularly branched; branchlets unequal, dilated upwards, very numerous, crowded, acute.—*Fr. Epicr. p.* 572. *Holms.* i. *p.* 113. *with fig. Sow. t.* 278. *Batt. t.* i. *A. Eng. Fl.* v. *p.* 173. *Krombh. t.* 53. *f.* 4. *Roq. t.* i. *f.* 1.

In woods.

964. Clavaria umbrina. *Berk.* "Umber Clavaria."

Pale umber, slightly branched; branches and branchlets cylindrical, obtuse, forked.—*Berk. Outl. p.* 279. *t.* 18. *f.* 4.

On mossy lawns. Coed Coch.

The habit is that of *C. fastigiata.* It has not, however, the slightest tinge of yellow.

965. Clavaria cinerea. *Bull.* "Cinereous Clavaria."

Fragile, stuffed, cinereous; stem thick, short, very much branched; branches and branchlets thickened, irregular, somewhat wrinkled, rather obtuse.—*Fr. Epicr. p.* 572. *Bull. t.* 354. *Grev. t.* 64. *Letell. t.* 708. *f.* 1. *Badh.* i. *t.* 15. *f.* 5. ii. *t.* 5. *f.* 5. *Cooke, B. F. t.* 17. *f.* 1. *Cooke exs. no.* 227. *C. coralloides* β. *cinerea, Eng. Fl.* v. *p.* 173.

In woods. Sept.

This appears to be a local species, very common in some places, and in others never to be found.

966. Clavaria cristata. *Holmsk.* "Crested Clavaria."

Tough, even, stuffed, white or dingy; branches dilated above, acute, incised, cristate.—*Fr. Epicr. p.* 572. *Holm. p.* 92. *with fig. Fl. Dan. t.* 1304. *f.* 2. *Grev. t.* 190. *Krombh. t.* 53. *f.* 13. *Pers. Com. t.* 4. *f.* 3. *var. Eng. Fl.* v. *p.* 174. *Bisch. f.* 3439. *Schnitz. Sturm. t.* 11.

In woods. [Mid. & Up. Carolina.]

Distinguished by its dilated, more or less crested, or fimbriated apices.—*M. J. B.* Spores oval, not truly white, with a suggestion of ochre, ·0002 × ·00027 in.

967. Clavaria rugosa. *Bull.* "Wrinkled Clavaria."

Tough, simple, or branched, thickened above, wrinkled, white or dingy; branches few, irregular, obtuse.—*Fr. Epicr. p.* 572. *Bull. t.* 448. *f.* 2. *Fl. Dan. t.* 1301. *Rabh. F. E. no.* 129. *Bolt.*

t. 115. *Sow. t.* 278. *Grev. t.* 328. *Krombh. t.* 54. *f.* 13-17. *Schæff. t.* 291. *var.* *Cooke, B. F. t.* 17. *f.* 3. *Berk. Outl. t.* 18. *f.* 3. *Eng. Fl.* v. *p.* 175. *Badh.* i. *t.* 15. *f.* 4. ii. *t.* 5. *f.* 6. *Cooke exs. no.* 228. *Smith. E. M. f.* 7. *Gard. Chron.* (1860) *p.* 217. *fig.* *Berk. exs. no.* 149.

In woods. Common. [Mid. Carolina.]

Generally simple, but occasionally furnished with a few short branchlets, which are incrassated, longitudinally rugose, and very obtuse.—*M. J. B.*

968. Clavaria Kunzei. *Fr.* "Kunze's Clavaria."

Rather fragile, very much branched from the slender cæspitose base, white; branches elongated, crowded, repeatedly forked, sub-fastigiate, even, equal; axils compressed.—*Fr. Epicr. p.* 573. *Bull. t.* 358. *f.* 1. *C.*

In woods. Rare. Sherwood Forest.

B. *Ochrosporæ*—spores yellowish or coloured.

969. Clavaria aurea. *Schæff.* "Golden Clavaria."

Trunk thick, elastic, pallid, divided into stout branches; branches straight, dichotomous, round, obtuse, numerous, somewhat toothed, yellow.—*Fr. Epicr. p.* 574. *Schæff. t.* 287. *Bull. t.* 222. *Ann. N. H. no.* 722. *Vent. S. M. f.* 112. *Krombh. t.* 53. *f.* 8.

In woods. Rare. Bristol. [United States.]

970. Clavaria formosa. *Pers.* "Beautiful Clavaria."

Trunk thick, elastic, whitish, much branched; branches elongated, orange-red; branchlets obtuse, yellowish.—*B. & Br. Ann. N. H.* (1865) *no.* 1031. *Pers. Ic. & Desc. t.* 3. *f.* 6. *Krombh. t.* 53. *f.* 37. *t.* 54. *f.* 21, 22. *Holms.* i. *no.* 13. *with fig.* *Batsch. f.* 48. *Harz. t.* 7. *f.* 6. *Barla. t.* 40. *f.* 4. *Cooke exs. no.* 230.

In woods, &c. Bathford Down. [United States.]

Spores buff, broadly fusiform, granulated, fleshy, brittle, cuts like *Fistulina.* Spores very large and handsome, elongated, oval, covered with papillæ, ·0006 × ·0003 in.

971. Clavaria abietina. *Schum.* "Fir-wood Clavaria."

Very much branched, ochraceous, trunk somewhat thickened, clothed with white down; branches straight, crowded, longitudinally wrinkled when dry; branchlets straight.—*Fr. Epicr.*

p. 574. *Grev. t.* 117. *Fl. Dan. t.* 2030. *f.* 2. *Eng. Fl.* v. *p.* 174. *Gard. Chron.* (1860) *p.* 871. *fig.*

In fir woods. Common. [Mid. Carolina.]

Easily known by its changing to green when bruised. Spores ochraceous. —*Eng. Fl.* Spores oval, greenish-yellow, ·00023 × ·00015 in. (*Fig.* 83.)

972. Clavaria flaccida. *Fr.* "Flaccid Clavaria."

Slender, very much branched, flaccid, ochraceous; trunk thin, smooth; branches crowded, unequal, converging, acute.—*Fr. Epicr. p.* 574. *Kl. exs. no.* 122. *Ann. N.H. no.* 154.

Amongst moss in woods. King's Cliffe.

Similar to *C. abietina*, but more delicate.

973. Clavaria crocea. *P.* "Saffron-yellow Clavaria."

Minute, slender, saffron-yellow; trunk naked, pallid; branches crowded, somewhat forked, as well as the similar branchlets.—*Fr. Epicr. p.* 575. *Pers. Ic. & Desc. t.* 11. *f.* 6. *Ann. N.H. no.* 367.

On the ground. Rare.

974. Clavaria grisea. *P.* "Grey Clavaria."

Firm; trunk thick, whitish; branches attenuated, somewhat wrinkled, obtuse, dingy-cinereous; branchlets unequal, obtuse, of the same colour.—*Fr. Epicr. p.* 575. *Berk. exs. no.* 150. *Krombh. t.* 53. *f.* 9-10. *Eng. Fl.* v. *p.* 173. *Barla. t.* 41. *f.* 1-2.

In woods. Rare. Appin. [Mid. Carolina.]

Known by its brownish spores.

975. Clavaria stricta. *P.* "Straight Clavaria."

Very much branched, pallid, brownish when bruised; stem somewhat thickened, branches and branchlets straight, even, adpressed, acute.—*Fr. Epicr. p.* 575. *Pers. Com. t.* 4. *f.* 1. *Fl. Dan. t.* 1302. *f.* 1. *Eng. Fl.* v. *p.* 174. *Kl. exs. no.* 1124.

In gardens. Rare. Kew. [United States.]

Stem rather slender, ascending, furnished at the base with rooting fibrillæ, firm, above 3 lines thick. Branches divided in an arcuate manner, then converging, opaque, generally pale yellow, brownish when bruised. Spores cinnamon.—*Fries.* Fragrant. Spores creamy-yellow, ·00015 × ·00024 in.

976. Clavaria crispula. *Fr.* "Flexuous Clavaria."

Very much branched, tan-coloured, then ochraceous; trunk

slender, villous, rooting; branches flexuose, multifid; branchlets of the same colour, divaricating.—*Fr. Epicr. p.* 576. *Bull. t.* 358. *f.* 1. *a, b. Ehr. Nat. Cur.* x. *t.* 14. *Ann. N. H. no.* 723. *Fl. Dan. t.* 2272. *f.* 1. *Bisch. f.* 3472.

At the base of trees. Rare. Woodnewton.

Spores creamy-yellow, ·00012 × ·00021 in.

Sect. 2. *Syncoryne*—simple, fasciculate at the base, cæspitose.

977. Clavaria purpurea. *Müll.* "Purple Clavaria."

Cæspitose, purple; clubs elongated, hollow, then compressed, simple, acute.—*Fr. Epicr. p.* 576. *Fl. Dan. t.* 837. *f.* 2. *Ann. N. H. no.* 368. *Berk. Outl. p.* 281. *C. rufa, Ann. N. H. no.* 155.

Amongst grass in pastures.

Usually of a dingy purple.

978. Clavaria rosea. *Fr.* "Rosy Clavaria."

Subfasciculate, fragile, roseate; clubs stuffed; tips at length yellowish, attenuated below, whitish.—*Fr. Epicr. p.* 577. *Sv. Bot. t.* 558. *Fr. Obs. t.* 5. *f.* 2. *Krombh. t.* 53. *f.* 21. *Eng. Fl.* v. *p.* 175.

In pastures, and amongst moss. Rare.

979. Clavaria fusiformis. *Sow.* "Spindle-shaped Clavaria."

(Fig. 9.)

Cæspitoso-connate, rather firm, yellow, soon hollow; clubs somewhat fusiform, simple, and toothed, even; base attenuated, of the same colour. —*Fr. Epicr. p.* 577. *Sow. t.* 224. *Bolt. t.* 110. *Eng. Fl.* v. *p.* 175. (*Fig.* 89.)

In woods. Common.

[United States.]

Yellow, smooth, about 3 in. high, many individuals collected into a fasciculate tuft, nearly erect, rather brittle, attenuated at either end; apex darker.—*Fries.*

980. Clavaria ceranoides. *Pers.* "Brown-tipped Clavaria."

Fasciculate, unequal, slightly divided above, yellow; apex brown.—*Pers. Syn. p.* 594. *Sow. t.* 235. *Eng. Fl.* v. *p.* 176.

In woods. Nov. Bagley Wood. Oxon.

Resembles in form some states of *C. rugosa*, but it appears to be very distinct.—*Eng. Fl.*

981. Clavaria inæqualis. *Müll.* "Unequal Clavaria."

Gregarious, subfasciculate, fragile, stuffed, yellow; clubs various, simple, or forked, contiguous below and of the same colour.—*Fr. Epicr. p.* 577. *Fl. Dan. t.* 873. (836?) *f.* 1. *Bull. t.* 264. *Sow. t.* 253. *lower figs. Huss.* i. *t.* 18. *Eng. Fl.* v. *p.* 176.

In woods amongst grass. Common. [United States.]

Somewhat tufted or gregarious, 1-3 in. high, of various sizes and forms, fragile, compressed, angular or channelled, often bifid, and variously cut and jagged at the apex, more or less ventricose in the centre, smooth, and mostly yellow, though occasionally whitish.—*Grev.* Spores white, ·00047 × ·00021 in.

982. Clavaria argillacea. *Fr.* "Clay-coloured Clavaria."

Fasciculate, fragile, pallid clay colour; clubs simple, various; stem yellow, shining.—*Fr. Epicr. p.* 577. *Fr. Obs. t.* 5. *f.* 3. *Schm. t.* 15. *Fl. Dan. t.* 1852. *f.* 2. *t.* 1966. *f.* 2. *Pers. Com. t.* 1. *f.* 4. *Kl. exs. no.* 1218. *Ann. N. H. no.* 370. *Harz. t.* 7. *f. a. C. flavipes, Ann. N. H. no.* 83.

In heathy ground. [Mid. Carolina.]

There is a variety with a white stem. The plant, moreover, is either dilated or cylindrical. The stem in this species is more distinct from the pileus than is consistent with the generic character.—*M. J. B.*

983. Clavaria tenuipes. *B. & Br.* "Slender stemmed Clavaria."

(Fig. 90.)

Small, gregarious, club inflated, wrinkled, pallid clay-colour; stem slender, flexuose, somewhat distinct from the club.—*B. & Br. Ann. N. H. no.* 369. *Ser.* ii. *vol.* ii. *t.* 9. *f.* 2.

On bare, heathy ground. Nov. Sherwood Forest. (*Fig.* 90.)

Not exceeding an inch in height. Head swollen, obovate, rugose, pale clay-coloured, about ½ in. high, rarely confluent with the stem, which is quite smooth, flexuous, and very slender.—*M. J. B.*

984. **Clavaria vermiculata.** *Scop.* "White-tufted Clavaria."

Cæspitose, fragile, white; clubs stuffed, simple, cylindrical, subulate.—*Fr. Epicr. p.* 577. *Fl. Dan. t.* 1966. *f.* 1. *t.* 775. *f.* 2. *Mich. t.* 87. *f.* 12. *Cooke, B. F. t.* 17. *f.* 4. *Eng. Fl. p.* 176. *Smith. E. M. f.* 4.

On lawns and short pastures. Common. [Mid. Carolina.]

"Looks like a little bundle of candles."

985. **Clavaria fragilis.** *Holmsk.* "Brittle Clavaria."

Fasciculate, very fragile; clubs hollow, rather obtuse, variable, attenuated below and white.—*Fr. Epicr. p.* 578. *Holms.* i. *p.* 7. *with fig. Bull. t.* 463. *f.* 1. *Sow. t.* 90. 232. *Mich. t.* 87. *f. b.* 10. 13. *Vaill. t.* 7. *f.* 5. *Fl. Dan. t.* 775. *f.* 2. *t.* 1783. *Bolt. t.* 111. *Eng. Fl.* v. *p.* 176. *Barla. t.* 41. *f.* 14-16. *Cooke exs. no.* 309.

In meadows, gardens, &c. [United States.]

Extremely brittle, occasionally yellow. Gregarious, subcæspitose, 1-3 in. high, sometimes forked, stuffed when young, round, straight, at length hollow, compressed, twisted, often rugose, attenuated, paler below, without a distinct stem; apex at length yellowish.—*Fries.*

986. **Clavaria fumosa.** *P.* "Smoky Clavaria."

Fasciculate, fistulose, fragile, smoky-coloured; clubs even, straight, subcompressed.—*Pers. Comm. p.* 76. *Fr. Epicr. p.* 578. *Krombh. t.* 53, *f.* 18. *Br. Bath. Trans.* 1860, *p.* 91. *Seem. Journ. Bot.* vii. *p.* 252.

In grassy places. Sept. Somerset, &c. [Mid. Carolina.]

Sect. 3. *Holocoryne*—simple, distinct at the base.

987. **Clavaria pistillaris.** *L.* "Large-clubbed Clavaria."

Simple, large, stuffed, fleshy, everywhere smooth, obovate-clavate, obtuse, yellow, then rufous.—*Fr. Epicr. p.* 578. *Huss.* i. *t.* 62. *Bull. t.* 244. *Sow. t.* 277. *Fl. Dan. t.* 1255. *Holms. p.* 12, *with fig. Sv. Bot. t.* 564, *f.* 1-2. *Krombh. t.* 54, *f.* 1-11. *Eng. Fl.* v. *p.* 175. *Ann. N. H. no.* 82. *Corda. Sturm. t.* 58. *Vent. S. M. f.* 114, 115. *Vent. t.* 41, *f.* 1, 3. *Fl. Boruss. t.* 395? *Bisch. f.* 3383.

In woods. Kent. King's Cliffe. [Mid. Carolina.]

Plant 6-12 in. high, varying somewhat in form, dull orange, dingy brown in decay.—*M. J. B.* Spores white, ·00043 × ·00023 in.

988. **Clavaria contorta.** *Fr.* "Contorted Clavaria."

Simple, bursting through the bark, stuffed, between spongy and fleshy, somewhat twisted, rugose, obtuse, pruinose, watery yellow.—*Fr. Epicr. p.* 579. *Holms. p.* 29, *with fig. Fl. Dan. t.* 1852, *f.* 1. *Ann. N.H. no.* 291. *Kl. exs. no.* 1125.

On fallen branches. Rare. [Up. Carolina.]

The erumpent habit easily distinguishes this curious species.—*M. J. B.*

989. **Clavaria Ardenia.** *Sow.* "Lady Arden's Clavaria."

Simple, very long, thickened upwards, hollow, apex obtuse and excavated, ferruginous, then bright brown, base tomentose, not rooting.—*Fr. Epicr. p.* 579. *Sow. t.* 215. *Eng. Fl.* v. *p.* 175.

On fallen branches. Rare.

Above a span high, flexuous below, gradually incrassated upwards, smooth, opaque, apex acute in the young plant, then obtuse and bursting.—*Fries.* Sometimes rooting amongst leaves, and attaining a height of 9 in.; hollow; the whole plant being a thin, inflated skin. Spores very large, white, oval, with an apiculus at one end, ·0006 × ·00035 in.

990. **Clavaria juncea.** *Fr.* "Thread-like Clavaria."

Gregarious, slender, filiform, flaccid, nearly equal, fistulose, acute, pallid, then reddish-brown, base creeping and fibrillose. —*Fr. Epicr. p.* 579. *Desm. exs. no.* 310. *Fl. Dan. t.* 1257. *Mich. t.* 87, *f.* 7. *Bull. t.* 463, *f. H. Ann. N.H. no.* 52.

Amongst leaves in woods.

991. **Clavaria acuta.** *Sow.* "Acute Clavaria."

Quite simple, straight, white, clubs distinct, acuminate, pruinose; stem cylindrical, equal.—*Fr. Epicr. p.* 580. *Sow. t.* 333. *Eng. Fl.* v. *p.* 177.

On soil in garden pots. [Low. Carolina.]

Solitary. Very variable in size, from a few lines to an inch or more in length.

992. **Clavaria uncialis.** *Grev.* "Greville's Clavaria."

Quite simple, stuffed, tough, straight, obtuse, smooth, contiguous below, attenuated.—*Fr. Epicr. p.* 580. *Grev. t.* 98. *Eng. Fl.* v. *p.* 177. *Berk. exs. no.* 297.

On dead stems of *Umbelliferæ.*

Gen. 46. **CALOCERA**, Fr.

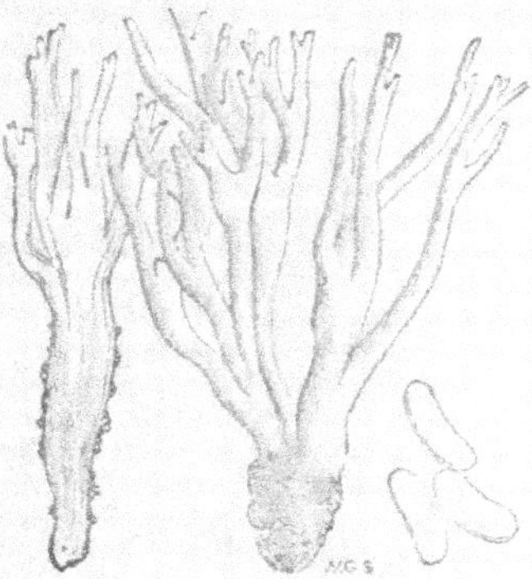

Fig. 91.

Gelatinous; sub-cartilaginous when moist, horny when dry; hymenium viscid. (*Fig.* 91.)

* Branched.

993. Calocera viscosa. *Fr.* "Clammy Calocera."

Branched, tough, rooting, even, linear, egg-yellow, branches straight, repeatedly dichotomous.—*Fr. Epicr. p.* 581. *Pers. Com. t.* 1, *f.* 5. *Schæff. t.* 174. *Eng. Fl.* v. *p.* 177. *Bail. t.* 27. *Kl. exs. no.* 131. *Corda. Icon.* v. *f.* 74.

On stumps in fir woods. [Mid. Carolina.]

Generally cæspitose, 1 in. or more high, root long, pale, branches round or compressed, equal, but little divided, known by its beautiful golden hue. —*Fries.* Spores white. (*Fig.* 91.)

** Cæspitose.

994. Calocera tuberosa. *Fr.* "Tuberous Calocera."

Cæspitose, simple, tough, even, linear, yellowish; base tuberous and rooting.—*Fr. Epicr. p.* 581. *Sow. t.* 199. *Eng. Fl.* v. *p.* 177.

On stumps.

Not found since the time of Sowerby. Root a thick, strigose, subglobose tuber, giving out two or three simple linear subacute receptacles from the same base.—*M. J. B.*

995. Calocera cornea. *Fr.* "Horny Calocera."

Cæspitose, rooting, even, viscid, orange-yellow; clubs short, subulate, connate at the base.—*Fr. Epicr. p.* 581. *Desm. exs. no.* 73. *Batsch. f.* 161. *Fl. Dan. t.* 1305, *f.* 2. *Sow. t.* 40. *Bull. t.* 463. *f.* 4. *Eng. Fl.* v. *p.* 178. *Bisch. f.* 3385.

On stumps, especially oak. Common. [United States.]

Springing from cracks; when fresh soft, when dry hard and horny.—*M. J. B.*

*** Simple, solitary.

996. Calocera stricta. *Fr.* "Straight Calocera."

Simple, solitary, elongated; base blunt, linear, yellow, even when dry.—*Fr. Epicr. p.* 581. *B. & Br. Ann. N. H.* (1865), *no.* 1032. *Scop. Ann.* iv. *t.* 1, *f.* 50. *Kl. exs. no.* 1121.

On ash. Oct. Belvoir Castle.

Differs from *C. cornea* in its scattered mode of growth and slender habit. Occasionally two individuals grow from the same spot, but they are never broadly confluent at the base, as in the common species.—*M. J. B.*

997. Calocera striata. *Fr.* "Striate Calocera."

Simple, solitary, tough, lanceolate, acute, yellow, striate when dry.—*Fr. Epicr. p.* 582. *Hoffm. Fl.* 9. *t.* 7, *f.* 1. *B. & Br. Ann. N.H.* (1866), *no.* 1140. *Bisch. f.* 3386.

On a prostrate trunk. Mar. Batheaston.

Very rare everywhere. Spores ·0003 × ·00025 in.

998. Calocera glossoides. *Fr.* "Soft Calocera."

Simple, solitary, somewhat tremellose, yellow; clubs incrassated, obtuse, compressed; stem round.—*Fr. Epicr. p.* 582. *Ann. N.H. no.* 371.

On decayed oak stumps. Rare. Leigh Wood, Bristol.

Composed of erect forked flocci. Spores oblong, oblique, somewhat incurved, attached by a short pedicle.—*B. & Br.*

Gen. 47. TYPHULA, Fr.

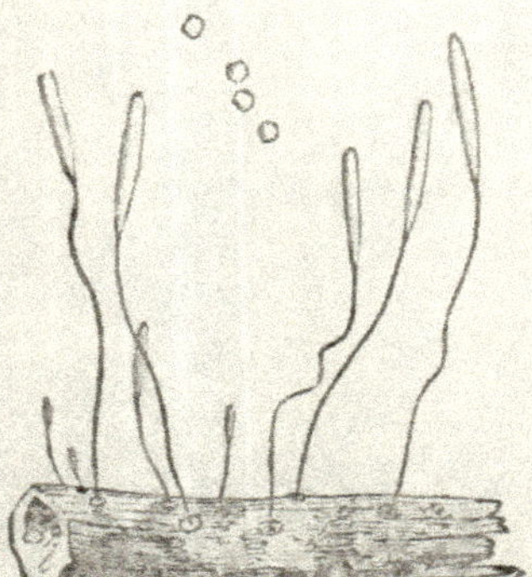

Fig. 92.

Stem filiform, flaccid; club cylindrical, perfectly distinct; hymenium thin, waxy. (*Fig.* 92.)

* With tubercle at the base.

999. Typhula erythropus. *Fr.* "Red-stemmed Typhula."

Simple. Club cylindrical, smooth, white; stem nearly straight, dark red, inclining to black.—*Fr. Epicr. p.* 585. *Fl. Dan. t.* 2030, *f.* 1. *Desm. exs. no.* 263. *Bolt. t.* 112. *Grev. t.* 43. *Berk. exs. no.* 24. *Eng. Fl.* v. *p.* 181. *Schnitz. Sturm. t.* 12. *Bail. t.* 27.

On dead stems of herbaceous plants. Common.

Often growing on some species of *Sclerotium*; 3 lines 1 in. high; stem often flexuous.—*M. J. B.* (*Fig.* 92.)

1000. Typhula gyrans. *Fr.* "Nodding Typhula."

Simple, white. Club cylindrical, smooth; stem pubescent, pellucid.—*Fr. S.M.* 494. *Epicr. p.* 585. *Fckl. exs. no.* 1290. *Batsch. f.* 164. *Br. Bath. Trans.* 1870, *p.* 92.

On straw, &c. [Mid. Carolina.]

1001. Typhula incarnata. *Fr.* "Flesh-coloured Typhula."

Simple. Club cylindrical, elongated, smooth, flesh-coloured, attenuated into the subpilose continuous stem.—*Fr. Epicr. p.* 585. *Willd. Ber. t.* 7, *f.* 17. *Kl. exs. no.* 1313. *Clavaria phacorrhiza, Grev. S.C. Fl. t.* 93.

On dead herbaceous plants.

1002. Typhula phacorrhiza. *Fr.* "Bulb-rooted Typhula."

Simple; club cylindrical, smooth, pallid; stem flexuose, smooth, brownish.—*Fr. Epicr. p.* 585. *Berk. exs. no.* 23. *Sow. t.* 233. *Eng. Fl.* v. *p.* 180 (*partly*).

On dead herbaceous plants, &c.

Attached to *Sclerotium complanatum* and *S. scutellatum.* Often hairy at the base, drawn out and distorted from peculiar circumstances of situation.

1003. Typhula muscicola. *Fr.* "Moss Typhula."

Simple, subfiliform, smooth, slightly incrassated upwards, white; stem not distinct.—*Fr. Epicr. p.* 585. *Pers. Obs.* ii. *t.* 3. *f.* 2. *Nees. f.* 154. *Bisch. f.* 3388.

On the larger mosses.

Perhaps more properly a *Pistillaria.* Sometimes not a line high.

** Without tubercle at the base.

1004. **Typhula Grevillei.** *Fr.* "Greville's Typhula."

Simple, white, club incrassated, obtuse; stem capillary, pilose.—*Fr. Epicr. p.* 585. *Grev. t.* 49. *Bisch. f.* 3382. *Sturm.* iii. 3. *t.* 25. *T. gyrans, Berk. exs. no.* 66, 151. *Eng. Fl.* v. *p.* 180.

On dead leaves. [Low. Carolina.]

1005. **Typhula filiformis.** *Fr.* "Thread-like Typhula."

Club incrassated, whitish; stem decumbent, somewhat branched, bright brown.—*Fr. Epicr. p.* 586. *Bull. t.* 448, *f.* 1. *Sow. t.* 387, *f.* 4. *Eng. Fl.* v. *p.* 181.

Amongst dead leaves.

Decumbent, creeping, free, subflexuous brown, cinereous brown, or brick-red.—*Eng. Fl.*

1006. **Typhula gracilis.** *B. & Desm.* "Slender Typhula."

Club simple or forked, pallid, acute; stem short, distinct.—*Berk. Outl. p.* 285. *Ann. N.H. no.* 84, *t.* 8, *f.* 1.

On putrid leaves.

Head rough with spores and little prominent bristles. Very near to *Isaria.* Pallid, one line or more high, simple or forked, rugged with the fruit-bearing cells, which are frosted with the spores, and interspersed sometimes with short bristles, of which some of the upper ones support a small spore; tips often acuminate, and then nearly barren. Stem short, smooth, or bristly. Spores elliptic, having a sparkling appearance under a lens.—*M. J. B.*

Gen. **48.** **PISTILLARIA,** Fr.

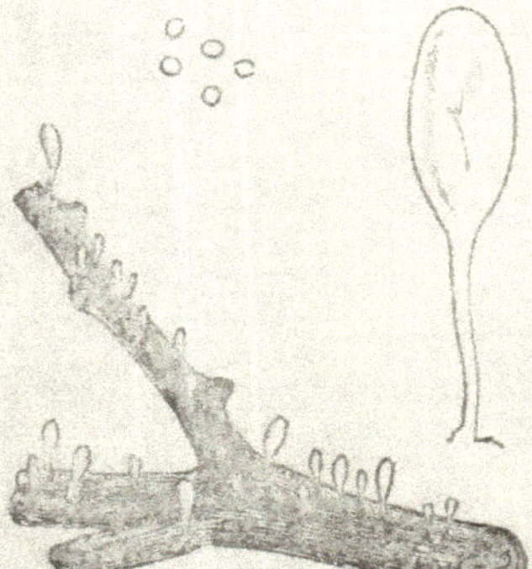

Fig. 93.

Club shaped, waxy, then horny. Structure cellular. (*Fig.* 93.)

1007. Pistillaria micans. *Fr.* "Glistening Pistillaria."

Obovate, obtuse, rose coloured; stem short, attenuated, whitish. —*Fr. Epicr. p.* 587. *Kl. exs. no.* 342. *Hoffm. Germ. t.* 7, *f.* 2. *Ehr. Ber. t.* 3, *f.* 2. *Eng. Fl.* v. *p.* 181. *Bisch. f.* 3438.

On dead thistles. Rare. Cambridge. [Mid. Carolina.]

Very minute, not a line high.

1008. Pistillaria culmigena. *Mont.* "Grass-stem Pistillaria."

Ovato-clavate, obtuse, pellucid, hyaline; stem distinct, very short.—*Fr. Epicr. p.* 587. *Mont. Ann. Sc. Nat.* 1836, *no.* 75, *t.* 12, *f.* 2. *Ann. N. H. no.* 85. *Berk. exs. no.* 152.

On stalks of grass. Jan.

1009. Pistillaria quisquilaris. *Fr* "Fern-stem Pistillaria."

Incrassated above, subcompressed, whitish, soft when recent, attenuated at the base, substipitate.—*Fr. Epicr. p.* 586. *Sow. t.* 334, *f.* 1. *Kl. exs. no.* 1312. *Berk. exs. no.* 25. *Eng. Fl.* v. *p.* 182.

On fern stems. Common.

Gregarious, 3-4 lines high, apex incrassated, sometimes flattened or bifid, quite even and smooth.—*Fries.* Often attached to a *Sclerotium.* (*Fig.* 93.)

1010. Pistillaria puberula. *Berk.* "Fibrous Pistillaria."

Obovate, ventricose, white; stem short, distinct, pellucid, tomentose.—*Berk. Outl. p.* 286. *Sow. t.* 334, *f.* 2. *P. ovata, Fr. Epicr. p.* 587. *Eng. Fl.* v. *p.* 181.

On dead *Pteris.* Rare. King's Cliffe.

Very minute, scarcely one line high; stem attenuated upwards, composed of many confluent fibres; receptacle obovate, but not broadly so.—*M. J. B.*

1011. Pistillaria pusilla. *Fr.* "Little Pistillaria."

Small, smooth, even, linear, white; stem scarcely distinct.—*Fr. Epicr. p.* 587. *Pers. Com. t.* 3, *f.* 6. *Eng. Fl.* v. *p.* 182.

On *Equisetum*, &c. Weymouth.

Slightly thickened upwards, not 1 line high, nodding when dry.—*M. J. B.*

1012. Pistillaria furcata. *Smith.* "Forked Pistillaria."

Clubs waxy, then tough, white or yellowish, compressed, broad at the apex, attenuated downwards, generally furcate and cæspitose.—*W. G. Smith, in litt.*

In greenhouses.

Clubs $1\frac{1}{4}$ in. high.

Order VI. TREMELLINI.

Whole plant gelatinous, with the exception occasionally of the nucleus. Sporophores large, simple or divided. Spicules elongated into threads.—*Berk. Outl. p.* 286.

Immarginate. Hymenium universal	*Tremella.*
Margined. Hymenium superior	*Exidia.*
Cup-shaped. Hymenium wrinkled	*Hirneola.*
Nucleus solid. Hymenium universal	*Næmatelia.*
Homogeneous. Sporophores clavate, bifurcate . . .	*Dacrymyces.*
Inflated. Hymenium smooth, then collapsed	*Apyrenium.*
Effused, thin, maculæform	*Hymenula.*
Patellæform. Hymenium discoid	*Ditiola.*

Gen. 49. **TREMELLA,** Fr.

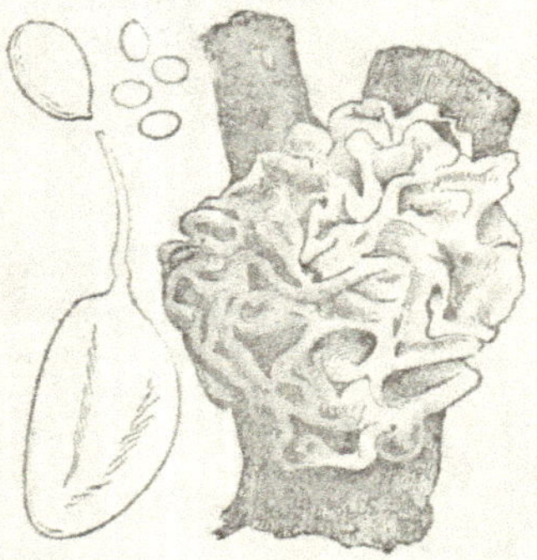

Fig. 94.

Gelatinous, tremulous, immarginate. Hymenium not papillate, surrounding the whole of the fungus.—*Berk. Outl. p.* 286. (*Fig.* 94.)

Sect. 1. *Mesenteriformes.*

1013. Tremella fimbriata. *Pers.* "Fringed Tremella."

Cæspitose, erect, corrugated, blackish-olive; lobes flaccid; margin incised, undulato-fimbriate.—*Fr. Epicr. p.* 588. *Bull. t.* 272. *Hoffm. t.* 7, *f.* 1. *Eng. Fl.* v. *p.* 215. *Berk. Outl. p.* 286.

On dead branches. Rare.

Of a soft, gelatinous consistence, almost watery within.

1014. Tremella frondosa. *Fr.* "Large pale Tremella."

Cæspitose; very large, even, pallid-yellow; base plicate; lobes gyroso-undulate.—*Fr. Epicr. p.* 588. *Bull. t.* 499, *f. T. Ann. N.H. no.* 810. *Berk. Outl. p.* 287.

At the base of living trees. Rare. Wothorpe.

When fresh of a peculiar pale pinkish-yellow, often attaining a very large size.

1015. **Tremella foliacea.** *P.* "Foliaceous Tremella."

Cæspitose, flaccid, even, diaphanous, undulated, flesh coloured cinnamon; base plicate; spores subelliptic.—*Bull. t.* 406, *f. A. a. Berk. Outl. p.* 287. *T. ferruginea, Eng. Bot.* 2*nd Ed. t.* 1452. *Eng. Fl.* v. *p.* 215. *Ann. N.H. no.* 13.

On old stumps. [United States.]

Very variable in colour, sometimes deep red-brown and sometimes violet. "Pliable and tender, becoming thin, shrivelled and shapeless when dry, reviving, though imperfectly, on the re-application of moisture; segments obtuse, lobed, and waved; surface finely pubescent or granulated; the granulations pale, giving the plant a velvet-like gloss, with brown, irregular specks, perhaps of a fructification among them."—*Eng. Bot.*

1016. **Tremella lutescens.** *Fr.* "Yellowish Tremella."

Cæspitose, tremulous, undulato-gyrose, white, then yellowish; lobes crowded, entire.—*Fr. Epicr. p.* 588. *Pers. Ic. & Desc. t.* 8, *f.* 9. *Bull. t.* 406, *C. D. t.* 499, *f. U. V. Berk. Outl. p.* 287. *Price. f.* 44. *Bisch. f.* 3403. *Bail. t.* 22.

On old stumps. [United States.]

Sect. 2. *Cerebrinæ.*

1017. **Tremella mesenterica.** *Retz.* "Orange Tremella."

Expanded, ascending, somewhat tough, plicato-undulate, smooth, orange.—*Fr. Epicr. p.* 588. *Jacq. Misc.* i. *t.* 13. *Schæff. t.* 168. *Eng. Bot.* 2*nd Ed. t.* 709. *Bull. t.* 174. *Huss.* i. *t.* 27. *Ann. Sc. Nat.* (1853), xix. *t.* 11. *Eng. Fl.* v. *p.* 216. *Berk. Outl. p.* 287. *Gard. Chron.* (1860), *p.* 953, *fig. Price, f.* 26. *Bot. Zeit.* 1859, *t.* 11, *f.* 22.

On sticks in woods, &c. Common. [United States.]

Varying considerably in size and form, sometimes quite flat and thin, but generally ascending and strongly lobed and plicate; when full grown consisting of branched, easily discernible filaments, surrounded by a dense stratum of spores. *(Fig.* 94.*)*

1018. **Tremella vesicaria.** *Bull.* "Bladdery Tremella."

Firm, bladdery, much waved and wrinkled, erect, pallid, very viscid within; sporophores globose; spores broad, oblong.—*Bull. t.* 427, *f.* 3. *Berk. Outl. p.* 287. *Eng. Bot. Ed.* ii. *t.* 2451. *Ann. N.H. no.* 724.

On the ground. Rare. [Pennsylvania.]

Spores ·0004 × ·00025 in.

1019. Tremella moriformis. *Berk.* "Mulberry Tremella."

Conglobated, sinuated, mulberry-black, opaque, firm.—*Berk. Outl. p.* 287. *Eng. Bot. Ed.* ii. *t.* 2451. *Price, f.* 21? *Dacrymyces moriformis. Fr. Epicr. p.* 592. *Eng. Fl.* v. *p.* 219.

On the ground. Rare. [Low. Carolina.]

Sessile in roundish or oblong tumid, sinuous masses of various size, not unlike mulberries in appearance, except being coal black. Internally of a deep rich purple, substance fleshy, attached by strong central roots. When dried between paper a violet stain is communicated to whatever the plant touches.—*Smith.*

1020. Tremella albida. *Hud.* "Whitish Tremella."

Expanded, tough, undulated, even, or somewhat gyrose, pruinose, whitish, at length brownish.—*Fr. Epicr. p.* 589. *Eng. Bot. t.* 2117. *Bull. t.* 386, *f.* A. *Eng. Fl.* v. *p.* 216. *Berk. Outl. p.* 287. *Price, f.* 50. *Bon. t.* 12, *f.* 246.

On dead branches. Common. [United States.]

It bursts through cracks in the bark, and then spreads itself in horizontal or clustered, rounded obtuse, scalloped masses, white, semi-pellucid, extremely gelatinous, and tender when young, afterwards turning yellowish.—*Smith.*

1021. Tremella intumescens. *Sow.* "Contorted Tremella."

Subcæspitose, rounded or conglomerate, soft, brown, when dry blackish-brown, obsoletely punctuate, somewhat tortuous and lobed.—*Fr. Epicr. p.* 589. *Berk. Outl. p.* 288. *Eng. Bot. Ed.* ii. *t.* 1870. *Eng. Fl.* v. *p.* 217.

On trunks of fallen trees. Apethorpe. [United States.]

In perfection in very wet weather only, when it forms numerous soft and pulpy clusters, twisted and tumid, like the intestines of some animal, of a darkish dull brown, but with a shining surface, obscurely dotted; inside paler and almost white, except that when cut longitudinally brown vertical streaks are discernible near the surface.—*Smith.*

1022. Tremella indecorata. *Somm.* "Dingy Tremella."

Sessile, rounded, moist, convex, plicate, opaque, black-brown, dingy.—*Fr. Epicr. p.* 589. *Kl. exs. no.* 822. *Ann. N.H. no.* 725, 810*. *Berk. Outl. p.* 283.

On willows. Mossburnford.

Dark pitchy brown when dry, dirty cinereous when swollen with moisture. —*M. J. B.*

Sect. 3. *Coryne*—erect, sub-clavate, subviscid.

1023. Tremella clavata. *P.* "Clavate Tremella."

Solitary, simple, incrassated, reddish flesh-colour, blackish at the base.—*Fr. Epicr. p.* 589. *Pers. Ic. Pict. t.* 10, *f.* 1. *Eng. Fl.* v. *p.* 217. *Berk. Outl. p.* 288.

On stumps. Rare. Appin.

About 1 in. high, 2 lines broad, blackish below, and slightly twisted.—*M. J. B.*

Tremella sarcoides. *Sm.* See *Bulgaria sarcoides*, of which it is a condition.

1024. Tremella tubercularia. *Berk.* "Horny Tremella."

Erumpent; stem short, cylindrical, head pileate, dirty white, nearly black when dry.—*Berk. Outl. p.* 288. *Tubercularia albida, Eng. Fl.* v. *p.* 354. *Coryne turbinata, Ann. N. H. no.* 165.

On fallen branches. Oct.

Left upon the wood when the bark falls off, when dry it has a peculiar, semi-transparent, horny appearance.

Sect. 4. *Phyllopta*—cartilaginous, depressed, or effused.

1025. Tremella torta. *Willd.* "Twisted Tremella."

Minute, round, depressed, gyroso-tuberculate, yellow or orange.—*Berk. Outl. p.* 288. *Ann. N. H. no.* 372.

On decorticated oak. Common.

Two or three lines across.

1026. Tremella versicolor. *B. & Br.* "Parasitic Tremella."

Minute, orbicular, orange, at length brown.—*Ann. Nat. Hist. ser.* ii. *vol.* xiii. *p.* 406, *no.* 726. *Berk. Outl. p.* 288.

On *Corticium nudum.* Feb.

Forming minute orange, tear-like, convex spots, on the hymenium of the *Corticium*, paler when young, at length assuming a rufous tinge. In young plants the delicate hyaline threads are terminated by four globules, which ultimately branch, forming moniliform threads.—*B. & Br.*

1027. Tremella viscosa. *P.* "Viscid Tremella."

Effused, resupinate, hyaline, at first white, undulated.—*Pers. Obs.* ii. *p.* 18. *Berk. Outl. p.* 288. *Ann. Nat. Hist. ser.* ii. *vol.* xiii.

t. 15, *f.* 4. *Corticium viscosum, Fr. Thelephora viscosa, Eng. Fl.* v. *p.* 171.

On dead wood.

We find globose sporophores, bearing three or four elongated sterigmata, and oblong, obliquely attached spores, which sometimes contain one or two nuclei.—*B. & Br.*

1028. **Tremella epigæa.** *B. & Br.* "Ground Tremella."

Effused, gelatinous, gyroso-plicate, white.—*Ann. Nat. Hist. ser.* ii. *vol.* 2, *p.* 266, *no.* 373. *t.* 9, *f.* 3. *Berk. Outl. p.* 289.

On the ground. Rare. Leigh wood, Bristol.

Spreading over the naked soil, on which it forms a thin white stratum, the surface of which is gyroso-plicate, and dusted with the white spores; the inner substance is very soft and gelatinous.—*M. J. B.*

Gen. 50. EXIDIA, Fr.

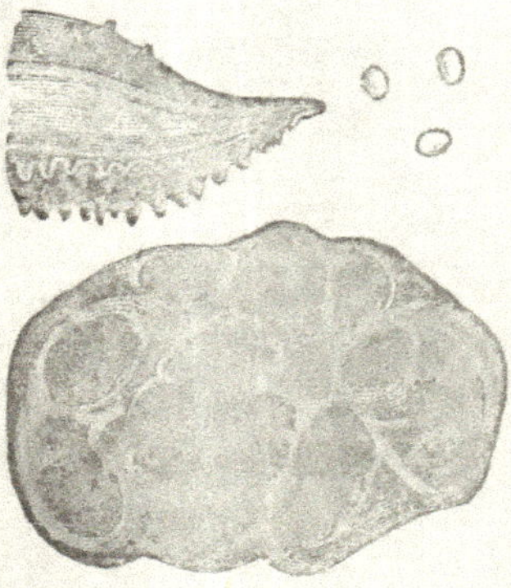

Fig. 95.

Tremulous, margined, fertile above and granular, barren below. —*Berk. Outl. p.* 289. *(Fig.* 95.*)*

1029. **Exidia recisa.** *Fr.* "Truncate Exidia."

Fig. 96.

Very soft, truncate, plane, costate, sub-repand, amber-brown, punctato-scabrous beneath; stem very short, excentric, oblique.—*Fr. Epicr. p.* 590. *Sturm. t.* 13. *Eng. Bot. Ed.* ii. *t.* 1819. *Eng. Fl.* v. *p.* 218. *Berk. Outl. p.* 289. *Bisch. f.* 3399. *Kl. exs. no.* 330.

On dead branches of willows. Common. [Low. Carolina.]

About 1 in. broad; spores oblong, obtuse, curved. *(Fig.* 96.*)*

1030. Exidia glandulosa. *Fr.* "Witches' Butter Exidia."

Effused, flattened, thick, undulated, blackish, spiculose with conical papillæ, cinereous beneath, and somewhat tomentose.—*Fr. Epicr. p.* 591. *Bull. t.* 420, *f.* 1. *Fl. Dan. t.* 884. *Eng. Bot. Ed.* ii. *t.* 2448, 2452. *Huss.* i. *t.* 42. *Eng. Fl.* v. *p.* 218. *Berk. Outl. p.* 289.

On dead branches of oak. Common. [United States.]

Varying in colour from whitish to brown, and deep cinereous, at length black; generally somewhat turbinate, slightly plicate below, much wrinkled above, sometimes thin; substance tender within, firmer towards the hymenium, composed of gelatine interlaced with very slender branched filaments, covered with oblong, obtuse, curved spores. Beneath rough like crape, with minute parallel papillæ.—*M. J. B.* (*Fig.* 95.)

1031. Exidia saccharina. *Fr.* "Larch Exidia."

Tuberculose, gyroso-undulate, thick, tawny-cinnamon, papillæ rare and scattered.—*Fr. Epicr. p.* 591. *Ann. N.H. no.* 811. *Berk. Outl. p.* 289. *Kl. exs. no.* 1611.

On larch. Rare. Mossburnford.

Gen. **51.** **HIRNEOLA**, Fr.

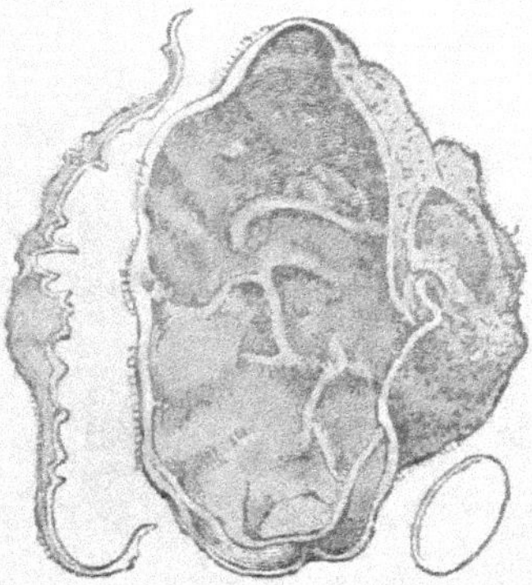

Fig. 97.

Gelatinous, cup-shaped, horny when dry; hymenium often more or less wrinkled; interstices even, without papillæ; outer surface velvety.—*Berk. Outl. p.* 289. (*Fig.* 97.)

1032. Hirneola Auricula-Judae. *Berk.* "Jew's-ear Hirneola."

Thin, concave, flexuose, blackish, venoso-plicate everywhere, tomentose beneath, cinereous-olive.—*Berk. Outl. p.* 289, *t.* 18, *f.* 7. *Huss.* i. *t.* 53. *Exidia Auricula Judae, Fr. Epicr. p.* 590. *Nees. Pl. Off. with fig. Bolt. t.* 107, *Tremella. Bull. t.* 427, *f.* 2. *Eng. Bot. Ed.* ii. *t.* 2147. *Batt. t.* 3, *f.* T. *Eng. Fl.* v. *p.* 217. *Corda. Sturm. t.* 6. *Harz. t.* 45.

On elder and elm. Common. [United States.]

1-3 in. or more broad; upper substance corrugated, the plaits branching from the middle part, where they are strongest, and somewhat convoluted, so as to give an idea of a human ear; when the plant grows on a perpendicular stump or tree it turns upwards.—*Smith.* (*Fig.* 97.)

Gen. 52. NÆMATELIA, Fr.

Fig. 98.

Nucleus solid, heterogeneous, covered with a gelatinous stratum, which is everywhere clothed with the hymenium.—*Berk. Outl. p.* 290. (*Fig.* 98.)

1033. Næmatelia encephala. *Fr.* "Flesh-coloured Nematelia."

Subsessile, pulvinate, plicato-rugose, pallid flesh colour, at length brownish.—*Fr. Epicr. p.* 591. *Willd. Bot. Mag.* i. *t.* 4, *f.* 14. *Eng. Fl.* v. *p.* 219. *Ann. N.H. no.* 292. *Berk. Outl. p.* 290. *Berk. exs. no.* 291.

On pine rails. Rare. Loch Lomond, Wales.
[Mid. & Up. Carolina.]

Solitary or clustered, more or less pulvinate; 4-6 lines broad and thick, firm, when fresh of a dead flesh colour, when dry reddish-brown; nucleus large, hard, white; base stem-like.—*Fries.* (*Fig.* 98.)

1034. Næmatelia nucleata. *Fr.* "Nucleate Næmatelia."

Sessile, flat, somewhat gyrose, yellowish-brown.—*Fr. Epicr. p.* 592. *Berk. Outl. p.* 290.

On rotten wood. Rare. [United States.]

Sometimes confounded with *Tremella albida*, from which it differs in the presence of a small white nucleus.—*M. J. B.*

1035. Næmatelia virescens. *Corda.* "Greenish Næmatelia."

Small, roundish, depressed, gyroso-tuberculate, or quite even, green.—*Ann. N.H. no.* 374. *Fl. Dan. t.* 1857, *f.* 1. *Dacrymyces virescens, Fr. Epicr. p.* 592. *Corda.* iii. *f.* 90. *Berk. Outl. p.* 290.

On furze branches. Common.

Gen. **53.** **DACRYMYCES,** Nees.

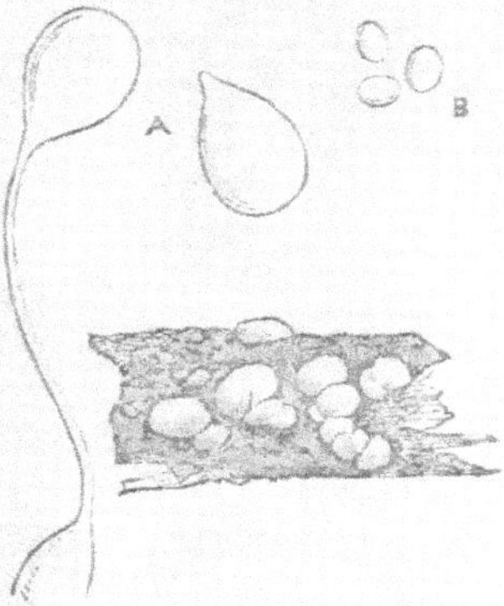

Homogenous, gelatinous. Conidia disposed in moniliform rows; sporophores clavate, at length bifurcate.—*Berk. Outl. p.* 290. (*Fig.* 99.)

Fig. 99.

1036. Dacrymyces violaceus. *Fr.* "Violet Dacrymyces."

Small, compact, somewhat compressed, gyrose, violet.—*Fr. Epicr. p.* 592. *Eng. Fl.* v. *p.* 219. *Berk. Outl. p.* 290.

On trunks of pear trees. Rare. [Mid. Carolina.]

Erumpent, gregarious; 3-4 lines long, 1 line thick, black when dry.—*Fries.* Very much like the tartar of port-wine.—*Relhan.*

1037. Dacrymyces sebaceus. *B. & Br.* "Waxy Dacrymyces."

Whitish, waxy, subrotund; spores ovate-triangular; filaments variously branched, clavate above, here and there resolved into globose conidia.—*Br. Bath. Trans.* 1870, *p.* 96.

On ash and maple twigs. Winter.

Conspicuous in wet weather, 2-4 lines broad; spores (·0005 × ·0003 in.) ·0125 × ·0075 mm. Besides the spores other bodies occur resembling those of a *Fusisporium*, which appear to grow from the same threads, but may possibly be parasitic on the *Dacrymyces.*—*C. E. B.* (*Fig.* 99.)

1038. Dacrymyces deliquescens. *Dub.* "Yellow Dacrymyces."

Pulvinate, slightly waved, and plicate yellow. Spores triseptate.—*Bull. t.* 455, *f.* 3. *Price, f.* 58. *Ann. Sc. Nat.* 1853, xix. *t.* 12, 13. *Ditiola nuda, B. & Br. Ann. N. H. ser.* 2, *vol.* ii. *p.* 267, *t.* 9, *f.* 4, *no.* 375 *& no.* 728. *Septocolla adpressa, Bon. f.* 274. *Berk. Outl. p.* 290.

On fallen pine branches. [Up. Carolina.]

Sometimes on pine rails, as well as *D. stillatus*, but easily distinguished from that by its larger size, more cæspitose habit, and paler yellowish colour. It often resembles very much a cæspitose, waved, yellow *Peziza*, growing in clusters, sometimes an inch or more in length. The spores are triseptate, slightly curved and obtuse.

1039. Dacrymyces stillatus. *Nees.* "Orange Dacrymyces."

Nearly round, convex, at length plicate, yellow, then orange, colour persistent; spores multiseptate.—*Fr. Epicr. p.* 592. *Grev. S. C. F. t.* 159. *Berk. Outl. t.* 18, *f.* 8. *Eng. Fl.* v. *p.* 220. *Cooke. exs. no.* 336.

On pine rails. [United States.]

Distinguished by its persistent orange colour from *D. deliquescens*, it is also smaller, more scattered, less depressed, and firmer. Generally barren.

1040. Dacrymyces chrysocomus. *Tul.* "Yellow-fir Dacrymyces."

Small, yellow, gelatinous, cup-shaped, at length turning pale. —*Berk. Outl. p.* 291. *Peziza chrysocoma, Bull. t.* 376, *f.* 2. *Eng. Fl.* v. *p.* 205.

On fir branches.

Gen. 54. APYRENIUM, Fr.

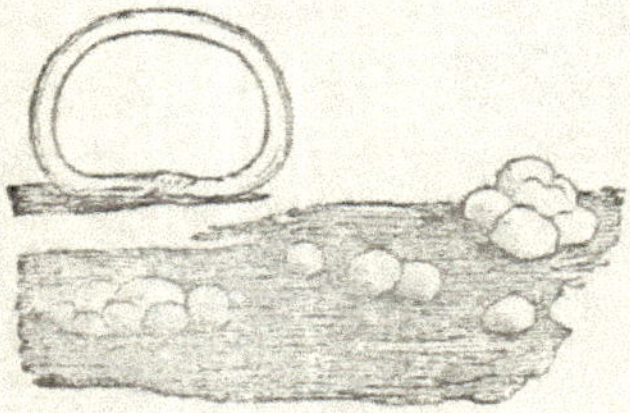

Fig. 100.

Stroma gelatinoso-carnose, fibroso-floccose, hollow, inflated; hymenium smooth, when dry collapsed, pubescent.—*Berk. Outl. p.* 291. (*Fig.* 100.)

1041. Apyrenium lignatile. *Fr.* "Wood-loving Apyrenium."

Subglobose, always hollow, mostly somewhat lobed, pallid yellowish, or reddish white.—*Fr. El.* ii. *p.* 39. *Berk. Outl. p.* 291. *Pyrenium lignatile, Eng. Fl.* v. *p.* 221. *Grev. t.* 276.

On rotten wood. Appin. (*Fig.* 100.)

1042. Apyrenium armeniacum. *B. & Br.* "Apricot-coloured Apyrenium."

Receptacle lobate, sub-gelatinous, apricot-colour; spores obovate, enucleate, borne at the tips of branched threads.—*B. & Br. Ann. N.H.* (1866), *no.* 1141, *pl.* ii., *f.* 2.

On oak sticks. Oct. Batheaston.

Spores ·0003 × ·0005 in. long. This may possibly be a condition of *Hypocrea gelatinosa*.

Gen. **55.** **HYMENULA**, Fr.

Effused, very thin, maculæform, agglutinate, between waxy and gelatinous.—*Berk. Outl. p.* 291.

1043. Hymenula punctiformis. *B. & Br.* "Point-like Hymenula."

Gelatinous, punctiform, pallid, somewhat undulated; spores elliptic.—*Ann. Nat. Hist. no.* 729. *Berk. Outl. p.* 291.

On decorticated fir poles. Sept. Batheaston.

Punctiform, gelatinous, dirty white or very pale umber, slightly tinged with yellow, ¼ line broad, slightly undulated, consisting of erect simple threads; spores minute (·0002 in.) ·005 mm. long. It has somewhat the appearance of *Peziza vulgaris*.—*B. & Br.*

Gen. **56.** **DITIOLA**, Fr.

Fig. 101.

Orbicular, margined, patellæform. Hymenium discoid, gelatinous, at first veiled.—*Berk. Outl. p.* 291. (*Fig.* 101.)

1044. Ditiola radicata. *Fr.* "Rooting Ditiola."

Disc nearly plane, golden-yellow; stem thick, villous, white, rooting.—*Fr. S.M.* ii. *p.* 170. *Fl. Dan. t.* 2338, *f.* 1. *Bisch. f.* 3375. *Bail. t.* 22. *A. & S. t.* 8, *f.* 6. *Eng. Fl.* v. *p.* 210. *Ann. N.H. no.* 729*.

On pine wood. East Bergholt. (*Fig.* 101.)

Family II. GASTEROMYCETES.

Hymenium more or less permanently concealed, consisting in most cases of closely-packed cells, of which the fertile ones bear naked spores on distinct spicules, exposed only by the rupture or decay of the investing coat or peridium.—*Berk. Outl. p.* 292.

The fructification is essentially produced within the surrounding tissues. A large portion are remarkable for the drying up of the hymenial tissues to such an extent that the cavity contains a dusty mass of spores, mixed more or less with threads, or the shrivelled remains of the constituent tissues, but this is not without exception. Some, again, are of a fleshy consistence when young, while others, in an early stage of growth, exhibit little more than an apparently inorganised mass of pulpy matter. One or two genera exhibit beautiful spiral threads. A few are edible.—*Berk. Introd. p.* 333.

Hymenomycetous—
- Subterraneous, naked or enclosed . . *Hypogæi.*
- Terrestrial. Hymenium deliquescent . *Phalloidei.*
- Peridium enclosing sporangia, containing spores . . . . *Nidulariacei.*

Coniospermous—
- Cellular at first. Hymenium drying up into a dusty mass of threads and spores . . . . *Trichogastres.*
- Gelatinous at first. Peridium containing at length a dusty mass of threads and spores . . . . *Myxogastres.*

Order VII. HYPOGÆI.

Hymenium permanent, not becoming dusty or deliquescent, except when decayed. Subterranean.—*Berk. Outl. p.* 292.

Analogous to Tuberacei in many particulars, except that the spores are *not* contained in asci.

Peridium adhering to creeping, branched fibres, which traverse its surface—
- Cells at first pulpy. Spores smooth. . . . *Melanogaster.*
- Cells at first empty. Spores smooth . . . *Rhizopogon.*

Peridium fleshy or thin. Cells at first empty—
- Without distinct base. Spores echinulate . *Hydnangium.*
- With absorbing base. Spores various . . . *Hymenogaster.*

Peridium cottony. Cells at first empty—
- Spores rough . . . . *Octaviania.*

Peridium separable. Cells at first empty—
- Substance cartilagino-glutinous. Spores minute . . . . *Hysterangium.*

Gen. 57. OCTAVIANIA, Vitt.

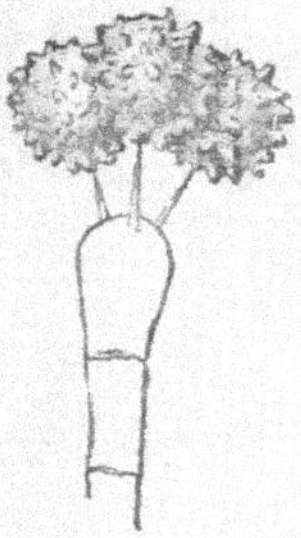

Fig. 102.

Peridium continuous or cracked, cottony, running down into the sterile base. Trama byssoid, easily divisible. Fruit-bearing cavities or cells at first empty. Spores rough.—*Vitt. Tub. p.* 15. *Tul. Hyp. p.* 77. *Berk. Outl. p.* 292. (*Fig.* 102.)

1045. Octaviania asterosperma. *Vitt.* "Star-spored Octaviania."

Globose, dirty white, then in parts, æruginous-blue and black; sterile base rather thick; spores spherical, deep ferruginous, echinate.—*Berk. Outl. p.* 292. *Tul. Hyp. t.* 11, *f.* 1. *Vitt. Tub. t.* 3, *f.* 7. *Tul. Ann. Sc. Nat.* xix. *t.* 17, *f.* 21. *Corda. Ic.* vi. *t.* 7, *f.* 64. *Corda. Anl. t. D. f.* 45, *no.* 5, 6.

Underground, adhering by the mycelium to twigs, &c. West of England.

The smell is just like the pungent odour of some Ichneumon or small bee. Spores (·0004 in.) ·0128 mm. (*Fig.* 102, *spores.*)

1046. Octaviania Stephensii. *Tul.* "Stephens's Octaviania."

Irregular, oblong, externally rufous, plicato-rugose at the base, cribrose, white within; milky, at length, when exposed to the air, rufous; spores globose, at length echinulate.—*Berk. Outl. p.* 292. *Tul. Hyp. t.* 21, *f.* 6. *Corda.* vi. *f.* 67. *Hydnangium Stephensii, Berk. Ann. N.H.* xiii. *p.* 352, *no.* 300.

Underground, or half buried. Aug. Clifton.

About ¾ in. diameter, oblong, attached by a branched fibrous root, smooth, not cracked, dark rufous, curiously plicate at the base, and cribrose; within white, yielding when cut a white milky fluid; substance when cut and exposed to the air soon acquiring a red tinge, which is not, however, permanent, and in young specimens vanishes almost entirely in drying, in which state the hymenium is cream-coloured; cells minute; spores at first irregularly globose, with a broad rugulose border, somewhat after the fashion of the young spores of *Scleroderma*, at length echinulate. This species is remarkable for its milky juice, smooth dark peridium, and plicate base. The smell was slight.—*M. J. B.* Spores ·0096 × ·0128 mm. (·00035 × ·0004 in.) diameter.

Gen. 58. MELANOGASTER, Corda.

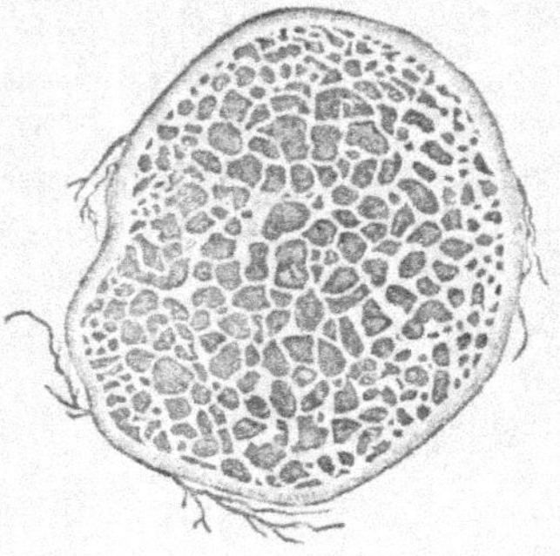

Fig. 103.

Peridium adhering to creeping branched fibres which traverse its surface, without any proper or distinct base; cells at first filled with pulp; spores smooth, mostly dark. —*Corda. Sturm.* iii. *p.* i. *Ic. Fung.* v. *p.* 23. *Tul. Hyp. p.* 92. *Berk. Outl. p.* 293. (*Fig.* 103.)

1047. Melanogaster variegatus. *Tul.* "Red Truffle."

At first ochraceous, then reddish-ferruginous, minutely downy; walls of the cells dirty white, yellowish or orange; pulp black; spores minute.—*Tul. F. Hyp. t.* ii. *f.* 4, *t.* xii. *f.* 6. *Bull. t.* 479. *Berk. Outl. p.* 293. *Vitt. Tub. t.* iii. *f.* 4. *Corda. Ic.* vi. *t.* 9, *f.* 91.

var. **Broomeianus.** Veins pale, sometimes becoming red when dry, sometimes unchangeable. *M. Broomeianus, B. Ann. N.H. no.* 301. *Tuber moschatum, Sow. t.* 426. *Berk. exs. no.* 285. *Tul. Ann. Sc. Nat.* xix. *t.* 17, *f.* 23. *Corda.* vi. *f.* 90.

Under beech trees, Lombardy poplars, &c. South West of England.

Sold in the market at Bath under the name of the Red Truffle, and eaten there in preference to the Common Truffle. In tufts of five or six together, and several of such tufts under each tree, half of them being in general exposed, and half beneath the soil; when fresh it is minutely tomentose, of a reddish ochre, which becomes less bright when handled or badly dried; the veins bright yellow in the typical form, pale in the variety, sometimes becoming red when dry, sometimes unchangeable; at first white within, then very pale yellow, at length fuliginous. The spores are elliptic and minute, without any papillæ, they contain one or two globose nuclei; when ripe spherical bodies of the size of the nuclei are often mixed with the spores.—*M. J. B.* Spores ·0064 mm. long, ·004 mm. broad (·00025 × ·00015 in.).

1048. Melanogaster ambiguus. *Tul.* "Stinking Melanogaster."

Very fœtid, globose, dirty olive, nearly even; walls of cells white, reddish when exposed to the air; pulp black; spores large, obovate. *Tul. Hyp. t.* 2, *f.* 5, *t.* 12, *f.* 5. *Berk. Ann. N. Hist. no.* 302. *Berk. Outl. p.* 293. *Corda. Ic.* vi. *t.* 9, *f.* 88. *Octaviana ambigua,*

Vitt. Tub. p. 18, *t.* 4, *f.* 7. *Hyperrhiza liquaminosa, Klot. Fl. Bor. t.* 468. *Lycoperdoides, Mich. t.* 98, *f.* 3.

Under fir trees. West of England. Apethorpe.

Known at once by its much larger ovate spores with a papilla at the apex, and its abominable smell, which resembles that of assafœtida. A single specimen in a room is so strong as to make it scarcely habitable. The walls of the cells when cut are whitish, but soon become red; this is not constantly the case.—*M. J. B.*

var. β. **intermedius.** Spores obovate, obtuse and even, very rarely slightly papillate.—*Berk. Ann. N.H. no.* 302.

This form, or more probably species, was found at Spye Park in August, by C. E. Broome. It is as large as M. *variegatus*, of which it has the bright rusty colour, but the spores are much larger, equalling in size those of the typical form of this species, though of a different form. There is scarcely ever the slightest indication of a papilla, and they are obovate, with a single globose nucleus. The smell is also similar. The walls of the cells are yellowish, and are red in dry specimens.—*M. J. B.* Spores ·013 × ·016 mm. long, ·008 mm. broad (·0005 × ·0003 in.). (*Fig.* 103, *section magd.*)

Gen. 59. HYDNANGIUM, Wallr.

Fig. 104.

Peridium fleshy or membranaceous. Sterile base none. Trama vesicular. Cells at first empty, then filled with spores. Spores echinulate.—*Tul. Hyp. p.* 74. *Berk. Ann. N.H.* xiii. *p.* 351. *Outl. p.* 293. *Corda. Ic.* v. *p.* 28. (*Fig.* 104.)

1049. **Hydnangium carotæcolor.** *Berk.* "Orange Hydnangium."

Oblong, rootless; peridium thin, rugulose, brick-red, orange within; spores subelliptic, pale, echinulate.—*Berk. Ann. N.H.* xiii. *p.* 351. *Berk. Outl. p.* 293, *t.* 20, *f.* 1. *Tul. Hyp. t.* 21, *f.* 4.

Under trees. Sept. Nov. Bristol.

Oblong, ¾ of an inch in diameter, externally slightly tomentose, pale orange-red, fleshy, but by no means deliquescent, rootless; peridium thin, at length rugulose, within minutely cellular; substance of a beautiful orange-red; cells hollow, clothed with obtuse bi-sporous sporophores, and slender cystidia; the cells are also traversed from wall to wall by slender occasionally branched threads. Spores subelliptic, strongly echinulate, supported on short but distinct sterigmata.—*M. J. B.* Colour exactly that of a carrot, communicating to paper a lemon-coloured stain. Spores ·0096 × ·0128 mm. long, ·007 × ·008 mm. broad (·0004 × ·0003 in.). (*Fig.* 104, *spores magd.*)

Gen. 60. HYSTERANGIUM, Vitt.

Peridium indehiscent, distinct, separable. Cavities at first empty. Substance cartilagineo-glutinous. Spores minute.—*Vitt. Tub. p.* 13. *Berk. Ann. N.H.* xiii. *p.* 350. *Outl. p.* 294. *Tul. Hyp. p.* 80.

1050. Hysterangium nephriticum. *Berk.* "Grey Hysterangium."

Depressed, springing from a white, flat, branched, membranous mycelium; peridium firm, elastic, distinct, tomentose, substance pale blue or grey, here and there greenish; cavities radiating from the base; spores minute, oblong, pale clay-colour.—*Ann. N. Hist.* xiii. *p.* 350, *no.* 298.

Under trees. Feb. Clifton.

About ½-1 in. across, gregarious, sometimes confluent, snow-white, downy, seated on a white, flat, branched mycelium, which penetrates deeply into the soil, and is attached at various points to the peridium; peridium firm, elastic, easily separating from the fructifying mass, but in the process of drying in young plants, adhering closely to it; in older plants often separating entirely; when rubbed or cut contracting sometimes a pale rufous tinge; substance firm, cartilagineo-glutinous, proceeding from the base and radiating into the mass, of a pale blue or grey in parts, with a green tinge; in very young specimens there is a tinge of very pale pink; cells irregular, minute, sometimes straight and radiating, clothed with very pale, argillaceous, oblong spores, and emitting from their walls irregular threads. As the plant dries the blue and green tints vanish almost entirely, and the mass is of a very pale clay-colour from the spores. The central mass contracts extremely, and the outer surface becomes more or less irregular. Smell at first like that of some *Hypericum*, then exactly that of a decaying puff-ball.—*M. J. B.* Spores ·0128 mm. long, ·0064 mm. broad (·0004 × ·00025 in.).

1051. Hysterangium Thwaitesii. *B. & Br.* "Thwaites's Hysterangium."

Subglobose, white, rufous when bruised; peridium membranaceous; spores oblong, apiculate.—*B. & Br. Ann. N.H. ser.* ii. *vol.* ii. *p.* 267, *no.* 377.

Under trees. Aug. Bristol.

Mycelium white, fibrillose, not much disposed to form membranous expansions, spreading for some distance. Sporangium globose, or slightly irregular, white, slightly silky, when rubbed or exposed to air assuming a rufous tinge. Peridium membranaceous, not so thick as in *H. nephriticum*, though, as in that species, it sometimes separates when dry; rufous when divided. Cells brownish-olive; spores oblong, apiculate, differently shaped from those of the other species.—*M. J. B.* Spores ·0192 mm. long, ·0064 mm. broad (·0006 × ·00025 in.).

Gen. 61. RHIZOPOGON, Tul.

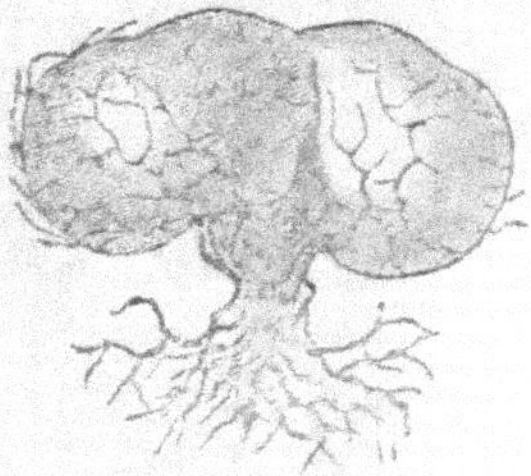

Fig 105.

Peridium continuous or cracked, adhering to creeping, branched fibres, which traverse its surface. Cavities distinct, at first empty. Spores smooth, oblong-elliptic.—*Tul. Hyp. p.* 85. *B. & Br. Ann. N.H.* xviii. *p.* 76. *Berk. Outl. p.* 294. (*Fig.* 105, *Rhizopogon luteolus.*)

1052. Rhizopogon rubescens. *Tul.* "Reddish Rhizopogon."

White, then reddish, and at length livid-olive, furnished with a few fibrillæ; substance very lacunose, dirty white, then olive; cavities always empty.—*Berk. Outl. p.* 294. *Tul. Hyp. t.* 2, *f.* i. *t.* 11, *f.* 4. *Melanogaster Berkeleyanus, Br. Ann. N. H.* (1845) *p.* 41. *Corda. Ic.* vi. *t.* 9, *f.* 90. *Sturm.* iii. *t.* 11.

In sandy fir woods. Chudleigh. [Low. & Mid. Carolina.]

This species grows gregariously in sandy fir woods; when young it is almost transparent, and resembles young *Cynophallus caninus*, being of a pure white, and furnished with white roots, which proceed from a mycelium that spreads sometimes an inch or two; in this state it turns pink on being touched; in a more advanced stage it is yellow, but even then it has here and there a pink tinge. The smell is very much like that of *Melanogaster ambiguus* when old, but when young it has an acid smell like that of sour ham. It rapidly decays into a brown, fœtid, pulpy mass.—*M. J. B.* Spores ·007-·009 mm. long, ·003 mm. broad (·00027 to ·00035 × ·00011 in.).

Gen. 62. HYMENOGASTER, Tul.

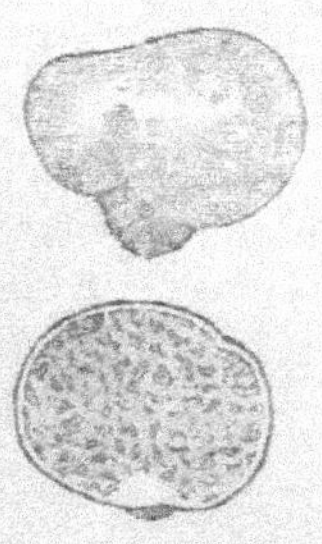

Fig 106.

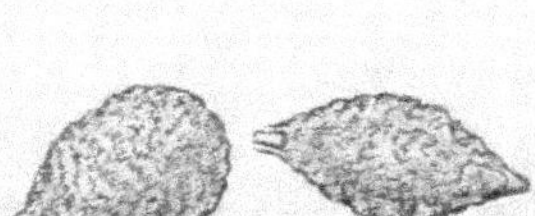

Fig. 107.

Globose, fleshy, firm, or rather soft. Peridium fleshy or thin, running down into an absorbing base. Cavities at first empty, radiating or irregular. Trama composed of elongated cells, but not of byssoid flocci, and therefore not easily separable. Spores various.—*Vitt. Tub. p.* 20. *Tul. Hyp. p.* 63. *Berk. Ann. N.H.* xiii. *p.* 346, xviii. *p.* 74. *Berk. Outl. p.* 295.

1053. Hymenogaster Klotschii. *Tul.* "Klotsch's Hymenogaster."

Obovate, fibrillose at the base, dirty white, within dull rufous ochre; spores small, elliptic, obtuse at either extremity, nearly even.—*Berk. Outl. p.* 295. *Tul. Hyp. t.* 10, *f.* 12. *H. albus, B. & Br. Ann. N. H. no.* 296. *Hymenangium album, Kl. Fl. Bor. t.* 466. *Rhizopogon albus, Eng. Fl.* v. *p.* 229. *Bail. t.* 27. *Kl. exs. no.* 1967.

Amongst soil. Glasgow.

Sowerby's *Tuber album*, t. 310, quoted in Eng. Fl. as above, is still uncertain. Spores ·016 mm. long, ·0095 mm. broad (·0005 × ·00035 in.).

1054. Hymenogaster muticus. *B. & Br.* "Cracking Hymenogaster."

Globose, quite white when young, then tinged with brown and cracked, pale yellow-brown within; spores obovate, oblong, very obtuse.—*B. & Br. Ann. N. H. ser.* ii., *vol.* ii., *p.* 267. *Berk. Outl. p.* 295. *Tul. Hyp. t.* 10, *f.* 7.

Under trees. Nov. Bristol.

About an inch in diameter, almost destitute of any absorbing base, globose, scarcely at all lobed. When young pure white, but changing with age, especially when rubbed, to brownish, and at length much cracked. Substance pale yellowish-brown, rather firm and dry; cells loose, but smaller than in some of the allied species, clothed with reddish-brown obovate oblong spores, which for the most part are quite obtuse, without the slightest trace of an apiculus, and contain two or three variously sized oil globules. Smell very slight. Distinguished from all its more immediate allies by its peculiar spores.—*M. J. B.* Spores ·023 mm. long, ·013 mm. broad (·0008 × ·0004 in.).

1055. Hymenogaster luteus. *Vitt.* "Yellow Hymenogaster."

Peridium very thin, soft and silky, white, then brownish, bright yellow within; spores even, ovate, or elliptic, oblong, yellow.—*B. & Br. Ann. N. H. no.* 294. *Tul. Hyp. t.* 1, *f.* 3. *Vitt. Tub. p.* 22, *t.* 3, *f.* 9. *Corda. Ic.* vi. *t.* 8, *f.* 76.

In woods. Rudloe, Wilts.

Distinguished by its bright permanently yellow hymenium, and smooth, papillate, very variable, often triangular spores. The tint varies according to the quantity of spores. Some specimens have but little scent; others, especially the larger ones, are powerfully fœtid.—*B. & Br.* Spores ·019-·023 mm. long, ·0096 mm. broad (·0007 to ·0008 × ·0004 in.).

1056. Hymenogaster decorus. *Tul.* "Comely Hymenogaster."

Roundish, dirty-white, here and there yellow, rather firm, within lilac-brown and at length blackish-violet; absorbing base obsolete; sporophores long, somewhat filiform; spores elliptic, obtuse or obtusely apiculate, rugulose, ochraceous, then brown. *Berk. Outl. p.* 295. *Tul. Hyp. t.* 10, *f.* 9. *Ann. Sc. Nat.* xix. *t.* 17, *f.* 4-8.

In woods. Epping Forest, Chudleigh, &c.

This is a much firmer species than *H. tener*, darker within, with larger spores; but it is especially distinguished by its elongated filiform sporophores, which project far beyond the surface of the hymenium.—*M. J. B.*

1057. Hymenogaster vulgaris. *Tul.* "Common Hymenogaster."

Roundish, irregular, dirty white, soon soiled, softish, within dirty white, then dark-brown; sterile base minute; spores oblong or lanceolate, oblong-acute, attenuated at the base, dark brown when mature; surface uneven.—*Berk. Outl. p.* 296. *Tul. Hyp. t.* 10, *f.* 13. *Corda. Ic.* vi. *t.* 8, *f.* 84, *t.* 13, *f.* 108.

In woods. Bristol. Apethorpe.

In general the internal substance changes from dirty white to pale reddish-brown, and then almost to black; sometimes, however, there is at first a slight tinge of pale tan. The spores are variable in form, but are never acuminate. —*M. J. B.* (*Fig.* 107, *spores.*)

1058. Hymenogaster pallidus. *B. & Br.* "Pallid Hymenogaster."

Smaller, rounded, depressed, nearly smooth, white, then dirty tan colour, rather soft, within white, then yellow, then pale brown; sterile base obsolete; spores lanceolate, acute, shortly pedicellate, rather tough.—*B. & Br. Ann. N.H.* xviii. *p.* 74. *Berk. Outl. p.* 296.

In a dry fir plantation. Cotterstock.

This species, which scarcely exceeds in size a horsebean, is nearly allied to *H. vulgaris*, but differs in its more acute spores as well as in colour. Spores ·032-·038 mm. long, ·013-·016 mm. broad (·0012 × ·0004 in.).

1059. Hymenogaster citrinus. *Vitt.* "Lemon-coloured Hymenogaster."

Rounded, gibbous, shining as if silky, lemon-coloured or golden-yellow, then rufous-black, of the same colour within; substance firm; spores lanceolate, apiculate, rugulose, reddish-brown, opaque.—*B. & Br. Ann. N.H. no.* 293. *Berk. Outl. p.* 296, *t.* 20, *f.* 2. *Vitt. Tub. p.* 21. *Berk. exs. no.* 284. *Tul. Hyp. t.* i. *f.* 1, *t.* 10, *f.* 3. *Corda. Ic.* vi. *t.* 9, *f.* 87.

In woods. Audley End. Wiltshire.

The yellow veins, subfusiform, rough, dark-coloured spores, the frequently coloured sporophores, and the cheese-like scent which communicates itself to everything which is near, are the criterions of this species. When young it is of a greenish-yellow, but this soon wears off when rubbed, or exposed to the air. The sporophores occasionally become of a much darker colour than the neighbouring cells, and have a resinous appearance.—*B. & Br.*

1060. Hymenogaster olivaceus. *Vitt.* "Olive Hymenogaster."

Globose, but angular; peridium whitish, then tinged with yellow, rufous when bruised; substance white, then of a dull buff, then rufous-olive, variegated with the white trama; spores pedicellate, mucronate, generally smooth.—*B. & Br. Ann. N.H. no.* 295. *Berk. Outl. p.* 296. *Vitt. Tub. t.* 5, *f.* 9. *H. populetorum, Berk. exs. no.* 304.

In woods. West of England.

Variable in size, from that of a hazel-nut to a walnut. Peridium at first white, slightly tinged with lemon-colour; cells at first white, gradually becoming of a dull buff, and then of a reddish grey or brown. Smell like that of *Lactarius theiogalus*. Spores ovate, shortly pedicellate, with an abrupt, elongated, sometimes irregular apex; in general smooth and transparent, and containing 2-3 nuclei, but sometimes slightly rugose, though by no means opaque, as in *H. citrinus*, from which it may be known by its reddish substance, larger cells, more transparent, paler and smoother spores, which are frequently more abruptly acuminate.—*M. J. B.*

1061. Hymenogaster tener. *Berk.* "Thin Hymenogaster."

Small, globose, soft, white, silky; substance pale pink, then greyish-umber; sterile base conspicuous, white; spores broadly elliptic, with a papillary apex, minutely warty.—*Berk. Ann. N.H. no.* 297. *Berk. Outl. p.* 296. *H. lilacinus, Berk. exs. no.* 305. *Tul. Hyp. t.* i. *f.* 4, *t.* 10. *f.* 1.

In woods. Spring and summer. West of England.

About the size of a bean or large hazel-nut; globose, soft and tender, white and silky externally; peridium thin, at length dingy, at first white within, but soon acquiring a delicate pink tinge, which, as the spores ripen, changes to an umber grey. Absorbing base white, very distinct; cells looser than in *H. olivaceus*; spores much smaller than in the neighbouring species, broad, elliptic, with a minute papilla, never acuminate, minutely verrucose. Smell like that of *Lact. theiogalus.*—*M. J. B.* This is one of the most distinct species, characterised by its small, widely elliptic, or subglobose spores. Spores ·016-·019 mm. long, ·0096-·0105 mm. broad (·0005-·0006 × ·00035-·0004 in.). (*Fig.* 107, *fungus and section.*)

1062. Hymenogaster Thwaitesii. *B. & Br.* "Thwaites's Hymenogaster."

Small, globose, firm, dirty white, here and there stained; substance brown; spores globose, rather rough, papillary.—*B. & Br. Ann. N.H.* xviii. *p.* 75. *Berk. Outl. p.* 297. *Tul. Hyp. t.* 10, *f.* 11.

In woods. Rare. Near Bristol.

The spores are far more globose than in any other species, and are either quite obtuse or minutely apiculate. The inner membrane of the spores often contracts, so as to present a very singular appearance. A few elongated spores are mixed with them, but the normal form is globose. They are larger than in *H. tener*, but smaller than in *H. decorus*.

1063. Hymenogaster pusillus. *B. & Br.* "Little Hymenogaster."

Very small, obovate or subdepressed, white; sterile base large; substance dirty white; cells large; spores pallid-rubiginous, short, broadly-elliptic, with a papillary apex, at length smooth. —*B. & Br. Ann. N. H.* xviii. *p.* 75, *no.* 5. *Tul. Hyp. p.* 73.

On mossy ground in woods. Rushton. Norths.

About 2 lines high, obovate or somewhat depressed, pure white, yellowish brown when dry, and then resembling strongly *Sclerotium complanatum*, nearly smooth; dirty white within, furnished with a large, distinct, absorbing base. Cavities of the hymenium large for the size of the fungus, clothed sparingly with the rust-coloured spores. Sporophores clavate, frequently forked or irregular, having two spores on rather long spicules. Spores short, minute, broadly elliptic, at first smooth, at length rather rough, obtusely apiculate. —*M. J. B.* Spores ·013-·016 mm. long, ·0096 mm. broad (·0004-·0005 × ·00035 in.).

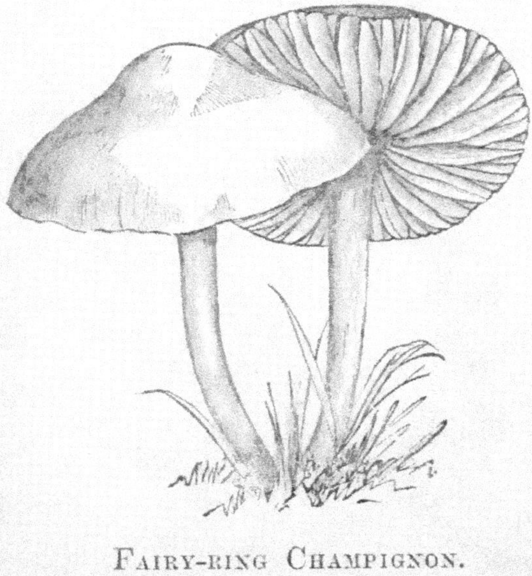

FAIRY-RING CHAMPIGNON.

Marasmius oreades.

Order VIII. PHALLOIDEI.

Volva universal, the intermediate stratum gelatinous. Hymenium deliquescent.—*Berk. Outl. p.* 297.

Pileus perforate, free . . . . *Phallus.*
Pileus imperforate, adnate . . . . *Cynophallus.*
Receptacle forming an ovate or globose network . *Clathrus.*

Gen. **63.** **PHALLUS**, Linn.

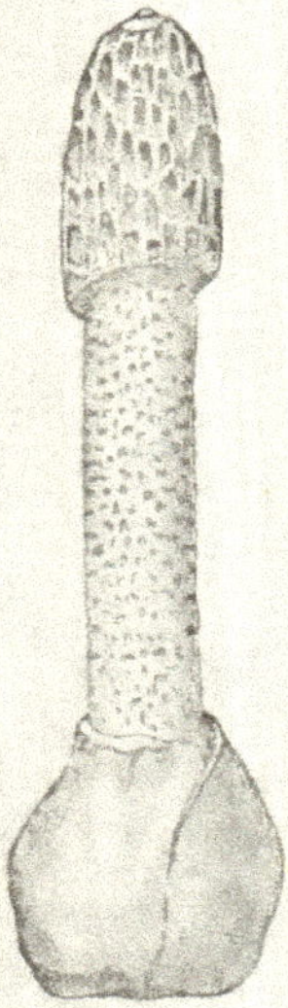

Fig. 108.

Pileus perforated at the apex, free all round, reticulate. Veil none. (*Fig.* 108.)

1064. **Phallus impudicus.** *Linn.* "Common Stinkhorn."

Pileus conical, reticulated ; margin of the reticulations nearly entire ; stem white, naked.—*Berk. Outl. p.* 297, *t.* 20, *f.* 3. *Grev. t.* 213. *Harz. t.* 65, 66. *Mich. t.* 83. *Bail. t.* 25. *Fl. Dan. t.* 175. *Schæff. t.* 196-198. *Bull. t.* 182. *Bolt. t.* 92. *Nees. f.* 259. *Fckl. exs. no.* 1270. *Smith, P.M. f.* 31. *Pay. f.* 551, 560. *Corda.* v. *f.* 50. *Eng. Fl.* v. *p.* 226. *Bisch. f.* 3330. *Phallus fœtidus, Sow. t.* 329.

In woods, &c. Common. Very fœtid. [United States.]

Uterus about as large as a hen's egg, consisting of two coats distended with jelly, besides which there is another delicate membrane immediately surrounding the pileus. Stem rapidly elongated, when full grown 6-8 in. high, 1 in. thick, hollow at first, closed at the apex, at length pierced.—*Eng. Fl.* (*Fig.* 108, *reduced.*)

1065. Phallus iosmos. *Berk.* "Toothed Phallus."

Pale reddish grey; pileus conical, reticulated, borders of the reticulations strongly toothed.—*Berk. Outl. p.* 298. *Curt. Brit. Ent.* x. *t.* 469. *Eng. Fl.* v. *p.* 227.

Sandhills. Lowestoft.

Scent something like violets at a distance, but very offensive when the plant is dried.—*Curt.*

Gen. 64. CYNOPHALLUS, Fr.

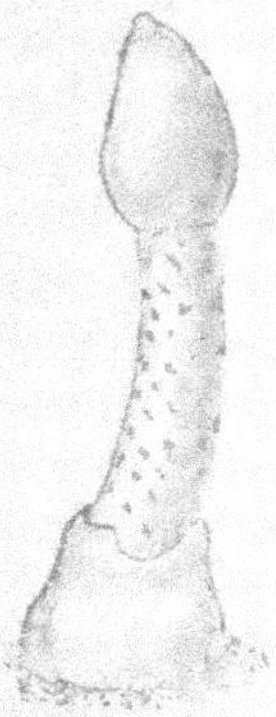

Pileus adnate, imperforate, uneven. Veil none.—*Fr. S. M.* ii. *p.* 284. *Berk. Outl. p.* 298. (*Fig.* 109.)

This genus differs from *Phallus* in the adnate and imperforate pileus, as well as in some other points.

Fig. 109.

1066. Cynophallus caninus. *Fr.* "Common Cynophallus."

Pileus continuous with stem, ovate, tuberculose, impervious, reddish.—*Curt. t.* 235. *Schæff. t.* 330. *Fl. Dan. t.* 1259. *Sow. t.* 330. *Nees. f.* 260. *Eng. Fl.* v. *p.* 227. *Bisch.* 3335.

Amongst decayed leaves in woods. Local.

Uterus about the size of a hazel nut; stem hollow, very pale orange; pileus covered with green scentless mucus, beneath which it is red and wrinkled.—*Eng. Fl.* (*Fig.* 109, *reduced.*)

Gen. 65. CLATHRUS, Mich.

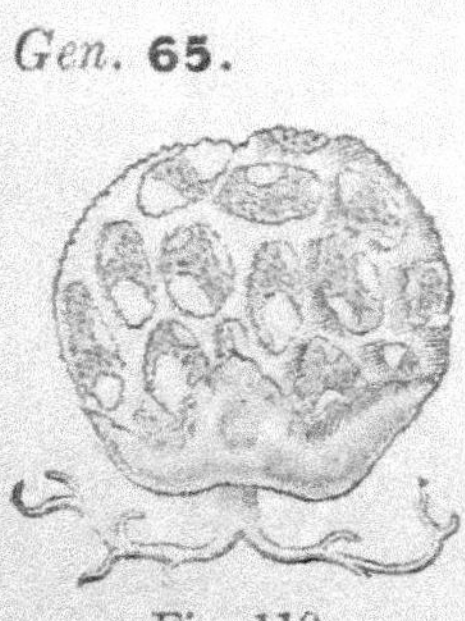

Stem none. Receptacle forming an ovate or globose network; branches of the network cellular within.—*Fr. S. M.* ii. *p.* 287. *Berk. Outl. p.* 298. (*Fig.* 110.)

Fig. 110.

1067. Clathrus cancellatus. *Linn.* "Latticed Stinkhorn."

Obovate, branches obliquely anastomosing, cancellate.—*Fr. S.M.* ii. *p.* 288. *Ann. N.H. no.* 304. *Huss.* i. *t.* 86. *Batt. t.* 2, *f.* E. *Pay. f.* 556-559. *Mich. t.* 93. *Nees. f.* 201. *Bull. t.* 441. *Tourn. t.* 329, *f.* B. *var. Cooke, B. F. t.* 20. *Corda.* v. *f.* 49. *Bisch. f.* 3638. *Bail. t.* 23. *Rabh. F. E. no.* 35.

In woods. Rare. Isle of Wight, Devonshire, Lyme Regis, South of Ireland, &c. [Georgia, U. S.]

Very beautiful, but extremely fœtid. Branches resembling sealing-wax, covered here and there with an olive sporiferous mass.—*M. J. B.*

(Fig. 110, reduced.)

Order IX. TRICHOGASTRES.

Peridium single or double. Hymenium at length drying up into a dusty mass of threads and spores.—*Fr. S.M.* iii. *p.* 3. *Berk. Outl. p.* 298.

Stalked—
- Receptacle pileiform; volva universal . . . *Batarrea.*
- Receptacle subglobose, peridium thin, outer coat separating . . . . *Tulostoma.*

Not stalked—
- Peridium thin—
  - Persistent, bark shelling off; no sterile base . . . . *Bovista.*
  - Vanishing above, bark becoming warty, with sterile base . . . . *Lycoperdon.*
- Peridium firm, central mass veined. Spores large, granulated . . . . *Scleroderma.*
- Peridium rigid, enclosing distinct cells filled with peridiola . . . . *Polysaccum.*
- Peridium carbonaceous, at length hollow . . *Cenococcum.*
- Peridium double, outer one splitting in stellate lobes . . . . *Geaster.*

Gen. **66** **BATARREA,** Pers.

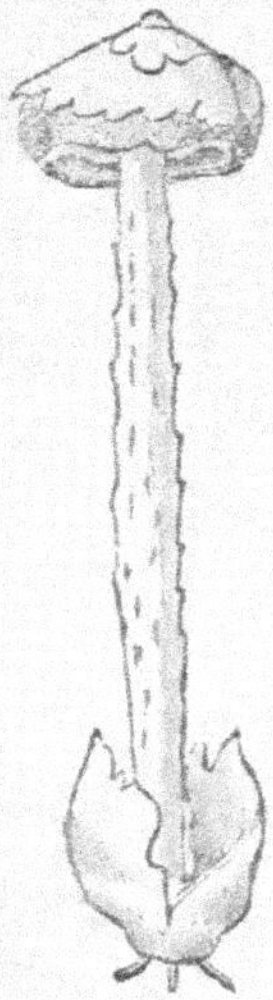

Fig. 111.

Volva universal, central stratum gelatinous. Receptacle pileiform, bursting through the volva, seated at the top of a tall stem.—*Berk. Outl. p.* 299.
(*Fig.* 111.)

1068. **Batarrea phalloides.** *P.* "Scarce Batarrea."

Stem equal. Spores brownish.—*Fr. S.M.* iii. *p.* 7. *Woodw. Phil. Trans.* v. 74, *p.* 423, *t.* 26. *Ann. N.H. no.* 303. *Smith. Spic.* i. *t.* 12. *Sow. t.* 390. *Pers. Syn. t.* 3, *f.* 1. *Nees. f.* 257. *Eng. Fl.* v. *p.* 298. *Hook. Journ.* 1843. *t.* 22, *f.* 1. *Bisch. f.* 3463. *Corda. Anl. t. E. f.* 50, *no.* 4-6.

On sandhills, or hollows of old trees. Rare. New Brighton. Dropmore.

Whole plant more or less of a brown hue. Exterior volva ovate, fleshy, dirty-white, inclining to brown, buried 6-8 in. in the sand, with a few dirty-white floccose hairs at the base, middle volva much thinner, and almost membranaceous, connected with the outer by mucilage, smooth within; inner volva internally villous, covered with very abundant yellow-brown dust-like seed; externally concave and smooth. Stem formed within the cavity of the interior volva, cylindric, straight, short, fleshy, filled with mucilage, but afterwards elongated upwards with wonderful force and quickness, and protruded through the soil, carrying with it almost the whole inner volva, adnate with its apex, and covered, with a portion of the outer coat torn off, in the same manner. Immediately after maturity it becomes dry, as also the volva; tubular within, and externally fibrous, and remains a long time bleached and tossed about by wind and rain.—*Smith.* (*Fig.* 111, *reduced.*)

Gen. 67. TULOSTOMA, Pers.

Peridium thin, papyraceous, the outer coat separating, distinct from the elongated stem. —*Fr. S.M.* iii. *p.* 41. *Berk. Outl. p.* 299. (*Fig.* 112.)

Fig. 112.

1069. Tulostoma mammosum. *Fr.* "Nippled Tulostoma."

Stem equal, subsquamose, mouth of peridium prominent, mammæform, entire.—*Fr. S.M.* iii. *p.* 42. *Ray. Syn. p.* 27. *Tourn. t.* 331, *f. E.F. Bull. t.* 294, 471, *f.* 2. *Sow. t.* 406. *Nees. f.* 130. *Fl. Dan. t.* 1740, *f.* 1. *Chev. t.* 10. *f.* 1. *Fckl. exs. no.* 1268. *Eng. Fl.* v. *p.* 305. *Pay. f.* 40, 42. *Bisch. f.* 3609, 3610. *Kl. exs. no.* 177.

On old walls, amongst moss. Local. [United States.]

It varies with a smooth and nearly solid stem, or subsquamose, with a central pith. A vertical section shows a groove round the top of the stem, and a cavity towards the top of the peridium, in consequence of the flocci being shorter above. Spores bright ferruginous.—*M. J. B.* (*Fig.* 112.)

Gen. 68. GEASTER, Mich.

Fig. 113.

Peridium double, outer distinct, persistent, bursting, and dividing into several stellite lobes.—*Fr. S.M.* iii. *p.* 9. *Berk. Outl. p.* 299. (*Fig.* 113.)

In one species the inner peridium is supported by several stems, and the orificesare numerous. This has led to its removal by some mycologists from this to a new genus. We prefer to retain it as a sub-genus. In the rest the orifice and support is single. None of the species are common.

Sub.-Gen. 1. MYRIOSTOMA—Orifices and peduncles numerous.

1070. Geaster coliformis. *P.* "Cullender Star Puff-ball."

Outer peridium multifid, expanded, inner supported by many short, slender stems; apertures numerous, ciliated.—*Pers. Syn. p.* 131. *Fr. S.M.* iii. *p.* 12. *Ray. Syn.* iii. *p.* 27. *Dicks. t.* 3. *f.* 4. *Sow. t.* 313. *Eng. Fl.* v. *p.* 299.

On the ground. Local. Norfolk. Suffolk.

Remarkable for its numerous peduncles and orifices. The peduncles are compressed, somewhat branched, and appear to bear a definite relation to the number of orifices.—*M. J. B.*

Sub.-Gen. 2. GENUINA—Orifice and peduncle single.

1071. Geaster fornicatus. *Fr.* "Vaulting Geaster."

Outer peridium subquadrifid, separating into two coats, connected at the tips of the divisions, and vaulted; mouth conical, plicato-sulcate.—*Berk. Outl. p.* 299. *Fr. S.M.* iii. *p.* 12. *Phil. Trans.* xliii. *t.* 2, *f.* 11, 12. *Blackst. t.* 2. *Buxb.* v. *t.* 28, *f.* 1, 2. *Batt. t.* 39, *f.* 1-4. *Bryant. f.* 15. *Sow. t.* 198. *Schæff. t.* 183. *Batsch. f.* 168. *Schmid. t.* 37. *Nees. f.* 128. *Eng. Fl.* v. *p.* 300. *Fckl. exs. no.* 1267. *Bisch. f.* 3635. *Kl. exs.* ii. *no.* 140.

On the ground and in hollow trees. [United States.]

The outer coat of the volva remains so firmly attached to the ground during the expansion of the plant that the inner separates, and is inverted and fixed by the tips of its stellate lobes, to those of the outer coat.—*Eng. Fl.*

1072. Geaster striatus. *D.C.* "Striate Geaster."

Outer peridium multifid, simple, expanded; interior subpedicellate; mouth prominent, conical, sulcate-striato.—*Fr. S.M.* iii. *p.* 13. *Mich. t.* 100, *f.* 3. *Gled. t.* 6, *f. upper. Eng. Fl.* v. *p.* 300. *Kl. exs. no.* 173. *Fckl. exs. no.* 1264.

Amongst sand. Great Yarmouth. [Cincinnati, U. S.]

This species differs from *G. limbatus* in the nature of the orifice, and from *G. Bryantii* in the want of the channel round the top of the stem.—*Eng. Fl.*

1073. Geaster Bryantii. *Berk.* "Bryant's Geaster."

Outer peridium coriaceous, expanded, multifid; inner pedicellate, with a groove round the top of the peduncle; mouth sulcato-plicate.—*Berk. Outl. p.* 300. *Eng. Fl.* v. *p.* 300. *Bryant. f.* 19. *Schm. Ic. t.* 37, *f.* 11-12. *Berk. exs. no.* 198.

Under yew trees, and on exposed fen banks.

Distinguished by the groove round the top of the peduncle and by the elongated plicate mouth.

1074. Geaster limbatus. *Fr.* "Bordered Geaster."

Outer peridium coriaceous, expanded, multifid; interior pedicellate; mouth fimbriato-pilose, depressed, rather acute.—*Fr. S.M.* iii. *p.* 15. *Sow. t.* 312. *Huss.* i. *t.* 2. *Ray. Syn. t.* i. *f.* i. *Buxb.* v. *t.* 29. *f.* 1. *Bryant. f.* 12, 13, 14, 16, 17. *Schmid. t.* 46. *Eng. Fl.* v. *p.* 301. *Bisch. f.* 3636, 3637. *Fckl. exs. no.* 1599.

On the ground. [Up. Carolina.]

The inner peridium is slightly constricted, and then swollen at the base, without any groove round the top of the peduncle, into which it passes gradually.—*Eng. Fl.*

1075. Geaster fimbriatus. *Fr.* "Fringed Geaster."

Outer peridium multifid, expanded, flaccid; interior sessile; mouth indeterminate, piloso-fimbriate.—*Fr. S.M.* iii. *p.* 16. *Mich. t.* 100, *f.* 1. *Berk. Outl. t.* 20, *f.* 4. *Sow. t.* 80. *Ann. N.H. no.* 378. *Schmid. t.* 43-53, *f.* 1-3. *Berk. exs. no.* 275, 209. *Rabh. F.E. no.* 165. *Cooke. exs. no.* 213. *Fckl. exs. no.* 1266.

In fir plantations. [Low. Carolina.]

The mouth is fimbriate, and not simply toothed as in *G. rufescens.*

1076. Geaster mammosus. *Chev.* "Nippled Geaster."

Outer peridium multipartite, rigid, hygrometric; laciniæ equal; interior sessile; mouth ciliate, acutely conic in a circular disc.—*Fr. S.M.* iii. *p.* 17. *Sow. t.* 401. *Mich. t.* 100, *f.* 3. *Bull. t.* 238, *f.* f, g, h? *Eng. Fl.* v. *p.* 301. *Ann. N.H. no.* 379.

On the ground. Rare.

This species is extremely rare. The Rev. M. J. Berkeley writes—"I have seen only the specimen figured by Sowerby."

1077. Geaster rufescens. *Fr.* "Reddish Geaster."

Outer peridium multifid, at length revolute; interior sessile, naked; mouth dentate.—*Fr. S.M.* iii. *p.* 18. *Bocc. t.* 305, *f.* 4. *Buxb.* ii. *t.* 49, *f.* 3. *Schæff. t.* 182. *Bull. t.* 471, *f.* 1. *Pay. f.* 469. *Fl. Dan. t.* 1433. *Ann. N.H. no.* 378.

In pastures. Leicestershire. Northamptonshire. [Carolina, U. S.]

The mouth appears to be irregularly toothed according to the "Outlines."

1078. Geaster hygrometricus. *P.* "Hard-coated Geaster."

Outer peridium multipartite, thick, rigidly inflexed when dry; inner sessile, sub-reticulate, bursting irregularly.—*Fr. S. M.* iii. *p.* 19. *Mich. t.* 100, *f.* 4-6. *Gled. t.* 6. *Bull. t.* 138 (*partly*), *f. a-d. Schmid. t.* 27, 28. *Sow. t.* 401. *Nees. f.* 127. *Bolt. t.* 179. *Kl. exs. no.* 341. *Eng. Fl.* v. *p.* 302. *Bisch. f.* 3632. *Fckl. exs. no.* 1263.

On the ground. Rare. Near Halifax. [United States.]

Variable in size, colour, and the surface of the inner peridium, which is sometimes reticulated, sometimes nearly smooth.—*Eng. Fl.* The hard, horny, outer peridium, and scurfy or reticulate, irregularly bursting, inner peridium, readily distinguish this species.—*M. J. B.*

1079. Geaster lageniformis. *Vitt.* "Flask-like Geaster."

Outer peridium splitting to the middle, in nearly equal acuminate laciniæ, inner stratum very thick, evanescent. Inner peridium sessile, flaccid, mouth determinate, plano-conic, ciliato-fimbriate, columella rather long, clavate.—*Vitt. Monog. Lycop. t.* 1, *f.* 2. *Payer. f.* 519, 520.

On the ground.

Specimens were exhibited at one of the meetings of the Horticultural Society of London. (*Fig.* 113, *reduced.*)

Gen. **69. BOVISTA,** Dill.

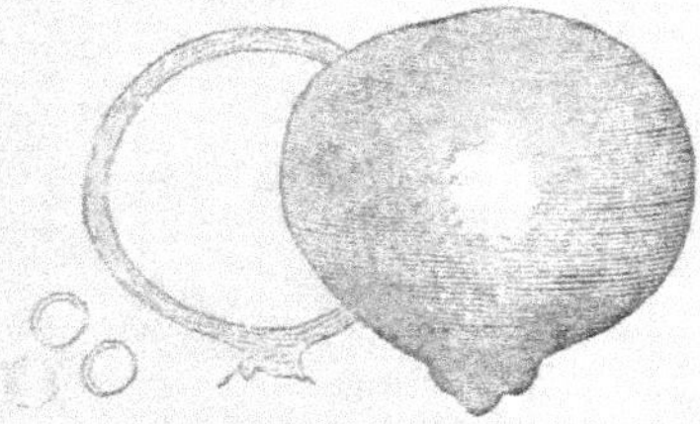

Fig. 114.

Peridium papyraceous (or sometimes corky), persistent; bark distinct, continuous, at length shelling off. Capillitium sub-compact, equal, adnate to the peridium on all sides; spores pedicellate.—*Fr. S. M.* iii. *p.* 21. *Berk. Outl. p.* 301. (*Fig.* 114.)

1080. Bovista nigrescens. *P.* "Blackish Bovista."

Subglobose, peridium papyraceous, tough, at length blackish-umber; bark even, entirely evanescent; capillitium dense, purple brown, as well as the spores.—*Fr. S. M.* iii. *p.* 23. *Berk. Outl. t.* 20, *f.* 5. *Bocc. t.* 306, *f.* 2. *Bolt. t.* 118. *Batsch. f.* 116. *Sow. t.* 331. *Eng. Fl.* v. *p.* 302. *Fckl. exs. no.* 1884. *Kl. exs. no.* 1410.

In pastures. Common. [United States.]

About 1½ in. broad.

1081. Bovista plumbea. *P.* "Lead-coloured Bovista."

Globose, peridium papyraceous, flexible, lead-coloured, bark subpersistent at the base, mouth narrow, capillitium and spores brown.—*Fr. S.M.* ii. *p.* 24. *Mich. t.* 97. *f.* 6. *Berk. Outl. t.* 20. *f.* 6. *Bull. t.* 192. *Eng. Fl.* v. *p.* 302. *Pay. f.* 20. *Corda. Ic.* v. *f.* 47. *Corda. Anl. t. C. f.* 36, *no.* 3-6. *Fckl. exs. no.* 1262.

In pastures. Common. [United States.]

Generally smaller than *B. nigrescens.* *(Fig.* 114.*)*

1082. Bovista ammophila. *Lev.* "Rooting Bovista."

Globoso-turbinate, tomentose, verruculose, white; mycelium cord-like, rooting. Spores globose, even, olivaceous, as well as the delicate capillitium.—*Lev. Ann. Sc. Nat. ser.* 3, ix. *p.* 129, *t.* 9, *f.* 5. *B. & Br. Ann. N.H. no.* 1033.

On the side of a wood. Sept. Denbighshire.

Easily recognised by the long cord-like root, and olivaceous spores.

Gen. 70. LYCOPERDON, Tourn.

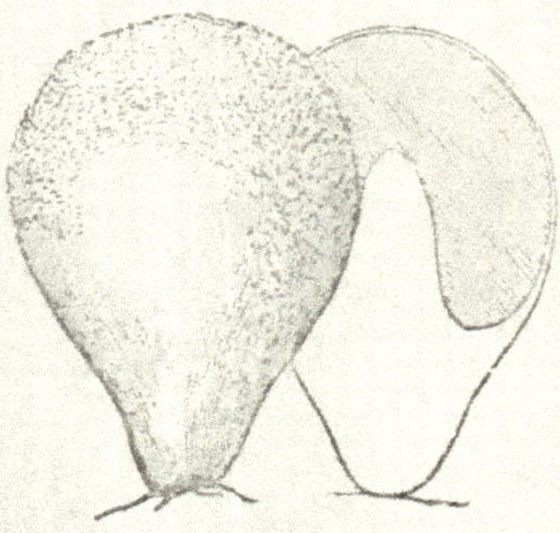

Fig. 115.

Peridium membranaceous, vanishing above, or becoming flaccid; bark adnate, subpersistent; breaking up into scales or warts. Capillitium soft, dense, adnate to the peridium, and sterile base.—*Fr. S.M.* iii. *p.* 27. *Berk. Outl. p.* 301. *(Fig.* 115.*)*

1083. Lycoperdon giganteum. *Batsch.* "Giant Puff-Ball."

Peridium very fragile above, and obtuse, cracking into areæ, evanescent, very widely open, bark floccose, rather distinct; capillitium vanishing, together with the dingy-olive spores.—*Fr. S.M.* iii. *p.* 29. *Grev. t.* 336. *Huss.* i. *t.* 26. *Ray. Syn. no.* 4, *p.* 26. *Schæff. t.* 191. *Bull. t.* 447. *Sv. Bot. t.* 294. *Batsch. f.* 165. *Fl. Dan. t.* 1920. *Sow. t.* 332, *upper fig.* *Nees. f.* 124, *C. Eng. Fl.* v. *p.* 303. *Smith, E.M. f.* 25. *Corda. Ic.* v. *f.* 40.

In pastures. Local. Esculent when young. [United States.]

Attaining a very large size; peridium soft and smooth, like kid-leather when young, when old dingy olive. Employed as an anæsthetic.

1084. Lycoperdon cælatum. *Fr.* "Collapsing Puff Ball."

Peridium flaccid above, collapsing, obtuse, dehiscent at the apex, at length open, cup-shaped; sterile stratum cellulose; inner peridium distinct all round; capillitium nearly free, collapsing; spores dingy-yellow.—*Fr. S.M.* iii. *p.* 32. *Ray. Syn.* iii. *p.* 26, *no.* 3. *Vaill. t.* 16, *f.* 4. *Schæff. t.* 189, 190, 186. *Nees. f.* 125. *Berk. Outl. t.* 20, *f.* 7. *Huss.* ii. *t.* 23. *Eng. Fl.* v. *p.* 303. *Harz. t.* 74. *Bisch. f.* 3604.

In pastures. Common. [Carolina. Maine, U. S.]

Remarkable for its spongy, blunt, obconic base, cavity above sublenticular. In consequence of the simple orifice the mass of flocci and spores does not fall out but collapses, until by decay the upper part of the fungus is ruptured. —*Eng. Fl.*

1085. Lycoperdon atropurpureum. *Vitt.* "Purple-spored Puff Ball."

Peridium flaccid, dingy-rufous, opening by a minute obtuse mouth; bark at first rough with minute spines; sterile base cellular, continuous with the capillitium; spores largish, pedicellate, brown-purple, echinulate.—*Vitt. Lyc. t.* 2, *f.* 6. *Berk. Outl. p.* 302. *Sci. Gos.* 1866, *f.* 252.

On downs. West of England.

Spores echinulate in this species, and in *L. saccatum.*

1086. Lycoperdon pusillum. *Fr.* "Little Puff Ball."

Peridium entirely flaccid, persistent, obtuse; mouth always narrowly dehiscent; bark even, then rimose with adpressed scales; sterile stratum obsolete, continuous with the capillitium; spores olive.—*Fr. S.M.* iii. *p.* 33. *Bolt. t.* 117, *f.* C. *Mich. t.* 97, *f.* 3. *Schæff. t.* 294. *Batsch. f.* 228, *var. Bull. t.* 435, *f.* 2. *Eng. Fl.* v. *p.* 304. *Sci. Gos.* 1866, *f.* 255. *Kl. exs. no.* 1635. *Fckl. exs. no.* 1261.

In pastures. [Low. & Mid. Carolina.]

A small species, sometimes not larger than a marble.

1087. Lycoperdon saccatum. *Vahl.* "Elongated Puff Ball."

Peridium lens-shaped or rounded, scurfy, obtuse, cracking into areæ, fugacious, very thin, as well as the adnate bark; capillitium compact, persistent; spores dingy-umber.—*Fr. S.M.* iii. *p.* 35. *Huss.* i. *t.* 14. *Bocc. t.* 306, *f.* 1. *Bisch. f.* 3605. *Fl. Dan. t.* 1139. *Sci. Gos.* 1866, *f.* 251. *Ann. N.H. no.* 210. *Cooke exs. no.* 214.

In thickets or their borders.

Easily known by the plicate folds on the under side of the peridium. Spores echinulate.

1088. Lycoperdon gemmatum. *Fr.* "Warted Puff Ball."

Peridium membranaceous, persistent, base narrow, opening with an umbonate mouth; bark farinaceous, adnate, covered with sub-spinulose warts; flocci in the centre forming a columella, persistent; spores yellow with a greenish tinge.—*Fr. S.M.* iii. *p.* 36. *Bolt. t.* 117. *Huss.* i. *t.* 54. *Vaill. t.* 12, *f.* 15, 16. *Mich. t.* 97, *f.* 1. *Batt. t.* 31, *f.* 4. *Fl. Dan. t.* 1120. *Bull. t.* 475, B-E. *Harz. t.* 27. *Chev. t.* 10, *f.* 2. *Schæff. t.* 184. *Eng. Fl.* v. *p.* 304. *Sci. Goss.* 1866, *f.* 253. *Bisch. f.* 3614.

In meadows, &c. Common. [Cincinnati. Maine, U. S.]

Very variable. Mouth prominent, umbonate from the club-shaped columella; spores small and smooth.

1089. Lycoperdon pyriforme. *Schæff.* "Pear-shaped Puff Ball."

Peridium membranaceous, persistent, subpyriform, opening with an umbonate mouth; bark innate, covered with very thin fugacious squamules, columella conical; spores greenish-yellow. —*Fr. S.M.* iii. *p.* 39. *Ray. Syn.* iii. *p.* 19, *no.* 7. *Huss.* i. *t.* 70. *Grev. t.* 304. *Schæff. t.* 189. *Bull. t.* 32, & *t.* 435, *f.* 3. *Fl. Dan. t.* 1680, *f.* 1. *Eng. Fl.* v. *p.* 304. *Sci. Goss.* 1866, *f.* 254. *Cooke, exs. no.* 215. *Fckl. exs. no.* 1260.

On decayed stumps. Common. [United States.]

Generally much tufted. Root white, branched, creeping; columella conical; spores small and smooth. *(Fig.* 115.*)*

Gen. 71. SCLERODERMA, P.

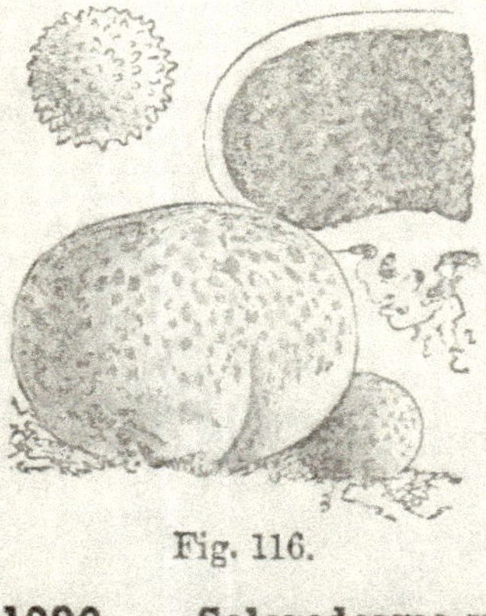

Fig. 116.

Peridium firm, with an innate bark, bursting irregularly; flocci adhering on all sides to the peridium, and forming distinct veins in the central mass; spores large, granulated.—*Berk. Outl. p.* 303. *Eng. Fl.* v. *p.* 305.

(*Fig.* 116.)

1090. Scleroderma vulgare. *Fr.* "Common Scleroderma."

Subsessile, irregular; peridium corky, hard, dehiscing indefinitely; inner mass bluish-black; spores dingy.—*Fr. S.M.* iii. *p.*

46. *Huss.* i. *t.* 17. *Fl. Dan. t.* 1969, *f.* 2. *Vaill. t.* 16. *f.* 8. *Bolt. t.* 116. *Bull. t.* 270. *Sow. t.* 268. *Eng. Fl.* v. *p.* 305. *Berk. Outl. t.* 15, *f.* 4. *Pay. f.* 506. *Schnz. t.* 14, *f.* 46-48. *Tuber solidum, With.* iii. *p.* 459. *Fckl. exs. no.* 1253.

On borders of woods. Common. [Maine, U. S.]

The larger form is generally of a yellowish hue, with the surface warty, or covered with squarrose scales, the smaller quite sessile, minutely warty, and of a bright brown. The spores are collected into little heaps separated by a few greyish flocci.—*Eng. Fl.* (*Fig.* 116.)

1091. Scleroderma bovista. *Fr.* "Thin-coated Scleroderma."

Subsessile, irregular; peridium thin, soft, dehiscing irregularly; bark sub-seceding; flocci yellow; spores dingy olive.—*Fr. S.M.* iii. *p.* 48. *Mich. t.* 99, *f.* 2. *Batsch. f.* 229. *Eng. Fl.* v. *p.* 306.

On sandy ground. [Low. Carolina.]

Known by its thinner peridium, and yellow flocci.—*M. J. B.*

1092. Scleroderma verrucosum. *Pers.* "Warty Scleroderma."

Substipitate; peridium rounded, subverrucose, thin above and fragile; inner mass purplish-black; flocci and spores brown.—*Fr. S.M.* iii. *p.* 49. *Grev. t.* 48. *Huss.* i. *t.* 17. *Bocc. t.* 305, *f.* 2. *Schæff. t.* 188. *Vaill. t.* 16, *f.* 7. *Mich. t.* 99, *f.* 3. *Bull. t.* 24. *Sow. t.* 311. *Nees. f.* 123. *Eng. Fl.* v. *p.* 306. *Fckl. exs. no.* 1254.

On sandy ground. [United States.]

Stem thick, lacunose. Care must be taken not to confound this with stipitate forms of the foregoing.—*M. J. B.*

Gen. 72. POLYSACCUM, D.C.

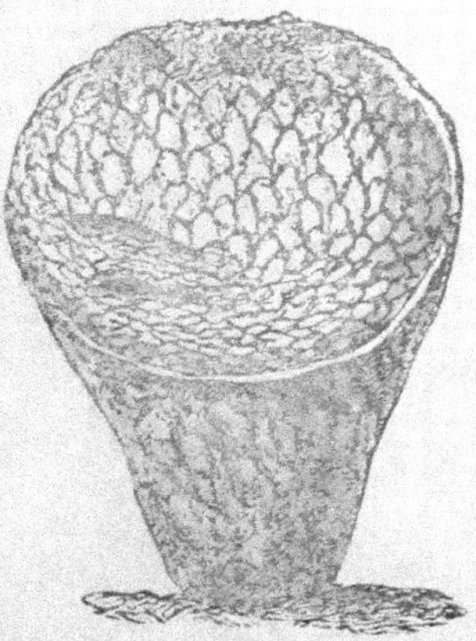

Fig. 117.

Common peridium simple, rigid, bursting irregularly; internal mass divided into distinct cells, filled with peridiola; spores mixed with the threads.—*Berk. Outl. p.* 304. *Eng. Fl.* v. *p.* 306. (*Fig.* 117.)

1093. Polysaccum olivaceum. *Fr.* "Olive Polysaccum."

Peridium roundish, olive, as well as the regular, minute peridioli; stem short, abrupt, almost rootless.—*Fr. S.M.* iii. *p.* 54. *Sow. t.* 425, *a. b. Berk. Outl. p.* 304.

On the ground. Very rare.

It is so extremely rare that neither the Rev. M. J. Berkeley nor ourselves have seen a single specimen. An allied species is found in Lower Carolina, U. S. *(Fig.* 117.*)*

Gen. **73. CENOCOCCUM,** Fr.

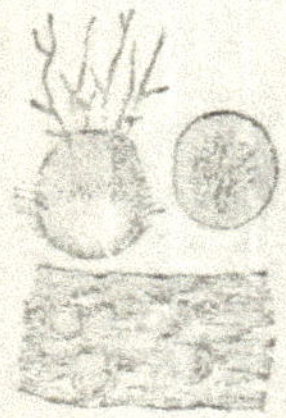

Fig. 118.

Peridium naked, thick, carbonaceous, indehiscent, at length hollow, with the walls dotted with dust-like spores.—*Berk. Outl. p.* 304. *Eng. Fl.* v. *p.* 307. (*Fig.* 118.)

1094. Cenococcum geophilum. *Fr.* "Ground Cenococcum."

Black, even, within of the same colour, or dark brown; spores subspherical, blackish, even (or sometimes reticulated?).—*Fr. S.M.* iii. *p.* 228. *Tul. Hyp. t.* 21, *f.* 8. *Lycoperdon graniforme, Sow. t.* 270. *Desm. exs. no.* 1021. *Bisch. f.* 3685. *Act. Turin.* 1843, v. *t.* 3, *f.* 5. *Fckl. exs. no.* 1072.

In woods where the soil is peaty. Common.

About the size of a vetch. Scattered upon the ground without any root. *(Fig.* 118.*)*

Order X. MYXOGASTRES.

At first pulpy, at length filled with flocci and dust-like spores. —*Berk. Outl. p.* 304.

Whole plant at first gelatinous. Mycelium often vein like, forming reticulated or anastomosing strata, but sometimes diffuse, giving rise to sessile or stipitate, free or confluent pendia, consisting of one or more membranes, inclosing, when mature, a dry mass of threads or plates, and spores; at length often bursting. Threads of various structure, sometimes containing one or more spirals.—*Berk. Introd. p.* 335.

Large, sessile, more or less indeterminate.
  Peridium double, externally warty or mealy . . . *Lycogala.*
  Peridium single.
    Externally naked, fugitive . . . . . . *Reticularia.*
    Externally floccose . . . . *Æthalium.*
  Peridium crustaceous.
    Spores surrounded by membranous folds . . *Spumaria.*
  Peridium thick, fleshy . . . . *Ptychogaster.*
Small, sometimes stalked, determinate.
  Threads not a prominent feature.
    Spores free.
      Peridium double, external smooth . . . *Diderma.*
      Peridium simple.
        Bursting irregularly.
          Scaly or floccose . . . . . . *Didymium.*
          Naked, smooth . . . . . . *Physarum.*
        Bursting longitudinally . . . . . *Angioridium.*
    Spores in groups.
      Peridium naked, or mealy . . . . . *Badhamia.*
  Threads congested.
      Peridium cup shaped, operculate . . . *Craterium.*
  Threads prominent, at length more or less exposed.
      Peridium delicate, evanescent.
        Threads springing from columella . . *Diachæa.*
        Threads springing from stem . . . *Stemonitis.*
        Threads dependent from disc . . . *Enerthenema.*
      Peridium veined from innate capillitium . *Dictydium.*
      Peridium persistent below.
        Capillitium netted, free above . . . *Cribraria.*
        Capillitium elastic, banded or nodulose . *Arcyria.*
      Peridium bursting irregularly.
        Threads free, spiral . . . . . . *Trichia.*
      Peridum bursting longitudinally.
        Threads of two kinds . . . . . . *Ophiotheca.*
      Peridium splitting horizontally.
        Threads few . . . . *Perichæna.*
  Threads obsolete.
      Peridium membranaceous.
        Bursting irregularly . . . . . . *Licea.*
        Splitting horizontally . . . . . . *Phelonitis.*

Gen. 74. LYCOGALA, Mich.

Fig 119.

Peridium composed of a double membrane, papyraceous, persistent, bursting irregularly at the apex, externally warty, or furfuraceous. Flocci delicate, adnate to the peridium.—*Berk. Outl. p.* 305. *Eng. Fl.* v. *p.* 307. (*Fig.* 119.)

1095. Lycogala epidendrum. *Fr.* "Stump Lycogala."

Sub-globose, blood-red then brownish, punctato-scabrous, mouth irregular, spores becoming pale.—*Fr. S.M.* iii. *p.* 80. *Fl. Dan. t.* 720, t. 2086, *f.* 2. *Bolt. t.* 119, *f.* 1. *Fckl. exs. no.* 1475. *Bull. t.* 503. *Sow. t.* 52. *Holms.* ii. *t.* 31. *Buxb.* v. *t.* 29, *f.* 2. *Mich. t.* 95. *Jacq. Misc. t.* 7. *Schæff. t.* 193. *Nees. f.* 97, 96. *Grev. t.* 38. *Moug. exs. no.* 85. *Eng. Fl.* v. *p.* 307. *Corda. Ic.* v. *f.* 40. *Bisch. f.* 3673. *Kl. exs. no.* 933.

On rotten stumps. Common. [Cincinnati, U. S.]

Varying much in colour and size, and the hue of the sporidia. The surface is rough with dot-like scurfy warts, and changes colour sooner than the pulpy mass within, which is often of the finest scarlet, and oozes out in large drops if the peridium is injured.—*Eng Fl.* (*Fig* 119.)

1096. Lycogala parietinum. *Fr.* "Paper Lycogala."

Hemispherical, punctate, bluish-black, lacero-dehiscent; spores yellow.—*Fr. S.M.* iii. *p.* 83. *Schrad. t.* 6, *f.* 1. *Pers. Ic. Pict. t.* 3, *f.* 4-5. *B. & Br. Ann. N.H. no.* 381.

On damp paper, basket work, &c. King's Cliffe.

Gen. 75. RETICULARIA, Bull.

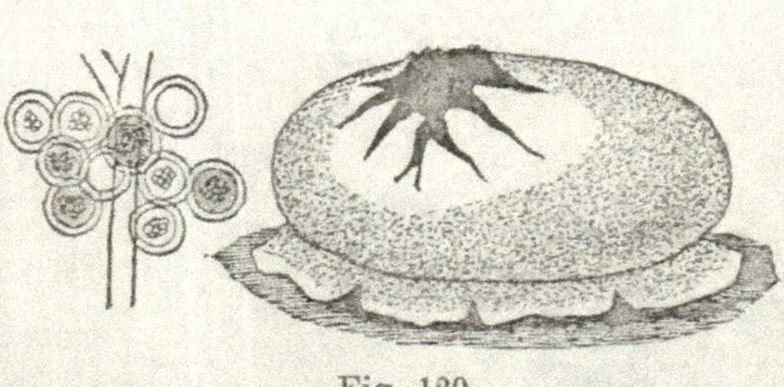

Fig. 120.

Peridium indeterminate, simple, thin, naked, bursting irregularly, fugitive. Flocci attached to the peridium, flat, branched, subreticulate.—*Berk. Outl. p.* 305. *Eng. Fl.* v. *p.* 308. (*Fig.* 120.)

1097. Reticularia maxima. *Fr.* "Large Reticularia."

Hypothallus effused, peridium very thin, tuberculose, white, then blackish-purple, flocci fasciculate, adnate to the base, spores black-purple.—*Fr. S.M.* iii. *p.* 85. *Eng. Fl.* v. *p.* 308. *Corda. Ic.* vi. *f.* 35. *Fckl. exs. no.* 1473.

On trunks of felled trees. [United States.]

1098. Reticularia applanata. *B. & Br.* "Flattened Reticularia."

Effused, delicate, olivaceous-brown, spores olive, echinulate.—*B. & Br. Ann. N.H.* (1866), *no.* 1142, *t.* 2, *f.* 3.

On fallen trunk, the surface of which had been charred. Nov. Ascot.

Resembling in habit *Licea applanata*. Surface reticulated, as in *R. maxima*. Spores 4-7 in. a fascicle, connate, echinulate, ·0005 in. diameter.—*B. & Br.*

1099. Reticularia atra. *Fr.* "Black Reticularia."

Sub-pulvinate, peridium very thin, subreticulate, flocci erect from the base, dendroid, divaricate, black, as well as the mature spores.—*Fr. S.M.* iii. *p.* 86. *Eng. Fl.* v. *p.* 308. *Kl. exs. no.* 1748. *A. & S. t.* 3, *f.* 3. *Lycop. fuliginosum*, *Sow. t.* 257.

On wood and bark of felled pines. [Mid. Carolina.]

1100. Reticularia umbrina. *Fr.* "Umber Reticularia."

Subpulvinate, peridium very thin, nearly even, silvery, then umber, flocci adnate to the base, erect, branched, umber as well as the spores.—*Fr. S.M.* iii. *p.* 87. *Fl. Dan. t.* 1976, *f.* 2. *Eng. Fl.* v. *p.* 308. *Mich. t.* 95. *f.* 1. *Gled. t.* 6. *Bolt. t.* 133, *f.* 2. *Bull. t.* 446. *f.* 4, *t.* 476, *f.* 1-3. *Sow. t.* 272. *Grev. t.* 106. *Sturm. t.* 38. *Nees. f.* 95. *Berk. Outl. t.* 20, *f.* 8.

On stumps, &c. [Mid. Carolina.]

When growing on a horizontal surface sometimes several inches broad; peridium before bursting of a beautiful silvery umber, passing beneath the mass of spores, and in favourable circumstances entirely separable from the matrix. From the base spring the compressed, branched, reticulated flocci, which are umber, like the spores, but shine with a golden or bronze-like lustre.—*Eng. Fl.* (*Fig.* 120.)

Gen. **76.** **ÆTHALIUM,** Link.

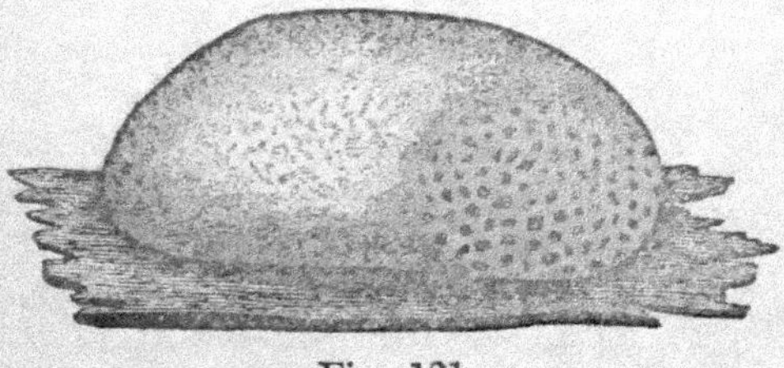

Fig. 121.

Peridium indeterminate, externally covered by a floccose evanescent bark, cellular within from the confluent interwoven flocci.—*Berk. Outl. p.* 306. *Eng. Fl.* v. *p.* 309. (*Fig.* 121.)

1101. **Æthalium septicum.** *Fr.* "Wood Æthalium"

Variously coloured, effused, external bark yellow, thin, deciduous; internal mass compact, black.—*Eng. Fl.* v. *p.* 309. *Fuligo violacea, Pers. Ic. Pict. t.* i., *p.* 1. *Pers. Syn. p.* 161. *Bisch. f.* 3631. *Schuzl. t.* 15, *f.* 57-58. *Kl. exs. no.* 1027.

In woods, on various substances. [United States.]
(*Fig.* 121.)

1102. **Æthalium vaporarium.** *Fr.* "Stove Æthalium."

Yellow, effused, in irregular masses; spores at length black. —*Pers. Syn. p.* 161. *Nees. t.* 8, *f.* 92. *Schæff. t.* 192. *Jacq. Misc.* v. *t.* 8. *Mich. t.* 96, *f.* 2. *Rabh. F.E. no.* 81. *Fckl. exs. no.* 1472. *Bolt. t.* 134. *Bull. t.* 380, *f.* 1, *t.* 424. *Sow. t.* 399, *f.* 1. *Grev. t.* 272. *Gard. Chron.* (1860), *p.* 409, *with fig. Eng. Fl.* v. *p.* 309 (*partly*).

In stoves, on bark. [United States.]

This species is always yellow, and is a great nuisance in hot-houses. The two species have long been confounded together, but Fries and Mr. Berkeley appear to be of opinion now that they are distinct, although the specific distinctions have not been well defined.

Gen. **77.** **SPUMARIA,** Fr.

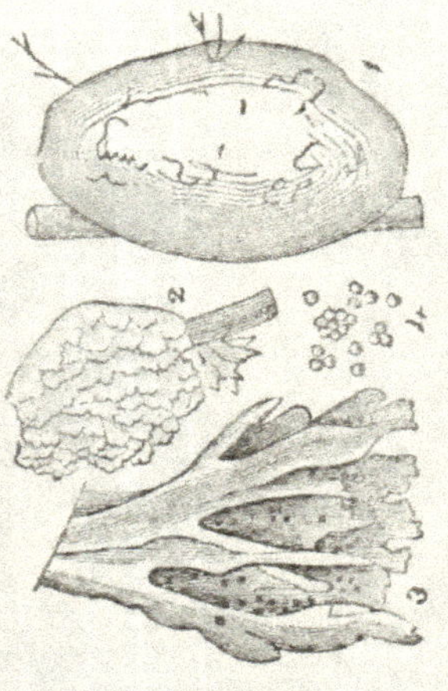

Fig. 122.

Peridium indeterminate, simple, crustaceous, flocculoso-cellular. Spores surrounded by membranaceous, ascending, often sinuous folds.—*Berk. Outl. p.* 306. *Eng. Fl.* v. *p.* 309.
(*Fig.* 122.)

1103. **Spumaria alba.** *D.C.* "White Spumaria."

Effused, whitish, the internal plicate membrane branched in a horn-like manner.—*Fr. S.M.* iii. *p.* 95. *Bot. Zeit.* 1848, *t.* 5, *f.* 1-6. *Fckl. exs. no.* 1471. *Batt. t.* 40, *f. G.H. Bull. t.* 326. *Nees. f.* 94. *Grev. t.* 267. *Fl. Dan. t.* 1978, *f.* 1. *Eng. Fl.* v. *p.* 310. *Sow. t.* 280. *Bisch. f.* 3630.

On living grass, &c.

In its young state having the appearance of a white froth, variable in size. At this period it is quite soft and pulpy, but in a few days it becomes of a firmer texture, the surface begins to scale off, to burst in the centre, and to emit a vast number of dark-coloured globose spores. When the spores have escaped, they are found to have been contained in numerous branched, horn-like, nearly erect, membranaceous folds, resembling irregular, imperfect, divided tubes.—*Grev.* (*Fig.* 122.)

Gen. **78.** **PTYCHOGASTER,** Ca.

Fig. 123.

Peridium thick, fleshy, sub-stipitate, lamelloso-cellulose within, strata irregular fertile and sterile mixed, cells composed of conglutinated flocci, which are simple and flexuous. Spores simple, acrogenous.—*Corda Ic.* ii. *p.* 24. (*Fig.* 123.)

1104. Ptychogaster albus. *Corda.* "White Ptychogaster."

Peridium rounded, soft, white, peduncle spurious, cells flexuous, unequal; spores ochrey-clay colour, very minute, ovoid, pellucid, mixed with the continuous flocci.—*B. & Br. Ann. N.H.* (1865), *no.* 1038. *Corda. Icon.* ii., *f.* 90. *Corda. Anl. t. C. f.* 34, *no.* 7-10.

On the ground, at the roots of firs. Aboyne, &c.

The affinities of this curious plant are doubtful, for it does not appear to be of the creamy consistence of *Æthalium* in any stage of growth. We have no better opinion, however, to give than that of Corda. Fries seems to think that it is a degeneration of *Polyporus destructor.*—*B. & Br.* (*Fig.* 123.)

Gen. **79.** **DIDERMA,** P.

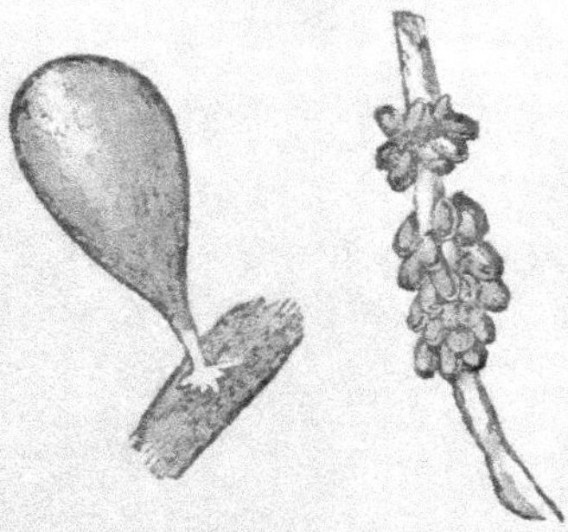

Fig. 124.

Peridium double, external distinct, crustaceous, smooth; internal delicate, evanescent, attached to the straggling flocci, with or without a columella.—*Berk. Outl. p.* 306. *Eng. Fl.* v. *p.* 310. (*Fig.* 124.)

A. *Stipitate*—stem distinct.

1105. **Diderma floriforme.** *P.* "Flower-like Diderma."

Yellowish or whitish; stem slender, peridium spherical, splitting in a stellate manner, reflexed; columella ob-conical; spores black-brown.—*Pers. Syn. p.* 164. *Fr. S.M.* iii. *p.* 99. *Bull t.* 371. *Eng. Fl.* v. *p.* 310.

On decaying trunks, &c. Autumn. [Mid. Carolina.]

Stems springing from a common thickish membrane.

1106. **Diderma umbilicatum.** *P.* "Umbilicated Diderma."

Whitish, stem obese, peridium sub-rotund, umbilicate beneath, split into laciniæ, at length patent; columella rufescent; spores purplish-black.—*Fr. S.M.* iii. *p.* 99. *Fl. Dan. t.* 1972, *f.* 1. *Eng. Fl.* v. *p.* 310.

On bark of trees, &c. Appin.

The columella is very large, white within, resembling strongly the nucleus of *Næmatelia*.—*Eng. Fl.*

1107. **Diderma citrinum.** *Fr.* "Lemon Yellow Diderma."

Lemon-yellow; stem firm, even; peridium hemispherical, squamulose, dehiscent; columella spurious; spores black-brown.—*Fr. S.M.* iii. *p.* 100. *Fl. Dan. t.* 1312, *f.* 1. *Eng. Fl.* v. *p.* 310.

On leaves of *Sphagnum.* Aug.—Oct. Inverary.

Scattered, each plant adhering by a separate membranaceous base; stem shortish, thickest below, when dry tawny-yellow. Peridium brownish, splitting irregularly in a stellate manner, covered under a lens with minute roundish white scattered scales.—*Eng. Fl.*

B. *Stipitate.*—stem spurious, somewhat confluent.

1108. **Diderma vernicosum.** *P.* "Varnished Diderma."

Peridia obovate, external thick, bay-brown, shining; internal yellow; stem thread-like, short, lax; spores blackish.—*Fr. S.M.* iii. *p.* 102. *Dicks.* i. *t.* 3. *f.* 6. *Sow. t.* 136. *Pers. Obs.* i. *t.* 3, *f.* 7. *Fl. Dan. t.* 1312, *f.* 2. *Nees. f.* 110. *Grev. t.* 111. *Eng. Fl.* v. *p.* 311. *Kl. exs. no.* 175.

On grass, twigs, moss, &c. [Carolina, Maine, U.S.]

(Fig. 124, cluster nat. size, peridium magnified.)

1109. Diderma spumarioides. *Fr.* "Effused Diderma."

Effused, crustaceous, cohering; peridia subrotund, or irregular; exterior white; interior ash-colour, often confluent in a cellulose crust, columella spurious, white, as well as the flocci; spores black.—*Fr. S.M.* iii. *p.* 104. *Mich. t.* 96. *f.* 2. *Bull. t.* 424, *f.* 2. *Sow. t.* 280. *Fl. Dan. t.* 1978, *f.* 2. *Eng. Fl.* v. *p.* 311.

On leaves, moss, &c.

The specimen before me has obovate-oblong, distinct peridia, stems arising from the hypothallus, a cylindrical central white columella, and flocci of the same colour, mixed with the spores. The stem is entirely formed from the hypothallus and hyaline.—*M. J. B.*

c. *Sessile.*

1110. Diderma lucidum. *B. & Br.* "Bright Diderma."

Subglobose, sessile, splitting in a somewhat stellate manner, bright reddish yellow, internally yellow, mass of fruit globose, black; flocci brown, triangular at the points of ramification, and yellowish; spores globose, black, very minutely echinulate.—*B. & Br. Ann. N.H. no.* 938, *t.* 15, *f.* 9.

On *Jungermanniæ* and moss.

Scattered or crowded, peridium subglobose, splitting in an irregular stellate manner. Spores (·0005 in.) ·0125 m.m. diameter. Smaller than *D. vernicosum*, in which the spores are inclined to be angular, and much paler under the microscope.

1111. Diderma Trevelyani. *Fr.* "Trevelyan's Diderma."

Sessile, ovate or globose; outer peridium splitting into many regular, linear, subreflexed, laciniæ; inner obsolete; columella minute; spores black. *Fr. S.M.* iii. *p.* 105. *Grev. t.* 132. *Eng. Fl.* v. *p.* 311.

On *Bryum ligulatum.*

In specimens communicated to Sowerby by Mr. Trevelyan there is a very short, but distinct cylindrical stem, the peridium at first appears under the lens like a coriander seed, pale-brown, with pallid striæ, which indicate the points at which it will split, and perfectly smooth. Within this is a distinct white inner peridium, lining it very closely, and probably in general breaking off with it. Flocci greyish. I can find no trace of a columella.—*M. J. B*

1112. Diderma Carmichaelianum. *Berk.* "Carmichael's Diderma."

Perfectly sessile, outer peridium brick-red, splitting into many revolute rays, inner white, intimately connected with the outer; columella large, spores black-brown.—*Eng. Fl.* v. *p.* 34.

On moss. Appin.

The columella resembles that of *D. umbilicatum.*

1113. Diderma nitens. *Klotsch.* "Shining Diderma."

Applanato-sessile, round, hemispherical, cæspitose, outer peridium crust-like, silvery white, brittle, inner very thin hyaline, columella none, spores black-brown.—*Klotsch. in Hook. Herb. Eng. Fl.* v. *p.* 312.

On bark. Appin.

1114. Diderma globosum. *Fr.* "Globose Diderma."

Sessile, globoso-hemispherical; outer peridium white, inner cinereous, columella globose, spores sooty-black.—*Fr. S.M.* iii. *p.* 106. *Mich. t.* 96, *f.* 6. *Bull. t.* 446, *f.* 2. *Pers. Disp. t.* 4, *f.* 4, 5. *Sturm. t.* 6. *Grev. t.* 122. *Chev. t.* 9, *f.* 28. *Eng. Fl.* v. *p.* 312. *Bisch. f.* 3629.

On dead leaves. Autumn. Common. [United States.]

Gregarious, sessile, minute, about a line in diameter, roundish, somewhat depressed, white, or greyish, the outer peridium fragile and evanescent in farinaceous particles; the inner one also fragile, grey, membranaceous. Columella large, white, roundish. Spores globose dark coloured, intermixed with filaments.—*Grev.*

1115. Diderma cyanescens. *Fr.* "Amorphous Diderma."

Sessile-adnate, sub-rotund, irregular, outer peridium thick, white, inner ash-colour, columella none, flocci and spores black-brown.—*Fr. S.M.* iii. *p.* 109. *Nees. f.* 105? *Eng. Fl.* v. *p.* 312.

On dead oak leaves.

Outer peridium crustaceous, white, like the shell of some small egg, inner peridium in the dry state brownish, except at the base, where it is adnate and rufous.—*Eng. Fl.*

1116. Diderma deplanatum. *Fr.* "Depressed Diderma."

Sessile, rounded, outer peridium thick, white, inner very thin, hyaline, columella and flocci none, spores black-brown.—*Fr. S.M.* iii. *p.* 110. *Hoff. F.G. t.* 9, *f.* 2. *Eng. Fl.* v. *p.* 312.

On dead oak leaves. Appin.

When the spores have fallen out, the base within is of a somewhat tawny tinge. There are a few flocci.—*Eng. Fl.*

1117. Diderma contextum. *Fr.* "Interwoven Diderma."

Sessile, crowded; peridia elongated, flexuose, outer lemon-coloured; inner whitish-yellow, columella none, flocci white, spores dingy.—*Fr. S.M.* iii. *p.* 111. *Sturm. t.* 39. *Berk. Ann. N.H. no.* 109. *Bisch. f.* 3624.

On dead grass, fern, &c. Wothorpe. [United States.]

Gen. **80.** **DIDYMIUM,** Schrad.

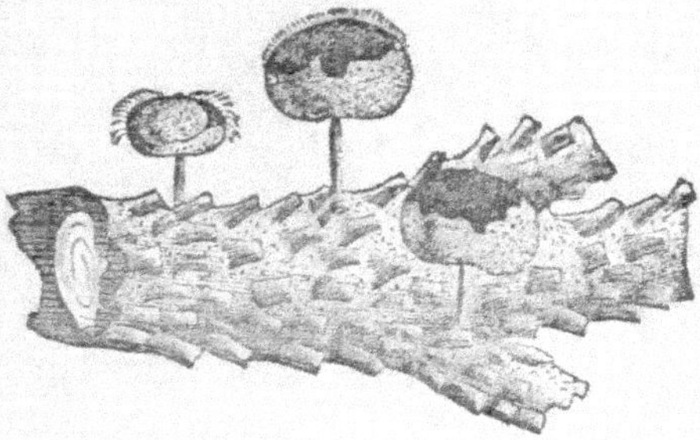

Fig. 125.

Peridium scaly or floccose, bursting irregularly. —*Berk. Outl. p.* 307. (*Fig.* 125.)

Inner peridium very delicate; membranaceous, bursting irregularly, externally clothed with the bark-like outer peridium, which breaks up into little furfuraceous scales or mealy down.—*Eng. Fl.* v. *p.* 312.

1118. Didymium melanopus. *Fr.* "Black-stemmed Didymium."

Peridium hemispherical, depressed, erect, farinose, plano-umbilicate beneath, grey; stem subulate, black, as well as the columella; spores dingy brown.—*Fr. S.M.* iii. *p.* 114. *Berk. Ann. N.H. no.* 382. *Bisch. f.* 3669.

On bramble. [United States.]

var. β. clavus. *Fr.* Stem substriate, peridium farinoso-villous, concave beneath, black.—*Ann. N.H. no.* 110, *A. & S, t.* 2, *f.* 2.

On various substances.

1119. Didymium hæmisphericum. *Fr.* "Hemispherical Didymium."

Peridium hemispherical, depressed, erect, with a whitish veil, plano-umbilicate beneath; stem short, thick, whitish; columella obsolete; spores sooty-black.—*Fr. S.M.* iii. *p.* 115. *Bull. t.* 446, *f.* 1. *Sow. t.* 12. *Fl. Dan. t.* 1972, *f.* 2.

On dead twigs, &c.

The curious flat subhemispherical peridia, with a broad shallow umbilicus beneath, and the short, dirty-white stem, are characteristic.—*Eng. Fl.*

1120. Didymium furfuraceum. *Fr.* "Scurfy Didymium."

Peridium lenticular, cernuous, flocculoso-farinaceous, whitish-cinereous, columella none; stem whitish, even; spores blackish.

—*Fr. S.M.* iii. *p.* 116. *B. & Br. Ann. N.H. no.* 734. *Fl. Dan. t.* 2092, *f.* 2.

On dead leaves (and oak branches ?). [United States.]

1121. Didymium tigrinum. *Fr.* "Spotted Didymium."

Peridium lenticular, erect, umbilicate beneath, black, covered with greenish-yellow furfuraceous scales; stem elongated, yellowish, columella brown, spores sooty-black.—*Fr. S.M.* iii. *p.* 117. *Schrad. t.* 6. *f.* 2, 3. *B. & Br. Ann. N.H. no.* 383. *Fl. Dan. t.* 1434, *f.* 1.

On decayed wood. [Mid. Carolina.]

According to the "Annals" this species has been found on mosses and Jungermanniæ.

1122. Didymium squamulosum. *A. & G.* "Scaly Didymium."

Peridium globose-depressed, umbilicate beneath, cinereous, covered with minute scales of the same colour, stem very short, even, white, columella white, spores brownish-black.—*Fr. S.M.* iii. *p.* 118. *A. & S. t.* 4. *f.* 5. *Eng. Fl.* v. *p.* 312. *Bisch. f.* 3676. *Kl. exs.* ii. *no.* 455.

On dead leaves, &c. [United States.]

1123. Didymium farinaceum. *Fr.* "Mealy Didymium."

Peridium subrotund, very thin, blackish, clothed with cinereous flocculose meal; stem short, brown-black, as well as the spores. —*Fr. S.M.* iii. *p.* 119. *Hall. t.* 48, *f.* 2. *Sow. t.* 240. *Schrad. t.* 5, *f.* 6. *Eng. Fl.* v. *p.* 313. *Fl. Dan. t.* 2094, *f.* 1. *Kl. exs. no.* 423, ii. *no.* 138. *Fckl. exs. no.* 1461.

On dead leaves, &c. [United States.]

(*Fig.* 125.)

1124. Didymium nigripes. *Fr.* "Black-stemmed Didymium."

Peridium globose, grey from the delicate meal with which it is clothed; stem elongated, rigid, even, black; columella obsolete, flocci and spores dingy-brown.—*Fr. S.M.* iii. *p.* 119. *Eng. Fl.* v. *p.* 313. *Sturm. t.* 42. *Bisch. f.* 3612. *Trichia alba, Purt. no.* 1113.

On rotten wood.

Remarkable for its dark, stiff, hair-like stem.

1125. Didymium pertusum. *Berk.* "Pierced Didymium."

Scattered; peridium white, mealy, depresso-globose, deeply but narrowly umbilicate; stem attenuated upwards, rufous; columella central, white; flocci brownish; spores brown-black.—*Eng. Fl.* v. *p.* 313. *Berk. Outl. p.* 307.

On dead herbaceous stems. Appin.

This approaches very near to *D. xanthopus*, but the columella is not truly stipitate, but only apparently so from the great depth of the umbilicus. —*M. J. B.*

1126. Didymium xanthopus. *Fr.* "Yellow-stemmed Didymium."

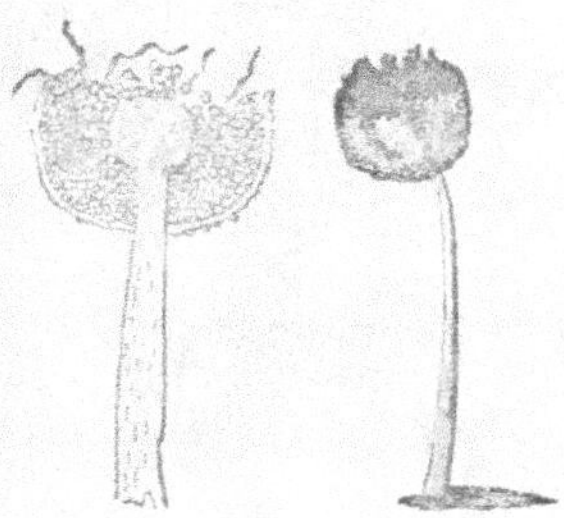

Peridium globose, brown, whitish-pruinose; stem elongated, even, yellow; columella stipitate, whitish, flocci and spores dingy brown.—*Fr. S.M.* iii. *p.* 120. *Sturm. t.* 43. *Berk. Ann. N.H. no.* 111. *Bisch. f.* 3682. *Kl. exs. no.* 737.

On dead leaves, (ivy &c.)

[United States.]

(*Fig.* 126.)

Fig. 126.

1127. Didymium leucopus. *Fr.* "White-stemmed Didymium."

Minute globoso-depressed, pale glaucous, stem very short, thick, pale, then brownish.—*Fr. S.M.* iii. *p.* 121 (*partly*). *Grev. Fl. Ed.* 454. *Eng. Fl* v. *p.* 313. *Fckl. exs. no.* 1462.

On dead beech wood. Autumn. Near Edinburgh.

[United States.]

Very minute, of an uncommonly stiff and dwarf aspect, filaments very few. Differs from Link's *P. leucopus* only in having a coloured stem.—*Grev.* Minute, globose, white, stem white, slightly entering the peridium, flocci white.—*Fries.*

1128. Didymium Sowerbeii. *Berk.* "Sowerby's Didymium."

Sub-fasciculate, peridium globose, dark grey, umbilicated beneath, stem slender, columella white.—*Eng. Fl.* v. *p.* 313. *Sow. t.* 412, *f.* 3.

On a decaying bulb in a parlour. London.

1129. **Didymium lobatum.** *Nees.* "Lobed Didymium."

Sub-sessile, peridium sub-rotund, or variable, somewhat lobed, black; clothed with whitish scurf, columella depressed, flocci and spores black-brown.—*Fr. S.M.* iii. *p.* 123. *Eng. Fl.* v. *p.* 314. *Nees. f.* 104. *Bisch. f.* 3684. *Fl. Dan. t.* 2094, *f.* 2.

On moss. [United States.]

1130. **Didymium congestum.** *B. & Br.* "Crowded Didymium."

Crowded, stems sub-membranaceous, hyaline; peridia obovate, elongated; spores black, variegated with white flocci.—*Ann. N.H. no.* 384. *Fl. Dan. t.* 1973, *fig.* 1, *lower fig.*

On dead leaves, grass, &c. King's Cliffe.
[N. Carolina, U.S.]

Forming crowded patches, very much resembling those of *Diachæa elegans*. Peridia obovate-oblong, cinerous, with a white mealy coat; stems hyaline, membranaceous, generally distinct, though crowded, springing from a thin subjacent membrane. Spores black, variegated with the white coarse, irregular, here and there lacunose flocci. The globose spores appear at first sight to be granulated, but on closer inspection the granules are found to arise from the disintegrated outer peridium.—*M. J. B.*

1131. **Didymium dædaleum.** *B. & Br.* "Spreading Didymium."

Stems short, coalescing; peridia connate, sinuate, dædaloid, pale reddish brown, as well as the stems, farinaceous; flocci white, spores purplish-black.—*Ann. N.H. no.* 385.

In a cucumber frame. April. Milton, Norths.

Spreading far and wide in little subglobose masses; stems reddish-brown, inclining to orange, connate, as if composed of a mass of little flat bran-like membranes; peridia connate, sinuated, forming a dædaloid mass of the same colour as the stem, but sprinkled with white meal, and having to the eye a greyish tinge from the contained spores, which are purplish-black, smooth, and globose, variegated with the white flocci, which are frequently forked, and vary greatly in width, being in parts broad, flat, and membranous.—*M. J. B.*

1132. **Didymium physarioides.** *Fr.* "Black Didymium."

Peridia crowded, subrotund, irregular, black; covered with a whitish powder, columella none, spores conglobated, blackish.—*Fr. S.M.* iii. *p.* 125. *Eng. Fl.* v. *p.* 314. *Kl. exs. no.* 176.

On rotten stumps, moss, &c. Appin. [Low Carolina.]

1133. Didymium cinereum. *Fr.* " Cinereous Didymium."

Adnate, peridia subglobose, whitish ; clothed with ashy-cinereous scurf, flocci reticulated, white ; spores black.—*Fr. S.M.* iii. *p.* 126. *Batsch. f.* 169. *Eng. Fl.* v. *p.* 314.

On bark and wood. Appin. [United States.]

Springing from white, gelatinous, serpentine threads. Inner peridium very delicate, reflecting prismatic colours ; flocci flat, white, irregularly reticulated.—*Eng. Fl.*

1134. Didymium serpula. *Fr.* " Flexuous Didymium."

Flattened ; peridium elongated, creeping, vein-like, flexuose, and reticulated, lead-coloured ; clothed with whitish scurf ; spores compact, black.—*Fr. S.M.* iii. p. 126. *Eng. Fl.* v. *p.* 314. *B. & Br. Ann. N.H. no.* 1035. *Fckl. exs. no.* 1463.

On leaves. Nov. Dec. Appin, Batheaston.

Gen. **81.** **PHYSARUM,** P.

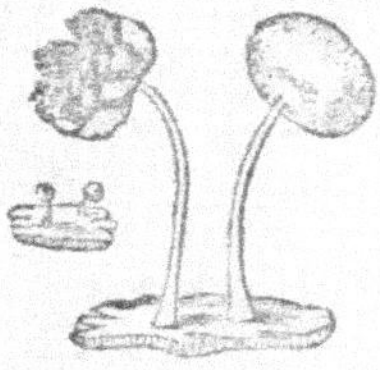

Fig. 127.

Peridium simple, membranaceous, very delicate, naked, quite smooth, bursting irregularly. Columella none.—*Berk. Outl. p.* 307. *Eng. Fl.* v. *p.* 314.

(*Fig.* 127.)

1135. Physarum nutans. *P.* " Nodding Physarum."

Peridium lenticular, umbilicate beneath, even, at length sub-squamulose, cernuous ; stem subulate, even, brownish, flocci very delicate, whitish, spores brownish-black.—*Fr. S.M.* iii. *p.* 128. *Eng. Fl.* v. *p.* 314. *Pers. Syn. p.* 203. *Bull. t.* 407, *f.* 3, *t.* 470, *f.* 1. *Fl. Dan. t.* 2096, *f.* 1. *Bisch. f.* 3616. *Rabh. F.E. no.* 40. *Fckl. exs. no.* 1457.

On decayed wood. [United States.]

var. β. **viride.** Peridium green.—*Eng. Fl.* v. *p.* 314. *Sturm. t.* 24. *Bull. t.* 407, *f.* 1. *Nees. f.* 108.

On decayed wood. [United States.]

var. γ. **aureum.** Peridium golden-yellow.—*Pers. Disp. t.* 1, *f.* 6. *Sturm. t.* 23. *Grev. t.* 124. *Fl. Dan. t.* 2096, *f.* 2. *Fckl. exs. no.* 1456.

On decayed wood. [United States.]

The stem when dry is longitudinally plicate. The flocci appear to be dark unless carefully cleared from the spores. (*Fig.* 127, *nat. size and enlarged.*)

1136. Physarum bulbiforme. *Schum.* "Bulb-like Physarum."

Peridium hemispherical, umbilicate beneath, erect, purple-black; stem attenuated, sulcate, whitish; flocci and spores brownish-black.—*Fr. S.M.* iii. *p.* 131. *Eng. Fl.* v. *p.* 315. *Fl. Dan. t.* 1974, *f.* 3.

On rotten wood.

1137. Physarum rubiginosum. *Chev.* "Rusty Physarum."

Peridium globoso-turbinate, rust-red, as well as the slender even stem; flocci reticulated, white; spores black.—*Fr. S.M.* iii. *p.* 137. *Chev. p.* 338. *Eng. Fl.* v. *p.* 315.

On trunks amongst moss. Appin.

The stem penetrates the peridium, but from the close adherence of the coat, not in such a manner as to form an evident umbilicus, nor distinct columella, and it is not paler than the peridium, nor is the hypothallus paler. The upper portion of the peridium is nearly white, as if bleached.—*Eng. Fl.*

1138. Physarum lilacinum. *Fr.* "Lilac Physarum."

Crowded; peridia sessile, obovate, even, lilac, or flesh coloured; flocci few, white; spores black.—*Fr. S.M.* iii. *p.* 141. *B. & Br. Ann. N.H. no.* 215.

On decayed wood. Nov. King's Cliffe.

The only English specimen was found on the smooth bark of a fallen oak twig.

1139. Physarum metallicum. *Berk* "Metallic Physarum."

Peridium subglobose, slightly depressed, a line or more in breadth, sessile (not adnate), quite smooth, very delicate, of a most beautiful metallic appearance, bursting irregularly. Flocci and spores pink-grey.—*Mag. Zool. & Bot. no.* 29, *t.* 3, *f.* 8.

On a decorticated stick. Nov. Clifton, Notts.

This most beautiful plant connects *Lycogala* with *Physarum*, in consequence of its bright-coloured sporidia. The peridium is, however, perfectly simple. —*M. J. B.*

1140. Physarum album. *Fr.* "White Physarum."

Peridia very delicate, subrotund, depressed, even, whitish; flocci few, delicate, loose, black, as well as the spores.—*Fr. S.M.* iii. *p.* 147. *Kl. exs. no.* 456. *Eng. Fl.* v. *p.* 316. *Lycogala minuta. Grev. t.* 40. *Fckl. exs. no.* 1459.

On various substances. Common. [Low. Carolina.]

Sporidia, globose, or sub-elliptic.

1141. Physarum atrum. *Fr.* "Black Physarum."

Aggregated, crowded, confluent, black, peridia very delicate, rounded; flocci none, spores black.—*Fr. S.M.* iii. *p.* 147. *Berk. Ann. N.H. no.* 216.

On fallen oak branches. King's Cliffe. [United States.]

Also a much smaller variety on cabbage stalks.

Gen. 82. **ANGIORIDIUM,** Grev.

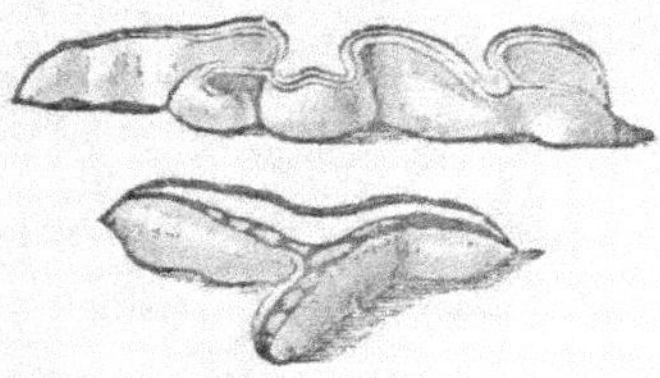

Fig. 128.

Peridium membranaceous, opening by a longitudinal fissure; flocci adhering to the peridium on all sides, reticulate, flat, ending above in the inner peridium.—*Berk. Outl. p.* 308. (*Fig.* 128.)

1142. **Angioridium sinuosum.** *Grev.* "Twisted Angioridium."

Peridia compressed, elongato-flexuose, venulose, whitish, cinereous, splitting in a labiate manner, flocci capillary, white, reticulated, spores black-brown.—*Grev. t.* 310. *Physarum sinuosum. Fr. S.M.* iii. *p.* 145. *Eng. Fl.* v. *p.* 315. *Bull. t.* 446, *f.* 3. *Sow t.* 6. *Pers. Ob.* i. *t.* 1, *f.* 2. *Bisch. f.* 3623. *Kl. exs.* ii. *no.* 761. *Fckl. exs. no.* 1466.

On various substances. [United States.]

Gregarious whitish. Peridium about ½ in. high, simple, sessile, papyraceous, somewhat rigid, fragile, rugulose, varying in form sometimes exactly like a roundish bivalve shell, at others lengthened out at each extremity in a creeping flexuose manner for a ½ in. or more, and either simple or divided. It is, however, always erect, and vertically compressed, the summit forming a sharp edge. When mature it bursts longitudinally, the two plates separating at the margin, sufficiently to allow the spores to escape. Spores globose, blackish, forming a compact mass.—*Grev.* (*Fig.* 128.)

Gen. 83. **BADHAMIA,** Berk.

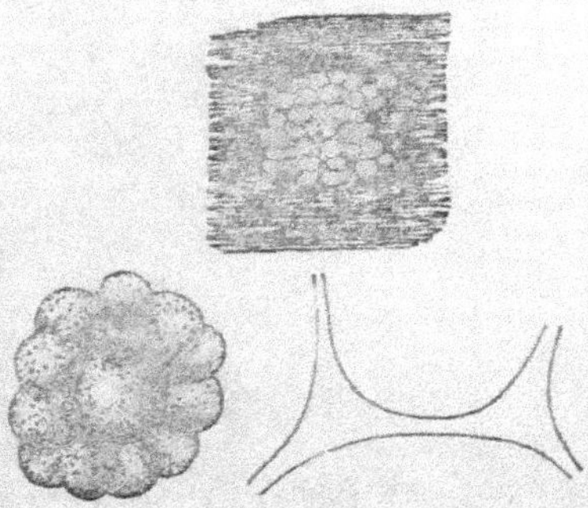

Fig. 129.

Peridium naked or furfuraceous. Spores in groups enclosed at first in a hyaline sac. —*Berk. Outl. p.* 308. *Linn. Trans.* xxi. *p.* 153. (*Fig.* 129.)

Peridium simple, externally naked, or very rarely subtomentose, apex at length opening with a lacerated fissure, flocci loosely reticulated, affixed to the walls of the peridium, here and there expanded in lamina, frequently triangular. Spores globose, or subangular, at first included in a common sac, at length free, conglobato-adnate.—*M.J.B.*

1143. Badhamia hyalina. *Berk.* "Hyaline Badhamia."

Peridia globose, inflated, very delicate, whitish, stems fasciculate, flaccid, ascending, rufous; flocci white; spores black.—*Berk. Linn. Trans.* xxi. *t.* 19, *f.* 3. *Physarum hyalinum. Fr. S.M.* iii. *p.* 139. *Eng. Fl.* v. *p.* 315. *Pers. Disp. t.* 2, *f.* 4. *Berk. Ann. N.H. no.* 213. *Fl. Dan. t.* 2093, *f.* 1.

On rotten wood. Appin. Lambley, Notts. [Mid. Carolina.]

1144. Badhamia fulvella. *Berk.* "Tawny Badhamia."

Peridia gregarious, sessile, globose, black, invested with a delicate tawny down; flocci whitish.—*Linn. Trans.* xxi. *p.* 154. *Ann. N.H. no.* 733.

On dead wood. East Bergholt, Suffolk.

Peridium very thin, black apparently, but yellow when divested of the spores. Gregarious, but not forming distinct patches, sessile, globose, clothed with very delicate, tawny down; mother-cells (·001 in.) ·025 m.m. diameter; spores (·0005-·00075 in.) ·0125-·018 m.m., black, forming a compact mass. Flocci often swollen in the middle, whitish. The habit is that of a *Didymium* rather than of a *Physarum*.

1145. Badhamia pallida. *Berk.* "Pallid Badhamia."

Peridia sessile, depressed, sub-lentiform, crowded here and there, or scattered, pallid-yellow; flocci yellow; spores large; granulate; central vesicle large.—*Berk. Trans. Linn. Soc.* xxi. *p.* 153, *t.* 19, *f.* 2. *Ann. N.H. no.* 732.

On decayed oak branches. March. East Bergholt.

At first exhibiting more or less effused cream-coloured patches, which gradually assume a yellow tinge, and from which arise a few irregular groups of yellow depressed peridia, some of which are confluent, somewhat wrinkled. Flocci evidently continued from the peridium, and of the same colour, branched, forming triangular spaces at the origin of the branches. Mother cells ·05 m.m. (·00175-·002 in.) diameter, spores slightly granulated, (.0005-·0008 in.) ·0127-·02 m.m. long, attached to a large central vesicle. The peridium consists of a membrane, rough with very minute granules, which become more dense where the flocci are produced. In old specimens the patches assume an olive tinge.

1146. Badhamia nitens. *Berk.* "Shining Badhamia."

Peridia subsessile, depressed, crowded, shining yellow, flocci yellow; spores externally strongly echinulate.—*Trans. Linn. Soc.* xxi. *p.* 153. *t.* 19, *f.* 1. *Ann. N.H. no.* 731.

On decayed oak branches. Feb. East Bergholt, Suffolk.

Forming little crowded orbicular patches, consisting of depressed sub-lentiform peridia of a bright persistent yellow, perfectly sessile, at length bursting above and dispersing their dark spores, so as to form a border resembling the stains produced by the sporidia of *Sphæria inquinans*. Flocci yellow, broad. Spores at first contained in a common vesicle, which bursts or is absorbed, and exposes them in the form of little globose branches, often supported by an articulated thread, strongly echinulate, externally smooth towards the common axis. Mother cells ·025-·04 m.m. (·001-·00175 in.) diameter; spores (·0004-·0005 in.) ·01-·0125 m.m.

1147. Badhamia utricularis. *Berk.* "Steel-blue Badhamia."

Peridia oblong, inflated, very delicate, steel-blue, when empty whitish; stems sub-adnate, flaccid, yellowish; flocci white; spores black.—*Berk. Linn. Trans.* xxi. *p.* 153. *Physarum utriculare. Fr. S.M.* iii. *p.* 139. *Bull. t.* 417, *f.* 1. *Berk. Ann. N.H. no.* 214. *Fl. Dan. t.* 2093, *f.* 2.

On wood. King's Cliffe.

1148. Badhamia inaurata. *Curr.* "Bright-yellow Badhamia."

Gregarious; peridia sessile, globose, or nearly so, bright yellow, $\frac{1}{24}$ in. across, covered with floccose yellow scales, opening by irregular fissures; sporidia subglobose, very minutely punctate, enclosed at first in hyaline sacs.—*Curr. Linn. Trans.* xxiv. *t.* 25. *f.* 8. *B. & Br. Ann. N.H. no.* 1034.

On *Jungermannia*. Oct. Paul's Cray Common.

Spores (·0004-·0006 in.) ·01-·015 m.m.

Gen. 84. CRATERIUM, Trent.

Fig. 130.

Peridium simple, papyraceous, rigid, persistent, closed at first with a decided operculum. Flocci congested, erect.—*Berk. Outl. p.* 308. *Eng. Fl.* v. *p.* 316. (*Fig.* 130.)

* Operculum distinct, chalky.

1149. Craterium pedunculatum. *Trent.* "Stalked Craterium."

Peridium cyathiform, subcernuous, chestnut, operculum firm, chalk-white: stem elongated, even, saffron-yellow; spores black. —*Fr. S.M.* iii. *p.* 150. *Eng. Fl.* v. *p.* 316. *Mich. t.* 86, *f.* 13. *Hoffm. Cr. t.* 2, *f.* 2. *Sturm.* iii. *t.* 9. *Nees. f.* 120. *Chev. t.* 4, *f.* 26. *Bisch. f.* 3666. *Kl. exs.* ii. *no.* 139. *Fckl. exs. no.* 1453.

On mosses, sticks, leaves, &c. [Mid. Carolina.]

Gregarious, stems capillary, equal, even, shining, base adnate to a very delicate, membranaceous, whitish hypothallus, soon vanishing. Peridium cup-shaped, somewhat nodding, dark bright brown; operculum plane, orbicular, seated below the prominent margin; flocci white; spores black, globose. (*Fig.* 130.)

1150. Craterium pyriforme. *Ditm.* "Pear-shaped Craterium."

Peridium pyriform, nearly erect, ochraceous, as well as the short even stem; operculum firm, chalk-white; spores black.—*Fr. S.M.* iii. *p.* 150. *Sturm. t.* 10. *Bisch. f.* 3667. *Pay. f.* 578. *Fckl. exs. no.* 1454.

On bark. Appin.

Constantly differing from *C. pedunculatum* in the form and colour of the peridium, and in the shorter stem. Peridium generally contracted above.

** Operculum circumscissile, parting from the peridium.

1151. Craterium minutum. *Fr.* "Little Craterium."

Peridium pyriform, erect, yellowish; operculum convex, of the same colour; stem short, even, rufescent; spores black.—*Fr. S. M.* iii. *p.* 151. *Eng. Fl.* v. *p.* 316. *Bull. t.* 484, *f.* 1. *Cyathus minutus. Sow. t.* 239.

On moss leaves, &c. Common.

Stem short, rather firm, equal, even, purplish expanding into the peridium, hypothallus orbicular, brownish; peridium always erect, pyriform, rufous, then yellow, apex at first rounded; operculum convex circumscissile, of the same colour, growing whitish. This is the commonest species.

*** Operculum very delicate, evanescent.

1152. Craterium leucocephalum. *Ditm.* "White-headed Craterium."

Peridium turbinate, erect, bright brown, growing pale, operculum very thin, evanescent; stem striate, bay; flocci white;

spores black.—*Fr. S.M.* iii. *p.* 153. *Eng. Fl.* v. *p.* 316. *Mich. t.* 86, *f.* 14. *Grev. t.* 65. *Cyathus cinereus. Purt. t.* 35. *Hoffm. Fl.* 9. *t.* 6, *f.* 1. *Fl. Dan. t.* 1314, *f.* 2. *Sturm. t.* 11. *Bisch. f.* 3665.

On various substances. [United States.]

Hypothallus, or orbicular spot, bay, soon obsolete; peridium top-shaped, at first bay, then becoming paler, yellowish, or whitish-mealy with age.

1153. Craterium mutabile. *Fr.* "Changeable Craterium."

Peridium sub-rotund, or turbinate, lacerated, erect; base, and short striate stem, golden-yellow, flocci yellowish; spores black. *Fr. S.M.* iii. *p.* 154. *Eng. Fl.* v. *p.* 316. *Fl. Dan. t.* 2087, *f.* 2, *Fckl. exs. no.* 1455.

On bark, moss, &c. July. Aug. Appin.

Peridium continuous, with the striate stem obovate above, and lacerated, at length more open and cup-shaped; scarcely any true operculum; stem short, thick, equal, or dilated upwards, sulcate. Colour of the whole fungus golden-yellow, the peridium at length becoming paler.

Gen. 85. DIACHÆA, Fr.

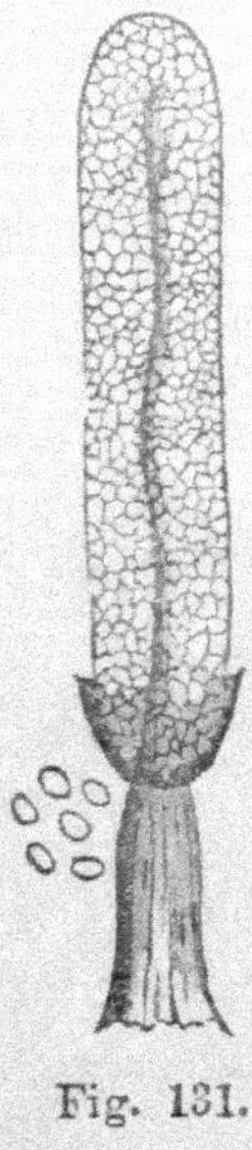

Fig. 131.

Peridium very delicate, simple, falling off in fragments. Capillitium, sub-reticulate, springing from a grumous pallid columella.—*Berk. Outl. p.* 308. (*Fig.* 131.)

1154. Diachæa elegans. *Fr.* "Elegant Diachæa."

Hypothallus persistent; peridium ovato-oblong, deciduous, violet or steel-blue; stem attenuated, thick, shorter than the peridium, white.—*Fr. S.M.* iii. *p.* 156. *Berk. Ann. N.H. no.* 112. *Bull. t.* 502, *f.* 2. *Corda. Ic.* v. *f.* 38. *Pay. f.* 582. *Kl. exs. no.* 1229. *Fckl. exs. no.* 1451.

On dead leaves, &c. King's Cliffe.

[United States.]

(*Fig.* 131.)

Gen. **86.** **STEMONITIS**, Gled.

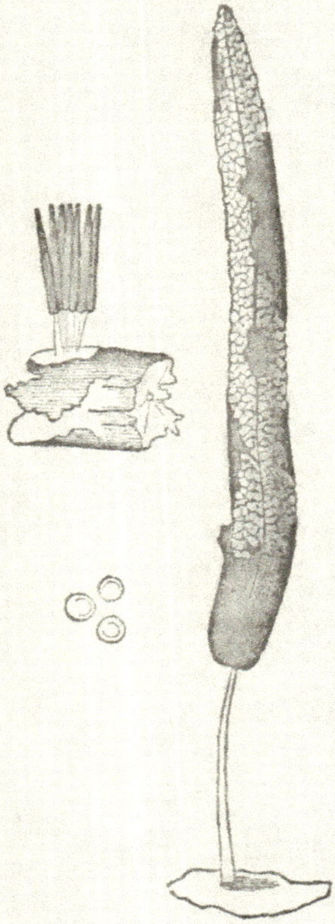

Fig. 132.

Peridium very delicate, simple, evanescent. Capillitium reticulate, springing from the dark penetrating stem.—*Berk. Outl. p.* 308. *Eng. Fl.* v. *p.* 317. (*Fig.* 132.)

1155. **Stemonitis fusca.** *Roth.* " Brown Stemonitis."

Fasciculate, hypothallus persistent, peridia very fugacious, cylindrical, as well as the capillitium; spores black-brown.—*Fr. S.M.* iii. *p.* 157. *Eng. Fl.* v. *p.* 317. *Nees. f.* 118. *Grev. t.* 170. *Mich. t.* 94, *f.* 1. *Ehr. S.B. f.* 5. *Jacq. Misc.* ii. *t.* 15. *Fl. Dan. t.* 659, *f.* 1, *t.* 2016, *f.* 2. *Bisch, f.* 3661. *Kl. exs.* ii. *no.* 457. *Fckl. exs. no.* 1449. *Trichia nuda. Sow. t.* 50. *Bolt. t.* 93, *f.* 1.

On rotten wood. Common. [United States.] (*Fig.* 132.)

1156. **Stemonitis ferruginea.** *Ehrb.* " Rusty Stemonitis."

Fasciculate, hypothallus persistent, peridia fugacious, cylindrical as well as the capillitium ; spores reddish, then ferruginous.—*Fr. S.M.* iii. *p.* 158. *Bull. t.* 477, *f.* 1. *Ehr. S.B. f.* 6 *A.B. Fl. Dan. t.* 2016. *f.* 1. *Bisch. f.* 3704. *Pay. f.* 580. *Fckl. exs. no.* 1448.

On old stumps. [United States.]

Similar to the foregoing, but the spores are much smaller, and of a different colour.

1157. Stemonitis typhoides. *D.C.* "Club-mace Stemonitis."

Gregarious, hypothallus evanescent, peridia fugacious, capillitium and spores brownish.—*Fr. S.M.* iii. *p.* 158. *Mich. t.* 94, *f.* 2. *Fl. Dan. t.* 216. *Schæff. t.* 297. *Batsch. t.* 30, *f.* 176. *Bull. t.* 477, *f.* 2. *Ehr. S.B. f.* 7. *Ann. N.H. no.* 113. *Kl. exs. no.* 923. *Fckl. exs. no.* 1450.

On rotten wood. [Low & Mid. Carolina.]

1158. Stemonitis ovata. *P.* "Ovate Stemonitis."

Scattered, peridium very fugacious, ovate, steel-blue, capillitium purplish, spores brown; stem semi-penetrating.—*Fr. S.M.* iii. *p.* 160. *Kl. exs. no.* 1132. *Eng. Fl.* v. *p.* 317. *Fckl. exs. no.* 1446. *Trichia alba. Sow. t.* 259.

On rotten wood. [United States.]

1159. Stemonitis obtusata. *Fr.* "Obtuse Stemonitis."

Scattered, peridium globose, fugacious, blackish; capillitium black-brown, stem slightly penetrating.—*Fr. S.M.* iii. *p.* 160. *Eng. Fl.* v. *p.* 317. *Fl. Dan. t.* 2091, *f.* 2.

On wood. Apethorpe, Norths. [United States]

At first white, then ruddy brown.

1160. Stemonitis pulchella. *Bab.* "Beautiful Stemonitis."

Very minute, hypothallus brownish; peridia scattered, evanescent; stem rather short, incrassated below, not reaching the apex; capillitium purplish, ovate-oblong, scarcely ventricose; spores purplish brown.—*Berk. Ann. N.H. no.* 217, *t.* 12, *f.* 11. *Bab. Abst. Linn. Trans.* 1839.

On *Pteris aquilina.* Sept. Leicestershire.

Extremely minute, not 1 line high, scattered, with a transparent horn-brown hypothallus; peridium extremely evanescent; stem vanishing a little below the apex, giving off filaments on every side; the free part rather short, smooth, dark, slightly incrassated below, capillitium ovato-oblong, purplish-brown; spores purple-brown.—*M. J. B.*

1161. Stemonitis physarioides. *A. & S.* "Coppery Stemonitis."

Peridium globose, obtuse, persistent, silvery, at length torn, capillitium sub-compact black-brown, stem long, semi-penetrating, brown-black.—*Fr. S.M.* iii. *p.* 162. *Sow. t.* 412, *f.* 3. *A. & S. t.* ii. *f.* 8. *B. & Br. Ann. N.H. no.* 386.

On mossy stumps. Northamptonshire.

[Carolina, Ohio, U. S.]

"Our specimens have a beautiful coppery tinge."—*B. & Br.*

1162. **Stemonitis violacea.** *P.* "Violet Stemonitis."

Peridium lenticular, steel-blue, fugacious, umbilicate beneath; capillitium whitish, lax, spores blackish, stem short semi-penetrating.—*Fr. S.M.* iii. *p.* 162. *B & Br. Ann. N.H. no.* 387.

On moss. Common.

1163. **Stemonitis arcyrioides.** *Somm.* "Violet Stemonitis."

Peridium globose, violaceous steel-blue, base somewhat persistent, capillitium globose; spores brownish; stem short, semi-penetrating.—*Fr. S.M.* iii. *p.* 162. *Ann. N.H. no.* 114. *Fckl. exs. no.* 1447.

On dead laurel leaves, &c.

Gen. 87. ENERTHENEMA, Bowm.

Fig. 133.

Peridium very delicate, simple, evanescent, except at the apex, where it is adnate with the dilated top of the penetrating dark stem. Capillitium dependent, attached to the dilated disc. Spores surrounded by a cyst.—*Bowm. Linn. Trans.* xvi. *p.* 151. *B. & Br. Ann. N.H. no.* 388. (*Fig.* 133.)

1164. **Enerthenema elegans.** *Bowm.* "Bowman's Enerthenema."

Peridium globose, very fugacious, at length cinereous, apex papillary from the excurrent stem. Capillitium and spores black-brown.—*Bowm. Linn. Trans.* xvi. *p.* 151, *t.* 16. *B. & Br. Ann. N.H. no.* 388, *t.* 11, *f.* 7. *Berk. Outl. t.* 1, *f.* 6. *C. Stemonitis papillata, Eng. Fl.* v. *p.* 317. *not Persoon.*

On rotton wood. [Low. Carolina.]

(*Fig.* 133, *thread and spores magnified.*)

Gen. **88.** **DICTYDIUM,** Schrad.

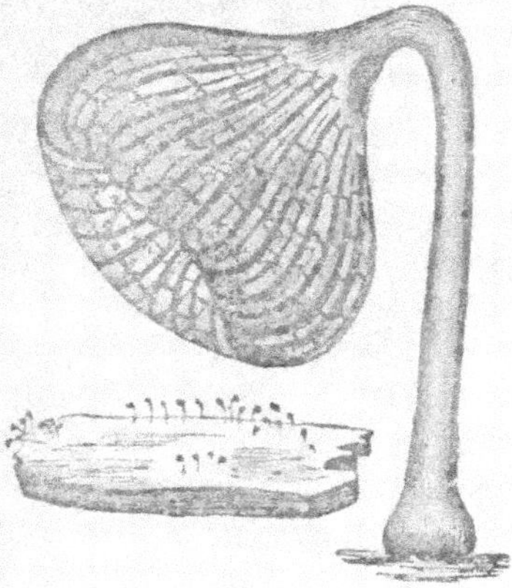

Fig. 134.

Peridium simple, very delicate, reticulated or veined from the innate capillitium.—*Berk. Outl. p.* 309. *Eng. Fl.* v. *p.* 317. (*Fig.* 134.)

1165. Dictydium umbilicatum. *Schrad.* "Depressed Dictydium."

Peridium cernuous, umbilicate, veins parallel, joined by others which are transverse; spores purplish-brown.—*Fr. S.M.* iii. *p.* 165. *Eng. Fl.* v. *p.* 318. *Batsch. f.* 232. *Schrad. t.* 4, *f.* 1. *Nees. f.* 117. *Grev. t.* 153. *Corda. Ic.* v. *f.* 36. *Bisch. f.* 3672. *Pay. f.* 573. *Kl. exs. no.* 820. *Fckl. exs. no.* 1445.

On rotten wood, pine stumps, &c. [United States.]
(*Fig.* 134.)

Gen. **89.** **CRIBRARIA,** Schrad.

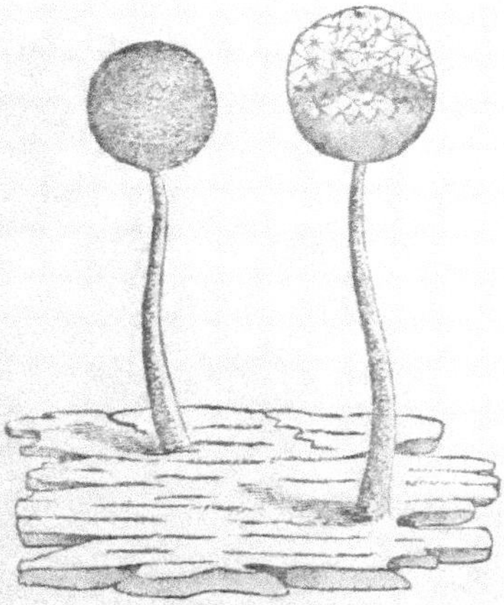

Fig. 135.

Peridium simple, persistent below, vanishing above. Flocci innate, forming a free network in the upper half of the peridium.—*Berk. Outl. p.* 309. *Eng. Fl.* v. *p.* 318. (*Fig.* 135.)

1166. Cribraria intermedia. *Berk.* "Sowerby's Cribraria."

Peridium globose, yellow, excipulum entire, stem pellucid, white, tapering upwards, spores yellow.—*Eng. Fl.* v. *p.* 318. *Sphærocarpus semitrichioides, Sow. t.* 400, *f.* 5.

On rotten wood.

1167. Cribraria intricata. *Schrad.* "Intricate Cribraria."

Peridium sub-rotund, nearly erect, reticulations unequal, spores dirty yellow.—*Fr. S.M.* iii. *p.* 173. *Schrad. t.* 3, *f.* 1.

On decayed fir stumps. July. Weybridge. [United States.]
(*Fig.* 135.)

1168. Cribraria argillacea. *Pers.* "Clay-coloured Cribraria."

Gregarious, clay-coloured, somewhat rounded; stem rather short, blackish, reticulations equal, spores clay-coloured.—*Pers. Obs.* i. *p.* 90. *Schrad. t.* 2, *f.* 1, 2. *B. & Br. Ann. N.H.* (1865) *no.* 1036. *Fr. S.M.* iii. *p.* 172. *Chev. t.* 9, *f.* 25.

On decayed branches and stumps of Scotch fir. Aboyne. [Mid. Carolina.]

Forming broad confluent patches, pouring out a large quantity of clay-coloured dust. The least beautiful of the genus, though when cleared from the spores, the plant is a pretty object under the microscope.—*M. J. B.*

1169. Cribraria aurantiaca. *Fr.* "Orange Cribraria."

Peridium spherical, somewhat nodding, tawny; reticulations equal; spores bright yellow.—*Fr. S.M.* iii. *p.* 174. *B. & Br. Ann. N.H.* (1865), *no.* 1037. *Pay. f.* 583. *Schrad. t.* 1, *f.* 3, 4. *Fl. Dan. t.* 2085, *f.* 1. *Corda Ic.* v. *f.* 35. *Bisch. f.* 3678.

On decayed branches of Scotch fir. Aboyne.

A very pretty, though minute species.

Gen. 90. ARCYRIA, Hill.

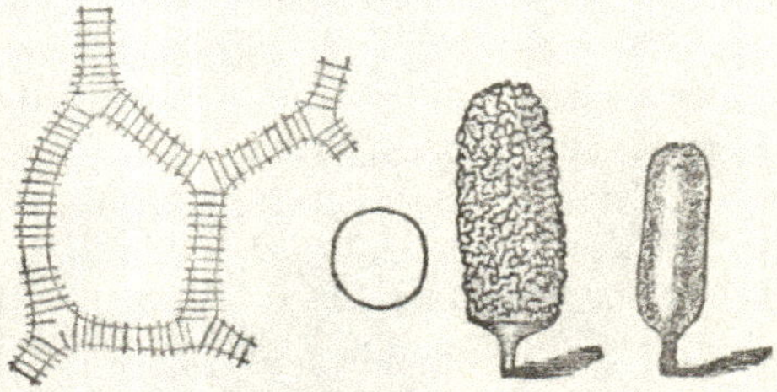

Fig. 136.

Peridium simple, upper portion very fugacious. Capillitium elastic. Flocci not spiral. —*Berk. Outl. p.* 310. *Eng. Fl.* v. *p.* 318. (*Fig.* 136.)

In this genus the threads of the capillitium have a row of little tubercles on one side only, or if not confined to one side, some of them are more strongly developed. In some instances they form rings round the threads.

1170. Arcyria punicea. *P.* "Splendid Arcyria."

Peridia crowded, stipitate, subovate, capillitium elongated; spores bright purplish vermillion.—*Fr. S.M.* iii, *p.* 177. *Eng. Fl.* v. *p.* 318. *Wig. Ann. Sc. Nat.* (1862), xvi. *t.* 16, *f.* 6-7. *Fckl. exs. no.* 1441. *Mich. t.* 94, *f.* 1. *Hall t.* 48, *f.* 6. *Fl. Dan.* 1364, *f.* 2. *Nees. f.* 114. *Grev. t.* 130. *Bull. t.* 368. *Batsch. f.* 177. *Clathrus denudatus. Bolt. t.* 93, *f.* 2. *Jacq. Misc. t.* 6. *Trichia denudata. Sow. t.* 49. *Purt. t.* 24, *f.* 2. *Kl. exs. no.* 932.

On rotten stumps. Common. [United States.]

1171. Arcyria incarnata. *P.* "Flesh-coloured Arcyria."

Peridia crowded, substipitate, ovate, capillitium elongato-effuse, flesh-coloured, as well as the spores.—*Fr. S.M.* iii. *p.* 178. *Eng. Fl.* v. *p.* 318. *Mich. t.* 94, *f.* 2. *Pers. Obs.* 1, *t.* 5, *f.* 4-5. *Sturm. t.* 44. *Fckl. exs. no.* 1442. *Wig. Ann. Sc. Nat.* (1862) xvi. *t.* 16, *f.* 8-9. *Bisch. f.* 3663. *Fl. Dan. t.* 2090, *f.* 1. *Schnizl. f.* 34-35.

On rotten wood. [United States.]

Smaller than *A. punicea*, and more shortly stipitate. In that the peridium is venose, in this veinless.—*Eng. Fl.* (*Fig.* 136.)

1172. Arcyria cinerea. *Schum.* "Grey Arcyria."

Gregarious, peridia stipitate, globoso-ovate, cinereous; capillitium ovato-cylindrical, glaucous, as well as the spores.—*Fr. S.M.* iii. *p.* 180. *Eng. Fl.* v. *p.* 318. *Bull. t.* 477, *f.* 3. *Pers. Disp. t.* 1. *f.* 2. *Fl. Dan. t.* 1975, *f.* 1. *Wig. Ann. Sc. Nat.* (1862) xvi. *t.* 16, *f.* 10-12. *Fckl. exs. no.* 1440.

On wood. Appin. [United States.]

1173. Arcyria nutans. *Fr.* "Nodding Arcyria."

Crowded; peridia cylindrical, capillitium very long, nodding; dirty yellow, as well as the spores.—*Fr. S.M.* iii. *p.* 180. *Eng. Fl.* v. *p.* 319. *Bull. t.* 502, *f.* 3. *Wig. Ann. Sc. Nat.* (1862) xvi. *t.* 16, *f.* 13-15. *Fckl. exs.* 1339. *Trichia nutans. Sow. t.* 260. *Purt. t.* 24, *f.* 1. *Arcyria flava. Grev. t.* 309. *Fl. Dan. t.* 2017, *f.* 1. *Kl. exs. no.* 421.

On rotten wood. [United States.]

1174. Arcyria umbrina. *Schum.* "Umber Arcyria."

Gregarious, peridia stipitate, ovate, umber, capillitium ovate, erect, ochraceous, as well as the spores.—*Fr. S.M.* iii. *p.* 181. *Fl. Dan. t.* 1975, *f.* 1. *Berk. Ann. N.H. no.* 389.

On decayed wood. Wothorpe, Norths. [United States.]

1175. Arcyria ochroleuca. *Fr.* "Ochrey Arcyria."

Scattered; peridia substipitate, globose, yellow; capillitium ovate, erect, pallid-ochraceous, as well as the spores.—*Fr. S.M.*

iii. *p.* 181. *Sturm. t.* 8. *Berk. Ann. N.H. no.* 115. *Wig. Ann Sc. Nat.* (1862) xvi. *t.* 16, *f.* 16. *Bisch. f.* 3692.

On decayed wood. Collyweston, Norths. [Mid. Carolina.]

Gen. **91.** **OPHIOTHECA,** Curr.

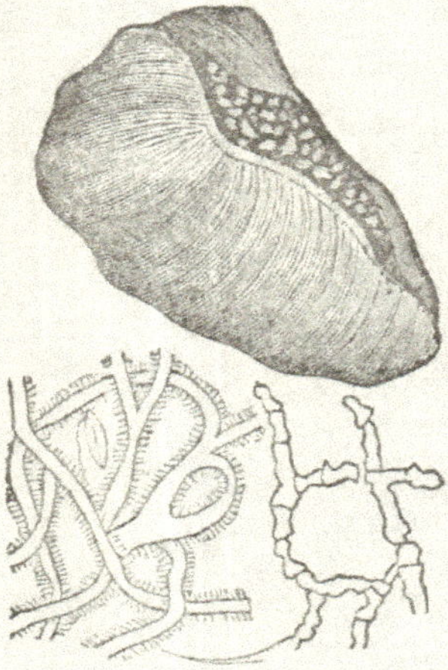

Fig. 137.

Peridium simple, bursting longitudinally. Capillitium twofold, one consisting of delicate hyaline threads, to which the spores are attached; the other of echinulate, thicker, branched filaments.—*Curr. Quart. Journ. Micr.* ii. *p.* 240. *Berk. Outl. p.* 310. (*Fig.* 137.)

1176. Ophiotheca chrysosperma. *Curr.* "Currey's Ophiotheca."

Peridium irregular, more or less serpentine, brownish. Fertile threads delicate transparent, barren threads somewhat reticulated, minutely denticulate, here and there swollen; spores yellow, elliptic, pointed at each end.—*Curr. Micr. Journ.* (1854), ii. *p.* 240, *t.* ix. *f.* 1-5, *vol.* v. *p.* 131.

On inner bark of a dead tree. (*Fig.* 137.)

Gen. **92.** **TRICHIA,** Hall.

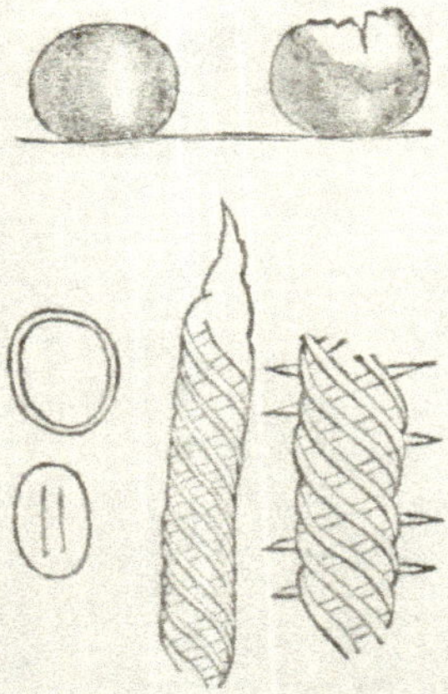

Fig. 138.

Peridium simple, persistent, membranaceous, bursting irregularly above. Threads spiral.—*Berk. Outl. p.* 310. *Eng. Fl.* v. *p.* 319. (*Fig.* 138.)

1177. Tricha rubiformis. *P.* "Reddish Trichia."

Fasciculate, peridia turbinato-cylindrical, steel-blue; stems short, confluent, red-brown, capillitium and spores purplish-red.—*Fr. S.M.* iii. *p.* 183. *Hall. t.* 48, *f.* 5. *Batsch. f.* 172. *Bull. t.* 502, *f.* 1? *Pers. Disp. t.* 4, *f.* 3, *t.* 1. *f.* 3. *Nees, f.* 112. *Fl. Dan. t.* 1365, *f.* 2. *Chev. t.* 9, *f.* 24. *Fckl. exs. no.* 1438. *Wig. Ann. Sc. Nat.*

(1862), xvi. *t.* 15, *f.* 12. *Curr. Micr. Journ.* iii. *t.* 2, *f.* 5, 6. *Trichia Neesiana. Corda. f.* 288. *Ann. N.H. no.* 218. *Bisch. f.* 3664.

On dead wood. Apethorpe. [United States.]

Most usually fasciculate, individuals sometimes solitary. Stems often very short, rubiginous, when confluent unequally sulcate, attenuated upwards. Peridia of a beautiful steel-blue, reddish, bay, &c., shining, nearly cylindrical, apex obovate, very obtuse, somewhat circumscissile, even, rugulose below. Capillitium elongated, echinulate, bright purplish-red, as well as the spores.

1178. Trichia pyriformis. *Hoffm.* "Pear-shaped Trichia."

Subfasciculate, peridia turbinato-pyriform, blackish-red, stems subelongated, tawny, capillitium saffron-tawny, as well as the spores.—*Fr. S. M.* iii. *p.* 184. *Hoffm. Cr. t.* 1, *f.* 1. *Eng. Fl.* v. *p.* 319. *Pers. Ic. Pict. t.* 12, *f.* 1, 2. *Curr. Micr. Journ.* iii. *t.* 2, *f.* 9, 10. *Sphærocarpus fragilis. Sow. t.* 279. *Purt. t.* 24, *f.* 3. *Wig. Ann. Sc. Nat.* (1862), xvi. *t.* 14, *f.* 12, 13. *Kl. exs. no.* 1026, 1632. *Fckl. exs. no.* 1437.

On rotten stumps. [United States.]

Stems racemoso-connate, often elongated, sometimes short, occasionally scattered and simple, with a membranaceous hypothallus. Peridia usually even, blackish-red, then bay-colour, sometimes with a ruddy tinge, opaque, oblong by mutual pressure, but in solitary individuals rounded. Threads very long, slender, echinulate.

1179. Trichia Ayresii. *B. & Br.* "Ayres' Trichia."

Crowded; peridia obovate, tawny-chestnut, shining; stems very short, connate; capillitium strongly echinulate, tawny saffron-yellow, as well as the spores.—*B. & Br. Ann. N.H. no.* 390.

On decayed wood. Oxfordshire.

Forming crowded masses. Peridia obovate, shining, of a bright tawny chestnut. Elaters of the capillitium thicker than in *T. pyriformis,* and strongly echinulate, tawny; spores globose, tawny.

1180. Trichia Lorinseriana. *Ca.* "Ribbed Trichia."

Subsolitary, stem long, dirty brown colour, flexuous, longitudinally ribbed with acute angular ridges, peridium turbinate or ovate, even above, smooth, pallid, irregularly ruptured in an operculate manner. Threads yellow, short, smooth; spores tetrahedral, yellow, diaphanous.—*Corda. Icon.* i. *f.* 288*d*. *Currey. Quart. Jour. Micr.* v. *p.* 129.

On wood. Jan. Weybridge.

Distinguished by the acutely fluted, long flexuous stem. "Spiral threads simple and detached, short, very pale yellow, with very delicate markings, each extremity of the thread tapering gradually to a very long thin point, the spiral markings not extending into the narrow extremities of the threads." —*Curr.*

1181. **Trichia serotina.** *Schrad.* "Late Trichia."

Scattered; peridium obovate, bay; stem brown, even; capillitium and spores yellowish.—*Fr. S.M.* iii. *p.* 184. *Eng. Fl.* v. *p.* 310. *Schrad. Jour.* 1779, *t.* 3, *f.* 2. *Fl. Dan. t.* 1680, *f.* 2. *Fckl. exs. no.* 1436.

On rotten wood. Appin. Bristol. [United States.]

1182. **Trichia fallax.** *P.* "Irregular Trichia."

Gregarious, peridia turbinate, at first vermillion-red, then clay-colour, plaited below as well as the stem, capillitium dusky-ochre, as also are the spores.—*Fr. S.M.* iii. *p.* 185. *Eng. Fl.* v. *p.* 319. *Schmid. Ic. t.* 33, *f.* 1. *Bull. t.* 417, *f.* 2. *Pers. Obs.* i. *t.* 3, *f.* 4, 5. *Nees. f.* 113. *Fl. Dan. t.* 467, *f.* 2, *t.* 2088, *f.* 3. *Jacq. Aust. t.* 299. *Wig. Ann. Sc. Nat.* (1862), xvi. *t.* 14, *f.* 14, 15. *Bisch. f.* 3674. *Kl. exs. no.* 931. *Fckl. exs. no.* 1435.

On rotten wood. [United States.]

Peridium at first globose, when adult top-shaped, even above and thin, circumscissile, firm below and plicate, as well as the stem. Colour dark and dusky yellow, sometimes shining, sometimes opaque. Spores ovate. When young of a beautiful vermillion-red, which, when dried prematurely, it sometimes retains, though often assuming a black hue.

1183. **Trichia clavata.** *P.* "Clavate Trichia."

Gregarious; peridium obovate, yellow, shining, even; stem rugose, of the same colour, capillitium and spores ochraceous. —*Fr. S.M.* iii. *p.* 186. *Eng. Fl.* v. *p.* 320. *Sturm. t.* 25. *Moug. exs. no.* 284. *Wig. Ann. Sc. Nat.* (1862), xvi. *t.* 15, *f.* 1-3. *Fl. Dan. t.* 2089, *f.* 1. *Bisch. f.* 3668. *Fckl. exs. no.* 1434. *T. pyriformis, Sow. t.* 400, *f.* 6.

On decayed wood. [United States.]

Stem constantly present, but variable, sometimes long and sometimes short, rugose, attenuated downwards, of the same colour as the peridium, or rufescent at the base. Peridium rather large, usually even, dehiscing irregularly; the lower part, which has a shining, transparent, skinny appearance, remains when the capillitium and spores have vanished, and in this state resembles a *Craterium.* "The threads form an extensive complicated capillitium, in which it is rarely, if ever, possible to trace a single thread from one extremity to the other, and their colour is darker than in *T. cerina.* The markings also are strongly defined."—*Curr.*

1184. **Trichia cerina.** *Ditm.* "Waxy Trichia."

Solitary, peridium egg-shaped, olivaceous wax-colour; stem elongated, dingy, spores globose, and as well as the threads of the colour of the peridium.—*Sturm.* i. *t.* 25. *Curr. Quart. Jour. Micr.* v. *p.* 127. *Trich. clavata* β. *olivaceus. Fr. S.M.* iii. *p.* 186.

On decayed wood. Sept. Near Swansea.

The threads are pale-coloured, and taper gradually to a very thin point at each extremity; the spiral markings are very delicate, and the threads themselves are simple, detached from one another, and of a definite and moderate length.—*Curr.*

** *Goniospora.*

1185. **Trichia nigripes.** *P.* "Black-stemmed Trichia."

Gregarious, peridia variable in form, even, yellowish, stem very short, blackish, capillitium and spores ochraceous-yellow.—*Fr. S.M.* iii. *p.* 186. *Bull. t.* 417, *f.* 2. *Pers. Ic. & Des. t.* 14, *f.* 3. *Fl. Dan. t.* 1313, *f.* 2. *Mich. t.* 96, *f.* 4. *Curr. Quart. Jour. Micr.* v. *p.* 128—iii. t. 2. *f.* 4. *Wig. Ann. Sc. Nat.* xvi. *t.* 15, *f.* 5-6. *Kl. exs. no.* 1025. *Fckl. exs. no.* 1433.

On rotten wood. Kent and Surrey. [United States.]

Threads rather short and obtusely pointed, smooth, slightly constricted between the spirals.

1186. **Trichia turbinata.** *With.* "Top-shaped Trichia."

Crowded; peridia obovate, sessile, even, ochraceous-tan colour, capillitium and spores ochre.—*Fr. S.M.* iii. *p.* 187. *Eng. Fl.* v. *p.* 320. *Hall. t.* 48, *f.* 7. *Fl. Dan. t.* 1313, *f.* 1. *Sow. t.* 85. *Kl. exs. no.* 762. *Wig. Ann. Sc. Nat.* (1862) xvi. *t.* 15, *f.* 6. *Clathrus turbinatus. Bolt. t.* 94. *f.* 3.

On rotten wood. Common. [United States.]

1187. **Trichia chrysosperma.** *D.C.* "Yellow-spored Trichia."

Crowded, peridia rounded, subsessile, cinnamon yellow, capillitum and spores ochraceous golden-yellow.—*Fr. S.M.* iii. *p.* 187. *Eng. Fl.* v. *p.* 320. *Batsch. f.* 173. *Bull. t.* 417, *f.* 4. *Trichia nitens. Grev. t.* 281. *Curr. Micr. Jour.* iii. *t.* 2, *f.* 1-3. *Wig. Ann. Sc. Nat.* (1862), xvi. *t.* 15, *f.* 13-17, *t.* 16, *f.* 1-5. *Fl. Dan. t.* 2089. *f.* 2.

On rotten wood. Common. [United States.]

Threads of a definite length, smooth, occasionally echinulate, terminating somewhat acutely.

Threads occasionally echinulate.—*Curr.* (*Fig.* 138.)

1188. **Trichia varia.** *P.* "Variable Trichia."

Scattered; peridia sessile, subrotund, or reniform, at length yellowish, capillitium and spores ochraceous.—*Fr. S.M.* iii. *p.* 183. *Eng. Fl.* v. *p.* 320. *Mich. t.* 95, *f.* 2. *Schæff. t.* 296. *Batsch. f.* 171. *Kl. exs. no.* 422. *Wig. Ann. Sc. Nat.* (1862) xvi. *t.* 15, *f.* 7-10. *Schnzl. t.* 14, *f.* 27-33. *Fckl. exs. no.* 1431.

On decayed wood. Appin. [United States.]

"Threads not distinguishable from those of *T. nigripes*, but I have sometimes found *T. varia* with echinulate threads."—*Curr.*

1189. **Trichia serpula.** *P.* "Reticulated Trichia."

Peridia creeping, vein-like, flexuous, and reticulated, yellow; capillitium and spores of the same colour.—*Fr. S.M.* iii. *p.* 188. *Eng. Fl.* v. *p.* 320. *Batsch. f.* 174. *Pers. Ic. & Des. t.* 12, *f.* 1. *Nees. f.* 111. *Curr. Micr. Jour.* iii. *t.* 2, *f.* 7-8. *Wig. Ann. Sc. Nat.* (1862) xvi. *t.* 16, *f.* 5.* *Fl. Dan. t.* 2089, *f.* 3. *Bisch. f.* 3622. *Trichia reticulata. Grev. t.* 266.

On rotten branches, leaves, &c. [United States.]

Peridium more or less bright yellow, sometimes bay, spores and flocci of a golden yellow, even more bright than in *T. chrysosperma*.—*Eng. Fl.*

Threads very long, sometimes branched, sparsely echinulate, obtusely pointed.

1190. **Trichia (?) flagellifer.** *B. & Br.* "Anomalous Trichia."

Globose, sessile, metallic; flocci flagelliferous at their tips; spores flesh-coloured.—*B. & Br. Ann. N.H.* (1866) *no.* 1143, *t.* 2, *f.* 4.

On spruce fir. Dec. Badminton.

Perfectly globose, but fixed only by a small portion of the surface, which slightly projects, smooth, bay, reflecting metallic tints like a *Physarum*; flocci divided above two or three times. Spores (·0003—·0004 in.) ·0075—·01 m.m. diameter. Perfectly distinct from every other *Trichia* by the colour of the spores and metallic coat, in addition to the flagelliform threads.—*B. & Br.*

This is certainly not a good *Trichia*, as the threads are attached to, and spring from, the inner surface of the peridium. It will more properly constitute the type of a distinct genus.

Gen. 93. PERICHÆNA, Fr.

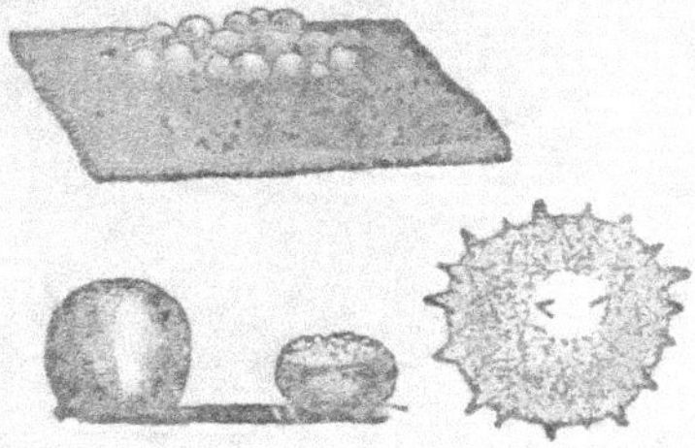

Fig. 139.

Peridium simple, submembranaceous, persistent, naked, often splitting horizontally in the middle. Flocci few, not spiral.—*Berk. Outl. p.* 311. *Eng. Fl.* v. *p.* 321.

(*Fig.* 139.)

1191. Perichæna abietina. *Fr.* "Fir wood Perichæna."

Peridia obovato-globose, bay black, more or less regularly splitting all round; flocci and spores yellow.—*Fr. S.M.* iii. *p.* 191. *Eng. Fl.* v. *p.* 321. *Sphærocarpus sessilis. Sow. t.* 258.

On fir wood.

There is an evident hypothallus, which is one of the peculiar characters of the species.—*M. J. B.*

1192. Perichæna populina. *Fr.* "Poplar Perichæna."

Peridia globose, depressed, yellow-brown, splitting all round, flocci and spores yellow.—*Fr. S.M.* iii. *p.* 191. *Eng. Fl.* v. *p* 321. *Grev. t.* 252. *Desm. exs. no.* 671. *Bull. t.* 417, *f.* 5. *Pers. Obs.* i. *t.* 6, *f.* 1-2. *Berk. exs. no.* 47.

On fallen poplars. [United States.]

Sometimes almost covering the tree. (*Fig.* 139.)

Gen. 94. LICEA, Schrad.

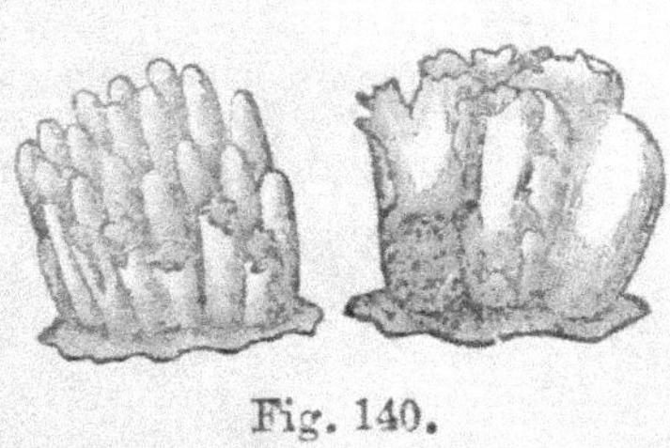

Fig. 140.

Peridium thin, membranaceous, even, bursting irregularly. Spores not mixed with the flocci.—*Berk. Outl. p.* 311. *Eng. Fl.* v. *p.* 321.

(*Fig.* 140.)

1193. Licea cylindrica. *Fr.* "Tubular Licea."

Equally effused, peridia linear, connate; spores earthy-ferruginous.—*Fr. S.M.* iii. *p.* 195. *Eng. Fl.* v. *p.* 391. *Batsch. f.* 175. *Bull. t.* 470, *f.* 3. *Kl. exs. no.* 349. *Nees. f.* 163. *Reticularia multicapsula. Sow. t.* 179. *Trichia meteorica. Sow. t.* 435.

On rotten wood. [Mid. & Up. Carolina.]

1194. Licea fragiformis. *Fr.* "Strawberry Licea."

Conglomerate; peridia linear, subconnate; spores umber.—*Fr. S.M.* iii. *p.* 196. *Eng. Fl.* v. *p.* 321. *Bull. t.* 384. *Nees. f.* 102. *Grev. t.* 308. *Chev. t.* 9, *f.* 23.

On rotten wood, &c. [United States.]

Very beautiful just before maturity, and resembling a strawberry.—*Eng. Fl.* (*Fig.* 140.)

1195. Licea applanata. *Berk.* "Flattened Licea."

Depressed, conglomerated; peridia very short, densely crowded, liver-brown; spores large.—*Berk. Hook. Lond. Jour.* iv. *p.* 67. *B. & Br. Ann. N.H. no.* 393.

On dead twigs of currant, &c.

Forming little thin, flat, distinct, rounded, or elongated patches, which are at first scarlet, and then liver brown. Peridia short, densely crowded, invisible to the naked eye. Spores large, broadly elliptic, with one or more nuclei, argillaceous, tinged with red, mixed with a few flexuous threads, very much larger than in *L. fragiformis* or *L. cylindrica.*—*M. J. B.*

1196. Licea perreptans. *Berk.* "Creeping Licea."

Effused, at length here and there conglomerated; peridia oblong, mostly distinct; spores purplish-black.—*Berk. Gard. Chron.* (1848), *p.* 451. *Ann. N.H. no.* 392. *Lycoperdon echiniformis. Sow. t.* 400, *f.* 1.

In a cucumber frame heated with spent hops. Rolleston. Staffordshire.

Hypothallus white, creeping far and wide, and protruding here and there masses of oblong peridia, which are mostly distinct, assuming gradually a reddish-brown tint, and in cases of premature exsiccation becoming black. Spores very abundant, purple brown, mixed with a few flocci. Of extremely rapid growth, which is like that of *L. fragiformis*; the spores, however, are quite different, and the mucilage never acquires the beautiful strawberry tint of that species.—*M. J. B.*

Gen. 95. PHELONITIS, Chev.

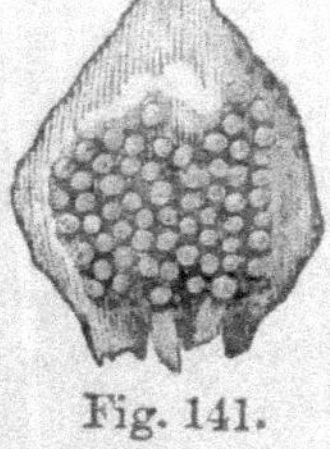

Fig. 141.

Peridium papyraceous, persistent, commonly splitting horizontally in the centre; spores large, rough.—*Berk. Outl. p.* 311. (*Fig.* 141.)

1197. Phelonitis strobilina. *P.* "Fir cone Phelonitis."

Aggregate, peridia rounded, red-brown, more or less circumscissile; spores dirty yellow, becoming pale.—*Perichæna strobilina. Fr. S.M.* iii. *p.* 190. *Eng. Fl.* v. *p.* 321. *A. & S. t.* 6, *f.* 5. *Sturm.* iii. *t.* 20. *Nees. f.* 101. *Chev. t.* 9, *f.* 22. *Grev. t.* 275. *Moug. exs. no.* 579. *Corda. Ic.* v. *f.* 30. *Berk. exs. no.* 292. *Fckl. exs. no.* 1469.

Between the scales of old cones of *Pinus Abies*. Appin.

(*Fig.* 141.)

Order XI. NIDULARIACEI. Tul.

Spores produced on sporophores compacted into one or more globose or disciform bodies, contained within a distinct peridium. —*Berk. Outl. p.* 311. *Tul. Ann. Sc. Nat.* 1844, i. *p.* 64.

Peridium cup-shaped, sporangia attached by a cord.
  Of three membranes . . . . *Cyathus.*
  Uniform, spongy . . . . *Crucibulum.*
Peridium globose, simple. Sporangia involved in mucus . *Nidularia.*
Peridium sub-hemispherical.
  Double; sporangium single, ejected . . . . . *Sphærobolus.*
  Single; sporangium papillæform . . . . . *Thelebolus.*
  Hyaline; sporangia large, grumous . . . . . *Polyangium.*

Gen. **96.** **CYATHUS,** Pers.

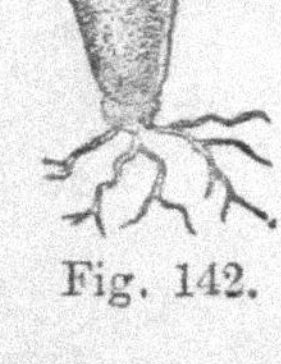

Fig. 142.

Peridium composed of three closely connected membranes, at length bursting at the apex, and closed by a white membrane. Sporangia plane, umbilicate, attached to the walls by an elastic cord.—*Berk. Outl. p.* 312. *Tul. Ann. Sc. Nat.* 1844, i. 65. (*Fig.* 142.)

1198. Cyathus striatus. *Hoffm.* 'Striate Cyathus.'

Obconic, truncate, broadly open, externally ferruginous, hirto-tomentose, internally lead-colour, smooth, striate; margin and corona thick, continuous; sporangia somewhat trigonous, whitish, broadly umbilicate; tunic above very thin, evanescent, beneath thicker and cottony, covered with a whitish meal; spores thick, oblong-elliptic.—*Tul. Ann. Sc. Nat.* 1844, i. *p.* 67, *t.* 3, *t.* 4, *f.* 1-3, *t.* 8, *f.* 1-12. *Hoffm. Cr. t.* 8, *f.* 3. *Nees. f.* 132. *Corda. Anl. t. D. f.* 42. *Nidularia striata. Holm.* ii. *t.* 2. *Sow. t.* 29. *Fr. S.M.* ii. *p.* 298. *Bull. t.* 40, *f. A. t.* 2, *f.* 3. *Peziza striata. Bolt. t.* 102, *f.* 2. *Schæff. t.* 178. *Gled. t.* 4. *Vaill. t.* 11, *f.* 4-5. *Mich. t.* 102, *f.* 2. *Bocc. t.* 301, *f.* 1. *Berk. Outl. t.* 2, *f.* 3. *Berk. exs. no.* 259. *Cooke. exs. no.* 311. *Fckl. exs. no.* 1247.

On sticks, fir cones, &c. [United States.]

1199. Cyathus vernicosus *D.C.* "Waxy Cyathus."

Campanulate, base narrowly subsessile, above broadly open, undulato-repand, externally pale ochre or cinereous, silky tomentose, at length nearly smooth, internally lead-coloured or brown, corona inconspicuous; sporangia pale blackish, even; tunic rather thick, continuous, with a scanty, cinereous meal; funiculum white.—*Tul. Ann. Sc. Nat.* 1844, i. *p.* 81, *t.* 5, *f.* 14-23. *Corda. Anl. t. D. f.* 42. *Link. Obs. t.* 2, *f.* 53. *Berk. Outl. t.* 21, *f.* i. *Berk. exs. no.* 258. *Cooke exs. no.* 312. *Fckl. exs. no.* 1246. *Nees. f.* 133, *B. Nidularia campanulata. Sow. t.* 26. *Holms.* ii. t. 3. *Paul. t.* 187, *f.* 7-12. *Bull. t.* 488, *f.* 1. *Hoffm. Cr. t.* 8, *f.* 2. *Fl. Dan. t.* 780, *f.* 1, *t.* 469, *upper fig. Peziza lentifera. Bolt. t.* 102, *f.* 1. *Gled. t.* 4. *Mich. t.* 102, *f.* 1. *Vaill. t.* 11, *f.* 6-7. *Bocc. t.* 301, *f.* 1. *Batt. t.* 3, *f. I.K.L.M.*

On the ground, especially stubble fields. Common.

[United States.]

(*Fig.* 142.)

Gen. **97. CRUCIBULUM,** Tul.

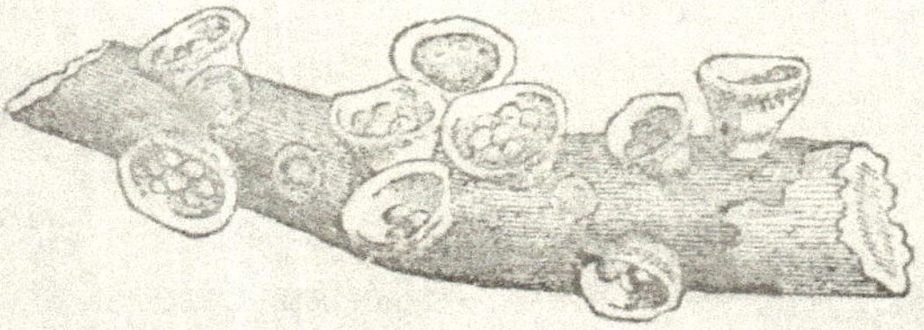

Fig. 143.

Peridium consisting of a uniform, spongy, fibrous felt, closed by a flat furfuraceous cover of the same colour. Sporangia plane, attached by a long cord, springing from a little nipple-like tubercle. —*Berk. Outl. p.* 312. *Tul. Ann. Sc. Nat.* 1844, i. *p.* 89.

(*Fig.* 143.)

1200. **Crucibulum vulgare.** *Tul.* "Common Crucibulum."

Peridium tawny tan-colour, thick, externally nearly even, internally quite even, smooth, shining; mouth quite entire, naked; sporangia pale ochre, at length whitish; spores minute, ovate. —*Tul. Ann. Sc. Nat.* 1844, i. *p.* 90. *Ray. Syn. 3rd ed. t.* 1, *f.* 2, *b. c. Mich. t.* 102, *f.* 3. *Gled. t.* 4. *Schæff. t.* 179. *Fl. Dan. t.* 105. *Hoffm. Cr. t.* 8, *f.* 1. *Bull t.* 40, *f. B.C. Nidularia lævis. Bull t.* 488, *f.* 2. *Sow. t.* 30. *Holms.* ii. *t.* 1. *Cyathus crucibulum. Nees. f.* 133. *Grev. t.* 34. *Desm. exs. no.* 766. *Corda. Anl. t. D. f.* 42, (10-18). *Berk. Outl. t.* 2, *f.* 1. *Berk. exs. no.* 167. *Fckl. exs. no.* 1248.

On fern, sticks, &c. [United States.]

(*Fig.* 143.)

Gen. 98. **NIDULARIA,** Tul.

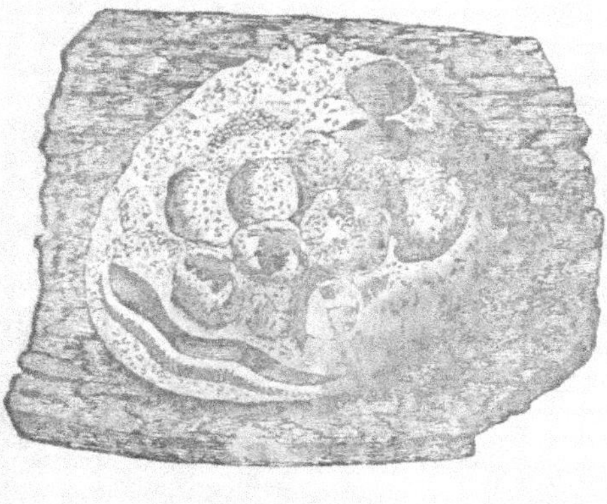

Fig. 144.

Peridium uniform, globose, of a simple membrane, at first closed, at length ruptured, or opening with a circular mouth; without a proper veil. Sporangia numerous, small, enveloped in mucus.—*Tul. Ann. Sc. Nat.* 1844, i. *p.* 92.

(*Fig.* 144.)

1201. **Nidularia pisiformis.** *Tul.* "Pea-shaped Nidularia."

Gregarious, subglobose, sessile, rootless, hairy, brownish. Sporangia subrotund or discoid dark brown; sporidia colourless, globose, or elliptical.—*Tul. Ann. Sc. Nat.* 1844, i. *p.* 100. *B. & Br. Ann. N.H. no.* 1039. *Curr. Linn. Trans.* xxiv, *t.* 25, *f.* 4-6 & 21-22. *Rabh. F. E. no.* 1328. *Granularia pisiformis. Roth. Ust. Ann. b.* 1, *s.* 6, *t.* 1, *f.* 1.

On pine chips. Weybridge. May—Oct. 1862.

Peridium subrotund, slightly flattened, varying in different specimens trom $\frac{1}{12}$ to $\frac{1}{4}$ in. across, brown or brownish white, woolly, tuberculate when ripe, from the pressure outwards of the sporangia; indehiscent, opening by irregular fissures; sporangia enveloped in jelly, subrotund, or disc-shaped, their outline forming a broad elipse (almost a circle) with a major axis of about $\frac{1}{20}$ of an inch, shining, of a rich dark brown colour, sometimes hollowed inwards on one side, but not umbilicate, and showing no trace of an elastic cord such as exists in *Cyathus.* Sporidia colourless, slightly varying in shape, globose, pear-shaped, or elliptical, produced on sterigmata, 0·0002-0·0003 in. across.—*F.C.* (*Fig.* 144.)

Gen. 99. **SPHÆROBOLUS**, Tode.

Fig. 145.

Peridium double, the inner at length inverted elastically, and ejecting a solitary subglobose sporangium.—*Berk. Outl. p.* 312. *Eng. Fl.* v. *p.* 231. (*Fig.* 145.)

1202. **Sphærobolus stellatus.** *Tode.* "Stellate Sphærobolus."

Globose, pale yellow; mouth regular, stellato-dentate.—*Berk. Outl. t.* 21, *f.* 2. *Eng. Fl.* v. *p.* 231. *Fckl. exs. no.* 1245. *Corda. Icon.* v. *f.* 48. *Bisch. f.* 3643. *Tul. Fung. Hyp. t.* 21, *f.* 11. *Rabh. F. E. no.* 36.

On sawdust, twigs, &c. Autumn. [United States.]

Plants at first connected by a web, at length smooth, subglobose, yellowish; outer peridium consisting of two substances, lined by the inner peridium, which is quite distinct and separated by some moisture, white, pellucid, and shining, at length both split together in a stellate manner, and the inner becomes suddenly inverted, while in general it still remains attached by the apices of the stellate margin, and the sporangium is shot forth to a considerable distance. Sporidia $\frac{1}{4000}$ in. long, elliptic or curved and irregular. The rays of the outer peridium are orange within.—*Eng. Fl.* (*Fig.* 145.)

Gen. 100. **THELEBOLUS**, Tode.

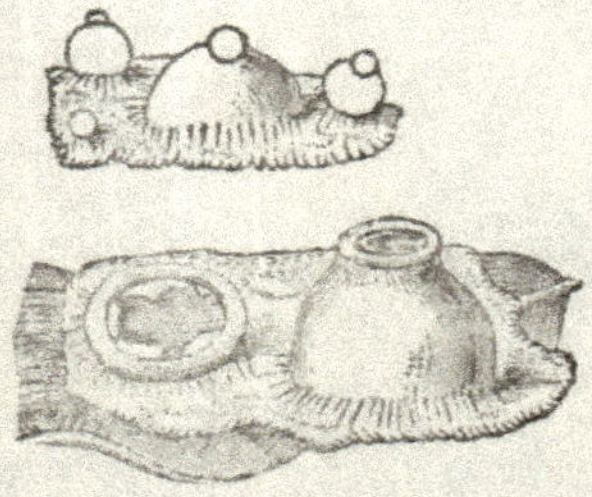

Fig. 146.

Peridium sessile, subrotund, urceolato-ventricose, mouth entire. Sporangium papillæform. Spores mucous.—*Fr. S.M.* ii. *p.* 307. *Eng. Fl.* v. *p.* 230. (*Fig.* 146).

1203. **Thelebolus terrestris.** *A. & S.* "Ground Thelebolus."

Hemispherical, saffron-yellow, crowded, seated on a dense tomentose subiculum.—*A. & S. t.* 2, *f.* 4. *Nees. f.* 364. *Ann. N.H. no.* 964. *Fckl. exs. no.* 643. *Bisch. f.* 3646. *Kl. exs.* ii. *no.* 718. *Corda. Anl. t. D. f.* 44, *no.* 9-11.

On fir leaves. Richmond, Yorks.

(*Fig.* 146.)

[THELEBOLUS STERCOREUS. *Tode.* Was inserted in English Flora on the authority of Loudon, and has not since been confirmed.]

Gen. **101.** **POLYANGIUM,** Link.

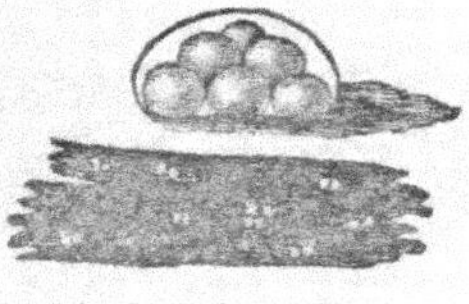

Fig. 147.

Peridium subhemispherical, hyaline, sporangia large in proportion, grumous within.—*Berk. Outl. p.* 312.

(*Fig.* 147.)

1204. **Polyangium vitellinum.** *Ditm.* "Egg-yellow Polyangium."

Minute, scattered; sporangia lemon yellow, sporangioles egg-shaped, orange.—*Ditm. Sturm. t.* 27. *Link. Obs. t.* 2, *f.* 65. *Berk. Outl. p.* 312. *Corda. Anl. t. C. f.* 40, *no.* 1-3. *Bisch. f.* 3628.

On fallen trunks. Rare. King's Cliffe.

[United States.]

(*Fig.* 147.)

Family III. CONIOMYCETES

Spores either solitary or concatenate, produced on the tips of generally short threads, which are either naked, or contained in a perithecium, rarely compacted into a gelatinous mass.—*Berk. Outl. p.* 313.

This family is distinguished by the vast predominance of the reproductive bodies over the rest of the plant, if not in size, at least in abundance, and from the ease with which in general they fall from the point of attachment, in consequence of which, as the name implies, they have a dusty appearance, and often soil the fingers of those who handle them. In some cases there is a decided perithecium or peridium; in others there is no approach to such an organ, and in very nearly allied productions, it may be either present or entirely absent. Many of the genera are doubtless conditions of higher forms. —*See Berk. Introd. p.* 315.

A.—Growing on dead or dying plants.
Subcutaneous.
Perithecium more or less distinct . . . *Sphæronemei.*
Perithecium obsolete or wanting . . . *Melanconiei.*
Superficial.
Fructifying surface naked.
Spores compound or tomiparous . . *Torulacei.*

B.—Parasitic on living plants.
Peridium distinctly cellular . . . . *Æcidiacei.*
Peridium none.
Spores subglobose, simple, or deciduous . *Cæomacei.*
Spores mostly oblong, usually septate . *Pucciniæi.*

Order XII. SPHÆRONEMEI.

Perithecium more or less distinct, free, or erumpent; spores basal or parietal, simple, or septate, sometimes oozing out by the contraction of the perithecial walls.—*Berk. Introd. p.* 330.

The structure of a greater part of them is much the same; an obscurely developed perithecium, minute sporophores, and microscopic spores. It is quite certain that a large portion of the so-called species of *Phoma*, *Leptostroma*, *Diplodia*, *Hendersonia*, *Cytispora*, *Septoria*, &c, are mere cases of dualism. All, indeed, are interesting, so far as ascertained dualism is concerned, or as far as there may be a prospect of showing that they are the spermatogonia or pycnidia of ascophorous species.—*M. J. B.*

A.—Spores oozing out in tendrils.
Perithecia delicate, simple.
Distinct.
Spores uniseptate or simple . . . *Ascochyta.*
Spores with a row of sporidiola . . *Darluca.*
Seated on discoloured spots.
Spores ovoid or oblong . . . *Phyllosticta.*

At length fissured.
Spores more or less globose . . . *Cheilaria.*
Perithecia more or less incorporated.
Spores oblong or thread-shaped . . *Septoria.*
Perithecia compound, or irregular.
Spores curved . . . . . . *Cytispora.*

B.—Spores oozing out in a globule.
Perithecia variable.
Spores minute . . . . . . *Sphæronema.*

C.—Spores not oozing out in globules or tendrils.
Perithecia carbonaceous.
With a papillate ostiolum.
Spores minute . . . . . . *Aposphæria.*
Perforated.
Spores simple . . . . . . *Sphæropsis.*
Spores uniseptate . . . . . . *Diplodia.*
Spores multiseptate . . . . . *Hendersonia.*
Spores fasciculate, fusiform . . . *Prosthemium.*
Fissured.
Spores simple, obovate . . . . *Clinterium.*
Cup-shaped, dimidiate . . . . . *Rabenhorstia.*
Cylindrical.
Spores long, flexuous . . . . *Acrospermum.*
Perithecia bristly.
Mouthless, thin.
Spores vermiculate . . . . *Vermicularia.*
Excipuliform.
Spores attenuated . . . . . . *Excipula.*
Spores aristate . . . . . . *Dinemasporium.*
Spores concatenate . . . . . *Myxormia.*
Perithecia membranaceous.
Not flattened.
Bursting irregularly.
Spores simple . . . . . . *Coniothyrium.*
Bursting longitudinally.
Spores uniseptate on branched sporophores . . . . *Cystotricha.*
Opening with a pore.
Spores simple . . . . *Phoma.*
Spores filiform appendiculate . . . *Dilophospora.*
Always covered.
Spores fusiform . . . . . *Cryptosporium.*
Spores crested . . . . . . *Neottiospora.*
More or less flattened.
Breaking off at the base.
Spores simple, minute . . . . *Leptostroma.*
Spores cylindrical, oblong . . . *Leptothyrium.*
Spores septate, aristate . . . *Discosia.*
Opening irregularly.
Spores curved . . . . . . *Pilidium.*
Gaping and innate.
Spores simple, linear . . . . . *Micropera.*
Irregular and wrinkled.
Spores minute . . . . . . *Melasmia.*
Spores large, obovate . . . . *Piggotia.*
More or less radiating.
Spores simple, fusiform . . . *Actinothyrium.*

Attached to creeping threads.
Spores simple or uniseptate . . *Asteroma.*
Perithecia spurious.
Simple, never deficient above.
Spores elongated . . . . . *Phlyctæna.*
Sometimes excipuliform.
Spores elongated . . . . . *Discella.*
Multicellular.
Spores minute . . . . . *Ceuthospora.*
Spores quaternate, filiform . . . *Eriospora.*

Gen. 102. CONIOTHYRIUM, Corda.

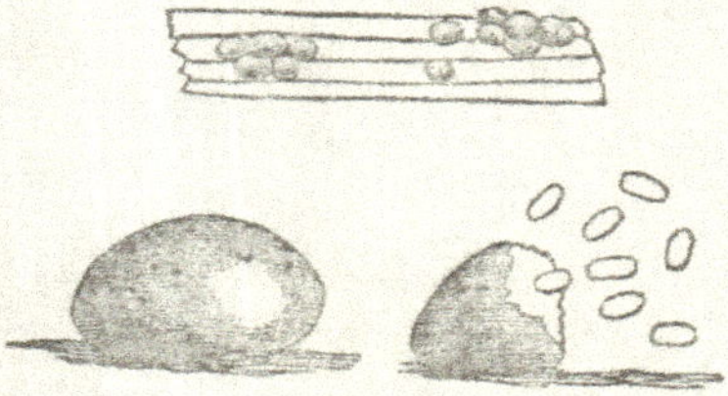

Fig. 148.

Perithecium membranaceous, bursting irregularly or transversely; spores simple, at length free.—*Berk. Outl. p.* 313. (*Fig.* 148.)

1205. **Coniothyrium glomeratum.** *Corda.* "Clustered Coniothyrium."

Tufts minute, black. Perithecia in heaps, convex, rugulose, brown; spores oblong, rounded at the extremities, colourless, hyaline.—*Corda.* iv. *f.* 108. *B. & Br. Ann. N.H. no.* 752.

On elm planks. Nov.

(*Fig.* 148.)

Gen. 103. LEPTOSTROMA, Fr.

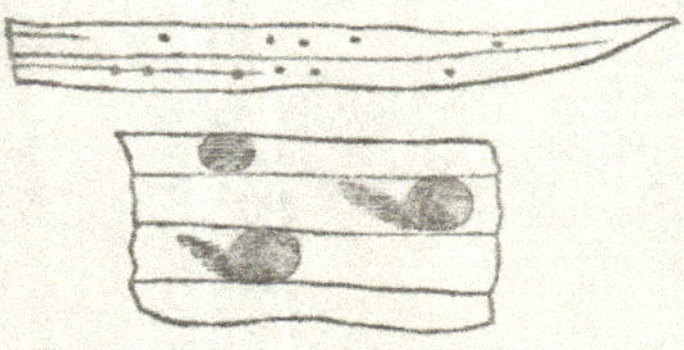

Fig. 149.

Perithecium membranaceous, flat, breaking off at the base; spores simple, minute.—*Berk. Outl. p.* 313. *Fr. S.M.* ii. *p.* 597. (*Fig.* 149.)

1206. **Leptostroma caricinum.** *Fr.* "Sedge Leptostroma."

Subrotund, unequal, thin, opaque, entirely falling off, and leaving a brown spot.—*Fr. Obs.* ii. *t.* 7, *f.* 4. *S.M.* ii. *p.* 598. *Eng. Fl.* v. *p.* 297. *Fckl. exs. no.* 186. *Kl. exs. no.* 383.

On leaves of *Carices.* [United States.]

The perithecium is extremely thin, and it leaves, when fallen off, a pale brown spot, surrounded by a little raised line. Other less perfectly defined spots, but of the same size, accompany the perfect plant, which are either old worn individuals, or an imperfectly developed state; occasionally in the centre of these there is a white spot.—*M. J. B.* (*Fig.* 149.)

LEPTOSTROMA JUNCINUM, Fr. (*Berk. exs. no.* 197) is undoubtedly the stylosporous condition of *Dothidea junci.*

LEPTOSTROMA FILICINUM, Fr. (*Cooke exs. no.* 334) is an incomplete condition of *Dothidea filicina* Fr.

LEPTOSTROMA VULGARE, Fr. is an imperfect state of *Hysterium commune,* Fr.

1207. Leptostroma litigiosum. *Desm.* "Minute fern Leptostroma."

Perithecia somewhat rounded, very minute, punctiform, scattered or clustered together, brown-black, sub-opaque, at length wholly seceding.—*Desm. Ann. Sc. Nat.* 1843, xix. *p.* 338. *Moug. exs. no.* 673. *Cooke exs. no.* 335.

On dead *Pteris aquilina.* [Low & Mid. Carolina.]

Much smaller than *L. filicinum.* Probably a condition of some ascigerous fungus.

1208. Leptostroma spireæ. *Fr.* "Meadow-sweet Leptostroma."

Conglomerate, connate, irregular, rugose, shining grey within, at length separating entirely at the base.—*Eng. Fl.* v. *p.* 298. *Cooke exs. no.* 333. *Berk. exs. no.* 46.

On dead stems of *Spiræa ulmaria.* Spring. Common. [Low. Carolina.]

Gen. 104. PHOMA, Fr.

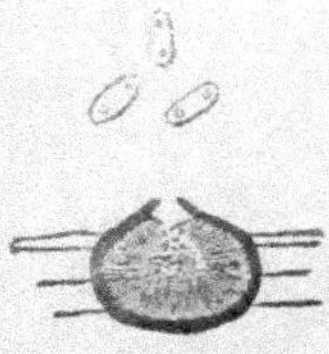

Fig. 150.

Perithecium punctiform or subglobose, often spurious, or incorporated with the matrix, discharging the minute simple spores by a small orifice at the apex. Spores mostly hyaline.—*Berk. Outl. p.* 314. (*Fig.* 150.)

Probably none of the species are autonomous, but they must be retained under this genus until satisfactorily referred to the higher forms to which they respectively belong.

Sect 1. *Chlorosporæ*—spores slightly coloured.

1209. **Phoma concentricum.** *Desm.* "Concentric Phoma."

Spots rounded, whitish, surrounded by a brown band, pseudo-perithecia numerous, concentrical, black, opaque; spores copious, very minute, subglobose.—*Desm. Ann. S.N.* xiii. *p.* 189. *Berk. Ann. N.H. no.* 197. *Depazea Agaves, Mont. Ann. Sc. Nat.* i. *p.* 344.

Common on leaves of *Yucca*. [Low. Carolina.]

Having the appearance of a *Phyllosticta* or *Depazea*. Spores (·005 m.m.) ·00019 in.

1210. **Phoma hederæ.** *Desm.* "Ivy Phoma."

Covered, black; spores hyaline, subglobose.—*Desm. exs. no.* 350. *Eng. Fl.* v. *p.* 284. *Berk. exs. no.* 90. *Fr. El.* ii. *p.* 119. *Sphæropsis Hederæ. Lev. Ann. Sc. Nat.* 1846. v. *p.* 296.

On small dead shoots of ivy.

Covered with the blackened epidermis, which is pierced with a ragged, round, or linear orifice. Spores blackish, not truly globose.—*M. J. B.*

Sect. 2. *Hyalosporæ*—spores hyaline.

1211. **Phoma asteriscus.** *Berk.* "Starry Phoma."

Unilocular, convex, pitch-brown, margin nebulose, spores oblong, sub-elliptic.—*B. & Br. Ann. N.H. no.* 394.

On dead stems of *Heracleum*. Nov.

Forming little pitch-brown, rather convex dots, with a paler cloudy narrow border. Mass of spores surrounded by a dark cellular stratum, consisting of hexagonal cells, confused with the matrix, but scarcely presenting a definite perithecium. Spores narrow-oblong, sub-elliptic, but by no means filiform.—*B. & Br.*

1212. **Phoma nothum.** *Berk.* "Bastard Phoma."

Perithecia spurious, here and there elevated below, spores obovate.—*B. & Br. Ann. N.H. no.* 395.

On dead plane twigs. Feb.

Pustules slightly raised; perithecia spurious, orbicular, the base protruding here and there into their cavity. Spores obovate, rather pointed at the narrow extremity.—*B. & Br.*

1213. **Phoma lingam.** *Desm.* "Cabbage Phoma."

Gregarious; perithecia irregular, convex, soon depressed and concave, rugose, black. Spores small, oblong, with a sporule at each extremity.—*Desm. Ann. Sc. Nat.* (1849), xi. *p.* 281. *Desm.*

exs. no. 1877. *B. & Br. Ann. N.H. no.* 395.* *Sphæria lingam, Tode. f.* 46. *Fr. S.M.* ii. *p.* 507.

On old cabbage stalks.

Spores about (·005 m.m.) ·00019 in.

1214. **Phoma radula.** *B. & Br.* "Rasp-like Phoma."

Perithecia delicate, broadly conical; spores oblong-elliptic. —*B. & Br. Ann. N.H. no.* 396.

On dead twigs of plane. Feb.

Sprinkled over the twigs, which renders it rough, like a little rasp or grater; epidermis split on each perithecium; perithecia delicate, composed of sub-hexagonal cells; spores minute, oblong-elliptic, with a sporule at either extremity, rarely an additional sporule in the centre.—*B. & Br.*

1215. **Phoma depressum.** *B. & Br.* "Depressed Phoma."

Perithecia spurious, much depressed above, stroma slightly thickened, olivaceous; spores oblong-elliptic.—*B. & Br. Ann. N.H. no.* 397. *Cooke exs. no.* 337.

On twigs of elm and *Robinia pseud-acacia.* Feb.

Scattered, forming little pustules pierced by the orifice; perithecia much depressed, spurious, covered by an olive-coloured stroma. Spores minute, oblong-elliptic, rather pointed at either extremity, towards which there is a sporule. Sometimes there is more than a single cell.—*B. & Br.*

1216. **Phomo eriophorum.** *B. & Br.* "Cottony Phoma."

Perithecia globose, free, at first pallid, at length blackish, tomentose below, springing from a similar mycelium.—*B. & Br. Ann. N. H. no.* 812.

On Spanish chestnuts.

Perithecia at first white, globose, clothed more or less with white or yellowish cottony down, like that of the mycelium from which they spring; at length dark, but when seen by transmitted light, reddish. Spores very abundant, white, slightly curved, ·00025 in. (·006 m.m.) long.—*B. & Br.*

1217. **Phoma samarorum.** *Desm.* "Ash-key Phoma."

Forming black spots, closely covered by the cuticle; perithecia convex, black, pierced; spores minute, oblong-elliptic.—*Desm. exs. no.* 349, 1875. *B. & Br. Ann. N.H. no.* 398. *Cooke exs. no.* 160.

On Samari of ash. Jan. Common.

Forming conspicuous black spots; cuticle closely applied to the perithecia; perithecia convex, black, pierced in the centre; spores minute, oblong-elliptic, with a sporule towards either extremity.—*B. & Br.*

1218. Phoma piceum. *B. & Br.* "Pitchy Phoma."

Hypophyllous; perithecia spurious, pitch-brown, convex, closely connected with the epidermis; spores oblong-elliptic.—*B. & Br. Ann. N.H. no.* 399.

On the under surface of dead rose leaves. Feb.

Scattered, pustules conspicuous, convex, pitch-brown; cuticle closely connected with the spurious perithecia; spores pure white, minute, oblong-elliptic, with a sporule at either extremity.—*B. & Br.*

1219. Phoma sticticum. *B. & Br.* "Pied Phoma."

Scattered; very minute; covered by the cuticle, which at length splits longitudinally; spores oblong-elliptic, with a sporule at either extremity.—*B. & Br. Ann. N.H. no.* 400.

On dead twigs of box. Feb.

1220. Phoma exiguum. *Desm.* "Little Phoma."

Perithecia numerous, scattered or approximate, small, rounded or ovate, opening with a pore, covered by the cuticle, brownish when moist, blackish when dry, and rather shining. Spores numerous, ovoid, very minute, hyaline.—*Desm. exs. no.* 1869. *B. & Br. Ann. N.H. no.* 400.*

On shoots of elder, &c.

Spores about $\frac{1}{200}$ m.m. Very different from *Sporocadus exilis*, Corda, and *Hendersonia exilis*, Lev., to which some authors have referred it.

1221. Phoma devastatrix. *B. & Br.* "Destructive Phoma."

Perithecia very minute, punctiform, black, globose; spores oblong, 2-3 nucleate.—*B. & Br. Ann. N.H. no.* 813.

On Lobelias. Aug.

This minute species, all but invisible to the naked eye, was most destructive in gardens in 1856. The perithecia are globose, and perforated with a minute round aperture; the spores are oblong, hyaline, containing from 2 to 3 nuclei ·0004-·00033 in. (·01-·008 m. m.) long.—*B. & Br.*

1222. Phoma microscopicum. *B. & Br.* "Microscopic Phoma."

Perithecia subglobose, scattered beneath the epidermis, which is blackened above the ostiola, spores oblong-elliptic.—*B. & Br. Ann. N.H. no.* 401.

On dead stems of *Potamogeton.*

Forming scattered, very minute dark brown dots on discoloured patches; beneath each dot is seated a distinct subglobose, smooth perithecium, with no visible mycelium, very slightly conical above, pierced with a round simple ostiolum. Spores oblong-elliptic, variable in size, having occasionally, but not constantly, a sporidiolum at either extremity.—*B. & Br.*

1223. Phoma nebulosum. *Berk.* "Cloudy Phoma."

Covered ; perithecia very minute, gregarious, forming interrupted, grey, cloud-like sub-longitudinal spots, ostiola rather prominent, acute.—*Berk. Outl. p.* 314. *Sphæria nebulosa, Pers. Syn. p.* 31. *Eng. Fl.* v. *p.* 256. *Nees. f.* 341. *Fr. S. M.* ii. *p.* 430.

On dead herbaceous stems. Common.

Easily known by its long grey patches, dotted with the ostiola.

1224. Phoma longissimum. *Berk.* "Very long Phoma."

Covered, black ; perithecia minute, running together into extremely long parallel rows, ostiola obsolete ; spores elliptical or slightly curved, with two nuclei.—*Berk. Outl. p.* 314. *Sphæria longissima, Pers. Syn. p.* 31. *Fr. S.M.* ii. *p.* 431. *Eng. Fl.* v. *p.* 256. *Curr. Linn. Trans.* xxii. *p.* 285.

On dead stems of *Umbelliferæ*, &c.

Known by the narrow, linear, black patches, extending from joint to joint.

1225. Phoma petiolorum. *Rob.* "Petiole Phoma."

Perithecia scattered, globose or ovate, black, covered by the epidermis, papillate, at length pierced with a terminal pore. Nucleus whitish. Sporidia minute, ovoid-oblong, with two nucleoli.—*Desm. Ann. des. Sc. Nat.* 1847, viii. *p.* 16. *West. & Wall. exs. n.* 471. *Cooke Seem. Journ.* iv. *f.* 13.

On petioles of *Robinia pseud-acacia.* Feb.

1226. Phoma glandicola. *Lev.* "Acorn Phoma."

Perithecia gregarious, erumpent, subglobose, smooth, black, surrounded by the lacerated epidermis. Ostiolum scarcely conspicuous. Spores minute, ovate, simple, pellucid.—*Lev. Ann. Sc. Nat.* 1846, v. *p.* 281. *Cooke Seem. Journ. Bot.* iv. *f.* 14. *Sporonema glandicola, Desm.*

On acorns which had lain some time on the ground.

[Low Carolina.]

Sect. 3. *Lignicolæ.* On bleached wood.

1227. Phoma inophilum. *Berk.* "Maple-plank Phoma."

Spots indeterminate, silky-shining ; perithecia oblong, spores oblong, very minute.—*Berk. Hook. Journ.* 1853, *p.* 40, *t.* 3, *f.* 4. *Ann. N.H. no.* 735.

On maple planks. Nov.

Forming shining patches, which contrast strongly with the rest of the surface; spores extremely minute, just distinguishable with a power of 250 diameters, ·0006 in. (·0015 m.m.) long; oblong, with a sporule at either extremity.—*M. J. B.*

1228. Phoma muciferum. *Berk.* "Mucous Phoma."

Perithecia scattered, oblong; spores very minute, involved in mucus.—*Berk. Hook. Journ. p.* 1853, *p.* 40, *t.* 3, *f.* 5. *Ann. N.H. no.* 736.

On elm planks. Nov.

Spores discharged from the base when ruptured in a cirrhiform string, extremely minute, oblong, with a nucleus at either extremity. The mucous substance in which the spores are involved is so little soluble, that they are not dispersed as in other species.—*M. J. B.*

1229. Phoma ulmicola. *Berk.* "Elm-plank Phoma."

Spots brown; perithecia rather crowded; spores small, elliptic, hyaline.—*Berk. Hook. Journ.* 1853, *p.* 40, *t.* 3, *f.* 3. *Ann. N.H. no.* 737.

On elm planks. Nov.

Forming little oblong brown patches. Spores ·0008 in. (·002 m.m.) long; nuclei obsolete.

1230. Phoma epileucum. *Berk.* "Bleached Fir Phoma."

Spots indeterminate; perithecia elongated; spores hyaline, rather large, oblong, without nuclei.—*Berk. Hook. Journ.* 1853, *p.* 40, *t.* 3, *f.* 2. *Ann. N.H. no.* 738.

On bleached pine planks. Dec.

Perithecia black, minute, elongated, following the direction of the fibres. Spores perfectly colourless, oblong, ·00015 in. (·0038 m.m.) long, sometimes slightly broader at one extremity, without any definite nuclei.—*M.J.B.*

1231. Phoma fibricola. *Berk.* "Fibre-loving Phoma."

Spots indeterminate; perithecia minute, elongated; spores ovate and elliptic, greenish.—*Berk. Hook. Journ.* 1853, *p.* 40, *t.* 3, *f.* 1. *Ann. N.H. no.* 739.

On oak, ash, and elm. Nov.

Perithecia mostly scattered, but sometimes forming distinct groups, elongated, following the course of the fibres; spores ovate or sub-elliptic, larger than in most species ·00023 in. (·006 m.m.) long, of a delicate olive green, without distinct nuclei.—*M. J. B.*

1232. Phoma bicuspidatum. *Berk.* "Two pointed Phoma.'

Spots indeterminate; perithecia elongated; spores large,

apiculate at either end, hyaline, binucleate.—*Berk. Hook. Journ.* 1853, *p.* 40, *t.* 3, *f.* 6. *Ann. N.H. no.* 740.

On pine planks. Dec.

Perithecia elongated, black, minute, following the direction of the fibres, at first scattered, at length often confluent. Spores ·0003 in. (·0076 m.m.) long, shortly fusiform, apiculate at either end, variable in size, and in the degree of acumination, hyaline, containing two sporules; seated on slender sporophores.—*M.J.B.*

Gen. **105.** **LEPTOTHYRIUM,** Kunze.

Perithecium flat, irregular, at length breaking off at the base; spores cylindrical, oblong, or irregular.—*Berk. Outl. p.* 314.

The species in this genus are also doubtfully autonomous.

1233. Leptothyrium juglandis. *Lib.* "Walnut Leptothyrium."

Hypophyllous. Spots orbicular, greyish; perithecia flattened, minute, rugose, brown; nucleus grey; spores ellipsoid.—*Lib. exs. no.* 164. *B. & Br. Ann. N.H. no.* 402. *Cooke exs. no.* 152. *Fckl. exs. no.* 201. *Cooke, L. F. no.* 60.

On half dead walnut leaves. Autumn.

1234. Leptothyrium fragariæ. *Lib.* "Strawberry Leptothyrium."

Epiphyllous. Spots indeterminate, reddish; perithecia flattened, rugose, shining, black; nucleus grey; spores cylindrical with 4-5 sporules.—*Lib. exs. no.* 162. *Cooke exs. no.* 153. *Cooke, L.F. no.* 62.

On strawberry and *Potentillæ.*

1235. Leptothyrium ribis. *Lib.* "Currant Leptothyrium."

Epiphyllous. Spots orbicular, minute, confluent, brown; perithecia flattened, red-brown; nucleus white; spores ovate, curved.—*Lib. exs. no.* 258. *Cooke exs. no.* 151. *Cooke, L. F. no.* 61.

On leaves of red currant. Autumn.

Gen. **106.** **ACTINOTHYRIUM,** Kunze.

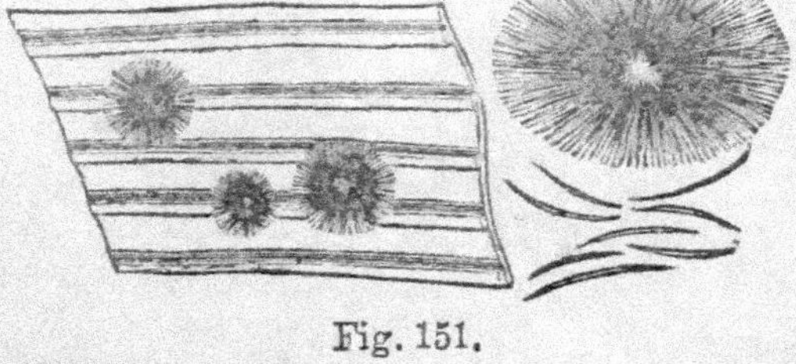

Fig. 151.

Perithecia orbicular, radiato-fibrous; spores fusiform, slender, simple —*Berk. Outl. p.* 315. *Eng. Fl.* v. *p.* 296. (*Fig.* 151.)

1236. Actinothyrium graminis. *Kze.* "Grass Actinothyrium."

Perithecia irregularly gregarious, orbicular, adnate, umbonate; margin radiating; spores slender, curved, fusiform.—*Kze. M.H.* ii. *t.* 2. *f.* 3. *Fr. S.M.* ii. *p.* 597. *Grev. t.* 218. *Moug. exs. no.* 637. *Eng. Fl.* v. *p.* 296. *Cooke exs. no.* 338. *Fckl. exs. no.* 555. *Bisch. f.* 3581. *Bail. t.* 15. *Pay. f.* 369.

On leaves and culms of grasses. Spring.

Forming little, round, very flat black spots, with a central umbo, of a close, radiating, fibrous structure. (*Fig.* 151.)

Gen. **107.** **CRYPTOSPORIUM**, Kunze.

Fig. 152.

Perithecium always covered by the cuticle, carnoso-membranaceous, at length pierced; spores fusiform, simple.—*Berk. Outl. p.* 315. (*Fig.* 152.)

1237. Cryptosporium Caricis. *Corda.* "Sedge Cryptosporium."

Perithecia very minute, scarcely conspicuous, hypophyllous, crowded, rounded, brown; spores fusiform, straight or curved, hyaline, brown.—*Corda. Sturm.* ii. *t.* 50. *B. & Br. Ann. N.H. no.* 403. *Fr. S.M.* iii. *p.* 482. *Bisch. f.* 3839. *Berk. exs. no.* 307.

On leaves of different *Carices.* (*Fig.* 152.)

Cryptosporium Neesii. Corda. has been proved to be a stylosporous condition of *Valsa suffusa*, Fr.

Gen. **108.** **SPHÆRONEMA**, Tode.

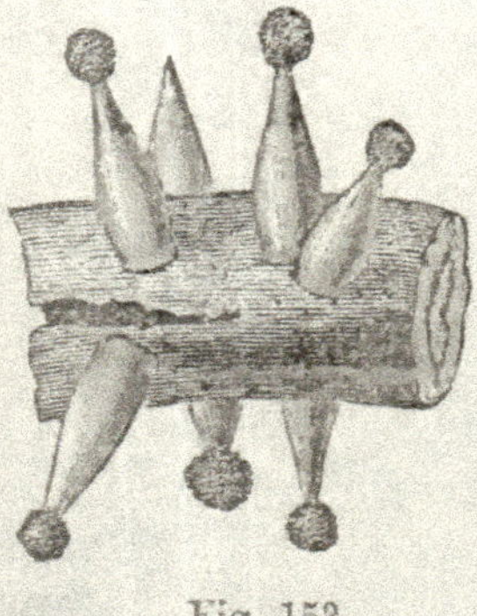

Fig. 153.

Perithecia free, opaque, or hyaline; spores minute, at length oozing out by the ostiolum, and forming a globule.—*Berk. Outl. p.* 315. *Eng. Fl.* v. *p.* 281. (*Fig.* 153.)

1238. **Sphæronema subulatum.** *Tode.* "Awl-shaped Sphæronema."

Perithecia grumous, between conical and subulate, acute, yellowish; globule paler.—*Fr. Obs.* i. *p.* 187. *Fries. exs. no.* 325. *Grev. t.* 189. *Tode. f.* 117. *Eng. Fl.* v. *p.* 281. *Fckl. exs. no.* 773. *Bisch. f.* 3532. *Bail. t.* 14.

On hard blackened *Agarics.* [Mid. Carolina.]

At first sight resembling a *Stilbum.* Varies considerably in form, being sometimes almost linear. (*Fig.* 153.)

1239. **Sphæronema vitreum.** *Corda.* "Glassy Sphæronema."

Perithecia minute, transparent, pale yellow, more or less inflated below, with a long neck, fimbriate; spores oblong, obtuse, or subtruncate; globule pale yellow.—*Corda.* i. *f.* 297. *S. blepharistoma. Berk. Mag. Zool. & Bot. no.* 57, *t.* 15, *f.* 4, *& no.* 196. *Berk. exs. no.* 189.

On *Russula adusta, Lactarii,* nettles, &c.

Perithecia scarcely exceeding half a line in height, often much more minute, varying greatly in form, but in general more or less inflated at the base, occasionally conico-subulate, often confluent, mostly furnished with a long, distinct, slender neck, the orifice of which is fringed with a single row of distinct filaments, which are the apices of those of which the perithecium is composed. Sporidia larger than in *S. subulatum,* flowing out and formi an elongated subpersistent pale yellow globule.—*B. & Br.*

1240. **Sphæronema leucoconium.** *B. & Br.* "White Sphæronema."

Gregarious; perithecia hyaline, plano-convex, depressed, rather irregular, seated on snow-white flocci; spores minute, elliptic.—*B. & Br. Ann. N.H. no* 405.

On decaying roots of beet. Nov. King's Cliffe.

Forming a thin stratum, consisting of minute, depressed, sub-hemispherical, or irregular white perithecia, simply pierced with a minute pore, and seated on branched white threads, of which a few spring from the sides. There is no papillæform or elongated ostiolum, but the convex perithecium is merely pierced in the centre.—*B. & Br.*

1241. **Sphæronema epimyces.** *Berk.* "Parasitic Sphæronema."

Gregarious, immersed in purplish spots, perithecia globose, papillate, black; nucleus white; spores —?—*Berk. Outl. p.* 315. *Sphæria epimyces. Fr. S.M.* ii. *p.* 499. *Berk. Ann. N.H. no.* 187.

On decayed *Corticium comedens*. Milton. Norths.

APOSPHÆRIA ACUTA. *Berk.* See *Sphæria coniformis.*—*Cooke exs. no.* 223. [United States.]

APOSPHÆRIA COMPLANATA. *Berk.* See *Sphæria complanata.*—*Cooke exs. no.* 224. [United States.]

Gen. 109. SPHÆROPSIS, Lev.

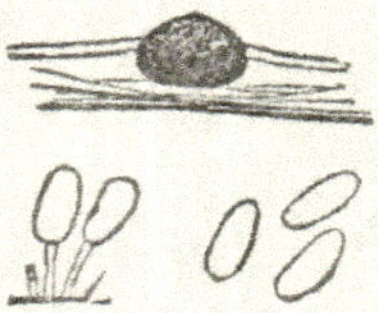

Fig. 154.

Perithecia distinct, carbonaceous; spores various, simple, escaping by a perforation at the apex.—*Berk. Outl. p.* 316. (*Fig.* 154.)

1242. Sphæropsis atrovirens. *Lev.* "Greenish-black Sphæropsis."

Scattered, at first greenish, then blackish; perithecia somewhat immersed, globose and ovate, disc erumpent, rugulose, at length torn.—*Sphæria atro-virens. A. & S. t.* 2, *f.* 1. *Kze. M.H.* ii. *t.* 1, *f.* 2. *Fr. S.M.* ii. *p.* 501, *in part. Eng. Fl.* v. *p.* 272.

On dead misletoe twigs.

SPHÆROPSIS CANDOLLII, *B. & Br.* is a stylosporous condition of *Sphærella Buxi. D.C.*—*Cooke exs. no.* 159. [Mid. Carolina.]

SPHÆROPSIS LEUCOSTIGMA, *B. & Br.* is a condition of *Sphærella Hederæ.*—*Sow.*

1243. Sphæropsis cylindrospora. *Desm.* "Straight-spored Sphæropsis."

Amphigenous, black, shining, punctiform; perithecia very small, numerous, densely scattered, globose, covered by the epidermis, opening by a pore, then collapsing and concave; spores hyaline, straight, cylindrical, obtuse at both ends.—*Desm. Ann. Sc. Nat.* 1849, *p.* 277. *B. & Br. Ann. N.H. no.* 418. *Diplodia Desmazierii. Gard. Fl. Forf. p.* 298.

On ivy leaves and petioles. Spring.

Remarkable for the linear straight spores, exceeding their diameter in length 6-7 times. The spots are far smaller than in mature specimens of *S. leucostigma.*—*B. & Br.* Spores (·025 m.m.) ·009 in. long.

1244. Sphæropsis Ralfsii. *B. & Br.* "Ralfs's Sphæropsis."

Perithecia scattered, punctiform, strongly collapsed; spores very minute, oblong.—*B. & Br. Ann. N.H. no.* 419.

On ivy leaves. Aberystwyth.

Scattered over the upper surface of the leaf, punctiform, black, strongly collapsed, and presenting the appearance of accurately defiued excipula; spores oozing out, on the application of moisture, from a central pore, extremely minute, oblong.

1245. Sphæropsis parca. *B. & Br.* "Sparse Sphæropsis."

Perithecia minute, collapsed; spores oblong, 4-5 longer than their diameter.—*B. & Br. Ann. N.H. no.* 420*.

On leaves of *Abies excelsa.* Jan. Wiltshire.

Scattered sparingly on the leaves; perithecia collapsed when dry, so as not to rise at all above the surface, black; spores oblong, sub-cylindrical, obtuse at either end, but often suddenly attenuated at one extremity, 4-5 times longer than their diameter.—*B. & Br.*

1246. Sphæropsis strobi. *B. & Br.* "Fir-needle Sphæropsis."

Perithecia minute, collapsed; spores linear, 6-7 times longer than their diameter.—*B. & Br. Ann. N.H. no.* 421.

On leaves of *Pinus strobus.* Mar. Wilts.

Very like *S. parca*, but scarcely so much collapsed. It differs in the longer, narrower spores, which are never attenuated suddenly.—*B. & Br.*

1247. Sphæropsis geniculata. *B. & Br.* "Oblique-spored Sphæropsis."

Perithecia globose, ostiolum conical, prominent; spores curved, equal, obtuse, 4-5 times longer than their diameter, fixed at an obtuse angle.—*B. & Br. Ann. N.H. no.* 421*.

On leaves of *Pinus strobus*, with *S. strobi.*

Perithecia globose covered by the epidermis, which they pierce by means of their prominent conical ostiola; spores cylindrical, curved, obtuse at either end, fixed at an obtuse angle obliquely to long delicate sporophores, sometimes there is a nucleus at either extremity.—*B. & Br.*

1248. Sphæropsis epitricha. *B. & Br.* "Byssoid Sphæropsis."

Perithecia globose, seated upon a furcato-ramose mycelium; spores oblong, three times longer than their diameter.—*B. & Br. Ann. N.H. no.* 422.

On dead stems of *Equisetum palustre.* Wilts.

Perithecia globose, seated beneath a discoloured cinereous spot, springing from forked septate threads, spores oblong, about three times longer than their diameter. The forked septate threads of the mycelium, with their obtuse apices, are very remarkable.—*B. & Br.*

1249. Sphæropsis mutica. *B. & Br.* "Smooth Sphæropsis."

Erumpent; perithecia globose, obtuse, more or less cæspitose, black, shining; spores very small, hyaline, elliptic, or obovate. —*B. & Br. Ann. N.H. no.* 422*.

On small branches of elder. Batheaston.

This has exactly the habit of a *Diplodia.*

1250. Sphæropsis menispora. *B. & Br.* "Long-spored Sphæropsis."

Concealed entirely beneath the cuticle, except the round ostiolum; perithecia ellipsoidal, black; spores very long, curved, acute at either end, containing many scattered, globose, pellucid nuclei.—*B. & Br. Ann. N.H. no.* 425.

On dead leaves of *Typha.* Spye Park, Wilts.

The nuclei are not arranged regularly in a single row, and therefore do not represent endochromes.

1251. Sphæropsis malorum. *Berk.* "Apple Sphæropsis."

Globose or subglobose, covered with the blackened cuticle; stroma blackish, ostiola erumpent, more or less strongly papillæform; spores greenish, elliptical, margined, granular.—*Berk. Outl. p.* 316. *Sphæria malorum. Eng. Fl.* v. *p.* 257. *Diplodia? malorum. Curr. Linn. Trans.* xxii. *t.* 49, *f.* 205.

On apples lying on the ground. Winter.

Spores ·0012 in. (·03 m. m.) long.

Sphæropsis arundinacea, *Lev.* is evidently a condition of *Sphæria arundinacea.—Sow.*

1252. Sphæropsis taxi. *Berk.* "Yew-leaf Sphæropsis."

Gregarious, covered with the epidermis, which becomes grey; perithecia sub-immersed, convex, black, at length piercing the epidermis by a pore; spores —?—*Berk. Outl. p.* 316. *Sphæria Taxi, Eng. Fl.* v. *p.* 272. *Sow. t.* 394, *f.* 6. *Cryptosphæria Taxi. Grev. t.* 13.

On dead yew leaves.

1253. Sphæropsis alismatis. *Curr.* "Water Plantain Sphæropsis."

Perithecia subglobose, chestnut-coloured. Spores colourless, bordered, elliptical, subglobose or turbinate, with sometimes the apparent remains of a peduncle.—*Curr. Linn. Trans.* xxii. *p.* 334.

On *Alisma plantago.*

Spores ·0004-·0005 in. (·01-·0125 m.m.) long.

Gen. 110. DOTHIORA, Fr.

Nucleus slowly developed, gelatinoso-grumous, black, immersed in an erumpent stroma, sub-carbonaceous externally, fleshy within, always astomous; spores pedicellate, obovate, simple.—*Berk. Outl. p.* 316.

1254. Dothiora pyrenophora. *Fr.* "Apple-twig Dothiora."

Erumpent, elliptic, plano-depressed, even, black, internally white.—*Dothidea pyrenophora, Fr. S.M.* ii. *p.* 552. *Berk. Ann. N.H. no.* 199. *Berk. exs. no.* 282.

On apple and pear twigs. [Low. Carolina.]

In my copy of Berkeley's British Fungi, No. 282, the spores are brown, uniseptate, and quite undistinguishable from those of a *Diplodia.*

1255. Dothiora sphæroides. *Fr.* "Ash-twig Dothiora."

Gregarious, subfasciculate, erumpent, irregularly angular, becoming plane, black, internally white.—*Dothidea sphæroides, Fr. S.M.* ii. *p.* 552. *Berk. Ann. N.H. no.* 198.

On ash twigs. Common.

Dr. Capron believes that he has traced this to a *Diplodia*, when mature.

Gen. 111. CLINTERIUM, Fr.

Perithecium erumpent, free, carbonaceous, bursting by fissures at the apex; nucleus gelatinoso-floccose; spores simple.—*Berk. Outl. p.* 316. *Fr. S.V.S. p.* 418.

1256. Clinterium obturatum. *Fr.* "Ling Clinterium."

Erumpent, nearly free, even, regular, black; rimoso-dehiscent, at length collapsed.—*Summ. V.S. p.* 418. *Berk. Outl. p.* 316. *Sphæria obturata. Fr. S.M.* ii. *p.* 495. *Fries. exs. no.* 128. *Eng. Fl.* v. *p.* 271.

On leaves of ling. Appin.

Gen. 112. ACROSPERMUM, Tode.

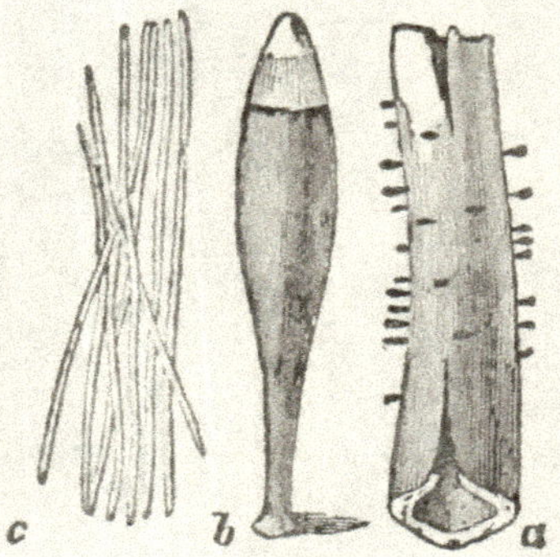

Fig. 156.

Perithecia cylindrical, free; spores long, asciform, flexuous, erect.—*Berk. Outl. p.* 317. (*Fig.* 156.)

1257. Acrospermum compressum. *Tode.* "Compressed Acrospermum."

Lanceolate or clavate, somewhat compressed, of an olivaceous black.—*Tode t.* 2, *f.* 13. *Fr. S.M.* ii. *p.* 245. *Berk. exs. no.* 270. *Grev. t.* 182. *Bisch. f.* 3406. *Eng. Fl.* v. *p.* 221. *Lib. exs. no.* 32. *Clav. herbarum. Pers. Com. t.* 3, *f.* 4. *Sow. t.* 253. *Moug. exs. no.* 671. *Clav. compressa. Purt. t.* 19, *f.* 3. *Fckl. exs. no.* 776.

On various dead herbaceous plants. [Low. Carolina.]

1½-2 lines high, at length concentrically grooved at the apex, when dry longitudinally sulcate and sometimes twisted.—*M. J. B.* (*Fig.* 156.)

1258. Acrospermum graminum. *Lib.* "Grass Acrospermum."

Scattered, minute, linear, blackish; perithecia cylindrical at the base, transversely undulated, annulate above, conical; spores very long, colourless.—*Lib. exs. no.* 33. *Corda.* iii. *f.* 73. *Berk. Ann. N.H. no.* 164. *Kl. exs. no.* 1553. *Fckl. exs no.* 777. *Bail. t.* 14.

On dead grasses.

The contents of the perithecia, which consist of very long linear bodies, are at length discharged at the apex.

Gen. 113. DIPLODIA, Fr.

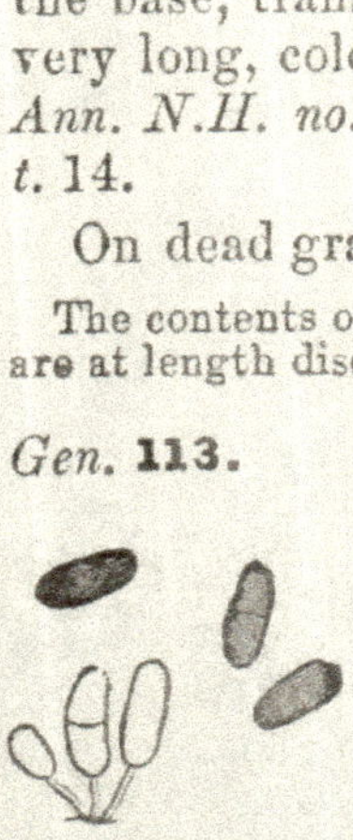

Fig. 157

Perithecia distinct, carbonaceous; spores uniseptate, escaping by a perforation at the apex.—*Berk. Outl. p.* 317. (*Fig.* 157.)

1259. Diplodia mutila. *Fr.* "Poplar Diplodia."

Black, stroma innate, perithecia confluent, globose; superior portion prominent, unequal, rugose; ostiola simple.—*B. & Br. Ann. N.H. no.* 407. *De. Not. Act. Tur.* 1845, vii. *Dec.* 4, *f.* 7. *Sph. mutila. Fr. S.M.* ii. *p.* 424.

On dead poplar twigs.

1260. Diplodia confluens. *B. & Br.* "Confluent Diplodia."

Perithecia confluent, spots small, depressed, somewhat collapsed; ostiolum obsolete.—*B. & Br. Ann. N.H. no.* 408. *D. mutila Desm. exs. no.* 1880.

On twigs of *Daphne Laureola.* July. Milton. Norths.

Forming small, often confluent spots, surrounded by the free raised cuticle; perithecia irregular, confluent, depressed, somewhat collapsed, with no evident ostiolum; spores oblong. Forms far larger patches than in *D. mutila.* —*M. J. B.*

1261. Diplodia cæspitosa. *B. & Br.* "Cæspitose Diplodia."

Cæspitose, black; perithecia globose, ostiolum papillæform; spores oblong.—*B. & Br. Ann. N. H. no.* 409.

On twigs of ivy. King's Cliffe.

Bursting in little black tufts through the cuticle; perithecia globose, black; spores pale-yellow, hyaline, oblong, with a broad distinct border; endochrome simple, without any distinct nuclei.—*B. & Br.*

1262. Diplodia vulgaris. *Lev.* "Common Diplodia."

Perithecia globose, innate, gregarious, covered with the cracked epidermis; ostiola prominent; contents white; spores bilocular. —*Lev. Ann. Sc. Nat. May* 1846, *p.* 291. *B. & Br. Ann. N.H. no.* 410. *Cooke exs. no.* 340.

On twigs of various trees. [United States.]

(*Fig* 157.)

1263. Diplodia herbarum. *Lev.* "Herbaceous Diplodia."

Caulicolous, erumpent, gregarious, perithecia oblong, convex, black, then irregularly depressed; spores oblong, uniseptate, contracted slightly at the septum, brown.—*Lev. Ann. Sc. Nat.* (1846) v. *p.* 292. *Sporocadus herbarum. Corda* iii. *f.* 63. *Cooke exs. no.* 339.

On stems of herbaceous plants. Common.

Sometimes scattered, commonly gregarious, often in lines beneath the cuticle, erumpent. Numerous species have already been described of this genus, which is doubtless but a condition of higher forms. The fruit differs so slightly in the species on different herbaceous stems, that we hesitate to characterise them as distinct.

1264. Diplodia ilicicola. *Desm.* "Holly-twig Diplodia."

Desm. Ann. Sc. Nat. 1838, x. *p.* 311. *Desm. exs. no.* 988. *Berk. Ann. N.H. no.* 206, *t.* 11, *f.* 7.

On dead holly twigs.

We have seen no published character of this species.

1265. Diplodia viticola. *Desm.* "Vine-twig Diplodia."

Desm. Ann. Sc. Nat. 1838, x. *p.* 311. *Desm. exs. no.* 989. *Berk. Ann. N.H. no.* 207. *Fckl. exs. no.* 541.

On vine branches. King's Cliffe. [Low. Carolina.]

We have met with no published character of this species.

1266. Diplodia paupercula. *B. & Br.* "Plane-twig Diplodia."

Perithecia at first covered, at length free, globose, with a prominent mouth; spores small, uniseptate.—*B. & Br. Ann. N.H. no.* 406*.

On dead twigs of plane. Batheaston.

Perithecia one or two together, at first concealed, at length exposed, globose, with a rather prominent orifice. Spores small, at first hyaline, elliptic or obovate, and falling off in that state, at length oblong, brownish, and uniseptate.—*B. & Br.*

1267. Diplodia æsculi. *Lev.* "Horse-chestnut Diplodia."

Perithecia innate, globose, black within, covered by the fissured epidermis. Sporidia elongated, opaque, brown and uniseptate.—*Ann. des Sc. Nat.* 1846, v. *p.* 290. *Fckl. exs. no.* 1563. *Cooke, Seem. Journ.* iv. *p.* 97.

On fallen twigs of *Æsculus Hippocastanum.* Feb.

1268. Diplodia Cowdellii. *B. & Br.* "Cotton Diplodia."

Perithecia free, globose, black, apices at length dehiscing; spores small, elliptic, uniseptate.—*B. & Br. Ann. N.H. no.* 406.

On damp cotton.

Forming dirty black spots on the matrix, but without any evident floccose stratum; perithecia globose, at length cracking above, black. Remarkable for its singular habitat and free mode of growth.—*B. & Br.*

1269. Diplodia fibricola. *Berk.* "Fibrous Diplodia."

Spots pallid or obsolete; perithecia minute, elongated; spores small, elliptic, somewhat constricted in the centre.—*Berk. in Hook. Journ.* 1853, *p.* 42, *t.* 3, *f.* 12. *Ann. N.H. no.* 741.

On Lombardy poplar. Nov. King's Cliffe.

Perithecia minute, more or less elongated, following the course of the fibres, rather delicate, easily lacerated, either scattered or disposed in distinct patches, sending off a few fibres from their base; spores minute, ·00025 in. (·006 m.m.) long, subelliptic, generally slightly constricted in the centre, pale yellow-brown, uniseptate, or very rarely acquiring a second septum.—*M. J. B.*

1270. Diplodia oospora. *Berk.* "Egg-spored Diplodia."

Spots olivaceous; perithecia minute, elongated; spores small, obovate, brown.—*Berk. Hook. Journ.* 1853, *p.* 42, *t.* 3, *f.* 11. *Ann. N.H. no.* 742.

On bleached willow. Nov. King's Cliffe.

Patches oblong, olive-brown from the fibres of the mycelium; perithecia minute, elongated; spores minute, obovate, yellow-brown, uniseptate, ·0003 in. long, ·00025 in. broad (·0076 × ·006 m.m.), much darker than in D. *fibricola*.—*M. J. B.*

1271. Diplodia tecta. *B. & Br.* "Covered Diplodia."

Perithecia covered, gregarious, raising the epidermis, the cuticle covering the ostiola, blackened and shining; spores large, oblong.—*B. & Br. Ann. N.H. no.* 411.

On dead leaves of cherry-laurel. Common.

The leaves are rough, with little elevated pustules disposed often in dry discoloured patches, marked in the centre with a shining black speck; spores oblong, endochrome simple (?).—*B. & Br.*

1272. Diplodia consors. *B. & Br.* "Laurel Diplodia."

Perithecia gregarious, covered; epidermis polished, becoming blackened, dehiscent in the centre, whitish; spores small, oblong.—*B. & Br. Ann. N.H. no.* 412.

On leaves of cherry-laurel. Common.

Forming broad patches, perithecia covered, indicated by small shining black dots, which open in the centre by an irregular orifice, the edges of which are white; spores only two-thirds the length of those of *D. tecta*, oblong-elliptic, uniseptate.—*B. & Br.*

1273. Diplodia arbuticola. *Fr.* "Uva-ursi Diplodia."

Gregarious, confluent, covered with the blackened epidermis; perithecia irregular, black, astomous; disc at length erumpent, opaque.—*Berk. Outl. p.* 317. *Sow. t.* 570, *f.* 6? *Sphæria arbuticola, Fr. S.M.* ii. *p.* 500. *Berk. Ann. N.H. no.* 189.

On *Arbutus uva-ursi* leaves. Scotland.

1274. Diplodia ilicis. *Curr.* "Holly-leaf Diplodia."

Gregarious, black; perithecia globose, rather prominent, covered; at length erumpent, dehiscing by fissures; spores elliptical, oblong, sub-globose, or turbinate, irregular, with a yellowish green tinge.—*Curr. Linn. Trans.* xxii. *no.* 343. *Sphæria ilicis. Fr. S.M.* ii. *p.* 501. *Eng. Fl.* v. *p.* 273.

On holly leaves.

Gen. **114. HENDERSONIA,** Berk.

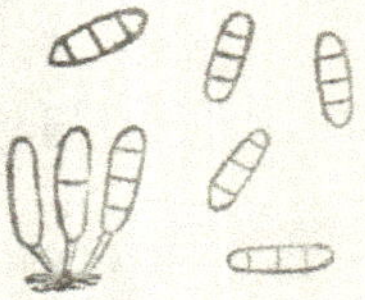

Fig. 158.

Perithecia distinct, spores 2-multiseptate, escaping by a terminal pore—*Berk. Outl. p.* 317. *Ann. N.H. no.* 208. (*Fig.* 158.)

1275. Hendersonia elegans. *Berk.* "Elegant Hendersonia."

Seated on a dark brown spot; perithecia shining, gelatinous within, spores 6-8 septate.—*Berk. Ann. N.H. no.* 208, *t.* 11, *f.* 9.

On culms of reed. April. Tansor. Norths.

Forming little dark brown spots in the centre of which is seated a single shining perithecium, the upper part of which causes a little projection above the surface; perithecia lined with a gelatinous stratum, which gives rise to long, broadly fusiform, pedunculate, colourless spores, with 6-8 dissepiments; articulations sometimes swollen, often quite even, each of the central ones containing a single large globose nucleus, with occasionally a few granules.—*M. J. B.*

1276. Hendersonia macrospora. *B. & Br.* "Large-spored Hendersonia."

Perithecia entirely concealed, spores straight, narrowly lanceolate, 5-8 septate.—*B. & Br. Ann. N.H. no.* 413.

On dead twigs of *Philadelphus coronarius.* Oct. Apethorpe.

Entirely concealed by the cuticle, which is very slightly raised; perithecia globose.

1277. Hendersonia arcus. *B. & Br.* "Box-twig Hendersonia."

Perithecia becoming naked, globose; under the microscope steel-blue; spores arcuate, incrassated in the middle, 3-septate. —*B. & Br. Ann. N.H. no.* 413*.

On box twigs. Batheaston.

Perithecia globose, at length naked, sub-gregarious, black, but when seen by transmitted light steel-blue. Sporophores branched; spores elongated, curved, swollen in the centre, attenuated at either extremity, hyaline, triseptate. Closely resembling in form and colour *S. pulicaris.*—*B. & Br.*

1278. Hendersonia mutabilis. *B. & Br.* "Changeable Hendersonia."

Pustules depressed, elliptic, cellular within, spores oblong-elliptic, 3-4 septate; articulations here and there longitudinally divided.—*B. & Br. Ann. N.H. no.* 414.

On dead twigs of plane. Batheaston.

Pustules small, scarcely bursting the cuticle, elliptic, black, with a few central cells, besides the large cell or perithecium, which occupies the whole of the pustule; the central cells are developed later than the main cell, so that the spores in the former are simple or uniseptate, while in the larger cell they have acquired a much larger size, and have 3-4 transverse septa with the articulations here and there divided.—*B. & Br.*

1279. Hendersonia sarmentorum. *West.* "Vine Hendersonia."

Perithecia immersed, flattened, dark brown, concealed by the epidermis, which is at length lacerated above the poriform ostiole. Sporidia brown, pear-shaped, obovate, elliptical or irregular, triseptate, with hyaline pedicels.—*West. Bull. de Brux.* xviii. *n.* 60, *fig.* 2. *Cooke Seem. Jour. f.* 15.

On dead twigs of vine. Feb. Highgate.

The sporidia are very variable in my specimens.

1280. Hendersonia corni. *Fuckel.* "Cornel Hendersonia."

Perithecia globose, at first covered by the epidermis, black; sporidia with long deciduous pedicels, oblong, sub-clavate, obtuse, four-celled, yellow, the cell next the stem hyaline.—*Fckl. exs. no.* 524. *Enum. Fung. Nassov. p.* 50, *no.* 416, *f.* 16. *Cooke Seem. Jour.* iv. *f.* 16. *S. (Hendersonia) Cornicola, D.C. Fr. S.M.* ii. *p.* 530. *Curr. Linn. Trans.* xxii. *t.* 59, *f.* 146.

On twigs of *Cornus.* Not uncommon. Feb.—May.

(*Fig* 158.)

1281. Hendersonia oreades. *Dur. & Mont.* "Oak-leaf Hendersonia."

Innate; perithecia small, globose, black, collected on pale spots, or disposed in a ring; spores shortly stipitate, ovoid, or oblong, transversely 2-3 septate.—*Dur. & Mont. Fl. Alg.* i. *p.* 571. *Desm. exs. no.* 1268. *Berk. Outl. p.* 318.

On half dead oak leaves.

HENDERSONIA ROBINIÆ, *West*, referred to *Sphæria elongata*. Fr.

HENDERSONIA POLYCYSTIS, *B. & Br. Ann. N.H. no.* 415. *Rabh. F.E., no.* 264, is a condition of *Diatrype lanciformis*. Fr.

HENDERSONIA STROBILINA, *Curr (Cooke exs. no.* 341*)* is a condition of *Dichæna strobilina*. Fr.

1282. **Hendersonia Stephensii.** *B. & Br.* "Bracken Hendersonia."

Perithecia irregular, in a single row beneath the brownish cuticle, which ruptures in a line; spores large, ovate, reticulato-cellular.—*B. & Br. Ann. N.H. no.* 502.

On dead stems of *Pteris aquilina*. Bristol.

Perithecia membranaceous, oblong, irregular, arranged in a single row beneath the cuticle, which exhibits little lanceolate brown spots above them, with a fissure down the centre. Spores large, ovate, with about three transverse septa, each division being again traversed by several vertical and transverse, or sometimes oblique partitions. The perithecia and spores are very remarkable.—*B. & Br.*

1283. **Hendersonia fibriseda.** *Berk.* "Birch-plank Hendersonia."

Perithecia sub-globose, minute, very delicate, blackish blue; spores elongated, flexuous, obtuse at either end.—*Berk. Hook. Journ.* 1853, *p.* 42. *t.* 3, *f.* 10. *Ann. N.H. no.* 743.

On birch planks. Dec. King's Cliffe.

Perithecia punctiform, sub-globose, seated on definite white spots, following the direction of the fibres; very delicate, pale blackish blue, especially at the edge, which consists of interwoven fibres. Sporophores short, obtuse; spores ·00015 in. long, ·0002 broad (·037 × ·005 m.m.) containing obscurely defined nuclei.—*M. J. B.*

Gen. 115. **DILOPHOSPORA,** Desm.

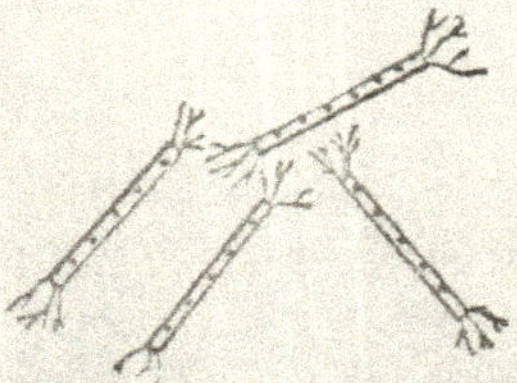

Fig. 159.

Perithecium rounded, closed, perforated; spores cylindrical, furnished at each end with radiating filiform appendages.—*Desm. Ann. Sc. Nat.* (1840) xiv. *p.* 6. (*Fig.* 159.)

1284. **Dilophospora graminis.** *Desm.* "Grass Dilophospora."

Perithecia minute, covered with a blackened crust, seriate, subconnate, globose, immersed in a whitish stroma, ostiola punctiform, black, disc white; spores straight, with 2-3 filiform appendages at each end.—*Gard. Chron.* (1862.) *Pay. f.* 256. *B. & Br. Ann. N.H. no.* 1040. *Desm. exs. no.* 1091. *Ann. Sc. Nat.* (1840) xiv. *t.* 1, *f.* 2. *Fckl. exs.* 558.

On sheaths and spike of *Alopecurus agrestis.*

The two or three glumes at the base are tolerably perfect, while the top looks as if it had been pinched up into a point when young, and afterwards charred. The outer coat is black and glossy, studded here and there with minute punctures, surrounded like a little eyelet hole, with a white border, which leads down to a subglobose cell, the walls of which are clothed with a white or greyish gelatinous mass of spores.—*M. J. B.*

(*Fig.* 159, *spores magnified.*)

Gen. 116. **DARLUCA,** Cast.

Fig. 160.

Perithecia delicate; spores containing a row of sporidiola, oozing out and forming a tendril. —*Berk. Outl. p.* 318. (*Fig.* 160.)

1285. **Darluca filum.** *Cast.* "Parasitic Darluca."

Gregarious, very minute. Perithecia globose, black, shining, pierced; spores hyaline, oblong, straight, containing four minute sporidioles.—*Berk. Outl. p* 318. *Hendersonia uredinæcola, Desm. Ann. Sc. Nat.* 1849, xi. *p.* 345. *Sphæria filum, Fr. S.M.* ii. *p.* 547.

On various *Uredines.*

The spores are about ·00055 in. (·016 m.m.) long. *Fig.* 160.

1286. **Darluca typhoidearum.** *B. & Br.* "Club mace Darluca."

Scattered, immersed; perithecia minute, globose, blackish-brown; ostiola naked, papillate, pierced; spores oblong, straight, rather obtuse at the ends, sub-fusiform, with four globose sporidioles.—*Hendersonia typhoidearum, Desm. Ann. Sc. Nat. June,* 1849. *exs. no.* 1891. *B. & Br. Ann. N.H. no.* 417. *Rabh. F.E. no.* 45.

On leaves of *Typha* and *Sparganium.* Feb. (*Fig.* 160.)

1287. **Darluca macropus.** *B. & Br.* "Sedge Darluca."

Perithecia depressed, somewhat collapsed; spores pedicellate, elongated, cylindrical, curved, with 3-6 sporidioles.—*Berk. Outl. p.* 318. *Hendersonia macropus, B. & Br. Ann. N.H. no.* 416.

On dead leaves of *Carices.* Jan. Wilts.

Perithecia entirely covered and pouring out their spores by a minute orifice, so as to make little black stains on the leaves; spores furnished with a long peduncle, cylindrical, but slightly attenuated at either end, many times longer than their diameter, somewhat curved.—*B. & Br.*

Gen. 117. VERMICULARIA, Tode.

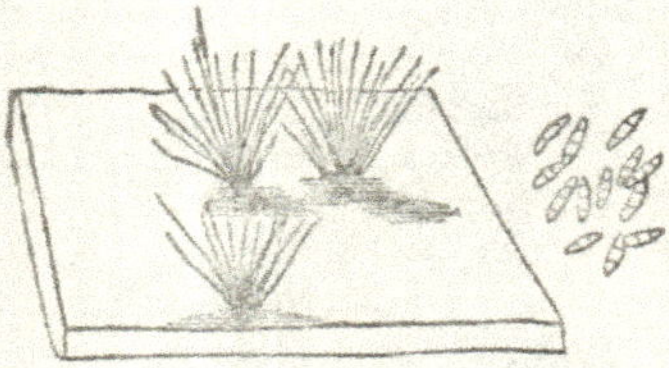

Fig. 161.

Perithecium thin, mouthless, generally bristly; spores vermiculate.—*Berk. Outl. p.* 318. (*Fig.* 161.)

1288. Vermicularia dematium. *Fr.* "Clustered Vermicularia."

Gregarious, perithecia plano-depressed, mouthless, black, strigose in the centre, with somewhat divergent hairs of the same colour; spores long, curved.—*Berk. Outl. p.* 318. *Sphæria dematium, Eng. Fl.* v. *p.* 274. *Fr. S.M.* ii. *p.* 505. *Fckl exs. no.* 570.

On dead herbaceous stems. [United States.]

At first covered by the epidermis, through which the hairs penetrate like a little brush, at length naked, the hairs frequently falling off.—*M. J. B.*

1289. Vermicularia trichella. *Grev.* "Ivy-leaf Vermicularia."

Scattered, perithecia ovate, very minute, mouthless, black, clothed at the top with very long divergent hairs.—*Grev. t.* 345. *Sphæria trichella, Fr. S.M.* ii. *p.* 515. *Eng. Fl.* v. *p.* 277. *Fckl. exs. no.* 569.

On dead ivy leaves.

Spores linear-oblong, septate. (*Fig.* 161.)

1290. Vermicularia atramentaria. *B. & Br.* "Inky Vermicularia."

Effused, gregarious, maculæform; spores straight, short: endochrome retracted to either end.—*B. & Br. Ann. N.H. no.* 430.

On decayed stems of potatoes. Common.

Forming large ink-black velvety patches, crowded with minute perithecia, clothed with long straight subulate bristles, connected at the base by intricate fibres creeping beneath the cuticle of the matrix. Spores minute, linear, rather short. Distinguished at once by its straight spores.

1291. Vermicularia circinans. *Berk.* "Circinating Vermicularia."

Spots orbicular, perithecia concentric, seated on a hyaline, articulated, radiating mycelium. Spores oblong, slightly curved, attenuated.—*Berk. Gard.Chron.* 1851, *p.* 595, *fig.* 1857, *p.* 53, *fig.*

On Nocera onions.

In round black spots, consisting of multitudes of distinct, extremely minute subglobose perithecia, clothed with long rigid black hairs, and sending off in every direction from the base flexuous hyaline articulated, often branched or anastomosing threads. The spores are slightly curved and attenuated at either end, though the tip is very obtuse. The endochrome is either retracted to either end, leaving a free space in the centre, or the whole mass is broken up into several round bodies.—*M. J. B.*

Gen. **118. DISCOSIA,** Lib.

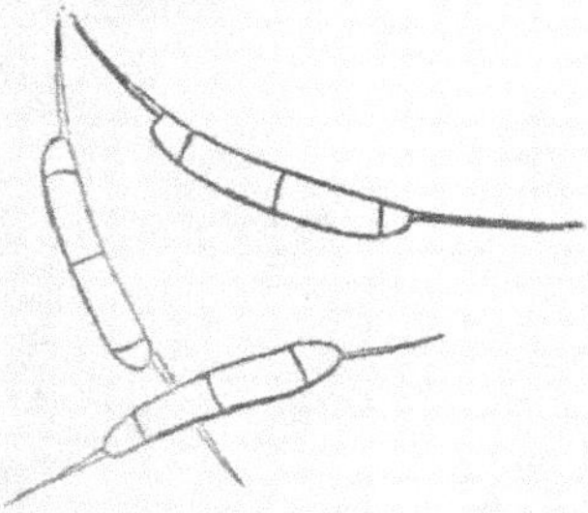

Fig. 162.

Perithecium flat, opening at the base; spores septate, obliquely aristate at either end.—*Berk. Outl. p.* 318. (*Fig.* 162.)

1292. Discosia alnea. *Lib.* "Leaf Discosia."

Gregarious, innate, orbicular, black, shining, at first convex, even, soon depressed round the dot-like ostiolum, at length collapsed and rugoso-plicate; spores triseptate, obliquely aristate at each extremity.—*Berk. Outl. p.* 318. *Sphæria artocreas, Tode.* ii. *f.* 72. *Fr. S.M.* ii. *p.* 523. *Eng. Fl.* v. *p.* 278. *Fckl. exs. no.* 452. *Kl. exs.* ii. *no.* 154. *Fries. t.* 8, *f.* 4-6. *De. Not. Act. Tur.* 1849, x. *f.* 2.

On dead leaves. Common. [United States.] (*Fig.* 162.)

Gen. **119. PILIDIUM,** Kunze.

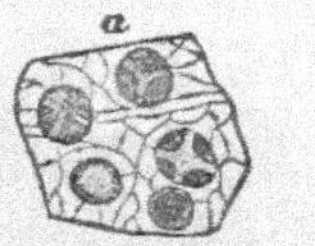

Fig. 163.

Perithecium scutellæform, smooth, shining, opening irregularly; spores curved, without appendages.—*Berk. Outl. p.* 318. (*Fig.* 163.)

1293. Pilidium acerinum. *Kze.* "Sycamore Pilidium."

Hypophyllous, hemispherical, black, splitting with from three to five acute teeth. nucleus white; spores fusiform.—*Kze. M.H.* ii. *p.* 92, *t.* 2, *f.* 5. *Fr. El.* ii. *p.* 136.

On dead sycamore leaves.

Externally resembling a *Phacidium*, but with different fruit. (*Fig.* 163.)

1294. Pilidium (?) carbonaceum. *Lib.* "Willow Pilidium."

Perithecia irregular, dingy-brown, crowded into broad patches, growing in a widely-effused more or less ambient subiculum; spores falciform, septate.—*B. & Br. Ann. N.H. no.* 442. *Cenangium fuliginosum, Fr. El.* ii. *p.* 23. *Eng. Fl.* v. *p.* 212.

On willow branches. King's Cliffe.

Not a good *Pilidium.*

Gen. **120.** **MELASMIA,** Lev.

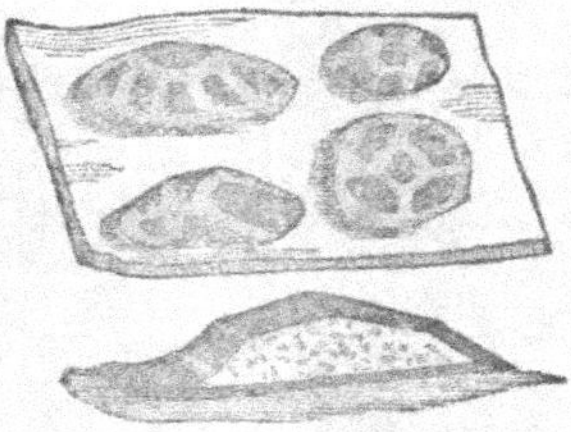

Fig. 164.

Perithecium membranaceous, dehiscent above, rather swollen, at length depressed and rugose, growing in a thin, spot-like, effused receptacle; spores simple.—*Berk. Outl. p.* 319. (*Fig.* 164.)

1295. Melasmia alnea. *Lev.* "Alder Melasmia."

Perithecia adnate, scattered, membranaceous, hemispherical, even, black, at length flattened and rugulose; spores elliptic-elongated, obtuse, straight or curved.—*Ann. Sc. Nat.* 1848, ix. *p.* 253. *Grev. t.* 146, *f.* 2. *Fr. S.M.* ii. *p.* 544.

On living alder leaves.

This plant presents exactly the aspect of *Discosia alnea*, but differs in the spores. (*Fig.* 164.)

MELASMIA ACERINA, *Lev.* is a condition of *Rhytisma acerinum.*

Gen. **121.** **PIGGOTIA,** B. & Br.

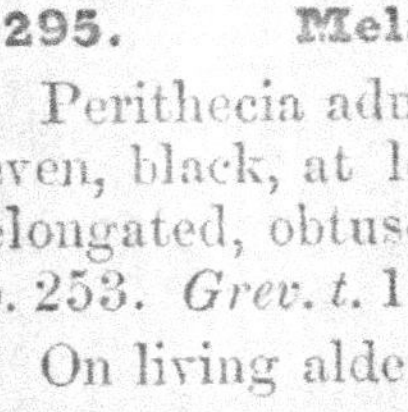

Fig 165.

Perithecium irregular, very thin, obsolete below, forming by confluence a wrinkled mass, bursting by a lacerated fissure; spores rather large, obovate, at length tomiparous. —*Berk. Outl. p.* 319. (*Fig.* 165.)

1296. Piggotia astroidea. *B. & Br.* "Stellate Piggotia."

Epiphyllous, black, perithecia slightly prominent, connate, forming small irregularly stellato-aggregate tubercles; spores broadly ovate, sporophores short, tomiparous.—*B. & Br. Ann. N.H. no.* 503, *t.* 5, *f.* 3. *Dothidea astroidea, Eng. Fl.* v. *p.* 287. *Asteroma ulmi, Grev. Fl. Ed. p.* 368.

On green leaves of elm.

Jet black, forming irregular, roundish, granulated, or wrinkled patches on the upper surface of the leaf, sometimes seated on a yellow spot, but frequently without any discoloured border; perithecia sub-orbicular where solitary, but soon confluent, though not making a uniform stratum, obsolete below, thin and shining above, bursting irregularly by a jagged orifice; spores oozing from the ruptures, and forming roundish discs, which at first look like the hymenium of some Peziza, broadly ovate, slightly constricted towards the obtuse base; sporophores short, at length tomiparous.—*B. & Br.* (*Fig.* 165.)

Gen. **122.** **SEPTORIA,** Fries.

Fig. 166.

Perithecia minute, more or less incorporated with the matrix; spores oblong and septate, or thread-shaped, and continuous, discharged in little tendrils.—*Berk. Outl. p.* 319. (*Fig.* 166.)

This is a very large and doubtful genus, but is retained here provisionally.

1297. Septoria ulmi. *Kze.* "Elm Septoria."

Spots brown, perithecia small, scattered; cirrhi dirty-white; spores nearly straight, subquadriseptate.—*Kunze M.H.* ii. *p.* 107. *Grev. t.* 112. *Eng. Fl.* v. *p.* 356. *Cooke. exs. no.* 207. *Fckl. exs. no.* 506. *Corda. Anl. t. F. f.* 54, *no.* 10, 11. *Berk. exs. no.* 214. *Cooke, L.F. no.* 63.

On elm leaves. Common. [United States.]

(Fig. 166.)

1298. Septoria heraclei. *Fckl.* "Hog-weed Septoria."

Epiphyllous; spots none; perithecia somewhat solitary, innate, brown, pierced; tendrils white; spores long, fusiform.—*Fckl. exs. no.* 515. *Ascoxyta heraclei. Lib. exs. no.* 51.

On fading leaves of *Heracleum.*

The spores are large, and very profuse, lying in white patches upon the leaves after they are expelled from the perithecia. Allied closely to *S. ulmi.*

1299. **Septoria oxyacanthæ.** *Kze.* "Hawthorn Septoria."

Spots purple; tendrils yellow; spores very long, 8-12 septate, curved.—*Kunze M.H.* ii. *p.* 109. *Eng. Fl.* v. *p.* 356. *Cooke exs. no.* 201. *Fckl. exs. no.* 500. *Kl. exs. no.* 456.

On living hawthorn leaves. [United States.]

1300. **Septoria aceris.** *B. & Br.* "Sycamore Septoria."

Hypophyllous; spots small; perithecia innate, minute, brown; tendrils small, pallid; spores long, straight, very distinctly septate. —*B. & Br. Ann. N.H. no.* 432. *Fckl. exs. no.* 499. *Ascoxyta aceris. Lib. exs. no.* 54.

On living sycamore leaves. Autumn.

1301. **Septoria salicella.** *B. & Br.* "Willow Septoria."

Beneath the cuticle; epidermis above the subglobose perithecia elevated; spores fusiform, triseptate, tendrils reddish, irregular.—*B. & Br. Ann. N.H. no.* 746, *t.* 15, *f.* 7.

On branches of willows.

Concealed by the cuticle, which is obscurely pustulate, in consequence of the presence of the subglobose perithecia; spores ejected in the form of pale pink tendrils, fusiform, ·00133 in. (·03 m.m.) long, triseptate.—*M. J. B.*

1302. **Septoria ægopodii.** *Desm.* "Gout-weed Septoria"

Epiphyllous; spots pale, perithecia globular, black, very visible on the under surface, spores long, curved.—*Desm. exs. no.* 616. *Eng. Fl.* v. *p.* 356. *Cooke exs. no.* 146.

On living leaves of *Ægopodium podagraria.*

1303. **Septoria lepidii.** *Desm.* "Crucifer Septoria."

Spots none; perithecia scattered or approximate, black, innate, slightly prominent, convex, at length pierced; tendrils white; spores elongated, linear, flexuous.—*Desm. Ann. Sc. Nat.* 1842, xvii. *p.* 110. *Desm. exs. no.* 1177. *B. & Br. Ann. N.H. no.* 431.

On *Lepidium Smithii.* Autumn.

After the spores are discharged, the mouths of the perithecia enlarge, and they collapse so as to have the appearance of a small black *Peziza.*

1304. **Septoria nodorum.** *Berk.* "Wheat-stalk Septoria."

Spots pale fawn-coloured, with a dark border, depressed, at length confluent; perithecia somewhat prominent; spores oblong, elongated, slightly curved, or irregular.—*Berk. Gard. Chron.* 1845, *p.* 601. *B. & Br. Ann. N.H. no.* 433.

On the joints of wheat stalks, just before the wheat is ripe.

Forming little discoloured depressed spots on the knots of the stem, especially the upper one, soon spreading till they invest the whole knot, pale fawn-coloured, studded with a number of minute, somewhat raised perithecia, which are at first reddish, eventually black.—*M. J. B.*

1305. Septoria hippocastani. *B. & Br.* "Horse chestnut Septoria."

Spots rufous; tendrils delicate; spores curved, flexuous, linear, simple.—*B. & Br. Ann. N.H. no.* 434. *Cooke exs. no.* 205.

On leaves of horse chestnut. Common.

Spots at first minute and scattered, then becoming confluent, and forming broad rufous patches; cirrhi delicate, pale; spores long, linear, simple, curved, flexuous.—*B. & Br.*

1306. Septoria lituus. *B. & Br.* "Twig Septoria."

Concealed by the cuticle, which is raised into minute pustules; perithecia depressed; spores filiform, curved at the apex, a little longer than the sporophores.—*B. & Br. Ann. N.H. no.* 744, *t.* 15, *f.* 5.

On smooth twigs.

Spores ·0015 in. (·037 m.m.) long.

1307. Septoria Ralfsii. *B. & Br.* "Apple Septoria."

Sub-cutaneous; epidermis above the perithecia elevated, centre of the pustules white; spores straight, multi-nucleate.—*B. & Br. Ann. N.H. no.* 745, *t.* 15, *f.* 6.

On decayed apples.

Forming black irregular patches, dotted with minute pustules, the centre of which is white. Spores ·00133 in. (·03 m.m.) long, with about six nuclei.

1308. Septoria insularis. *B. & Br.* "Ivy leaf Septoria."

Spots brown, distinct; epidermis above the perithecia elevated, centre of the pustules white; spores filiform, slightly curved.—*B. & Br. Ann. N.H. no.* 747, *t.* 15, *f.* 8.

On half dead ivy leaves.

Forming large definite umber-brown spots, which are rough from the presence of the concealed perithecia, with a white spot in the centre of each pustule; spores filiform, slightly curved ·0015 in. (·038 m.m.) long.—*B. & Br.*

1309. Septoria Badhamia. *B. & Br.* "Vine-leaf Septoria."

Perithecia sub-conglomerate, brown; spores clavate, elongated, slightly thickened.—*Cooke exs. no.* 206. *B. & Br. Ann. N.H. no.* 748, *t.* 15, *f.* 9.

On vine leaves. Oct. Common.

Forming little brownish specks on either side of the leaf, consisting of a few sub-conglomerate perithecia; spores oblong, clavate ·002 in. (·05 m.m.) long; endochrome sometimes retracted to one end, containing a few minute granules, very rarely there are one or two septa.—*B. & Br.*

1310. Septoria polygonorum. *Desm.* "Polygonum Septoria."

Epiphyllous; spots small, rounded, tawny, with a purplish border; perithecia innate, very minute, pale-brown, pierced, at length concave; spores linear, curved, with numerous sporules. —*Desm. Ann. Sc. Nat.* 1842, xvii. *p.* 108. *Desm. exs. no.* 1171. *B. & Br. Ann. N.H. no.* 749.

On living *Polygonum.* Autumn.

The spores are unequal in length, from (·025-·03 m.m.) ·0009-·001 in.

1311. Septoria convolvuli. *Desm.* "Bindweed Septoria."

Epiphyllous; spots orbicular, then confluent and irregular, dingy brown or whitish; perithecia innate, minute, blackish-brown, pierced; spores elongated, linear, curved or straight.—*Desm. Ann. Sc. Nat.* 1842, xvii. *p.* 108. *Septoria convolvulicola, Ann. N.H. no.* 195. *S. fuscella, Berk. M.S. Cooke, exs. no.* 127. *Kl. exs. no.* 1862. *Cooke. L.F. no.* 65.

On living bindweed. Summer.

Spores ·001-·0015 in. (·03-·04 m.m.) long.

1312. Septoria cornicola. *Desm.* "Dogwood Septoria."

Spots orbicular, greyish, circumscribed by a darker line; perithecia scattered, rounded, depressed in the centre.—*Desm. Ann. Sc. Nat.*. *Sphæria cornicola, Fr. S.M.* ii. *p.* 530. *Berk. Mag. Zool. & Bot. no.* 54. *Cooke exs. no.* 136. *Berk. exs. no.* 185. *Cooke L.F. no.* 64.

On leaves of dogwood. Common.

In Berkeley's "Outlines" this is said to be the *Hendersonia cornicola* of Currey, evidently by a slip of the pen, since the *Hendersonia* is found on the twigs, and is a very different thing (agreeing with Currey's description) from the *Septoria* on the leaves.

1313. Septoria heterochroa. *Desm.* "Varicoloured Septoria."

Spots scattered, small, rounded, greyish-brown, then white, with a brown border; perithecia few, brown, at length black, pierced, concave when dry; spores linear, slender, straight or curved.—*Ann. Sc. Nat.* 1847, viii. *p.* 22. *Sphæria (Depazea) vagans, Fr. S.M.* ii. *p.* 532. *Berk. Ann. N.H. no.* 105. *Berk. exs. no.* 188. *Cooke exs. no.* 140.

On leaves of *Lamium album,* Mallow, &c.

1314. Septoria stemmatea. *Berk.* "Cowberry Septoria."

Epiphyllous, gregarious; perithecia globose, minute, seated upon rounded bleached spots.—*Sphæria (Depazea) stemmatea, Fr. S.M.* ii. *p.* 528. *Berk. Ann. N.H. no.* 192.

On living leaves of *Vaccinium Vitis Idea.*

1315. Septoria graminum. *Desm.* "Grass Septoria."

Spots oblong, pallid, surrounded by a more or less distinct darker line; perithecia obscurely disposed in lines, immersed; spores linear, straight, or curved.—*Desm. Ann. Sc. Nat.* 1843, xix. *p.* 339. *Sphæria (Depazea) graminicola, Berk. exs. no.* 186. *Ann. N.H. no.* 103. *Cooke, exs. no.* 208.

On grass. [Low. Carolina.]

The perithecia are so minute as scarcely to be visible to the naked eye.

1316 Septoria hederæ. *Desm.* "Ivy Septoria."

Spots dirty-white, surrounded by a broad brown border; perithecia gregarious, globose, naked, opaque, at length black; spores linear, slender, straight.—*Desm. exs. no.* 341. *Ann. Sc. Nat.* xix. *p.* 340. *Sphæria hederæcola, Fr. S.M.* ii. *p.* 528. *Eng. Fl.* v. *p.* 279. *Moug. exs. no.* 663. *Cooke. exs. no.* 126. *Fckl. exs. no.* 503.

On ivy. Common.

1317. Septoria populi. *Desm.* "Poplar Septoria."

Spots white, or greyish, with a brown border; perithecia hypophyllous, scattered, depressed, soon splitting all round; spores elongated, obtuse, curved, uniseptate.—*Desm. exs. no.* 1731. *Ann. Sc. Nat.* 1843. xix. *pp.* 345. *Sphæria frondicola, Fr. Obs.* ii. *t.* 5, *f.* 6, 7. *S.M.* ii. *p.* 529. *Eng. Fl.* v. *p.* 280. *Moug. exs. no.* 369. *Cooke exs. no.* 145. *Kl. exs. no.* 1958.

On poplar leaves. Autumn.

1318. Septoria thecicola. *B. & Br.* "Capsule Septoria."

Superficial, convex, collapsing, rugose; spores very delicate linear, straight.—*Berk. Intell. Obs.* 1863, *p.* 9, *fig.* 1. *Sphæropsis thecicola, Berk. Ann. N. H. no.* 424.

On thecæ of *Polytrichum piliferum.* Aberdeen.

Perithecia black, scattered, convex, at length collapsing, opening by a definite orifice; spores of various lengths.

1319. Septoria princeps. *B. & Br.* "Beech Septoria."

Perithecia large, depressed, papillate, covered by the epidermis; spores cylindrical, oblong, 5-6 septate, hyaline.—*B. & Br. Ann. N.H. no.* 940, *t.* 15, *f.* 11.

On beech sticks. Batheaston.

Spores ·002 in. (·05. m.m.) long, cylindrical, oblong, with about seven or eight endochromes, hyaline, oozing out in an irregular mass.

1320. Septoria pyricola. *Desm.* "Pear-leaf Septoria."

Epiphyllous; spots greyish white, scattered, roundish or irregular; perithecia few, minute, rather prominent, black, pierced at the apex; tendrils whitish; sporidia elongated, curved, containing several nucleoli.—*Ann. Sc. Nat. ser.* 3, xiv. *p.* 115. *Cooke Seem. Journ.* iv. *f.* 27. *Depazea pyricola, Desm. exs. n.* 721. *Septoria pyri, Cast. Cat. Pl. de Mars, p.* 194. *Septoria dealbata, Lev. Ann. Sc. Nat. ser.* 3, ix. *p.* 249 *(partly).*

On leaves of apple and pear. Oct. Common.

1321. Septoria viburni. *West.* "Guelder-rose Septoria."

Epiphyllous; spots roundish or irregular, becoming whitish in the centre, with a brownish border; perithecia minute, semi-emergent, black, pierced at the apex; tendrils white; sporidia cylindrical, obtuse at their extremities, containing from 5 to 7 nucleoli. — *West. Bull. de Brux.* 1852, xix. *part* iii. *p.* 121. *Bell. Cat. Crypt. Namur, n.* 350. *Cooke Seem. Journ.* iv. *p.* 97. *Cooke exs. no.* 300.

On leaves of *Viburnum opulus* and *V. lantana.* Oct.

1322. Septoria unedinis. *Rob.* "Arbutus Septoria."

Epiphyllous; spots small, numerous, irregular, whitish, with a broad purplish margin; perithecia few, scarcely prominent, blackish, convex, then collapsing and becoming concave; sporidia elongated, slender and curved.—*Desm. Ann. Sc. Nat. ser.* 3, iii.

1847, *p.* 20. *Pl. Crypt. exs. Ed.* i. *no.* 1713. *Cooke Seem. Journ.* iv. *p.* 97, *f.* 24. *Sphæria unedinicola, Eng. Fl.* v. *p.* 279. *Cooke exs. no.* 135. *Cooke L.F. no.* 69.

On leaves of *Arbutus unedo.* Oct. Nov. Common.

1323. Septoria hydrocotyles. *Desm.* "Flukewort Septoria."

Epiphyllous; spots irregular, rufous or brownish, then pallid; perithecia minute, innate, pierced with a terminal pore; tendrils whitish; sporidia linear, curved, containing numerous opaque nucleoli.—*Ann. Sc. Nat. ser.* 2. xvii. *p.* 109. *Pl. Crypt. exs. Ed.* i. *no.* 1175, *Ed.* ii. *no.* 675. *Cooke Seem. Journ.* iv. *p.* 97, *f.* 31. *Cooke exs. no.* 134.

On leaves of *Hydrocotyle vulgaris.* Summer. Common.

1324. Septoria ficariæ. *Desm.* "Figwort Septoria."

Amphigenous; spots roundish or confluent, pallid, cinereous in the centre, with an irregular brownish margin; perithecia innate, very small, black, convex, at length plane; tendrils white; sporidia linear, straight, or curved.—*Ann. Sc. Nat. ser.* 2, xv. *p.* 135. *Pl. Crypt. exs. Ed.* i. *no.* 1087. *Cooke Seem. Journ.* iv. *p.* 97, *fig.* 26. *Rhabdospora ficariæ, Mont. Fl. Alg.* i. *p.* 596. *Cooke exs. no.* 131.

On leaves of *Ranunculus Ficaria.* Common.

1325. Septoria menyanthes. *Desm.* "Bogbean Septoria."

Amphigenous. Spots tawny-rufous, irregular; perithecia very minute, of the same colour, pierced with a terminal pore; tendrils white; sporidia linear, straight or curved, nucleoli scarcely distinct.—*Ann. Sc. Nat. ser.* 3, xx. *p.* 89, 1853. *Desm. exs. Ed.* i. *no.* 2178, *Ed.* ii. *no.* 1828. *Cooke Seem. Journ.* iv. *p.* 97. *Ascochyta menyanthis, Lib. exs. no.* 251. *Lasch. Rabh. exs. no.* 860.

On fading leaves of *Menyanthes trifoliata.*

1326. Septoria clematidis. *Rob.* "Clematis Septoria."

Amphigenous; spots greyish, with a brownish border, rounded, angular or irregular; perithecia on the upper surface, very minute, innate, scarcely prominent, pallid-brown, pierced with a terminal pore; tendrils whitish; sporidia elongated, curved or flexuose, with numerous nucleoli.—*Desm. Ann. Sc. Nat. ser.* 3, xx. *p.* 93

(1853). *Desm. exs. Ed.* i. *no.* 2186, *Ed.* ii. *no.* 1836. *Cooke Seem. Journ.* iv. *p.* 97. *Cooke exs. no.* 132. *Cooke L. F. no.* 66.

On leaves of *Clematis vitalba.* Summer and Autumn. Common.

1327. Septoria epilobii. *West.* "Willow-herb Septoria."

Amphigenous; spots olivaceous, irregular or angular, limited by the veins of the leaves, or confluent; perithecia on both surfaces, very small, brown, pierced with a terminal pore; tendrils white, very delicate; sporidia elongated, slender, straight, curved, or flexuose, with numerous nucleoli.—*Bull. de Brux.* 1852, xix. *part* iii. *p.* 120. *Bell. Cat. Crypt. Namur. no.* 324. *Cooke Seem. Journ.* iv. *p.* 97. *Desm. Ann. Sc. Nat. ser.* 3, xx. (1853), *p.* 94. *Desm. exs. Ed.* i. *no.* 2188, *Ed.* ii. *no.* 1838.

On living leaves of *Epilobium.*

1328. Septoria rosarum. *West.* "Rose-leaf Septoria."

Epiphyllous; spots small, round, scattered, pallid, surrounded by a purplish border; perithecia rare, semi-emergent, blackish; tendrils whitish; sporidia flexuose, cylindrical, obtuse at the extremities, with from 3 to 6 nucleoli.—*Bull. de Brux.* 1851, *p.* 396. *Cooke Seem. Journ.* iv. *p.* 97. *Septoria rosæ,* β. *minor, West. and Wall. exs. no.* 426.

On living leaves of roses in gardens.

1329. Septoria sedi. *West.* "Orpine Septoria."

Epiphyllous; spots circular, greyish; perithecia numerous, minute, nearly black, scattered over the spots pierced with a terminal pore; tendrils white; sporidia linear, usually straight or slightly curved, with about five nucleoli.—*Bull. de Brux. ser.* 2, ii. *no.* 107. *West. & Wall. exs. no.* 943. *Cooke Seem. Journ.* iv. *p.* 97. *f.* 29. *Cooke exs. no.* 133. *Ascochyta sedi, Lib. exs. no.* 249.

On leaves of *Sedum telephium.* Sept.

1330. Septoria sorbi. *Lasch.* "Mountain Ash Septoria."

Epiphyllous; perithecia minute, aggregate, semi-innate, nearly black. Sporidia elliptic, slightly pointed at the extremities, so as to be almost almond-shaped.—*Lasch. Klotsch. Herb. Myc. no.* 459. *Cooke Seem. Journ.* iv. *p.* 97, *fig.* 25. *Cooke exs. no.* 128. *Cooke L.F. no.* 67. *Fckl. exs. no.* 509. *Depazea sorbicola. Rabh. exs. no.* 548.

On leaves of *Sorbus aucuparia.* Autumn. Common.

1331. Septoria fraxini. *Desm.* "Ash-leaf Septoria."

Epiphyllous; perithecia minute, black, semi-innate, clustered together in irregular spots. Sporidia cylindrical, truncate at the extremities, containing numerous nucleoli.—*Desm. exs. no.* 1086. *West. Bull. de Brux.* xviii. *no.* 76. *Fr. El.* ii. *p.* 119. *no.* 3. *Bisch. f.* 3517. *Cooke Seem. Journ.* iv. *p.* 97. *Cooke exs. no.* 202. *Fckl. exs. no.* 507. *Septoria Badhami, var.* β. *Fraxini. Awd. Rabh. exs. no.* 852.

On leaves of ash. Common.

In habit it differs from *S. Sorbi*, in which the perithecia are aggregated about the margin of the leaves, and also from that of *S. Badhami*, with which some authorities have associated it. This is probably only a condition of *Sphærella inæqualis.*

1332. Septoria chelidonii. *Desm.* "Celandine Septoria."

Amphigenous; spots grey, whitish, or of a brownish tint; perithecia innate, minute, nearly black, pierced with a large apical pore; tendrils yellowish; sporidia elongated, linear, straight, or curved, with several nucleoli.—*Desm. exs. no.* 1176. *Cooke Seem. Journ.* iv. *p.* 97. *Ascochyta chelidonii. Lib. exs. no.* 57. *Spilosphæria chelidonii. Rabh. exs.* 552. *Cooke exs. no.* 204.

On leaves of *Chelidonium majus.*

1333. Septoria scabiosæcola. *Desm.* "Scabious Septoria."

Amphigenous; spots orbicular, of a violet-brown, marked in the centre with a white point, which bears the solitary perithecium containing the elongated sporidia.—*Ann. Sc. Nat.* 1853. xx. *p.* 96. *Cooke Seem. Journ.* iv. *p.* 97. *Depazea scabiosæcola. Desm. exs. ed.* i. *no.* 722, *ed.* ii. *no.* 179. *Sphæria lichenoides, var. scabiosæcola? De Cand. Fl. Fr. Ascochyta scabiosæ. Rabh. exs. no.* 1253. *Spilosphæria scabiosæ. Rabh. exs. no.* 557.

On leaves of *Scabious.* Autumn. Common.

1334. Septoria scleranthi. *Desm.* "Knawel Septoria."

Spots obliterated; perithecia densely scattered, rather prominent, convex, black. Ostiole minute, conical. Sporidia linear, slightly curved, nucleoli scarcely distinct.—*Bull. Soc. Bot. Fr.* 1857, *p.* 861. *Desm. exs. ed.* ii. *no.* 689. *Cooke Seem. Journ.* iv. *p.* 97, *fig.* 30.

On all parts of *Scleranthus annuus.* Summer and Autumn.

1335. Septoria gei. *Desm.* "Avens Septoria."

Amphigenous; spots orbicular or irregular, brown at first, cinereous when dry, with a purplish-brown margin. Perithecia on the upper surface, very minute, numerous, brownish-black, sometimes arranged along the veins of the leaves, at first hemispherical, becoming at length concave. Sporidia linear, flexuose. —*Ann. Sc. Nat.* 1843, xix. *p.* 342. *Cooke Seem. Journ.* iv. *p.* 97. *Cooke exs. no.* 138. *Sphæria lichenoides, var. geicola. De Cand. Fl. Fr. p.* 149. *Sphæria (Depazea) vagans geicola. Fr. S.M.* ii. *p.* 532. *Acrotheca gei, Fuckel, Enum. p.* 43.

On leaves of *Geum urbanum.* Autumn.

1336. Septoria lysimachiæ. *West.* "Moneywort Septoria."

Epiphyllous; spots indeterminate, brown; perithecia minute, scattered, terminated by a pore; tendrils whitish; sporidia linear, straight, with numerous nucleoli.—*Bull. de Brux.* 1852, iii. *p.* 120. *Bell. Cat. Crypt. Nam. no.* 333. *Cooke. Seem. Journ.* iv. *p.* 97. *Cooke exs. no.* 142. *Fckl. exs. no.* 513. *Ascochyta lysimachiæ. Lib. exs. no.* 253.

On leaves of *Lysimachia nummularia.*

1337. Septoria castanæcola. *Desm.* "Chestnut-leaf Septoria."

Amphigenous; spots tawny, indeterminate; perithecia on the under surface, brownish-black, minute, numerous, somewhat innate, pierced with a terminal pore; tendrils whitish; sporidia elongated, slender, curved.—*Ann. Sc. Nat.* 1847, viii. *p.* 26. *Cooke Seem. Journ.* iv. *p.* 97. *Cooke exs. no.* 129. *Fckl. exs. no.* 508. *Kl. exs. no.* 1957. *Cooke, L. F. no.* 68.

On fading leaves of *Castanea vesca.* Sept. Common.

It is very probable that this is only a condition of *Sphærella sparsa* or *Sphærella maculæformis.*

1338. Septoria ribis. *Desm.* "Currant-leaf Septoria."

Amphigenous; spots numerous, small, irregular and angular, of a pale brown or purple colour; perithecia innate, very small, blackish-brown, convex, pierced with a large apical pore; tendrils flesh colour, or roseate; sporidia elongated, linear, containing numerous nucleoli.—*Mem. Soc. des Sc. de Lille,* 1842. *Cooke Seem. Journ.* iv. *p.* 97, *f.* 32. *Cooke exs. no.* 130. *Fckl. exs. no.*

498. *Desm. exs. no.* 1179. *Ascochyta ribis, Libert. exs. no.* 53. *West. and Wall, exs. no.* 92. *Phlæospora ribis, West. Bull. de Brux,* 1850, *p.* 20.

On leaves of black currrant. Common.

1339. Septoria alnicola. *Cooke.* "Alder Septoria."

Spots pallid, brown or tawny, rounded, about one-fourth of an inch in diameter; perithecia minute, scattered over the spots, semi-innate, black, pierced at the apex; sporidia oblong, straight or curved.—*Cooke Seem. Journ.* iv. *p.* 97, *f.* 23. *Cooke exs. no.* 203.

On living leaves of *Alnus glutinosa.* Autumn.

1340. Septoria lavandulæ. *Desm.* "Lavender Septoria."

Spots on both surfaces, numerous, bleached, rounded or irregular, with a purplish margin; perithecia on the upper surface, few, very small, black, globose, pierced, cup-shaped when dry; spores linear, straight or curved.—*Desm. Ann. Sc. Nat.* 1853, xx. *p.* 86. *Cooke exs. no.* 139.

On fading lavender leaves. Summer.

Spores (·025 m.m.) ·009 in. long.

1341. Septoria urticæ. *Desm.* "Nettle Septoria."

Spots on both surfaces; ochraceous, rounded, or irregular; perithecia very minute, epiphyllous, numerous, brown, pierced; spores elongated, slender, curved or flexuous.—*Desm. Ann. Sc. Nat.* 1847, viii. *p.* 24. *Cooke exs. no.* 137.

On nettle leaves. Summer.

Spores (·04 m.m.) ·0015 in long.

1342. Septoria astragali. *Desm.* "Milk-vetch Septoria."

Epiphyllous; spots irregular, greenish-grey, then tawny; perithecia few, globose, slightly prominent, black, pierced; spores very long, flexuous, multiseptate (?).—*Desm. Ann. Sc. Nat.* 1843, xix. *p.* 345. *Cooke exs. no.* 141. *Cooke L. F. no.* 70.

On leaves of milk-vetch (*Astragalus*). Autumn.

1343. Septoria virgaureæ. *Desm.* "Golden-rod Septoria."

Epiphyllous; spots orbicular or irregular, bleached, whitish, and brown, variegated; perithecia innate, minute, convex, nearly black, mouth widely open; tendrils white; spores very long, linear, nearly straight or flexuous.—*Desm. Ann. Sc. Nat.* 1842, xvii. *p.*

109. *Cooke exs. no.* 144. *Ascochyta virgaureæ, Lib. exs. no.* 55. *Rabh. exs. no.* 1321.

On leaves of *Solidago virgaurea.*

Spores (·1·05 m.m.) ·0035-·002 in. long.

Gen. 123. PHYLLOSTICTA, Pers.

Perithecia few and minute, innate; pierced with a terminal pore, seated on discoloured spots; nucleus gelatinous; sporidia ovoid or oblong, straight, minute, ejected in tendrils.

It is doubtful whether any satisfactory characters have yet been indicated to separate this genus from *Septoria.*

1344. Phyllosticta atriplicis. *Desm.* "Goose-foot Phyllosticta."

Amphigenous; spots orbicular, whitish, with a tawny or brownish margin, scattered or confluent; perithecia on the upper surface, very minute, numerous, globose, innate, brownish-black, pierced at the apex; tendrils yellowish-white; sporidia cylindrical, obtuse, straight or curved, and somewhat torulose, with from three to five nucleoli.—*Ann. des Sc. Nat.* 1851, xvi. *p.* 298. *Cooke Seem. Journ.* iv. *p.* 97. *f.* 22. *Sphæria (Depazea) vagans, atriplicicola, Fr. S.M.* ii. p. 582. *Cooke exs. no.* 148. *Cooke L. F. no.* 71.

On leaves of *Atriplex* and *Chenopodium.*

1344a. Phyllosticta cirsii. *Desm.* "Thistle Phyllosticta."

Epiphyllous; spots roundish or irregular, numerous, whitish with a brown margin; perithecia innate, black; sporidia very minute, oblong, with two nucleoli.—*Ann. Sc. Nat.* 1847. viii. *p.* 31. *Cooke Seem. Journ.* iv. *p.* 97.

On leaves of *Cirsium arvense.* Sept.

1345. Phyllosticta viciæ. "Vetch Phyllosticta."

Epiphyllous; spots white, rounded, with a purplish margin; perithecia minute, aggregate, black, with a terminal pore; tendrils white; sporidia ellipsoid with two, sometimes three nucleoli. —*Cooke Seem. Journ.* iv. *p.* 97. *Ascochyta viciæ, Lib. exs. no.* 356. *Phyllosticta Ervi? West. Bull. des Brux.*

On leaves of *Vicia sepium.* Oct.

1346. **Phyllosticta ruscicola.** *D.R. and Mont.* "Butcher's Broom Phyllosticta."

Amphigenous; spots pallid, with a reddish-brown margin; perithecia scattered over the spots, covered by the epidermis, globose, black; sporidia oblong.—*Fl. Alg.* i. *p.* 611. *Mont. Syll.* *p.* 279. *Desm. Ann. Sc. Nat.* 1847, viii. *p.* 32. *Desm. exs. no.* 1634. *West. Bull. de Brux.* vii. *p.* 23. *Cooke Seem. Journ.* iv. *p.* 97.

On the phyllodia of *Ruscus aculeatus.* Autumn.

1347. **Phyllosticta cytisi.** *Desm.* "Laburnum Phyllosticta."

Spots few, round or irregular, grey, with a brown margin; perithecia epiphyllous, black, numerous; sporidia ovoid-oblong, with two nucleoli.—*Ann. Sc. Nat.* 1847, viii. *p.* 34. *Desm. exs. no.* 1861. *Cooke Seem. Journ.* iv. *p.* 97. *Cooke exs. no.* 150.

On fading leaves of *Cytisus Laburnum.* Autumn.

1348. **Phyllosticta sambuci.** *Desm.* "Elder Phyllosticta."

Epiphyllous; spots whitish, solitary, or confluent, and disposed in a line; perithecia innate, minute, few, brownish-black, pierced with a terminal pore; nucleus whitish; sporidia ovoid-oblong, with two nucleoli.—*Ann. Sc. Nat.* 1847, viii. *p.* 34. *Desm. exs. no.* 1638. *Cooke Seem. Journ.* iv. *p.* 97, *f.* 28.

On fading leaves of elder. Autumn.

1349. **Phyllosticta primulæcola.** *Desm.* "Primrose Phyllosticta."

Spots occupying both surfaces of the leaves, large, blanched, oftentimes with a yellowish border; perithecia epiphyllous, numerous, rather prominent, globose, black, shining; sporidia subglobose, very small.—*Ann. Sc. Nat.* 1847, viii. *p.* 130. *Desm. exs. no.* 1629. *Cooke Seem. Journ.* iv. *p.* 97. *Cooke exs. no.* 147.

On fading leaves of *Primula vulgaris.* Autumn. Common.

1350. **Phyllosticta limbalis.** *Pers.* "Box-leaf Phyllosticta."

Spots oval or oblong, ivory white, with a discoloured margin, generally at the edges of the leaves; perithecia rare, blackish, scattered, sometimes confluent; spores oblong, hyaline, with three or four nucleoli.—*Pers. Champ. Comest. Cooke Seem. Journ.* iv. *p.* 97. *Depazea buxicola. Fr. S.M.* ii. 528. *Fckl. exs.*

no. 429. *Sphæria lichenoides var. buxicola. De Cand. Welw. Crypt Lusit. no.* 21.

On living box leaves. Oct.

1351. Phyllosticta erysimi. *West.* "Sauce alone Septoria."

Spots blanched, rounded, with a linear dark brown margin; perithecia numerous, black, scattered about the centre of the spot; ostiole poriform; sporidia oval, hyaline, containing two nucleoli at the extremities.—*West. Bull. de Brux.* 1863, *no.* 21. *Cooke Seem. Journ.* iv. *p.* 97.

On leaves of *Erysimum alliaria.* Autumn.

1352. Phyllosticta violæ. *Desm.* "Violet Phyllosticta."

Amphigenous; spots whitish, rounded, scattered, or confluent; perithecia innate, numerous, microscopical, brown; tendrils white; spores very minute, straight, sub-cylindrical.—*Desm. Ann. Sc. Nat.* 1847, viii. *p.* 29.

On violet leaves. June. July.

Spores ·01 m.m. long.

1353. Phyllisticta vulgaris *var.* **Loniceræ.** *Desm.* "Honey-suckle Phyllosticta."

Spots on both surfaces, scattered, rounded, or irregular, olive brown, grey, or whitish; perithecia immersed, globose, then depressed, amber colour then brown, pierced; spores minute, cylindrical, straight, obtuse.—*Desm. Ann. Sc. Nat.* 1849, xi. *p.* 350. *Cooke exs. no.* 149. *Cooke L.F. no.* 72.

On honeysuckle leaves. Autumn.

Gen. 124. CHEILARIA, Libert.

Perithecia sub-globose, dehiscing with a fissure; nucleus gelatinous; sporidia more or less globose, ejected in tendrils.

1354. Cheilaria arbuti. *Desm.* "Arbutus Cheilaria."

Epiphyllous; spots minute, dark-coloured; perithecia minute, crowded, black, shining, roundish-oblong, dehiscing by a longitudinal fissure; nucleus at first whitish, ultimately blackened; sporidia ovoid, minute, with two nucleoli.—*Ann. Sc. Nat.* 1846, vi. *p.* 68. *Cooke Seem. Journ.* iv. *p.* 97. *Dothidea arbuti, Duby. Bot. Gall.* ii. *p.* 717.

On leaves of *Arbutus unedo.* Jan.

1354a. **Cheilaria coryli.** *Rob.* "Hazel-leaf Cheilaria."

Amphigenous; spots irregular, rufous; perithecia hypophyllous rarely epiphyllous, innate, membranaceous, sub-gregarious, very small, roundish, pallid brown, dehiscing with a longitudinal fissure; nucleus white; sporidia hyaline, oblong, somewhat truncate, wedge-shaped, or fiddle-shaped.—*Desm. Ann. Sc. Nat.* 1853, xx. *p.* 226. *Desm. exs. ed.* ii. *no.* 80. *Cooke Seem. Journ.* iv. *p.* 97. *Cooke exs. no.* 154.

On leaves of *Corylus avellana.* Autumn.

Gen. **125.** **ASCOCHYTA,** Lib.

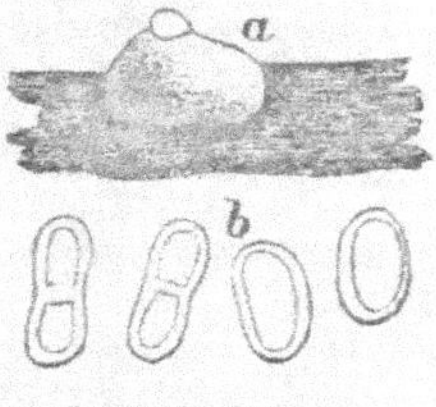

Fig. 167.

Perithecia distinct, delicate; spores oozing out, uniseptate, or simple.—*Berk. Outl. p.* 320. (*Fig.* 167.)

1355. **Ascochyta pisi.** *Lib.* "Pea-pod Ascochyta."

Spots somewhat rounded, excavated, fawn-coloured, margin brown; perithecia sub-central, very delicate, brownish; mouth round; spores oblong, uniseptate, contracted in the middle.—*Berk. Outl. p.* 320. *Sphæria (Depazea) concava. Berk. Ann. N.H. no.* 194, *t.* 11, *f.* 3. *Fckl. exs. no.* 487.

On pea pods.

Forming little round fawn-coloured pits, studded in the centre with the short sub-cirrhiform masses of spores. Spores oblong, contracted in the middle, uniseptate, with occasionally a single nucleus in each cell.—*M. J. B.* (*Fig.* 167.)

1356. **Ascochyta pallor.** *Berk.* "Pallid Ascochyta."

Spots pallid, sub-rotund; perithecia scattered, immersed, pallid; epidermis rather prominent above the obsolete ostiola; spores linear, curved slightly.—*Berk. Outl. p.* 320. *Sphæria (Depazea) pallor. Berk. Ann. N.H. no.* 193, *t.* 11, *f.* 2.

On living bramble shoots. May.

Forming sub-rotund, sometimes confluent, pale spots, sprinkled with little elevated dark-bordered dots, which indicate the perithecia; perithecia extremely delicate, pale fawn-coloured, filled with linear slightly curved spots, much larger then in *Cytispora*, some of which contain an obscure row of nuclei.

1357. Ascochyta dianthi. *Berk.* "Pink-leaf Ascochyta."

Perithecia irregular, conglomerate; spores spathulate, sometimes divided into two parts, containing a few globose granules. —*Berk. Outl. p.* 320. *Sphæria (Depazea) dianthi A. & S. t.* 6, *f.* 2. *Berk. exs. no.* 187. *Berk. Ann. N.H. no.* 104, *t.* 7, *f.* 5. *Fckl. exs. no.* 490. *Kl. exs. no.* 863.

On living pink leaves, &c.

1358. Ascochyta rufo-maculans. *Berk.* "Brown-spot Ascochyta."

Spots orbicular, red-brown; perithecia emergent, free, of the same colour; spores oblong, simple, constricted in the centre. —*Berk. Outl. p.* 320. *Septoria rufo-maculans. Berk. Gard. Chron.* 1854, *p.* 676, *with fig.*

On grapes.

Forming an orbicular spot of a sienna brown, preserving constantly a definite outline. This spot separates readily from the subjacent pulp, in consequence of a copious crop of mycelium, the threads of which form the radii of a circle. The surface is rough with little raised orbicular reddish perithecia arranged concentrically; spores varying from ·0008 to ·0065 in. (·02 to ·15 m.m.) In age the perithecia fall away, leaving a little aperture, the border of which is often stained black.

Gen. **126. CYSTOTRICHA,** B. & Br.

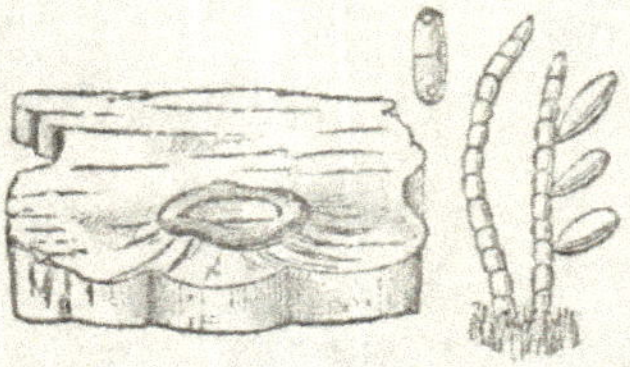

Fig. 168.

Perithecia bursting longitudinally; sporophores branched, articulated, beset here and there with oblong, uniseptate spores.—*Berk. Outl. p.* 320. *B. & Br. Ann. N.H. no.* 448. (*Fig.* 168.)

1359. Cystotricha striola. *B. & Br.* "Seriate Cystotricha."

Perithecia punctiform or linear, often forming little rows, black, with a reddish tinge; disc reddish; sporophores highly developed, greatly elongated, bearing one or two branches above, articulate from the base, sub-moniliform, articulations about as long as broad, giving off here and there oblong pellucid spores, at first simple, at length uniseptate.—*B. & Br. Ann. N.H. no.* 448, *t.* 12, *f.* 10.

On decorticated wood.

It has nearly the structure of *Tubercularia*, with the addition of a perithecium, the sporophores being closely articulate. (*Fig.* 168.)

Gen. **127.** **NEOTTIOSPORA,** Desm.

Perithecia concealed, with a central perforation; spores hyaline, crested.—*Berk. Outl. p.* 320. (*Fig.* 169.)

Fig. 169.

1360. **Neottiospora caricum.** *Desm.* "Sedge Neottiospora."

Amphigenous; perithecia scattered, minute, rusty brown, at length umber, nestling in the parenchyma of the leaf, covered by the blackened cuticle; tendrils orange; spores minute, subhyaline.—*Desm. Ann. Sc. Nat.* 1843. xix. *p.* 346. *Desm. exs. no.* 1338. *B. & Br. Ann. N.H. no.* 435. *Rabh. F.E. no.* 42. *Sphæria caricina. Desm. exs. no.* 717.

On dead leaves of *Carices.*

Remarkable for the appendage of short hyaline threads, with which the spores are furnished at one extremity. (*Fig.* 169.)

Gen. **128.** **EXCIPULA,** Fr.

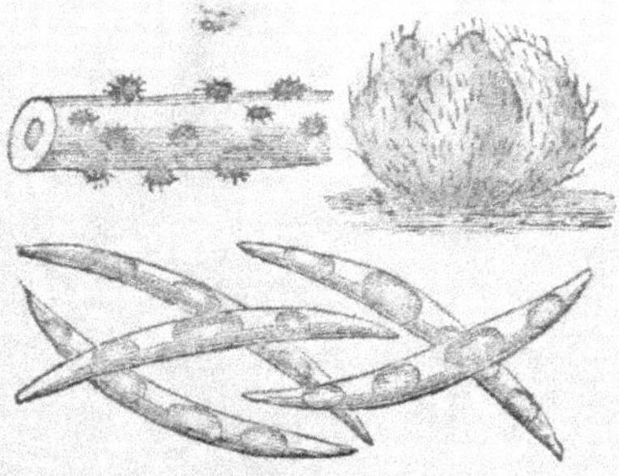

Perithecia delicate, hispid open above (excipuliform); spores hyaline, attenuated, but not appendiculate.—*Berk. Outl. p.* 321. (*Fig.* 170.)

Fig. 170.

1361. **Excipula strigosa.** *Fr.* "Grass Excipula."

Innate, sessile, flattened, concave, strigose, black, disc pale; spores fusiform, curved, accuminate.—*Fries exs. no.* 136. *Eng. Fl.* v. *p.* 296. *Peziza strigosa. Fr. S.M.* ii. *p.* 103. *Corda. Icon.* iii. *f.* 78. *Lib. exs. no.* 349. *Kl. exs. no.* 1236.

On culms and leaves of grass. (*Fig.* 170.)

1362. Excipula macrotricha. *B. & Br.* "Furze Excipula."

Perithecia hispid, hairs long, straight; spores minute, lunulate.—*B. & Br. Ann. N.H. no.* 444.

On dead furze branches.

Perithecia larger than in the other species, coarsely hispid, hairs long, their inner tube separating easily from the outer.

1363. Excipula chætostroma. *B. & Br.* "Ash-key Excipula."

Gregarious, convex, cinereous, everywhere penetrated by black bristles; spores lunate, sub-fusiform.—*B. & Br. Ann. N.H. no.* 445, *t.* 11, *f.* 2.

On dead ash keys. Somerset.

Minute, convex, black; disc rough with the long inarticulate bristles, which everywhere penetrate its substance; spores on rather long, fasciculate, or connate sporophores, lunate, subfusiform, acute at either extremity, pale; endochrome granulated, green under the microscope.—*B. & Br.*

1364. Excipula fusispora. *B. & Br.* "Clematis Excipula."

Minute, very black, invested with rigid bristles; spores fusiform, multiseptate, middle articulations darker.—*B. & Br. Ann. N.H. no.* 814, *t.* 9, *f.* 1.

On bark of *Clematis vitalba.* Jan. Batheaston.

Forming very minute black specks, perithecia clothed with dense, slightly waved, continuous setæ; spores curved, fusiform, ·002 in. (·05 m.m.) long, multiseptate, the two extreme articulations hyaline, the others rather darker, and generally containing a globose nucleus.—*B. & Br.*

Gen. **129. DINEMASPORIUM,** Lev.

Perithecia excipuliform, delicate, hispid; spores hyaline, aristate at either extremity. —*Berk. Outl. p.* 321. (*Fig.* 171.)

Fig. 171.

1365. Dinemasporium graminum. *Lev.* "Grass Dinemasporium."

Perithecia scattered, hairy, with simple, black bristles; spores cylindrical, obtuse, curved, aristate.—*Lev. Ann. Sc. Nat. May*, 1846, *p.* 274. *B. & Br. Ann. N.H. no.* 446. *Excipula graminum. Berk. exs. no.* 328. *Lib. exs. no.* 348. *Corda. Icon.* iii. *f.* 79. *Fckl. exs. no.* 204.

On leaves of grasses.

var. **herbarum.** *Cooke.* Larger than the typical form, but hardly differing in fruit.—*Cooke exs. no.* 279.

On stems of nettle, &c.

An allied species of this genus occurs in South Carolina, U.S. (*Fig* 171.)

Gen. 130. MYXORMIA, B. & Br.

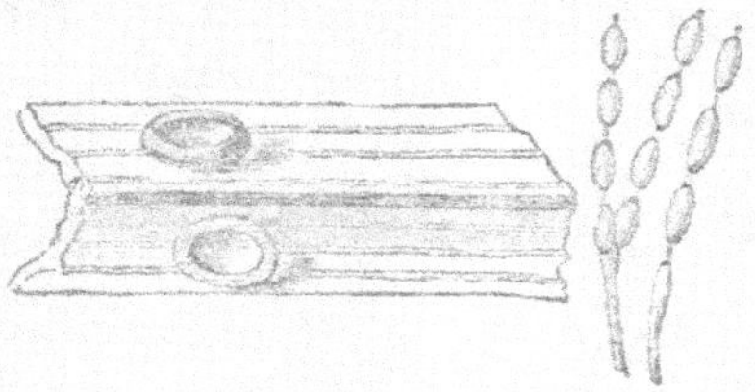

Fig. 172.

Perithecium composed of flocci with free apices, open above; spores concatenate, involved in gelatine.—*Berk. Outl. p.* 321. *B. & Br. Ann. N.H. no.* 447. (*Fig.* 172.)

Allied to *Excipula*, but separated from it by habit, by the absence of flocci, and above all by its concatenate spores. The spores collectively are very gelatinous.

1366. Myxormia atro-viridis. *B. & Br.* "Black Green Myxormia."

Perithecia excipuliform, scattered, minute, quite smooth, formed of long, closely-packed narrow cells; sporophores filiform; spores linear-oblong, concatenated.—*B. & Br. Ann. N.H. n.* 447, *t.* 12, *f.* 9.

On dead leaves of grass. Dec. Batheaston.

Spores connected by a very delicate thread, which frequently breaks off with them, containing one or more globose nuclei, generally one at either end, involved in gelatine, forming a black green mass, resembling strongly the fructifying stratum in the genus *Phallus*. (*Fig.* 172.)

Gen. 131. PROSTHEMIUM, Kunze.

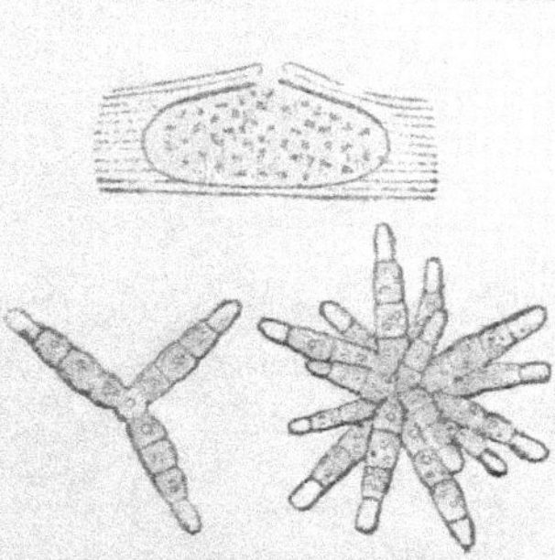

Fig. 173.

Perithecia carbonaceous; spores fasciculate, fusiform, septate, attached to articulated threads.—*Berk. Outl. p.* 321. *Eng. Fl.* v. *p.* 297. (*Fig.* 173.)

1367. Prosthemium stellare. *Riess.* "Stellate Prosthemium."

Perithecia sub-lentiform, black, covered; spores brown, 12-20 connate in a stellate manner, at length ejected in tendrils.—*Riess. Bot. Zeit.* 1853, *p.* 130, *t.* 3, *f.* 28-31. *B. & Br. Ann. N.H. no.* 939, *t.* 15, *f.* 10.

On alder. West of England. (*Fig.* 173.)

Prosthemium betulinum, *Kze.* is a condition of *Massaria siparia.*

en. 132. ASTEROMA, D.C.

Fig. 174.

Perithecia flat, with no determinate orifice, attached to creeping branched threads; spores simple, or uniseptate.—*Berk. Outl. p.* 321. *Eng. Fl.* v. *p.* 288. (*Fig.* 174.)

1368. Asteroma reticulatum. *Berk.* "Reticulated Asteroma."

Epiphyllous, black, sub-seriate, the cells joined by free longitudinal creeping, somewhat branched fibrillæ.—*Berk. exs. no.* 41. *Eng. Fl.* v. *p.* 288. *Dothidea reticulata. Fr. S.M.* ii. *p.* 560. *Sturm.* iii. *t.* 13. *Moug. exs. no.* 982. *Asteroma polygonati D.C. Mem. Mus. t.* 4, *f.* 5. *Fckl. exs. no.* 464.

On dead leaves of *Convallaria majalis.* King's Cliffe.

1369. Asteroma ulmi. *Kl.* "Elm-leaf Asteroma."

Fibrillæ very delicate, much branched, radiating, sub-dichotomous, flexuous, seated on a brownish spot.—*Klotsch. Hook. Herb. Eng. Fl.* v. *p.* 289. *Cooke L.F. no.* 74. *Cooke exs. no.* 155.

On living elm leaves. Scotland.

1370. Asteroma prunellæ. *Purt.* "All-heal Asteroma."

Epiphyllous, fibrillæ pitch black, straight, radiating in fascicles from a central tubercle, cells minute, sub-central—*Baxt. exs. no.* 79. *Eng. Fl.* v. *p.* 289.

On green leaves of *Prunella vulgaris.*

It has the appearance of a minute *Hutchinsia*, spread out upon the leaf, with its knob-like root in the centre.—*M. J. B.*

1371. Asteroma padi. *Grev.* " Bird Cherry Asteroma."

Radiating, much branched, the branches arcuate, brown, with a central silvery line; spores at length oozing out, linear, very minute, slightly curved.—*Grev. Loud. Hort. B. p.* 459. *Eng. Fl.* v. *p.* 289. *Ann. N.H. no.* 201* *t.* 11, *f.* 4.

On leaves of *Prunus padus.* Scotland. (*Fig.* 174*b.*)

1372. Asteroma rosæ. *D.C.* " Rose leaf Asteroma."

Epiphyllous; spots purplish, fibrils radiating from the centre; perithecia scattered, blackish; spores consisting of two obovate cells attached by their broader ends, and each containing two nuclei.—*Lib. exs. no.* 61. *Berk. Ann. N.H. no.* 202, *t.* 11, *f.* 5. *Asteroma radiosa. Berk. exs. no.* 314. *Fries. El.* ii. *p.* 151. *Cooke exs. no.* 156. *Cooke L.F. no.* 73.

On rose leaves. Autumn. Common. [Low Carolina.] (*Fig.* 174*a.*)

ASTEROMA VERONICÆ. *Desm.* (*Berk. exs. no.* 193) is an early condition of *Capnodium sphæricum*, Cooke, as traced by Dr. Capron, of Shere.

Gen. 133. RABENHORSTIA, Fr.

Conceptacle thin, sub-carbonaceous, cup-shaped, dimidiate, above covered with the adnate cuticle, celluloso-loculose within, ostiolum simple; nucleus gelatinous.—*Berk. Outl. p.* 322.

1373. Rabenhorstia rudis. *Fr.* " Laburnum Rabenhorstia."

Crowded or scattered, furnished with a black, effused, ambient crust; perithecia covered, villoso-furfuraceous, dingy-black, at length dimidiate from the peeling off of the epidermis; nucleus pale whitish rose colour.—*Fr. El.* ii. *p.* 98. *Eng. Fl.* v. *p.* 270.

On dead twigs of *Laburnum.*

1374. Rabenhorstia tiliæ. *Fr.* "Lime Rabenhorstia.."

Scattered; perithecia covered, smooth, black, somewhat pitcher-shaped, dimidiate, neck erumpent, unequal, black.—*Sphæria tiliæ. Fr. S.M.* ii. *p.* 485. *Eng. Fl.* v. *p.* 269. *Nees. f.* 339. *Fckl. exs. no.* 582. *Moug. exs. no.* 660. *Sphæria subsecreta. Sow. t.* 373, *f.* 8.

On dead twigs of lime.

Gen. 134. CYTISPORA, Fr.

Perithecia irregular, or compound and radiating; spores minute, mostly curved, oozing out from a common spot in the form of globules or tendrils.—*Berk. Outl. p.* 322. *Eng. Fl.* v. *p.* 281.

All the species of *Cytispora* are merely conditions of different species of *Valsa*, &c. The following are given in Berkeley's outlines:—

Cytispora rubescens. Fr. On dead twigs of *Rosaceæ*.
Cytispora chrysosperma. Fr. On dead poplar.
Cytispora carphosperma. Fr. On dead twigs of *Rosaceæ*.
Cytispora leucosperma. P. On various trees.
Cytispora fugax. Fr. On dead willows.
Cytispora Hendersonii. B. & Br. On twigs of *Rosa arvensis*.
Cytispora pinastri. Fr. On fallen pine leaves.
Cytispora guttifera. Fr. On dead willow twigs.

Gen. 135. MICROPERA, Lev.

Perithecia innate, membranaceous, gaping above, without any common ostiolum; spores simple, linear.—*Berk. Outl. p.* 322.

1375. Micropera drupacearum. *Lev.* "Cherry Micropera."

Perithecia pustulate, innate, sub-cylindrical, deformed by mutual pressure; ostiola white; spores curved above.—*Lev. Ann. Sc. Nat. May*, 1846, *p.* 283. *Kl. exs. no.* 1960. *B. & Br. Ann. N.H. no.* 437. *Pers. Ic. Pict. t.* 20, *f.* 1. *Fckl. exs. no.* 638.

On dead branches of cherry. King's Cliffe.

Probably not autonomous. Tulasne states it is the Pycnidia of *Dermatea Cerasi*.

Gen. 136. DISCELLA, B. & Br.

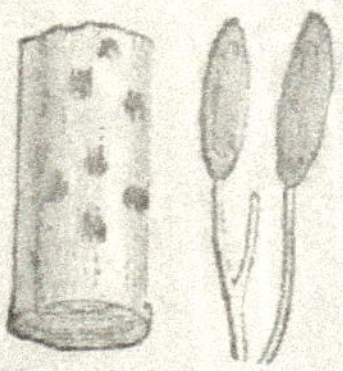

Fig. 175.

Perithecium spurious, nearly simple, sometimes obsolete above, or entirely wanting, and hence excipuliform; spores elongated, simple, or uniseptate.—*Berk. Outl. p* 323. *B. & Br. Ann. N.H. no.* 426. (*Fig.* 175.)

The perithecium is so little distinct from the stratum of sporophores, that it is frequently difficult, in examining a slice under the microscope, to say that it exists, though the two together are sometimes of considerable thickness, neither is the limit between the external cells and those of the matrix very accurately defined. In the same species it is sometimes entirely wanting above, and the sporophorous stratum merely covered by the cuticle, which at last splits, and exposes the excipuliform disc, while in other cases the spurious perithecium extends all round, being intimately blended with the cuticular cells. The cavity is essentially simple, but there is sometimes a slight fold or two below, showing a tendency to become multicellular, occasionally the centre is vacant, and the perithecium then forms an irregular ring.—*B. & Br.*

1376. Discella carbonacea. *B. & Br.* "Black Discella."

Perithecium black; spores elongated, subfusiform, pale yellow-green by transmitted light, uniseptate.—*Ann. N.H. no.* 426, *t.* 12, *f.* 8, *d. Phacidium carbonaceum, Fries. exs. no.* 210. *Berk. exs. no.* 44. *Fckl. exs. no.* 1100 (*partly*). *Stilbospora microsperma, Johnst. Fl. Ber.* ii. *p.* 192.

On dead sallow twigs. Common.

Forming small scattered disc-like spots, covered with the cuticle, which splits from the centre, and ultimately separates. Perithecia black, generally excipuliform, but sometimes extending all round, and then bursting above with the cuticle.

1377. Discella Desmazierii. *B. & Br.* "Blue-spored Discella."

Perithecia soft, externally hyaline, internally bluish; sporophores elongated; spores fusiform, simple, indigo-blue.—*Ann. N.H. no.* 427, *t.* 12, *f.* 8 *a.*

On twigs of lime. Norths.

Forming scattered discs, which however are blacker than in *D. carbonacea*, from the spores being darker. Perithecium delicate, hyaline next to the matrix, then blue, obsolete above; sporophores elongated, strongly developed, sometimes forked; spores of a beautiful indigo-blue, truly fusiform, though not much elongated, without any septum, distinctly bordered, larger than in *D. carbonacea.*—*B. & Br.* (*Fig.* 175.)

1378. Discella platyspora. *B. & Br.* "Broad-spored Discella."

Perithecia small, for the greater part deficient above, sporophores short, stout, deciduous as well as the oblong, broad, obtuse spores.—*Ann. N.H. no.* 428.

On dead twigs of plane. Batheaston.

Forming rather minute, slightly raised pustules, perithecia but slightly developed, generally, if not always deficient above; sporophores short, obtuse, simple, often breaking off with the oblong, obtuse spores, the cavity of which is simple, but the contents decidedly granular, so as at first to give a granulated aspect to the outer wall—*B. & Br.*

1379. Discella microsperma. *B. & Br.* "Small-spored Discella."

Perithecia black, pallid under a lens; spores minute, oblong, simple.—*B. & Br. Ann. N.H. no.* 429, *t.* 12, *f.* 8 *e. Berk. exs. no.* 44 (*partly*).

On dead sallow twigs.

Resembling strongly *D. carbonacea*, but somewhat larger, and distinguished at once by the minute, oblong, simple spores, several times smaller than in that species. In some pustules the perithecia open by a minute fissure, the lips of which being elongated by the oozing out of the spores make a spurious ostiolum.—*B. & Br.*

1380. Discella abnormis. *B. & Br.* "Abnormal Discella."

Perithecia globose, spurious, pierced above with a round pore; spores shortly fusiform, yellow-brown, uniseptate.—*B. & Br. Ann. N.H. no.* 429*.

On shoots of elder. Batheaston.

Perithecia small, entirely covered with the cuticle, globose, confused with the matrix. Approaches the type of *Diplodia.*

Gen. 137. PHLYCTÆNA, Desm.

Perithecium spurious, simple, never deficient above; spores elongated.—*Berk. Outl. p.* 323.

1381. Phlyctæna vagabunda. *Desm.* "Common Phlyctæna."

Spots none, or very minute, brown, fibrillose; pseudo-perithecia numerous, scattered; spores hyaline, curved, elongated, linear, somewhat obtuse, with 7-9 sporules.—*Desm. Ann. Sc. Nat.* 1847, viii. *p.* 16. *Desm. exs. no.* 1624. *B. & Br. Ann. N.H. no.* 753. *Lib. exs. no.* 248. *Moug. exs. no.* 1086.

On dead teazle stems, &c.

1382. Phlyctæna Johnstonii. *B. & Br.* "Johnston's Phlyctæna."

Spots rather broad; pseudo-perithecia brown; sporophores flexuous, ample; spores elongated, curved, nodulose in the middle.—*B. & Br. Ann. N.H. no.* 639*.

On dead *Senecio Jacobæa.* Berwick.

Spores several times longer than in *P. vagabunda*, the sporophores highly developed, and towards the centre of the spores there is generally a distinct knot, and frequently the outline is more or less irregular.—*B. & Br.*

Gen. 138. CEUTHOSPORA, Fr.

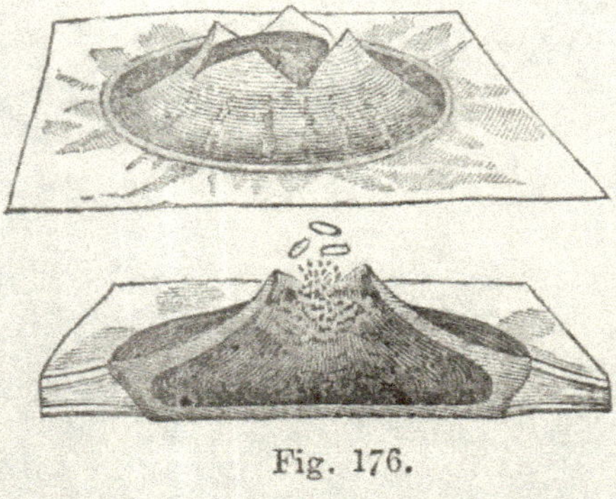

Fig. 176.

Perithecium spurious, innate, stromatiform, multicellular; spores ejected from one or more orifices. —*Berk. Outl. p.* 323. (*Fig.* 176.)

1383. **Ceuthospora lauri.** *Grev.* "Laurel Ceuthospora."

Unilocular, brownish-black, obtusely conic splitting into 3-4 acute erect laciniæ; spores minute.—*Grev. t.* 254. *Eng. Fl.* v. *p.* 283. *Sphæria lauri. Sow. t.* 371, *f.* 4. *S. hederæ* β. *lauri. Fr. S.M.* ii. *p.* 521. *Cooke exs. no.* 157. *Berk. exs. no.* 89.

On dead leaves of cherry laurel. (*Fig.* 176.)

Ceuthospora phacidioides, *Grev.* (*Cooke. exs. no.* 156) is an imperfect condition of *Phacidium ilicis.*

Gen. 139. ERIOSPORA, B. & Br.

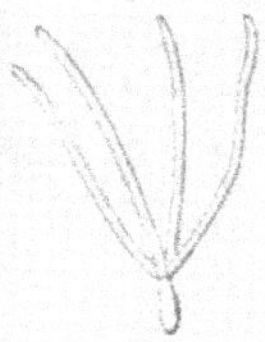

Fig. 177.

Stroma multicellular; spores ejected by a common orifice, quaternate, filiform, seated on short sporophores.—*Berk. Outl. p.* 323. *Ann. N.H. no.* 438. (*Fig.* 177.)

1384. **Eriospora leucostoma.** *B. & Br.* "White mouthed Eriospora."

Spots pitch brown; stroma depressed, cells variable, subglobose; spores very long, filiform.—*B. & Br. Ann. N.H. no.* 438, *t.* 11, *f.* 1.

On dead leaves of *Typha.* Feb. Wilts.

Spots pitch brown, very thin and diffused towards the edges, not a line broad, marked in the centre with a punctiform, white-bordered, pulverulent aperture; stroma depressed; cells varying in number, generally globose, but sometimes from the confluence of one or more depressed; spores very long, filiform, so delicate that they wave from the minute currents formed by the evaporation of the water in which placed for examination, at first seated four together on short cylindrical sporophores, but soon falling off.—*B. & Br.* (*Fig.* 177.)

Order XIII. MELANCONIEI.

Perithecium obsolete or altogether wanting.

Spores oozing out in a black mass.
- Simple . . . . *Melanconium.*
- Endochrome divided . . . . *Stegonosporium.*
- Septate . . . . *Stilbospora.*
- Septate and stellate . . . . *Asterosporium.*

Spores pedunculate.
- Septate, not crested . . . . *Coryneum.*
- Septate, crested . . . . *Pestalozzia.*
- Simple, collected in tufts . . . . . . *Cheirospora.*

Spores oozing out in tendrils.
- Coloured.
  - Of two kinds . . . . *Nemaspora.*
  - Of one kind . . . . *Myxosporium.*
- Hyaline.
  - Of one kind . . . . *Glœosporium.*

Gen. **140.** **MELANCONIUM,** Link.

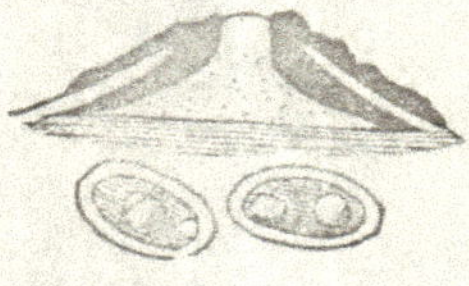

Fig. 178.

Spores simple, oozing out in a dark mass.—*Berk. Outl. p.* 323. *Eng. Fl.* v. *p.* 357. (*Fig.* 178.)

Not autonomous.

1385. **Melanconium bicolor.** *Nees.* " Two-coloured Melanconium."

Stroma elevated, prominent, white ; spores compact, subglobose, olive, or olive brown.—*Nees. t.* 2, *f.* 27. *Berk. Mag. Zool. & Bot. no.* 37. *Cooke exs. no.* 349. *Fr. S.M.* iii. *p.* 488. *B. & Br. Ann. N.H. no.* 250. *Didymosporium elevatum. Fr. S.M.* iii. *p.* 486. *Melanconium sphœroideum. Eng. Fl.* v. *p.* 358. *Didy. betulinum. Grev. t.* 273. *Kze. exs. no.* 157. *Corda.* i. *f.* 33-34. *Fckl. exs. no.* 84. *Bisch. f.* 3835.

On birch. [United States.]

(*Fig.* 178.)

1386. **Melanconium magnum.** *Berk.* " Large Melanconium."

Spores oval or sub-ovate, not septate.—*Berk. Outl. p.* 324. *Stilbospora magna. Eng. Fl.* v. *p.* 357. *Nemaspora carpinea.*

Baxt. exs. no. 76. *Nemaspora magna. Grev. t.* 349. *Sow. t.* 376. *Corda.* iii. *f.* 58. *Fckl. exs. no.* 87. *Pringsh. Jahrb.* ii. *t.* 28, *f.* 19.

On walnut and hornbeam, [Up. Carolina.]

Sometimes covering the whole trunk, the spores oozing out in long tendrils.

1387. Melanconium sphærospermum. *Lk.* "Round-spored Melanconium."

Stroma none; spores erumpent, scarcely compact, globose, pellucid, blackish.—*Fr. S.M.* iii. *p.* 489. *Berk. Ann. N.H. no* 251. *Rabh. F.E. No.* 179. *Fckl. exs. no.* 86. *Bot. Zeit.* 1859, *t.* 11, *f.* 5. *Stilbospora sphærosperma. Pers. Obs. t.* 1, *f.* 6. *Kze. exs. no.* 102.

On reeds. Tansor, Norths. [United States.]

Gen. **141.** STEGONOSPORIUM, Corda.

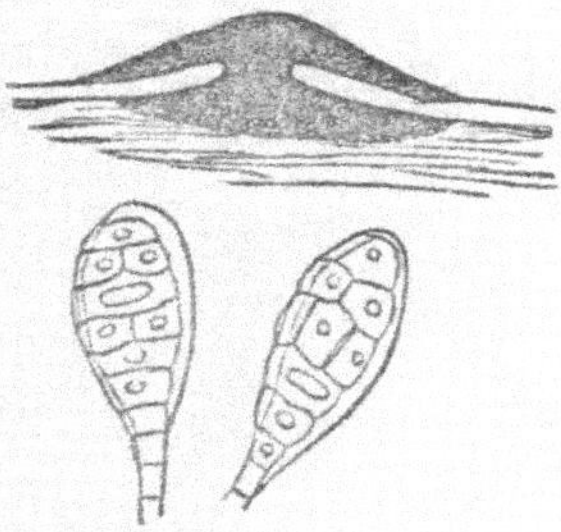

Fig. 179.

Spores unilocular, the endochrome transversely septate, or cellulose, oozing out in a black mass.—*Berk. Outl. p.* 324. (*Fig.* 179.)

Not autonomous.

1388. Stegonosporium cellulosum. *Corda.* "Cellular Stegonosporium."

Pustules effused, black; spores sub-pyriform, longitudinally cellulose and transversely septate.—*Corda. Ic.* iii. *f.* 62. *Kl. exs.* ii. *no.* 148. *Fres. t.* 7, *f.* 53-57. *Curr. Micr. Journ.* iv. *t.* 11, *f.* 10-25.

On dead branches.

See *Valsa vestita*, of which this is a secondary fruit. (*Fig.* 179.)

Gen. **142.** STILBOSPORA, Pers.

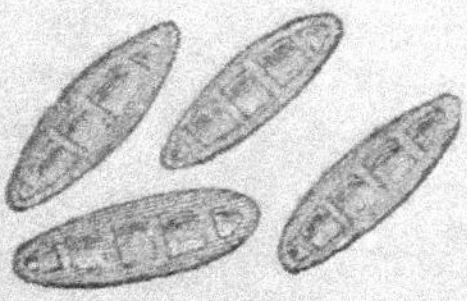

Fig. 180.

Spores septate, oozing out in a black mass.—*Berk. Outl. p.* 324. *Eng.Fl.* v. *p.* 356. (*Fig.* 180.)

Scarcely autonomous.

1389. **Stilbospora ovata.** *Pers.* "Ovate Stilbospora."

Stroma scarcely any; spores ovate, triseptate, septa sometimes obsolete.—*Pers. Obs.* i. *t.* 2, *f.* 2. *Eng. Fl.* v. *p.* 357. *Grev. t.* 212. *f.* 2. *Fr. S.M.* iii. *p.* 485. *S. pyriformis, Hoffm. F. G.* ii. *t.* 13, *f.* 2. *Fries. exs. no.* 214. *Corda.* iii. *f.* 61. *Bisch. f.* 3890.

On dead twigs. [United States.]

1390. **Stilbospora angustata.** *P.* "Narrow Stilbospora."

Stroma scarcely any; spores cylindrical, 4-5 septate.—*Fr. S.M.* iii. *p.* 485. *Berk. Mag. Zool. & Bot. no.* 36.

On *Cornus sanguinea.* [United States.]

(*Fig.* 180.)

1391. **Stilbospora macrosperma.** *P.* "Large-spored Stilbospora."

Stroma scarcely any; spores oval-oblong, quadriseptate.—*Pers. Disp. t.* 3. *f.* 13. *Nees. f.* 17. *Fckl. exs. no.* 82. *Sporidesmium, Corda. Sturm. t.* 21. *Bisch. f.* 3879. *Schnzl. t.* 12, *f.* 16-18. *Fres. t.* 7, *f.* 46-52. *Hook. Journ.* 1851, iii. *t.* 9, *f.* 9. *Pay. f.* 254. *Rabh. F.E. no.* 180.

On oak branches, &c. [Mid. Carolina.]

The stylosporous fruit of *Sphæria (Massaria) inquinans.*

Gen. **143.** **ASTEROSPORIUM,** Kunze.

Spores stellate, septate, oozing out in a black mass.—*Berk. Outl. p.* 324.

(*Fig.* 181.)

Fig. 181.

1392. **Asterosporium Hoffmanni.** *M. & N.* "Star-spored Fungus."

Stroma floccose or grumous; spores stellate, septate, brownish, or slightly coloured.—*Moug. exs. no.* 669. *Fres. t.* 5, *f.* 10-13. *Curr. Micr. Jour.* iv. *t.* 11, *f.* 1-9. *Stilbospora asterosperma, Pers. Syn. p.* 96. *Hoffm. F.G.* ii. *t.* 13, *f.* 3. *Fr. S.M.* iii. *p.* 484. *Eng. Fl.* v. *p.* 356. *Cooke exs. no.* 211. *Fckl. exs. no.* 81.

On twigs of beech. Common. [Mid. Carolina.]

Easily known by the stellate spores. (*Fig.* 181.)

Gen. **144.** **CORYNEUM**, Kunze.

Spores separate, seated on a cushion-like stroma.—*Berk. Outl. p.* 324. *Eng. Fl.* v. *p.* 355. (*Fig.* 182.)

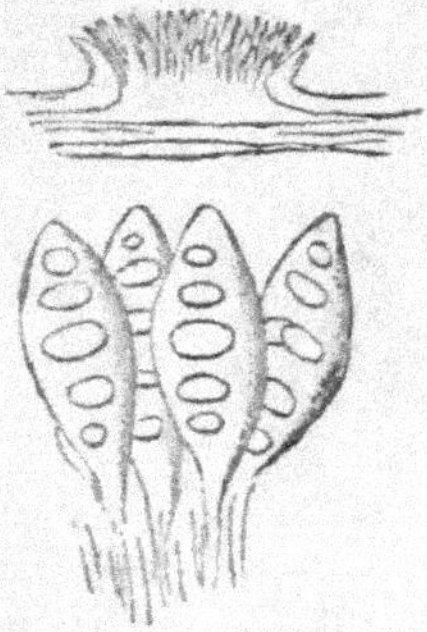

Fig. 182.

1393. **Coryneum macrosporum.** *Berk.* "Large-spored Coryneum."

Disc slightly depressed; spores fusiform 7-12 septate, pellucid above, greatly elongated, and curved back.—*Eng. Fl.* v. *p.* 355. *Rabh. F.E. no.* 75. *Sporidesmium vermiforme. Fres.* ii. *t.* 6, *f.* 56-58.

On beech twigs.

Spores ·0065 in. (E.C.) This is said to be the Conidia of *Melogrammæ oligospora.*

1394. **Coryneum pulvinatum.** *Kze.* "Pulvinate Coryneum."

Disc sub-rotund, pulvinate, convex, spores oblong, obtuse, brown; sporophores cylindrical.—*Kunze. M. H.* i. *t.* 2, *f.* 19. *Moug. exs. no.* 574. *Eng. Fl.* v. *p.* 355. *Fr. S.M.* iii. *p.* 474. *Fckl. exs. no.* 1654. *Bon. t.* 12, *f.* 240.

On dead sycamore. [Mid. Carolina.]

Spores ·003 in.

1395. **Coryneum disciforme.** *Kze.* "Discoid Coryneum."

Pustules disc-like, flattened; spores clavate, sporophores attenuated.—*Kunze. M. H.* i. *p.* 76, *f.* 18. *B. & Br. Ann. N.H. no.* 450. *Pay. f.* 356. *Bisch. f.* 3893. *Cooke exs. no.* 351. *Rabh. F.E. no.* 278. *Bon. t.* 12, *f.* 239.

On dead birch.

var. β. **ellipticum.** *B. & Br.* Bursting transversely through the bark, large, elliptic, pulvinate; stroma thick white, black towards the edges, consisting of closely packed elongated cells; spores fusiform, multiseptate, articulations slightly constricted; endochromes granular, containing generally two transversely arranged globules.—*Ann. N.H. no.* 450.

On trunks of birch. King's Cliffe.

1396. Coryneum compactum. *B. & Br.* "Compact Coryneum."

Minute, at first covered, at length exposed; spores broadly fusiform, slightly obtuse, nuclei concatenate.—*Ann. N.H. no.* 449.

On dead twigs of elm. March. Wraxall.

[Upper Carolina, U.S.]

Forming minute scattered pustules, at first quite covered by the cuticle, at length exposed; stroma convex, spores pedunculate, widely fusiform, slightly obtuse, 4-5 septate, nuclei large, connected with one another.—*B. & Br.*

1397. Coryneum Kunzei. *Corda.* "Kunze's Coryneum."

Erumpent, disciform, black, stroma placentæform, brown within; spores fusiform, acute at each end, septate, brown, with a terminal, colourless apiculus.—*Corda. Icon.* iv. *f.* 131. *Kl. exs. no.* 1360, ii. *no.* 779. *Berk. exs. no.*

On dead oak twigs.

Spores ·0025-·003 in. (E.C.) The sporophores are very persistent and long.

1398. Coryneum microstictum. *B. & Br.* "Small-spored Coryneum."

Covered; stroma obsolete; spores minute, shortly lanceolate, 2-3 septate.—*B. & Br. Ann. N.H. no.* 451. *Sporocadus rosæola. Rabh. exs. no.* 1166.

On dead twigs of rose, vine, *Kerria*, &c.

Scattered over the twigs, and always concealed beneath the cuticle, which cracks in the centre of each little pustule; stroma obsolete; sporophores elongated; spores minute, brown, shortly lanceolate, with two or three septa. This has much the habit of a *Hendersonia*, but there are no perithecia.—*B. & Br.*

1399. Coryneum macrospermum. *B. & Br.* "Naked Coryneum."

Stroma minute, pulvinate; flocci forked above; spores subcylindrical, 4-5 septate, extreme articulations hyaline.—*B. & Br. Ann. N.H. no.* 941. *t.* 15, *f.* 12. *Didymosporium macrospermum Corda.* vi. *f.* 17. *Fckl. exs. no.* 83.

On elm poles. Jan. Batheaston.

Forming little scattered spots on the surface of the wood; stroma cellular; thread cylindrical, equal, forked above.

1400. Coryneum umbonatum. *Tul.* "Umbonate Coryneum."

Erumpent, black, disciform, umbonate in the centre; stroma cellular, brown; spores oblong, on slender sporophores.—*Tul.*

Carp. ii. *t.* xv. *f.* 9. *Corda. Anl. t. G. f.* 69, *no.* 11-13. *Bisch. f.* 3859. *Nees.* ii. *f.* 31. *Corda. Icon.* iii. *f.* 92. *Steganosporum elevatum. Reiss. Bot. Zeit.* 1853, *t.* 3, *f.* 24-27. *Fckl. exs. no.* 95. *Kl. exs. no.* 1853.

On oak twigs.

Conidiiferous condition of *Melanconis umbonata* Tul. The spores are very broadly fusiform on slender sporophores, the endochrome divided into four or five transversely elliptical portions, scarcely coloured ·0017-·002 in. (*Fig.* 182.)

Gen. **145.** **PESTALOZZIA**, De Not.

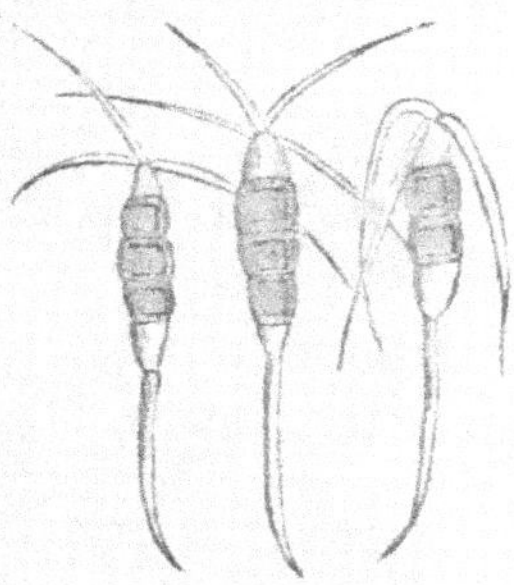

Fig. 183.

Spores septate, seated on a long peduncle, crested above.—*Berk. Outl. p.* 324. (*Fig.* 183.)

1401. Pestalozzia Guepini. *Desm.* "Camellia Pestalozzia."

Amphigenous, black, scattered; spores fusiform, pedicellate, hyaline at each extremity, 3-4 septate; crowned with 3-4 very slender, hyaline, divergent setæ.—*Desm. exs. no.* 1084. *Ann. Sc. Nat.* 1840, xiii. *p.* 182. *Corda. Anl. t. F. f.* 58, *no.* 8, 9, *t.* 4, *f.* 1-3. *Fckl. exs. no.* 522. *Pay. f.* 361.

On *Camellia* leaves. [Low. & Mid. Carolina.]

(*Fig.* 183.)

1402. Pestalozzia funerea. *Desm.* "Cypress Pestalozzia."

Pustules black, scattered, erumpent. Spores fusiform, shortly pedicellate, hyaline at each extremity, 4-septate, crowned above with 3-5 filiform hyaline, short, straight, divergent appendages.—*Desm. Ann. des Sc. Nat.* 1843, xix. *p.* 335.

On twigs and branches of cypress. (Dr. J. Lampray.)

1403. Pestalozzia lignicola. *Cooke.* "Wood Pestalozzia."

Perithecia semi-immersed, laterally compressed, black; ostiola elongated from lateral pressure; spores cylindrical, obtuse, triseptate, the cell at each end hyaline, intermediate cells brown; setæ 2-4 hyaline, simple; sporophores very long.

On chips. Shere.

This has the appearance of a Lophiostomous *Sphæria*, and is quite distinct from anything we find described.

Gen. **146.** **CHEIROSPORA,** Fr.

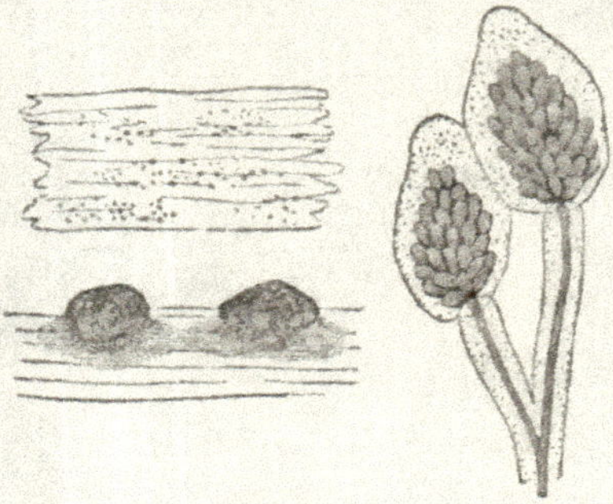

Spores collected in bundles at the tip of hyaline, filiform sporophores, forming moniliform threads.—*Berk. Outl. p.* 325. (*Fig.* 184.)

Fig. 184.

1404. **Cheirospora botryospora.** *Fr.* "Cluster-spored Cheirospora."

Gregarious, punctiform, black, opaque, oozing when moist in a tremelloid mass; stroma hyaline, gelatinous; sporophores dichotomous or branched; spores minute, oblong, collected in subglobose heads at the tips of the sporophores.—*Fr. S.V.S. p.* 499. *B. & Br. Ann. N.H. no.* 441*. *Hyperomyxa stilbosporoides. Corda.* iii. *f.* 89. *Stilbospora botryospora. Mont. Ann. Sc. Nat.* 1837, *t.* 18, *f.* 5. *Myriocephalum. Fckl. exs. no.* 96-97. *Curr. Micr. Journ.* iv. *t.* 11, *f.* 1-9. *De Not. Micr. Ital.* iii. *t.* 10. *Fres. Beitr. t.* 5, *f.* 1-9.

On beach and ivy twigs. Common.

There appears to be no specific difference between the form on beech twigs and that on ivy. (*Fig.* 184.)

Gen. **147.** **NEMASPORA,** P.

Spores coloured, oozing out in large tendrils; spores of two kinds, some minute, others filiform, with a strong curvature.—*Berk. Outl. p.* 325. *Eng. Fl.* v. *p.* 355.

These species are only conditions of Sphæriaceous fungi.

1405. **Nemaspora crocea.** *P.* "Orange Nemaspora."

Nucleus pallid, spores (at length) curved, very slender, orange.—*Pers. Syn. p.* 109. *Eng. Fl.* v. *p.* 355. *Fries. exs. no.* 107. *Moug. exs. no.* 177. *Desm. Ann. Sc. Nat.* xix. *t.* 5, *f.* 3. *Sphæria profusa. Sow. t.* 377. *Libertella faginea. Desm. Ann.*

Sc. Nat. xix. *t.* 5, *f.* 5. *Cooke exs. no.* 212. *Fckl. exs. no.* 634. *Corda. Icon.* i. *t.* 6-7. *Fres. t.* 4, *f.* 35-39. *Bisch. f.* 3885.

On beech trunks. Common. [United States.]

In an imperfect state it is a mere gelatinous mass of minute globose conidia. The perfect spores are strongly curved.—*M. J. B.*

1406. Nemaspora rosæ. *Desm.* "Rose Nemaspora."

Spores curved into a semi-circle, very slender, orange.—*Fr. S.M.* iii. *p.* 479. *Eng. Fl.* v. *p.* 356. *Libertella rosæ. Desm. Ann. Sc. Nat.* xix. *t.* 5, *f.* 6.

On rose and lilac.

Gen. **148. MYXOSPORIUM,** De Not.

Spores coloured, minute, of one kind, forming tendrils.—*Berk. Outl. p.* 325.

1407. Myxosporium orbiculare. *Berk.* "Orbicular Myxosporium."

Spores very minute, oblong, pale vinous red, discharged in slender tendrils.—*Berk. Outl. p.* 325. *Cytispora orbicularis. Berk. Ann. N.H. no.* 106, *t.* 7, *f.* 6.

On gourds.

Forming orbicular patches. In a vertical section there is an appearance of perithecia, but in the horizontal section this is scarcely observable; in general confluent, with one or two orifices to each group.

MYXOSPORIUM COLLICULOSUM. *Berk.* (*Sow. t.* 409) is evidently nothing more than the spermogonia of *Ræstelia cancellata.*

MYXOSPORIUM PARADOXUM. De Not. according to Tulasne, is the pycnidia of *Trochila craterium.*

Gen. **149. GLÆOSPORIUM,** Mont.

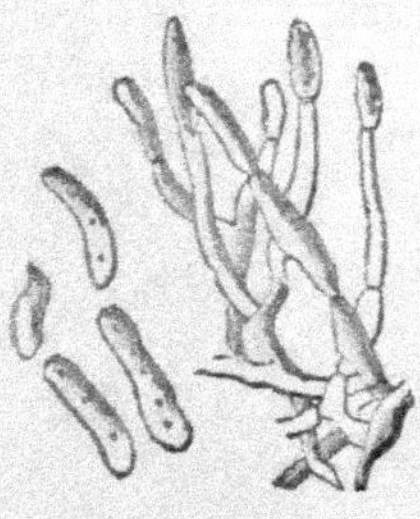

Fig. 185.

Spores hyaline, simple, of one kind, oozing out in the form of tendrils.—*Berk. Outl. p.* 325. (*Fig.* 185.)

1408. Glæosporium concentricum. *B. & Br.* "Concentric Glæosporium."

Minute, white, disposed concentrically; spores numerous, cylindrical, truncate, pellucid, oozing out and forming little heaps.—*B. & Br. Ann. N.H. no.* 441. *Cylindrosporium concentricum, Grev. t.* 27. *Uredo cylindrospora. Eng. Fl.* v.*p.*384.

On living cabbage leaves.

Spores produced beneath the cuticle, and forming little heaps by oozing out, as in other species.

1409. Glæosporium labes. *B. & Br.* "Poplar-leaf Glæosporium."

Spots indefinite, brown; spores sub-pyriform, obsoletely uniseptate, sub-cirrhose.—*B. & Br. Ann. N.H. no.* 440. *Asteroma labes. Berk. exs. no.* 346. *Ann. N.H. no.* 203, *t.* 11, *f.* 6.

On living poplar leaves. Jul.

Forming irregular brown patches, scattered or occupying almost the whole of the upper surface of the leaf, the stroma when held up to the light is found to be disposed in a fibrillose form; spores forming short tendrils, subpyriform, with an obscure septum (not always visible) at the contracted part of the spore. The spores in the fresh plant show little granules, generally disposed in two patches.—*M. J. B.*

1410. Glæosporium læticolor. "Salmon-coloured Glæosporium."

Spots depressed, centre white, with a black ring, pustules circinating, tendrils pale red, spores oblong, the endochrome retracted at either end.—*Berk. Gard. Chron.* 1859, *pp.* 604.

On peaches and nectarines.

At first appearing as dark specks with a bleached centre, at length the white spot and dark ring become more clearly defined, seated in the centre of a regular circular depression, the borders of which are pale. The whole surface of the depression studded with little salmon-coloured warts, disposed more or less in circles, from which issue little curled tendrils of salmon-coloured spores; spores oblong $\frac{1}{1300}$ in. long, with their contents retracted to either end.

1411. Glæosporium fructigenum. "Fruit Glæosporium."

Pustules concentric, of two forms, one opening in a stellate manner, with apical spores, the other opening by a pore, with the spores forming a gelatinous tendril.—*Berk. Gard. Chron.* 1856, *pp.* 245, *fig.*

On apples.

Studding the fruit with pearl-like specks, bursting through the cuticle, and swelling above it in the form of little flat cushions. Sometimes single, more frequently surrounded by a more or less perfect ring. Each plant consists of a branched inosculating mycelium, giving rise to simple or forked subfastigiate, irregular threads, each tip surmounted by an oblong, curved, or irregular spore ('001 in.) m.m. long. Afterwards the cuticle is raised in little shining transparent pustules, and a tendril of minute spores, precisely like the previous ones, issues from them. (*Fig.* 185.)

1412. Glæosporium umbrinellum. *B. & Br.* "Little brown Glæosporium."

Spots irregular, angular, brown; spores pallid.—*B. & Br. Ann. N.H.* (1866), *no.* 1144, *t.* 3, *f.* 5.

On fallen oak leaves. Oct. Batheaston.

Forming minute brown spots; spores binucleate, '0004-'0006 in. ('01—'015 m.m.) long, supported on long, often forked sporophores, at length oozing out in the form of a pale irregular tendril.—*B. & Br.*

1413. Glæosporium ficariæ. *Berk.* "Pilewort Glæosporium."

White; spores irregularly oblong, slightly curved.—*Cylindrosporium ficariæ, Berk. exs. no.* 212. *Ann. N.H. no.* 135.

On *Ranunculus ficaria.* Common.

Oozing out in tendrils, and forming irregular white patches on the green leaves.

Order XIV. TORULACEI.

Perithecium altogether wanting. Fructifying surface naked. Spores compound, or arising from repeated division (tomiparous), very rarely reduced to a single cell.—*Berk. Outl. p.* 325.

Spores tomiparous
  Simple
    Flocci straight . . . . *Torula.*
    Flocci concentric . . . . *Speira.*
    Didymous . . . . *Bispora.*
    Multiseptate.
      not enclosed . . . . *Septonema.*
      at first enclosed in the flocci . . . . *Sporochisma.*
Spores radiating, multiseptate . . . . . *Bactridium.*
Spores spirally involute, articulated . . . . *Helicosporium.*
Spores irregular, multicellular
      conglutinate . . . . *Coniothecium.*
      not conglutinate . . . . *Sporidesmium.*
      Flattened, tongue shaped . . . . *Dictyosporium.*
Spores collected in fours.
    Quadriarticulate crested . . . . *Tetraploa.*
Spores bilocular, epiphytal . . . . *Acalyptospora.*
Spores unicellular.
    Rough, parasitic . . . . *Echinobotryum.*
    Smooth, arising from the matrix . . . . *Gymnosporium.*

Gen. **150.** **TORULA,** Pers.

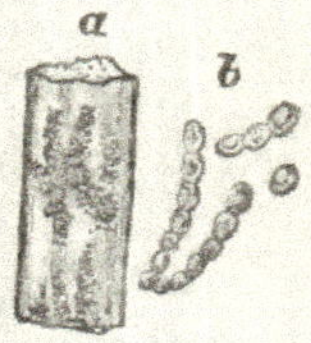

Fig. 186.

Spores tomiparous, simple.—*Berk. Outl. p.* 326. (*Fig.* 186.)

1414. Torula monilioides. *Cd.* "Beaded Torula."

Spores oblong-elliptic, flocci sub-effused, erect, aggregate, simple, jet black.—*Eng. Fl.* v. *p.* 359. *Corda, Sturm. t.* 38. *Bon. t.* 2, *f.* 58.

On sticks. Appin.

1415. Torula ovalispora. *Berk.* "Oval-spored Torula."

Spores broadly oval, pale, minute; flocci densely aggregate.—*Eng. Fl.* v. *p.* 359. *Conoplea cinerea, Pers.*

On wood. Common.

Forms little flat, roundish, at length confluent patches, of a brownish-black hue, with sometimes a glaucous bloom externally.

1416. Torula pulvillus. *B. & Br.* "Cushion-like Torula."

Tufts pulvinate, flocci compact, straight, branched; joints oblong, slightly constricted.—*Ann. N.H. no.* 463.

On dead twigs of oak, bursting in little tufts through the bark. March. Apethorpe.

Tufts cushion-shaped, half a line broad, compact, black; flocci straight, slightly branched, often suddenly diminishing in size, and again incrassated, consisting of numerous slightly constricted oblong joints; endochrome containing a single nucleus.—*M. J. B.*

1417. Torula pulveracea. *Corda.* "Powdery Torula."

Tufts olivaceous-black or sooty, oblong, parallel, thick, with a blackish spurious stroma, threads of spores branched; spores oblong ovate, olive, smooth, with nuclei.—*Corda.* ii. *p.* 8, *t.* 9, *f.* 38. *Fckl. exs. no.* 68. *Cooke exs. no.* 347.

On fallen sticks, &c.

Forming thick oblong sooty tufts, which are often confluent in a large patch, pulverulent, and of a brown or olive-black colour, not the jet-black of many other species. The spores are more brown than olive, with usually one or two nuclei.

1418. Torula stilbospora. *Corda.* "Willow Torula."

Tufts erumpent, pulverulent, elongated, confluent, very black; flocci unequal, branched or simple, flexuous; spores sub-quadrate, sub-equal, connate, brown.—*Corda. Sturm* iii. *t.* 46. *Corda. Icon.* v. *f.* 13. *Rabh. F.E. no.* 79 *&* 882.

On willow branches. Batheaston, &c.

1419. Torula abbreviata. *Corda.* "Short-threaded Torula."

Tufts black, confluent; flocci abbreviated, 3-4 spored; spores very minute, globose, greyish, semi-pellucid.—*Corda. Icon.* i. *f.* 130.

var. β. **sphæriæformis.** *B. & Br. Ann. N.H. no.* 464.

On decorticated branches of *Pinus sylvestris.* Wraxall.

Instead of being widely diffused, this variety presents little sphæria-like tufts, and has a highly developed hyphasma, consisting of forked threads, at the apices of which the short chains of spores are fixed.—*B. & Br.*

1420. Torula basicola. *B. & Br.* "Creeping Torula."

Hyphasma creeping, branched, here and there rising; fertile flocci short, 5-7 articulate, fastigiate; articulations not constricted, at length separating, the last very obtuse.—*Ann. N.H. no.* 465, *t.* 11, *f.* 4.

On stems of peas and *Nemophila auriculata.*

Black, effused; hyphasma here and there rising from the general mass, and giving off fascicles of short fastigiate fertile threads, consisting of 5-7 articulations. Each endochrome has usually a single nucleus.—*B. & Br.*

1421. Torula hysterioides. *Cd.* "Hysterium-like Torula."

Tufts linear, abbreviated, often parallel, black; flocci erect, crowded (adherent), equal, filiform, yellowish; spores quadrangular, terete, pellucid.—*Corda. Icon.* i. *f.* 139. *B. & Br. Ann. N. H. no.* 751. *Rabh. F. E. no.* 282.

On poles, &c.

Easily distinguished under the microscope by the flocci having a tendency to adhere to each other, side by side.

1422. Torula cylindrica. *Berk.* "Cylindrical Torula."

Effused, threads not moniliform; spores fasciated.—*Berk. Eng. Fl.* v. *p.* 359.

On sticks.

Spores united four together, into short, equal, cylindrical flocci, which resemble in some states those of *Arthrinium.* It appears like a thin black wash on the bark of sticks.—*M. J. B.*

1423. Torula herbarum. *Lk.* "Herbaceous Torula."

Spores globose, green, then black; flocci aggregate, not strongly moniliform.—*Link. Sp.* i. *p.* 128. *Corda, Sturm. t.* 48. *Eng. Fl.* v. *p.* 359. *Cooke exs. no.* 362.

On stems of herbaceous plants, especially *Umbelliferæ*. Common. [United States.]

Forming flat sooty patches, variegated with olive-green; spores fasciated. (*Fig.* 186.)

1424. Torula graminis. *Desm.* "Grass Torula."

Tufts very small, subrotund or oval, brownish black; flocci simple, decumbent, opaque; spores globose, deciduous.—*Desm. Ann. Sc. Nat.* 1834, ii. *t.* 2, *f.* 6. *Desm. exs. no.* 169. *B. & Br. Ann. N.H. no.* 134. *Fckl. exs. no.* 69.

On dry leaves of *Carices*. Colleyweston.

1425. Torula plantaginis. *Cd.* "Plantain Torula."

Hypophyllous, effused, indeterminate, tomentose, black; hyphasma creeping, filamentous, branched; flocci erect, brown, fasciculate, flexuose, simple, rarely forked; spores subquadrate, smooth, brown, nucleate.—*Corda.* iii. *t.* 1, *f.* 14. *B. & Br. Ann. N.H. no.* 252. *Kl. exs. no.* 1764. *Fckl. exs. no.* 65.

On leaves of Plantain. Stibbington, Hants.

"I find exactly the same barren creeping threads of a perfectly distinct structure from the torulose threads as Corda. I suspect that further observations will show that this fungus has distinct spores."—*M. J. B.*

1426. Torula sporendonema. *B. & Br.* "Cheese Torula."

Flocci somewhat branched, woven together into pulvinate red tufts; spores globose.—*Ann. N.H. no.* 462. *Rabh. F.E. no.* 849. *Sporendonema casei, Desm. Ann. Sc. Nat.* xi. *p.* 246. *Moug. exs. no.* 998. *Eng. Fl.* v. *p.* 350. *Bull. t.* 504, *f.* 2.

On cheese and rat's dung.

This has exactly the structure of *Torula*, and certainly has not the spores contained in a tube.—*M. J. B.* We have also found it on old and decaying glue.

Torula Eriophori. *Berk.* is *Gonatosporium puccinioides*. See *Ann. N.H. no.* 236, 519.

Sporendonema Muscæ. *Fr.* *Empusa muscæ. Cohn.* See *Saprolegniei.*

Gen. **151.** **SPEIRA,** Corda.

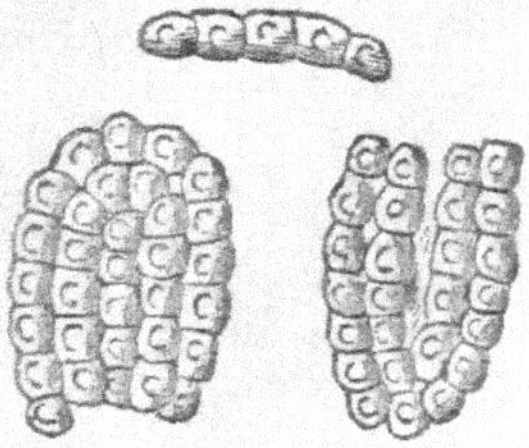

Fig. 187.

Flocci concentric, at first connate, forming plates, at length breaking up. Spores simple. Stroma none.—*Corda. Icon.* i. *p.* 9.

(*Fig.* 187.)

1427. Speira toruloides. *Corda.* "Torula-like Speira."

Tufts irregular, elongated, brown; threads connate in laminæ; spores quadrangular, yellowish, pellucid.—*Corda. Icon.* i. *f.* 140. *B. & Br. Ann. N.H. no.* 1041. *Pay. f.* 295. *Corda. Anl. t. B. f.* 5. 7.

On dead herbaceous plants. Batheaston. (*Fig.* 187.)

Gen. **152.** **BACTRIDIUM,** Kunze.

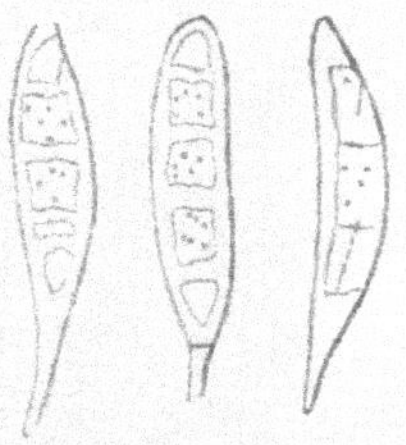

Fig. 188.

Spores radiating, coloured or hyaline, oblong, multiseptate.—*Berk. Outl. p.* 326. (*Fig.* 188.)

1428. Bactridium flavum. *Kze.* "Yellow Bactridium."

Tufts irregular, usually subglobose, compact, yellow; spores oblong-ovate, obtuse; hyphasma somewhat branched, sparingly septate.—*Kze. M.H.* i. *t.* 1, *f.* 2. *Bon. t.* 2, *f.* 47. *Berk. exs. no.* 327. *Rabh. F.E. no.* 372.

On elm stumps. [United States.] (*Fig.* 188.)

1429. Bactridium helvellæ. *B. & Br.* "Parasitic Bactridium."

Tufts confluent, very thin, microscopical, effused; flocci somewhat erect, branched sparingly; spores clavate, or clavately pear-shaped, 2—at length 6-7 septate, colourless.—*B. & Br. Ann. N.H. no.* 816, *t.* 9, *f.* 3. *Didymaria helvellæ. Corda.* vi. *f.* 24.

On the hymenium of *Pezizæ.* Dec. Batheaston.

Spores at length 5-7 septate, ·0025 in. long. Corda's figure represents the early stage of growth; at length it acquires several septa.

1430. Bactridium atrovirens. *B.* "Black-green Bactridium."

Flocci forked, pellucid; spores lanceolate, 1-2 septate, dark-green.—*Eng. Fl.* v. *p.* 350.

On stumps. Winter. Apethorpe.

Forming a thin, dark, black-green, minutely granulated stratum; flocci white, so slender and transparent as to be seen only with some difficulty; spores lanceolate, with one or more, frequently two, septa.—*M. J. B.*

Gen. 153. HELICOSPORIUM, Nees.

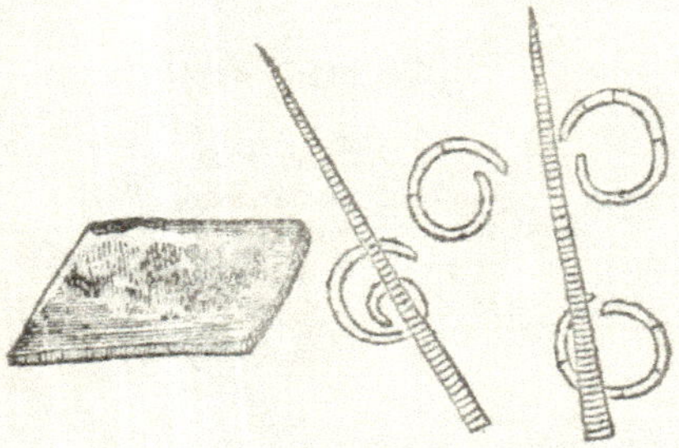

Fig. 189.

Parasitical; spores filiform, articulated, spirally involute.—*Berk. Outl. pp.* 326. *Eng. Fl.* v. *pp.* 335. (*Fig.* 189.)

1431. Helicosporium vegetum. *Nees.* "Oak Helicosporium."

Flocci black; distant, subulate, spores pale greenish, spiral, septate, pellucid.—*Nees. f.* 69. *Berk. Ann. N.H. no.* 229. *Kl. exs. no.* 1433. *Corda. Sturm. t.* 16.

On decayed oak branches, &c. Rockingham Forest. (*Fig.* 189.)

1432. Helicosporium pulvinatum. *Fr.* "Pulvinate Helicosporium."

Threads cæspitoso-pulvinate, very slender, branched, septate at their apices; spores yellow green.—*Fr. S.M.* iii. *p.* 354. *Eng. Fl.* v. *p.* 335. *Helicotrichum pulvinatum. Nees. f.* 15.

var. β. **effusum.** Effused, very thin, spores whitish.—*Berk. Eng. Fl.* v. *p.* 335.

On old chips, &c.

Forming a very thin black stratum, following the inequalities of the wood; flocci branched; branches patent, articulated; articulations about as long as broad; apices pointed, pellucid, terminated by the minute closely involute, extremely fugacious spores, which consist of about three volutions, and as many articulations, volutions at first so close that the spores appear globose, and their true nature might easily be overlooked.—*M. J. B.*

Gen. **154.** **BISPORA,** Corda.

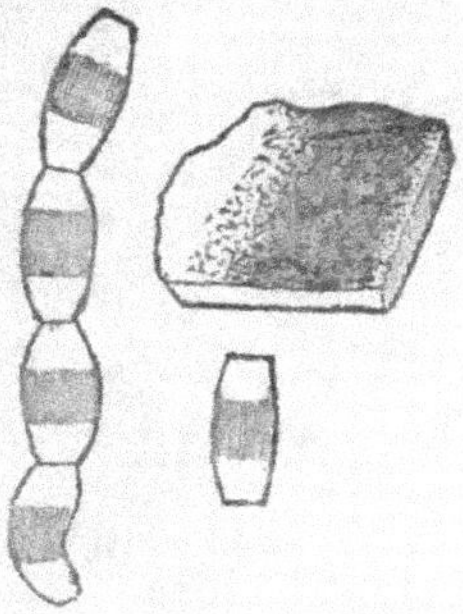

Fig. 190.

Flocci tomiparous, moniliform, composed of didymous spores.—*Berk. Outl. p.* 326. (*Fig.* 190.)

1433. Bispora monilioides. *Cd.* "Beaded Bispora."

Flocci aggregate; spores oval, obtuse, barrel-shaped.—*Corda, Icon.* i. *f.* 143. *Fres. t.* 6, *f.* 46-54. *Torula antennata. Pers. M.E.* i. *p.* 21. *Berk. exs. no.* 215. *Eng. Fl.* v. *p.* 359. *Monilia antennata. Grev. t.* 255. *Fckl. exs. no.* 74. *Cooke exs. no.* 346.

On old stumps. Common. [Mid. Carolina.]

Forming intense black velvety patches on the cut surface of stumps, chips, &c. (*Fig.* 190.)

Gen. **155.** **SEPTONEMA,** Corda.

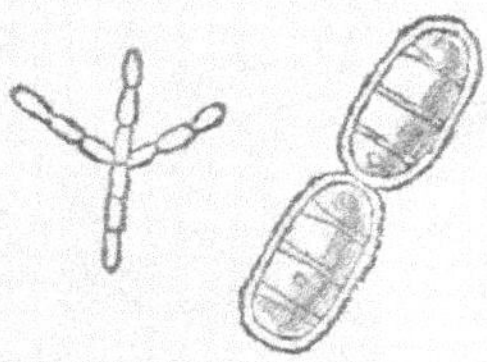

Fig. 191.

Flocci tomiparous, moniliform, composed of multiseptate spores.—*Berk. Outl. p.* 327. (*Fig.* 191.)

1434. Septonema spilomeum. *Berk.* "Point-like Septonema."

Sori small, punctiform; threads branched; articulations oblong-elliptic, rather rough, triseptate.—*Berk. Hook. Journ.* 1845, iv. *p.* 310, *t.* 12, *f.* 5. *B. & Br. Ann. N.H. no.* 466.

On old fence rails. Guernsey. [U. Carolina, Ohio.]

Forming little scattered sori about the size of a poppy seed; threads branched. articulations oblongo-elliptic, triseptate, one or more of the septa occasionally containing an oil globule, border of articulations pellucid, rough with little scabrous prominences. Very distinct in the punctiform habit, and in the nature of the articulations.—*M. J. B.* (*Fig.* 191.)

1435. Septonema irregulare. *B. & Br.* "Irregular Septonema."

Effused, thin black, irregular; spores oblong.—*B. & Br. Ann. N.H. no.* 942, *t.* 15, *f.* 13.

On living apple twigs. Apethorpe.

Forming a very thin, cloud-like, black stratum; very irregular, sometimes exhibiting continuous threads under the microscope, sometimes distinct, spores ·0007-·0001 in. long.

1436. Septonema elongatispora. *Preuss.* "Long-spored Septonema."

Tufts effused, whitish; flocci erect, branched; spores sub-cylindrical, apiculate, variable in length, 1-2 septate, pellucid, colourless.—*Sturm.* vi. *p.* 72, *t.* 36. *B. & Br. Ann. N.H. no.* 1059.

On nettle stems. Oct. Batheaston.

1437. Septonema concentricum. *B. & Br.* "Concentric Septonema."

Sessile, superficial, scattered or confluent, orbicular, at first entirely white, then the centre or disc ochraceous; flocci concatenate, radiating from the pulvinate, compact, fibrous, pallid stroma; spores straight, continuous, white, of two kinds.—*Rabh. F.E. no.* 777.

On pine and larch chips. Dec.

Tufts ·01-·035 in. broad. Spores ·0007 × ·00015 in. mixed with others ·001 × ·0003 in.—*B. & Br.*

Gen. **156. SPOROCHISMA,** B. & Br.

Flocci erect, simple; outer membrane tough, inarticulate; endochrome at length emergent, breaking up into quadriseptate spores.—*Berk. Outl. p.* 327. *Ann. N.H. no.* 467. (*Fig.* 192.)

The affinities of this genus are clearly with *Torula*, the circumstance of the endosporous mode of fructification being apparent rather than real. The outer membrane is very tough, and does not break up into separate portions with the spore. It is, in fact, a *Septonema* enclosed in an additional membrane—*M. J. B.*

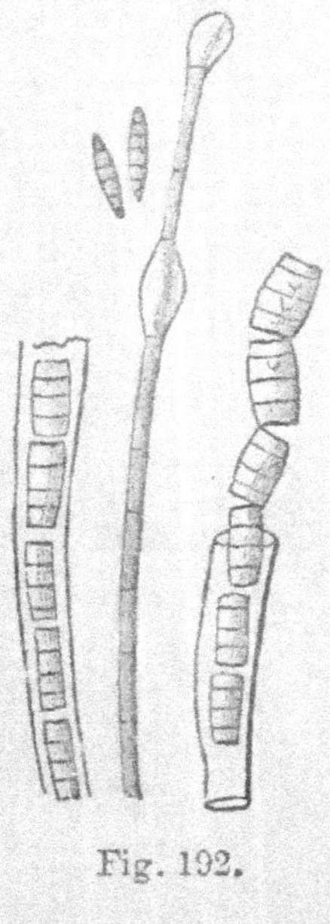

Fig. 192.

1438. Sporochisma mirabile. *B. & Br.* "Curious Sporochisma."

Effused, black, velvety; flocci erect, simple; endochrome breaking up into cylindrical, quadri-articulate spores.—*Gard. Chron.* 1847, *p.* 540. *Ann. N.H. no.* 467. *Berk. Intr. f.* 74*a*. *Fres. t.* 6, *f.* 26-28.

On beech.

Forming a black velvety stratum; flocci erect, simple, tapering towards the base; external membrane tough, inarticulate; endochrome breaking up into cylindrical quadri-articulate spores, at length escaping from the ruptured thread, each joint having frequently a single nucleus.—*B. & Br.*

(*Fig.* 192.)

Gen. **157.** **SPORIDESMIUM,** Link.

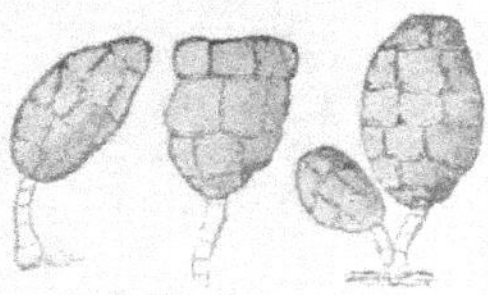

Fig. 193.

Spores mostly irregular, pluricellular, springing immediately from the obscure mycelium, rarely borne upon a distinct peduncle, more rarely uniseptate.—*Berk. Outl. p.* 327.

(*Fig.* 193.)

1439. **Sporidesmium polymorphum.** *Corda.* "Many-shaped Sporidesmium."

Tufts black, effused, powdery, opaque; spores pedicellate, oblong, black-brown, opaque, cellular; peduncle filiform, septate, or irregularly cellulose, brown.—*Corda. Icon.* i. *f.* 119. *B. & Br. Ann. N.H. no.* 452.

On decaying oak. Feb. Wraxall.

Remarkable for its closely septate peduncle. (*Fig.* 193.)

1440. **Sporidesmium alternariæ.** *Cooke.* "Paper Sporidesmium."

Tufts irregular, dendritic, bright dark brown; hyphasma creeping, profuse, filiform, hyaline, branched, sparsely septate; spores irregular, ovate, sub-pyriform, or cylindrical, one or more septate, with transverse divisions, brown.—*Sporidesmium polymorphum var. chartarum. Cooke exs. no.* 329.

On varnished wall paper. Jan.—May.

This can scarcely be a form of *S. polymorphum* from the nature of the peduncles; the hyphasma is too much developed for a good *Sporidesmium.* I am disposed to regard it as a condition of *Alternaria chartarum.* Preuss. (Sturm. vi. t. 49.) Mr Broome and myself have seen distinct indications of a moniliform arrangement of spores, under an inch objective, but the attachment seems so slight that we could not verify this with higher powers. Never having seen specimen or description of *Sporidesmium chartarum,* B. & C. (from Mid. Carolina, U.S.), I cannot be certain that this is distinct. —*M. C. C.*

1441. Sporidesmium antiquum. *Corda.* "Compact Sporidesmium."

Tufts black, tomentose, very broad, irregularly expanded; spores congested, joined in fascicles, erect, polymorphous, cellulose; hyphasma rooting, branched, filamentous, cellulose, brownish.—*Corda.* iii.*f.* 11. *B. & Br. Ann. N.H. no.* 453.

var. β. **compactum.** *B. & Br. Ann. N. H. no.* 453.

On hard wood. Wraxall.

More compact than the typical form as figured by Corda, and composed of smaller cells.

1442. Sporidesmium pyriforme. *Corda.* "Pear-shaped Sporidesmium."

Effused, black; spores obovate, at first septate, then cellulose, brown, semi-pellucid, 2-4 celled; peduncle hyaline, colourless, short or elongated, and filiform, flaccid.—*Corda.* i.*f.* 116. *B. & Br. Ann. N.H. no.* 454.

On decayed boards. July. Shropshire.

It forms a thick crust-like stratum.

1443. Sporidesmium melanopum. *B. & Br.* "Black-patch Sporidesmium."

Spores subglobose, supported by a cellular base, forming a stratum with the crowded tufts.—*Ann. N.H. no.* 455. *Spiloma melanopum, Ach. Meth. t.* i.*f.* 3. *Eng. Bot.* (*2nd ed.*), *t.* 2358.

On bark of apple trees. Common. [Up. Carolina.]

Forming broad black patches, made up of many smaller spots, spores subglobose, very opaque, apparently simple, but really composed of numerous cells, supported by a cellular base, which varies much in length and breadth.

1444. Sporidesmium scutellare. *B. & Br.* "Scutellate Sporidesmium."

Sori scutellæform; spores broadly obovate, cellular; supported by a short cellular base.—*B. & Br. Ann. N.H. no.* 456.

On larch bark.

Sori scattered, minute, scutelliform; spores obovate, evidently cellular, springing from a cellular stroma, and supported by a few variously arranged cells, which are sometimes reduced to merely one.—*B. & Br.*

1445. Sporidesmium lepraria. *B. & Br.* "Black Sporidesmium."

Spots effused, very black; spores irregular, without any distinct base.—*Berk. Hook. Journ.* 1853, *p.* 43. *t.* 3, *f.* 9. *Berk. Intr.*

f. 18*a*. *Ann. N.H. no.* 750. *Lepraria nigra, Eng. Bot.* (2*nd ed.*), *t.* 2409. *Coniothecium effusum, Corda.* i. *f.* 21. *B. & Br. Ann. N.H. no.* 459.

On exposed planks and rails. Common. [Carolina, U.S.]

Forming broad black persistent patches, sometimes it occurs in distinct black specks, which wear the appearance of little oblong perithecia. The spores are extremely irregular, of no definite shape, and without any distinct base.

1446. Sporidesmium uniseptatum. *B. & Br.* "Two-celled Sporidesmium."

Spores obovate, uniseptate, shortly pedicellate, cæspitose; lower articulation shorter.—*B. &. Br. Ann. N.H. no.* 815, *t.* 9, *f.* 2.

On *Clematis vitalba.* Jan. Batheaston.

Forming minute dark specks, consisting of obovate, uniseptate, shortly pedicellate spores, (·0005 in.) ·0127 m.m. long, the lower articulation of which is much the shorter and narrower. As seen by transmitted light they have a slight vinous tinge.—*B. & Br.*

1447. Sporidesmium opacum. *Corda.* "Opaque Sporidesmium."

Somewhat effused, irregular, very black, opaque; spores very shortly pedicellate, polymorphous, oblong, cuneate, ovate, or elliptical, 2-4 celled, at first brown pellucid, then black, opaque; peduncle colourless.—*Corda.* i. *f.* 115. *B. & Br. Ann. N.H. no.* 1145, *t.* 3, *f.* 6.

On stumps of Wych elm. Mar. St. Catherine's.

When young forming small round cinereous tufts, sparingly scattered over the wood.—*B. & Br.*

1448. Sporidesmium lobatum. *B. & Br.* "Lobed Sporidesmium."

Stem articulated, hyaline below, divided above in subquaternate, subglobose articulations.—*B. & Br. Ann. N.H.* (1866), *no.* 1146, *t.* 3, *f.* 7.

On fir sticks. April. Lucknam.

Forming minute black, pulvinate tufts. At first simple and strongly swollen above. The upper articulation then divides, and ultimately gives off the spores, which are (·0006 in.) ·015 m.m. long. The whole plant is ·001 in. high.

1449. Sporidesmium abruptum. *B. & Br.* "Abrupt Sporidesmium."

Pulvinate, very shortly stipitate, confluent with the spores, which are oblong, septate, with unequal articulations.—*B. & Br. Ann. N.H. no.* 1042, *t.* 14, *f.* 8.

On dead wood. March.

Forming little pulvinate tufts, externally resembling a villous *Sphæria*. Spores oblongo-clavate, confluent with the stem, septate, the lower articulation and the uppermost short, the second from the top very long. Spores (·0025 × ·0006 in.) ·06 × ·015 m.m.

Sporidesmium fungorum. *Berk.* See *Sphæria epochnum, B. & Br.*

Gen. 158. CONIOTHECIUM, Corda.

At length naked; spores multicellular, irregular, conglutinate. —*Berk. Outl. p.* 327.

Neither of the British species are autonomous.

Coniothecium amentacearum, *Corda.* a condition of *Valsa salicina, Fr.*

Coniothecium betulinum, *Corda.* a condition of *Diatrype lanciformis, Fr.*

Gen. 159. DICTYOSPORIUM, Corda.

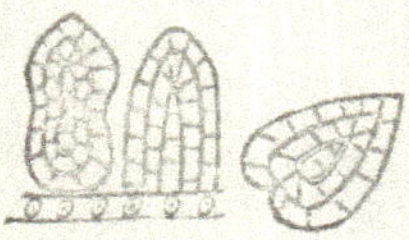

Fig. 194.

Spores linguæform, erect, plane, cellular; cells sub-concentric.—*Berk. Outl. p.* 328. (*Fig.* 194.)

1450. Dictyosporium elegans. *Corda.* "Elegant Dictyosporium."

Tufts black, effused; spores tongue-shaped, acute above, or rounded, rarely contracted in the middle, base then attenuated or cordate; cells diaphanous, yellowish, walls becoming thickened, brownish or black.—*Corda.* ii. *f.* 29. *B. & Br. Ann. N.H. no.* 458. *Pay. f.* 255. *Corda. Anl. t. B. f.* 4, *no.* 7-9.

On barked oak trees. Feb. Somerset. [Low. Carolina.] (*Fig.* 194.)

Gen. **160.** **TETRAPLOA,** B.& Br.

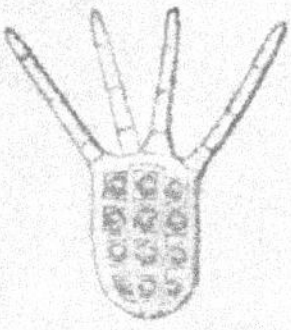

Fig. 195.

Spores mostly quadri-articulate growing together in fours, and each crowned with a jointed bristle.—*Berk. Outl. p.* 328. *Ann. N.H. no.* 457. (*Fig.* 195.)

This genus is represented by one species, which is so rare that no opportunity has occurred of watching its growth. It appears to be a kind of compound *Sporidesmium*.

1451. **Tetraploa aristata.** *B. & Br.* "Bearded Tetraploa."

Stratum olive-black; spores oblong, quadriarticulate, connate in fours, each with an articulate seta of the same length.—*B. & Br. Ann. N.H. no.* 457, *t.* 11, *f.* 6.

On grass. King's Cliffe.

Forming a thin olive-black stratum, consisting of generally quadriarticulate oblong spores, growing four together and perfectly connate, each crowned with an articulate seta as long as itself. The quadriaristate bodies may either be regarded as made up of four spores or as spores formed of four parallel rows of cells, each row being terminated by a bristle.—*B. & Br.* (*Fig.* 195.)

Gen. **161.** **ECHINOBOTRYUM,** Corda.

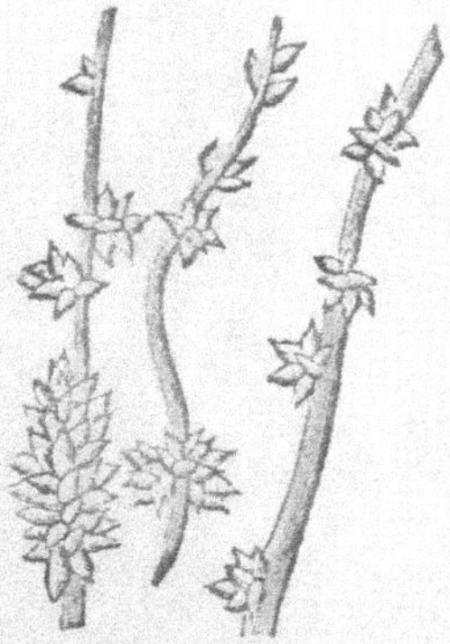

Fig. 196.

Parasitical; spores unicellular, stellato-fasciculate, ovate, acuminate, rough. —*Berk. Outl. p.* 328. (*Fig.* 196.)

1452. **Echinobotryum atrum.** *Corda.* "Black Echinobotryum."

Tufts at first stellate, then irregularly expanded, black; spores fawn coloured, ovate-oblong, narrowed at the base, warted, warts produced above into long obtuse points, which are brown.—*Corda. Sturm.* i. *t.* 26. *Bon. t.* 10, *f.* 218*d*. *Corda. Icon.* iii. *f.* 6. *B. & Br. Ann. N.H. no.* 124, 457*. *Corda. Anl. t. B. f.* 3, *no.* 5, 6, 7. *Kl. exs. no.* 1585.

Parasitic on black moulds (*Pachnocybe.*) Milton. King's Cliffe.

The spores have the appearance of fascicles of minute perithecia. (*Fig.* 196.)

Gen. 162. GYMNOSPORIUM, Corda.

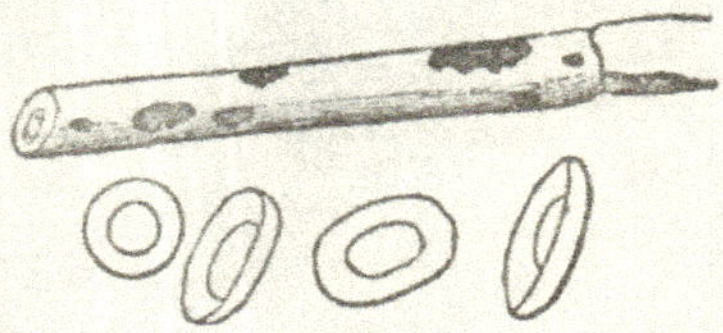

Fig. 197.

Mycelium very obscure; spores unicellular, arising apparently from the matrix.—*Berk. Outl. p.* 328.

(*Fig.* 197.)

1453. Gymnosporium arundinis. *Corda.* "Reed Gymnosporium."

Immersed, then naked, livid; spores oval, lens-shaped, or rounded, margin depressed, diaphanous, livid-yellow; nucleus obovate or globose, brownish.—*Corda. Icon.* ii. *f.* 1. *Berk. Outl. p.* 328. *Corda. Anl. t. B. f.* 3. *no.* 8-11. *Curr. Micr. Journ.* 1857, *t.* 8, *f.* 35-37.

On reeds. (*Fig.* 197.)

Gen. 163. ACALYPTOSPORA, Desm.

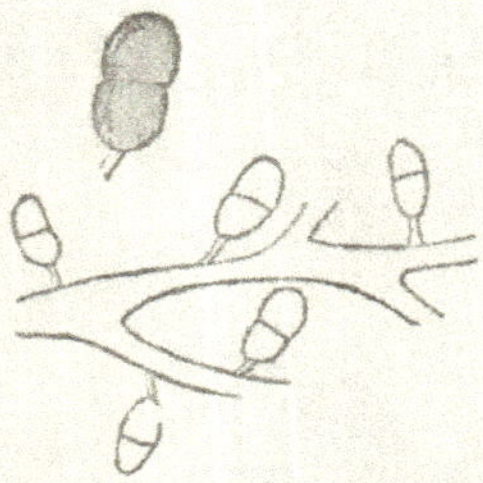

Fig. 198.

Spores epiphytal, superficially innate, didymous, stipitate, not collected in heaps; stroma none.—*Desm. Ann. S.N.* 1848, x. *p.* 342.

(*Fig.* 198.)

By some authors this genus is included in *Pucciniæi*; it is clearly intermediate between *Torulacei* and *Pucciniæi*, but, as it appears to us, more closely allied to the former than the latter.

1454. Acalyptospora nervisequia. *Desm.* "Nerve Acalyptospora."

On both surfaces; spores seriate along the nerves, red-brown, shining, ovoid or oblong, obtuse, scarcely constricted; epispore smooth; stem thick, rather long, fragile, colourless.—*Desm. Ann. Sc. Nat.* 1848, x. *p.* 343. *Ann. N.H. no.* 1043.

On living and dead leaves of elm.

Looking like a short, obtuse *Puccinia* with one to three septa, and a short pellucid stem. In every stage of growth free. It closely resembles a gland. —*B. & Br.* (*Fig.* 198.)

CPSIA information can be obtained
at www.ICGtesting.com
Printed in the USA
LVHW100559210323
742065LV00002B/102

9 783382 126957